George E. Ellis

Memoir of Sir Benjamin Thompson, Count Rumford

With notices of his daughter

George E. Ellis

Memoir of Sir Benjamin Thompson, Count Rumford
With notices of his daughter

ISBN/EAN: 9783742801784

Manufactured in Europe, USA, Canada, Australia, Japa

Cover: Foto ©Raphael Reischuk / pixelio.de

Manufactured and distributed by brebook publishing software
(www.brebook.com)

George E. Ellis

Memoir of Sir Benjamin Thompson, Count Rumford

MEMOIR

OF

SIR BENJAMIN THOMPSON,

COUNT RUMFORD,

WITH NOTICES OF HIS DAUGHTER.

By GEORGE E. ELLIS.

PUBLISHED IN CONNECTION WITH AN EDITION OF RUMFORD'S COMPLETE WORKS.

BY THE

American Academy of Arts and Sciences,

BOSTON.

———

PUBLISHED FOR THE ACADEMY
BY
CLAXTON, REMSEN, AND HAFFELFINGER,
819 & 821 MARKET STREET,
PHILADELPHIA.

TO

JACOB BIGELOW, M. D.

My dear Sir: —

IN inscribing this volume with your name, without having asked your permission to do so, I must seek your indulgence after the act.

There is no name which, more fitly than yours, could be thus brought into connection with the subject of the volume. As the first incumbent of the Rumford Professorship in Harvard College, you paid a most felicitous and discriminating tribute, in your Inaugural Address, to the distinguished man who founded that Professorship by a generous endowment, and by making the College his residuary legatee. You initiated and directed a method of fulfilling the duties of your office in strict accordance with the wishes and purposes of Count Rumford, especially with a view to those ends of practical public good which he so ardently and successfully pursued. Your published lectures, The Elements of Technology, have recently had the title which you assigned to them adopted by an Institution of highest promise with us in its field and objects. This Institution, also, you most happily inaugurated.

You presided for seventeen years over the American Academy of Arts and Sciences with an ability and urbanity of which the Fellows expressed to you their heartiest appreciation when you declined to be longer a candidate for that position; where also you had to direct the administration of another generous trust confided by Count Rumford to the Academy.

Your lengthened life and professional devotion, while they have brought you to stand now as the oldest and most esteemed physician in the city of your residence, have likewise permitted you to indulge your taste and genius in the broadest culture of the many provinces of literature, art, and science in which you are an authority.

I may not put into print the epithets and encomiums attached to your name by those who come nearest to you in the wide circles of your friendship and personal intercourse.

Most respectfully yours,

GEORGE E. ELLIS.

PREFACE.

THE circumstances which led the writer to the preparation of the following Biography of Count Rumford may properly be mentioned here.

In one of a series of letters with which I was favored by my much-esteemed friend, the Hon. Robert C. Winthrop, — also my associate on the Council of the Academy, — during his last European tour, was a passage which I here copy. The letter was dated Munich, August 19, 1867.

"You have not forgotten how much there is here to remind an American of his own country. No one could drive in the beautiful English Garden (as it is called) without remembering with pride that it was originally laid out by Benjamin Thompson, Count Rumford, who would almost seem to have been driven from his native land (by unjust suspicions and prejudices, as I have always feared) in order to give him a wider sphere for doing good to mankind. We have never done honor enough to his memory in America. Is there any portrait of him at Harvard, where he endowed so valuable a Professorship? I do not remember any. [Mr. Winthrop for the moment forgot the excellent portrait of the Count, the gift of his daughter, which hangs in Massachusetts Hall, Cambridge.] There ought to be a statue of him somewhere in America. I am glad to find that there is to be one here. At the foundry here, a day or two since, I found them actually engaged in casting one to adorn one of the squares of Munich. This foundry itself is a most interesting place to Americans. The museum connected with it contains the original models of all the statues which have been cast here. There I found .... But, after all, I think the Rumford statue gave me the greatest satisfaction. It is a tardy act of justice to one who did really great things for the world, as well as for Bavaria. His Essays on Pauperism, and his plans for its relief and prevention, would alone entitle him to the blessing of mankind. Almost everything which is valuable in our modern systems of charity may be traced in his writings. When we add all that he did for science, and for the advancement of science, at the Royal Institution in London, and at Harvard, and at our American Academy, his claim to a statue seems to be far less equivocal, to say the least, than that of many of those who have lately received such commemoration. I trust we shall have a portrait of him, one of these days, in the gallery of our Historical Society, if nowhere else."

As I could not have a more fitting introduction to this volume than is found in that most just tribute to Count Rumford, so admirably expressed, so I most

gratefully acknowledge that my share in this work came
of my possession of the letter which contained the
above matter. I had the letter, just received, in my
pocket, while attending one of the regular meetings
of the Academy. And it so happened, likewise, that
among the matters of business which occupied the
meeting was a report of progress from the Rumford
Committee of the Academy, in the trust assigned to
them of collecting and editing the works of our eminent benefactor. Knowing that I had with me something so appropriate to the matter then in hand, I
read to the Academy the above extract from the letter
of our associate. I mentioned, likewise, that I had
in my house and had recently been reading with
great interest the contents of a very valuable manuscript volume, loaned to me by its owner, my valued
friend, George Rumford Baldwin, Esq., of Woburn,
in which he had carefully copied the correspondence
of Count Rumford with his father, the late Colonel
Loammi Baldwin, and many other papers of biographical use. I suggested that possibly the Rumford Committee might find help in examining these
documents. A proposition was then made and urged,
that I be requested to furnish a biographical memoir
of the Count as introductory to the edition of his
Works. Though surprised at the request, and wholly
unprepared to comply with it, I consented to entertain and consider it. I had no other expectation or
purpose, in finally acceding to it, than that all which

I should need to do in the case would be to gather from published sources the materials for a brief prefatory paper, which should give the dates and principal events and labors of the Count's career. In undertaking to do only this, the search and inquiry which were necessary led on to further investigations, rewarded by such an amount of authentic and interesting documents as in the view of the Rumford Committee justified the assigning of an additional volume for the memoir. As will be noticed by the reader, the new material used in the following pages is mostly of manuscripts gathered from public and private sources. I have indicated these sources either in the text or the notes of this volume.

The Life of Count Rumford contributed by Professor Renwick to Sparks's Library of American Biography, allowing for its necessary compactness, is a very excellent performance. The writer, I suppose, had the use of some of the Baldwin manuscripts above referred to. Professor Pictet, in some letters of his published in the *Bibliothèque Britannique*, furnished the substance of the matter which appears in the biographical sketches of Count Rumford contained in the Encyclopædias and Biographical Dictionaries, all of which are imperfect, and which repeat the same errors, trivial and important. Colonel Baldwin's series of four articles on the Count's life and labors, published in two volumes of the Literary Miscellany, while the Count was living, have a particular value.

Besides the acknowledgments that will be found in the following pages, made to friends for whose aid and suggestions I am under obligations to them, I must make here a special mention of the kind and helpful assistance, sympathy, and information which I have received from Mr. George Rumford Baldwin of Woburn, Massachusetts; Mr. Joseph B. Walker, of Concord, New Hampshire; Dr. H. Bence Jones, of London, Secretary of the Royal Institution of Great Britain; Mons. Jules Marcou, of Paris; and Mr. G. Henry Horstmann, United States Consul at Munich.

A search which I was privileged to make among the effects of Sarah, Countess of Rumford, in Concord, New Hampshire, was rewarded, as will be seen, by the discovery of much curious and interesting matter.

I hardly need to add, that, though I have done this work as a labor of love in the service, as well as at the request, of the American Academy of Arts and Sciences, I alone am responsible for any errors which it may contain, and for the statements and opinions expressed in it.

G. E. E.

CONTENTS.

CHAPTER I.

CHAPTER IV.

CHAPTER V.

CHAPTER VI.

CHAPTER VII.

CHAPTER VIII.

CHAPTER IX.

CHAPTER X.

APPENDIX.

LIFE OF COUNT RUMFORD.

CHAPTER I.

Benjamin Franklin and Benjamin Thompson. — Ancestry and Family of Thompson. — His Birth. — Death of his Father. — His early Education. — His own Account of his early Years. — His Friends and Guardians. — His School Days. — Apprenticeship at Salem. — Accident. — Return to Woburn. — Memoranda. — Apprenticeship in Boston. — Medical Student. — School-Teacher. — Marriage. — Military Commission. — Farmer.

MASSACHUSETTS, during the second period of its history, — when, as a Province, it received its chief magistrate and the authority for its administration of government from the mother country, — gave birth to two men the most distinguished for philosophical genius of all that have been produced on the soil of this continent. They were Benjamin Franklin and Benjamin Thompson. They came into life in humble homes, within twelve miles of each other, under like straits and circumstances of frugality and substantial thrift. They both sprang from English lineage, of an ancestry and parentage yeomen on the soil on either continent, to be cast, as their progenitors had been, upon their own exertions, without dependence upon inherited means, or patronage, or even good fortune. Born as subjects of the English monarch, they both, at different periods of their lives, claimed their privileges as such, visiting their ancestral soil, though under widely unlike circumstances, and there winning fame and distinction for services to humanity. We almost forget the occasion which parted them in the sphere of politics, because they come so close together in the more engrossing and beneficent activity of their genius.

I cannot learn that these two eminent men, with so much that was common between them in their interests and pursuits, ever met together, or sought each other's acquaintance, or even recognized each other's existence, though they were contemporaries for more than thirty years, were both in Europe — the one in England, the other in France — for six of those years, and were intimate in friendship or correspondence with some of the same distinguished persons.

In the best work of their several lives they sought to do, and eminently succeeded in doing, what should prove effective of good to their common humanity in the ordinary interests of existence, without distinction of class, and without a view to any personal ends of thrift or glory. Nor is there ground or occasion for any broad distinction in our estimate of the moral character or of the private life of these two eminent men. Neither of them had in his early, nor even in his later, years that rigid purity of principle which insured that all his domestic relations should be such as would admit of record, according to the good New England usage, on the few blank leaves between the Old and the New Testament in the family Bible. There are details concerning both these Benjamins of a sort which their biographers must pass unmentioned, thankful if only they can be referred to foreign soil and foreign customs.

The services of Franklin as a patriotic statesman lift him on a higher pedestal. Yet two widely discordant opinions have been held and expressed as to the general effect on the qualities of nobleness and unworldliness of character, as illustrated in New England, of his calculating, prudential, and thrift-bringing philosophy. If, according to what we shall find was the judgment of one of Benjamin Thompson's most intimate friends, — his eulogist, also, — we shall see reason to admit that he did not really love his fellow-men, and could not yield even his own self-will and conform his own personal habits to the ordinary conditions of sympathetic intercourse, we may be led to recognize all the more gratefully his patient, persistent, and ingenious industry, given in so many ways to ends of true benevolence.

Benjamin Thompson came on both sides of his parentage from the original stock of the first colonists of Massachusetts Bay. When, in his thirty-first year, he had attained such distinction in England as to receive the honor of knighthood from King George III., he was naturally concerned to provide himself with proper armorial bearings, and, if possible, to appropriate such as might already be attached to the name which he bore. He could not have done better than to adopt a device which, as we shall soon see, was the product of his own youthful ingenuity alike in designing and in engraving, and equally characteristic of his nature, circumstances, and prospects in life. But he seems to have forgotten this, and to have aimed higher, in this instance failing in his flight. His emblazoned diploma of arms is now before me in all its original glory and beauty, with its rich adornments, and the proper attestations of Garter and Clarenceux kings in heraldry, and their well-protected seals, enclosed in tin casings. The Knight himself must have furnished the information written on that flowery parchment.

In it he is described as "Son of Benjamin Thompson, late of the Province of Massachusetts Bay, in New England, Gent: deceased, and as of one of the most ancient families in North America; that an island which belonged to his ancestors at the entrance of Boston Harbor, near where the first New England settlement was made, still bears his name; that his ancestors have ever lived in reputable situations in that country where he was born, and have hitherto used the arms of the ancient and respectable family of Thompson, of the county of York, from a constant tradition that they derived their descent from that source," &c.

The new knight was mistaken in this account of himself, so far as relates to the man whose name is still borne by the island in our harbor. That name was derived from one David Thompson, whom the first charter colonists to our bay found already seated here, and who was regarded as an interloper. He belonged to a mysterious class of men, described as the "Old Planters," who occupied many of the headlands and some of the islands of the bay, and could show no rights of possession. This Thompson died in Dorchester before 1638, leaving an infant son.

Before the son of this Thompson had grown to manhood, indeed almost as soon as we hear of the father, the ancestors of the subject of this memoir were already in occupancy on the main-land. The head of the family

Birthplace of Benjamin Thompson, in North Woburn, Massachusetts.   Page 5

here may have come from York, in England, though the fact is not on record. His first paternal ancestor, James Thompson, was of Winthrop's company, and at the age of thirty-seven was in Charlestown, in 1630. He was one of the first settlers of that portion of the original bounds of the town which, running more than ten miles up into the country, was soon set off as a separate precinct under the name of Woburn. Here the family with numerous descendants and branches continued till the birth of our subject, as many that sprung from the first comer do to this day. He himself was a man of worth, position, and trust in an arduous enterprise, being one of the "selectmen" of the town, and he lived nearly to the age of ninety.

Captain Ebenezer Thompson and Hannah Convers were the grandparents, Benjamin Thompson and Ruth Simonds were the father and mother, of our subject ; the mother being the daughter of an officer who performed distinguished service in the French and Indian War, which was in progress at the time of the birth of his eminent grandson. The parents were married in 1752, and went to live at the house of Captain Ebenezer Thompson. Here, under his grandfather's roof, the future Count Rumford was born, March 26, 1753, in the west end of the strong and substantial farm-house which is still standing a few rods south of the meeting-house in North Woburn. This house was, till quite recently, occupied by the Count's first cousin, the widow of Willard Jones.*

The father of our subject died November 7, 1754, in his twenty-sixth year, leaving his wife and her child, hardly twenty months old, to the care and support of

* Sewall's History of Woburn, p. 190, &c.

the grandparents. In March, 1756, when the child was three years old, his widowed mother was married to Josiah Pierce, Jr., of Woburn. Mr. Pierce took his wife and her child to a new home, which, now removed, stood but a short distance from the old homestead, opposite the present conspicuous and venerable Baldwin mansion.

The *Biographie Nouvelle*, in its article on Count Rumford, says that he would have been left in his infancy to absolute destitution, had not his grandfather taken pity on him. The article in the *Encyclopædia Britannica* says that the child's step-father banished him from his mother's house almost in his infancy. Chalmers's Biography substantially repeats the statements. These are drawn from, and are supposed to be warranted by, certain particulars given by M. A. Pictet, in the *Bibliothèque Britannique*. Pictet was an intimate, confidential, and admiring friend of Count Rumford, and has recorded much very interesting information concerning him which can be got from no other source. I shall have occasion by and by to draw largely and gratefully from that information. Meanwhile, it is in place here to say that while M. Pictet was on a visit to England in 1801, he spent several days in the house of Count Rumford, at Brompton Row, as his guest, and was wont to draw from him confidentially particulars of his life, of which he took notes for subsequent publication.

I anticipate the relation of this friendship and its results so far as to translate from Pictet such matter as has been made the basis of the at least over-colored statements that have been referred to. It will be noticed by the error in the first paragraph following, that Pictet, though he might have been a close listener, was not a perfectly accurate reporter of his friend's communications.

"Sir Benjamin Thompson, Count Rumford, whom half Europe takes to be an Englishman, was born in North America in 1753. His family, of English origin, was long settled in New Hampshire, and lived in a place formerly called Rumford, and now Concord, and owned land there before the war of Independence.

"'If the death of my father,' he said to me one day, 'had not, contrary to the order of nature, preceded that of my grandfather, who gave all his property to my uncle, his second son, I should have lived and died an American husbandman. This was a circumstance purely accidental, which, while I was still an infant, decided my destiny in attracting my attention to objects of science. The father of one of my companions, a very respectable minister, and, besides, very enlightened, (by name, Bernard,) gave me his friendship, and, of his own prompting, undertook to instruct me. He taught me algebra, geometry, astronomy, and even the higher mathematics. Before the age of fourteen, I had made sufficient progress in this class of studies to be able without his aid, and even without his knowledge, to calculate and trace rightly the elements of a solar eclipse. We observed it together, and my computation was correct within four seconds. I shall never forget the intense pleasure which this success afforded me, nor the praises which it drew from him. I had been destined for trade, but after a short trial my thirst for knowledge became inextinguishable, and I could not apply myself to anything but my favorite objects of study. I attended the lectures of Dr. Williams, and afterwards those of Dr. Winthrop, at Harvard College, and I made under that happy teacher a sufficiently rapid progress.'

"'But at the age you then were,' said I to him, 'is a young man the master of his own actions? How could you follow so, without opposition, the sort of instinct which carried you towards a vocation so different from that which had been destined for you!'"

"'Ah!' he replied, 'shortly after the death of my father my mother contracted a second marriage, which proved for her a source of misfortunes. A tyrannical husband took me away from my grandfather's house with her. I was then a child; my grandfather, who survived my father only a few months, left me but a very slender subsistence. I was then launched at the right time upon a world which was almost strange to me, and I was obliged to form the habit of thinking and acting for myself, and of depending on myself for a livelihood. My ideas were not yet fixed; one project succeeded another, and perhaps I should have acquired a habit of indecision and inconstancy, perhaps I should have been poor and unhappy all my life, if a woman had not loved me, — if she had not given me a subsistence, a home, an independent fortune.'

"'I married, or, rather, I was married, at the age of nineteen. I espoused the widow of a Colonel Rolfe, daughter of the Rev. Mr. Walker, a highly respectable minister, and one of the first settlers of Rumford. He was already connected with my family. He had made three voyages to England on matters of public interest. He was a very cultivated man, and of a most generous character. He heartily approved of the choice of his daughter, and he himself united our destinies. This excellent man became sincerely attached to me; he directed my studies, he formed my taste, and my position was in every respect the most agreeable that could possibly be imagined.'

" Here a pang of feeling checked him. I dropped the subject till the next day. Such are my notes.

" Unexpected circumstances drew him from this peaceful retreat, and snatched him from those favorite studies which would probably have formed the principal occupation of his life, in order that he might play a part on the great stage of the world, for which he would not seem to have been prepared." *

* Marc Auguste Pictet was born in 1752, in Geneva, where he died in 1825. He was highly distinguished as a philosopher in Natural Science, and as a statesman and man of letters, founder of the Society of Physics at Geneva, and member of the French Institute and the Royal Society. In 1796, with his brother Charles, and

There are several matters in this relation which will call for remark further on. At present we are concerned with those sentences in it which reflect upon Thompson's relatives, especially his step-father, — charges of neglecting, wronging, or ill-treating him in his early years. Baron Cuvier, who was a very intimate friend of Count Rumford in the latter part of his life, and who delivered an *eloge* upon him before the French Institute, said in it something very similar to the above, the authority for which must be supposed to be either a communication from the Count himself, or the assertions made by Pictet.

Cuvier said: "Rumford has informed us himself that he should probably have remained in the modest condition of his ancestors if the little fortune which they had to leave him had not been lost during his infancy. Thus, like many other men of genius, a misfortune in early life was the cause of his subsequent reputation. His father died young. A second husband removed him from the care of his mother, and his grandfather, from whom he had everything to expect, had given all he possessed to a younger son, leaving his grandson almost penniless. Nothing could be more likely than such a destitute condition to induce a premature display of talent,"* &c.

Now, if these statements and imputations really rest upon positive assertions made by him whom they con-

---

F. G. Maurice, he planned and edited the voluminous periodical work, the *Bibliothèque Britannique*, which, in 1816, became the *Bibliothèque Universelle*.

His ten letters, embracing his tour in England, Ireland, and Scotland, were republished in a volume at Geneva. The above extract in the text is translated from his ninth letter, dated London, 15th August, 1801. (Vol. XIX. *Science et Arts.*)

* Cuvier's Eloge. A translation of this Eloge appeared in the Boston Daily Advertiser of the 18th and 19th October, 1815.

cern, it might seem unnecessary and unreasonable to go behind them and dispute them. Yet we know for a certainty that they do contain errors, and there is room for supposing that Count Rumford's friends might have misunderstood him, and that, being both of them Frenchmen, they may themselves have erred in a matter of sentiment, by exaggerated expressions. It is possible, too, that, looking back from his state of popular celebrity, comfort, and affluence, the Count himself may have seen the hardships of his early years as unrelieved.

It is certain, however, that there is exaggeration or over-coloring in what is reported as having come from his lips. Young Thompson was born in the same state of life, and to the same conditions of labor and personal dependence, as those of his ancestors for several generations, who, tilling their acres, cutting their lumber and fuel, and working at their varied trades, had won the means of a frugal subsistence, and maintained the respectable position of New England yeomen. True, it was a misfortune to him that he lost his father before he was two years old. But he had an excellent mother, who never neglected him, but seems to have treated him with a redoubled love. His own letters to her from abroad, after he had achieved his great distinctions, — letters continued to the close of her life and full of affection, — and the munificent pecuniary provision which he made for her, will be duly recognized in the course of this biography, as showing the tender and grateful regard of the son for the mother.

As to the "tyrannical step-father" who "removed him from the care of his mother," I have sought in vain for a shadow of a reason to justify the harsh epithet, and have evidence·that disposes of the other charge as purely fictitious. Josiah Pierce, Jr., appears to have been a kind and faithful husband, and, as has been said, he took his wife's child with her to a new home. They had afterwards four children. Her first child by this new husband, Josiah Pierce, 3d, about four years younger than Benjamin Thompson, grew up with him as a playmate, and in after life corresponded with him. The son of this half-brother of Thompson, the Hon. Josiah Pierce, of Gorham, Me., had heard nothing from his father that would warrant an imputation of the sort we are considering.*

It was not usual among the self-respecting groups of New England households, — the staple of the thrifty country towns of those days, where there was a minister that had authority, where neighbors had mutual oversight, and the law and its officers had cognizance of private relations now released from its control, — it was not usual that a fatherless child should be wronged in property rights, or even in domestic privileges. Indeed, so far was young Thompson from being neglected or misused in his early years, that it seems from the facts to be now related of his boyhood and apprenticeship, he was, for one in his place, unusually favored by friends and by fostering help. There were evidently many of his kindred, and of those who were not of his kindred, who were interested for him. It is to be considered,

* In Volume XXXIII. of Silliman's American Journal of Science, &c., p. 11, is a "Sketch of the early History of Count Rumford, in which some of the Mistakes of Cuvier and others of his Biographers are corrected"; by John Johnston. Read before the Natural History Society of the Wesleyan University, June 30, 1837. The writer does correct some mistakes, but makes others. This article introduces a letter from the Hon. Josiah Pierce, in which he says, " My grandmother (Rumford's mother) lived in my father's house for seven years previous to her death, which occurred June 11, 1811."

too, that he exercised the patience and sympathy of his friends somewhat severely, till the bent of his genius, asserting and proving itself, offered a more favorable interpretation of what had appeared in him as fickleness, inconstancy of purpose, and even a determined unwillingness to apply himself to any routine and rewarding work.

It may be as well to mention here one of the earliest and most valued and steadfast friends of young Thompson, his townsman and neighbor, and confidential intimate in boyhood, though his senior, the sharer with him in his early scientific tastes and pursuits, his supporter in the severe trouble which attended his opening manhood, and his correspondent and agent while abroad. This was the late Colonel Loammi Baldwin, of Woburn, a very distinguished officer in the early part of the Revolutionary War, and afterwards the most eminent engineer in our country, whose enterprise in the Middlesex Canal was the great work of its time. He was born January 10, 1744, nine years before Thompson, and died October 20, 1807, nearly seven years before his friend. It is to his interest in young Thompson from his boyhood, which led him to preserve papers of that period, as well as those which related to his mature years, that the biographer is very largely indebted. His only surviving son, George Rumford Baldwin, Esq., also a very eminent civil engineer, has kindly allowed me the free use of these papers of his father.

The paternal grandfather, his maternal uncle, Joshua Simonds, the step-father, and the maternal grandfather, successively the responsible guardians of the child and youth, had in view, as a matter of course, to educate and train him for their own respectable way of living, leaving to his own development and use of opportunities the chance of rising, as so many children around him and under similar circumstances with himself had risen, to any more conspicuous position. The lands which had been allotted to his progenitor, in the first settlement of the town, had of course been divided from time to time in the partition of his estate among the steadily increasing number of his descendants. But some of them had added to their respective shares, and clearing and tillage had made portions of the original acres more valuable than the whole had been. The child's grandfather had died previously to October 16, 1755, for the agreement among his heirs, including that of the guardians of a minor son and of Benjamin, the grandson, bears that date.

By this instrument, it was provided that his mother, Ruth, should have the improvement "of one half of the garden at the west end" of the house where her child and she had been living with his grandparents, and "the privilege of land to raise beans for sauce." The guardian of her child's minor uncle was likewise to "give the said widow eighty weight of beef, eight bushels of rye, two bushels of malt, and two barrels of cider for the present year"; while she also had the "liberty of gathering apples to bake, and three bushels of apples for winter, yearly and every year." (See Appendix.)

When the boy was taken to his step-father's, Mr. Pierce, according to the custom of the time and community, covenanted with the child's guardian for an allowance of two shillings and fivepence, old tenor, per week, for maintenance, till his step-son should be seven years old.

If Pictet and Cuvier received an impression from the

Count that any wrong had been done him in his childhood by his grandfather's unequal distribution of his
estate, their informant failed to explain to them the different usage which prevailed in New England from that
followed in Europe in the partition of property on the
decease of the head of a family.

The Rev. Samuel Sewall, the faithful historian of the
town of Woburn, coming of a family which has given
three chief-justices to Massachusetts, might well be
supposed to hold the laws of his native State in reverent
regard. His impartiality, therefore, is to be recognized
in the fidelity with which he represents the shortcom-
ings of that town, in some periods of its history, in
evading the statutes which so carefully provided for the
interests of a common-school education for all children.
But at the time in which Benjamin Thompson was in
his early pupilage, the town was particularly favored in
having for a village school-teacher an accomplished and
faithful man, Mr. John Fowle, a graduate of Harvard
College in 1747. It is evident from the handwriting
of Thompson when he was only thirteen years of age,
from the spelling and the almost faultless grammatical
expressions in his letters and compositions before he
had reached manhood, and from his skill in accounts,
that he had not only had remarkable native powers, but
that he had also been the subject of careful and thorough
training. His chirography was clear, strong, and elegant, and it remained the same through his life. Nor
was his style one whit inferior in terseness, exactness,
and simplicity to that of Franklin. The high authority
of Mr. George B. Emerson has been given for the assertion, that, under the mode of instruction through which
young Thompson and his contemporaries enjoyed the

opportunities provided by law in Massachusetts, there was afforded a better training, and to better results, than are realized now from all our elaborate provisions for public education.*

Thompson, like other youths, was entitled only to a "grammar-school education," that is, to be taught to read, to spell, to write, to construct sentences grammatically, and to understand the rules of arithmetic. The range was a narrow one compared with that which is professedly covered now. But the lessons that were taught, and the way of teaching them, were such as to quicken the faculties, and to excite, if it was latent in the pupil, a desire for more, while affording him help to attain it. There was also an able and faithful minister in young Thompson's parish, the Rev. Josiah Sherman, a part of whose official duty it was to exercise a supervision over the village school and over fatherless children. There were no manuals for English grammar in those days, and as a substitute was found in a Latin text-book, a bright pupil incidentally acquired "an entrance" into that tongue.

Thompson indicated from his early years an inconstancy and indifference to the homely routine tasks and the rural employments which were required of him, while, at the same time, he exhibited an intense mental activity, a spirit of ingenuity and inventiveness, and was found seeking for amusement in things which afterwards proved to lead him to the profitable and beneficent occupations of his mature life. He showed a particular ardor for arithmetic and mathematics, and it was remembered of him, afterwards, that his playtime, and some of

* Lecture in Historical Course before the Lowell Institute, on "Education in Massachusetts: Early Legislation and History," February 16, 1860.

his proper worktime, had been given to ingenious mechanical contrivances, soon leading to a curious interest in the principles of mechanics and natural philosophy. His guardians, of course, undertook, as their responsibility, to engage him in the practical drudgery of country life, that he might be fitted for work which would promise direct results. So far as they found they were likely to fail in this purpose, they would regard him as indolent, flighty, and unpromising.

He was also, for a while, a pupil in a school at Byfield, under the charge of a family connection. In 1764, when he was eleven years old, he was for a time put under the tuition of Mr. Hill, an able teacher in Medford, a town adjoining Woburn. Thus it would seem that the youth, for one born in his sphere of life, was not neglected. There is abundant evidence, likewise, that many kind friends were interested in him before he began to draw others to serve his aims. Young Baldwin alone was invaluable to him.

It being plain to his guardians that he was either too good or too unpromising material out of which to make a thriving farmer, the alternative was to train him for a merchant or trader. To this end, on October 14, 1766, he was apprenticed to Mr. John Appleton of Salem, an importer of British goods, and a dealer in all the miscellaneous articles which formed the stock of a warehouse in so flourishing and rich a place as, that town then was. Mr. Appleton was a man of great respectability, and did a large business. I have before me a bill for goods bought from the store, receipted by Thompson when he was fourteen years old, which, for grace of penmanship, mercantile style, and business-like signature, might be regarded as proving that the youth had found his proper position. He lived in his master's family as a member of the household. But there is something better than tradition to warrant the inference that his heart was not in his employment. Instead of watching for customers over the counter, he was apt to busy himself with tools and instruments which he had hid away under it. And, when the sound would not betray him, he ventured to play his fiddle, — for he was a skilful musician, and passionately fond of music of every kind.

The following document, relating to the apprenticeship of young Thompson with Mr. Appleton, has a claim to be introduced here on that ground, if not, also, as an illustration of the exercise of the right of private judgment in the art of spelling and in the use of capital letters.*

"To Mr. John Appleton in Salam.

Medford, June ye 26: 1767.

"Mr Appelton, Sir, these lins left us all well, as I hope they may find you. Thompson has wrote to me diuers times about his affairs, and he saith he is Contented, and hath Sum priuyledge of trade for him Self, and that you, Sir, would let him haue Sum fish to Ship, if I would send you an order for them : acordingly I send one inclosed. Pray Sir, if he Shipeth any thing, See it insured in a proper manner. Sir, if Den Sends to Sea and dont make Pay, let me haue Notis of it. Pray, Sir, tak Spechal Care about the Company he keeps, and I should be glad to know the General Run of his behauour, both as to trade and Company : and if you will fauour me with an acount there of, I shal tak is as fauour. As to his Cloath, I Exspect his

---

* The original manuscript was communicated at a meeting of the Massachusetts Historical Society, in October, 1864, by the Amherst Librarian, the late Dr. John Appleton, to whose grandfather it was addressed, and is published in the Proceedings of the Society for that year, pp. 4, 5.

Mother will giue me and a Count there of. Sir, I hear you liue
Shingel as yet, but dont Exspect it will be so long. Sir, Remem-
ber me to Ben? and to M? West. No more at this time. So
I Remain yours to Serue,

     "JOSHUA SIMONDS."

John Sparhawk Appleton, of Salem, the son of the
gentleman to whom the above letter is addressed, has
appended to it the following: "Benjamin Thompson
(afterwards Sir Benjamin, and Count Rumford) was
apprenticed to John Appleton, merchant, Salem, October 14, 1766, with whom he continued until about
October, 1769, as appears by some memoranda sent
to Professor Levi Hedge, Cambridge, this 25th March,
1817."

In a memoir of the late Francis Peabody, President
of the Essex Institute in Salem, communicated to
that body by Hon. C. W. Upham, a very interesting
reference is made to the temporary residence of young
Thompson in that town. Mr. Upham traces that very
laborious and flourishing institution back through a
series of organizations, all having scientific and literary
objects in view, to a social evening club, formed about
the middle of the last century to promote literature and
philosophy. Beginning at that date, Salem and its
neighborhood was the home of many prominent men,
distinguished for enterprise in commerce and for attainments in law, science, and manufacturing skill, whose
names are now famous in the history of the past. Mr.
Upham suggests that the lad of thirteen years, from the
farm in Woburn, must have found, from his genius
for observation and the improvement of opportunities,
some efficient impulse and help for his future course
in the place of his service. His employer, though

keeping a retail variety-store, after the style of that day, under the same roof with his dwelling-place, on the south side of Essex Street, was also engaged in commercial pursuits. His apprentice had open eyes and ears for all that was to be seen or heard, in store or house, from customers or visitors; and his mechanical and chemical propensities were well known. Doubtless he was employed by others in the preparation of the fireworks, in glorification over the repeal of the Stamp Act, in the composition of which he met with so severe an accident. The properties of gunpowder were then, as they continued to be, a favorite matter for his studies and experiments.[*]

In his confidential relation of the incidents of his early life to Monsieur Pictet, it will be remembered that the Count, as reported by his friend, spoke of a very respectable and enlightened minister, "Mr. Bernard," who gave him such efficient patronage and such impulse in his mathematical studies. Many who have followed with interest the career of Thompson, meeting with this name of Bernard, copied from Pictet's statement in sketches of Count Rumford's life, supposing it to refer to the minister of his native town, have been puzzled in identifying him. The name, in his case, as in that of one of our royal Governors, Sir Francis Bernard, and of his son Thomas, a very intimate friend of Rumford's, in London, was confounded with Barnard. It was in Salem, not in Woburn, that young Thompson found this friend. The Rev. Thomas Barnard was the minister of the First Church in Salem from 1755 to 1776. His eldest son, Thomas, after graduating from Harvard in 1766, taught school in Salem, and was

ordained as minister of the North Church there in
1773. Both of these ministers were men of marked
ability and fine scholarship, took part in founding or
purchasing, successively, the "Social Library," the
" Kirwan Library," and the " Philosophical Library,"
represented now by the "Salem Athenæum," and gave
much attention to scientific pursuits. The Appleton
family, and of course young Thompson as a member of
it, worshipped with the congregation of the elder Barnard. The son coming to teach in Salem in the same
year in which Thompson began his apprenticeship there,
and having a younger brother who was one of Thompson's "companions," we find in the facts a full explanation of the assertion of M. Pictet. Thompson was
a handsome and engaging youth, of evidently bright
faculties. The interest of his minister was thus drawn
to him, and he probably received the aid and encouragement of the new teacher. It was thus that he was
" taught algebra, geometry, astronomy, and even the
higher mathematics," so that before the age of fifteen
he was able to calculate an eclipse.

The subjoined letter, from the boy to his friend in
Woburn, contains one word of faulty grammar, which,
as unusual with him, is to be accounted as a slip of the
pen : —

"SALEM, Nov. 12, 1768.

" DEAR SIR, — I did not go to Mr. Derby's after them Pis
tols till yesterday, but he had not got them, having sent them
home some time before (for they were not his). But he told me
another man had got them who lived up in Danvers about a
mile. Upon this I rode up to this man, but he had sent them
home to the owner, about two or three days before, who lives at
Beverly. This man saith that the price is four dollars. The
Barrels are very good, the locks but ordinary. If you conclude

BOOK-PLATE ENGRAVED BY BENJAMIN THOMPSON ABOUT 1768

[PAGE 21]

to take them, I can get them at that price, but I don't think much under.

Votre tres humble Serviteur, Monsieur,
B: THOMPSON.

To MR. LOAMMI BALDWIN, *Woburn.*

We must regard the perseverance of the youth in going, in his spare time, in so many directions, to hunt up "them Pistols," as an offset to the inelegance in describing them.

His skill and ingenuity, which are said to have been remarkable in this exercise of them, were constantly put to use by the boys of his acquaintance, in engraving upon the handles of their knives and other implements the names and certain devices of their owners. Doubtless, also, his facility in this work was improved by elder persons in marking silver. Indeed, he was an able and accurate draughtsman, and an accomplished designer. I have before me a copy of an engraved plate, wrought by him when in Salem, three inches and five eighths long by two inches and seven eighths broad. From the lopped bough on one side of an old and topless tree is suspended a shield, and from a green shoot on the other side a square and compass. The shield, inscribed " B. Thompson," is beautifully proportioned, and traced with all the heraldic accompaniments. On the upper right-hand corner an open eye is looking from a quarter of a radiated sun, below which is a ship in full sail. Beneath the shield is a young lion couched, an open and a closed book, a sword, and another compass. This work seems to have been intended for a book-plate.

Like other geniuses in mechanical inventions, excepting only that, being brighter than many of them,

Thompson's delusions came in early youth and were sooner outgrown in manhood, he experimented upon the desideratum of a machine which should realize "perpetual motion." He even thought he had been successful in contriving one. He had the privilege of making occasional visits to his family in Woburn, generally of brief duration, and his conveyance was necessarily upon his own feet, and the time taken was not to interfere with his duties to his employer. His friend Baldwin records * that Thompson walked one night from Salem to Woburn, in order to show him parts of this wonderful instrument of wheels, and to explain its mechanical powers. The friend, however, adds that he "was never able to gain any information concerning the principles upon which it was expected to act."

Though the young apprentice was well understood in Salem to be a dabbler in a great many pursuits and occupations, with tools and experiments and mechanics and chemistry, which did not appertain to his calling with his employer, it does not appear that he failed of rendering him due service. He undoubtedly had an aversion to the business, while compelled by supposed necessity to commit himself to it. His apprenticeship covered a period of intense popular excitement over the preliminary events leading to the Revolutionary War. The youth must have heard the heated discussions of the time, and been more or less initiated understandingly into the merits of the issue which was soon to open, disastrously as it at first seemed to bear on his own personal experience. His employer was among the signers of the non-importation agreement, by which the mercantile and trading class in the Province sought to

* In the "Literary Miscellany," Cambridge. Vol. I. pp. 353-361.

express their resentment, in conformity with the popular feeling against the oppressive measures of the British Ministry. This agreement, which the watchful patriots took care should be strictly kept even by those who might have reluctantly entered into it, of course so affected the business of Mr. Appleton as to make the services of Thompson less necessary to him. In the mean while the boy, more engaged, we must venture to say, in his scientific experimenting than in the cause of demonstrative patriotism, came very near to losing his eyesight, if not also his life, by an alarming accident. He had undertaken to prepare some fireworks for use in a public jubilation over the news of the repeal of the Stamp Act. While grinding his materials in a mortar, a terrific explosion, probably caused by some grains of sand in the compound, involved his head, hands, and breast in its fearful consequences. He suffered a long confinement and much pain, and was regarded as very fortunate in escaping permanent injury.

The following correspondence shows that young Thompson was at home, probably in a state of convalescence, at the time of its date : —

"WOBURN, Aug. 14, 1769

" MR. LOAMMI BALDWIN,

" SIR, — Please to give the Direction of the Rays of Light from a Luminous Body to an Opake, and the Reflection from the Opake Body to another equally Dense and Opake; viz! the Direction of the Rays of the Luminous Body to that of the Opake, and the direction of rays by reflection to the other opake Body.   Your, &c.

" BENJ! THOMPSON.

" N. B. From the Sun to the Earth, Reflected to the Moon at an angle of 40 Degrees."

"WOBURN, Aug! 16, 1769.

" MR. BENJ. THOMPSON,

" SIR, — It is almost impossible to describe the directions the rays pass. Suppose one was at the Equinoctial Line, at twelve o'clock. At that place then I imagine that the rays of the Sun would pass directly straight to the eye of the beholder. But suppose the Sun to be just arising, then I imagine that the rays would pass in a curve line, and so grow straighter as it rises higher in the horizon. The reason is, I conjecture, owing to the Vapours that ascend out of the earth. I would prove it thus. Take a bowl and put a dollar in it, and then carefully filling it with fair water, till it seems to be heaped as it will do if the brim was dry, and go off to a distance that brings your eye level with the top of the bowl, and you can see the dollar in the bottom of the bowl; and that air nigh the ground is something of the same nature is the opinion of

" Your Humble Servant,

" LOAMMI BALDWIN."

" WOBURN, August 16th, 1769.

" MR. LOAMMI BALDWIN,

" SIR, — Please to inform me in what manner fire operates upon Clay, to change the Colour, from the Natural Colour to red, and from red to black, &c.; and how it operates upon Silver, to change it to Blue.

" I am your most Humble, and Obedient Servant,

" BENJͣ THOMPSON.

" God save the King."

" WOBURN, Aug! 1769.

" MR. LOAMMI BALDWIN

" SIR, — Please to give the Nature, Essence, Beginning of Existence, and Rise of the Wind in General, with the whole Theory thereof, so as to be able to answer all Questions relative thereto.

" Yours,

" BENJ. THOMPSON."

The following is written on the back of the above: —

"WOBURN, Aug! 11th, 1769.

"SIR, — There was but few beings (for Inhabitants of this world) created before the airy Element was: so it has not been transmitted down to us how the Great Creator formed the matter thereof. So I shall leave it till I am asked only the Natural cause, and why it blows so many ways in so short a time as it does."

In the autumn of 1769, Thompson was sent to Boston, to engage in a business similar to that which he had been learning at Salem. He was put as an apprentice clerk with Mr. Hopestill Capen, a dry-goods dealer. Here he had as a fellow-apprentice the late Samuel Parkman, who became, after the Revolutionary War, one of the largest and richest merchants of Boston. Thompson records the beginning of his attendance on a French school, held in the evening, on October 27, 1769. He remained in this situation till the spring of the following year, and would appear then to have left it from the falling off in the business of his employer, who had also entered into the non-importation agreement.

I have seen it stated as a matter of fact by one of Count Rumford's biographers, in a sketch already referred to,* that young Thompson, while in the employ of Mr. Capen, was present on the 5th of March, 1770, on the occasion known to fame and popular oratory as "the Boston Massacre"; when the hated soldiery, representing, in our capital, the cause of tyranny, goaded by the jeers and insults of a street crowd of boys and men, fired into it and killed four victims. It is said that Thompson "was there found, sword in hand, among the most eager to attack those whom he considered the

* American Journal of Science. Vol. XXXIII. p. 14.

enemies of his country." There may be tradition to authenticate this statement, which came as from a trustworthy source to the writer of it. But I know of no documentary attestation of it.

Fortunately there is preserved a very interesting and suggestive relic, which Mr. Thompson left behind him in his abrupt departure from his home, for reasons soon to be stated, and which is very significant of the tastes and occupations of his youth. It is a memorandum-book of substantial linen paper, with parchment cover and a brass clasp, some leaves of which have been cut out, thirty-six of those it may have originally contained being still left. This memento is now before me; and the fragmentary information and the curious matter of its contents may be turned to a profitable account. *

The contents of the book are, as will be seen, very miscellaneous, giving tokens of the bent of genius of the youth, with anticipatory hints of the characteristics and occupations of his mature life. The boy in this case was certainly father of the man. About fifty of the seventy-two remaining pages have upon them some sketch or record; the others, unfortunately, being blank. Twenty of the pages at the beginning and the end of the book contain a most extraordinary variety of sketches and etchings with pen and pencil, some of them being colored by paints. A portion of these are but rude and of faint outlines; but others of them give evidence of a skilful and accurate draughtsman, with an eye for proportions, with correct perspective and a cunning hand. There are caricature sketches of human physiognomy and forms, — men and women, young and

* The book belongs to Joseph B. Walker, Esq., of Concord, N. H., a descendant of the father of Count Rumford's first wife. I am indebted to Mr. Walker's courtesy for the privilege of using the book, as for other valued favors.

old, grave and gay ; a full figure, with laughing countenance, strongly marked, and outstretched arm, entitled
" My Dear Democritus "; the figure of a wigged and
spectacled preacher, which, it is to be feared, represents,
not reverently, the Rev. Mr. Sherman of Woburn, in
whose meeting-house, it will appear, he paid the hire of
a seat ; an old-fashioned gentleman in grotesque courtly
costume, with cane, tie wig, and plumed hat, entitled
" Harry Modiste," pointed at from behind by a railing
jester, asking, " Ha! you red nose, how will you sell
your wig? by the Cord?" — a winged cherub; a female
form with an ass's head, holding an open hymn-book,
singing; a swordsman, and two fencers in attitude.
There is a sketch of an old-fashioned corner dwelling-
house, with a shop under it, which may be that of
Mr. Appleton in Salem, or of Mr. Capen in Boston.
There is an etching of a group, called " A Council of
State," including a jackass and twelve human heads,

with a variety of most expressive caricature features.
In this sketch the roguish artist seems to have anticipated an innovation of our own times, as he has introduced both a young and an old woman into this Council, with two other faces that may belong to either sex.
There is an admirably drawn psalm-book, open and
showing the notes of a tune, and a well-shaded scroll.
There are boats and ships, a table with bottles and
glasses, pistols, Indian tomahawks, and human bones.
Here is indeed a boyish medley, but indicating a
wonderful versatility.

The earliest entry of a more serious character is
without date, and contains a recipe for making rockets, &c., giving the proportions of powder, sulphur,
saltpetre, and charcoal for rockets of different sizes,
with the following directions, accompanied by ink-
drawn sketches : —

"The Composition for middle-size Rockets, may serve for
Serpents and for Raining Fire. Composition for Stars — 4 oz.
Saltpetre, 2 oz. Brimstone, 2 oz. Powder, ground fine and made
into a paste, and rolled into little balls, and then on dry gunpowder dust, then dry them. The Tail of the Rocket should be
seven times as long as the Rocket itself.

"A Compound Rocket has a head filled with Serpents,
Crackers, Stars, &c., or fire-balls, or any combustibles, having
a piece of leather covered over the top of the Rocket, with
small holes burnt through the middle of it, to let the fire
through to the Crackers, &c., having some dry ground powder
in the head.

"A double Rocket is one placed above another, with goose
quill placed from the lower to the bottom of the upper one.

"To make a Report: When you have filled the Rocket
within about two inches of the top, thrust down a piece of
leather about the bigness of the hole of the Rocket, and punch

it full of holes in the middle with a bodkin, then strew a little dust of powder ground fine, and fill the rest up with unground powder, and stop up the remaining part with leather or paper, and stop it up."

The recipe closes with the somewhat irrelevant reflection: " Love is a Noble Passion of the Mind. LOVE."

The first entry in the book that bears a date is as follows : " Boston, October 27th, 1769. This evening entered French School to Learn the French Language, at six pounds, fifteen shillings, Old Tenor, *per* Quarter Anni, to go every evening except Sunday; deducting the time I am absent." This is followed by a table of dates reaching through November, and showing ten occasions of absence to eighteen of attendance. Thompson was then in his seventeenth year, and an apprentice to Hopestill Capen in the dry-goods trade in Boston. He records the purchase, on December 21, 1769, of two and a half yards of black cloth, and his indebtedness to Hiram Thompson, his uncle, for rent of a part of a pew from August 1, 1770. He had a settlement with this kinsman on November 11, 1771, offsetting pew-rent and the use of a horse to Reading and Boston by charges against Hiram for cutting and carting fire-wood. He had similar transactions in fuel with his step-father, Josiah Pierce, and with James Snow. His loads were generally small ones, seldom more than half a cord each, showing that while he needed thus to earn money, he did not like any long job of the kind. He received a pound, old tenor, per cord. On April 6, 1771, he made a contract with Abraham Alexander to cut and cord for him seven or eight cords at nine shillings per cord.

These economical entries are very pleasantly diversified by the following " Directions for the Back Sword ": —

"1. To put yourself in a proper posture of Defence, viz!
hold your Sword firm in your Right hand, with your point
elevated as high as your Antagonist's head, and your hilt a
little depressed, bringing your sword to range with your Antagonist's body and with his eyes: then step forward with your
right foot about a foot, forming a square with your two feet:
then stand upright and take your distance, just so as to touch
your Antagonist's breast: then bend your left knee, which will
bring your body in a proper Posture of Defence." (From Mr.
McAlpine).

This is illustrated by a sketch in ink of two fashionable combatants engaged in the exercise.

The following entry carries much interest with it : —

*" An Account of what Expence I have been at towards getting an
Electrical Machine.*

		£	s.	d.
" 1771.	July.— ½ pd. brass wyer	0	5	0
	1 yd. Iron wyer		1	3
	1 pd. 7 oz. Pewter to make bullets, &c.			
	pd. Cowdry for 3 bells	1	10	0
Aug.	To Baldwin's Horse to Reading.			
" 12	To Cash paid for old Brass,	0	9	3
	To 1 Book Brass Leaf	0	2	6
" 16	To Cash paid for 1 yd Brass wyer	0	2	6
do	1 book Leaf Brass	0	2	6
do	2 Oil Bottles	0	5	3
do	½ pd. Copper Filelings	0	2	6
do	½ oz. Silver Brons	0	9	0
do	1½ oz. Shell Lac	0	7	6

```
                                                              £   s   d
1771.  Aug.ᵗ 16 To Cash ½ gill Laquer                         o   5   o
               do      1 Varnishing Brush          .          o   3   o
               do      3 oz.ᵗ Aqua Fortis                     o   7   6
          To 2 phials, 1 for Laquer, the other for
               Aqua Fortis                                    o   2   6
     "   23 Paid for Mr. R. Baldwin's horse to go to
               Cowdry for Brass Work                          o   4   6
          To Stuff to make a Wheel,
               p.ᵈ             LOAMMI BALDWIN."
```

Young Thompson at this time began the study of medicine with Dr. Hay.

A debit and credit account is then opened with Dr. John Hay, of Woburn, beginning in February, 1771. Young Thompson credits the Doctor for a pair of leather.gloves, for Mrs. Hay's knitting him a pair of stockings, for a small quantity of gum benzoine, and " By my Board, from Dec.ᵗ 15th, 1770, to June 15th, 1772, at 40 Shillings, Old Tenor, *per* Week, being 78 Weeks, — £156 o. o." This indebtedness of the young medical pupil is offset to the amount of £108 by as promiscuous and miscellaneous a list of materials in payment as ever found entry on the ledger of a country variety-store, or in barter traffic. Small sums of cash, in eight payments, not amounting in the aggregate to two pounds, are interspersed with considerations of this sort, leading us to marvel over the ingenuity of young Thompson in gathering resources:

" To Ivory for Smoke Machine: parcels of Butter, Coffee, Sugar and Tea; parcels of various drugs, camphor, contryerva, gum benzoine, arsenic, calomel and rhubarb: one half a white sheep skin: leather: brass wire; white oak timber: to sundry lots of wood; to other lots ' delivered while I was at Wilmington, and left by me when I was at Wilmington the last time ': ' to a Blue Huzza Cloak bought of Zebediah Wyman, and paid for by fifteen and a half cords of wood': a pair of knee buckles: a Chirurgical Knife: 'to a Cistern (a Musical Instrument),' and 'to the Time I have been absent from your house, nineteen weeks at Forty Shillings: and to the time my Mother washed for me.'"

Two periods of absence were doubtless those in which the youth was replenishing his funds by keeping school at Wilmington and Bradford, as appears by the following entry on another page.

"*Time of my Absence from Board at Dr. Hays.*

"From June the 12th, 1771 To—— whilest I was at Cambridge attending Mr. Winthrop's Lectures. From Dec! the 9th, 1771, to Feb! the 5th, 1772, keeping School at Wilmington. From March the —, 1772, to April —, 1772, six weeks and three days, keeping School. On a Journey to Pepperell, three days. On a Journey to Bradford, June the 2d, 1772, absent from Monday morning, before Breakfast, to Friday Night after Supper."

These entries indicate the frugality and the rigid conditions of scrupulous economy and careful calculation by which the youth in the period of his pupilage was compelled to adjust his expenses to his means, while he was dependent upon his own earnings.

Another entry, without date, acquaints us with the exertion and effort on his own part, added to the outlay for materials above transcribed, which he devoted to the construction of his electrical machine.

"*An Account of what Work I have done towards Getting an Electrical Machine.*

"Two or three days work making Wheele.

"One half days work making pattern for Small Conductor.

"Making pattern for Electrometer.

"One half day and a horse from hence to B. Tays, then to W. Youngs, from thence to Icb! Richardsons, to try to get Machine made.

" Four Journeys down to Ich? Richardsons Shop.

" Three Journeys to Cowdreys.

" One Journey to Boston, Aug⁴ 16th, as I think."

A heading is made over a column for the entry of the pecuniary estimate of these specifications, but no sums are set down. It would have interested us to be told what valuation he fixed for a day of his own time.

But young Thompson was at this time a student of medicine and anatomy. The article devoted to him as Count Rumford, in the *Nouvelle Biographie Générale*, very properly describes him before he left this country as " Chimiste et Physicien [Physicist] Américain." The memorandum-book has its full share of entries recognizing his interest and his devotion to the professional studies for which he was making his home with Dr. Hay. Besides a few entries in cipher which may be regarded as containing professional secrets, there are medical recipes, in the approved cabalistic style, for the composition of doses, pills, and clysters. The ingredients of a special preparation are set down as " for Phillis Walker," in which assafœtida enters alike at the beginning and at the end. As these recipes have doubtless been very much improved upon; it is hardly advisable to copy them here. The pupil's interest and skill in anatomy are attested by an all too faithful drawing of the body of a malformed and monstrous infant, with a whole page of minute description "of the following Cut," dated April 16th, 1771, — "a Club-foot," " a Compleat hare-lip," and " toes growing in pairs," being the least revolting among the aberrations noted.

An undated entry gives the following arrangement for the disposal of his time during each period of twenty-four hours. Beginning at eleven o'clock at night, —

" From eleven to six, Sleep. Get up at Six o'clock and wash my hands and face. From Six to eight, exercise one half and study one half. From eight till ten, Breakfast, Attend Prayers, &c. From ten to twelve, Study all the time. From twelve to one, Dine, &c. From one to four, study constantly. From four to five, Relieve my mind by some Diversion or Exercise. From five till Bedtime, follow what my inclination leads me to ; whether it be to go abroad, or stay at home and read either Anatomy, Physic, or Chemistry, or any other book I want to Peruse."

This is followed by the ensuing account of his occupations on each week-day for two weeks.

" Monday and Tuesday, Anatomy. Wednesday, Institutes of Physic. Thursday, Surgery. Friday, Chemistry, with the Materia Medica. Saturday, Physic one half, and Surgery one half.

" Monday, Anatomy. Tuesday, Anatomy one half, and Surgery one half. Wednesday, Surgery. Thursday, Institutes of Physic. Friday, Physic. Saturday, Chemistry with the Materia Medica."

When any man, young or old, thus methodically disposes the days of the week and the hours of each day with reference to systematic study and culture in pursuing various branches of knowledge, not neglectful of the laws of health and the necessity of relaxation, we may be sure that he will make, if he be not already, a true philosopher. The fact, also, that Thompson had to teach while he was himself learning, would make it certain that he would do both to better purpose. In boarding around for short periods with successive families in many country towns, — the fashion for the district schoolmaster of those times, — he largely increased his knowledge of men and things.

The Hon. C. W. Upham, of Salem, informs me,

that when in 1818-19, as a college student, he taught
school in a district of Wilmington, following Thompson at a distance of forty-seven or forty-eight years,
the oldest people there very well remembered their
distinguished and eccentric master of the former age.
Strange stories were told of certain athletic and gymnastic
performances and feats, not to say tricks, in which he
sometimes exercised himself and his scholars, within the
walls as well as outside. In the winter of 1770, Thompson was confined five weeks with a fever.

Going back a little from some of the later contents
of these memoranda, particular reference must be made
to the envied privilege which young Thompson enjoyed
in attending some of the scientific lectures at Harvard
College. He refers to his temporary absence from Dr.
Hay's as beginning June 12, 1771, on occasion of
such attendance, and he seems to imply that he lived,
during the interval, at Cambridge. He may have found
lodging and board there for a short time. But it has
always been affirmed that so ardent was his desire thus
to gratify his scientific passion, that, while compelled to
make his visits to Cambridge consistent with duties in
Woburn, he walked, with his friend Baldwin, over the
distance, some eight miles or more. Some time before this, Mr. Baldwin, not being a student at the
College, had sought, and through the interest of a
friend in Boston had obtained, the privilege of attending upon Professor Winthrop's lectures there. He
secured the same privilege for his younger friend. We
may be sure that among those whose names were on the
class-lists there were none who more valued this rich
opportunity, or turned it to better account, than these

volunteers. It was in summer weather, and the walk, if a long one, was agreeable, — by shady roads and green fields, and easy hills and pleasant ponds. When the friends returned home, they were in the habit of repeating the experiments which they had witnessed, and of trying others, with rude apparatus of their own contrivance. It was as a grateful return for the favors he had thus enjoyed at the College that Count Rumford gave to it the endowment which founded the Professorship that bears his name, to be fitly mentioned in its proper place.

Pictet must have again misapprehended his friend as mentioning " Dr. Williams " as preceding Professor Winthrop at Cambridge. Thompson could not have heard the former as a lecturer in the College. The Rev. Samuel Williams, to whom probably the reference is made, succeeded Winthrop in the Professorship in 1780, when Thompson was not in the country. He was called to that position from the pastorship of the Church in Bradford. As Thompson had taught school in that town, he may have there received instruction from the scientific minister.

The following letter must interpret itself to the reader. I can throw no light upon the occasion of it.

" Woburn, May 4, 1770.

" Sir, — I just received your letter dated this day, the sequel of which signifies your uneasiness with my conduct together with a number of other persons concerned with me in rehearsing part of a play. I am not sensible we have transgressed the laws of this Province. I have heard an argument related for and against the thing by persons well acquainted with Law : the person for it (as I was informed) brought his antagonist to acknowledge that there was such a hole in that law, that any moderate performer of plays might easily creep through, and that it is only meant (he supposed) to prevent extravagances, such as public Theatres erected, stage-players and actors maintained, and frequent performances of plays, and the like. How far he was right I can't say. For my share, I was not conscious that I had violated the law, or have done anything in the affair that tends to corrupt the good morals of the people. And as that was a real affair that happened between a king and his subjects that we repeated, which our present times resemble so much, we thought our time well spent in representing to a few people the bad consequences attending a misled king.

" And men of the most refined sense and learning look upon well-wrote plays to be very improving. Our present Majesty, George the third, together with his Brother, Prince Edward, and two sisters, Princesses Augusta and Elizabeth, have acted upon the Stage, where his Majesty, in a prologue, spoke thus : —

> " ' Wise Authors say, let youth in earliest age,
> Rehearse the poet's labours on the Stage ;
> Teach our young hearts with generous fire to burn,
> And feel the virtuous sentiments we learn,' &c.

" It seems he justifies and highly approves of them by his large Donations and frequent attendance, &c.

" I have not had opportunity to communicate the contents of your letter to those of the Society, but shall embrace the first opportunity proper for such an affair. And it is probable that you will hear something from us as a Society yet, and there is not a doubt with me but it will be to your entire satisfaction. Meanwhile, I believe you may rest assured that there will not be any further performances at present, by this Society.

" As I suppose you do not mean to seek an occasion against us, but only to act faithfully in your office, as I hope I have not given you reason to do it out of ill-will to me, nor would I believe you would do it on such principles, so, hoping that what's past will not destroy the understanding between us,

" I remain your well-wisher, friend, and humble servant,
" L. BALDWIN "

Most friendships among young persons of either sex are subjected to occasional disturbances of feeling arising from misunderstanding or the crossing of plans. They generally are of a trifling character, and are most apt to originate in connection with pleasure-parties. The following correspondence seems to cover an incident of this sort, in a fishing-excursion at Nahant.

" Mr. Baldwin,   " Woburn, June 4th, 1770.

" Sir, — Having received your favour of this afternoon, I find a Question proposed to me, in answer to which I say — first — I acted wrong in leaving Mr. Johnson's house before you were ready. But as to slighting your company or friendship, I can truly say I never meant it, and had I not expected you would have overtaken us, I never would nor should have left the house without you. But you may say I had no reason to expect you to overtake me. — In answer to that, I say, I knew nothing of your affairs in the boat, among the fish, but what I gathered from Mr. A. Thompson's talk when he came up. He said he would eat his dinner and tackle the horses in the carriage and go along. Dr. Hay said he would eat his dinner with him and go along slowly, for his horse was very dull. He said you would overtake him before he got to Lynn town, as you would have nothing to do but to eat your dinner and set out after.

" I considered no more of the matter, but ate my dinner with him, went and got the horses, brought yours to the door and paid part for his keeping, and left word with Mrs. Johnson to receive the rest, and set out, not doubting but you would overtake me.

" I see no reason why you was so much more affronted with me than with Dr. Hay, except the trouble you took to procure me a horse (which I own was very kind). But you was at much trouble, I should think, in taking care of the Doctor's fish, in gutting and cleaning them, wetting and nastying yourself with them. Be that as it may — but to return.

" As to my talk after our return from Nahant, you must

judge of it as of a person in anger, as I suppose we both were, and I believe no person on earth can answer for all they say when in anger. I believe if I had been in your place I should have been angry; but this I must affirm, that what reason I have given you to be affronted with me, it was not through any dislike to your company, or in any way wilfully to affront you, but entirely through inadvertence and unthoughtfulness. For if I had thought a moment it would have been just as well to have stopped till you was ready, and then both of us have overtaken the Doctor. But as I did not do it, 't is impossible to do it now.

"And thus I think I have answered your question to me; and if you think me worth your further notice, I shall be very glad to hear further from you, as soon as shall suit your convenience. And I shall conclude with subscribing myself,

Sir, your friend and humble servant,

BENJ^ THOMPSON.

"Mr. Thompson,

"Sir, — I have just received your letter, by hand of your little Brother [Josiah Pierce, 3d]. The sequel of which (if sincerely, sentimentally wrote, and not from some private view dormant to me) is almost to my entire satisfaction. And had it been offered the day after we were at Nahant, it had prevented anything further than a reprimand, which my then present exasperated state must have discharged. You quere why you are so much more to blame than the Doctor. I consider that I did not expect that you were going to make up with me on the Doctor's account, but only on your own. So I understood only with you. But the Doctor must think differently from what he said the other day, before I shall think of him as I did before. And if he catches me so again before he has made me some satisfaction for what is past I 'll not blame him. But not to detain you with my intentions with regard to the Doctor, I shall proceed to inform you, if my company is agreeable to you, you are welcome, and any apartment in my house at present — You may wonder at this last expression. But I expect to have an apartment that I can't admit my brother into, at certain times, before long.

"But not forgetting the first proposed question, I answer that I am ready to join in such a Society with you, and shall attend upon it as far as my business will permit — which calls for me now. So I must conclude, acknowledging myself your reconciled friend, and

"Humble servant,

"L. BALDWIN.

"Woburn, June 5, 1770."

The letter which succeeds is without date, but must have been written before the preceding had been received. The variance between the friends could not have been a very deep, nor a permanent one.

"Mr. Baldwin,

"Sir, — Some time before our unhappy difference we talked of forming a Society amongst us, for propagating learning and useful knowledge by means of questions to be proposed to a certain number of persons, and each person to bring his answer to said question proposed.

"And I don't doubt but by this means we might render ourselves very useful to one another, and I see no just cause why our late difference should be any impediment to this affair. But if my being one in said Society be the reason for your not joining, I shall be very sorry to be the cause of depriving you of so much pleasure as will naturally accrue to one of your genius.

"Sir, I should be extremely glad if you would favor me with a line or two (since I am denied talking with you) with your sentiments on the affair, and your answer to this. In so doing you will oblige,

"Your most humble servant,

"BENJ^a THOMPSON.

"P. S. — I have made the book to enter the questions and answers in.

"Yours, &c., B. T.

"To him I thought once I might call

"my friend, Mr. L. BALDWIN."

The place, unnamed, where Thompson, in his memoranda, records that he taught school "six weeks and three days," was doubtless the pleasant town of Bradford, on the Merrimack. Here he was so well esteemed for faithful services that he was sent for to Concord, New Hampshire, higher up the same river, by Colonel Timothy Walker, and offered a situation in a school of a higher grade, which would secure him a permanent position. Concord, under its Indian name of Penacook, had been claimed on its settlement by the English as being within the bounds and jurisdiction of Massachusetts. As such it had been incorporated, in 1733–34, as a town in Essex County, Massachusetts, under the name of Rumford, probably from a town of that name, generally called Romford, about twelve miles from London, whence some of the original settlers in the New England wilderness had emigrated. The name has interest for us, as it was chosen by Benjamin Thompson for a title when he was made a "Count of the Holy Roman Empire." The name of the town was changed to Concord, to mark the restoration of harmony after a long period of agitation as to its provincial jurisdiction and its relations with its neighbors. It was gratitude which prompted Thompson to make the name of Rumford titular, and, as we have seen, he expressed most tenderly and reverently his sense of obligation to the venerated minister of the place, — his patron, guide, and father-in-law.

Thompson had reason for this gratitude and sense of obligation. Had he fallen upon peaceful times, and made his native country his home for life, the propitious start which he received in Concord and the friends which there made his family circle would have secured his high position and success.

The Rev. Timothy Walker, the first minister of Concord, New Hampshire, himself a native of Woburn, and connected already with the Thompson family, had joined the fortunes of the early settlers in 1730 as their spiritual guide, and continued in their service as such till his death, September 2, 1782, after a ministry of fifty-two years. He was one of that class of ministers, characteristic of New England from its colonization down nearly to our own times, who, while holding a position and authority officially and conventionally supreme among the people of a settlement, proved worthy of esteem, and used their influence for unqualified good. Mr. Walker was the most honored citizen of Concord, as well as its beloved minister, and he has been honored in the line of his descendants. He had been thrice sent on missions to England on business connected with the disputes about the jurisdiction of the town and province, and had there impressed the legal counsel which he employed, and the tribunal before which he was heard, in a manner that insured his success. He also used his opportunities abroad for observation and acquisition, so as to enhance his influence at home. His son, Colonel Timothy Walker, a lawyer, was also a man of talent and position.

But next to the minister, just previous to Thompson's visit to Concord, Colonel Benjamin Rolfe held place and power in the village. He was the squire, was rich and public-spirited. He is distinguished as having been the first owner and driver of a curricle and · a pair of horses in New Hampshire, always excepting the Governor's at Portsmouth. Colonel Rolfe having lived as a bachelor till he was about sixty years old, then married Sarah, the daughter of the Rev. Timothy Walker, she being at the time about thirty. Unfortunately, some of the interleaved almanacs in which the good minister was in the habit of entering his official acts and matters of church record have been lost, and thus we are left in ignorance of some dates which would interest us. The Concord town records say that Sarah Walker was born October 6, 1739. She was married to Colonel Rolfe in 1769. They had one son, afterwards Colonel Paul Rolfe. The father died December 21, 1771, in his sixty-second year, leaving to his widow and son a large estate. He built a fine house at the so-called "Eleven Lots," since known as the Rolfe House. It was here that his widow, as the wife of Count Rumford, lived, and on the 19th of January, 1792, died at the age of fifty-two.

When Benjamin Thompson went to Concord as a teacher he was in the glory of his youth, not having yet reached manhood. His friend Baldwin describes him as of a fine manly make and figure, nearly six feet in height, of handsome features, bright blue eyes, and dark auburn hair. He had the manners and polish of a gentleman, with fascinating ways, and an ability to make himself agreeable. So diligently, too, had he used his opportunities of culture and reading that he might well have shined even in a circle socially more exacting than that to which he was now introduced. We may anticipate here the conclusion to which the review of his whole career will lead us, — that, as boy or man, he was never one to allow an opportunity of advancement to escape him. He seems to have given satisfaction as a teacher. The traditions that linger in the older homes at Concord, like those at Wilmington, include a large element of reminiscences of certain accomplishments and activities of the young teacher which were not of a strictly official character. He was skilled in vaulting and other athletic feats, and he won very early in his life the repute of gallantry.

When Count Rumford, looking back from the achievements and honors of his foreign career, told his friend Pictet of his deep indebtedness to the Rev. Mr. Walker for kindly oversight and counsel, for fostering patronage, and for fatherly love, his thoughts must have turned into feelings as he tenderly recalled some happy scenes and hours in that country parsonage. There, and to the house of the younger Walker, Thompson often went to give account of his pedagogueship and to enjoy social pleasures. There, too, and at other places, he would meet the daughter and sister in her early widowhood. He told Pictet that she married him, rather than he her. The tradition is that she facilitated what is often to the young man the difficult crisis in a relation which is easy before and after that crisis is past. An engagement was speedily effected between the parties with the entire approbation of the reverend father.

The before-mentioned curricle, left among the effects of Colonel Rolfe, was now put to service. The lady invited the young teacher, who was no longer to preside over a school, to accompany her on an excursion to Boston, a drive of over sixty miles, she having friends on the way whose hospitality was sure. She took care, with his own efficient co-operation, to have him furnished in Boston with all that was requisite at that time for fashionable array, including the offices of tailor and hair-dresser. Of course the color of his garments was his own favorite scarlet, ominous of the ill esteem into which he was soon to fall as too friendly to those whose military garb was of that hue. Tradition reports, that as the pair, not yet married, were on their homeward way, the lady ordered the curricle to stop at the door of Mrs. Pierce's house, the mother of her companion. That mother, being as yet ignorant of the change that had come over the fortunes of her son, was amazed at the apparition at her humble doorway, and especially at the gorgeous and extravagant array of her son, the village schoolmaster, and the not idle, but unprofitably busy experimenter. She is reported to have given vent to her surprise in the rebuking question, "Why, Ben! my son, how could you go and lay out all your winter's earnings in finery?" The tradition continues that the mother, hesitating somewhat about the character of her son's female companion and the explanation given by her, was finally, through the intervention of Dr. Hay, made to understand the circumstances of the case. She still wished time to think upon it, but on the next day gave her consent. (See Appendix.)

Thompson said that he was married "at the age of nineteen." Here, again, the loss of the minister's almanac leaves us in ignorance of a date. Benjamin Thompson and Mrs. Sarah Walker Rolfe were married previously to January 18, 1773. Their daughter, and only child, Sarah, late Countess of Rumford, was born October 18, 1774, in the Rolfe mansion. I have found one date given for the marriage as "about November, 1772," and it probably did take place then, or nearer the close of that year. At that time Thompson would have been but four or five months short of twenty years of age, while his wife would have been thirty-three. This disproportion of years might have proved infelicitous in itself, had not a more serious misfortune soon resulted in a separation between them. Whether we are to recognize in this disparity of the parties one reason for the seeming indifference of the husband when in exile to the wife whom he had left at home, must be referred to the judgment of the reader.

Mrs. Thompson, through her former husband, had made acquaintance at Portsmouth with Governor Wentworth and others in prominent society there. Thither she took her new husband on their marriage tour, and he soon became known to the Governor. The probable date of this bridal tour furnishes another reason for believing that the marriage of Mr. Thompson took place in November, 1772. On the 13th of the month there was a grand military muster and review at Dover, ten miles from Portsmouth, of the officers and soldiers of the Second Provincial Regiment of New Hampshire. Governor Wentworth and some of his Council, with many gentlemen and ladies from Portsmouth, attended it with considerable display and ceremony. The Rev. Dr. Belknap, the admirable historian of New Hampshire, and then the minister of Dover, preached on the occasion a sermon which was thought by the officers worthy of the press, and it was published at their request. The festivities, which began in Dover, were transferred for their continuance to Portsmouth. The tradition has always been that Mr. Thompson here attracted the attention of the Governor at the review, was introduced to him, and was on the day following a guest at his table. For the good fortune, if such it really were, which thus secured to him a questionable honor, he was indebted, as we shall find that he also was eleven years afterwards on the continent of Europe, to his fine appearance as he rode on horseback, as a spectator of a military review. Portsmouth was then the centre of much wealth and refinement. It had a mercantile class engaged in extensive business. Its crown officers, with others in government employ, and their associates in the administration of local affairs, made an aristocracy of influence and fashion. It was a time of growing alienations and fermenting discords, and the more prominent or influential the position of any individual, the more necessary was it for him to commit himself to a side, and, having done so, to act and speak as no longer neutral. Governor Wentworth recognized in young Thompson, not only the representative of a family already prominent in the public and social life of his Province, but also a man of unmistakable promise, and of qualities that would be likely to work vigorously for any interests which he should espouse, especially if they were identified with his own. He determined, therefore, to make him an object of marked favoritism. A vacancy having occurred in a majorship in the Second Provincial Regiment of New Hampshire, Governor Wentworth at once commissioned Thompson to fill it. It was only as a matter of patronage from the royal Governor that the receipt of such a commission might be supposed to cool the spirit of patriotism in the young officer. It was not the place, but the source and manner of his elevation to it, that made it embarrassing to its possessor in his subsequent course. His fellow-officers found no difficulty, when the time of trial came, in deciding whether they were to engage for or against the liberty of their native land.

But this sudden elevation of Thompson, without military knowledge or experience, without even any personal claim, over men in the line of fair promotion who had seen actual service and had won their position, was a piece of simple folly on the part of the Governor; and it was an act of weakness, if not of pure vanity, in Thompson to accept it, though it is affirmed that he had not asked it. He had himself not yet come of legal age, and he was lifted over veterans, — the military men with well-known titles, as lieutenants and captains, in different country towns, when those titles were something more than tavern or roadside compliments. The young officer became the subject of jealous feeling and of hostile criticism. Every subordinate, as well as many of his superiors, were soon found to be his effective enemies.

He made frequent calls upon the Governor, and it is evident that he appreciated and improved his opportunities. The following letter to his friend the Rev. Mr. Williams, of Bradford, afterwards Professor at the College, indicates the high spirits in which Thompson returned from one of his visits to Portsmouth.

"Concord, Monday, Jan'y 18th, 1773.

"Dear Sir, — Last Friday I had the honour to wait upon his Excellency, Governour Wentworth, at Portsmouth, where I was very politely and agreeably entertained for the space of an hour and a half. I had not been in his company long before I proceeded upon business, viz. to ask his Excellency whether ever the White Mountains had been surveyed. He answering me in the negative, I proceeded to acquaint him that there was a number of persons who had thought of making an expedition that way next summer, and asked him whether it would be agreeable to his Excellency. He said it would be extremely agreeable, seemed excessively pleased with the plan, promised to do all that lay in his power to forward it, — said that he had a number of Mathematical instruments (such as two or three telescopes, Barometer, Thermometer, Compass, &c.) at Wentworth House (at Wolfeborough, only about 30 miles from the mountains), all which, together with his library, should be at our service. That he should be extremely glad to wait on us, and to *crown all* he promised, if there were no public business which rendered his presence at Portsmouth *absolutely necessary*, that he would take his tent equipage and go with us to the mountain and tarry with us, and assist us till our survey, which he said he supposed would take about 12 or 14 days !!! — !! — !!!!!

"My dear Mr. Williams, is not this a sweet gentleman? one exactly suited to our taste, — how charming! how condescending! how easy and pleasant in conversation! But you can form no adequate idea of him till you have been in his company. But to proceed. His Excellency asked me what gentlemen I thought would be likely to go. I told him I had mentioned it to several, but more especially to *Mr. Williams of Bradford, who was a gentleman famous for his Mathematical Genius,* &c., &c., &c., &c. His Excellency answered that he had no particular acquaintance with you, but that he had heard of you as being a great Mathematician! and Philosopher! and should be extremely glad of your company and assistance in the affair. And further! he desired me to give his compliments to you, and desire you to attend.

"But stop! I will not tell you any more till you come and see me as you promised; then we will lay the whole plan of operation, and I will tell you a charming secret, — something you would give the world to know. 'T is nothing about Magnetism, nor Electricity, nor Optics, nor Evaporation, nor Flatulances, nor Earthquakes. No, but 't is something twice as pretty! something entirely new; but it can't be revealed

except in the town of Concord. And I do solemnly protest
by the third joint of St. Peter's great toe, that unless you come
and see me this winter, you shall never know this grand
Arcanum.

"There will be an ordination at Hopkinton next week on
Wednesday, and 't is only six miles from our house. Pray,
try and come, so as to attend, if possible. If not, come as soon
as you can, for 't is charming sleighing as ever was known.

"Mrs. Thompson's Compliments to you and your lady, and
begs you would give us the Pleasure of waiting on you both at
Concord very soon.

"Interim, we both remain Yours and Your Lady's most
Obedient

"Humble Servt,
"BENJ. THOMPSON." *

One might imagine the something "new" and "so
pretty" here referred to was a father's proud trophy
of a babe. But this could not be.

We may suppose that Major Thompson, with his
versatility of talent, would not neglect any means of
qualifying himself in knowledge and practice for a military career. . As we shall see, when on his way ten years
afterwards to offer his services as a soldier to the Austrians, he confesses to having been passionately engaged
with ardor for martial work. I am inclined to think
that the entry in his memorandum-book, already copied,
of "Directions for the Back Sword," is a memorial of
his purpose and effort to train himself in the use of
weapons as became a field-officer. He may have taken
lessons from the Mr. McAlpine to whom he credits
those directions, as I find the advertisements of that
teacher in the New Hampshire Gazette of the dates

* Copy of a letter of Benj. Thompson to Rev. Samuel Williams, LL. D., then
at Meredith, N. H. I am indebted for this letter to Mr. Jos. B. Walker of Concord.

corresponding to Major Thompson's commission. Mr. Donald McAlpine appears to have been an itinerant practitioner, having pupils at Portsmouth, Newbury-port, and several other places.

In his essay on his Experiments in Gunpowder, made in England in 1778 and 1779, Thompson speaks of himself as having been "for many years" engaged in practical investigations of that subject. It would appear that this was his first really scientific labor. The knowledge and skill which he professed when he first experimented abroad are evidences of what he had already done here at Salem, Woburn, and Concord, and afterwards, for a short time, in the camp of the New England forces at Cambridge.

For a brief interval Thompson comes before us as a gentleman farmer, with a zeal exceeding that of the husbandmen around him who were content to cultivate native crops. He had broad acres to till, and employed many laborers, among them some deserters from the British regiments in Boston.

Here we have Thompson as a farmer.

"Concord, July 17th, 1773.

" Mr. L. Baldwin,

" Sir, — As I am engaged in husbandry I have a mind to try some experiments in that way, and as my Mother informs me you are about to send to England for some Garden-seeds, — against the spring, — I should be extremely obliged if you would send the enclosed memorandum (or, rather, a copy of it) to London, so that I may have the seeds mentioned therein (or as many of them as can be had) as early in the spring as possible. You may depend upon the cash for them as soon as they arrive, together with an ample reward for your trouble and expenses.

" Please to write for them to come as soon as possible, for I have 18 or 20 acres of land to lay down to grass in the spring, and shall want the grass-seed very much and very early.

" Last evening I had the pleasure to receive a letter from his Excellency Governor Wentworth, in which, among others, is the following Paragraph, viz. ' The many unexpected affairs of business that have hitherto employed me has consumed so much of my time this summer, that I am compelled to give up my proposed tour to the White Hills for this year. But I shall be very glad to see you at Wolfboro' at any time it may suit your convenience, as I hope to get my family there by the last week of August,' &c.

" Thus you see we are disappointed this year ; perhaps next may prove more favorable.

" I received your letters *per* Mr. Sables, but had not opportunity to write by him.

" Mrs. Thompson sends compliments (and we trust by this time congratulations would not be improper) to you and your Lady. [They were just in season for a child born June 22d.]

" Have nothing new — so must conclude with telling you the old story over again — viz! that I am with great truth and esteem

" Your real friend and Humble Servant,
" BENJ^a THOMPSON.

" To Mr. Baldwin, Merchant in Woburn."

" Concord, August 21, 1774.

" Dear Sir, — I have been extremely busy this Summer, or I should have given myself the pleasure of coming to see you, but have not been able to get away as yet.

" The seeds which you were so kind as to send to England for on my behalf, I will come or send for as soon as I can conveniently, when I will pay you, together with ample satisfaction for my not sending for them sooner. I should have sent a hand on purpose for them, but the season of their usefulness was past for this year before I received advice of their arrival.

" I know you must be extremely altered, or a Philosophical and Mathematical Correspondence would be very agreeable to

you. I have, therefore, taken the liberty tó propose the following Problem, which I send you not so much for the difficulty as
the oddness of the Solution.

"A certain Cistern has three Brass-Cocks : one of which will
empty it in 15 minutes, one in 30 minutes, and the other in
60 minutes. Qu? How long would it take to empty the Cistern if all three of the Cocks were to be opened at once?

"If you are fond of a correspondence of this kind, and will
favour me with an easy question, Arithmetical or Algebraical, I
will endeavour to give as good an account of it as possible. If
you find out an answer to the above immediately, I hope you
will not take it as an affront, my proposing anything which you
may think so easy, for I must confess I scarce ever met with
any little notion that puzzled me so much in my life.

"You must give me leave to complain a little of your unkindness in not letting me have so much as one line by so good
an opportunity as Mr. Richardson. You used to profess friendship for me, I really thought it was not mere profession only.
And I cannot but have charity for you yet. I suppose business
—the cares of the world—prevented. Pray, don't fail to let
me hear from you as often as possible. And believe me Really
to be your Sincere friend, and

"Humble Servant,
"BENJ: THOMPSON.

"P. S.—Please to make mine and Mrs. Thompson's compliments to your Parents and Lady.

"To MR. LOAMMI BALDWIN, Merchant in Woburn."

It would have been natural, and according to the
common precedents of the time and of the community
in which he lived, for this promising and well-supported
young man to have looked for civil office, first as a
representative of Concord in the Provincial Assembly
of New Hampshire, and then as one of the Governor's
Council. But he would have needed what he seems
not to have secured or enjoyed, the hearty confidence

and attachment of the common people, to have obtained any office in their gift. The time was near at hand when he found that patronage from any other quarter than that of the people was at least a disadvantage, not only as a bar to popular favor, but also as a reasonable ground of suspicion.

It is pleasant, however, to close this chapter of the biography of Benjamin Thompson, leaving him at the first stage of success in a course which was to be splendidly illustrated by distinctions and titular honors. As to the shadows which we are now to trace as gathering around his opening manhood, we may study them either in their own disagreeable aspects, or as subsequent incidents and acts tend to drive them, if not into oblivion, at least into a considerate and softened estimate of their relatively unimportant character.

CHAPTER II.

Revolutionary Portents. — Division of Parties. — Governor Wentworth. — Thompson's Visits to Portsmouth. — Military Review. — Intimacy and Favor with the Governor. — Commissioned Major. — Jealousies and Enmities. — Accused of Toryism. — Meditated Outrage. — Flight from Concord. — Refuge in Woburn, Charlestown, and Boston. — His Petition and Examination. — Letters to Mr. Walker. — Visits the Camp. — Seeks Employment. — Departure. — Newport. — Secret Residence in Boston. — Sent to England. — Confiscation of his Property. — Proscribed.

THE genius of which young Thompson had given such early and marked tokens might possibly have found at the time a sphere for its development and culture in his native country, either in peace or in war. The revolutionary struggle which began with his opening manhood, continuing for seven years, and closing with heavy exactions upon all men of mental vigor and executive faculties in the arduous work of organizing an infant republic, would certainly have afforded for him a field in which he would as certainly have engaged his eminent abilities and won high distinction. It seemed as if accident, or rather the influence of circumstances independent of, and even in opposition to, his own avowed inclinations, decided for him the issue whether he should side with his native country or against it in its war of freedom. Happily for him, however, and for us, the great work of his life and his services to humanity lead us away from battle-fields, and from the limitations of what is called patriotism.

It is probable, on the other hand, that the bent of Thompson's genius, and the qualities of his natural character and temperament, needed a foreign field for their most favorable and congenial exercise. Like Franklin, he knew that he would meet with a fuller appreciation, and find a stimulus and an efficient patronage, only in the fellowship of men who had talent, means, and leisure for scientific inquiries and pursuits.

It becomes necessary now to set down a matter-of-fact statement of the circumstances which led Thompson to abandon his home, leaving behind him his wife, to whom he owed so much, and whom he was never to see again, and his infant child; deserting, likewise, the cause of his native country, though with no purpose at the time, as it would appear, of taking part against it. I shall content myself with a relation of those circumstances, not interposing any judgment of my own as a plea in his defence or as a verdict of condemnation. The circumstances will have interest in themselves, illustrating very pointedly, in the case of an individual, an episode of history which bore with great severity upon the fortunes of large numbers.

Young Thompson was essentially a courtier. He manifested in early manhood the tastes, aptitudes, and cravings which prompt their possessor, however humbly born, and under whatever repression from surrounding influences, to push his way in the world by seeking the acquaintance and winning the patronage of his social superiors, who have favors and distinctions to bestow. Conscious of possessing talents and capacities which would make the labors of a country farmer, or even of a pedagogue, distasteful, as well as inadequate for him, he would hardly be a congenial companion for those around him. The facility with which he adapted himself to court-life in Europe, to intimacies with nobles, to the ways of fashion, and to the culture of the intellectual classes, reflects back upon his early years the certainty that he could not have been popular with his townsfolk and neighbors, or even a sociable companion with his own kin. He was regarded from his boyhood as being above his position; and while his inconstancy of occupation gave him the repute of an idler and a dreamer, his dabblings with science were not interpreted as promises of a fruitful and serviceable life. He had also a noble and imposing figure, with great personal beauty, and with those whose acquaintance he cultivated he was most affable and winning in his manners. He had never been really indolent, but was ever seeking to rise. Doubtless, in the rustic labor which in his boyhood took him by himself into the forest to chop a load of wood and to team it to the market, to meet the frugal expenses of his livelihood, he kept his mind engaged upon the philosophy of even that work. We may be sure that he learned to wield the axe with scientific skill, and to economize his blows, while all the facilities of sledding, and logging, and adjusting a load would be acquired by experiment. The traditions already referred to of his extraneous performances in gymnastics while a school-teacher, fail to report to us what we may reasonably imagine, — that he was the most diligent and acquisitive pupil in his own school, and that there was no instructive book in the village, or in the not scanty library of his father-in-law, who had thrice been a sojourner in England, whose contents had not attracted him.

His marriage, enabling him to give over the necessity of school-keeping, furnished him the leisure and the means for making excursions at his pleasure. Besides his acquaintance with Governor Wentworth at Portsmouth, he had also, on visits with his wife to Boston, been introduced to Governor Gage, and several of the British officers, and had partaken of their hospitalities. Two soldiers who had deserted from the army in Boston, finding their way to Concord, had been employed by him upon his farm. Thinking they would do better to return to their ranks and their comrades, they had sought for the intervention of their employer to secure them immunity from punishment. Thompson addressed a few lines for this purpose to General Gage, asking, at the same time, that his own agency in their behalf should not be disclosed.

I can find no positive and direct evidence of any unfriendly or unpatriotic act done by Mr. Thompson, or even of any speech of such a character attributed to him. None such is upon record. His friend, Colonel Baldwin, stood by him, as would appear, confidently and heartily. But his brother-in-law, the Hon. Timothy Walker, next to his father the most influential man in Concord, with other friends, by advising his leaving that town, help us to conjecture what may have been the facts of the case, though no witness ever appeared to testify against him when opportunity was given. Besides his acquaintance with the royal governors, the patronage he had received from one of them,

the intimacy in which he was supposed to stand with
the other, the return of the deserters, and any degree
of unpopularity which he may have had with his towns-
men, Thompson had probably spoken his mind with
some freedom, in a way to check the rising spirit of
the people, in palliation of the measures of the King
and ministry, and in distrust of the ability and success
of the resistance which was to be made. This, I am
inclined to think, was the extent of his "Toryism,"
aggravated by his youth, and perhaps not relieved by
any modesty of utterance, caution, or deference. There
were inflammable materials around him. There were
very many older and far more conspicuous men than
himself who, in the earliest stage of the revolutionary
struggle, were forced against their own inclinations to
take side with the royalist party, because they had
spoken some hasty or deliberate words of hesitancy,
and had been roughly treated for them.

The actual rupture into hostilities against the British
authority and arms had come suddenly, especially in
New Hampshire, where, notwithstanding, it was decisive. Governor Wentworth had himself been quite
popular in his Province. Before he had succeeded his
uncle in his office, he had been strongly opposed to
every measure of Great Britain which was regarded as
encroaching upon our liberties. He had even been
sent to England as the agent of the Assembly to procure the repeal of the Stamp Act; and he had shown
a great deal of public spirit in his efforts and measures
to improve the Province by opening and settling its
interior and fostering its rising college. Mr. Thompson
might well allege, as he did, the fact that Governor
Wentworth, when he made him his friend, was warmly

esteemed. But he was nevertheless faithful to his official trust when the royal authority was defied, though he acted most unwisely and blindly.

Yet some of the foremost men in all the Colonies — men of intelligence, rectitude, high character, and unquestionable patriotism — hesitated as to the rightfulness or the policy of the first measures which initiated the Revolution. Some such honestly doubted whether the colonists had real, substantial grievances, and if, having such, they ought not to seek quite different means of redress. We can afford in these days, and in the calmness of our retrospect, to distinguish between the facts of history and the rhetoric of demonstrative orators. We certainly must distinguish between the grounds for hesitancy and mistrust which influenced wise and honest men who were obliged to take a side before actual hostilities opened, and the character of the struggle as it went on. The exasperation of feeling which followed upon the successive measures and acts of the British government and forces, in burning our towns and seaports, and employing mercenary troops, and in other outrages, doubtless made many of the " Tories " regret their loyalty, while at the same time it intensified the popular acrimony against them.

Ten years before the outbreak of hostilities there had been even an era of good feeling, in the New England Colonies especially, towards the British monarchy and ministry. The Indian and French War, in which Thompson's own kin had many of them done good service, had happily freed the frontier towns of all the apprehensions and horrors of savage inroads, and the treasuries of the other settlements from the exactions of .a military force for their defence. Though the

Colonies themselves had contributed men and money to this tedious and costly warfare, yet the exchequer and the soldiery of England had furnished the forces without which we should have been powerless. When the Prime Minister, Grenville, in 1764, called the agents of our Colonies together in England, he said to them that the burden left by the French war was a debt of seventy-three millions sterling. The protection we had received, of course, excited a feeling of gratitude among our people, and the more loyal among them thought that their share in the cost of government was light, and that it was compensated. In 1763, Mr. James Otis, afterwards to be known as the leading patriot, in his address as Moderator of the first town meeting held in Boston after the peace, said: " No other constitution of civil government has ever yet appeared in the world so admirably adapted to the preservation of the great purposes of liberty and knowledge as that of Great Britain. Every person in America is, of common right, by acts of Parliament and the laws of God, entitled to all the essential privileges of Britons. The true interests of Great Britain and her Colonies are mutual; and what God in his providence has united, let no man dare attempt to pull asunder." Duties had been reduced, and now the odious Stamp Act had been repealed, and the colonists had assurance that their last and fundamental grievance, of taxation without representation, would be redressed.

Our candor, therefore, in these days, must persuade us to allow that there were reasons, or, at least, prejudices and apprehensions, which might lead honest and right-hearted men, lovers and friends of their birthland, to oppose the rising spirit of independence .as

inflamed by demagogues, and as foreboding discomfiture
and mischief. They feared that we should suffer the
worst of the strife, and that the sort of government we
should be likely to have as the alternative of a monarchy would probably make us largely the losers. Yet
the utterance of such views, if only as misgivings, might
in many places be equally impolitic and dangerous.

As has been already said, there is no record, or even
tradition, of unwise or unfriendly expressions dropped
by Mr. Thompson which could be used against him
even when he challenged proof of his alleged disaffection to the cause of his country. However, he was
young, and he had an independent spirit. His military
promotion by pure favoritism, and, what he insisted was
simply an act of humanity, his seeking immunity for
two returning deserters, were enough in themselves to
assure him jealous enemies. But silence and neutrality
were then as hazardous as speech or opposition directed against the popular enthusiasm. He therefore
became a suspected person in Concord, where there
were watching enemies and tale-bearers, as well as jealous Committees, who soon brought their functions to
bear in a most searching and offensive way against all
who did not attend the popular assemblies. It was as
well known as it was observable that Thompson took
no part in these. What more he did or said, or failed
of doing or saying, must be left, as before remarked, to
conjecture. Yet it must have been something which
irritated or displeased, something which could be turned
into the material for exciting a mob, with the risk of
rude, if not violent, treatment, exhibited at the time in
the favorite process of tarring and feathering a politi-
cally obnoxious person. Thompson's family connec-

tions, beginning with the minister and the squire of the town, were, of course, the most powerful set among the inhabitants; and if they were unable to vindicate him and protect him from outrage, and if even his brother-in-law and other friends advised him to quit the place, — though he did not seek counsel from his venerated father-in-law, — we may well infer that his apprehensions were not vain, whatever his own consciousness of rectitude.

There was something exceedingly humiliating and degrading to a man of an independent and self-respecting spirit in the conditions imposed at times by the "Sons of Liberty," in the process of clearing himself from the taint of Toryism. The Committees of Correspondence and of Safety, whose services stand glorified to us through their most efficient agency in a successful struggle, delegated their authority to every witness or agent who might be a self-constituted guardian of patriotic interests, or a spy or an eaves-dropper, to catch reports of suspected persons. A case transpired in Mr. Thompson's neighborhood of which he doubtless had knowledge. The British troops in Boston being without barracks, and the carpenters of that and the surrounding towns being unwilling to build them, Governor Gage had applied to Governor Wentworth to send him workmen from New Hampshire for that service. The latter engaged secret agents to execute this commission. But the story leaked out, and the Committee of Ways and Means at Portsmouth took up the matter vigorously, and so thoroughly searched it as to discover one of the Governor's secret agents in this business, Nicholas Austin. The "Sons of Liberty" summoned the delinquent before them on the

8th of November, 1774, and compelled him to make, on his knees, the following confession : —

"Before this company I confess I have been aiding and assisting in sending men to Boston to build Barracks for the soldiers to live in, at which you have reason justly to be offended, which I am sorry for, and humbly ask your forgivness ; and I do affirm, that for the future I never will be acting or assisting in any wise whatever, in Act or Deed, contrary to the Constitution of the Country ; as witness my hand.

"NICHOLAS AUSTIN." *

Benjamin Thompson was not the man to subject himself to any such humiliating treatment. He, however, knew very well, that the military commission which he had received — though, it is said, without his having asked for it — from the partiality of Governor Wentworth, while it had provoked the enmity of older men who had real claims for military promotion, had also led him to be classed with the partisans of that magistrate just as the popular feeling was most inflamed against him. He had occasion to fear any indignity which an excited and reckless country mob, directed by a secret instigation, might see fit to inflict upon him, whether it were by arraying him in tar and feathers, or by riding him upon a rail to be jeered at by his former school-pupils. The actual and visible agents in inflicting such degrading insults were not generally the neighbors and former companions of an obnoxious person, but were such volunteers, whether in their own proper garb or disguised as Indians, as were easily rallied from adjoining towns. If ill-usage stopped short of these extremes, the condition of escape and security was, as has been given in the case of Austin, a public

* New Hampshire Gazette, Portsmouth, November 11, 1774.

recantation, unequivocally and strongly expressed, involving a confession of some act or word in opposition
to the will of the popular party, and a solemn pledge
of future uncompromising fidelity to it. Major Thompson insisted from the first, and steadfastly to the close
of his life affirmed, that he was friendly to the patriot
cause, and had never done or said anything which could
be truthfully alleged as hostile to it. He demanded,
first in private, and then in public, that his enemies
should confront him with any charges which they could
bring against him, and he promised to meet them, while
he also offered to render any service for which he was fitted in the popular interest. He resolved, however, that
he would not plead except against explicit charges, nor
invite indignity by self-humiliation. We must draw
our own inferences here, whether by convincing ourselves that the popular distrust of him was unerring in
its discernment and surmise, and had good reason on
its side, or that he was the innocent sufferer from un-
toward circumstances. If the people of Concord and
the jealous regimental officers of New Hampshire were
responsible for depriving the patriot cause of an effective military or executive servant, they may claim
credit for furnishing Europe with a very eminent and
practically useful philosopher.

Major Thompson was summoned before a Committee
of the people in Concord, in the summer of 1774, to
answer to the suspicion of "being unfriendly to the
cause of Liberty." He positively denied the charge,
and boldly challenged proof. The evidence, if any
such was offered, — and no trace of testimony, or even
of imputation, of that kind is on record, — was not of a
sort to warrant any proceeding against him, and he was

discharged.   This discharge, however, though nominally an acquittal, was not effective in relieving him from popular distrust and in assuring for him confidence. Probably his own backwardness to avow sympathy and make professions in accordance with the wishes of his enemies left him still under a cloud.   A measure less formal and more threatening than the examination before a self-constituted tribunal was, as a matter of course, secretly planned by the excited people.   This was a visit to his comfortable home, the most conspicuous residence in the village.   It was carried into effect in November, 1774.   A mob gathered, at the time agreed on, around this dwelling, and after a serenade of hisses, hootings, and groans, demanded that Major Thompson should come out before them.   The feeling must have been intense, and was of a nature to feed its own flame.   Had Thompson been within, he would inevitably have met with foul handling.   The suspicion that he was hiding there would have led to the sacking of his dwelling and the destruction of his goods, though the daughter of their venerated minister was its mistress, and she was the mother, not only of Thompson's infant, but of the only child of their former most distinguished townsman, Colonel Benjamin Rolfe.   Mrs. Thompson and her brother, Colonel Walker, came forth, and with their assurance that her husband was not in the town, the mob quietly dispersed.

Having received a friendly warning that this assault was to be made upon him in the shape of an inquisitorial visit at his house, and taking the advice to which reference has been made, Mr. Thompson had secretly left Concord just before.   He thought it was to be only a temporary separation from the place, from all his friends there, from his wife and his infant child. He was never to see that pleasant home again, nor any one of those whom he left there, except that he had a brief and troubled visit from his wife and infant, and met the latter again only after an interval of twenty-two years. He was himself, when he fled, midway in his twenty-second year. He had made a hasty effort to collect some dues which belonged strictly to himself, but he scrupulously avoided taking with him anything that belonged to others, or even to his wife. What of his own he left there we shall see was soon subjected to the process of confiscation.

Thompson at first sought refuge in his former home at Woburn, with his mother, in the house to which she had moved with her second husband, opposite the Baldwin Mansion, — a security to which, as we shall find, he was to be indebted for another release from the dealing of a mob. Here, for a short time, he sought to occupy himself in quiet retirement with his favorite pursuits of philosophical study and experiment, especially on the properties of gunpowder. But popular suspicion found means to visit its odium upon him here, and he was kept in a continual state of anxiety. Seeking a new place of refuge, he found temporary shelter in Charlestown, with a friend, nine miles from Woburn and one from Boston, — divided from the latter place, with which he could easily hold intercourse, only by a river. This position, when it became known, was not likely to reassure confidence in him. (See Appendix.)

While in Charlestown, Major Thompson addressed the following letter to his father-in-law, at Concord.

" December 24th, 1774.

" REVEREND SIR, — The time and circumstances of my leaving the town of Concord have, no doubt, given you great uneasiness, for which I am extremely sorry. Nothing short of the most threatening danger could have induced me to leave my friends and family; but when I learned from persons of undoubted veracity, and those whose friendship I could not suspect, that my situation was reduced to this dreadful extremity, I thought it absolutely necessary to abscond for a while, and seek a friendly asylum in some distant part.

" Fear of miscarriage prevents my giving a more particular account of this affair; but this you may rely and depend upon, that I never did, nor (let my treatment be what it will) ever will do, any action that may have the most distant tendency to injure the true interest of this my native country.

" I most humbly beg your kind care of my distressed family; and I hope you will take an opportunity to alleviate their trouble by assuring them that I am in a place of safety, and hope shortly to have the pleasure of seeing them. I also most humbly beseech your prayers for me, that under all my difficulties and troubles I may behave in such a manner as to approve myself a true servant of God and a sincere friend of my country.

" To have tarried at Concord and have stood another trial at the bar of the populace would doubtless have been attended with unhappy consequences, as my innocence would have stood me in no stead against the prejudices of an enraged, infatuated multitude, — and much less against the determined villany of my inveterate enemies, who strive to raise their popularity on the ruins of my character. My friends would have been deemed unfriendly to the cause of Liberty, and my defence would have been treated with contempt and disdain. It would have been vain for me to have pretended to curb the fury or calm the rage of this popular whirlwind; but I must have been cast, and condemned to suffer punishments equal to the blackness of my supposed transgressions.

" The plan against me was deeply laid, and the people of Concord were not the only ones that were engaged in it. But others to the distance of twenty miles were extremely officious on this occasion. My persecution was determined on, and my flight unavoidable. And had I not taken the opportunity to leave the town the moment I did, another morning had effectually cut off my retreat."

There is a tradition, which I have not been able to authenticate, that either at this time or nearly a year afterwards, while Thompson was concealed in some friendly refuge in Boston, he received a visit from his father-in-law, who urgently appealed to him to return to his home. There is no evidence within my reach that the two ever met again. But on the 9th of January following the date of the above letter, the Rev. Mr. Walker addressed him a reply, the tenor of which we know only from the response which it drew from his son-in-law. The relations of the latter were becoming more and more embarrassing, on account of his visits to Boston and the intimacy which he appeared to seek with the British officers; though, as there had not yet been any decisive outbreak, he might have expected that the rupture would be averted. Mr. Walker had urged his return to Concord, and had coupled with the appeal a suggestion that he should be prepared, in doing so, to make some sort of recognition of the grounds under which his patriotism had been doubted and his conduct brought under suspicion. We may infer from this advice, that the wise and esteemed minister had misgivings, at least, about the discretion of his son-in-law; and from the answer written by the latter we may also infer, that, regarding the advice as proposing a confession or recantation, he was determined to stand on his dignity or his sense of perfect innocence, and refuse to make it. He might have shrunk from the full demands of truth, or he might have feared the risk of hypocrisy. His answer was as follows: —

"HON^D SIR,—Last evening I had the pleasure to receive your kind Letter of the 9th instant, for which I return many thanks.

" As to my return to Concord, it is what I most ardently desire and wish for, could I do it with safety. But in the present distracted state of affairs, I fear I could have no security that might be depended on, especially if things should proceed to such extremities as they at present bid fair to do. And as to any concessions that I could make, I fear it would be of no consequence, for I cannot, possibly, with a clear conscience, confess myself Guilty of doing anything to the disadvantage of this Country, but quite the reverse.

" As to Mrs. Thompson's coming to live with me, I apprehend that it will be so far from embarrassing my affairs, that it will lessen my expenses, — as Mrs. Clark will let us have house-room sufficient for our small family for a very trifle, and we can live upon our own provisions, which can easily be brought from Concord in a sled ; and as to wood, I have enough of that on land of my own, which my Father Pierce will transport for me on easy terms.

"And as Mrs. Thompson's Company is almost the only thing that can be any alleviation of my present troubles, and as my being absent from her is the greatest unhappiness of my present situation, I hope I shall be so happy as to obtain your consent for her leaving Concord."

In compliance with this earnest appeal, his wife, with her infant, joined him at his mother's home in Woburn, though it required of them a ride of more than fifty miles in midwinter. They remained with him till the last of May, 1775, after which he never again saw his wife. My friend, Mr. George Rumford Baldwin, the only surviving son of Colonel Baldwin, informs me that he has been told that, at the time, Major Thompson was mostly with the army at Cambridge, — though I think it must have been at an earlier time, probably in March, 1775, — while he was at his mother Pierce's house in New Bridge Village, Woburn, a military company, perhaps a body of practising minute-men, came to arrest him when he was temporarily confined by illness. His friend, Colonel Baldwin, whose mansion was opposite, seeing the men halt, at once suspected their object, and determined to try to protect·Thompson. He made a speech to the company, saying that he well knew his friend's principles and feelings, and that he was not inimical to the American cause, but might have appeared so in consequence of having been disappointed of the promotion he desired. After pleading in behalf of Thompson to the extent of his ability, he remarked to the men that they must be greatly fatigued by their march, and that he would be much gratified if they would cross over to his barn (which was the nearest building, and opposite the Pierce house), and that he would then bring out what he might have for their refreshment. They accepted the invitation, and were so generously treated with food and liquor that their errand was overlooked, and they returned without molesting Thompson, though they had previously twice sent in their summons that he should present himself, whether sick or well.

Whether this incident transpired at the earlier or the later date, it shows that Major Thompson had not overcome the animosity against him. While his wife and child were with him the skirmishes at Concord, Massachusetts, and Lexington occurred, in which it has been said, on what authority I cannot learn, that Thompson bore arms with the Massachusetts yeomen in resisting the British inroad.

We have another letter which was sent to the Rev. Mr. Walker while his daughter was still with her husband.

" Woburn, May 11th, 1775.

" Rev⁰ Sir,—Since Mrs. Thompson has been at Woburn she has been very unwell, which has prevented her coming to Concord this week as was proposed. But as soon as she gets well enough she will set out. As to my returning to Concord, it is what I have most earnestly desired ever since I left home, and nothing but a sense of danger has prevented my doing it long ago. And now the advice I receive from different people, who appear equally to be my friends, relative to my going back, is so intirely different that I scarcely know what to do or what course to take. If I can be assured of safety and restored to that friendship and esteem of my fellow Countrymen which I trust no action of mine has ever forfeited, I will, with the greatest pleasure and alacrity, return to Concord; and the good People of that Town in particular, and of the Country in general, may rely on my best endeavours to serve them. And if ever I have done anything which in the event has turned out to the damage of this Country, I am sincerely and heartily sorry therefor. But as to confessing myself guilty of doing anything with a design to injure them, it is what I can never do without doing violence to my Conscience and committing a crime in reality which I do not choose to be guilty of.

" I have not a single doubt of your sincere friendship and affection for me, and believe you would not on any account advise me to anything contrary to my safety and interest. But many Persons from Concord tell me that neither you nor your son are so well acquainted with the minds of the People respecting myself as many others, and advise me by no means to return at present. Among these are Col. Stickney and Capt. Chandler.

" To return to Concord and be kept a Prisoner in the Town, or to be treated with coldness and indifference for crimes which I feel myself intirely innocent of, would be to me even worse than my present situation. But if the People of Concord will be so kind as to'assure " [The rest is wanting.]

Soon after writing this letter, Major Thompson was arrested and confined in Woburn. It has been said that he himself courted this proceeding as the only means likely to result in securing him a fair decision of his case.

There appears among Colonel Baldwin's papers a document which is here copied.

" Woburn, May 16th, 1775.

" GENTLEMEN, — Major Benjamin Thompson of Concord, in the Province of New Hampshire, having been taken up and confined in the Town upon suspicion of being inimical to the liberties of this Country, and his Excellency General Ward having ordered, agreeable to advice of Congress, that the Committee of Correspondence for this Town be a Court to inquire into that Matter :

" This is therefore to desire that all persons under your command, or otherwise belonging to the Province of New Hampshire, or elsewhere, that can give evidence in this affair, may appear at the Meeting-house in the first Parish in Woburn, on Thursday, the 18th inst. May, at Two o'clock, P. M., and they shall be heard.

" We are, Gentlemen, Your Humble Servants,

" To COL. JOHN STARK,   SAMUEL WYMAN,
    LT. COL. WYMAN,   ROBERT DOUGLAS,
    MAJOR ANDREW McCLARY,   DR. SAMUEL BLOGGET,   } Com^tee of Corre-spon."
    CAPT. ABBOT HUTCHINS,   LOAMMI BALDWIN,
    CHANDLER BALDWIN,   TIMOTHY WINN.
    GERRISH AND CLOUGH,
      of New Hampshire.

The above-named " Committee of Correspondence " had been chosen at a town meeting, February 1, 1773. At a meeting on January 4, 1775, twenty-one men had been chosen as a " Committee of Inspection," and on

April 17, 1775, a body of fifty "minute-men" had been provided for. Thus watchful was the oversight of suspected persons and the cause of Liberty.

It seemed as if the worried man were now in a fair way to obtain a hearing.

In Colonel Baldwin's Diary, under date of May 18, 1775, is the following entry : —

"Thursday in afternoon went to Woburn to sit as one of a Committee of Correspondence upon Major Thompson, who was taken up as a Tory, but, finding nothing against him, adjourned till next Monday."

And the following occurs in another place, which seems to refer to the same occasion as it is of the same date : —

"At a Court of Inquiry into the conduct of Major Thompson of Concord, New Hampshire, convened at the Meeting-House of the First Parish in Woburn, on Thursday, the 18th of May, 1775, at 2 o'clock, by the Committee of Correspondence of said Town."

Until after the affair at Concord and Lexington, while it was evident that matters were coming to a crisis, intercourse between Boston and the adjoining country was substantially open, though the capital was under military rule, and the yeomen of the neighboring towns, organized as minute-men, were on the watch night and day for alarms. But after the British troops had returned from their inroad, entrance to Boston or exit from it was attended with difficulty. General Gage, who had himself married an American lady, and was the owner of land here, appears to have thought, till he was recalled to England, that the quarrel between the colonies and the mother country might yet be adjusted; and it seems plain that Major Thompson, on his visits to Boston, felt the influence of the General upon himself. But with predilections, as he still insisted, for the cause of his native country, he determined to make an effort to obtain a hearing before the Committee of the Provincial Congress then sitting at Watertown, which exercised the functions of government. He therefore addressed the following letter to his friend Baldwin.

"WOBURN, 19th May, 1775.

"DEAR SIR,—The enclosed Petition I beg you would do me the honour to present to the Committee of Safety, and accompany it with your influence. As my only design is to convince the world of my innocence, and silence the clamours of my enemies, and as I know this method is agreeable to your mind, I doubt not but the prayer of the Petition will be granted. But if the Committee of Safety *will not* have anything to do in the affair, but insist upon it that the Committee of Correspondence for the Town of Woburn shall make an end of the matter, yet I would most earnestly beg to have Concord and the adjacent Towns have notice of the time and place of the further examination, in order that this may be a final settlement. And if the Committee of Safety, or, otherwise, the Committee of Correspondence, will make out a proper notification for that purpose, I will at my own expense immediately forward it to Concord.

"You cannot be insensible that my present confinement is very disagreeable, therefore I hope you will endeavour that the day of Trial may be appointed as soon as may be consistent with giving my accusers sufficient notice to appear. I am, Dear Sir, Your real friend and Humble Servant,

"BENJ: THOMPSON.

"P. S.—The Bearer, Mr. Thomas, comes to Cambridge on purpose to deliver this, and I beg he may return as soon as possible.

"To MAJOR LOAMMI BALDWIN, Head Quarters, Cambridge."

The petition enclosed to Mr. Baldwin was as follows:—

"*To the Honourable the Committee of Safety for the Colony of Massachusetts Bay.*

"The Petition of Benjamin Thompson, Esq., of Concord, in the Province of New Hampshire, humbly sheweth : —

"That on Monday, the 15th inst., your petitioner was taken up and confined in this Town, upon suspicion of being inimical to the liberties of this Country ; and that in consequence of his being taken up, the Committee of Correspondence for the Town, after having given public notice of the time and place of hearing, and desired all persons that could give evidence to attend, proceeded to an examination of the affair, agreeable to the recommendation of the Honourable Provincial Congress. But as no person appeared to lay anything of consequence to his charge ; and as the Committee were not pleased either to acquit or condemn him ; and as his own personal safety, as well as the quiet and satisfaction of the public, but more especially of the people of New Hampshire, depends on his having an acquittance after the most public, thorough, and impartial examination, — your petitioner humbly prays that the Committee of Safety would be pleased to take the matter into consideration, and examine the same ; and that they would be pleased to give notice of the time and place of hearing, not only to the people of New Hampshire, and others that are in the Army at Cambridge, or elsewhere, but also that the public in general, and the inhabitants of the Town of Concord, in the Province of New Hampshire, and the adjacent Towns in particular, be desired to attend or send in depositions of what they know relative to the affair.

"And your petitioner, as in duty bound, shall ever pray, &c.

"BENJ. THOMPSON.

"Woburn, May 19, 1775."[*]

May 20, 1775, Colonel Baldwin makes the following entry : —

"Saturday, I presented a Petition to the Committee of Safety, sent me by Major Thompson, and brought by Alexander

[*] Force's American Archives, 4th Series, Vol. II. pp. 647, 648.

Thomas, which Petition the Committee referred to the Congress, where we went and sent it in to them sitting at Watertown Meeting-house. We dined at Leonard's; so the matter was deferred for the present."

We must remind ourselves that this was at one of the most critical and anxious stages in the course of events which resulted in opening the Revolutionary War. Large bodies of minute-men and soldiers from all the New England Provinces were gathered in Cambridge, and on the hills in its neighborhood, under the command of General Ward. The Provincial Congress was in session, overwhelmed with business, as it had assumed full legislative functions independently of the control of the royal Governor or his subordinates. The people had in their town meetings resolved to recognize the authority of this Congress and to pay their taxes to the treasurer appointed by it, while they helped by other popular measures to confirm and increase that authority. The object was to confine the British forces to the peninsula of Boston, leaving them no exit but by the sea, and, if possible, to embarrass that. This made it necessary to guard and fortify nearly a whole circle of territory, extending round from the heights of Dorchester to those of Chelsea. Aspirants for commissions in the American army were numerous and in warm rivalry. If Major Thompson were, as he affirmed, impatient to assume his military office, or to secure a higher one, we can well imagine how he must have fretted under the confinement which not only restrained his liberty and subjected him to indignity, but also threatened to be an insuperable obstacle to his attainment of his object. If his after course was largely decided by resentment and the sense of having been outraged, we must look for the occasion of it now and here. He thus conveys his thanks to his friend.

"Woburn, May 2d, 1775.

"DEAR SIR, — I am to return you many thanks for your kindness in presenting my petition to the Committee of Safety, and your further care and trouble in laying it before the Congress. I must intreat your further assistance in this affair, and hope that it will one time or other be in my power to make a suitable return for all your kindness.

"Mr. Thomas now waits upon you to know what the Congress are determined to do respecting me ; and I shall wait with impatience for his return.

" I would beg leave to congratulate you upon your promotion in the Army, and I would at the same time congratulate the Public upon the same occasion.

"I am, Sir, with real Regard and Esteem,
"Your friend and Humble Servant,
"BENJ^ THOMPSON.

"To COLONEL BALDWIN, Head Quarters, Cambridge."

Either from pressure of business, or under the persuasion that Woburn was the proper place for a hearing of the cause, the Committee of the Provincial Congress did not see fit to entertain Major Thompson's petition. He had further reason for resentment and chagrin, when, after subjecting himself to the trouble and expense of summoning any witnesses who might see fit to appear against him, and after securing a hearing of the case in his native town, the result was as dilatory and as undecisive as the documents next given will show.

" *Woburn (Massachusetts) Committee.*

" Whereas the Committee of Correspondence for the Town of Woburn, authorised by the honourable Provincial Congress to examine into the principles and conduct of any person suspected of being inimical to the liberties of this Country, have examined Major Benjamin Thompson, of Concord, in the Province of New Hampshire, being brought before them, suspected of being thus inimical. And whereas the said Committee have summoned certain evidences, who they supposed could give light into the matter, to attend, which evidences failed of so doing: This is therefore to inform all persons who are knowing to the said Major Thompson's conduct, that the Committee have adjourned to Monday the 29th day of May next, at three o'clock, afternoon, at the meeting-house, where said evidences are desired to attend, as the Committee think themselves bound to dismiss and recommend the said Thompson, unless something more appears against him than what they have heard.

"SAMUEL WYMAN, *Chairman.*

"May 24, 1775." "

"*Massachusetts Provincial Congress, May* 25, 1775.

"The Petition of Benjamin Thompson to the Committee of Safety was read, and ordered to subside." †

The action in the town of Woburn on the hearing of the case, as preserved in a record in Colonel Baldwin's papers, is thus related : —

" Major Benjamin Thompson of Concord, in the Province of New Hampshire, having been taken up and confined in this Town upon suspicion of being inimical to the liberties of this Country: And we, the Committee of Correspondence for the Town of Woburn, (being duly authorised by a vote of the Hon. Provincial Congress to hear and Determine upon this matter,) after having given public notice of the time and place of examination, and desired all persons that could give evidence respecting that affair to attend ; and after having strictly and impartially examined into the affair, do not find that said Thompson in any one instance has shown a Disposition unfriendly to American Liberty : But that his general behaviour has evinced

* Force's American Archives, 4th Series, Vol. II. p. 701.   † Idem, p. 813.

the direct contrary: And as he has now given us the strongest assurances of his good intentions, we recommend him to the Friendship, Confidence, and Protection of all good People in this and the neighboring Provinces — Colonies.

"Woburn, in the Province of Massachusetts Bay, 19th May, 1775."

The meeting-house was crowded on the occasion, and the accused pleaded his own cause and managed his own defence. There does not appear to have been any examination of witnesses. Such reports, surmises, or charges as any one present chose to repeat or suggest personally or through hints to the Committee were met by Thompson, and by him ascribed to envy or jealousy. It has been said by one who has argued in his cause,* that, though the Committee reached this favorable decision, they refused to secure him a public acquittal, the reason assigned being, that if they gave a copy of their proceedings to Thompson for publication, it would offend his opponents, as seeming to condemn them. He adds that Thompson's feelings were greatly exasperated at this injustice.

The statement hardly seems probable. A result reached and announced in a thronged meeting in a village church, after such a deliberate hearing, could hardly be prevented from becoming matter of notoriety. Yet Thompson himself complains, as we shall see in another letter to Mr. Walker, of injustice from the Committee. The inference drawn by Mr. Johnston is, that the above vindication of Thompson was written by one of the Committee, but was not allowed, as the accused desired, to be communicated to the public. He says that as a postscript to the original report of the Committee of Vigilance is added what follows: —

* John Johnston. See note on p. 11.

"This may certify that when Major Thompson was examined before the Committee of Correspondence for the town of Woburn, (being brought before them on suspicion of being inimical to American liberties,) the affair of the return of four deserters from Concord, in New Hampshire, to Boston, in which said Thompson was supposed to be instrumental, and also his conduct relative to the Concord donation, — sending a load of peas to Boston, — and an undue connection or correspondence with Gov. Wentworth, were matters which were laid to his charge against him, which were thoroughly examined into, and in every particular the Committee received full satisfaction from said Thompson."

If this favorable but suppressed judgment on his case was indeed only the unsuccessful verdict of a friend present at the examination, we may well conclude that that friend was Baldwin. Himself a man of thorough sincerity and rectitude and a warm patriot, his championship is Thompson's best vindication.

The sense of a wrong which was becoming too aggravating for longer patient endurance expresses itself in this request of Thompson to his friend.

"Cambridge, May 30, 1775.

"Sir, — I should take it as a great favour if you would apply to the Honourable Provincial Congress, and withdraw a Petition which I preferred to the Honble the Committee of Safety, on the 19th of May inst., through your hands.

BENJ^a THOMPSON.

"Major Loammi Baldwin."

Major Thompson was after this released from confinement, and of course left free to go where he would, at the risk of meeting still unappeased enemies, and suffering such treatment as any combination of them might visit upon him. That he did not return to Concord, New Hampshire, and with such credentials as he could present for his security, and a reasonable degree of reliance upon the support of his friends, attempt resolutely to face down his calumniators, is to be referred to the one or the other of these two reasons. Either he felt that there was no reasonable hope that he should succeed in this courageous attempt, and that if he were allowed to remain at home it would be as a suspected person smarting under a sense of wrong, to lead an aimless and miserable life; or else he really desired and expected that he might yet obtain a place of honor and service in the patriot army. He lingered about the camp. He devoted himself zealously to the study of military tactics. He continued his experiments on gunpowder. He strolled between Woburn, Medford, Cambridge, and Charlestown, learning whatever his inquisitive and observing mind could appropriate. But there was one set of men whom he never could conciliate, who mistrusted his purposes and cast upon him lowering looks as they met him about the camp. These were the general and field officers from New Hampshire, who looked upon him as a dandy and an upstart at least, if not also as at heart a traitor. They would not associate with him, still less confide in him.

Major Baldwin records under date of June 4, 1775: —

"Sunday, A. M., went to Meeting: after Meeting at noon went down to see the Men-of-War fire, &c. to Lechmere Point, and viewed Boston, &c. Major Thompson and Lieut. Reed was my company."

"June 13. Tuesday, A Manifesto came out from General Gage. We are in expectation that the Troops will be out soon. I am poorly with a cold. Major Thompson went to Woburn."

It was to avert and oppose that expected *sortie* of the

British troops from Boston, that on the following Saturday, June 17, the fortifications were thrown up on the heights of Charlestown by a detachment of New England soldiers, sent from Cambridge by General Ward, just before midnight on Friday, resulting in the Battle of Bunker Hill, of which it has been generally believed that Major Thompson was at least a spectator.

As the College buildings at Cambridge were now used as barracks, Colonel Baldwin records on the 15th, "They are beginning to remove the Library." The books were transported to Concord, Massachusetts, some eighteen miles into the country. Major Thompson assisted in this labor, glad thus to recognize his obligations to the College.

Mr. Johnston, above quoted, as writing from information communicated to him by the son of Thompson's eldest step-brother, says that, after the battle at Charlestown, Thompson was favorably introduced by some officers at Cambridge to General Washington, who had just assumed the command; and that, had it not been for the opposition of some of the New Hampshire officers, he would have had the place in the American artillery corps which was given to Colonel Gridley.

The following letter of Thompson's was found in a file of Colonel Baldwin's papers. Its probable date was August, 1775.

"DEAR SIR, — I observed in the General Orders of Sunday last that each Sargent and Corporal in the Army was to wear an *Epaulet* to distinguish them from the Commissioned Officers and from the private soldiers. I herewith send you samples of some which I apprehend will answer the end, and if you will be so kind as to get them approved of by the General, and engage any considerable number for me, you may depend on having them done in the best manner and with the utmost despatch, as there is a considerable number of Women here who will immediately go to work upon them. Whether it is proper or not to shew them to General Washington, I leave to your judgement. I apprehend the price ought to be somewhere about 15/, or perhaps as low as 13/6, if a large number were engaged.

" If it shall be thought proper for the Sargent Majors to wear one or two red Silk Epaulets, instead of a worsted one, I can easily supply them.

" Please to give my compliments to Col. Gerrish, and present him with one of the red cockades which the bearer will give you as a present from his and your much

Obliged and most Obedient Servant,
" BENJAMIN THOMPSON.

" *Wednesday Morning.*

" To Col. Baldwin, Camp before Boston."

Only one other letter written on this side of the ocean remains to be given from the pen of Benjamin Thompson. It is impossible to read it without emotion. The writer was twenty-two years of age, but the letter has the vigor of the maturest manliness. Its firm and bold chirography is in keeping with its sentiments and with the forcible language in which they are expressed. It is addressed to his father-in-law.

" Woburn, August 14th, 1775.

" Hon[d] Sir, — I have your favours of the 16 and 29 May, which I should have answered long since, but have waited for an opportunity of conversing with you Verbally. But as I see no prospect of having such a long-wish'd-for interview, I shall trouble you with one more of my Letters.

" I am not so thoroughly convinc'd that my leaving the Town of Concord was wrong (considering the circumstances at that time) as I am that it was wrong in me to do it without your knowledge or advice. This, Sir, is a step which I always have repented, and for which I am now sincerely and heartily sorry, and ask your forgiveness. What infatuation could induce me to take a step of so much importance without previously consulting you upon the affair, I am at a loss to imagine. But be assured, Sir, that tho' you was not privy to my going off, yet I did not do it without the knowledge and advice of many others whom I really thought my friends, and among the rest you will give me leave to name your Son as the chief, who not only gave it as his opinion that it was for the best, but also furnished me with a Horse to make my escape, and money to the amount of 20 Dollars to bear my expenses, and promised to take care of my affairs in my absence. Into his hands I committed all my Notes and papers of consequence; saving only a few Notes to the amount of about £ 300, which I left with Mrs. Thompson, the chief of which, I am informed, he has since gotten into his possession.

" My situation at that time was peculiarly critical. I knew I had a number of enemies in the Town whose Personal and inveterate malice nothing would satisfy, and found by fatal experience that they had it in their power to raise the cry of the populace against me; and to persuade them that what they laid to my charge (Viz: being instrumental in procuring a pardon for some Deserters) was not only in itself a crime of the blackest dye, but that I did it with an express design to injure the Country, and assist in enslaving it; in fine, that I was an enemy to the cause of America, and deserved the severest punishments. 'Tis true all did not coincide in this opinion, and I was peculiarly happy in having my Brother Walker's approbation of my conduct. But notwithstanding he thought me innocent, yet he dared not appear in my behalf; he saw the current was against me, and was afraid to interfere.

" When I was brought to trial, my friends (knowing in what a light my crime was look'd upon by the populace) advised me to plead *not guilty*. I did so, but found, instead of quieting the disturbances, it only served to heighten the clamours against me, 'till at length I found it absolutely necessary that something should be done for my *personal security*. My friends advised me to leave the Town 'till the storm should be abated, which they doubted not would be in a short time. I neither doubted the abilities nor scrupled the sincerity of my friends, and accordingly followed their advice. But the event has not proved equal to my expectations, for the storm, instead of subsiding, has increased, and the popular disturbances have grown into such a flame as I fear nothing but my blood will extinguish.

"Had the People of Concord looked upon Banishment as a punishment equal to my crimes, they would not surely have refused my *very reasonable request* for Liberty to pass to that Town and to repass to Cambridge unmolested, if affairs could not be amicably settled so that I might live at home in peace and safety. I did not claim any merit from any examination I had passed through here. I did not attempt in the least to palliate those offences I am charg'd with by mine enemies, but only wished to meet my accusers on equal ground. And I think their refusal of this request not only affords a melancholy presage of what I am to expect from them, but will clearly demonstrate to the World upon what principles *these men* act who, under pretence of 'defending their Liberties and priviledges, and asserting the rights of mankind,' are depriving individuals of every *idea of freedom*, and are exercising a *Tyranny* which an *Eastern Despot* would blush to be Guilty of.

"As to my being instrumental in the return of some Deserters, by procuring them a pardon, I freely acknowledge that I was. But you will give me leave to say that what I did was done from principles the most unexceptionable — the most disinterested — a sincere desire to serve my *King* and *Country*, and from motives of *Pity* to those unfortunate Wretches who had deserted the service to which they had *voluntarily* and so *solemnly* tyed themselves, and to which they were desirous of returning. If the designed ends were not answered by what I did, I am sincerely and heartily sorry. But if it is a Crime to act from principles like these, I glory in being a Criminal.

"But as to the other 'Known' and 'Obnoxious facts' which you mention, Viz. 'maintaining a long and expensive correspondence with G——r W——th,' or 'a suspicious correspondence, to say the least, with G——rs W——th and G——e,' I would beg leave to observe, That at the time that Governor Wentworth first honored me with his notice, it was at a time when he was as high in the esteem of his people in general as ever was any Governor in America,—at a time when even Mr. Sullivan himself was proud to be thought his friend. And as from the first commencement of our acquaintance 'till I left Concord he never did anything (to my knowledge) whereby he forfeited the affection and confidence of the Public, I cannot see why a correspondence with him should be obnoxious; or that the *length* or *expensiveness* of it should be thought an object of *public attention*,—that merited *Public Censure*. 'T is true, Sir, I always thought myself honored by his friendship, and was ever fond of a correspondence with him,—a correspondence which was purely private and friendly, and not Political, and for which I cannot find in my Heart either to express my sorrow or ask forgiveness of the Public.

"As to my maintaining a correspondence with Governor Gage, this part of the charge is intirely without foundation, as I never received a Letter from him in my life; nor did I ever write him one, except about half a dozen lines which I sent him just before I left Concord may be call'd a Letter, and which contained no intelligence, nor anything of a public nature, but was only to desire that the Soldiers who returned from Concord might be Ordered not to inform any person by whose intercession their pardon was granted them.

"But this is not the only groundless charge that has been brought against me. Many other crimes which you do not mention have been laid to my charge, for which I have had to answer both *publicly* and *privately*. Mine enemies are indefatigable in their indeavours to distress me, and I find to my sorrow that they are but too successful. I have been driven from the Camp by the clamours of the New Hampshire People, and am again threaten'd in this place. But I hope soon to be out of the reach of my Cruel Persecutors, for I am determined to seek for *that Peace* and *Protection* in foreign Lands and among strangers which is deny'd me in my native country. I cannot any longer bear the insults that are daily offered me. I cannot bear to be looked upon and treated as the *Arban* of Society. I have done nothing that can deserve this *cruel usage.* I have done nothing with any design to injure my countrymen, and cannot any longer bear to be treated in this barbarous manner by them.

" And notwithstanding I have the tenderest regard for my Wife and family, and really believe I have an equal return of Love and affection from them; though I feel the keenest distress at the thoughts of what Mrs. Thompson and my Parents and friends will suffer on my account, and though I foresee and realize the distress, poverty, and wretchedness that must unavoidably attend my Pilgrimage in unknown lands, destitute of fortune, friends, and acquaintance, yet all these Evils appear to me more tolerable than the treatment which I meet with from the hands of mine ungrateful countrymen.

" This step, I am sensible, is violent, but my case is desperate. I have nothing to expect from mine Enemies, and my friends are afraid to appear for me. And I see no prospect of being able either to return to Concord, or even to stay here much longer in peace and safety. A reconciliation upon honorable terms is of all others the thing most to be desired. But you must allow me to say, that my present situation, notwithstanding it is thus dreadful, is to be preferred to a reconciliation (supposing it possible) upon the terms of my making an acknowledgement. The crime which is alleged against me (Viz! being an enemy to my Country) is a crime of the blackest dye, — a crime which must, if proved against me, inevitably entail perpetual infamy and disgrace upon my name. If I confess myself Guilty, will mine Enemies, will the World, think me innocent ? — or will even the Charity of my very friends attempt to exculpate me when I accuse myself ?

" Whatever prudence may dictate, yet Conscience and Honor, God and Religion, forbid that my Mouth should speak what my Heart disclaims. I cannot profess my sorrow for an action which I am conscious was done from the best of motives.

If the event has proved contrary to my expectations, or if I can be persuaded that I have acted upon mistaken principles, I am ready not only to Express my sorrow, but to do it in the most open and public manner. But 'till this can be the case, 'till I can be fully persuaded that I have really *done* wrong, I cannot be persuaded to acknowledge that I *have* done so.

"I am extremely unhappy to differ from you in opinion in anything, but more especially in an affair of so much consequence as the propriety of my returning to Concord upon the terms mentioned in your Letter. But I hope that the reasons which I have now given, added to the inimical disposition which the Committee have lately shown towards me, will serve in some measure as an excuse for my not following your advice in this affair.

"Believe me, Sir, I always have had, and still retain, the highest veneration for your judgement, and the most sincere and dutiful affection for your Person; and hope that the unhappiness of my present deplorable situation will not be increased by incurring your displeasure. Be assured, Sir, I mean not to offend, and hope that no offence will be taken.

"I am too well acquainted with your Paternal affection for your Children to doubt of your kind care over them. But you will excuse me if I trouble you with my *most earnest* desires and intreaties for your *peculiar* care of my family, whose distressed circumstances call for every indulgence and alleviation you can afford them.

"I must also beg a continuance of your Prayers for me, that my present afflictions may have a suitable impression on my mind, and that in due time I may be extricated out of all my troubles. That this may be the case, that the happy time may soon come when I may return to my family in peace and safety, and *when every individual in America may sit down under his own vine, and under his own Fig-tree, and have none to make him afraid* is the constant and devout wish of

"Your dutiful and Affectionate Son,

"BENJ: THOMPSON.

"Revd Tim^y Walker."

Major Thompson was not the only person in those troubled times that had occasion to charge upon those espousing the championship of public liberty a tyrannical treatment of individuals who did not accord with their schemes or views. Probably in our late war of Rebellion his case was paralleled by those of hundreds in both sections of our country, who with halting and divided minds or unsatisfied judgments were arrested in the process of decision by treatment from others which put them under the lead of passion. The choice of a great many loyalists in our Revolution would have been wiser and more satisfactory to themselves had they been allowed to make it deliberately, — an impossibility under the circumstances. So far as I have means of knowing, this letter was the last communication which Thompson ever made to his father-in-law or to his wife, directly or indirectly. This statement, however, and the inferences which might be drawn from it, are to be accepted only as negative evidence, for letters may have been written and received of which there is no record or tradition, and letters may have been written which were never received by the parties to whom they were respectively addressed. It was comparatively easy, during the war, for persons in England and in this country who belonged to the same side in interest and sympathy to correspond with each other, taking the risks of the sea, of privateering, and of capture. But for those who belonged to the contending parties, separated by the ocean, correspondence was more embarrassed.

Certainly all the claims and promptings of natural love are fully and tenderly indulged in that heart-written letter. Filial gratitude and veneration, and a young husband and father's yearnings struggle in it with the alternate expression of a deep and harrowing sense of unjust treatment and unmerited obloquy. One can hardly suppress the wish that the good old minister might have survived to know the philanthropic labors and the peaceful honors of his son-in-law. It is to be feared, however, that he to whom Thompson owed so much, and for whom he dropped a tear and yielded to deep emotion when speaking confidentially to Pictet about his obligations, went to his honored grave without any further word from his son-in-law, though he probably had tidings of him.

Thompson was preparing to do effective service in the British army in this country at the very time when the aged minister sunk peacefully to rest in his parsonage at Concord, September 2, 1782.

From the facts and documents which have been thus presented at length, a reader who cares to make a moral estimate of the course pursued up to this stage by Major Thompson, and of his subsequent action, must form his judgment. Candor will make an allowance on the score of his youth and the influence of the circumstances amid which he was compelled to reach a decision. It is remarkable that his two most intimate friends in later life have given us, seemingly as deductions from his own confidential statements, reasons for inferring that his heart was from the first on the side of the royalist party. The following is a translation from the narrative of Pictet, in continuation of that already given : —

"At the commencement of the troubles in America which preceded and brought about the war of Independence, Thomp-

son, then twenty years old, was bound in friendship with the
Governor of the Province, who was his compatriot and a
supporter of the government. The civil and military trusts
with which, while still so young, he had already been invested,
continued to attach him to the royalist party by duty and gratitude. When the party in opposition had sway in his Province,
he was compelled to abandon his home and to seek an asylum
in Boston, then occupied by the English troops. . . . . Thompson was received with distinction by the British commander,
and called to raise a regiment for the King's service. But the
course of the war having brought about the evacuation of Boston
in the spring of 1776, he went then to England, and was made
bearer of important despatches for the government."

Cuvier's report, in his Eloge, is to this effect: After
having referred to the incident by which "at the age of
nineteen, the hand of a rich widow had made the poor
scholar, at the moment when he least expected it, one of
the most considerable men in the colony," Cuvier adds: —

"Having taken side with the royalist party during the troubles
in America, the populace of Concord were so enraged against
him that he found it requisite to take refuge in Boston, leaving
his wife behind him pregnant of a daughter. The former he
never saw again; the latter joined him for the first time when
twenty years of age.
"One of the first triumphs of Washington was to compel
the British troops to evacuate Boston on the 24th of March,
1776, and Mr. Thompson was the official bearer of this disastrous intelligence to London."

Now it is hardly probable that the then Count Rumford in confidential narration to his friends intended to,
or did, disclose a secret which he had up to that time
kept to himself, — that he had from the first been a
royalist. He knew too well what he had left in writing
on this side of the water, and remembered too well the

confidence and friendship reposed in him by Mr. Baldwin, to make such statements concerning that period of his life before he left Concord. I have found no reason for doubting that, if Thompson had been treated in a conciliatory manner after his examination, and had been gratified in his desire to have a position in the American army, he would have faithfully served his native country. Nor do I imagine that under any circumstances he would have proved an Arnold. That he was deeply wounded in spirit and irritated in temper when he formed his plan of exile either to some distant part of this country or abroad is very evident. But that this sense of wrong, or irritation, excited in him a vengeful purpose, is not shown by anything known to have been said by him, nor is it necessarily indicated by what he did. Neither is there any evidence that when Major Thompson left Woburn, according to the intention which he frankly communicated to his father-in-law, he had resolved to join the ranks of the enemy, or even to seek their civil protection. Pictet, in a paragraph which I have omitted from the above quotation, says that Thompson left his home in November, 1773, and Cuvier says that his daughter was not born till after his departure. These errors as to matters of fact may persuade us that both Pictet and Cuvier erred also in matters of inference as to the early predilections of Thompson for the royalist cause. Probably circumstances and the opening of opportunities, more than any settled purpose, decided the course of this forlorn and ill-treated young husband and father, adrift on the world, when he found himself, loosed from all home ties, beginning to wander in distracted times.

There was really nothing secret or disguised in the plans which he formed for seeking " in a foreign land and among strangers," at the risk of homelessness and poverty, the peace and protection which he could not find in his own dwelling. He did not privately steal away. He remained in and about Woburn two months after writing his last letter to Mr. Walker, in which he so deliberately avowed his intentions. He settled his affairs with his neighbors, collecting dues and paying debts, well assured that his wife and child would lack none of the means of a comfortable support. Having thus made all his preparations, he started from Woburn, October 13, 1775, in a country vehicle, accompanied by his step-brother, Josiah Pierce, who drove him near to the bounds of the Province, on the shore of Narragansett Bay, whence young Pierce returned. Thompson was taken by a boat on board the Scarborough, British frigate, in the harbor of Newport. (See Appendix.)

What Major Thompson said or did to secure himself a favorable reception from the commander of the vessel, — whether he sought refuge as a persecuted sufferer, or proffered service as a new-won friend, there are no means at this time for knowing. The vessel itself very soon came round to Boston, and he came in her in some capacity. Here he remained till the evacuation of the town by the British forces, of which event he was undoubtedly the bearer of tidings to England, in despatches from General Howe. Here the work of conversion, slow or protracted, was completed ; and henceforward we are to know Benjamin Thompson, till the close of the war, as in council and in arms an opponent of the cause of liberty for his native land. He must have done appreciable service in the four or five months of his new apprenticeship in Boston, in order. to have won so soon the place of an official in the British government

It has come down distinctly in the family of the Rev. William Walter, D. D., as I learn from a granddaughter, that during Thompson's stay in Boston he was a somewhat secret inmate of that clergyman's family in their house in South Street. Dr. — then Mr. — Walter, a graduate of Harvard College in 1756, was Rector of Trinity Church in Boston, having been ordained by the Bishop of London. There is a vague tradition that the Rev. Mr. Walker contrived to have an interview — quite an unsatisfactory one — with his son-in-law while he was thus a guest of Mr. Walter. It may have been so. But the jealousy of any intercourse between the town and the suburbs when occupied respectively by the hostile armies, and the difficulties thrown in the way of such intercourse, render this alleged interview doubtful, and, unless sought by both parties, improbable. I am inclined to believe that Mr. Walter and Thompson were fellow-passengers to England. They were thenceforward intimate friends. At the peace, Mr. Walter came to Sherburne, Nova Scotia, as a Doctor of Divinity, and there exercised his clerical functions, having received a large grant of land from the crown. He returned to Boston in 1791, and was chosen Rector of Christ Church. I find mention of him till his death, in 1800, in letters of Count Rumford, as a confidential friend with whom he corresponded. Unfortunately, the Count's numerous letters to him have not been preserved.

Of course there was much interest and curiosity among the friends and relatives of Major Thompson to learn his whereabouts after his departure. They could hear only rumors like the following.

Mrs. Baldwin wrote to her husband at the camp at Cambridge, under date from Woburn, January 15, 1776 : —

"Mrs. Pierce [mother of Thompson] has heard that you said you knew that Major Thompson was in Boston. She gives her compliments, and begs that if you know anything where he is, be so kind as to let her know ; she is in pain to hear."

And again,

"Woburn, Feb. 7, 1776.—I must inform you that Brother Cyrus saw Mr. Parkman,—informs him that our famous Major Thompson is in Boston, a clerk for a Major—— [name illegible). Mrs. Thompson is in Woburn."

After the army had gone with General Washington to New York, Colonel Baldwin, who was on duty there, wrote to Mrs. Baldwin from the

"Camp at Mile Square, about five miles north of King's Bridge, and near General Lee's Head-quarters, October 22d, 1776. I have had no opportunity to find out whether Major Thompson is with the enemy or not."

The first trustworthy information received about Major Thompson by his friends was that communicated in letters from London by American refugees there resident. These letters made known his rapid advancement in a career in which we must soon trace him.

Mr. George R. Baldwin copied, in 1858, the following papers, which he obtained at that time from Cyrus Thompson, Esq., grandson of Justice Samuel Thompson, named in them. They have an historical and personal interest.

" *Confiscation Papers of Benj^a^ Thompson, Absentee. Commonwealth of Massachusetts, Middlesex, ss.*

" To Messrs. BARTHOLOMEW RICHARDSON, JR., NOAH EATON,
and ABIJAH THOMPSON, all of Woburn, in the County of
Middlesex aforesaid, Greeting :

" Whereas it has been represented that Benjamin Thompson,
late of Woburn, Physician, now an Absentee, hath fled from
his habitation to the Enemies of the United States for protection, leaving behind him real and personal Estate of more than
Twenty Pounds in value, and that he hath been absent from his
usual place of abode more than three months :

" Pursuant, therefore, to a Law of this State in' such cases
provided, and the authority to me therein given, I do hereby
authorise and empower you, the above-named three Persons,
a Committee to receive and examine the claims of the several
Creditors to the Estate of the said Absentee ; and you are hereby
allowed three months' time from the date hereof, in which
time to transact the said business. You are in all cases to
proceed by the same rules as are by law prescribed for insolvent
Estates, and to report to me your doings at the end of the said
three months, and in all things deal impartially as you are
sworn, and you are to notify Wm Hunt, Esq., to contest the
claims before you.

" Given under my hand and seal of office, this fifth day of
September, A. D. 1781.

" OLIVER PRESCOTT, Prsd.

BARTH. RICHARDSON, } Sworn before me, SAM^t^ THOMP-
" Decr 4. NOAH EATON,   } son, Justice of the Peace."
ABIJAH THOMPSON. }

" *A List of the Claims exhibited and allowed agst. the Estate of
Benjamin Thompson, late of Woburn, Absentee.*

" To Hannah Flagg, by Legacy
    Principal   £ 26 13 4
    Interest due on the Same   35 8 0   £ 62 1 4
  This Legacy was ordered to be paid to the said
  Hannah Flagg in the Testament of Capt. Eben-

7

ezer Thompson, deceased, Grandfather to said
Absentee.

	£	s.	d.
To Mary Carter's Account	£0	12	0
To Loammi Baldwin on Note and Acc.ᵗ	4	13	6
To Timothy Walker, Jr., note dated Aug. 16ᵗʰ, 1774, with interest for the same	117	16	0
To Timothy Walker, Jr., other note, dated Dec.ʳ 14ᵗʰ, 1774, with interest for the same	8	6	7
To Timothy Walker, Jr., another note dated Nov. 2ᵈ, 1774, with interest	2	2	10
Cost of Advertising	0	12	0
Time expended by the Commissioners	4	10	0
To Jonathan Randall for expense at Sundry times, when examining the claims	0	12	0
To Samuel Thompson for Journey in part to Cambridge for Commissioners 4/, Fees 4/	0	8	0
Swearing the Commissioners and lodging the return	0	6	0
Fees paid	0	3	3
	£212	3	3

" WOBURN, 4ᵗʰ Dec.ʳ 1781.

" BARTHᵂ RICHARDSON, ⎫
NOAH EATON,   ⎬ *Commissioners.*"
ABIJAH THOMPSON, ⎭

" MIDDLESEX, 12 Dec. 1781. — Exhibited upon oath by Samuel Thompson, Esq., Attorney to one of the principal Creditors, who likewise attested that the claims were contested by William Hunt, Esq., Attorney for the Commonwealth, and I have examined the same and do allow thereof.

"OLIVER PRESCOTT, *J. Prob.*"

" *The account of the Committee of Correspondence and Safety, &c. for the Town of Wilmington for the year* 1779.

" The Committee aforesaid charge themselves with the Rent of Land of Benj. Thompson, an Absentee, for the year aforesaid, amounting to

	£	s.	d.
	£18	0	0
Said Comᵗᵗ crave an allowance for their cost and trouble	8	0	0
Balance in favour of the Estate,	£10	0	0

" *Account as above for the year* 1780.

" The Committee aforesaid charge themselves with the Rent of Lands which did belong to Benjamin Thompson, an Absentee, for the year 1780, said Land lying in Wilmington aforesaid, amounting to   £ 135   0   0

    Said Com^{ttee} crave an allowance in their discharge
     as follows : viz.

For Advertisement 18/, Expenses at Vendue £ 12 18   £ 13   16   0
Committee' Time, and Leases,   12   12   0
Journey to Cambridge and Expenses to Boston to pay
    Balance to the Treasurer,   12   0   0
Probate fees,   4   11   0
                                  £ 43   0   0

" MIDDLESEX, 3d May, 1780. — Having examined this account and sworn Deacon Benjamin Jaquith, Chairman of the Committee, I allow thereof.

" OLIVER PRESCOTT, *J. Prob.*"

Major Thompson had been named among the proscribed in the Alienation Act passed by the State of
New Hampshire in 1778.

CHAPTER III.

IN one of his letters to his father-in-law, on a previous page, Benjamin Thompson had written, "I never did, nor (let my treatment be what it will) ever will do, any action that may have the most distant tendency to injure the true interests of this my native country." Any one who should assume — as I do not — to maintain the consistency between this solemn pledge and the agency to which Major Thompson immediately and zealously committed himself on his arrival in England would have to fashion for him an argument which, however plausible, would be subtle and casuistical. He would need to undertake to prove that Mr. Thompson had persuaded himself that "the true interests of his native country" were not to be secured by resisting British authority and achieving its political independence, but would be realized by allowing that authority, with whatever limitations and conditions, — graciously defined after submission had been exacted, — to be permanently restored over the revolting Provinces. It might be a part of this plea to show that, when he left America, Major Thompson had· become satisfied that the resources of this country were unequal to success in the struggle; and that when he reached England he was so impressed by the tokens of the royal and ministerial ability to subdue a rebellion, that he was willing to help bring about what was seemingly inevitable.

As I would not offer such a plea for the subject of this memoir, neither will I disguise or palliate the fact that he threw his whole efficiency — doubtless also his pride and ambition — into the service of the British ministry. He must have said or done something at once to secure his ready welcome, and must have so improved upon the opportunity which that afforded him as to win confidence and to secure position and influence. The smart of indignation at the injustice which he conceived he had borne, and the contempt exhibited by the patriots in rejecting his proffered services, might either have combined with or yielded to the lures of patronage and distinction. Thenceforward the rustic youth became the companion of gentlemen of wealth and culture, of scientific philosophers, of the nobility, and of princes. The kind of influence which he at once began to exert, and the promotions which he so soon received in England, answer to a class of services rendered by him of a nature not to be misconceived.

Pictet, proceeding with his report of the confidential disclosures of his friend from the point at which we left them, wrote the following : —

"They had not in England at that time much exact information about the state of the country, all whose ties to the mother land had been ruptured for many years. Thompson thoroughly understood the matter. He could give trustworthy intelligence about the topography, and about the events of the war in which he had played a part. He was not slow in winning the confidence of the Secretary of State for the Colonies. Some time after his arrival in London he was appointed Secretary of the Province of Georgia, — an office, however, which he never filled. He remained in London attached to the Colonial Office."

When, soon after the peace, the members of the successive administrations and parliaments of Great Britain looked back over the long series of mortifying blunders, mishaps, and discomfitures connected with the management of the war, there was one conviction which, as an explanation or a palliation, offered them chief relief, though in itself hardly a consolation, namely, that they had all along been working in the dark. They were made aware of the entire ignorance, and of the wholly misleading knowledge, so called, of this country, its geography, its people, their feelings, purposes, and resources, under which the war had been conducted. This ignorance was felt in itself to have been culpable, though the reason of it had been mainly indifference, if not arrogant contempt. Means of information had been within the reach of the government. Franklin and other provincial agents had offered to enlighten the ministry. Whole drawers of despatches and other important papers relating to the American Colonies had lain unopened in government offices. · Indeed, the first knowledge which some of the custodians of those papers and many more recent historical and political essayists obtained about important documents hid away in those offices came to them through the requests sent in for the privilege of examining them by investigators like Mr. Sparks, who crossed the ocean for that purpose.

The receipt in England of the intelligence that the British army, after having been cooped up in Boston for nine months, had been compelled by Washington to evacuate it by their ships, and that a whole fleet of store-vessels and transports on their way to Boston to relieve the army were likely, one by one, to fall into the hands of the Yankees, furnishing them with just the munitions and goods which they most needed, caused an intense excitement and dismay. The intelligence of the evacuation was made public in the London Gazette of May 3, 1776, though, during the storm which the announcement raised in Parliament, suspicions were thrown out that the ministry had had earlier knowledge of the mortifying fact which they had concealed.

It would be pleasant to think that Major Thompson bore the tidings of that significant prognostication of the course of the war. That, however, could hardly be regarded as the reason for his welcome from Lord George Germaine, to whom he would have carried the despatch, nor for his immediate admission to a desk in the Colonial Office. He, of course, proffered, and showed he could impart, "information," as Pictet learned from himself. That a youth of twenty-three years should thus at once be relied upon and rewarded

for service of that kind was in perfect consistency with
the mode in which affairs were then managed. No
doubt " topography " was the matter of his first conversation with Lord George and the youth had only
to fall back upon his school lessons.

The head of the Department himself was wholly incompetent for the place, and was but a blunderer. It
was in keeping with either the comic or the tragic element in his management that he should have accepted
so young an adviser, and have extended to him so large
a confidence, so well rewarded. Lord George had
been received into office as a prominent and effective
agent in the subjugation of the American Colonies,
having been made Secretary on November 10, 1775.
He was desirous, by complete subserviency to the
schemes of the King and ministry, of retrieving his own
previously damaged reputation as a soldier. And we
may reasonably infer, that, as a condition of securing
his patronage and confidence, Thompson must have
shown that the information he could impart and the
counsels he should suggest would lie midway between
those given by such advisers as had previously been
listened to or set aside by the ministry. There were
honest, wise, and every way competent men, Americans
and Englishmen, within easy reach of the administration, and indeed proffering their counsels and warnings,
who knew much more, and saw far more keenly into
the horoscope of probable events, than did Thompson.
But their advice, so far as it involved forebodings, or
even deliberation and caution, was rejected by the
ministry as unwelcome, because given in the interest
of the rebellion. Others there were, like the refugee
officers of the crown and other loyalists, who had been

driven hence by an angry populace. These were ready
to sustain the contemptuous opinions of a few members
of the Parliament on the side of the ministry, that
resolute measures on the part of the King, and a few
regiments of British soldiers, would soon extinguish the
threatening flame. The advice of the former class was
rejected in scorn; that of the latter class had been
found misleading, and dangerously falsified by the attempts to follow it. Thompson must have found his
cue in substantially pursuing a midway course. Cuvier, referring to his first presenting himself before the
Minister with his despatches, says: "On this occasion,
by the clearness of his details and the gracefulness of
his manners he insinuated himself so far into the
graces of Lord George Germaine that he took him
into his employment." An intelligent and observing
witness on the spot, who had known Thompson as an
apprentice-boy in Salem, and who is by and by to be
quoted, tells us that the young man soon became such
a favorite with Lord George that he was daily in the
habit of breakfasting, dining, and supping with him at
his lodgings; while it soon came to be known among
the American refugees in England, that rills from the
fountain of favor and patronage flowed through Thompson, and that he himself was becoming rich and conse-
quential. There is but one fair construction to be put
on these facts. In accordance with the strain of what
has previously been said about Thompson's espousal
of the unpatriotic side in our war, if it were a matter
of importance to ascertain how and in what way he
committed himself to the King's service, and what was
the nature of the information or advice imparted by
him, we should have in the main to depend wholly

upon inferences. With his great natural abilities and his spirit of observation, not forgetting his own appreciation of himself, he might have been a really valuable counsellor to those who rejected such as were more wise and such as were more reckless. He may have satisfied himself that the rebellion would, in any event, stop short of securing the independence of the Colonies, and have looked upon himself as a mediator on the side of the stronger party, aiming in a friendly antagonism to secure the real interests of the weaker party. Besides his clerkship, his first civil appointment, as he informed Pictet, appears to have been as Secretary of the Province of Georgia, — in which position, however, he would seem to have done nothing, simply because there was nothing to be done in it. The British authority was nominally restored in that Province by the return of the Governor, Sir James Wright, July 20, 1779. But it was a short and barren restoration. The loyal-ists there, who had been beguiled by the royal proclamation into a belief that an end had come to their troubles, had occasion soon after to rue their confidence, when orders came from England, in 1782, that the royal authority should be abandoned there, — orders which included, of course, an abandonment of the loyalists themselves, and a surrender of their property to confiscation. In vain did they offer to the King's general the assurance that they would still hold the Province for him if he would give them a single regiment of foot to assist the Georgia Rangers. We may be sure that Thompson's secretaryship, if rewarded, was ineffective. We may be sure, too, that the first occupation of Thompson, apart from the discharge of his duties as a private secretary and a subordinate official in his Department, would be to make the most and the best of his opportunities in acquainting himself with the British metropolis and in seeking introductions alike to men in public station and to those engaged in scientific pursuits. Nothing of interest would escape his keen observation, and no means of personal improvement or acquisition, through men or things, would fail to yield him advancement. It was a place for the country youth to indulge his genius, and for the aspirant for thrift and fame to gratify his ambition. He happened, as did Franklin a little earlier, upon a time and stage of development when science and philosophy were making a marked transition in their methods, from the speculative to the experimental process. Thompson's genius was eminently practical and experimental, and he showed a most cautious painstaking in the most minute processes and conditions with which he applied the tests of experiment. After he had given some considerable time to peering round and through the metropolis, as his position naturally prompted him he turned his attention to certain improvements in economy, utility, and efficiency in connection with military details. He was so situated that his suggestions would readily obtain a hearing and attention. He advised and procured the adoption of bayonets for the fusees of the Horse-Guards, to be used in fighting on foot. He continued his experiments on gunpowder, with greater facilities at his command for extending them and making them yield to the severest tests of science. The range and character of his social intimacies formed within the next year or two show how diligently and successfully he cultivated the acquaintance of men of station and distinction. His manners with such were always fascinating and ingratiating. In the autumn of the year 1777, on account of his sufferings from impaired health, Mr. Thompson went to Bath, where he spent some time in using the waters. Here he resumed and continued his favorite scientific experiments, especially a series of them to test the cohesive force of different bodies. In July, 1778, he was the guest of Lord George Germaine at his country-seat at Stoneland Lodge. Here, with the assistance, as he tells us, of the Rev. Mr. Ball, Rector of Withyham, he undertook experiments "to determine the most advantageous situation for the vent in fire-arms, and to measure the velocities of bullets and the recoil under various circumstances. I had hopes, also, of being able to find out the velocity of the inflammation of gunpowder, and to measure its force more accurately than had hitherto been done." *

On Thompson's return to London from Bath, he communicated the results of his investigations into the cohesion of bodies to Sir Joseph Banks, President of the Royal Society. Being thus self-introduced as a scientific inquirer to that eminent man, he was soon on most intimate terms with him, and became one of his nearest circle of friends. It was not in 1778, as stated by his biographers, but in 1779, that Thompson was elected a Fellow of the Royal Society. His certificate for election describes him "as a gentleman well versed in natural knowledge and many branches of polite learning." †

He very soon became one of the most active and hon-

* An Account of some Experiments upon Gunpowder, &c.

† History of the Royal Society &c. By Charles Richard Weld, Esq. Vol. II. p. 212.

ored members of the Society, always attending its meetings when he was in London. In order that he might pursue his experiments on gunpowder with great guns, he sought, and readily obtained, the most favorable opportunity with extraordinary facilities for so doing. In the Essay already quoted he thus refers to an occasion which also enabled him to engage in sea-service : —

" During a cruise which I made, as a volunteer, in the Victory, with the British fleet, under the command of my late worthy friend Sir Charles Hardy, in the year 1779, I had many opportunities of attending to the firing of heavy cannon ; for though we were not fortunate enough to come to a general action with the enemy, as is well known, yet, as the men were frequently exercised at the great guns and in firing at marks, and as some of my friends in the fleet, then captains (since made admirals), as the Honourable Keith Stewart, who commanded the Berwick of 74 guns, — Sir Charles Douglas, who commanded the Duke of 98 guns, —and Admiral Macbride, who was then captain of the Bienfaisant of 64 guns, were kind enough, at my request, to make a number of experiments, and particularly by firing a greater number of bullets at once from their heavy guns than ever had been done before, and observing the distances at which they fell in the sea, — I had opportunities of making several very interesting observations, which gave me much new light relative to the action of fired gunpowder."

He also made a study of the principles of naval artillery, which he contributed as a chapter to Stalkartt's Treatise on Naval Architecture, published in 1781. He likewise devised a new code of marine signals which has not been made public. The period and the state of things in which he thus devoted his genius to practical science were peculiarly suited to procure him a full appreciation.

The Annual Register, in its chronicle of promotions

for the year 1780, records that in September, " B. Thompson, Esq., was made Under-Secretary of State for the Northern Department." The oversight of all the practical details for recruiting, equipping, transporting, and victualling the British forces, and of many other incidental arrangements, was thus committed to him. Though he discharged the duties of this office in person but little more than one year, his influence would naturally be felt while the administration of which he was a subordinate remained in power. The tenor of his counsels has not transpired, nor are we sufficiently well informed about the matter to say whether he had any special theory, plan, or policy; whether he was a prime originator, or only a subservient agent, of measures the results of which could have afforded but little satisfaction to those who were responsible for them. If he often attended the debates in Parliament, as doubtless he did, he had full opportunities of watching how the tide turned to ebb at the very moment before it seemed to have reached a full flood; and if he was discerning in the interpretation of signs, he must have known that his official service would be brief. As we shall see, he availed himself of a graceful occasion for resignation, most probably in full foresight of an alternative method of release. The exercise of his genius and the way in which he could best serve his fellow-men — that being afterwards the great aim of his life — lay in a direction quite different from his present employments. No one, therefore, biographer or critic, need be concerned to plead for him in an office where success would have been worse than failure. He first signed official papers October 27, 1780.

Thompson has left an interesting token of his officiousness in the service of King George III. in one of the manuscript volumes in the British Museum in London. That king showed a most commendable zeal in collecting a library of all the books and papers which came from, or which would throw light upon, the American Colonies from their first planting to his own time. A large portion of this collection came through the hands of George IV. into the national repository. In it is a small quarto volume containing a series of letters from Dr. Franklin to the Rev. Dr. Cooper, an eminent minister in Boston, upon American politics, from 1769 to 1774, with Dr. Cooper's answers; and also some letters from Governor Pownall to Dr. Cooper. There is added "a short history of those letters, or an account of the manner in which they happened to fall into the hands of the present proprietor of them," Mr. Thompson.

From this "account" it appears that when Dr. Cooper left Boston, after the battle of Bunker Hill, to find refuge in the country, as his effects, which he took with him, would be subject to search, he committed these valuable papers to the care of his friend, Mr. Jeffries, one of the selectmen of the town, who was then confined by sickness. Mr. Jeffries consigned them to a trunk containing things of his own. When he too left Boston, forgetting what had thus been intrusted to him, he left the trunk in charge of his son, Dr. Jeffries, who, remaining in the town, was in sympathy with the royalist party. At the evacuation of Boston he took the papers with him to Halifax. "From Halifax he brought them with him to London in January last [1777], and made a present of them to Mr. Thompson, who now presumes most humbly to lay them at his Majesty's feet [George III.] as a literary as well as a political curiosity." *

While the war was in progress, Mr. Thompson was brought into constant and intimate relations with the refugees or loyalists who had sought in England for protection against popular indignation and violence in this country, which steadily increased with the exasperation excited by every new measure of hostility adopted by the mother country. Being himself so well provided for, and in a situation of influence, where his patronage was effective, he undoubtedly found his position in this respect one of embarrassment and annoyance. There were several centres in England where these refugees gathered for companionship and mutual comfort. Bristol sheltered very many of them, but London was the place of their thickest concourse. The condition of most of the exiles was deplorable in the extreme, and many of the more magnanimous of them learned abroad a true love for their native country by suffering for it, if in another way, hardly any less in feeling than they would have suffered had they remained exposed to the dislike and gibes of their own fellow-citizens. Such of these refugees as had no means of their own and no wealthy friends — the case with all but a very few of them — beset the home government with their piteous appeals for aid, and the overburdened treasury was drawn upon for pensions and gratuities to keep them from starvation. Every one of them who could establish a claim for any loss incurred by his loyalty on this side of the water was eager to press his demands. In one year the grants made to them amounted to some £80,000. At the close of the war,

* Collections of Massachusetts Historical Society, 3d Series, Vol. VIII. pp. 278, 279.

under the constraints of ministerial reform and economy, this sum had shrunk to £18,000, and many of the exiles were compelled to face the alternative of returning to America to meet the humor of their now independent countrymen, or of remaining under humiliating circumstances amid equally unsympathizing people in England. So far as the relations between these refugees and Mr. Thompson can be traced, I find no evidence that he failed to do, in any case, what duty and friendliness required of him. If there was a seeming exception to this in a case now to be mentioned, it is very easy to relieve the imputation.

One of the most forlorn and disconsolate of these exiles was Samuel Curwen, of Salem, Massachusetts, who had been a Deputy Judge of Admiralty and Provincial Impost Officer in the service of the crown, as well as a county magistrate for thirty years. He had abundant property, but, being obnoxious for lack of spirit or confidence, on the breaking out of hostilities he had fled to Philadelphia, and from thence had sailed to England, remaining there through the war, but returning here unmolested at its close. He was a refined and sensitive man, desponding over his separation from wife and home and his fear of want, as he had reached the borders of old age. He received a gratuity of a hundred pounds, and was put on the Treasury list for an annual pension of the same amount.

The following extracts from Judge Curwen's journal have an interest in themselves in connection with Mr. Thompson.* Having chosen his residence in London, where he was intent to hear all the feverish rumors of

* The Journal and Letters of Samuel Curwen, &c. By George Atkinson Ward, 4th edition. Boston, 1864.

each day on the war, he writes under date of November 14, 1780: —

"Arriving at home, William Cabot drank tea with me, S. Sparhawk came in afterwards, and abode two hours; from whom I heard the first account of Arnold's intentional withdrawing himself and four or five thousand troops under his command from Congressional service to the Royal standard at New York, the failure of this scheme of treachery, and his lucky escape from his enemies' hands. From him also the relation of the seizure of Mr. Laurens's papers, late President of the Congress, and now a prisoner in the Tower; giving an account of the desperate situation of their affairs, with complaints of failure of their resources, and their inability to support the war any longer without loans from Holland, France, or Spain. The above comes from Benjamin Thompson, a native of Massachusetts, (formerly an apprentice to my next-door neighbor in Salem, Mr. John Appleton, an importer of British goods,) now Under-Secretary in the American Department."

Curwen records next year, April 19, an unsuccessful attempt to call on Mr. Thompson at his lodgings, Pall Mall.   On May 23 he writes : —

"On returning home, found a letter from Arthur Savage, informing me of Mr. Thompson's compliments and wish to see me at eleven o'clock to-morrow at his lodgings.

"May 24 [1781]. — Went early, in order to be at Mr. Benjamin Thompson's in time, and being a little before, heard he was not returned from Lord George Germaine's, where he always breakfasts, dines, and sups, so great a favorite is he.   To kill half an hour, I loitered to the Park through the Palace, and on second return found him at his lodgings; he received me in a friendly manner, taking me by the hand, talked with great freedom, and promised to remember and serve me in the way I proposed to him [probably the securing the continuance of his allowance unreduced]. Promises are easily made, and genteel delusive encouragement, the staple article of trade, belonging to the courtier's profession. I put no hopes on the fair appearances of outward behavior, though it is uncandid to suppose all mean to deceive. Some wish to do a service who have it not in their power ; all wish to be thought of importance and significancy, and this often leads to deceit. This young man, when a shop-lad to my next neighbor, ever appeared active, good-natured, and sensible ; by a strange concurrence of events, he is now Under-Secretary to the American Secretary of State, Lord George Germaine, a Secretary to Georgia, inspector of all the clothing sent to America, and Lieutenant-Colonel Commandant of horse dragoons at New York ; his income arising from these sources is, I have been told, near seven thousand a year,* — a sum infinitely beyond his most sanguine expectations. He is, besides, a member of the Royal Society. It is said he is of an ingenious turn, an inventive imagination, and, by being on one cruise in Channel Service with Sir Charles Hardy, has formed a more regular and better-digested system for signals than that heretofore used. He seems to be of a happy, even temper in general deportment, and reported of an excellent heart ; peculiarly respectful to Americans that fall in his way."

On July 27, and on August 3 and 4, Judge Curwen was disappointed in his attempts to find Mr. Thompson, either at his lodgings or at the Treasury. But the following entry in the journal, under August 11, indicates even a more grievous disappointment when he did find him : —

"After one hour's waiting, admitted to Mr. Thompson in the Plantation Office ; he seemed inclined to shorten the interview, received me with a courtier's smile, rather uncommunicative and dry. This reception has damped my ill-grounded hopes, derived from former seeming friendly intentions to pro-

* It is hardly probable that Major Thompson received anything like the sum above named as his annual emolument. Evidence enough will appear from his own pen and those of others, in the following pages, that he was neither mercenary nor avaricious. He never was lavish in expenditure for himself.

mote my views; this, my first, will be my last attempt to gain advantages from a courtier of whom I never entertained favorable impressions."

The Judge, in a letter to a friend, dated November 25, 1781, writes: "Our townsman, Mr. Fisher, holds a quartered precarious office, at, I fancy, less than half its real income, under, and returnable to, Mr. Thompson, when he shall come back, which I doubt not will be in the spring or summer following." The absence of Mr. Thompson here alluded to was doubtless on occasion of his military errand to America, soon to be related. Had Judge Curwen been the only applicant for such intercessory help as his favored young countryman was known to be able to extend, no doubt he would have left this "courtier" in better humor. But the Under-Secretary was so often called upon for similar favors that he learned to put his handsome features in fitting expression, and to frame avowals and promises which had their fullest meaning for the eye and the ear. It was, however, a trying experience for the venerable Salem magistrate thus to stand before the "shop-lad" of whom he may once have purchased soap or shoe-buckles.

Another of the more distinguished refugees in London who was very intimate with Mr. Thompson was Dr. Sylvester Gardiner, of Boston. Having studied medicine in London and Paris, he was established here before the war as a physician and druggist. He had acquired immense wealth, and was honored as a noble, public-spirited, and popular man. As one of the partners in the "Plymouth Purchase," so called, on the Kennebec, he owned one twelfth of the property, and had been assiduous and enterprising in improving and settling it. He is said to have owned a hundred thousand acres in Maine. Being in close social intimacy with the royal party in Boston at the opening of hostilities, he was regarded as unfriendly to the cause of liberty. Still he wished to remain here and share the fortunes of his countrymen. He would have done so, had not a young wife persuaded him, at nearly the age of seventy, to go off with the British forces to Halifax at the evacuation. This was, of course, the ruin of his fortunes by confiscation. When he came back to Boston, in 1785, to try to reclaim something from the wreck by a petition to the Legislature, he alleged that on his forsaking the town he had intentionally left for the benefit of his countrymen in their need a very full storehouse of drugs and medicines. These Washington had tried to appropriate for the army, but the sheriff of Suffolk got the start of him.

Doubtless Dr. Gardiner and Mr. Thompson had been acquainted with each other here. In the following reply which the Under-Secretary of State addressed to this impoverished refugee, the "plan" referred to may concern either some suggestion for the conduct of the war, or for providing for the clamorous demands of the loyalists, who had to take the Secretary's office on their way to the Treasury.

"Pall Mall Court, Feby. 24, 1780.

"Dear Sir, — I return you many thanks for the excellent plan you have been so good as to send me. I have shown it to my Lord George Germaine, who approves of it very much. And I am directed by his Lordship to return you his thanks for the trouble you have had in preparing it. He is fully convinced of its utility, and would be very glad to see it carried into execution.

" I am sorry to inform you that nothing has yet been done at the Treasury respecting your Petition. I have often inquired after it, and I shall continue to do everything in my power to forward it. But just at this moment their Lordships are so extremely busy with Parliamentary matters that it is next to impossible to get them to attend to anything else. But as soon as the present hurry is a little over, I would hope they will take the Petitions of the American sufferers into consideration; and you may rest assured that your Petition will be among the very first that are laid before them.

" I am, Dear Sir, with great regard and respect,

" Your most Obedient,

" And most faithful, humble Servant,

" B. THOMPSON. .

" Doctor Gardiner."

It is suggestive to think of Mr. Thompson as having in hand, and inquisitively scanning, the official papers seized with Henry Laurens, the late President of our Congress, when he was captured, in the summer of 1780, by a British frigate near Newfoundland, on his way to Holland as our Minister Plenipotentiary. Laurens was then in the Tower, and his papers, which he had thrown overboard on his capture, but which were fished up by a seaman, made piteous exposure of the needs of his countrymen. Thompson, it seems, divulged their secrets. He was soon after to have a meeting with Laurens under other circumstances. There were many curious surprises in those days, which required that Americans meeting in Europe should keep full command of courteous manners.

It is probably safe to accept the reason and motive assigned by Cuvier as the promptings which induced Mr. Thompson to seek active military service in the royal army, and in that capacity to return to his native country to fight, as he had already counselled, against her cause of independence. He might have felt the impulse, whether of conviction, self-respect, or the plea of consistency, to show the sincerity of the course he had been pursuing in the quiet of his official bureau by exposing his life for the same object, and thus proving that he was a loyal and grateful subject of his King. There is this, however, to be said on the side of the possible magnanimity of his conduct, — that he formed the purpose of coming here in command as an officer of the British army at the very darkest and most hopeless stage of the war as regarded the prospects of the royal cause. The King and the administration had been thwarted. The majority in Parliament was shifting against them. England found herself involved by sea and land with our French allies. The surrender of Burgoyne, to be soon followed by the capitulation of Cornwallis, had discomfited even the most arrogant and contemptuous enemies of the Colonies. Exhaustive levies and reckless appropriations had dispirited the people, and held up to them the prospective burdens of overwhelming debt and excessive taxes. The subjugation of America had to be recognized as delusive, — as, in fact, an impossibility. Whether disappointment, stung into vengeance, might yet inflict a few more heavy blows against the opening life of a new nation, or whether discord might be introduced among its constituent parts, or, finally, whether more or less of the territory of North America should still be held by the crown, were as yet contingent. Thompson's political prospects were — for the time, at least — identified with those of his head and patron, Lord G. Germaine. The latter felt that the last hope of subjugating the Colonies

hung upon the fate of Cornwallis. Sir M. W. Wraxall *
has given a striking sketch of the incident when the
news of the Earl's capitulation on October 19 was
brought to the Secretary, with whom he dined on the
day mentioned.

"On Sunday the 25th [November], about noon, official
intelligence of the surrender of the British forces at Yorktown
arrived from Falmouth at Lord George Germaine's house in
Pall Mall. Lord Walsingham, who had been Under-Secretary of State in that Department, happened to be there. Without communicating it to any other person, Lord George, for
the purpose of despatch, immediately got with him into a
hackney coach, and drove to Lord Stormont's residence in
Portland Place. Having imparted to him the disastrous information, and taken him into the carriage, they instantly proceeded to the Chancellor's, and, on consultation, determined to
lay it before Lord North. The First Minister's firmness, and
even his presence of mind, gave way for a short time under
this awful disaster. I asked Lord George afterwards how he
took the communication. 'As he would have taken a ball in
his breast,' replied Lord George. 'For he opened his arms, ex-
claiming wildly, as he paced up and down the apartment during a few minutes, O God! it is all over!'"

Doubtless Thompson had formed strong personal relations with Lord George, from such close intimacy with
him, not only in the office, but at his house in Pall
Mall, and in frequent visits to him at his seat at Dray-
ton. Perhaps Thompson foresaw, even more clearly
than many others, what was to be the probable issue of
the struggle in America, and provided for himself the
alternative which, poor as it proved, we are soon to find
him accepting. He was on this side of the ocean when,
in February, 1782, the forced resignation of his patron

* Historical Memoirs of my own Time. Vol. II. p. 99, &c.

was accepted, as a temporary dalliance of Lord North with his own fate, which was to be a little longer deferred.

The humiliations which successively were visited on the schemes and enterprises of the ministry reflected reproaches upon themselves which they sought to shift upon secretaries and subordinates, as having been incompetent blunderers. Cuvier says — and Mr. Thompson alone could have been a qualified informant — that, as Under-Secretary of State for thirteen months, "he had been disgusted by the want of talent displayed by his principal, for which he had himself not unfrequently been made responsible." It was too much to expect that the ministry and their secretaries, who had conducted the war, should be the agents for devising and ratifying terms of peace. Interest, therefore, was concentrated upon the Cabinet, with the knowledge that a rupture there could alone bring the problem to a solution. When the mortifying intelligence of what had occurred at Yorktown and Gloucester reached England, king and ministry still stood by each other, and the majority in Parliament still confirmed their policy, though with a halting decision. But the opposition in Parliament made Lord George the target of their assaults, as it was within his Department that the measures which had proved so impotent in the direction of Colonial affairs had been administered. The Premier, Lord North, abandoned him, and he resigned, — receiving, however, some special marks of the King's favor in pensions and a peerage. Viscount Sackville, as he was now entitled, had, in his turn, in foresight of his resignation, an opportunity to reward so faithful a friend as he had found in his Under-Secretary. Accordingly

Major Thompson, who had always clung to that title, though its provincial commission gave him no rank in the regular army, was now honored with the commission, in the British army, of a Lieutenant-Colonel. It was to forces already organized, or in fragmentary bodies supposed to admit of being rallied into new vigor, in America, that Thompson's commission applied. His pay was 24 *s.* 6*d.* per diem.

But the officer, though at the age of twenty-eight not yet a veteran, wished for, and meant to do, full military duty. He needed a command. Where should he find a regiment? He provided for himself, and resolved to secure a following from those who, in his native land, had willingly espoused the cause of the King against their own country. They called themselves loyal Americans. For the most part they were a sorry company, the most desperate and hated in their mode of warfare and in their subserviency, and the bitterest sufferers in the wreck of the cause to which, in principle or in malignity, as the case may have been, they had given themselves. The ranks of the " Loyal American Regiments," gathered in full or only in a skeleton form in New York and in the Southern Provinces, were held to the royal side by a very slender allegiance, influenced in part by fear, and in part by the stronger attraction of pay in English coin above · that of a paper currency. They, however, found it very easy to shift to the American side; and perhaps a majority of them had been so impartial as to serve in .the course of the war with equal merit, principle, and efficiency in both armies.

Yet it was not so easy for the officers of these regiments of loyalists to pass from one side to the other.

For them consistency and notoriety were pledges that they might perform acceptable service. Their self-committal gave them a claim to royal gratitude to be met only by exchanging their provincial commissions for others which should raise them to and confirm them in honorable positions in the regular army of Great Britain, with opportunities for promotion, pay, half-pay, and pensions accordingly.

Thompson himself said that he "went out to America to command a regiment of cavalry which he had raised in that country for the King's service." * .But little could be done in England for that enterprise, except the procuring of commissions and funds. The work was to be accomplished here, and Thompson essayed it.

True to his devotion to scientific experiment in the subject which he had investigated from his boyhood, Thompson so far redeemed what in our eyes must be regarded as the inglorious purpose of his sea voyage. He says : —

"His Majesty having been graciously pleased to permit me to take out with me from England four pieces of light artillery, constructed under the direction of the late Lieutenant-General Desaguliers, with a large proportion of ammunition, I made a great number of interesting experiments with these guns, and also with the ship's guns on board the ships of war in which I made my passage to and from America." †

Pictet gives us the following account from his friend's confidential communication of this incident in his life : —

"The regiment of cavalry called the King's American Dragoons was raised at this time in his native country by his friends and agents, and he was then commissioned as its Lieutenant-Colonel Commandant. This circumstance led him to

* Essay on Gunpowder.   † Ibid.

leave England for a return to America to serve with his regiment. He had intended to land at New York, but contrary winds compelled him to disembark at Charleston [South Carolina]. Obliged to pass the winter there, he was made commander of the remains of the cavalry in the royal army which was then under the orders of Lieutenant-General Leslie. This corps was broken up, and he promptly restored it and won the confidence and attachment of the commander. He led them often against the enemy, and was always successful in his enterprises.

" That which is called good fortune and success in war is achieved amid many scenes deeply saddening for a kind heart. The sort of engagements to which he was drawn multiplied these harrowing scenes. It was a war of posts and a civil war at the same time. So there was much of danger and fatigue with little glory, and the spectacle of a people reduced to desolation and despair. Such was his position at that time. I have seen his eyes filled with tears when he told me certain anecdotes relating to those times and to his military career. A German painter has undertaken to represent one of these scenes, which makes one shudder, and which I have not now heart or time to describe to you."

Pictet would seem in this last sentence to refer to some picture shown him by his friend, then Count Rumford, drawn by description and narrative furnished by the latter to some German artist. I have been the more ready to quote the sentiment which the Swiss friend connects with his statement of facts, because, though it may be a little overstrained, I should be glad to believe that the larger part of it was to be credited to Pictet's informant. There were indeed some peculiarly sad and harrowing circumstances connected with the desultory warfare in our Southern Provinces; but I have not been able to identify Colonel Thompson as an actor in, or even as a spectator of, many of them.

Neither have I succeeded. further than in approximating to the dates at which Thompson sailed from England and arrived at Charleston. It was undoubtedly stress of weather which carried him thither, rather than to Long Island, New York, where the remnant of the corps of dragoons which he was to command was quartered. Curwen, as we have seen, writes of having had an interview with Thompson in London, August 11, 1781, and then writes of him as absent under date of November 25, 1781. Between these dates, probably about October 4, Thompson, who had before received his commission, had left England. He was in Charleston early in January, 1782. He has left, however, but faint traces of his visit there, and but one signal event of the many which Pictet reports is attached to his name.

The following brief extracts from American papers of the time, published on the royal side, help us to a few facts relating to Colonel Thompson : * —

Rivington's New York Gazette, January 5, 1782. — " The British fleet of forty-odd sail, under convoy of the Rotterdam, of 50 guns, Astrea, 32, and Duke de Chartres, 16, with Lord Dunmore, destined for this port, was safe arrived at Charleston."

January 9. — " The Quebec [which left Cork, the great depot for provisions, October 29] a convoy has anchored in New York Harbor. They left the Rotterdam and Astrea's fleet of victuallers and store-ships, &c. at Charleston, where they arrived from Cork ten days before the Quebec convoy got thither."

New York Mercury, January 16, 1782. — " The fleet which sailed from this port for South Carolina, 25th ult., was seen on

* I am indebted to the kindness of Mr. Henry Onderdonk, Jr., of Jamaica, L. I., in communicating to me these extracts.

the 4th inst., by his Majesty's frigate Blond, since arrived here, off Cape Fear, with a favorable wind for Charleston.

"On Sunday last arrived his Majesty's Ship Rotterdam, James Knowles, Esq., commander, which sailed from Charleston the same day the Blond left it. Colonel Thompson, of the King's American Dragoons, late Under-Secretary of State for the American Department, and a number of gentlemen of rank, who came passengers in the above-mentioned ship, remain at Charleston."

Rivington, January 19, 1782. — "We are informed that Lord Dunmore had a grand reception at Charleston, on his arrival there."

Supposing Thompson to have arrived in Charleston on or before January 1, we might infer that he did not leave England until after the news had arrived there of Cornwallis's surrender, if Curwen had not written of him as absent on the same date referred to in the extract given above from Wraxall. At any rate, Thompson must have learned at once, as he landed on this continent, that the war waging here by Great Britain was rather a defensive than an offensive one.

. Tarleton, in his History of the Campaigns of 1780 and 1781 in the Southern Provinces, does not come far enough down to cover his presence. In the autumn of 1781 the remnant of the British army in the South had been driven by Greene into Charleston, South Carolina. There, and at Savannah and on John's Island, — the only places in the region left in their possession, and these too held by the aid of vessels, — the British forces were hemmed in and found it difficult to hold their ground. Their discomfiture had rallied the hopes of the patriots. Hundreds of halting, time-serving waiters on the fortunes of the war, within the former British lines, now put themselves under the protection of the Legislature

which was convened at Jacksonborough by Governor
Rutledge. This was watched over by Greene's advance.
General Leslie, the British commander at Charleston,
baffled in all his enterprises, was at his wits' end, and
had reason to apprehend starvation, the main security
against which was to be found in successful inroads into
the country. In vain did he issue his proclamations to
rally Tories and provisions. He must have welcomed
the weather-bound new-comer who told Pictet that he
made himself so serviceable. By a bold movement in
January, 1782, Major Craig, who with a small British
force was in command on John's Island, was driven
into Charleston by a body of Greene's army, with the
loss of a few prisoners and stores. Becoming desperate
in their need of supplies, in a skirmish on one of their
sorties they had been repulsed by Marion's Brigade
near Monk's Corner. Marion, soon after filling his
seat in the Legislature, left his brigade in command of
Colonel Horrey. An attack was made upon him by a
larger force under Colonel Thompson, near the Santee,
and though Marion came in season to take part in the
action, he had the mortification of witnessing the discomfiture of his little band with the loss of men and
munitions. This is the only conspicuous action which
our own historian has credited to Thompson while at
the South.*

A few other brief extracts from Rivington, containing information collected from ports below New York,
contain for us hints of Thompson's activity.

Under date February 18: "A detachment of the royal Americans went on service, supposed against Greene."

* Memoirs of the War in the Southern Department of the United States. By
Henry Lee. Washington, 1827. p. 397.

Richmond, March 9. — "A person who left the Southern army, February 13, says Lieutenant-Colonel Thompson has taken command of the British cavalry under Colonel Leslie."

Philadelphia, March 27. — "A considerable force of cavalry and infantry, commanded by Colonel Thompson, sallied out from Charleston on the side opposite the American camp, and surprised and dispersed a party of militia on Feb. 24 and 25. The British retreated before Greene could send reinforcements."

Charleston, March 2. — "Lieutenant-Colonel Thompson moved on Sunday, Feb. 24, from Daniel's Island, with the cavalry, Cunningham's and Young's troops of mounted militia, Yagers, and volunteers of Ireland, with one three-pounder, and a detachment of the Thirtieth Regiment. By the spirited exertions of his troops, and by the Colonel's mounting the infantry occasionally on the dragoon horses, he carried his corps thirty-six miles without halting. [Having secured the American scouts to prevent information being given.] He drove in Horrey's regiment. They were pursued by Major Doyle with mounted militia. On seeing the enemy, Colonel T—— sounded a charge and dashed forwards. Marion's marque and men refreshed our soldiers. Colonel T—— marched back, driving the cattle, &c. The admirable conduct of the officer who commanded can only be equalled by the spirit with which his orders were executed." (Rivington, April 17.)

"This series of actions took place at Warnham Bridge, and at Tydeman's house."

In the war of posts, of desultory skirmishes, and of inroads into the farming regions for plunder, to which the struggle at the South was reduced, there was indeed little opportunity for Thompson to win laurels. He undoubtedly made use of his energetic and methodical skill in doing what he could to organize and discipline such unpromising materials as he had before him. It is to be remembered that he was only accidentally on the spot, and had no permanent command there. The dragoons at the head of which he intended to place him-self, or rather that remnant of the corps which escaped coming under the full terms of the capitulation at York-town, were on Long Island, New York, awaiting his coming. As to the pathetic scenes which Thompson was called to witness, and at the narration of which, in the Frenchman's rehearsal, he wept, he might have seen similar ones at the beginning of the war, before he left his native country. No doubt there were enough of them, and they were harrowing enough to distress one of a philanthropic heart. But without meaning to intimate that there was any exaggeration in the reference to so many peculiarly distressing incidents, I feel re-lieved in avowing that in faithfully searching after the real occurrences which they imply I have been unsuc-cessful in finding them.

Charleston was evacuated December 14, 1782, but before that event had taken place, and in the middle of the spring of that year, Thompson had sailed for New York. What Pictet received from his own lips is to be inferred from the following report of it : * —

"Honored with the esteem of the army, and with the most flattering recommendations from General Leslie for the Com-mander-in-Chief, Thompson started in the spring of 1782 for New York, where he took the command of his regiment. Prince William Henry, Duke of Clarence, third son of the King, who reviewed his corps, committed the colors to him with his own hand. General Clinton was succeeded towards autumn by Carlton, who also extended to Thompson his friendship and confidence. He gathered into his corps the feeble remains of two regiments which had been engaged through the war, and was sent to Huntington, an advanced post of the army on Long Island, where he passed the winter."

* Bibliothèque Britannique. Vol. XX.

I am able to fill up with some interesting details what M. Pictet presents in this condensed form. Doubtless Thompson showed to his friend the commendatory document from General Leslie, as he did the originals of other papers. The order issued from Leslie's headquarters, as given in Rivington's Gazette, is as follows:—

"Davis House, March 1, 1782.

"Lieutenant-General Leslie desires Lieutenant-Colonel Thompson and the officers and soldiers of the cavalry and infantry who served under his command will accept his best thanks for the services performed by them on the late expedition. The Lieutenant-General cannot too truly express to the army the opinion he entertains of the merit of Lieutenant-Colonel Thompson's conduct upon the occasion, and of the spirited behavior of the troops. The constancy with which they supported the fatigues of a long and very rapid march claims his approbation, no less than their exertions in presence of the enemy."

Under date of April 13, 1782, Rivington announces:—

"New York. — On Thursday arrived from South Carolina, the Earl of Dunmore, Colonel Thompson, who lately effected a successful attack upon the Rebels in South Carolina, and many other officers of the army arrived in town from thence on Tuesday evening and yesterday."

The New York Mercury of April 16 gives this announcement:—

"Thursday last, arrived at Sandy Hook, in ten days from Charleston, South Carolina, a fleet of forty-five sail, of navy and army victuallers (most of which arrived at that place last fall) from Europe), under convoy of his Majesty's ships Carysfort, Duke de Chartres, Astrea, Charlestown, and Grana. When the fleet left Charleston, the garrison was very healthy and well supplied with all sorts of provisions. General Greene, with an army of about two thousand men, being at thirty miles' distance. In the fleet came passengers, his Excellency the Earl of Dunmore, Governor of Virginia, Colonels Small and Thompson, and several other gentlemen of high rank."

It would be agreeable to be able to recognize here any effort made by Colonel Thompson to communicate with the members of his own family, or even with his friend Baldwin, in New Hampshire or Massachusetts, now that he was again so near them. I cannot say that he did not make such an effort, but I have been unable to find any trace or token of it. The attempt would have been attended with difficulties, though these were by no means insurmountable. Constant intercourse was kept up across Long Island Sound between the British troops in New York, and neutrals, loyalist sympathizers, and time-servers in Connecticut, and contrivance and money would have effected the object had it been one of strong desire. I am forced to the conclusion that Thompson was either indifferent to or alienated from his family. But of this something more will be said in another connection.

It is somewhat derogatory to the fair fame of Thompson, to have to connect him with the following recruiting bulletin for filling up the thinned ranks of his command.

In Rivington's Royal Gazette, for July 24, 1782, we find this tempting advertisement for attracting recruits for the " King's American Dragoons."

" Any likely and spirited young lads who are desirous of distinguishing themselves by serving their King and country, and who prefer riding on horseback to going on foot, have an opportunity of gratifying their inclinations : ten guineas to volunteers, or five to any one who brings a recruit, and five to the recruit. For the convenience of those who may come from the continent by the way of Lloyd's Neck, an officer will constantly remain at that post."

The particulars which fidelity to the truth of history now requires to be set forth as they appear in our local annals, though they do not add to, but must be regarded as detracting from, the repute of our distinguished countryman, may still be found to possess an interest in themselves. Pictet's gush of sentiment, original or sympathetic, can hardly be considered as giving them any dignity. Colonel Thompson, however, is entitled to the benefit of the suggestion already intimated, that the military operations of Great Britain in this country at the time were continued certainly without any hope of, and possibly without much reference to, the subjugation of the Colonies. Through her war against us England had become involved in hostilities with the Continental powers of Europe, which made the ocean perilous for her naval armaments and transports, and threatened her other colonial possessions. It is therefore possible that Colonel Thompson may at this period have felt that he was serving his King and government in a cause which did not necessarily involve further distress for his native country.

Mr. Henry Onderdonk, Jr., in his laborious and miscellaneous gatherings for illustrating historical incidents connected with the war on Long Island, gives me valuable aid in tracing Colonel Thompson in this part of his inglorious campaign.*

* Documents and Letters Intended to Illustrate the Revolutionary Incidents of Queen's County; with connecting Narratives, explanatory Notes and Additions. By Henry Onderdonk, Jr. New York, 1846. Also, Revolutionary Incidents of Suffolk and Kings' Counties; with an Account of the Battle of Long Island, &c. By Henry Onderdonk, Jr. New York, 1849. These are volumes of great value and interest to the historical student. The quotations in the text are made from pp. 149, 150, of the former book, and from pp. 107, 261 – 264 of the latter.

Mr. Onderdonk makes the following extract from Rivington's Royal Gazette, of August 7, 1782, — a journal printed in New York while it was occupied by the British army : —

"Presentation of colors, Thursday, August 1, to the King's American Dragoons, under Colonel Benjamin Thompson, at camp, about three miles east of Flushing, consisting of four complete troops mounted, and two dismounted. The regiment was formed on advantageous ground in front of the encampment, having a gentle declivity to the south, with two pieces of light artillery on the right. About sixty yards in front of the regiment was a canopy twenty feet high, supported by ten pillars. East of which was a semicircular bower for the accommodation of spectators. The standards were planted under the canopy.

"At one o'clock the Prince, with Admiral Digby, General Birch, Hon. Lieutenant-Colonel Fox, of 38th, and Lieutenant-Colonel Small of 84th, and other officers of distinction, came on the ground, and received the usual salutes (the trumpets sounding and the music playing 'God save the King!'), and posted themselves in the canopy. The regiment passed in review before the Prince, performing marching salutes. They then returned, dismounted, and formed in a semicircle in front of the canopy. Their chaplain, the Rev. Mr. Odell, delivered an appropriate address. After which the whole regiment, officers and men, kneeled and laid their helmets and arms on the ground, held up their right. hands, and took a most solemn oath of allegiance to their sovereign and fidelity to their standard, the whole repeating the oath together. The chaplain then pronounced a solemn benediction. The regiment rose, and returned to their ground, and fired a royal salute. They then mounted, and saluted the standard together. As soon as the consecrating and saluting the standard was over, the Prince came forward to the centre of the regiment, received the colors from Admiral Digby, and presented them with his own hand to Lieutenant-Colonel Thompson, who delivered them to the eldest cornets.

On a given signal the whole regiment, with all the numerous spectators, gave three shouts, the music played 'God save the King!' the artillery fired a royal salute, and the ceremony was ended."

The scion of royalty who officiated on this rather demonstrative than brilliant occasion was his Royal Highness Prince William Henry, the King's third son, aged nearly seventeen, afterwards King William IV. He had sailed on board the Prince George, under Admiral Digby, to qualify himself for rank in the Royal Navy.

An ox was roasted whole, to grace this occasion. " He was spitted on a hickory sapling, twelve feet long, supported on crotches, and turned by handspikes. An attendant dipped a swab in a tub of salt and water to baste the ox and moderate the fire." Each soldier then sliced off for himself a piece of the ill-cooked beef.

The same local annals contain several specifications of grievances, which may be set forth in the terms that the writers have chosen for expressing them.

The first printed charge and complaint brought against the conduct of. Colonel Thompson while in command at Huntington are found as given by Hon. Silas Wood, the first historian of Long Island.[*]

Mr. Wood lived in Huntington, and represented the temper and the remembered grievances of the inhabitants. His account, which is interesting, as well as sharply pointed, is as follows : —

"From 1776 to 1783 the island was occupied by British troops. They traversed it from one end to the other, and were stationed at different places during the war.

---

[*] A Sketch of the First Settlement of the Several Towns on Long Island; with their Political Condition to the End of the American Revolution. By Silas Wood. Revised Edition. Brooklyn, N. Y., 1828. pp. 85-90.

" The whole country within the British lines was subject to martial law ; the administration of justice was suspended ; the army was a sanctuary for crimes and robbery, and the grossest offences were atoned by enlistment. Many of those who had served as officers in the militia, or as members of the town and county committees, fled into the American lines for safety. Some of the most active of those who remained at home were taken to New York, and suffered a long and tedious imprisonment ; others were harassed and plundered of their property ; and the inhabitants generally were subject to the orders, and their property to the disposal, of the British officers. They compelled the inhabitants to do all kinds of personal services, to work at their forts, to go with their teams on foraging parties, and to transport their cannon, ammunition, provisions, and baggage from place to place, as they changed their quarters, and to go and come on the order of every petty officer who had the charge of the most trifling business.

" In April, 1783, Sir Guy Carlton instituted a Board of Commissioners for the purpose of adjusting such demands against the British army as had not been settled. The accounts of the people of the town of Huntington alone for property taken from them for the use of the army, which were supported by receipts of British officers, or by other evidence, which were prepared to be laid before the Board, amounted to £7,249 9s. 6d., and these accounts were not supposed to comprise one fourth part of the property which was taken from them without compensation. These accounts were sent to New York to be laid before the Board of Commissioners, but they sailed for England without attending to them, and the people from whom the property was taken were left, like their neighbors who had no receipts, without redress. During the whole war the inhabitants of the island, especially those of Suffolk County [in which was Huntington], were perpetually exposed to the grossest insult and abuse. They had no property of a movable nature that they could, properly speaking, call their own ; they were oftentimes deprived of the stock necessary to the management of their farms, and were deterred from endeavoring to produce more than a bare subsistence by the apprehension that a surplus would be wrested from them, either by the military authority of the purveyor or by the ruffian hand of the plunderer.

"Besides these violations of the rights of person and property, the British officers did many acts of barbarity for which there could be no apology. They made garrisons, storehouses, or stables of the houses of public worship in several towns, and particularly of such as belonged to the Presbyterians. In the fall of 1782, at the conclusion of the war, about the time the provisional articles of the treaty of peace were signed in Europe, Colonel Thompson (since said to be Count Rumford), who commanded the troops then stationed at Huntington, without any assignable purpose except that of filling his own pockets, by its furnishing him with a pretended claim on the British treasury for the expense, caused a fort to be erected in Huntington, and without any possible motive, except to gratify a malignant disposition by vexing the people of Huntington, he placed it in the centre of the public burying-ground, in defiance of a remonstrance of the trustees of the town against the sacrilege of disturbing the ashes and destroying the monuments of the dead."

The historian proceeds to show how much more of "cruelty and oppression" the people of the island, after the peace, had to suffer from their own Legislature, by legal inflictions and fines, and the denial of their claims for damages, for what they had done through compulsion of the British military force, including the imposition upon them of a tax of £37,000 "for not having been in a condition to take an active part in the war against the enemy!" These latter charges, however, are aside from our present purpose, except as they illustrate the miseries of war, and show, as the historian pleads, "that an abuse of power was not peculiar to the British Parliament."

The next historical annalist of Long Island, bearing a name very nearly the same as that of the subject of his severity, Benjamin F. Thompson, Esq.,* repeats the substance of the above charge against Colonel Thompson, as made by Wood, and adds that, instead of listening to the entreaties and remonstrances of the inhabitants, "he compelled them to assist in pulling down the Presbyterian Church to furnish materials for the building of the fort."

This namesake of the Colonel brings the further allegation against him, that on his return to England "he received the enormous sum of £30,000 sterling for his military services, and was also knighted by the King." I may as well make an exhaustive exhibition of the reproach heaped upon Colonel Thompson by those who have had occasion to chronicle the matter; so I will quote a third repetition of the censure, with aggravations, from a later historian of Long Island, Mr. Nathaniel S. Prime.†

After copying in an early part of his volume what has been above transcribed from Wood, and affirming that no town on the island suffered so much as Huntington from the insolence and outrages and oppression of the Tories and the British soldiers, Mr. Prime continues : —

"The seats in the house of God were torn up, and the building converted into a military depot. The bell was taken away, and though afterwards restored, it was so injured as to be useless. Subsequently (1782) when the contest was virtually ended, the church was entirely pulled down, and the timber used to erect block-houses and barracks for the troops. And to wound the feelings of the inhabitants most deeply, these structures were erected in the centre of the burying-ground, the

* The History of Long Island, from Its Discovery and Settlement, &c. By Benjamin F. Thompson. Second Edition. 1843. Vol. I. pp. 211, 478.

† A History of Long Island, from its first Settlement by Europeans to the year 1845, &c. By Nathaniel S. Prime. New York, 1845. pp. 65, 66, 151.

graves levelled, and the tombstones used for building their fire-places and ovens. The writer has often heard old men testify, from the evidence of their own senses, that they had seen the loaves of bread drawn out of these ovens with the reversed inscription of the tombstones of their friends on the lower crust.

"The redoubtable commander in these sacrilegious proceed-ings was Colonel Benjamin Thompson, a native of Massachu-setts, and the same man that was afterwards created by the Duke of Bavaria and known to the world as Count Rumford. But his acts in this place have given him an immortality which all his military exploits, his philosophical disquisitions, and scien-tific discoveries, will never secure to him among the descendants of this outraged community."

Mr. Prime says that his grandfather, "the aged pastor of the congregation," was peculiarly obnoxious to the British as an "old rebel," and that when the soldiers first came to the place they treated him with special indignity, littering the stable with valuable books from his library. Some of these books were lying before the historian as he wrote, "with the impress of the same savage hands." The Rev. Ebenezer Prime, the min-ister here referred to, died in 1779, so that Colonel Thompson was not a party to this offence.

I have not assumed the championship of Colonel Thompson as a soldier, even independently of his espousal of the side in which he appears against his native country. He may have been responsible for all that is here charged against him as a matter of fact, but there are no adequate grounds for ascribing to him malignity of motive in the acts done under his com-mand. The people of Long Island suffered especial hardships and exactions during the Revolutionary strug-gle. After the disastrous affair to our forces which occurred there so early in the war, the Island, like New York, remained in the possession of the British forces, naval and military, till the peace. Part of the inhabitants of the Island had begun very vigorously on the popular side, and many of the real patriots had fled to the main. Those who were compelled to remain under a sincere or a forced and unwelcome allegiance to the crown had to meet the usual conditions of the occupancy of a spot which was substantially a station and centre of hostile military operations. The Island was the resting-place for the British regiments when not on active duty. They were quartered there for the very great convenience of embarking, when needed, on any expedition, south or north. Colonel Thompson does not appear to have had any special duty assigned to him on the Island, but was merely quartered there from having nothing to do elsewhere. In the winter the troops gave over campaign work, came into winter-quarters on the Island, and built huts and barracks, and excavated the side-hills to get comfortable shelter and sleeping-places. The town of Huntington runs through nearly the centre of the Island, from the sea-coast to opposite the town of Norwalk, Connecticut, on the Sound. At Lloyd's Neck, near Huntington, was a fort to protect the British wood-cutters against the whale-boatmen from the mainland, who came out at night to strip the country. Firewood and boards for huts were very scarce and difficult to obtain. There was constant depredating from across the Sound, and also sharp smuggling between wily Yankees, the soldiers, and the disaffected islanders.

The fort that Colonel Thompson built was doubtless intended chiefly as a winter shelter for his troops;

and the meeting-house — not by any means the only one destroyed by the British troops for fuel — was stripped from necessity. There was a similar fort built on a similar rise of ground at Oyster Bay for the like twofold purposes of shelter and protection against Yankees.

Mr. Onderdonk writes me that he has "seen the elevated conical hill in Huntington, around the base of which the road winds. It was just the place for a fort. It strikes the eye of the stranger at once, as he is about entering the town. When I saw it, about 1842, it was filled with tombstones. Many of those disturbed by military necessity were doubtless what we call field-stones, with the initials and the year of death rudely cut on them."

Colonel Thompson's presence is noted again in a piece of news which reached Fishkill from Long Island on December 5, 1782. "The enemy are fortifying Huntington. They have pitched on a burying-ground, and have dug up graves and gravestones, to the great grief of the people there, who, when they remonstrated against the proceeding, received nothing but abuse."

As we have seen, Colonel Thompson is made to bear the reproach of this outrage, aggravated by the charge that he compelled the remonstrating people themselves to assist in demolishing their church, in order to furnish materials for his fort.

On December 18, 1782, Thompson's corps — "the remains of the Queen's Rangers, and Tarlton's Legion (five or six hundred)" — were reported as being "at Huntington to protect the trade with the mainland." His force is afterwards stated as "five hundred and eighty effectives."

An inhabitant of Stamford, Connecticut, reported that

"On December 1 he was at Huntington, passing for an inhabitant, and passed within four rods of the front of the fort which faces the north. It is about five rods in front, with a gate in the middle; it extends a considerable distance north and south: the works were altogether of earth, about six feet high, no pickets or any other obstruction of the works, except a sort of ditch which was very inconsiderable, some brush-like small trees fixed on the top of the works in a perpendicular form; he was told it encompassed near two acres of ground. It is built on a rising ground, and takes in the burying-ground; the meeting house they have pulled down. The troops consist of Thompson's regiment, the remains of the Queen's Rangers, and the Legion, being five hundred and fifty effectives. They are quartered as compact as possible in the inhabitants' houses and barns, and some hutted along the sides of the fort, which makes one side of the hut. The inhabitants of Huntington do suffer exceedingly from the treatment they receive from the troops, who say the inhabitants of that county are all rebels, and therefore they care not how they suffer."

There is one other sharp historical criticism in our Revolutionary literature relating to Colonel Thompson, a reference to which will close our account with him in his military career against his native country.

It will have been observed in the extracts made above, that the corps commanded by him is described as made up in part of "the remains of the Queen's Rangers." The corps of Hussars known under that name through the war was at first wholly composed of American loyalists, raised mostly in Connecticut and the neighborhood of New York, and was especially odious to the patriots. Its largest force, at its most flourishing fortunes, was about four hundred men. Captain

John Graves Simcoe had been, in October, 1777, commissioned to the command of the Rangers by Sir William Howe, with the provincial rank of Major. He rose in that command to the rank of Lieutenant-Colonel, attaining by real service the military grade which, as he knew, Thompson had got by favoritism. The corps had been diminished by dissension and desertion, while it had been from time to time replenished by heavy bounties and by disaffected and mercenary men who proved disheartened or faithless in the patriot cause. A portion of the corps was at Yorktown to share in the mortification of the surrender there. When it became known that Cornwallis had proposed a cessation of hostilities, in order to arrange terms for giving up the posts of York and Gloucester, with his whole army, Simcoe, knowing well what treatment would await the deserters and the miscreants in his own corps from the rank and file of the patriot forces, and from the rage of the populace, sought permission from the British commander, if the treaty were not finally signed, to allow his Rangers to try to escape in some of the boats which the traitor Arnold had built. Simcoe hoped that a great part of the remnant of his corps might thus cross the Chesapeake, land in Maryland, and make their way to New York. Earl Cornwallis approved the scheme as ingenious and desirable, but could not himself sanction its being carried into effect, as the whole army must share one fate. The measure, however, was effected under a deception. The Earl in his capitulation had reserved a vessel, the Bonetta, for taking his sick to New York. Simcoe proving to be "in a dangerous state of health," making "a sea voyage the only chance by which he could save his life," went off in this vessel, with as many of the Rangers and of deserters in other corps as she would hold. They were to be exchanged, on their convalescence, as prisoners of war. Sir Henry Clinton allowed Simcoe to sail immediately for England on his arrival at New York, and there in December, 1781, the King gave him the same rank in the regular army which he had held as a provincial. Captain Saunders, soon arriving from Charleston, took command of that portion of the corps which reached New York in the Bonetta.

It was this precious constituency — once, as Simcoe insists, constituting the forlorn hope of the British army — that formed a part of Colonel Thompson's command. Simcoe's disgust is unconcealed at "the severe mortifications which Captain Saunders and the officers who were with him had to experience" when the following order from the Adjutant-General's office was received. It was reported to Simcoe, with the comments which follow, while he was in England.

" ADJUTANT-GENERAL'S OFFICE, March 31, 1783.

" Sir, — Lieutenant-Colonel Thompson having received orders to complete the regiment under his command by volunteers from the different provincial corps, and to raise in like manner four additional companies of light infantry for a particular service, the Commander-in-Chief desires you would give all possible assistance to Lieutenant-Colonel Thompson and those concerned with him in the execution of this business by encouraging the men belonging to the corps under your command to engage in this service; and his Excellency directs me to assure you that neither the officers nor others who may remain with you in the corps shall suffer any loss or any injury to their pretensions by the diminution of your numbers arising from the volunteers who may join the corps under the command of Lieutenant-Colonel Thompson. It is to be understood, that, though the men wanted for this service are to engage as soon as possible, yet they are not to quit the regiments to which they at present belong till further orders.

"OL. DELANCY, &c."

(Addressed to Captain Saunders.)

Simcoe, in his chagrin at this transfer to Thompson of a corps which his own self-esteem put at so conspicuous an estimate for service, ascribes the outrage to the fact that Sir Henry Clinton, the late Commander-in-Chief, who well knew the merits of the Rangers, had recently been recalled to England, and been succeeded by Sir Guy Carlton, who had not learned to regard them so highly.

The "particular service" for which Thompson's command was probably intended, I infer to have been a projected enterprise for the defence of Jamaica, which, it was understood, was about to be threatened by an expedition under D'Estaing. The announcement of the treaty of peace, which was soon made, rendered the intended enterprise unnecessary, and, as we shall see, put an end to Thompson's career here. But the comment with which, as Simcoe says, the order of the Adjutant-General was reported to him in England conveys a sting, the bitterness of which we can account for only by inference. It was as follows : —

"I will only say that though as military men they could not publicly reprobate and counteract this unjust, humiliating, and disgraceful order, yet, conscious of their superiority both in rank in life and in military service to the person whom it was meant to aggrandize, they could not but sensibly feel it. I am sorry to say that some of the Rangers, being made drunk, were induced to volunteer it. The arrival of the last packet, as it took away the pretence of their being for ‘some particular service,’ has put a total stop to this business. The warrant, I am told, specified that when this corps was completed and embarked, they were from that time to be on the British establishment." *

Governor Carlton issued, on August 17, 1783, the following disbanding order, which shows incidentally the provision made for the purpose of removing the most odious of those who had served in the British ranks from the retribution so much dreaded by them if they should be left to the mercy of the Legislature and the people of the nation that had achieved its independence.

"King's American Rangers, Queen's Rangers, [with ten other provincial regiments named,] and all men who wish to be discharged in America, are to hold themselves in readiness to embark for Nova Scotia, where they will be disbanded, unless they prefer being disbanded in New York. A non-commis-

* " A Journal of the Operations of the Queen's Rangers, from the End of the Year 1777 to the Conclusion of the Late American War." By Lieutenant-Colonel Simcoe. This journal, privately printed by the author in 1787, was published in a new edition by Messrs. Bartlett and Welford, New York, in 1844. The extracts above are from this reprint, pp. 255-57. Personal vanity and superciliousness characterize this egotistical journal. "Mr. Washington," as the conceited writer chooses always to call the American commander, was the especial object of his petty spite, and chiefly for his course in the case of Major André. Let the following specimen suffice. "In the length of the war, for what one generous action has Mr. Washington been celebrated? What honorable sentiment ever fell from his lips which can invalidate the belief, that, surrounded with difficulties and ignorant in whom to confide, he meanly sheltered himself under the opinions of his officers and the Congress in perpetrating his own previous determination? And, in perfect conformity to his interested ambition, which, crowned with success beyond human calculation in 1783, to use his own expression, 'bid a last farewell to the cares of office, and all the employments of public life,' to resume them at this moment (1787) as President of the American Convention!'" &c. As I transcribe these sentences, I happen to sit where, on raising my eyes, I see at a few rods' distance the majestic work of Ball, the equestrian statue of Washington, in the Public Garden. A small cur-dog is looking up at it, though I cannot hear that he barks. It should be added that Simcoe, when he was afterwards Governor of Canada, exhibited more of courtesy to the representatives of the nation which with his light corps of depredators he had sought to vanquish.

sioned officer will have two hundred acres of land, and a private one hundred acres, in Nova Scotia. The soldiers can go to England or stay in America.

"The King's American Dragoons, Colonel Thompson, have permanent rank in America."

Colonel Thompson, by leave of absence dated April 11, returned direct to England, ready for any further military service which might be required of him, and indeed earnestly bent upon engaging in it; as we learn, from an avowal made by him soon afterwards, that he had now conceived a passion for it. He at once solicited to be employed with his regiment in the East Indies, but the peace dispensed with the necessity. Either his actual services in command, or the incidental influence and value of his extraordinary organizing and executive abilities in military affairs, helped by the personal charm which always advanced him, had won for him the highest esteem and favor of General Carlton. The General having made distinguished mention of him in his despatches to the King, his Majesty, on this recommendation, advanced him to a colonelcy, though he had held the rank of Lieutenant-Colonel but two years. He was thus secured half-pay on the British establishment for the remainder of his life.

The following is given by Pictet as the letter from the British Secretary of State to General Carlton, authorizing the promotion of Thompson, copied from the original, as shown by the last-named to his friend.

"Lieutenant-Colonel Thompson having been particularly distinguished by you in the appointment to the command of the corps of provincial troops intended to be sent upon service in the West Indies, (which corps, had it embarked, would, agreeably to the King's commands signified by the late Secretary of

State in his letter of the 3d of January last, have been placed upon the British establishment,) and as it appears by your letter of the 15th of June that his conduct has met with your full approbation, and that you consider him to be an officer possessing an uncommon share of merit in his profession, the King, for these reasons, has consented to his being appointed, by commission from you, Colonel of the King's American Dragoons upon the American provincial establishment."

" WHITEHALL, 8th August, 1781.

Pictet informs us — again, of course, receiving his information directly from Thompson — that the first solicitude of the latter on his arrival in England was to respond to the confidence which the American officers had reposed in him that he would be the most effective agent for securing to them compensation for the sacrifices which they had incurred in their loyalty to the mother country. Thompson had peculiar influence and facilities for pressing these claims. Yet the responsibility which he had assumed was in many respects embarrassing and irksome. The fifth article of the Treaty of Peace was generally regarded as meanly sacrificing the interests of the loyalists, as it covenanted only that the American Congress, which declared itself to be powerless in the case except in the way of advice, should propose to the States a relaxation of the severities and a relieving of some of the penalties against that odious class of exiles. The advice, of course, was mainly ineffective.

Failing of adequate redress through the provision in the Treaty, the loyalists importuned Parliament with their piteous complaints and demands.

As to the compensation of £30,000 received by Colonel Thompson, as alleged by the indignant annalist of Long Island, the assertion is simply preposterous. There was an army of suppliants and mendicants for whom the justice and mercy of Parliament were besieged, not without strong opposition, through many of its sessions. Benjamin West's allegorical picture of the reception of the American refugees in England had in it many elements of the purely ideal. Before Thompson had reached England on his return, a Parliamentary commission had already been revising the list of pensioners and their allowances; and by their award in June, 1783, a sum of less than fifty thousand pounds had been distributed among nearly seven hundred loyalists. The claimants and their urgency so increased as to engage a permanent commission for seven successive years. That Thompson should have received the lion's share to such an exorbitant excess in this distribution would have been altogether unlikely, even if he had had pre-eminent claims for losses incurred, or for great services performed. He had really left but very little of his own behind when he first abandoned his birthplace. He had had a lucrative post in England, and his military services here were abundantly remunerated by promotion and a permanent position on the British establishment. The whole tenor of his life, his generosity, and his public and private munificence, secure him against the imputation either of greed in getting or of selfishness in hoarding money. Cuvier said of him most truly, that he lavished his own money to teach others how to save theirs.

I am glad to be able to close at this point the reference which I have had to make to the influence and efforts exerted by Major Thompson, both in a civil and a military capacity, adverse to the cause of American independence. I have allowed myself to use some harsh and deprecatory terms concerning this period in his career, and concerning the policy and measures of the British government to which he seems so strenuously to have committed himself. Personal and general considerations have alike induced me to write as I have done. It is to be remembered that Thompson, up to the time when he finally left Woburn, had steadily and positively affirmed his attachment to the cause in whose behalf his friends, neighbors, and fellow-countrymen were putting themselves in armed opposition to the British power. We have not only his disclaimer of any act or word at variance with the popular enthusiasm, but his reiterated professions of full sympathy with it. Add to this, also, the well-established fact, that he had through his friend Baldwin, and by his own direct appeals, sought a command in the American army while in camp in and around Cambridge. I have not authenticated a traditional report that he petitioned Washington himself to that effect. Nor can I certify to — though I think very probable — the statement made by the late Colonel Samuel Swett, in his pamphlet on the Bunker Hill battle, to the effect that Thompson was chagrined at his disappointment in not obtaining the place given to Gridley in the artillery service. It is enough for us to know, as we do, that some of those, apparently well-informed persons, who had heard Major Thompson on his trial and on other public occasions, as well as in private, use the strongest language in asserting his patriotism, very soon after heard of him as on familiar and confidential terms with the British officers in Boston, and as making himself of use to them. If, too, as there is reason to believe, he was lurking in secrecy for many months in that town between his coming to it from Newport and its evacuation, rumors and hints of what could not be regarded otherwise than as dishonorable in his course could hardly fail to reach his old acquaintances. His readiness to act as bearer of despatches, and then to be the servant and adviser of the British War-Minister, and soon his colleague in office, and then to enlist and command a most odious class of troops in the service of what was regarded as tyranny, complete the grounds on which his countrymen at the time would condemn him, — those grounds being furnished entirely by himself. The constancy of Baldwin's friendship accrues to the credit of Baldwin himself. Till Thompson had won a name of honor and renown in other ranges of his genius, and indeed even after his benevolent projects had done · so much to offset reproach, there were many in this neighborhood who spoke of him with indignation and scorn. Nor can the plea advanced for him of having been driven by unjust suspicion and ill-usage, and by the withholding from him of a coveted promotion, to turn against an imperilled cause which he had professed in his heart to love, be of much weight in his defence. (See Appendix.)

Having thus pronounced upon him as in opposition in act to himself and his convictions, I may add to such praise as is due to him as a good soldier, quick and true and bold in action, and faithful to the government which he served, the higher tribute, that from the hour when the war closed he became, and ever continued to be, the constant friend and generous benefactor of his native country. The engraving on the opposite page is from a painting of Thompson as a British officer, taken at this time.

CHAPTER IV.

AS a commissioned officer of high rank in the British army, now on half-pay, though without an occasion for his active services, Colonel Thompson, of course, needed a special permission to enable him to leave the kingdom, if only for travel, and still more if he had any purpose of seeking military employment under another power. He readily obtained leave of the King to visit the Continent. He had two leading objects in view. One was of pure curiosity, connected with a search for means of self-improvement and opportunities of advancing the general welfare of his fellow-men. His other aim was the gratification of a military ambition,— a temporary passion, it would seem, caught from his recent occupations in the Bureau and in the camp. Looking out for an opportunity of exercising this ambition, he hoped to find a chance to serve as a volunteer in the Austrian army against the Turks.

He left England in September, 1783, with no anticipation of the ultimate result of what was to him in intent mainly a trial of fortune. On his passage across the channel for Calais, chance seems to have given him two fellow-voyagers who might well occupy his curiosity and interest either on a long or a short transit. One of these was Henry Laurens, a former President of the American Congress, recently released from the Tower of London, after more than a year's confinement, as a sort of exchange for the paroled General Burgoyne. Reference has already been made to Colonel Thompson's official knowledge and his free disclosure of the contents of the papers which had been taken from the person of this state prisoner on his capture. There may have been no lack of courtesy between these two representatives of a pacified strife, and there was much matter of large interest that might well engage them in animated conversation. Yet there could have been but little of cordiality or sympathy between them.

The other fellow-voyager was the historian Gibbon, who had just lost his place at the Board of Trade. Thompson was transporting with him some fine English horses. These, it seems, by their restlessness and stamping, excited the anxiety and dread of Gibbon lest they might cause the vessel to founder. Pictet says that Thompson informed him that Gibbon had confessed his fright on this occasion in a letter to Lord Sheffield, found in the published correspondence. Pictet adds, on the same alleged authority, that Gibbon signified to his Lordship the profound impression made upon him by Thompson in their brief intercourse, describing him by three epithets, as "the Soldier, the Philosopher, and the Statesman, Thompson." It is to be hoped, as a cover for Thompson's modesty, that, happening to have the interesting volume at hand, he playfully referred to it in conversation with his guest, and left him to copy the reference instead of repeating the compliment himself. But if so, Pictet must have copied carelessly. As there is a vivacity in the letter of Gibbon here quoted, I will transfer to my pages that portion of it which has interest for us. It is dated Dover, September 17, 1783.

"Last night the wind was so high that the vessel could not stir from the harbor; this day it is brisk and fair. We are flattered with the hope of making Calais Harbor by the same tide in three hours and a half; but any delay will leave the disagreeable option of a tottering boat or a tossing night. What a cursed thing to live in an island! this step is more awkward than the whole journey. The triumvirate of this memorable embarkation will consist of the grand Gibbon, Henry Laurens, Esq., President of Congress, and Mr. Secretary, Colonel, Admiral, Philosopher Thompson, attended by three horses, who are not the most agreeable fellow-passengers. If we survive, I will finish and seal my letter at Calais. Our salvation shall be ascribed to the prayers of my lady and aunt, for I do belie.e they both pray. . . . . .

"Boulogne, next day. — Instead of Calais, the wind has

driven us to Boulogne, where we landed in the evening, without much noise and difficulty. . . . . Laurens has read the pamphlet, and thinks it has done much mischief. A good sign!" *

The pamphlet here referred to was Lord Sheffield's Observations on the Commerce of the American States.

Pictet continues to report from his own notes of conversations with his friend, and in what follows is probably almost literally correct.

"Here begins a new epoch in the career of my illustrious friend, and a purely accidental circumstance had a decisive influence over his destiny. He arrived at Strasburg, where the Prince, Maximilian of Deux Ponts, now [1801] Elector of Bavaria, then Field-Marshal in the service of France, was in garrison. This prince, commanding on parade, sees among the spectators an officer in a foreign uniform, mounted on a fine English horse, whom he addresses. Thompson informs him that he comes from serving in the American war. The Prince, in pointing out to him many officers who surround him, says, 'These gentlemen were in the same war, but against you! They belonged to the Royal Regiment of Deux Ponts, that acted in America under the orders of Count Rochambeau.'

"They engaged in conversation which became very animated. Colonel Thompson, being invited to dine with the Prince, met at the table a number of French officers whom he had encountered on the field in America. They talked at length of the events of this war. The Colonel produced his portfolio, which contained exact plans of the principal engagements, the forts, the sieges, and an excellent collection of maps. One and another recognized the place or the interesting incident which was recalled to him. They conversed a long while, and separated promising to meet again. The Prince was passionately devoted to his profession and intensely eager for information. He invited the Colonel for the next day. They resumed with

---

* The Autobiography and Correspondence of Edward Gibbon, the Historian. Reprint of the original edition. London: Alexander Murray and Son. 1869. pp. 301, 302.

the same zest the conversation of yesterday. When at last the traveller took leave, the Prince engaged him to pass through Munich, and gave him a friendly letter to the Elector of Bavaria, his uncle.

"The season was advanced, and he was in haste to reach Vienna. He had purposed to stop at Munich two or three days at most; but he passed there five days, and then did not leave but with regret a city where the tokens of the regard of the Sovereign and the attentions of different classes of society were extended to him with that frank cordiality which so eminently distinguishes the Bavarian nation. He received equally at Vienna the most flattering welcome, and was presented at court, and mingled in the first society. There he passed a part of the winter, and, learning that the war against the Turks was not to be carried on, he yielded to the attractive memories of Munich, and, passing through Venice, where he stopped some weeks, and by the Tyrol, he returned to Brompton by the end of the winter of 1784."

There is an ingredient from the imagination, or from a confused memory, or, it may be, from the conviviality of a banquet in the quarters of military officers, in a part of the relation thus made by Pictet. That any of the French or Bavarian officers whom Colonel Thompson met at Strasburg had been directly opposed to him in any of the same actions in our Revolutionary War, is an assumption for which I can find no grounds in matters of fact. There is some confusion likewise in such documentary and historical references as we have to the individual whose attention on parade is said to have been first drawn to Colonel Thompson.

Dr. Samuel Abbot Green, of Boston, while walking upon a quay in Paris, in 1867, noticed in a second-hand book-stall a manuscript journal purporting to have been written by "Comte G. de Deux Ponts." It had been well preserved and handsomely ornamented, and covered a hundred and fifty-two pages. The journal and three letters following it related to a military campaign in America. On returning to Boston, Dr. Green translated and carefully annotated this manuscript, and published it with an Introduction, in 1868, under the title of " My Campaigns in America. A Journal kept by Count William de Deux Ponts, 1780–81. Translated from the French Manuscript." * This journal, the careful editor thinks, was written by one of two brothers — Christian the Colonel, and William the Lieutenant-Colonel, of the Royal Regiment Deux-Ponts — who were among our French allies in the siege of York. He regards them as illegitimate sons — by a French mother, once a *danseuse*, afterwards Baroness von Forbach — of Christian, Count Palatine, and Duke of Deux-Ponts-Birkenfield. At his death his dukedom passed successively to his two nephews, Charles Augustus and Maximilian, — the latter of whom became in 1799 Elector, and in 1805 King, of Bavaria. It was this Maximilian whose interest was attracted to Colonel Thompson as a British officer at Strasburg, and who was the medium of introducing the latter to his uncle, then Elector. He had not been in the American campaigns, and therefore was not the writer of the journal. He was, however, the prince referred to by Pictet who made known to the French officers, among whom probably was the diarist, an officer who had served in the British army in our war. They might well have with them, if Thompson had not, the field-plans and maps of several sites and ac-

* Dr. Green, having been for more than three years the surgeon of the Twenty-Fourth Regiment of Massachusetts Volunteers in the war of the Rebellion, was able most felicitously to inscribe his publication to the officers and men who were in service in some of the places mentioned in its pages.

tions; and of these Thompson would have perfect knowledge officially, if not from personal observation. It would be very agreeable for those who had come out sound in limb from the recent struggles to recount the incidents of them at hospitable tables. The French officers could not have found a better-informed or a more communicative companion to tell them whatever might gratify their curiosity.

M. Pictet does not inform us where the following incident of sentiment and moralizing, which he relates, occurred. It is reported as taken down from his friend's lips.

"I owe it," said he to me, one day, "to a beneficent Deity, that I was cured in season of this martial folly. I met, at the house of the Prince de Kaunitz, a lady, aged seventy years, of infinite spirit and full of information. She was the wife of General Bourghausen. The Emperor, Joseph II., came often to pass the evening with her. This excellent person conceived a regard for me; she gave me the wisest advice, made my ideas take a new direction, and opened my eyes to other kinds of glory than that of victory in battle."

It was well, therefore, that he could not fight against the Turks. Colonel Thompson had received from the Elector an earnest invitation to enter into his service in a joint military and civil capacity. It was the very year in which Bavaria was a prize in contest between the imperial Continental powers, — Austria, Prussia, and Russia, with France in abeyance only to wait a later opportunity, intriguing and bargaining for a territory which, under changing dynasties and disputed successions of dukedoms and palatinates, could hardly be said to be either independent or in vassalage. The Elector, Charles Theodore, whom we are henceforward to regard

till his death, in February 16, 1799, as the confidential
friend and the ardently grateful patron of Thompson,
committed himself to the protection of Prussia. He
sent his contingent to the army of the empire in the
French Revolution, and being a prince whose aims were
high, and whose interest in the welfare of his subjects
was sincere, as he foresaw the troublous times of that
mighty convulsion, he seems to have desired to set his
own dominions in order by removing abuses and introducing various economical improvements.

The discerning mind of the Elector had detected in
his few days' interviews with his mercurial guest the
versatility and the ability which were so marked in him,
and appreciated the training of his thirty years of life
in the workshop, the Cabinet, and the field. Pictet says
that he also corresponded with Thompson during his
stay at Vienna. The pressing request of the Elector
was undoubtedly welcome to Thompson, but he would
need to have the permission of the King of England
before he could entertain it. He therefore returned to
London to seek for that permission. The King not
only granted Thompson the favor for which he applied,
but also conferred on him the honor of knighthood on
February 23, 1784.* I copy here the Grant of Arms
to Sir Benjamin, before referred to, as the best token of
the position to which he had now attained.†

"To all and singular to whom these Presents shall come,
Isaac Heard, Esquire, Garter Principal King of Arms; and
Thomas Lock, Esquire, Clarenceux King of Arms of the

---

* Annual Register for the Year, p. 114.

† The original parchment, perfect and unsullied, with all its seals, is in the possession of Mrs. James F. Baldwin of Boston, widow of the executor of Countess Sarah
Rumford.

South, East, and West Parts of England, from the River Trent Southwards, send Greeting : Whereas it appears by a Memorial recorded in the College of Arms, that Sir Benjamin Thompson of St. James's, Westminster, Knight, Colonel of the King's American Regiment of Light Dragoons, and Fellow of the Royal Society of London, late Under-Secretary of State of the Province of Georgia, and Colonel of a Regiment of Militia in the Province of New Hampshire, in North America, Son of Benjamin Thompson, late of the Province of Massachusetts Bay, in New England, Gent., deceased, is of one of the most antient Families in North America; that an Island which belonged to his Ancestors, at the Entrance of Boston Harbour, near where the first New England Settlement was made, still bears his Name; that his Ancestors have ever lived in reputable Situations in that Country where he was born, and have hitherto used the Arms of the antient and respectable Family of Thompson of the County of York, from a constant Tradition that they derived their Descent from that Source. And Whereas, at a very early Period of the late Troubles in North America, the said Sir Benjamin Thompson having engaged warmly in support of the British Government in that Country, and in the course of the War been distinguished for his good Conduct and Bravery in the Line of his Profession, and recently received a very honorable Mark of His Majesty's Approbation and Favor, the Most Honorable Charles Howard, Esquire, commonly called Earl of Surrey, Deputy, with the Royal Approbation to his Father, the Most Noble Charles, Duke of Norfolk, Earl Marshal and hereditary Marshal of England, hath been pleased by Warrant under his Hand and Seal, bearing date the twenty-third Day of April last, to authorise and direct Us to grant and confirm to the said Sir Benjamin Thompson such Variations in the Armorial Bearings of Thompson as may distinguish him and his Descendants from all others of the Name. Know ye, therefore, that We the said Garter and Clarenceux, in pursuance of his Lordship's Consent, and by Virtue of the Letters Patent of our several Offices, to each of Us respectively granted under the Great Seal of Great Britain, do by these

Presents grant and confirm to the said Sir Benjamin Thompson, in testimony of his Merits and Services, the Arms distinguished as follows ; that is to say: Per Fess Argent and Sable, a Fess embattled, counter-embattled, counter-changed between two Falcons, in chief of the second beaked, membered, and belled Or, and a Horse passant in base of the first. And for Crest on a Wreath of the Colours, A Mural Crown Or, thereon a Mullet of six points Azure, and between the Battlements four Pine Buds Vert as the same are in the Margin hereof more plainly depicted, to be borne and used forever hereafter by him, the said Sir Benjamin Thompson, Knight, and his Descendants, with due and proper Differences according to the Laws of Arms, without Let or Interruption of any Person or Persons whatsoever. In Witness whereof We, the said Garter and Clarenceux Kings of Arms, have to these Presents subscribed our Names and affixed the seals of our several Offices, this thirty-first Day of May, in the twenty-fourth Year of the Reign of our Sovereign Lord George the Third, by the Grace of God King of Great Britain, France, and Ireland, Defender of the Faith, &c., and in the Year of our Lord One thousand seven hundred and eighty-four."

With a continuance of his half-pay as a British officer, and with a title of honor, both of which would be sure to win him consideration on the Continent of Europe, this soldier of fortune entered, at Munich, in the spring of 1784, on the service of the Elector. In the vigor of his manhood, and now with a trained ambition, perhaps quickened by the splendid career of his countryman Franklin, he had great opportunities and abilities to improve and increase them.

We derive the best and most authentic account of the many and various and most remarkable labors to which Sir Benjamin Thompson devoted himself so assiduously and continuously in the service of the Elector from his own incidental references to them, as well as from the

results of them as given in his Essays. These labors
ranged from subjects of the homeliest nature in their
bearings upon the thrift, economy, and comfort of life
for the poorest classes, through enterprises of wide-
extended and radical reform and comprehensive benevolence, up to the severest tests and experiments in
the interests of practical science. Eleven years were to
pass before he returned to England, — then, too, only for
a visit, for the purpose of publishing the rich results of
all his devoted and multiplied efforts. He was most
favorably situated, alike amid circumstances calling for
and admitting of his wonderful reformatory and benevolent zeal, and with just such patronage and sympathy
from the head of the government as would secure for
his schemes the means for giving them full and favorable trial. The Elector was from first to last his constant friend, never thwarting him, never holding back
his aid; but, on the contrary, ready always to advance
every plan of his, and to espouse his views when ques-
tioned or opposed by other counsellors.

When, on the 1st of July, 1796, Sir Benjamin signed
the Dedication of his Essays for publication in London,
— that Dedication, of course, being by permission, —
"To His Most Serene Highness The Elector Palatine,
Reigning Duke of Bavaria, &c.; &c., &c," he gratefully
acknowledges his obligations thus : —

"In requesting permission to dedicate to your most Serene
Electoral Highness these Essays, I had several important objects in view. I was desirous of showing to the world that I
had not presumed to publish an account of public measures and
institutions, planned and executed in your Electoral Highness'
dominions, — by your orders and under your immediate authority and protection, — without your leave and approbation.

11

I was also desirous of availing myself of the illustrious name of a Sovereign eminently distinguished by his munificence in promoting useful knowledge, and by his solicitude for the happiness and prosperity of his subjects, to recommend the important objects I have undertaken to investigate to the attention of the Great, the Wise, and the Benevolent. And lastly, I was anxious to have an opportunity of testifying, in a public manner, my gratitude to your most Serene Electoral Highness for all your kindness to me ; and more especially for the distinguished honour you have done me by selecting and employing me as an instrument in your hands of doing good."

I have thus anticipated the felicitous consummation of great labors and enterprises of benevolence, and of a devoted friendship founded upon the relations of patron and agent in the doing of them, as a proper preface to a brief account of those labors in detail.

On the arrival of Sir Benjamin, the Elector appointed him colonel of a regiment of cavalry, and General Aide-de-Camp, in order that he might be in immediate contact with himself. A palatial edifice was furnished for his residence in Munich, shared between himself and the Russian Ambassador, with a military staff and a proper corps of servants. Sir Benjamin especially prided himself upon the blood horses which he had brought with him from England. His fine appearance when mounted on parade is frequently noticed. His imposing figure, his manly and handsome countenance, his dignity of bearing, and his courteous manners, not only to the great, but equally to subordinates and inferiors, made him exceedingly popular. This finished courtier and favored child of fortune — favored both by native gifts and by opportunities — needed no transformation within or without to adapt himself to circumstances. He had not exactly, as Cuvier says of him at this critical stage in his life, "just issued from the forests of the New World." He had passed his thirtieth year, having spent nearly one decade of his life amid scenes, objects, and companionships advanced by a considerable grade in civilization, culture, and refinement above those with which he was now to be conversant. Nor, indeed, had his American home been in a wilderness. He had known men and women in Salem, Cambridge, and Boston who would not have appeared to disadvantage in any European society. His position, surroundings, and duties, as well as his official and personal relations, differed much from those of Franklin, about the same time at the court of France. But the elder philosopher accomplished his great work no more successfully than did Sir Benjamin his, nor would the former more patiently or more effectively have perfected than did the latter the details and enterprises of so many by no means inviting but most beneficent schemes.

Sir Benjamin very rapidly acquired a mastery of the German and French languages. Like a true practical philosopher, also, he gave the whole force of his inquisitive and comprehensive mind to the preliminary work of informing himself generally, and in minute particulars, about everything that concerned the dominions of the Elector. The relations of the Electorate to other powers, within and outside of the empire; its population and their employments; its resources and the means of their development; the abuses and evils which admitted of remedies, and the method of applying them,—all found in him as curious and intelligent an investigator as could have been chosen among the select few most concerned to examine them. If, as a military man, he might have been prompted to excite and guide in his sovereign any ambitious schemes for extending his domains or securing a fuller independence of control by the great powers, he would have been precluded from everything of this sort by the then established order of affairs, which left Bavaria only a chance to lose, with no prospect of gain from any conceivable change. Sir Benjamin very soon learned that the development of resources and the reform of abuses were the emergent needs of the Electorate, and would furnish an abundant and rewarding field for his special abilities. The Bavarian princes ever since the Reformation had found their apparent security and prosperity to be identified with allegiance and devotion to the Roman Church and Catholicism. The Electorate was under the oppressive influence of a priesthood, and the people, submitting to their dictation, acquiesced in the thriftlessness and the burdens thus imposed upon them. The very name of Munich or *München*, derived from *Monks*, carries with it an historical fact which had made a mark deep and permanent in the capital of the Electorate. As Cuvier says, " Its sovereigns had encouraged devotion and made no stipulation in favor of industry. There were more convents than manufactories in their States ; their army was almost a shadow, while ignorance and idleness were conspicuous in every class of society." There was no State in Christendom at the time which offered a fairer field for the economical and reformatory enterprise of a man with the genius and proclivities of Sir Benjamin Thompson, with a training in the frugal and thrifty ways of New England during the second stage of its own development.

He never seems to have become involved, either in

his private relations or in the most radical and revo-
lutionizing of his schemes, with any religious animosities. Besides his frequent avowals of a religious faith,
and his devout references to God in connection with
his scientific and benevolent pursuits, he often speaks
of himself as an avowed Protestant, and as finding no
opposition or loss of regard on that score.

It may be as well to mention here the titular, military, civil, and academic honors which so rapidly and
lavishly were bestowed upon Sir Benjamin while residing
in Bavaria. By request of the Elector, the King of
Poland, in 1786, conferred on him the Order of Saint
Stanislaus, the statutes of Bavaria not then allowing
of his receiving the Bavarian orders. In a journey
to Prussia, in 1787, he was made a member of the
Academy of Berlin. He was also admitted to the
Academies of Science at Munich and Mannheim. In
1788 the Elector made him Major-General of cavalry
and Privy Councillor of State. He was also put
at the head of the War Department, with powers and
directions from the Elector to carry into effect the
schemes which he had been maturing for the reform
of the army and the removal of mendicity. In the
interval between the death of the Emperor Joseph and
the coronation of Leopold II., the Elector profited by
the right going with his functions as Vicar of the Empire to raise Sir Benjamin, in 1791, to the dignity of a
Count of the Holy Roman Empire, with the Order of
the White Eagle. That he should have selected as his
title marking this distinction the former name of the
New England village in which he had first enjoyed the
favors of fortune, shows that he was not alienated in
heart from his native land, and that he gladly associated

the memory of it with his own personal advancement. There were many to say of him, during the remainder of his life, that he was even vainly fond of his titles, and claimed the social position which his services secured to him as at least an equivalent for the noble birth and the inheritance of land which ordinarily carry with them titular honors independently of character or achievement. This is true. He prized the mark of dignity which was attached to his name, and was gratified that he could transmit it to his daughter. The inheritors of such shadowy titles should be the first to manifest their approbation that a substance is occasionally secured to them as being won by merit.

With the united offices of Minister of War, and Minister or Superintendent of Police, and Chamberlain of the Elector, Sir Benjamin combined administrative and executive functions which substantially covered every department of public service. Some traditionary or conventional prejudices or proprieties withheld the Elector from seeking or accepting such advice from his own Council as he felt more free to ask and receive from a foreigner who had won his title to consideration. It might, of course, be foreseen that such privileges as were granted to Thompson, however judiciously and unselfishly improved to public ends of beneficence, would excite against him jealousies, if not opposition, from some on whose supposed prerogatives he might infringe. Though later in his career in Germany, and under a change in the headship of the government, he did not, as we shall see, escape his share in a common experience of this kind, he seems to have encountered the very least of it at the time when it would have been most disagreeable and embarrassing to him. Rather did he find sympathy and aid, and that to a somewhat remarkable degree, in the officials and subordinates, civil and military, and even ecclesiastical, in his very radical dealing with abuses.

The richly embellished city of Munich, on which, with its tripled population, dating after the middle of this century, the munificent King Louis lavished his patronage of art, is a very different place from what it was in the last quarter of the last century, when Thompson was its most distinguished and influential citizen. The curse of all the States of the Continent at that time, as it has since been, was the standing army with its incessant recruiting by conscription. The rural population, which should have tilled the fields and pursued the manifold labors of domestic and mechanical industry, was drained of its element of vigor, and then demoralized, by the return into it from time to time of its furloughed or relieved bands of lazy loiterers, incapacitated for, while they despised, work. Thompson soon found that the root of all the difficulties which he aimed to reach and remove lay in this matter of the army. But he had to proceed with caution, as he already had knowledge that the worst abuses have always the most unprincipled and malignant supporters interested in their undisturbed allowance. In none of the incidents of his remarkably diversified life, and in none of his vast, comprehensive, and benevolent undertakings, does the character of Thompson show itself to higher advantage, on the score of wisdom, patient effort, and magnanimity, than in the course which he pursued in Bavaria, dealing with enormous evils in the spirit of prudence and mildness, while still with a thoroughness of remedy. He spent

four full years at Munich before he ventured to put on
trial either of the great reforms, or to initiate either of
the great institutions, which he had been quietly planning. The pay of the soldiers being but threepence
a day, their arms, clothing, and quarters being of the
meanest sort, yet involving wasteful expense, and the
system of tactics and discipline being unnecessarily
burdensome, as well as inefficient, he made reform in
these matters the object of his most earnest efforts.
The officers, who regarded themselves as the owners of
the common soldiers, as if themselves masters of slaves,
were likely to withstand all innovations. Thompson
showed a marvellous tact in winning some of the least
indifferent of these officers to co-operate with him in a
way which seemed to indicate that they themselves were
instigating a reform. There was a foundry for cannon
at Mannheim, and here Thompson made some of his
first experiments on heat. He built another foundry
at Munich, with greatly improved machinery.

We are to remember, while recognizing the subjects
and the methods of his economical reforms, that, when
pursuing them, he never failed to aid them all by his
severest scientific experiments.

Though, when we come shortly to sketch some of the
more remarkable results of these four years of preparation in the Institutions established by him in Bavaria,
we might suppose that the work had been necessarily so
absorbing that Thompson must have given over his
favorite philosophical pursuits, we must set this inference aside. Science and philosophy, in his view, lay at
the foundation of all reformatory, economical, and
benevolent enterprises, however homely the matters
which they concerned. In all the Institutions which he

successfully planned, he introduced, indeed he depended mainly upon, some facilities of process, or means of diminishing expense, which he had mastered by his own severely scientific investigations. In the Philosophical Transactions of the Royal Society, published periodically in England, during his first eleven years' absence on the Continent, are found papers of his, for the most part addressed to his friend, Sir Joseph Banks, the President. They record Thompson's Experiments on Heat; Experiments on the Production of Dephlogisticated Air from Water, with various Substances; Experiments made to determine the Positive and Relative Quantities of Moisture absorbed from the Atmosphere by Various Substances under Similar Circumstances; Further Experiments on Heat; An Account of a Method of measuring the Comparative Intensities of the Light emitted by Luminous Bodies; and An Account of some Experiments on Colored Shadows. These had appeared in print before his return to England. His membership of the Scientific and Literary Academies of Berlin, Munich, and Mannheim also required of him to keep himself in communication with their officers or members. Indeed, he was attaining his high repute as a philosopher while he was most engrossed in seemingly inconsistent labors. Thompson's first experimental Institution was the Military Workhouse at Mannheim. This he undertook and established under some peculiar difficulties and obstacles, additional to those for which he was prepared. He regarded it as only partially successful, and he improved upon it greatly in the one at Munich. The marshes of Mulhau, near Mannheim, which till then had been only unwholesome bogs, worthless for culture and ruinous to the health of the inhabitants of the city, were connected by embankments, surrounded by a mole, and transformed into a fertile garden, devoted to the industry of the garrison. The corresponding Military Academy at Munich was founded in 1789. A military cordon was formed, as is soon to be more particularly stated, in order to free the country from vagabonds.

In his first and most elaborate economical Essay, which gives an account of his Establishment for the Poor at Munich, "together with a detail of various public measures connected with that Institution, which have been adopted and carried into effect for putting an end to mendicity, and introducing order and useful industry among the more indigent of the inhabitants of Bavaria," Sir Benjamin recognizes very pleasantly and gratefully, and not without a degree of complacency, his confidential relations with the Elector. We must allow, however, for the eleven years of severe disciplinary work which had passed, up to the date of the publication of his Essays, in order to justify his tone, like that of a well-worn veteran, if not a mentor. He begins thus: —

" Among the vicissitudes of a life chequered by a great variety of incidents, and in which I have been called upon to act in many interesting scenes, I have had an opportunity of employing my attention upon a subject of great importance, — a subject intimately and inseparably connected with the happiness and well-being of all civil societies, and which, from its nature, cannot fail to interest every benevolent mind, — it is the providing for the wants of the Poor, and securing their happiness and comfort by the introduction of order and industry among them."

Sir Benjamin recognizes, as so many philanthropists

and statesmen have done since, and — never with more
perplexity and baffled wisdom — are doing now, the terrible problems presented by pauperism in every state,
however otherwise flourishing. In his time he might
well say that the subject had not been investigated with
any just degree of interest or success. To him belongs
the high honor of a leader in gaining a direct and most
practical mastery of its painful and often revolting details, and in devising as efficient a system for prevention, abatement, and remedy of its evils as has ever
been proposed and put on trial. The prevalence of
indolence, misery, and beggary in almost all the countries of Europe at that time was painfully realized and
mourned over by all who gave the subject but a superficial consideration. Yet there was no harmony of
opinion, and very little co-operation in effort for the
removal of these evils, even among those who most
lamented them. Within a short time after Sir Benjamin had left England for Munich, a society was formed
in London for bettering the condition of the poor.
One, if not more, of his most intimate friends, Thomas
Bernard, Esq., was the leading spirit of this enterprise.
He corresponded with Thompson while he was in Bavaria, and, as we shall afterwards have occasion to note,
this friendly intercourse in one good cause guided and
facilitated another and most signal undertaking of
Thompson's in England.

He was able to say that what he had to offer on the
subject of pauperism was not speculation, but the genu-
ine result of actual experiments made on a very large
scale, and under peculiarly interesting circumstances.
He thinks that the account which he offers will furnish
amusement, as well as useful information. Not for-

getting that he was a military man, he feels bound to explain the way and the motives which engaged him in an object seemingly foreign to his profession. This explanation is found in the connection which proved to exist between the many different measures for the promotion of the public welfare which had occupied him.

He says that, among the various public services which the Elector asked of him, he was particularly charged with the arrangement of his military affairs in introducing a new system of order, discipline, and economy among his troops. Knowing very well the injury to the population, morals, manufactures, and agriculture of a country which accrued from the maintenance of a standing military force, he divined that the most practicable mode of relief from, or of a limitation of, this mischief, would be found "in making soldiers citizens, and citizens soldiers." The situation of the soldier was to be made as easy, agreeable, and eligible as possible; his pay was to be increased, he was to be comfortably and even elegantly clothed, allowed all liberty consistent with order and subordination, with simpler military instruction, and to be relieved of all obsolete and useless customs. His quarters and barracks were to be made neat and clean within, and attractive on the outside. Schools were to be established, in all the regiments, for teaching reading, writing, and arithmetic. And not only the soldiers, but their children, and the children of the neighboring peasants, were to be taught here gratuitously; school-books, paper, pens, and ink being furnished by the Sovereign. With true Franklinian economy, Thompson adds that the paper which had thus served one use would really come free of cost for such use to the government, as it might serve afterwards for making cartridges.

Regarding habitual idleness, especially that of soldiers in their quarters, as most fatal to morals, Thompson's scheme comprised not only schools of instruction, but also houses of industry. The soldiers and their children were to have the raw material for various kinds of work furnished them, when off duty, and they were to dispose of the results of their labor without accounting to anybody. Besides being allowed to retain their old uniforms, they were supplied gratis with working-suits of strong canvas. It was found that they could earn by their industry between three and four times as much as their pay. The soldiers were put to employment as laborers in all public works, like making and repairing roads, draining marshes, and repairing the banks of rivers; while a band of music would often be provided to inspirit their work, and sports, games, and various amusements were encouraged for their holidays. Paid officers were sent to oversee them when detached in working parties. A large number of the soldiers in garrison were allowed to be absent in rotation at their country homes for ten and a half months in each year, where they might mingle with the peasantry, help recruiting, and apply themselves to agriculture and manufactures. The regimental garrisons were made permanent, that soldiers might be near their homes, — a measure that was very advantageous on account of the scarcity of husbandmen. It was through the soldiers trained in the garrisons to industry and skill that Thompson expected to extend useful improvements over the whole country. Though in some parts of the Elector's domains agriculture was carried to great perfection at that time, yet it was very backward in Bavaria, very many improvements not having been introduced, many profitable plants being unknown, the potato, clover, and turnip being scarcely to be seen, and the rotation of crops neglected.

Thompson planned a military garden in connection with each garrison for the special purpose of introducing the culture of potatoes. These were exclusively appropriated to the non-commissioned officers and privates, each one having a bed of three hundred and sixty-five square feet, which was his, and the produce of which he could dispose of, so long as he would till it. Neatly gravelled alleys between these cultivated plots, made them pleasant places of resort. The agreeable and beneficent results of these arrangements were realized sooner, and even more widely, than the planner of them could have hoped. Indolent soldiers became model laborers, proud of their task and its fruits. They were seen collecting manure in the streets, besides using what was furnished them. Little gardens fashioned by the soldiers on their furloughs sprang up all over the country, as each one carried home with him garden-seeds and potatoes. The use of the latter, as of many other vegetables for food, became universal. The officers, meanwhile, were ordered to give the soldiers every facility, and never to exact any emolument from them.

Besides the direct objects of improving the condition and raising the character of the soldiers which were effected by the measures thus described, Sir Benjamin had in view a further purpose, in securing a very potent agency for advancing the most difficult and comprehensive of all his benevolent schemes. He intended

to make use of these reformed soldiers in grappling
with and suppressing the enormous evils connected
with mendicity in Bavaria. This was, at the time, a
stupendous and organized system of abuses, which,
gradually growing upon the tolerance of the government and the people, had reached such proportions, and
had established itself with such a vigorous power of
mischief, as to be acquiesced in as irremediable. There
were, indeed, laws in each community which provided
for the support of the poor, but they were utterly ineffective. Beggars and vagabonds, the larger part of
whom were also thieves, swarmed all over the country,
especially in the cities. These were not only natives,
but foreigners. . They were of both sexes and all ages.
They strolled in all directions, lining the highways,
levying contributions with clamorous demands, entering houses, stores, and workshops to rob, interrupting
the devotions of the churches with their exactions, and
extorting everywhere through fear what they failed to
get by importunity. These swarms of mendicants and
freebooters were in the main composed of stout, strong,
healthy, and able-bodied persons, who preferred an easy
life of indolence to any kind of industry. They had
become the terror and the scourge of the country.
"These detestable vermin had recourse to the most
diabolical arts and the most horrid crimes in the prose-
cution of their infamous trade." They would steal,
maim, and expose little children, and compel them to
extort by their piteous appeals a fixed sum for a day's
gatherings, with the threat of an inhuman punishment
if they failed. Every attempt to suppress this system
of outrages having been thwarted, the community had
learned to submit and conform to it as admitting of no

relief; and this wretched tolerance seemed to double the number of these vagabonds, while it raised beggary into a profession. Even herdsmen and shepherds, tending their flocks by the wayside, were in the habit of levying contributions on passers-by, and their opportunity to do this was had in view in fixing the rate of their wages from their employers. Farm children, too young to labor, were improved as mendicants, — and a traveller seemed to have his road lined with outstretched hands.

The beggars formed a caste in the cities, with professional rules, assigning to them beats and districts, which were disposed of by regulations in case of the death, promotion, or removal of the proprietors. Sometimes a fight decided the contested right to a district. Even matrimonial alliances between the mendicants, and the entail of the privileges of the profession on the children born of these bargains, were a recognized usage. Thompson observed that the profession of a beggar was a training for thievery, and that there was really no difference between the ways used for extorting gifts and the being subjected to actual plundering. He tells us that after the measures which are to be described as instituted by him had taken effect, out of the population of Munich, then about sixty thousand, as many as two thousand six hundred beggars were seized in a single week.

These measures were deliberate, wise, thorough, and effective. They were admirably planned and carried into the most minute details. Four regiments of cavalry were cantoned in Bavaria and the adjoining provinces, so that even every village had a patrol party of three, four, or five mounted soldiers daily coursing from one station to another. They were forbidden to stop at any peasant's house for victuals, or to demand forage. Officers and subalterns stationed at centres in the cantonments were so distributed that they could inspect these patrolmen, and a general officer, after visiting all the cantonments, was to have his headquarters at Munich. Printed instructions requiring regular returns from the lowest up to the highest of the ranks and the staff were furnished, and extreme care was taken to prevent any collision or conflict between the civil authorities and the military. The soldiers were also to convey government messages, to guard the frontiers, to prevent smuggling, to assist at conflagrations, and to pursue and apprehend all malefactors. The inhabitants of each district were to be at the expense of providing simple quarters for the soldiers, but the cost was so carefully restricted that the whole charge for the whole country for one year was but £2,727.

This cantonment of the cavalry was but one preparatory measure planned for effecting what had been resolved on, — a general and simultaneous seizure of all the beggars in the capital, to begin with. A distinction was to be made, from the first, between the disposal and treatment of aged and infirm mendicants and the restraints designed for the sturdy and ablebodied beggars. Contributions of money voluntarily made by the inhabitants were essential, to obtain which they must be drawn to approve the plan and to trust in its success. This condition it was not easy to secure; for though the inhabitants, tormented by mendicity, would most readily help any measure promising to remove it surely, they had been over and over again disappointed by fruitless essays to that end. Thompson determined to carry out his scheme before asking general pecuniary aid for it, and also to enlist in it people of the highest rank. He organized a most efficient bureau as a police over the poor, in order to provide relief for the necessitous and the opportunities of profitable industry for the well and strong. His committee was constituted of the respective presidents of the Council of War, the Council of the Supreme Regency, the Ecclesiastical Council, and the Chamber of Finances. To these was added one additional councillor from each of these departments, and offices were provided for meetings, with a secretary, accountant, and clerk, and the police guards were under the direction of the committee. The members were all without pay, and the employees were remunerated from the Treasury, so as not to draw upon the Poor Fund, which was intrusted to a public banker of the city, Monsieur Dallarmi.

The city was divided into sixteen districts, in which every dwelling, palace or hovel, was numbered; and a committee of charity was appointed for each, headed by a respectable citizen, assisted by a priest, a physician, a surgeon, and an apothecary, all serving without pay, to look after the worthy poor. A connection was established by rotation between these district committees and the central committee. There were many vested funds, grants, and bequests which had for years been nominally consecrated to charity, but as most of these had been reduced, wasted, or misapplied, Thompson determined wisely not to excite the opposition or odium which he might incur by claiming them. He looked for support from the Sovereign, from the Treasury, from subscriptions, legacies, and small revenues.

To provide raw material, help, oversight, interest,

and stimulus for engaging common beggars seized in the streets and highways in the pursuits of useful industry, was a formidable task, next in order, to exercise Sir Benjamin's resources. How could persons bred up in lazy and dissolute habits, regardless of decency, and callous to any sense of shame, be turned into happy and thrifty workers? *Precepts* and *punishments* would be sure to fail, but they might be taught *habits.* Thompson ventured to reverse the maxim that people must be virtuous if they would be happy, and he essayed to make his wretched beggars happy as a step towards making them virtuous. He therefore devised for them comforts and appliances to soften their hearts and make them docile and grateful. His experience led him to write down the ejaculation, "Would to God that my success might encourage others to follow my example! If it were generally known how little trouble, and how little expence, are required to do much good, 'the heartfelt satisfaction' which arises from relieving the wants and promoting the happiness of our fellow-creatures is so great that I am persuaded acts of the most essential charity would be much more frequent, and the mass of misery among mankind would consequently be much lessened."

Thompson says he had learned from the brute creation, from beasts and birds, that cleanliness is the first condition of comfort. He had noticed, also, that all the great lawgivers and founders of religions had had regard to the influence of cleanliness on the moral nature of man, thinking the soul defiled and depraved by everything unclean. He adds, "Virtue never dwelt long with filth and nastiness; nor do I believe there ever was a person scrupulously attentive to cleanliness who was a consummate villain." He had now to deal with men and women who had become habituated to being covered with filth and vermin, and who had slept in their rags in the streets and hedges. They should have a neat and commodious building, well warmed and lighted, with healthful and palatable food and good beds. Teachers, materials, and utensils should enable them to work, and the pay for it should be their own. There should be no harsh language, no ill-usage. The founder was able to say, after a five years' operation of his scheme, that not a blow had been given even to a child, while thrift had so abundantly followed from it, that even extra rewards had been granted to the deserving.

Consulting economy in every stage of his enterprise, Thompson avoided, what to most schemers in similar undertakings would have seemed essential, the building of an edifice, at considerable cost, with reference to the improvements and conveniences which he desired. In one of the suburbs of Munich, on the other side of the Iser, called Au, was a deserted structure, once a manufactory, then falling into decay. He caused this to be thoroughly repaired and enlarged, adding to it a kitchen, refectory, and bakehouse, with workshops for carpenters, smiths, turners, and other mechanics needed for making and repairing all the tools and machinery which would be requisite in the establishment. Large halls were provided for spinners of flax, hemp, cotton, wool, and worsted, with an office attached to each for a clerk or overseer of the department. Through a window connecting each hall with its office, raw materials, finished work, and accounts for labor done, were given to and received from each workman. Another series of halls was fitted up for weavers in all the departments, and for clothiers, cloth-shearers, dyers, saddlers, wool-sorters, carders, combers, knitters, seamstresses, &c., as also dwelling-rooms, magazines, store-rooms for all assorted materials and goods, and rooms for the officers. There was likewise a spacious drying-hall, where eight pieces of cloth might be stretched at once. A running stream was availed of for a fulling-mill, a dyer's shop, and a wash-house. The building, which was square, enclosing a paved court, was carefully and even elegantly painted, and arranged, without and within, to make it attractive. Over the principal gate was an inscription denoting the purpose of the establishment, and over the passage into the court letters of gold on a black ground proclaimed the warning, "No alms will be received here." Over the doors of the various apartments were inscribed their uses.

The building being prepared with tools, materials, and utensils for work, Sir Benjamin proceeds to tell us how he got his inmates. New Year's Day had from time immemorial been the beggars' holiday in Bavaria. They were out in full force to receive and to exact alms. Their philanthropic patron and reformer chose that day for inaugurating his own establishment. It was the 1st of January, 1790. We cannot but be very forcibly impressed by the amount and kind of influence and authority which Sir Benjamin had personally secured to himself, when we reflect upon the resoluteness, the almost arbitrary and autocratical character of his way of proceeding in this matter, and consider, too, that every one concerned, from the Sovereign down to the beggars themselves, so far from thwarting him, appeared to fall under his lead. Here was a foreign resident in a

strange country, of a language not his own, himself
not yet thirty-seven years of age, who had spent but
little more than four years of his residence to such
purpose as to be able to bring the whole military and
civil powers of the government, at his own dictation,
to grapple effectively with the most gigantic of the evils
of a demoralized community. No Eastern monarch
ever had a vizier to represent his delegated despotism
for effecting results that would compare in amount or
extent with the beneficence of the measures which found
their agent in the Elector's American counsellor.

On the morning of New Year's Day, then, the officers and non-commissioned officers of the three regiments of infantry in garrison were directed to station
themselves at appointed posts in the streets, and to wait
for further orders. To relieve his bold undertaking
of the odium it might have risked if carried through
wholly by the military power, Thompson had at the
same time assembled at his lodgings the field-officers
and all the chief-magistrates of Munich, and begged
them to accompany him with their full sympathy and
aid, as he proceeded that morning to execute his plan
of seizing upon every beggar in the town, that the
strong among them might be put to work, the helpless provided for, and the city be thoroughly relieved
of its worst nuisance. All whom he thus appealed to
heartily consented to attend him and aid him. He
himself was paired off with the chief-magistrate, and
each field-officer with an inferior magistrate. The
moment they had got into the streets a beggar extended his hand and asked alms. Thompson, setting
an example which he desired all his companions to
imitate, laid his own hand gently upon the shoulder

of this first vagabond, and told him that from that day begging would no longer be permitted in the streets of Munich. The mendicant was committed to a sergeant with orders to take him to the Town Hall, where he was told that he would be provided for in one way if he was really helpless, and in another way if he was not. To his own act Thompson added some rallying words to his associates to overcome their reluctance to what might seem a derogatory proceeding to any of them, and assured them that there could be no disgrace in assisting "in so useful and laudable an undertaking." With such alacrity and thoroughness was the work accomplished, that the magistrates and soldiers had seized upon every beggar, — not a single one remaining at large.

When the motley mass of mendicants had been gathered in the Town Hall, their names were taken down on prepared lists, and they were sent off for a time to their own private haunts, with instructions to present themselves on the next day at the "Military Workhouse" already provided in the Au. They were promised there comfortable, warm rooms, a warm dinner daily, and remunerative work if they would labor. They were likewise assured that a committee would inquire into the condition, wants, and ability of each of them, with a view to granting them permanently all needful aid. The same measures were then followed up in the suburbs by patrols of soldiers and police.

Thompson was greatly aided in his work by the circulation all over the city of an address and appeal to the inhabitants, prepared by his hearty coadjutor, Professor Babo, a distinguished literary man in Munich. Many of these circulars were carried by Thompson himself to the doors of the principal citizens, with printed blanks containing the forms for an elaborate system of regular voluntary subscriptions. The city was again districted for this purpose, and the plan was so thoroughly contrived that pledges by name or anonymous gifts acknowledged in the Munich Gazette, or the contents of alms-boxes, all under the oversight of the committees, seemed to engage the generosity of all citizens. The reasonable motive was urged, that systematic benevolence, besides being alone effective, was also much cheaper than enforced and desultory almsgiving.

Provision had to be made for some embarrassments attendant upon the comprehensiveness of this system. Several public establishments in Munich, like the schools for poor students, orders of Sisters of Charity, the Hospital for Lepers, and others, had been long privileged to make periodical appeals from house to house. To avoid collision and jealousy, an equivalent to these former resources of such institutions was provided from the public treasury. Then, too, the vested rights of German apprentices to beg on their travels — a custom attended with many abuses — had to be restrained and regulated, as did also the privilege granted to sufferers from fire to go about with a government license asking for aid. In fact, the oversight and removal of mendicity required safeguards in every direction. When the wretched objects of Thompson's resolute measures, deprived of their former range and liberty of mendicancy, · were thus gathered into a central asylum, he had an administrative and executive task to accomplish to which only his own wonderful powers and skill would have been equal. He was to provide profitable work for them. He was to change all their habits of life. He was to bring under rules of cleanliness, thrift, and order the most unpromising subjects of such discipline. Yet he accomplished all he undertook, and he did it with signal success. All through his life and in all his private and public relations *Order* was with him almost a deified principle. He carried order into everything. He exacted order of everybody. He did make his pauper asylum a workhouse of remunerative industry, the inmates of which were really happy. For a series of years the institution was so successful that besides producing all the clothing needed for the Bavarian troops a large supply from it was sold to the public, and even to other countries. At one period there accrued from it to the Electorate a profit of ten thousand florins in a year. Though at first some of the inmates felt the constraint and restlessness of their new condition, there never was any mutinous conduct among them. Cheap materials which they could not waste — hemp, flax; and wool — first engaged their unskilled hands. A system almost like mechanism was introduced into all the details of the establishment. True to his leading aim of economy, Thompson constructed and arranged the kitchen, which daily provided a warm and nutritive dinner for from a thousand to fifteen hundred persons. So highly did Sir Benjamin pride himself on this special accomplishment of his, which he brought to bear in sundry culinary feats in many southern cities of the Continent, and in Great Britain and Ireland, that he procured certificates from great functionaries testifying to the incredibly small amount of fuel used in his apparatus. Four and a half pennies' worth of fuel cooked a dinner

for a thousand persons. Thompson pledged himself
to prove that he carried economy even further in a
kitchen which he had made in a hospital at Verona.
Many out-patients, as we now call them, — many poor
persons who received work from the establishment
without being inmates of it, were regularly provided
with food from it. As the meat-shops of the city had
long been laid under exacting contributions by the
mendicants, Thompson found their now relieved trades-
men gladly ready, at his suggestion, to keep tubs la-
belled " For the Poor," in which they would daily de-
posit scraps suitable for soups. The bakers also made
a similar composition for their own relief.

Apologizing for a lack of orderly arrangement in the
matter of his Essay, though to general readers it seems
to be wonderfully methodical, Thompson proceeds to
describe in particulars the whole organization, routine,
and discipline of his establishment. He yields often
to an overflow of sentiment, proving that he mingled
in his martinet-like stiffness of regulation much of very
tender and considerate feeling. He tells us how he
encouraged a spirit of industry, pride, self-respect, and
emulation, finding help even in some trifling distinctions in apparel. Some children who were too young
to be trusted with any material for mechanical work
were placed on benches around the hall where older
children were at labor, till, in the irksomeness of the
position, they cried to be allowed to do something, if
it were only to turn a wheel by foot or hand. Some
trifling reward encouraged them on from step to step
in their progress.

Here, then, Thompson had in successful operation
two economical and benevolent institutions. The first,

initiated in 1789 as the Military Workhouse, not dependent upon charity, but substantially self-supporting as a manufactory for clothing the army; and the Institution for the Poor, occupied in 1790, and drawing its resources from the benevolent that its profits might accrue to the relief of the poor and the protection and education of their children.

The spinning and weaving of wool, linen, and cotton were carried on with great, systematic, and profitable enterprise in the Military Workhouse at Munich, which furnished the clothing for fifteen Bavarian regiments. Its profits for six years exceeded a hundred thousand florins. The troops of the Palatinate, and those of the Duchies of Juliers and Bergen, were furnished from a similar establishment at Mannheim. This had been in operation some months before its corresponding institution had been opened at Munich, and, being Thompson's first experiment, he improved much upon it in the second. When he came to publish a second edition of his first Essay, he was compelled to announce that his Military Workhouse at Mannheim had been set on fire and totally destroyed during the siege of that city by the Austrian troops.

None of our numerous ethical essays contain more healthful, just, or fitly expressed reflections upon the exercise of the benevolent feelings and the pure happiness which comes from doing good to others, than does the closing part of Thompson's sketch of his establishment for the poor. He was the daily witness of its benefits, and the daily recipient of the gratitude of its inmates, — beggars raised to self-respecting industry, abandoned women reformed to an enjoyment of a pure life, little children shedding tears of joy to welcome their

benefactor. Thompson says that the fear of being re-
proached for personal vanity shall not withhold him
from mentioning some of the marks of public gratitude,
esteem, and consideration which he received. On one
occasion, when he was dangerously ill, the poor of
Munich went publicly in a body, in procession, to the
cathedral, and put up public prayers for his recovery.
And again, when four years afterwards they learned
that he was in a similar condition at Naples, they, of
their own accord, set apart an hour each evening, after
they had finished their work in the Military Workhouse, to pray for him. On his return, after an
absence of fifteen months, the subjects of his benevolence gave him a most affecting reception. He, in
response, provided for them a *fête* in the English
Garden, where eighteen hundred poor people of all
ages enjoyed themselves, in presence of above eighty
thousand visitors. Thompson asks his reader not to
be impatient with him for thus expressing his feelings.
He says : —

"Let him figure to himself, if he can, my situation, sick in
bed, worn out by intense application, and dying, as everybody
thought, a martyr in the cause to which I had devoted myself;—
let him imagine, I say, my feelings, upon hearing the confused
noise of the prayers of a multitude of people who were passing
by in the streets, upon being told that it was the Poor of Munich, many hundreds in number, who were going in procession
to the church to put up public prayers for me ; — public prayers
for me! — for a private person ! — a stranger ! — a Protestant !
— I believe it is the first instance of the kind that ever happened ; and I dare venture to affirm that no proof could well be
stronger than this, that the measures adopted for making these
poor people happy were really successful. And let it be remembered that this fact is what I am most anxious to make
appear in the clearest and most satisfactory manner."

It will be understood that while actual beggars were thus provided for in the House of Industry, the zeal of their benefactor took in also all the indigent in Munich, who, though they had never begged, needed aid, food, and care. Measures were instituted which wisely and effectively ministered to them. Thompson expresses his warm thanks to the clergy who had so heartily co-operated with him, though a Protestant, in all his measures of reform and benevolence. Of course, efforts were made by him, and plans were matured, for securing that what he had been doing for Munich should serve as an impulse and a guide for like measures and institutions over the whole country. He himself made many excursions and journeys with these objects in view; and in all his travels, wherever his route took him, he interested himself in introducing social, economical, and mechanical improvements.

Having met with such marked success in the hard and exacting work of practical reform, Thompson felt himself warranted in devoting his next Essay to dealing with the "Fundamental Principles on which General Establishments for the Relief of the Poor may be formed in all Countries." There is an admirable medium kept in this Essay between the sentimental vein, which engages the feelings, and the strain of experimental wisdom, which would guide the judgment to directly beneficent results. The suggestions which it presents, and the methods and rules which it proposes, might be adopted this year, after all the gatherings of experience, as promising a satisfactory solution — if such is possible — to the problem offered to the civilized world in pauperism.

The author engages with that sad and hopeless kind

of poverty exhibited by those who are positively incapable of self-support, and which requires continuous charitable assistance and relief. The aid which such indigent persons need from others cannot be provided by compulsory legal exactions; it must be contributed by benevolent and humane promptings. This voluntary provision will require organizations to gather and administer it. Persons of the highest social rank must put themselves foremost, and must combine with those who belong to the middle classes, to institute an elaborate system of oversight and relief. The objection likely to arise from the enormous expense which may be supposed to be involved in such a scheme must be met by the bold and easily demonstrable statement, that the cost of such a well-devised system will always be much less than that visited on a community by beggary, with its concomitant of thieving. The system will require the districting of a town, and the numbering of the houses, with a careful examination into the condition and circumstances of every indigent person. Thompson here plants himself, as he always did in every great or little matter that interested him, upon his divine principle of Order. Arrangement, method, provision for the minutest details, subordination, co-operation, and a careful system of statistics will facilitate and make effective any undertaking, however burdensome or comprehensive. Humanity, kindness, and wisdom are capable of dealing with the huge evils of pauperism. The objects of this benevolence when thus cared for must be made, skilfully and resolutely, to contribute as far as possible to the efforts made for their own relief. They must be set to industrious occupations. To make the burdens of providing for

them as tolerable as they may be, all the best scientific
and mechanical improvements must be introduced in
workshops and kitchens, in the selection and cooking
of food, and in all the economy of administration. He
would rely largely upon the donations and bequests of
the rich, and would maintain that the endowment of
well-ordered institutions would prove more effectual
than the forms of private charity.

As each of Thompson's benevolent schemes involved
this great object of economy, he was led to find the
next subject of his investigations in the selection and
preparation of Food, especially for the poor. When he
came to publish his Essay on that subject in London,
in 1796, it was a time of general scarcity, and consequently of anxiety and alarm. The House of Commons and the Board of Agriculture were earnestly
engaged with measures for relieving distress and avert-
ing an apprehended famine. He begins his Essay, as
usual, with the easy and obvious practical philosophy
of his subject. He refers us to the principles and
method by which animals and plants are nourished.
The newly discovered fact that water, instead of being
a simple substance, might be decomposed, is turned to
instruction on this point. He enlarges upon the pleasant maxim that the food which is most palatable is
likely to be also the most nutritious. He proves that
very little solid food is essential or healthful, even to
the most laborious persons, and shows how vegetables,
skilfully cooked, may be alike nutritious and palatable.
He deals most judiciously with what we may call his
new vegetable, the potato. He gives rules for the
construction of public kitchens, and very methodical
recipes, tables, and statistics of the most economical

a id agreeable food for the diet of soldiers. The nutritive qualities of different kinds of food and of vegetable soups are elaborately investigated and tabulated. The courtly Count seems almost to show himself to us in the apparel and with the apron of an artist in one of his own kitchens, when he deals with the matter of Indian meal, and pleads for cakes, dumplings, bread, and especially "Hasty-Pudding," to be made from it. Memories of his boyhood's home in Woburn, of the yellow maize of autumn, of husking-parties, and of his mother's substantial provisions for a youthful appetite, must have come tenderly over him as he fondly argued for this staple of the white and the red men of America. An exiled loyalist, Sir William Pepperell, then living in London, was an intimate friend of Thompson's, and this friend had an American countrywoman in his kitchen. The philosopher, not satisfied, it would seem, to trust wholly to her native skill, gave her some directions and oversight of his own for preparing an "Indian pudding" as a treat for his friends. He adds much useful information about macaroni, barley, and rye-bread. I have noticed in various Parliamentary documents and public journals of the time how highly his advice and efforts were appreciated in that time of scarcity and apprehension.

Thompson made up another Essay by gathering together sketches of four of his subordinate schemes which he devised as incidental to the larger ones. These were, first, a military academy, in which a thorough practical education should be furnished, not exclusively, but mainly for youths designed for soldiers. It was planned for one hundred and eighty *élèves*, distributed in three classes. The first of these was to be composed of thirty orphans, or children of inferior civil and military officers, from eleven to thirteen years of age, remaining, free of cost, for four years. The second class was to include sixty sons of the poorer nobility, from eleven to fifteen years of age, at a small monthly charge. The third class received ninety pupils, gratuitously, as able and promising children, showing uncommon abilities, from the lowest ranks of society. The rules of admission and discipline were rigid, and the administration was to be economical.

The second scheme had in view the improvement of the breed of horses and horned cattle in Bavaria and the Palatinate. This was in the interest of his military and agricultural reforms. He imported some fine stock to be gratuitously distributed over the country; but he tells us that the success of the enterprise did not meet his expectations.

The third scheme aimed to resist an enormous abuse, by which poor functionaries, supernumerary clerks, and others on small pay, which from their poverty they had to anticipate, were subjected by Jewish usurers to an exaction of five per cent per month as interest on an advance. Thompson brought about an arrangement at the Military Pay Office by which the advance was made at five per cent a year.

The fourth of these incidental schemes, which, as subsidiary to one of his larger establishments, he was obliged to advance only as such subordination would allow, might of itself have been a leading enterprise with him. In making his arrangements for a military cordon, extending over the country, as a measure essential to his plan for seizing upon all vagabonds and mendicants, he had recognized the advantage to be gained by giving permanency to some temporary provisions which he had then felt to be necessary. He formed and matured a plan to facilitate a military patrol of the whole country. This required permanent stations for soldiers, and, in order that the soldiers should not be idle, he proposed to keep them employed on the repair of roads and highways, and also to provide for them comfortable tenements at their stations, so that they need not levy contributions of food and forage upon the inhabitants. This scheme, as its author devised it, included the opening and improving of military roads, with distances carefully marked by milestones, and the planting of trees on the sides. Very little was done towards carrying out this proposition.

Leaving out of view the philosophical science which undoubtedly, like a conscious or unconscious subsidiary motive, excited and aided the Count in all these comprehensive plans of beneficence, we must certainly regard them in their sum and effect as equalling the results accomplished by any other single benefactor of mankind. It is indeed hard to believe of him, as not only Cuvier but others have said, that he really did not love his fellow-men. Cuvier, in recognizing the scientific passion and the social distinction which aided and rewarded the benevolent and economical labors of Count Rumford, applies to him in pleasantry what Fontenelle said of Dodard, — who, in his rigid observance of the fasts of the church, turned the process into a means of scientific experiment on the effects of abstinence and asceticism on himself, — that he was the first man who took the same path for getting into heaven and into the French Academy.

Till within the last two years there has been but one monumental memorial in Munich, which, by bearing the name of Rumford, associates him in this way with the city of which he was so conspicuous a benefactor. Even this inscribed memorial would not indicate to an American visitor that it was a tribute to one of his own countrymen. I refer to the monument erected during his life by some of the principal citizens of Munich, in the so-called " English Garden," as an expression of public gratitude to the Count for his suggestion and supervision of that admirable design. This work of his was undertaken in 1790. In the northeasterly environs of Munich was a wild and neglected region of forest and valley, which had formerly been a hunting-ground of the Elector, but at the time was unsightly and dreary. Sir Benjamin conceived the project of converting this region, with the permission of the Elector, into pleasure-grounds, a park, and fields for making improving experiments in agriculture. He surrounded it with a road or drive of a circuit of six miles, on which, at proper intervals, were erected cottages and farm-houses for laborers employed on the grounds. Walks, promenades, grottos, a race-course, and other attractions, diversified the extensive stretch of territory. With the earth scooped out in preparing a small lake, he built up an elevated mound. A refreshment saloon, handsomely furnished, and a Chinese pagoda, were among the conveniences and adornments; and Sir Benjamin exercised all his ingenuity in perfecting the details of his plan so as to render the Garden attractive as a place of resort to the higher classes, and a place of carefully guarded amusement to the common people.

While he was absent in England in the autumn of
1795, and without his knowledge, the memorial tribute
just referred to was prepared and set up.

It stands within the Garden, and is composed of
Bavarian freestone and marble. It is quadrangular,
its two opposite fronts being ornamented with *basso-
rilievos* and bearing inscriptions. The side fronting
the principal roadway shows two figures, representing
the Genius of Plenty leading Bavaria and strewing her
path with flowers. Under these is a block of polished
marble with this German inscription, now nearly ob-
literated : —

LUSTWANDLER, STEH !

DANK STAERKET DEN GENUSS :

EIN SCHOEPFERISCHER WINK KARL THEODOR'S

VOM MENSCHENFREUND RUMFORD

MIT GEIST GEFUEHL UND LIEB GEFASST,

HAT DIESE EHEMALS OEDE GEGEND

IN DAS WAS DU NUN UM DICH SIEHEST

VEREDELT.

The above may be paraphrased [not translated] as
follows : —

" Pause, saunterer! The enjoyment [which this place affords]
is heightened by gratitude. A suggestive hint of Charles Theodore, seized on with genius, taste, and love by Rumford, the
friend of mankind, has transformed this once waste spot into
what thou now seest about thee."

On the opposite side of the memorial is a bust of
Count Rumford, in Bavarian alabaster, which, at the
time, was thought to be a good likeness; and under
this another block of polished marble bears the following inscription : —

IHM
DER DAS SCHMÄHLICHSTE ÖFFENTLICHE UEBEL,
DEN MÜSSIGGANG UND BETTEL TILGTE,
DER ARMUTH HÜLF' ERWERB UND SITTEN,
DER VATERLANDSCHEN JUGEND
SO MANCHE BILDUNGSANSTALT GAB.
LUSTWANDLER GEH,
UND SINNE NACH IHM GLEICH ZU SEYN
AN GEIST UND THAT
UND UNS
AN DANK.

Which may be rendered : —

To him who rooted out the most disgraceful public evils, —
Idleness and Mendicity: who gave to the Poor, relief, occupation, and good morals, and to the Youth of the Fatherland so
many schools of Instruction. Go, Saunterer! and strive to
equal him in Spirit and Deed, and us in Gratitude.

The Institutions which the Count had established,
and which, after 1791, were in full experimental trial,
were of a kind to make him alike assiduous in their
management and anxious lest, from any oversight of
his own, they should meet with embarrassment or failure. Of course, as a very wise and discerning man, he
had expected to meet opposition, alike from ignorance,
jealousy, and envy. This he now began to encounter.
He showed great discretion and magnanimity in dealing
with it. But care and perplexity from so many exacting
labors began to wear upon his health. He did not
spare himself either mental or physical exertion, but he
was always thoughtful about preserving his constitution
unimpaired, and he applied rigidly to himself his rules
of dietetics. He habitually abstained from wines and
spirituous liquors, drinking only water, and was regarded as whimsical about his food.

The dangerous illness to which reference has already been made in connection with his own account of the manifestation of sympathy in his behalf by his beneficiaries compelled him at length to seek relief and change of place. The Elector granted him leave to travel for some time, according to his inclination, upon the Continent. But before leaving Munich, doubtful if he might live to return, the Count rendered in to the Elector an exact account of the principal results of the four years of his administration, compared with the four years preceding his entrance into office. He left Munich in the spring of 1793, and, being absent sixteen months, returned there in August, 1794, having in the interval suffered another serious illness at Naples. He planned kitchens for economy of food and fuel in Verona and many cities, superintended their construction, and provided for gathering statistics of the saving effected. He seems to have been heartily welcomed, and allowed full scope and tolerance for his schemes, by the ecclesiastical and other authorities having those institutions in charge. It is somewhat noteworthy to mark how acquiescingly, and even deferentially, those who are generally so jealous of their own prerogatives, and especially of the abuses to which they are accustomed, conformed themselves to the Count's experimental projects. Throughout his published writings are very many references to the sympathy and courtesy on which he thus drew, while high officials gladly supplied him with their affidavits as to the incredible saving effected in fuel, and the nutritive and palatable qualities of some rather feebly organized soups.

In November, 1793, while stopping at Florence, he made some of his long-continued and varied experiments on heat in presence of Lord Palmerston, who was then in that city. He was at Naples in the beginning of the next year.

He returned to Munich in a state of slow convalescence. Being unable to resume the management in detail of all the affairs of his various Institutions, as well as of his military department, he was obliged to content himself with exercising a general superintendence. He was constantly watchful to conciliate to his undertakings all opponents who were simply ignorant or prejudiced. Hoping, as it proved with good reason, that the manifest results of his reformatory efforts wholly to suppress public mendicity and to make the poor in a measure self-supporting by organized industry would certify to his unselfishness and his practical wisdom, he never, so far as I can discover, offered a plea on his own behalf, or vindicated his motives. From first to last the Elector advanced all his schemes, admiring his philosophical genius and grateful for his administrative aid. Spending the year after his return from his travels in Munich in this comparative quiet, he worked diligently in his study upon those literary productions the subject-matter of some of which has been above presented. I have already spoken of his admirable style, his simple, direct, and forcible way of expressing himself. Without the ornaments of rhetoric his Essays have many graces, and are well freighted with important truths fittingly set forth. When, soon after their publication and very extensive circulation, they were remarked upon in the ephemeral journals of Great Britain, I have noticed, in several instances, that they were criticised as often prolix and abounding in repetitions. Lord Brougham, in

an article on Popular Science, in the London Quarterly
Review for April, 1849, comments with sharpness upon
the different faults of some philosophers and some com-
mentators in respectively failing to clear up the ob-
scurities in their subjects, or in over-explaining and
tediously illustrating easy texts. He commends Franklin and Cobbett as admirable examples, in that, remembering the toil and difficulty with which they had
overcome the embarrassments attending their unaided
investigation of abstruse subjects, they had taken special pains to make those subjects easy and plain to their
readers. At the same time his Lordship thus finds
matter of ridicule in the Essays of Rumford : —

"The scientific works of Count Rumford abound in
examples of the ludicrous extent to which sensible men
will sometimes carry their exposition of matters known
to everybody. In one of his economic treatises he
gives a receipt for a pudding, and then a page of description how to eat it. The concluding sentence will
serve for a specimen: 'The pudding is to be eaten
with a knife and fork, beginning at the circumference
of the slice [in a cavity of the centre of which he had
directed that a piece of butter be left to melt] and
approaching regularly towards the centre, each piece
of pudding being taken up with the fork and dipped
into the butter, or dipped into it in part only, as is
commonly the case, before it is carried to the mouth.'"
This does indeed seem trifling, as his Lordship asserts ;
but the Count's whole minute description is pertinent,
as it really makes a difference how the "Indian Pudding" is eaten. The Count himself apologizes for his
details, alleging "the importance of giving the most
minute and circumstantial information respecting the

manner of performing any operation, however simple it may be, to which people have not been accustomed."

This was incident to the writer's purpose, to make himself intelligible and to communicate his views, when they were far from being the commonplaces of knowledge, to persons of ordinary capacity. These Essays, which have strangely dropped out of common appreciation during the last two generations, are to be regarded as the fruits of the author's period of rest after ten years of arduous and manifold labor in Bavaria and the Palatinate. The first five of them were written out in Munich, in the main as they were first published in London, some additional notes and tables being added in subsequent editions.

Rumford left Munich on his return to London, after an absence of eleven years, in September, 1795. The principal object of his visit was, as has been said, that he might publish his Essays. But he had another leading end in view. He had many warm friends and admirers as well as scientific correspondents in England, with whom he had kept up constant intercourse, communicating his experiments, as we have seen, to the Royal Society, — his membership of which always enlisted his pride and obligation of constant service. Undoubtedly, too, could he have had equal consideration in England, and have felt that he was as highly appreciated there for official dignity, if not with social rank, he would have preferred a residence in it. He sought, in this visit, to draw the attention of the English nation to the measures of public and domestic economy which he had conceived and realized in Germany. Unfortunately, on his arrival he was the victim of an outrage which, besides the grievous loss that it entailed, seems to have caused him some bitterness of feeling, from a suspicion which it roused in him. He thus refers to this painful experience. In his account of his Experiments on Gunpowder, he had promised at some time to give to the public the results of some other experiments which he had been making for several years upon the strength of various bodies. But he was obliged to add in a note: —

"Since writing the above, I have met with a misfortune which has put it out of my power to fulfil this promise. On my return to England from Germany, in October, 1795, after an absence of eleven years, I was stopped in my post-chaise, in St. Paul's Churchyard, in London, at six o'clock in the evening, and robbed of a trunk which was behind my carriage, containing all my private papers, and my original notes and observations on philosophical subjects. By this cruel robbery I have been deprived of the fruits of the labours of my whole life, and have lost all that I held most valuable. This most severe blow has left an impression on my mind which I feel that nothing will ever be able entirely to remove. It is the more painful to me, as it has clouded my mind with suspicions that never can be cleared up."

Rumford's friend, Colonel Baldwin, writing before he had knowledge of this misfortune, says that the Count "has prepared, for his own amusement, a short sketch 'of the vicissitudes of a life checkered by a great variety of incidents.'"[*] As this sketch, which would have had a profound interest, has never appeared, and is not now known to be in existence, we may infer that it was with the other private papers, the loss of which the Count thus deplores. We can only conjecture the nature of his suspicions which aggravated that loss as possibly referring to the jealousy of some rival, or the

---

[*] Literary Miscellany, Vol. II. p 33.

pique of some enemy ready to do the Count a wrong in his repute or in his feelings. He refers to the same misfortune again in his Essay on the Management of Fire. The register of his experiments on this subject was so voluminous that he had left it at Munich, otherwise it would have shared the fate of his other papers. To the statement of this fact he subjoins the remark : " I have many reasons to think that these papers are still in being. What an everlasting obligation should I be under to the person who would cause them to be returned to me ! "

On his arrival in England, Lord Pelham, his very warm friend, then Secretary for Ireland, gave Rumford a pressing invitation to visit that Island. The Count willingly responded, and went there in the spring of 1796, spending there two months. He at once employed himself in introducing into the hospitals and workhouses of Dublin many important improvements, and in heating a church by steam. He left there a collection of models for a number of useful mechanical inventions. His friend Pictet, who followed in his track some four years afterwards, says that these interesting objects were the first to engage his attention in his visit to the Dublin Society, and he furnishes an account of them for the *Bibliotlieque Britannique.*

Very marked attentions and honors were lavished upon Count Rumford in Ireland. The Royal Academy there, and the Society for the Encouragement of Arts and Manufactures, elected him an honorary member. After he had left the country he received an address of thanks from the Grand Jury of Dublin, an official letter from the Lord Mayor of the city, and one from the Viceroy of Ireland. These documents, which I have not been able to recover, Rumford showed to Pictet, who describes them as filled with the most flattering expressions of esteem and gratitude. On his return to London the Count superintended the changes which he had before advised in the arrangements and kitchen economy of the Foundling Hospital in London, and deposited in the Bureau of Agriculture many ingenious models of useful machines. The Annual Register for 1798 * thought of importance enough for insertion in its pages " An Account of the Kitchen fitted up at the Foundling Hospital under the Direction of his Excellency Count Rumford."

In connection with the visit he was making in England, the Count had sent for his daughter to come from America and meet him there.

* Page 397.

CHAPTER V.

IT is pleasant to be able, at this point, to introduce an episode in this narrative directly connecting the now famous Count Rumford with the country of his birth, where he had been known as Benjamin Thompson, and with those who survived here of his kindred and early friends. I have been fortunate in the collection, from various sources, of materials to illustrate and to give even a lively interest to this portion of the narrative. The labors to which Rumford had devoted himself in Germany had been so engrossing that his whole mind and thought must have been concentrated upon them. It would hardly surprise us, therefore, if we were left to infer that he had been comparatively uninformed about many important events transpiring in his native country at the most critical periods of its constitutional development. But he seems not to have been in ignorance of its public affairs nor of its distinguished men in politics or science. On the other hand, though reports of the eminence to which he had attained and of the philosophical genius to which he had given exercise were, of course, current in America, it was not till the publication of his Essays that his real achievements were known.

When Benjamin Thompson sailed from this country, he left behind him, as we have seen, his wife and infant daughter. The latter having been born October 18, 1774, was thus by absence deprived of a father's care at about the same age as that in which he himself had been bereft by the death of his own father. It has been affirmed in more than one sketch of Count Rumford's life, that his family heard and knew nothing of him till the close of the Revolutionary War. Even if there be no positive evidence in refutation of this statement, — and in the want or loss of writings covering that period of time I am not able to produce such evidence, — the assertion would in itself seem a preposterous one. The public services upon which Mr. Thompson entered at once on his arrival in England; the constant intercourse which he had with a great many refugees from Boston and Salem and other places, with several of whom he must have had a previous acquaintance at home; and his own official duties which required him to be a party to a correspondence with military men and royalists on this side of the water, — must certainly have kept his relatives and old neighbors perfectly informed about himself. How far and in what way he may have kept himself acquainted, by exchange of messages or letters, with those naturally most dear to him, and with their fortunes during the war, there is now extant no sufficient means for deciding. Communications of that kind were difficult and embarrassing. Perhaps the severance of his domestic and civil ties was attended for a short time with soreness of feeling and apparent alienation. The embitterment of the strife as the war advanced, — caused by the prostration of this country, — the havoc and ruin which were so wide-spread, the contemptuous spirit and the ruthless animosity which dictated the successive hostile measures of Great Britain, and the employment of foreign mercenaries against us, made the progress of the conflict more and more effective in destroying or in impeding the expression of anything like kindly sentiments between the parties.

I have deferred the introduction of the following letter — which, as its date will show, was written between two and three years before the Count left Munich for his visit to England — because it seems to be in itself but a fragment of a correspondence which was apparently resumed by Colonel Baldwin shortly before. This reply, as well as the reference made in it to the letter that called it forth, would lead us to infer that it was a resumption of the friendly intercourse between the parties, which, beginning in childhood, was interrupted by the exile of Thompson. From some memoranda of Colonel Baldwin's I infer, also, that his friend had made pecuniary remittances to his mother and daughter annually, through some mercantile acquaintance in Boston, before Baldwin himself became the medium for their transmission, as I find by an entry in his diary, dated October 7, 1793, that he then was. The letter from Baldwin which called forth the ensuing reply was dated November 10, 1792, and, as I have said, would indicate that it was the reopening, on his own part, of the suspended correspondence. "As to the main business of Mr. Stacey's journey," to which the Count refers, he having been the bearer of both the letters, the natural inference which we should draw would be, that that gentleman was a suitor for the hand of the daughter. She had many such, but I can learn nothing further of the matter, if Mr. Stacey were one of them. The reader will be struck alike by the earnestness with which the Count, longing to revisit his native country, asks if he may safely do so, — knowing, as he well did, how bitter had been the feeling against many returning refugees, — and by the strong terms of endearment and veneration with which he speaks of his mother.

"Munich, 18th January, 1793.

Dear Sir, — I received by the hands of Mr. Stacey your letter of the 10th November, for which I beg you would accept my best thanks. It gave me very sincere pleasure to hear from you, and to learn from Mr. Stacey that you were in good health when he left America, and surrounded by all the enjoyments of domestic happiness, and distinguished by the Esteem and Respect of your fellow-citizens. Neither time nor distance, nor change of habits and circumstances, have in the least abated that affectionate regard which I conceived for you at a very early period of my life, and I shall ever feel myself peculiarly interested in everything which relates to your prosperity, and shall be much gratified by every proof of your friendly recollection. I am very much obliged to you for your kind attentions to my Daughter. I hope she will ever conduct herself in such a manner as to merit your esteem, and to justify the good opinion you have expressed of her.

" As to the main business of Mr. Stacey's journey, I must refer you to my Daughter, to whom I have written fully upon the subject. As I have no wish but for her happiness, I think she must be satisfied with the advice I have given her, and I have no doubt but she will receive it as it is meant, and cheerfully follow it.

" As to my situation in this country, I must refer you to Mr. Stacey, who can give you the fullest information in respect to it. He will tell you how sick I am of the bustle of Public affairs, and how earnestly I long and hope for deliverance.

" You could hardly conceive the heart-felt satisfaction it would give me to pay a visit to my native country. Should I be kindly received ? Are the remains of Party spirit and political persecutions done away? Would it be necessary to ask leave of the State ?

" It is possible you may see me at Woburn before you are aware of it. I wish exceedingly to be personally acquainted with my Daughter. I wish to know her real character, and how I must go to work to lay a solid foundation for her future happiness. I wish once more to have the satisfaction of seeing my most kind and affectionate mother. I wish to prove to her how dear she is to me, and how grateful I am for all her goodness to me. My dear, beloved Parent! What would I give to see her, were it but for one hour! I should be much obliged to you for any accounts you may from time to time send me of her situation, and of others, my friends, in your neighborhood. Desiring to be remembered to all those of my old acquaintance who interest themselves in my welfare, I am, my dear Sir, with unfeigned Regard, and much Esteem,

" Yours, most affectionately,

" B. THOMPSON.

" To Col. Loammi Baldwin, &c., &c.
 Woburn, near Boston, N. America.
 By Mr. Stacey."

14

Thus the tone and language in which Count Rumford is found whether to continue or to renew his intercourse with his family and friends here, in the first of his communications after the war which has been preserved, would not indicate even that the intercourse had been indifferently or passionately suspended; for they are characterized by affection, and imply a full knowledge of matters which might be expected to interest him. He seems to take up again with the strongest natural feeling the relationships of son and father, as will abundantly appear.

The Count's honored and revered father-in-law, the Rev. Timothy Walker, had, as we have seen, received from him, in tender terms, the charge of wife and infant when the young parent hurriedly and secretly went from his home to go he hardly knew whither nor for how long an absence. That venerable clergyman, the chief man in patriotism and in common esteem in Concord, died, as I have said, after a ministry of fifty-two years, on September 2, 1782. His daughter, the wife of Count Rumford, lived to know of her husband's great fame and advancement, and died January 19, 1792, aged fifty-two years. Her abundant property and her continuance in her own comfortable home secured her every worldly advantage. Frequent entries in Colonel Baldwin's diary refer to visits at his home in Woburn, made for months at a time, by Sally Thompson, — as the daughter was familiarly called, — and to the payment to her of the proceeds of bills of exchange for considerable amounts sent to her by her father. In the diary, under date of January 29, 1796, is the following: " Friday, ten o'clock, Sally Thompson, daughter of Sir Benjamin Thompson, sailed from Boston in the . . . . ,[*] Captain Oliver, for London, to see her father, who has come from Munich to meet his daughter in London." She was then in her twenty-second year. She took with her the following letter from Colonel Baldwin : —

"Woburn, 26th of January, 1796.

"Dear Sir Benjamin, — When I received your much esteemed favor of the 18th of January, 1793, by the hand of Mr. Stacey, I expected ere this to have seen you in America, and participated in the pleasure which must have arisen on meeting your friends and recognizing in person your amiable daughter. I have often anticipated such an event with real pleasure, but I find it is like to happen otherwise. Your daughter informs me that she has your permission to visit you in London, and shall take passage in the . . . . , Captain Oliver, who will sail in a day or two. Her sudden departure, and business of pressing importance which calls me from home, afford me time only to say that it is with a mixture of pleasure and concern that we part with Sally at this time. So long a voyage through this northern region during the sun's retreat must be unpleasant. But the object of the journey is the first and greatest that can exist ; it certainly justifies the undertaking, which God grant may be prospered. The companions on board are strangers, but appear friendly, and the circumstance of there being one passenger of her own sex makes it much more agreeable. Mr. Fraizer is very obliging, and gives up his state-room for Sally's accommodation, and has been pleased to say to me that he will afford her every assistance in his power during the voyage, and on their arrival will take her to his own house until her father provides otherwise for her.

"I know Sally will render suitable returns for all favors, and (sickness excepted) make herself agreeable to her fellow-passengers, as she always conducts with the greatest propriety, and has the esteem of all her acquaintance. She has been attentive to your mother, who expresses much affection for Sally,

[*] The vessel was named the Charlestown.

and has assisted in her education ; and your daughter has improved greatly on the opportunities she has had. She possesses
a noble mind, and wants nothing but the aid of her father to
make her accomplished. . . . . I am sure you will not hesitate at
bestowing upon her every blessing a parent can impart. Your
daughter will be the bearer of this, and will sail to-morrow
(weather permitting). The season is advanced, but the weather
easy and fine. I shall feel anxious until I hear of her arrival.
Pray, write me by the very first opportunity.

"In answer to your inquiry, I can say that it is my opinion
that you can freely return to America, either with or without
official leave from the State, as you may choose ; and that you
would realize a hearty welcome from all your old friends and
citizens in general. I can say for one, that there is not a person on earth that I should rejoice so much to see. . . . . Sally
will be able to inform you particularly what your mother's situation is, and that of many other of your friends ; but I trust you
will yet return. Pray, come and see your kind mother. Make
us a visit, if you do no more.

"I am, dear Sir Benjamin, with much respect and esteem,
　　　"Your most obedient servant,
　　　　　　　　　"LOAMMI BALDWIN.
"Sir Benjamin Thompson, Knt."

The Count returned the following in reply : —

"London, 16th March, 1796.

"My Dear Sir, — I return you many thanks for your
friendly letters which I received by my Daughter, and I beg
you would accept my warmest acknowledgments for all the
kindness you have shown to my Daughter for the many years
she has been known to you.

"Her gratitude to you is without bounds, and she says nothing on earth will ever make her forget your goodness to her. I
do not despair of being able, at some future period, to express to
you in person, by word of mouth, the sense I entertain of your
kindness to my dear Child. You will not expect that I should
attempt to describe the pleasure I felt at seeing my dear Girl,

after an absence of twenty years! Such interesting events may be conceived, but cannot be described. No language could paint the agitation of my mind upon seeing before me a being whose existence had always appeared to me like the vision of a dream.

"As Sally means to write to you herself, I shall leave it to her to inform you of the courageous resolution she has taken, to go with me to Bavaria. God grant she may be happy there! She will likewise tell you whether she likes me as well as she expected, and whether I am kind to her. As to myself, all I can say is, that I like her very much indeed. She is just what I wished to find her,—an unaffected, cheerful, pleasing, amiable, Good Girl.

"We shall probably stay in England about two months longer, and shall then set off for Munich, from which place you shall hear from me. In the mean time, accept my best wishes for your health and prosperity.

"I am, Dear Sir, with unfeigned Regard and Esteem,

"Yours, most affectionately,

"RUMFORD.

"To Colonel Loammi Baldwin,
Woburn, near Boston, Massachusetts."

This letter may properly come in the order of its principal topic.

"Woburn, 28th June, 1796.

"My dear Count,—It has given me inexpressible satisfaction, on reading your kind letter of the 26th of March last, to find that your daughter is safe arrived; so much natural affection and love are met. It must be gratifying in the highest degree to meet your dear and only child, whom you had seen but for a moment in the first stage of her existence; and although she might have seen her father, yet her organs were too tender and undefined to retain the least idea of him, — more than twenty-one years have passed since you thus met before. Scenes tender like this are not for the pen to describe, they .

dissolve the soul into liquid joy, and mingle a divine affinity. I participate most feelingly in the joy of this event. God grant you both a long and happy existence! I know you will continue to be pleased with your amiable daughter. She is really a fine girl. She was beloved by everybody when she was here, and I only regret, and this I do sincerely, that it was not in my power to pay more attention to her education and happiness than I did. Her enterprising disposition made up for part of my neglect, but she is now in the immediate care of one who will do everything for her. She acknowledges in expressions of tenderness how affectionately you received and loved her.

"We are not disappointed in hearing that your daughter has resolved to accompany you to Bavaria. We have only to consider whose daughter she is, and everything good and great are the ideas that succeed. I long for the period to arrive when you shall make a visit to your native country. Thousands are ardently desirous of seeing you here.

"Mrs. Baldwin, although unknown, desires to be named to you in terms expressive of the happiness she feels on the kind reception you gave her dear friend, Miss Thompson, whose welfare is ever near her heart. Give our best love to Sally, and tell her that we all think and speak of her often, and hope erelong to see her again in this country.

"I wish for an opportunity to acquaint you with the many enterprises and various improvements going forward in this country, but time will not permit.

"I am, with much respect and esteem,

"My dear Count, your most affectionate friend,

"LOAMMI BALDWIN.

"Sir Benjamin Thompson,
    Count of Rumford."

It would seem, from the above, that it had been intended that the daughter should merely make a visit to her father while he was superintending the publication of his Essays in England, and that her going to reside with him for a time in Bavaria was an afterthought. She was abroad a little more than three years and a half. Mr. Baldwin enters her re-arrival in Boston in his diary under date of October 10, 1799, and refers to her return in a letter to her father of November 4, to be copied in another connection.

The following letter from Miss Sally to Mrs. Baldwin, announcing her arrival in England, must be erroneously dated, according to her statement of a six weeks' passage.

"London, March 5, 1796.

"DEAR MRS. BALDWIN,—I improve the first opportunity to acquaint you of my safe arrival, and kind reception by my father. We had a tedious passage of six weeks. I began to fancy the hand of Providence against me. But all fatigue and anxiety are now at an end, since my dear father is well, and loves me. Till I see you I shall think very often upon you and the Colonel, whose kindness to me I shall ever remember with gratitude. I have a thousand things to say. I have only time to tell you how sincerely I want to see you. I often reflect with much pleasure upon the happy days and months I have spent in your family. Neither time, nor absence, nor any situation of life, ever so exalted, will make me forget my good friends in America; and be assured there is none I esteem more highly than you. I will thank you to give my respects to the Colonel, &c.

"I am your affectionate
"SARAH THOMPSON.
"MRS. BALDWIN, Woburn."

In 1793 or 1794, Miss Thompson was introduced, by a daughter of the Revolutionary patriot, Robert Treat Paine, to the family of the Rev. Dr. Joseph Willard, President of Harvard College, in Cambridge. She made a most agreeable impression on them, and became thenceforward a most welcome guest on long and frequent visits. Before joining her father in England, as well as after her arrival, she had informed him of her obligations to this excellent family, which doubtless prompted him to write the following letter to President Willard.

"London, 25th March, 1796.

"REVEREND SIR, — The affectionate manner in which my daughter speaks of you, and of your kindness to her, has shown me how good you have been to her; and though I have not the pleasure of being personally known to you, I cannot help taking the liberty of writing to you, to express the obligations I feel myself under to you for your friendly attentions to my child. Though I have not the honor of being personally acquainted with you, I am no stranger to the respectable character you bear; and nothing could have been more pleasing to me than to find that my daughter had found means to attract your notice, and to merit your approbation and friendship.

"Excuse the liberty I take in troubling you with this letter, and do me the justice to believe that it is with much esteem and regard I have the honor to be, Sir, your much obliged and most obedient servant,

"RUMFORD." *

Here is another letter from Miss Sally, as, for a reason to be soon given, she is daily in expectation of leaving England, with her father, for Germany.

"London, June 13, 1796.

"MY DEAR MRS. BALDWIN, — I cannot quit England without writing once more to my dear friend, although I have not yet received letters from you in return to the ones I wrote you upon my first arrival here. I do not believe you think of me so often as I do of you, for I am sure there is not a day, nor hardly an hour, that I do not think of you. I hope by this time, my dear Mrs. Baldwin, that your canal-hurry is a little over. But

---

* Memoirs of Youth and Manhood. By Sydney Willard. Cambridge. 1855. Vol. I. p. 156.

I fear it is not, for it is such an immense undertaking that it is impossible it should be already finished. I am very happy, I should think it very strange if I was not. For I have one of the best of fathers, that seems desirous to do everything that will contribute to my happiness. We shall set off for Germany in a few days, and after I arrive there I shall write you again, to tell you how I like, and by that time I hope to receive letters from you and Colonel Baldwin.

" We should have been gone long before this time to Germany if some business had not called my father to Ireland.

" I enjoy very good health, and am very happy. I should think it strange if I was not to be. I am indulged in everything I wish, and I am under the protection of a parent that I have not only reason to love, but to be proud of. On his account I receive every polite attention that I could wish, and had I his merit, I should feel that I deserved it. But this you know, my dear Mrs. Baldwin, that *good-nature* is the chief I have to recommend me, and which, to do myself justice does not fail to secure me friends wherever I go.

" Believe me to be your affectionate

" SARAH THOMPSON.

" To Mrs. Marshat Baldwin."

It will be noticed by the following letter of the Count's to Colonel Baldwin, mainly on business, that the writer's kind intentions included his mother's other children.

" London, 20th July, 1796.

" My dear Sir, — As I am informed by my Daughter that you have hitherto been so good as to assist me in making my little remittances to America, by drawing her Bills, &c., I take the liberty to request you would give your assistance to my dear Mother, in procuring and sending to her the annual allowance of thirty Pounds sterling, which for several years past I have given her, and which she has received through the hands of my Daughter. I therefore request you would, upon the receipt of this letter; draw a set of Bills of Exchange *in your own name*, on the house of Sir Robert Herries & Co., Bankers, St. James St., London, for Thirty Pounds sterling, at thirty days sight, taking care to date this set of Bills the 26th of March, 1796 (my Birth Day).

"I also request you would draw on the said Sir Robert Herries & Co. (who are my agents in London, and who have my directions to accept and pay these Bills) every succeeding year, on the 26th of March, for the like sum of Thirty Pounds sterling, for the same purpose, and apply it in the same manner: that is to say, that you would pay it into the hands of my dear Mother, which I desire she would receive as a small token of my filial affection, and of my gratitude for all her goodness to me.

"In case of my Mother's death, it is my request that the annual amount of this allowance may be equally divided among my Mother's four children by her husband, Mr. Josiah Pierce.

"Begging you would excuse the liberty which I take with you, and assuring you of my most sincere regard and esteem, I remain, with unalterable affection,

"Dear Sir, Yours most Sincerely,

"RUMFORD.

"During my stay in England, I have published a volume of Essays, which I have sent to you under cover to my friend, Doctor Walter, of Boston. I wish they may meet with your approbation. I do not despair of seeing you in America in the course of a year or two. My Daughter, who is very well, desires her best compliments to you and to Mrs. Baldwin. She is just setting out with me for Germany. She does not seem disposed to leave me, and I am delighted to have her with me.

"The Honble. Col. Baldwin, Member of the Senate, &c.
    Woburn, near Boston, Massachusetts."

I am able to give Colonel Baldwin's reply.

"WOBURN, December 26, 1796.

"MY DEAR COUNT, — I have received your favor of the 20th of July last, wherein provision is made for furnishing your kind mother with a gratuity of £30 sterling, a year. I shall cheerfully undertake to perform the part which you have requested of me, in order to effect your benevolent purpose; and in pursuance thereof I have made your honored mother acquainted with the arrangements, and agreeably to your instructions have drawn the first set of exchange for £30 sterling on your new agents, Sir Robert Herries & Co., dated 26th March, 1796, and have delivered the same to Jonathan Porter (in whose favor the draft is made) in lieu thereof, and to replace the draft your daughter made in my favor for the same on your late agent, Richard Armstrong, Esq., dated 23d of October, 1795, who refused payment thereof, as appears by my letter of the 5th instant, with the protest and papers accompanying it. However, I do not mean that this shall operate to the injury of your mother.

"Please to accept my sincere thanks for the volume of your Essays which I have received through the hands of our good friend, Doctor Walter. I consider it a work of inestimable merit. It is very much admired by all who have had opportunity to peruse the few copies which have arrived in this country. The author is more frequently spoken of than ever, and daily inquiry is made, when he will return to or visit his native country.

"Permit me again, with the most cordial affection, to invite your attention to an object in which the wishes of so many unite. Mrs. Baldwin desires to be remembered with particular affection to your daughter.

"With much esteem, I have the honor to be, my dear Count,

"Your most sincere friend, and humble servant,

"LOAMMI BALDWIN.

"SIR BENJAMIN, Count of Rumford."

"The above letter was forwarded by Dr. Welsh's son of Boston, going to Berlin, in Prussia."

I have already had occasion to mention the late
James F. Baldwin, of Boston, one of the sons of
Count Rumford's friend, who, inheriting the scientific
genius and taste of his honored father, employed his
engineering skill in the introduction of the Cochituate
water into this city. Holding the most intimate relations with Sarah Thompson all through her life, having
her frequently as a guest in his family, managing her
affairs and acting as her executor, I find from the correspondence which passed between them, and which I have
before me, that he had for her a high regard. He was,
of course, aware of her marked peculiarities of character, and as a man of excellent discernment could hardly have expected that she should have been without
them, or have viewed and treated them otherwise than
he did, considering what had been her experiences and
fortunes from her infancy to old age. Towards the
close of her life she wrote a sketch of a considerable
portion of its most interesting period for the wife of
Mr. Baldwin, also her warmly attached friend. I am
allowed to have, and to use according to my own judgment, this piece of autobiography. I may not, perhaps, use it wisely in making such large extracts from
it in the ensuing pages. But as there is no one among
the living who will be troubled by its disclosures, except,
it may be, by some of its incongruities with Philosophy,
I venture to print much of its contents, as illustrating
one of the ever varied and ever interesting exhibitions
of human nature under peculiar circumstances of opportunity and experience. I may say in explanation of its
style and matter, that though there had been an intention
and effort to secure to Sally the best education which
could then be obtained by one situated as she was,

there was something so fragmentary and desultory in her school training as to secure to her from it very imperfect results. She had now for two or three years been in correspondence with her father, and her letters had been of such a character as to have raised his expectation of her accomplishments higher than were realized when they met. It was said that her teacher, Mrs. Snow, helped her in the composition of these letters.

The manuscript has a wrapper inscribed, " The history of my life : begun at Paris, in, possibly, 1842, and ended in May, 1845." It is entitled, " Memoirs of a Lady, written by herself." Indulging in the sentimental vein common in her girlhood among female writers and correspondents, she takes the name of " Serafena," and addresses herself to Mrs. Baldwin, by whose request she was induced to give this account of some particulars of her life. Her experience, she says, had led her through so many strange scenes, with rapid changes, beginning when she was four years old, that she might easily refer it to supernatural agency. The absence of her father, and her mother's illness, led to her being sent away from Concord, at the age just mentioned, to the care of an aunt. She was put in charge of a female slave, to whom she was much attached, who left her at her relative's, the indulgent mother of " many young children badly brought up " Her little companions engaged her in rude and dangerous plays; in one of which, having been severely burned, she was taken back to her mother. On account of that mother's long invalidism the child was left very much to herself, and her early education was defective, the effects of which she felt through life. She gives an account of her grandfather Walker, and of

the peculiarities of his substantial parsonage, which was
a garrison house.   This leads her to refer to those rem-
nants of the Indian tribes which occasionally made
troublesome visits to the place in her childhood, though
they were so wisely and kindly treated by the minister
and his wife that some of them once rescued him from
extreme peril.   From his three voyages to England on
business of the town, the minister was careful to bring
home attractive presents for the red men and their
squaws.   Sarah yields to a touch of romance in describing her rides upon a pony, and her lonely meditations in pleasant woods.

The young lady had much of her father's skill in
etching and drawing.   Three of her sketches are found
on the pages of the manuscript before me.   I have
caused them to be copied as accurately as possible from
the original, without any additional touches from the
artist.   Indeed, the copies hardly do justice to the
spirit and vigor of the originals.   On one of her
visits to her aunt with the " naughty children," an
incident occurred which she describes as " very dangerous to our morals, getting us into the way of telling
stories."   They had partaken of a surreptitious repast
in the dairy, and happening to go in to the aunt and
mother with the tokens of it around their mouths,
were accosted thus: " ' My little dears, I think you
have been at the cream!'   'No!' exclaimed one,
echoed by all.   ' But look ye in the glass,' said my
aunt."

On the next page is Sally's representation of the scene.

The writer, however, bears testimony to the fact
that when her young companions grew up they were
very excellent persons.

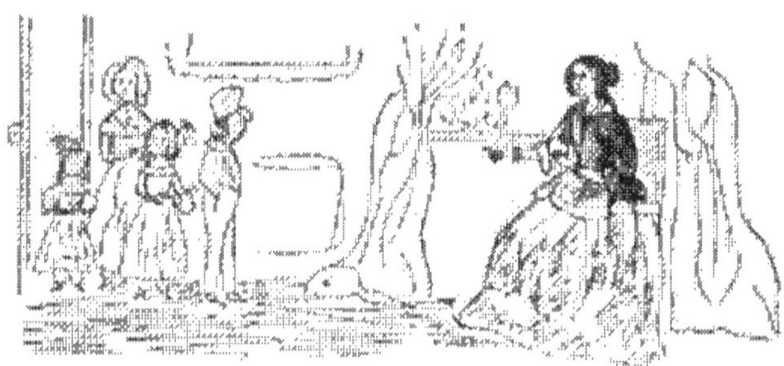

During her childhood her mother's invalidism made her familiar with the sick-chamber, and there is really an exquisite delicacy of drawing in Sally's delineation of this scene.

She was sent, for two or three seasons, to Mrs. Snow's boarding-school in Boston, that she might be taught dancing and other accomplishments, and she made many agreeable acquaintances in the town. Her mother, with recovered health and with tender kindness, during the long winter evenings would read and tell stories to her and her half-brother, Paul Rolfe. It would hardly be fair to the daughter to suppress the

following passages, though the admission of tnem seems
to be at the expense of the father.

"Peace, liberty, independence, are proclaimed throughout
the United States of America, enlivening the spirits and glad-
dening to all hearts.   Alas! those forsaking their country, deserting its divine cause, are now excluded this joy and blessing."

"It is true, we read thus in the papers: 'His Majesty,
George III., King of Great Britain, has conferred on Colonel
Benjamin Thompson the order of Knighthood, for services
rendered his country.'"

"Vain honors!   Is that a sufficient recompense for a separation from friends, from all that is dear on earth?   Ask these
favored ones who received like honors, if they can ever after
look into their hearts and pronounce themselves perfectly
happy!"

Sarah represents herself as living under the most
happy circumstances of a country life till the death of
her fond mother committed her to the care of strangers,
and a severe sickness prostrated her.   Her memory was
at fault when she represents her age at fourteen at her
mother's death; and the winter ride on horseback, which
took her out of her native State to dwell with strangers, was doubtless, for a time at least, to the friendly
home of the Baldwins in Woburn.   She describes her
voyage across the ocean with skill and feeling.   She
not only had the incidents of "dreadful winds followed
by calms," but the disturbance of a love-passage, — in
which, however, by her own account, she did not participate.   She "was enticed into the gambling game of
loo"; was exposed to the addresses of a young captain, "who, as the word goes, fell in love with me, or,
probably, at sea, having few adventures, took a fancy
for a flirtation, — fortunately, in no way or shape returned."

" Though destitute of proper earthly protection I seemed favored by a divine Providence, in the midst of temptations remaining unshaken. Playing this horrible game of *los*, and always winning it, gave me not the least inclination to continue it. Thus, I say, with all our troubles, there is a kind Providence, and ways pointed out to us if we will but pursue them."

She was wind-bound for three weeks off the Scilly Isles.

" My protectors were a Captain and Mrs. Bennet, and a Mr. Frasier of London; on arriving, I was to go to his house, where I was to meet my father, Baron Thompson. The Bennets were of Boston. Mrs. Bennet and I walked all around the Island of St. Mary's, picking up pebble-stones on the sea-shore; but we had to have recourse to our old method of passing time, that of playing cards. The captain coming from his ship, the commandant (so-called) of the place, besides an officer, joining us, — the only people we saw, as may be said, companionable in the place, — we would be set down daily at some round gambling game. It is said of people beginning to play, that they are generally lucky. Undoubtedly it is the case, tempted by his satanic Majesty. For myself, I won all the time; winning at least the cost of my passage twice over of the captain. But when we got to London my father would not let me take any of the money; yet he or I must have paid it had I lost."

The party landed at Portsmouth, and took post-chaises for London.

" Count Rumford, my father, having passed several preceding years at Munich, in Bavaria, had come to England to have published some of his Essays. He took the opportunity to send for me, my mother being dead, and I requiring protection. Many were the scenes he had passed through after leaving me as an infant, and erroneous were the ideas I had formed of him, particularly of his appearance; we having had only a small profile of him in shade, giving ever an imperfect idea of the person.

15

Indeed, so different from what I had thought were his looks, that I could hardly fancy him the person I sought after, would willingly have run from him, and ended in a violent fit of crying, which he did not consider as a compliment, asking me afterwards what I meant by it. To secure love to my father was the playfulness of his character (at times), — witness his laughter, quite from the heart, nothing made up about it; the expression of his mouth, ornamented with the most finished pearls, was sweetness itself. But to see him accidentally, he did not strike one as handsome, or very agreeable, though not exactly to the contrary. At the time I met him, having been ill, he was very thin and pale, — again a reason of my disappointment. My opinion of him was naturally romantic, perhaps, as young people's often are. I had heard him spoken of as an officer. I had attached to this an idea of the warrior, with the martial look, possibly the sword, if not the gun, by his side. His profile being in black, made me suppose him dark in complexion, possibly sunburnt; in short, in stature, size, and looks the perfect warrior. Yet my mother often spoke of him as carroty, his hair being red; but later not so, a very pretty color. My father pretended I looked better than he expected to find me. It is true he had had a most unfavorable likeness of me in a small miniature.

" Though it was a trying scene to meet, yet it was nothing to finding out each other's disposition in the end, and my father began with being much alarmed about me. He himself resided in a large hotel in Pall Mall, but could not have me with him, putting me to board not far off, at a Mrs. Lackington's. He had brought his valet, Aichner, with him, and for me a maid, by the name of Anymeetle, both Germans. I was to be presented to Lord and Lady Palmerston, Sir Charles Blagden, Sir William Pepperell and family (Americans), and other of his friends. My dress, it was thought, required looking into, and I was sent with my maid for purchases. Cloaks being fashionable, materials were bought for one. It being to be trimmed with lace, I returned to my father with some of the most elegant London afforded, we having by chance gone to a very dear, fashionable shop. Nothing could equal my father's surprise but mine at his. I had never the care of my own things, my mother doing all that; nor had I the least real knowledge of the value of money. The lace was bought because I thought it was handsome, and it pleased me. To make matters worse, before he had got over his surprise about the lace, I showed him at least half a dozen of beautiful new pairs of shoes I had bought, besides several other things. My father, without having a particle of avarice in his character (he never laid up money, or anything of that sort), had order in the extreme, and these purchases of mine looked much like disorder and extravagance, — not the case, however, inexperience only. It would be difficult to imagine the effect it had on my father, he viewing me, undoubtedly, as lost forever if a stop was not put to it, if not himself ruined."

" This was nothing to my having made a courtesy out of place to a housekeeper. The circumstance was as follows, but must be somewhat explained.

" Different customs, though trifling, excite interest. An American miss of certain pretensions, approaching or accosting a superior, places the feet in position, and, drawing them back, makes a low courtesy. The English custom is, to draw one foot carelessly back, making a courtesy, not near so low a dip (so called), not going back far enough to lose hold of hands mutually given for the celebrated shake. Nor with real fashionables is there any dip at all, going bolt upright, giving the hand, sparing even the epithets, Madam, Sir, or Miss, and with answers, to inquiries of health, of Yes or No. In France the young person approaches slowly, with apparent diffidence, with a slight motion of the head, looking steadfastly with a smile at the person they are to meet; and when the other with open arms comes forward, as when receiving a child first running alone, and much in the same manner, bestows caresses, with the difference of a degree more ceremony towards the miss than the child it being thought indecorous to express the same warmth of feeling. The forehead of the young lady is destined to receive the caress. In these trifles are to be seen

the characteristics of the three nations, — the humility of the
Americans, the dignity of the English, and the graceful good-
humor of the French.

"I could make one of the humble courtesies, and was thought
to acquit myself well.   My father having taken me with him in
going to pay a visit to a lady, a particular friend of his, not finding her at home, inquires for the housekeeper, having a message to leave.   Whether it was that I did not rightly comprehend the word *housekeeper*, we having few people of that description in the New England States, — people of first fortune
and family performing that office for themselves, — or whether,
from inattention, I did not hear the word, I cannot say, but
on entering, disengaging my arm from that of my father, placing
my feet in position and drawing back to allow myself a comfortable sweep, I made one of my very best, lowest courtesies.
And this to a *housekeeper!*   Than this, the affair of the lace,
most likely, was not more cutting to my father's feelings.

"Poor man! he had occasion to tremble for another circumstance.   I, having been promised to go with him to the Italian
Opera, was, unfortunately, to be with a party of high fashionables.
After, I suppose, weighing matters well, instead of retracting his
promise, he concludes to lecture me.   Whatever my impressions
of the music, I was to make no observations; preferring, it
seems, insipidity to an improper remark.   This music being
an acquired taste, and I having had the advantage of only that
which was most simple and natural, it is true I was not enchanted.   I much preferred — *within myself*, of course — old
Black Prince's fiddle, of Concord; particularly when a rosy lad,
leading to the floor of the dance his still more rosy partner, looking sternly, said peremptorily, ' Make your fiddle speak, Prince.'

"In consequence of the Baron's taking a trip to Ireland, I
was put to a boarding-school at Barnes's Terrace, kept by the
Marquise of Chabann.   She, her husband and family, were
French emigrants.   My stay was much shorter there than I
could have wished, I being very happy, — three months only, —
my father then returning from Ireland and making preparations
to go to Bavaria, obliging me to quit.   Madame de Chabann

give us a holiday for amusement before separating. Those with whom I was the most intimate wrote me letters not to be read before arriving at Munich. There were only twelve young ladies taken, most of them noble. Miss Byron was my particular favorite, and friend. There were peculiarities of parentage in common to us both, but I was not unfortunate and disgraced like herself. She had a father she never saw, her mother she saw seldom, and her grandfather, the Duke of Leeds, who supported her, would not see her. I have since heard of this young lady, and learned she had been properly established in life, though I never again met her. Thus, from my roving life, if I had friends I was deprived of them. A very beloved one I had in Mrs. Snow's school in Boston, Miss Porter, after our separation there I never met again. These are only a few of the many I could mention. The Marquis and Marchioness of Chabann and family I met again in Paris, restored to their fortune and consequence.

"The fine appearance of English ladies on horseback, German ladies riding differently, induced my father to buy a couple of English side-saddles, designing one for the Countess of Nogarola, a particular friend of his, the other for me, in hopes of putting the English method of riding in fashion in Munich. I was sent to Ashley's riding-school to take lessons. I was surprised at it, thinking myself all-sufficient in the art, yet I found there was much to be learnt. The mounting, dismounting, manner of sitting, holding the reins, the whip even, walking the horse, putting him on the gallop, the trot. Yet with all due deference to Baron Thompson's opinion and taste for riding, joined with many others, I beg leave to differ, — not approving of ladies' riding. While graceful, it is dangerous.

"My father's friend, Lady Palmerston, observed to him one day, in my hearing, that I did not appear to be struck with their fine edifices or architecture in general. This was turned into a joke by him, saying, it was a characteristic of savages; that they did not — or appeared not to — take notice of things. I, bridling up, told her Ladyship that I had seen beautiful paintings and drawings in America of buildings in England and in

London, but I had found nothing like them here, all being
covered with smoke, and that was why I admired nothing. I
secretly applauded myself for having given so sharp an answer.
People of any character after a while get conformed to circumstances. My father observing one day, to friends present, that I
was extremely docile and obedient to him, I burst into a laugh,
saying, he was not to imagine it was all free-will and pleasure.
My father was fond of having his own way, even, as I fancied,
to despite me; but, as an excuse for him, he had led the life of
a bachelor ever after twenty.

" It is well known to be a disadvantage, in many respects, for
males and females to have little or no control. His wish for
implicit obedience from me, and my early indulgence, as I may
say, from a mother, made us at times not get on so well, at all
events rendering me extremely unhappy. My stay in London
at this time was not of long duration, but from the novelty of
scenes and the multiplicity of ideas seemed to be so. Our
society being the first, my advantages were great, and might
lead to happiness if always to be continued; much the contrary, if otherwise. The first society has a charm which leaves
a void difficult to be filled up when deprived of it.

" My father was often at the Royal Society, and intimate
with its President, Sir Joseph Banks. I would be invited to the
dinners Sir Joseph gave to the select ones of his royal learned
Society. Through the kindness and civility of Lady and Miss
Banks, his wife and sister, I several times found myself one of
their party. Lady Banks was so kind, and most likely out of
civility to my father she would allow me to be with her for
days together, taking me about with her, letting me see things,
— in short, trying to amuse me. I recollect she took me to a
Lord Mayor's ball, where I saw the princes and royal family for
the first time. As may be supposed, the select dinners of the
Royal Society were highly interesting, and where, I think,
ladies were seldom or never admitted. I was allowed to accompany Lady and Miss Banks as a mere nobody; but this did not
prevent my making observations which never have been and
never will be forgotten. The idea of very learned people

suggests that of pedantry. At these dinners there was nothing of the kind, differing only from other refined societies when remarks were made to convey perhaps new ideas, discoveries, or highly entertaining instruction, sometimes there being no such talk at all. In our every-day companies we consider talking (incessantly) of the greatest consequence, and lucky if all do not talk together and no one is heard."

I must here interrupt the gossip in the pleasant narrative of the daughter to recognize the graver occupations of her father. It would seem that he had fixed no particular limit for his stay in England, and that, as we shall have to notice soon, an emergent necessity called him hurriedly back to Bavaria before he had completed the work he had in view. Of the Count's writings, which are called by him Essays, there are, in all, eighteen. The publication of these extended through many years, the last of them having appeared in 1812. But the beginning of the series properly dates its publication in July, 1796. The following proud array of titular honors appears attached to his name on his first title-page : —
"Benjamin Count of Rumford, Knight of the Orders of the White Eagle and St. Stanislaus : Chamberlain, Privy Counsellor of State, and Lieutenant-General in the service of his Most Serene Highness the Elector Palatine, Reigning Duke of Bavaria; Colonel of his Regiment of Artillery, and Commander-in-Chief of the General Staff of his Army; F. R. S. Acad. R. Hiber. Berol. Elec. Boicœ, Palat. and Amer. Soc." He lived to win and display many more scientific and academic honors. The third London edition of his first Essays was published in 1798. An American edition appeared in Boston, in three volumes, in 1798 and 1799. The

Count himself sent several copies to his friends in this country. A fifth edition of three volumes appeared in London in 1800. In 1802 a fourth volume was added, containing many of Rumford's Philosophical Papers, and this was issued again the next year. His Essays on the Treatment of Pauperism were published separately in London in 1851, and again in 1855. His works were at once translated into German and French.

During this period of his stay in England, making excursions to Ireland and Scotland, as we learn from his daughter's narrative, the Count was in the full enjoyment of his social and scientific distinction. Undoubtedly this was to himself the most satisfactory period of his life. His fame was now established on claims and services which partook equally of scientific and philanthropic contributions to the welfare of humanity. Farther on in his career we shall find that an element of embitterment and antagonism entered into his experience and his relations with some of his contemporaries and scientific associates, and led him to narrow the range of his intercourse, even to a degree of isolation and self-seclusion. But while in England on this visit, and on the even more important one which he made two years afterwards, he seems to have found an unqualified pleasure in his work in the appreciation of it by the public, and in the respect and attentions exhibited towards him by very many persons of the highest social rank. He certainly was fond of such attentions. He was deferential to rank and station, and craved intercourse on confidential terms with many of the nobility, no doubt persuaded that his talents and the uses for which he employed them made him a peer of those whom birth, fortune, or circumstances had lifted in the social scale. Franklin—to outward seeming, at least—was more indifferent than was Rumford to the prestige and assumptions of the aristocracy. Yet we should give to the latter the benefit of judging him by a principle of his own, which, in his following of it, may have furnished him with a disinterested motive. That principle was that all reforms and improvements must be directed with an aim to relieve and help the common people, and that a prime condition for a successful application of them was to engage for them the sympathetic interest of the privileged, the nobility, and the wealthy.

Incident to his very laborious and ardent efforts for cheapening the production and preparation of nutritive food, and indeed as the essential condition for success in those efforts, the Count devoted himself most zealously to the study and the mechanical improvement of all the apparatus connected with fireplaces and chimney-flues. When he first published his Essay on "Chimney Fire-places, with Proposals for improving them to save Fuel; to render Dwelling-houses more Comfortable and Salubrious, and effectually to prevent Chimneys from Smoking," the Count was able to say that he "had not had less than five hundred smoking chimneys under his hands." Of course the announcement was an advertisement of himself as an expert in a rather uninviting occupation. But he was so zealous and unwearied a worker in such economical reforms that he never refused to give his services, whether in palace, poor house, or farmer's cottage. His first experiment in London was tried in Lord Palmerston's house, in Hanover Square. Then he took in hand the chimneys of the house where the Board of Agriculture held its

meetings, and which, being frequented by-people from
all parts of Great Britain, he hoped would be another
advertisement of his improvement. He did the same
for the chimneys of Devonshire House, and for the
dwellings of Sir Joseph Banks, the Earl of Besborough,
the Countess-Dowager Spencer, Melbourne House,
Lady Templeton's, Mrs. Montague's, Lord Sudley's,
the Marquis of Salisbury's, and a hundred and fifty
others in London. He instructed a firm of bricklayers
in his method so as to give them constant employment.
He found that the saving of fuel which he effected,
while gaining increased warmth, amounted to from one
half to two thirds. He made use of his own room in
the Royal Hotel, Pall Mall, for trying experiments in
the construction of fireplaces and chimney-flues; and he
enlisted the co-operation of Mrs. Hempel, the owner
of a large pottery in Chelsea, for manufacturing the
parts of new materials in her line, and of Mr. Hopkins,
the King's ironmonger, for materials in his line, to aid
in carrying out his own designs. Giving very simple
and intelligible information about the philosophical
principles of combustion, ventilation, and draughts, he
prepared careful diagrams to show the proper measurements, disposal, and arrangements of all the parts of a
fireplace and a flue, at the same time announcing that
he had no purpose to take out a patent for any of his
inventions or improvements, but left them wholly free
to the public. The cure of smoking chimneys and the
economy of heat were found to depend upon much the
same improvements applied to the construction of fireplaces. He noticed that, in most of those which he
examined, the heat which was radiated so as to warm an
apartment was scarcely a fifth part of what was gen-

erated by the fuel, all the rest passing off by the chimney. He fixed upon an angle of one hundred and thirty-five degrees as the one that ought to be formed between the sides of the fireplace and the back of it, and decided that the back should be one third of the breadth of the front opening, and be carried up perpendicularly till it joins the breast, and leave the throat of the chimney about four inches wide. The historian of the Royal Society, its assistant secretary and librarian, writing in 1848, says in a note:[*] "One of the earliest of Rumford's stoves, or fireplaces, is that set up under the Count's immediate superintendence in my office in the Royal Society. It is by far the best fireplace which I have seen." The Count did not neglect the interests and comfort of the sooty chimney-sweepers, so important a class in the London of those days.

In a poem entitled "The Pursuits of Literature," by Thomas James Mathias, (erroneously ascribed in Watt's Bibliotheca Britannica to William Gifford) the first part of which was published in May, 1794, and which, in spite of its prosiness and its dull satire, was so popular as to have reached the seventh edition of all its four parts in London in 1798, and to have been reprinted in Philadelphia two years afterwards, occurs the following tribute to Rumford, perhaps the best thing in the whole work : —

> "Yet all shall read, and all that page approve,
>   Where public spirit meets with public love.
>   Thus late, where poverty with rapine dwelt,
>   Rumford's kind genius the Bavarian felt,
>   Not by romantic charities beguiled,
>   But calm in project, and in mercy mild;
>   Where'er his wisdom guided, none withstood,
>   Content with peace and practicable good;

[*] Weld's History, &c.   Vol. II. p. 113.

"Round him the laborers throng, the nobles wait,
Friend of the poor and guardian of the State."*

The poet, referring in a note to the then recently published Essays, says: "I hope the directors of the interior government of this country will have the sense and wisdom to profit from this most valuable and important work, whose truly philosophic and benevolent author must feel a joy and self-satisfaction far superior to any praise which man can bestow." In another note, on the word "mercy" in his text, the poet says that grace is "a distinguishing feature in all the Count's plans for the relief of the poor, the idle, the abandoned, and the wretched. The mode of conferring mercy and apparent kindness is not always mild and merciful."* The poet's high encomiums on Count Rumford are the more observable, as in his numerous and elaborate notes, covering more than half his pages, he delights to launch his satires against the Royal Society and its members, especially the Count's intimate friend, Sir Charles Blagden. In another of his Poems, "The Shade of Alexander Pope," Mathias, in a complimentary allusion, makes a reference to the figure of the Count which indicates the effect of labor and illness on his health and former robustness.

"Through air, fire, earth, how unconfined we range!
What veil has Nature? and what works are strange?
All mark each varied mode of heat and light,
From the spare Rumford to the pallid Knight."†

As the Count returned to London from his frequent long or short journeys, taken in behalf of his friends or for the introduction and supervision of his own contrivances, his attention was always curiously and anxiously engaged by the clouds of smoke which hung over

* Pursuits of Literature, Philadelphia Ed., p. 192.   † Ib. p. 34.

the metropolis, and which covered all its prominent edifices with a dingy and sooty mantle. He saw in that smoke the unused material which was turned equally to waste and a means of annoyance and insalubrity. He said, playfully, yet in the sincerity of a true economical philosophy, that he would bind himself, if the opportunity were allowed him, to prove to the citizens, that from the heat and the material of heat which were thus wasted he would agree to cook all the food used in the city, warm every apartment, and perform all the mechanical work done by means of fire. There have been many wise and skilful experiments since his day, and many scientific papers have been prepared on the loss and the nuisance represented by that same smoky atmosphere of London. But probably no one has intermeddled with it more effectually than did he who first turned full attention to the philosophy of light and heat.

"The Rumford Roasters," so called, came into extensive use in Great Britain, and were imported into this country, very many of them being set up in Boston and the neighboring towns in the best houses. The Roaster, if not the first, was the most scientific, ingenious, and effective apparatus of the kind which, by its arrangement of flues for conveying hot air around the food in the oven, as well as by economizing fuel, allowed of the preparation of many articles by one fire, and greatly facilitated the labors and added to the comfort of the cook. The families which practised a generous hospitality found it to be a most welcome addition to their culinary arrangements. There was at one time, so to speak, an enthusiasm and an epidemic excitement about it. Count Rumford's Essays on Food and its

Preparation, and on Fuel, were widely circulated here, both in copies of the English edition, which he sent to his many friends, and in the Boston reprint. The simplicity, homeliness, and experimental good sense of the subject-matter of their text, and the admirable diagrams and the plates which illustrated them, made them intelligible to all readers, and prompted a general desire to put his improvements under practical trial. They were especially popular in Salem, where many of the flourishing citizens had occasion to recall over their dinners the apprentice-boy in Mr. Appleton's store. The distinguished minister of the First Church in that town, Dr. Prince, the successor to young Thompson's friend Barnard, himself a most successful cultivator of experimental science, is said to have set up the first Rumford Roaster in his own house, at the beginning of the century; it remained in constant use there till within ten years, when the house was sold.

A curious anecdote is told in connection with the "Roaster," in a charming biography of one of the eminent men of Massachusetts of the last age, — that of Chief-Justice Theophilus Parsons, by his son, the Law Professor of the same name. The biographer says that his father had imported, in or about 1807, a complete set of the apparatus, and having had it placed in his upper kitchen, was very proud of it. He found that from its novelty and the ignorance of his cook it required for a time his own oversight, when at last, by his patient instruction of his servant, everything went well. On the strength of the new cooking apparatus he had invited a large dinner-party, and the Roaster proved equal to the occasion. Judge and Mrs. Sever, of Kingston, excellent people of the old school, were among his guests,

— she being stiff and precise in formality and brocade. The water through the aqueduct from Jamaica Plain, another improvement, had also been recently introduced into the Chief-Justice's house, and on the day of the dinner-party, owing to some derangement, had required his attention. He had come from court with his mind engaged by an interesting insurance case, which he had been trying, about a schooner. The Chief-Justice had a marked peculiarity of memory. His hold on mere names seemed to be as weak as his grasp of everything else was strong, and sometimes, in moments of abstraction, he would make strange mistakes. On this occasion, the company being seated, after grace was said, as he took the carving-knife in hand, he addressed the stately Mrs. Sever across the length of the table, with this remarkable announcement, " Mrs. Schooner, all the food on this table was cooked in the aqueduct." His wife, dropping from her hand the fish-knife, cried out in consternation, " Lord's sake, Mr. Parsons, what *do* you mean ?" *

In casting my eyes over the last importation of a batch of books from London, for one of our public libraries, after writing the preceding pages, I was struck with an inscription on the cover of one of them as follows: " Fuel in Cooking." On opening to the title-page, I read, "On the Extravagant Use of Fuel in Cooking Operations, together with a short account of Benjamin, Count of Rumford, and his economical systems, and numerous practical suggestions adapted for domestic use. By Frederick Edwards, Jr. London : Longman, Green, & Co., 1869." It is the third

* Memoirs of Theophilus Parsons, Chief-Justice of the Supreme Judicial Court of Massachusetts, &c., pp. 161, 162.

publication of the author on the same subject. He recognizes the valuable services rendered by Count Rumford at the beginning of this century, the important improvements which he introduced, and the enthusiasm and gratitude which he called forth so widely over the kingdom in great houses and in humble homes. He regrets that indifference, carelessness, and wastefulness, have allowed his valuable, salutary and economical inventions and arrangements to fall into disuse and oblivion, and zealously pleads for their revival. The book is illustrated by plates and directions which would almost lead one who was resting for an hour from recording the life of Count Rumford to imagine that his fading memory was being revived by one who shared his interest in culinary economy. I also .see, almost daily, passing through our streets, an express wagon which bears the inscription, " Rumford Food Laboratory." It is in the service of an establishment in the main thoroughfare of this city, which announces in its advertisements that it will furnish cooked provisions daily, nutritive, hot, and cheap, to lonely lodgers, or to families without cook or kitchen.

During this transient residence of less than one year in England, busily occupied as he was in a variety of interesting and important occupations, scientific and economical, Count Rumford, by what was for the time a most munificent endowment, provided in both hemispheres for the incidental connection of his own name, perpetually, with the progressive pursuit of his own favorite study in the philosophy of light and heat. If we look to the lines of the sightless Milton for the most exquisite and touching utterances of poetry on the " co-eternal " element of light, we must assign to

Rumford an unrivalled honor for his prose treatment of the *created* element. There is almost a soaring into the realm of poetry in his references to it. He regarded it as one of the subjects most engaging for human thought, and in connection with the study of optics, and in applications to artificial inventions for the household, as well as for advancing astronomical science, as promising steady revelations to reward the search of the philosopher. There was something almost of an over-trustful confidence in his belief, assured to us by the terms of his endowments, that some discovery or improvement would be made in the subjects of Light and Heat as often as once in each period of two years for an indefinite future, and that, too, on either hemisphere of the earth, of a nature to justify the award of a valuable gold medal to a long series of prospective benefactors of mankind. Of course his object was to engage special study, and to turn investigation and experiment towards those subjects. The medal was to be an honorary recognition, not a pecuniary reward of success in those branches of science. Yet while Rumford did not forbid that a mere theorizer upon them should be a candidate for his prize, he had in view, as always, what would best "promote the good of mankind."

His correspondence on his endowments, and a sketch of the administration of them, may properly be introduced by the following letter: —

"To Sir Joseph Banks, Bart., K. B., P. R. S., &c., &c., &c.

"London, 12th July, 1796.

"Sir,—Desirous of contributing efficaciously to the advancement of a branch of science which has long employed my attention, and which appears to be of the highest importance to mankind, and wishing at the same time to leave a lasting testi-mony of my respect for the Royal Society of London, I take the liberty to request that the Royal Society would do me the honour to accept of one thousand pounds stock in the funds of this country, which I have actually purchased, and which I beg leave to transfer to the President, Council, and Fellows of the Royal Society, to the end that the interest of the same may be, by them and by their successors, received from time to time for ever, and the amount of the same applied and given once every second year as a premium to the author of the most important discovery, or useful improvement, which shall be made or published by printing, or in any way made known to the publick, in any part of Europe during the preceding two years, on Heat or on Light ; the preference always being given to such discoveries as shall, in the opinion of the President and Council, tend most to promote the good of mankind.

" With regard to the formalities to be observed by the President and Council in their decisions upon the comparative merits of those discoveries which, in the opinion of the President and Council, may entitle their authors to be considered as competitors for this biennial premium, the President and Council of the Royal Society will be pleased to adopt such regulations as they in their wisdom may judge to be proper and necessary.

" But in regard to the form in which this premium is conferred, I take the liberty to request that it may always be given in two medals, struck in the same die, the one of gold and the other of silver, and of such dimensions that both of them together may be just equal in intrinsic value to the amount of the interest of the aforesaid one thousand pounds stock during two years ; that is to say, that they may together be of the value of Sixty Pounds Sterling.

" The President and Council of the Royal Society will be pleased to order such device or inscription to be engraved on the die that they shall cause to be prepared for striking these medals, as they may judge proper.

" If, during any term of years, reckoning from the last adjudication, or from the last period for the adjudication of this

Premium by the President and Council of the Royal Society, no new discovery or improvement should be made in any part of Europe relative to either of the subjects in question (Heat or Light) which in the opinion of the President and Council shall be of sufficient importance to deserve this premium, in that case it is my desire that the premium may not be given, but that the value of it may be reserved, and, being laid out in the purchase of additional stock in the English funds, may be employed to augment the capital of this premium. And that the interest of the same, by which the capital may from time to time be so augmented, may regularly be given in money, with the two medals, and as an addition to the original premium at each such succeeding adjudication of it. And it is further my particular request, that those additions to the value of the premium arising from its occasional non-adjudication may be suffered to increase without limitation.

"With the highest respect for the Royal Society, of London, and the most earnest wishes for their success in their labours for the good of mankind,

"I am, &c.,

"RUMFORD."

Undoubtedly the founder of this premium was influenced, at least in his selection of the method of it, by the fact that the Royal Society already had in trust a fund of one hundred pounds bequeathed by Sir Godfrey Copley, in 1709, "to be laid out in experiments or otherwise." The Society voted, in 1736, "To strike a gold medal of the value of £5, to bear the arms of the Society, as an honorary favor for the best experiment produced within the year."

The Copley medal had been awarded to Benjamin Franklin in 1753, for "Curious Experiments and Observations on Electricity." Rumford himself received the same medal in 1792, for "Various Papers on the Properties and Communication of Heat."

In accepting the munificent endowment of the Count, the Society, through the Council, requested the President to return their sincere thanks to the donor; and at the same time, as some range of uncertainty was left in the interpretation of terms, and questions might arise as to restriction or comprehension of subjects to be recognized in the award, he was instructed to inquire how far improvements or discoveries in optics and chemistry might come under the Count's views.

This request drew from Rumford the following communication he having in the interval returned to Bavaria: —

"Munich, April 26, 1797.

"My Dear Sir, — In your last letter, you expressed a wish that I would write to inform you how far, in my opinion, discoveries in Optics, and improvements in Chemistry by the agency of fire, ought to be considered as being so connected with light or heat as to be taken into consideration in the adjudication of the premium I have founded for encouraging the investigation of those branches of philosophical enquiry, and improving the useful arts which depend on them. Though I am quite willing to leave this question to the decision of the Royal Society, and shall certainly be perfectly satisfied with whatever they may determine respecting it, either as a general regulation, or in any particular case which may occur; yet, as you have done me the honour to call on me for my opinion, I think it my duty to comply with your request by communicating to you my ideas on the subject.

"I think that the premium should be limited to new discoveries tending to improve the theories of Fire, of Heat, of Light, and of Colours, and to new inventions and contrivances by which the generation and preservation and management of heat and of light may be facilitated. In as far, therefore, as chemical discoveries or improvements in optics answer any of

MOSCERE QUÆ VIA ET CAUSSA
PRÆMIUM
OPTIME MERENTI
EX INSTITUTO
BENJ. A RUMFORD
S.R.I. COMITIS
ADJUDICATUM
A
REG SOC LOND

those conditions, they may, I think, fairly be considered as being within the limits assigned to the operation of the premium. The objects, however, which I had more particularly in view to encourage, are such practical improvements in the generation and management of heat and of light as to tend directly and powerfully to increase the enjoyments and comforts of life, especially in the lower and more numerous classes of society.

"I am, &c.,

"RUMFORD."

Before this letter had been penned, a committee of the Council of the Society, consisting of Sir Charles Blagden, Mr. Joseph Planta, and Dr. Combe, had been appointed, "to consider and report upon a design for a medal." Subsequently, Sir Joseph Banks, Dr. Gray (Secretary), and Count Rumford, who had been chosen into the Council, were added to the Committee, who, on the 4th of April, 1799, delivered in a Report with the following Resolution: —

"*Resolved*, That the device on the obverse be a tripod with a flame upon it. And that the inscription round the same be part of the 773d verse of the Vth Book of Lucretius (*De Rerum Natura*): —

'*Noscere quæ vis et causa.*'

"That the inscription on the reverse be as follows: —

'*Præmium optime merenti ex instituto Benj. a Rumford, S. R. L. Comitis: adjudicatam a Reg. Soc. Lond.*'

"That the diameter of the Medal do not exceed three inches. That Mr. Milton be employed in sinking the dies of the said Medal." *

The Report of the Committee was accepted by the Council, and the Resolution was approved, to be carried into immediate execution. But from some unexplained

* The device on the obverse was suggested by Mr. Smirke.

delay it was not until the 2d of April, 1802, — nearly six years after Rumford had made his gift, — that the Council received the impressions from the dies ordered from Mr. Milton. These "were approved, and orders were given for striking one gold and one silver medal from the same, according to the regulations prescribed by the Council." The cost of sinking the dies was £105, which sum was paid out of the funds of the Society. The engraving which I have procured of this first style of the Rumford Medal is copied from that in Weld's History.

It was with a most graceful courtesy, as well as in conformity with the strictest construction of the terms of the premium, that the first award of it was made to its founder. The minutes of the Council of the Society state, that on the 11th November, 1802, "the allotment of the gold and silver medals on Count Rumford's foundation was taken into consideration, and the letter respecting his donation was read, and it appearing that no discovery lately published, on the subjects to which they are limited, is of equal merit with those of the Count himself, it was unanimously resolved, by ballot, that the said medals be given to Benjamin, Count Rumford, for his various discoveries on the subject of heat and light."

The next who received the medals was John Leslie, in 1804, for " Experiments on Heat." The premium was awarded in 1806, 1810, 1814, 1816, 1818, 1824, 1834, 1838, 1840, 1842, and 1846, and thenceforward regularly in alternate years.

Up to 1846, several biennial periods having elapsed in which no award was made, the Rumford fund, through the accruing dividends, had increased from

£1,000 to £2,430. At that date, therefore, the receiver of the prize, in accordance with the terms of the trust, obtained a gold medal of the value of .£60, one of silver, of the value of £4, and a money balance of about .£80.*

It will not be inappropriate for me to copy here a list of the awards of this medal which I have gathered from the journals of the Royal Society.

Date of Award.

1802. Benjamin Rumford. For his various Discoveries respecting Light and Heat. (*Phil. Trans.* 1803.)

1804. John Leslie. Experiments on Heat.

1806. William Murdock. Publication of the Employment of Gas from Coal for the Purpose of Illumination. (*Phil. Trans.* 1809.)

1810. Étienne-Louis Malus. Discovery of Certain Properties of Reflected Light.

1814. William Charles Wells. Essay on Dew.

1816. Humphry Davy. Papers on Combustion and Flame. (*Phil. Trans.* 1817, 1818.)

1818. David Brewster. Discoveries relating to the Polarization of Light. (*Phil. Trans.* 1819.)

1824. Augustin-Jean Fresnel. Development of the Undulatory Theory, as applied to the Phenomena of Polarized Light: and for his various Important Discoveries in Physical Optics.

1834. Macedonio Melloni. Discoveries relative to Radiant Heat.

1838. James David Forbes. Experiments on the Polarization of Heat.

1840. Jean Baptiste Biot. Researches in and connected with the Circular Polarization of Light.

---

* For all the above particulars relating to the Rumford fund and medal, at the disposal of the Royal Society, I am indebted to the admirable history of that venerable institution, by Charles Richard Weld, Esq. London. 1848.

Count Rumford was probably well aware of the contention and ill-feeling that had arisen in the Royal Society, some years before, because those who administered the trust for the Copley Medal considered foreigners equally

BENIAMIN AB RVISBORG S ROM IMP COMES INSTITVIT
MDCCXCVI

entitled with Englishmen to be candidates for its award. Sir Gilbert had neither restricted nor expressly extended the terms of his bequest in that regard. Rumford, in emphatic language, made the whole of Europe, continent and islands, the field for such stimulation of rivalry, and such recognition of desert, as might attach to his premium of tenfold intrinsic value. It will be seen from the list that has been given, that ten of the twenty-four distinguished men who have received his award from the Royal Society have been foreigners, Mr. Wells being of America. The fact has a significance when taken in connection with the well-known effort which is required of Englishmen, whether men of science, or statesmen, or private persons, to extend their impartiality beyond their own country.

It is remarkable that the Count, after having liberally provided funds for medals in the award of two learned bodies, should a few years afterwards, when drawing his plan and publishing his proposals for his own Royal Institution, have introduced into them an express prohibition of all premiums and rewards.

A new die for the Rumford Medal of the Royal Society has since been adopted, from which Dr. H. Bence Jones has kindly sent me a copy, as shown in the engraving. The head of Rumford which is engraved upon it is copied from a portrait of him painted in Munich, which hung in the Count's house at Brompton, and which was presented to the Society by his daughter, in December, 1831.

The Count's correspondence with reference to his endowment in this country begins with the following letter: —

"London, July 12, 1796.

"To the Hon. John Adams, President of the American
Academy of Arts and Sciences.

"Sir, — Desirous of contributing efficaciously to the advancement of a branch of science which has long employed my
attention, and which appears to me to be of the highest importance to mankind, and wishing at the same time to leave a lasting testimony of my respect for the American Academy of Arts
and Sciences, I take the liberty to request that the Academy
would do me the honour to accept of Five Thousand Dollars,
three *per cent* stock in the funds of the United States of North
America, which Stock I have actually purchased, and which I
beg leave to transfer to the Fellows of the Academy, to the end
that the interest of the same may be by them, and by their
successors, received from time to time, forever, and the amount
of the same applied and given once every second year, as a
premium, to the author of the most important discovery or useful improvement, which shall be made and published by printing,
or in any way made known to the public, in any part of the
Continent of America, or in any of the American Islands, during the preceding two years, on Heat, or on Light; the preference always being given to such discoveries as shall, in the
opinion of the Academy, tend most to promote the good of
mankind.

"With regard to the formalities to be observed by the Academy in their decisions upon the comparative merits of those
discoveries which in the opinion of the Academy may entitle
their Authors to be considered as competitors for this biennial premium, the Academy will be pleased to adopt such
regulations as they in their wisdom may judge to be proper
and necessary.

"But in regard to the form in which this Premium is conferred, I take the liberty to request that it may always be given
in two medals, struck in the same die, the one of gold and the
other of silver, and of such dimensions that both of them
together may be just equal in intrinsic value to the amount of
interest of the aforesaid Five Thousand Dollars stock during

two years : that is to say, that they may together be of the value of Three Hundred Dollars.

"The Academy will be pleased to order such device or inscription to be engraved on the die they shall cause to be prepared for striking these medals, as they may judge proper.

"If during any term of two years, reckoning from the last adjudication, or from the last period for the adjudication of this Premium by the Academy, no new discovery or improvement should be made in any part of America, relative to either of the subjects in question (Heat or Light), which, in the opinion of the Academy shall be of sufficient importance to deserve this Premium, in that case, it is my desire that the Premium may not be given, but that the value of it may be reserved, and by laying out in the purchase of additional stock in the American funds, may be applied to augment the capital of this Premium ; and that the interest of the sums by which the capital may, from time to time, be so augmented, may regularly be given in money with the two medals, and as an addition to the original Premium at each succeeding adjudication of it. And it is further my particular request, that those additions to the value of the Premium arising from its occasional non-adjudication may be suffered to increase without limitation.

"With the highest respect for the American Academy of Arts and Sciences, and the most earnest wishes for their success in their labours for the good of mankind,

"I have the honour to be, with much Esteem and Regard, Sir, Your most Obedient, Humble Servant,

"RUMFORD."

His intended donation was first announced by this letter from Count Rumford read at a meeting of the Academy, November 9, 1796, accompanied by the gift of a volume of his Essays, and of what is described in the records as his " bust," though it was a small bass-relief profile. The delay in the receipt of the proper papers, and in the negotiation connected with the transfer of the funds, caused chiefly by the capture of a vessel on board of which were the necessary legal documents, of course deferred the proper and decisive action of the Academy in recognizing, as they appreciated, Count Rumford's noble endowment. Compared with the gifts which previously to that time had been made by individuals to Harvard College, and by Dr. Franklin to provide medals for scholars in our public schools, and a loan fund for the encouragement of worthy mechanics, — which latter provision remains still accumulating to be appropriated, as it never yet has been, according to the wishes of the donor, — Count Rumford's donation had a character of munificence. The members of the Academy regarded it as the most helpful and encouraging recognition which their Institution had received during the sixteen years of its existence. The correspondence of our few learned and scientific men, who were then pursuing their high aims under great disadvantages, recognizes with enthusiasm and congratulation this auspicious incident, and finds in it an impulse and a motive for activity and zeal in its work.

The Academy had been instituted and incorporated in the year 1780, midway in the war of our Revolution, amid all the distractions and exactions of that trying period. While the whole community was burdened by taxation and the exorbitant prices of the articles of prime necessity, and while it might seem that the thoughts and time of all intelligent men would have been engrossed by giving to public affairs all the interest they could spare from their private concerns, a few men of cultivated and generous minds devised the plan of this Institution. It is a very singular fact, that all the most distinguished of the now existing and flourishing learned bodies of Christendom originated and were organized under similar circumstances, in periods of distraction and strife. The Royal Society of London was an incorporation, in 1661, of a society of gentlemen interested in scientific objects, who had been meeting for many previous years to encourage and help one another in their pursuits. It was amid the heated and alienating strifes of political and religious animosity inflaming all classes of the people, that those who loved science and high culture, and were within easy reach of intercourse, gathered in a little coterie in London. They realized that, if they would mutually tolerate and enjoy each other's presence and sympathy in their professed objects, they must carefully exclude all recognition of the distractions outside of their fellowship. As one of the foremost of them, Dr. Wallis, writing of the year 1645, quaintly says of their coming together, "when (to avoid diversion to other discourses, and for some other reasons) we barred all discourses of divinity, state affairs, and of news, other than what concerned our business of Philosophy." The French National Institute, established in 1796, offered a similar refuge from the embitterments of revolutionary times for those who could subordinate their party or polemical divisions to a zeal for researches and labors which would accrue to the welfare of a common humanity.

Count Rumford had been elected a Foreign Honorary Member of the Academy on May 29, 1789.

The first recognition which the Academy made to Count Rumford of his purposed benefaction was through the following letter, which I copy from the original on the files.

"Sir,—At a meeting of the American Academy of Arts and Sciences, the 9th instant, were communicated by the President your very acceptable favors of the 12th July. In reply to which, permit me the honor to request your acceptance of the thanks of the Academy for your very polite and obliging present of the first volume of your ingenious and useful Essays, and for the pleasing and elegant profile of their Author. I am also charged by the Academy to give you every possible assurance, not only of the lively emotions of gratitude inspired by your generous and truly noble proposal of transferring to the Academy, for the important purposes expressed in your letter, five thousand dollars of the three *per cent* stock of the United States, but likewise of their conscious obligation and cheerful readiness sacredly to apply the interest of the same as directed by the munificent donor. Excuse my adding, that the Academy is sensibly affected, not only by the liberality of this appropriation, but by the delicate manner in which it is made.

"Supposing it possible, though not probable, that you might be unacquainted with the method of transferring American stocks, the President suggested the expediency of enclosing an abstract of the mode of making transfers at our offices. Accordingly, I waited on Mr. Appleton, the Loan Officer in this State, and from his letter have transcribed the enclosed extract.

"Agreeably to Mr. Appleton's ideas I have also taken the liberty of naming two gentlemen in the vicinity of Boston who will be happy to execute your orders, if empowered to transfer the stock aforesaid to the 'American Academy of Arts and Sciences,' either jointly or severally, as you may think proper, viz., the Rev. Joseph Willard, D. D., of Cambridge, and the Hon. Loammi Baldwin, Esq., of Woburn, both in the county of Middlesex. These gentlemen, or either of them, would, I doubt not, faithfully and cheerfully discharge the trust, whether the stock were issued from the office in Boston or from any other office in the United States. But if some other gentleman will be more agreeable to you, sir, he will be so to the Academy. I have, however, to ask your pardon of this freedom, as my only object is to facilitate the business.

" I ought not to trespass further on your patience. But I knew not how to close without acknowledging the obligations imposed on me, and I think on the world, by your late publications. Some of your former ingenious and philosophical communications to the Royal Society I read with great delight. But your Essays have filled me with transport. Such philanthropy, so well directed zeal, and such unwearied diligence in promoting the common good of mankind, more especially of the indigent and helpless, bespeak a godlike mind, and command the warmest gratitude and most sincere respect of every benevolent mind. It is a happiness, a great happiness, even to th'.k that there is on earth a man who can and will interest himself so efficaciously, and in so great a variety of ways, for the good of the human species. Your unprecedented success also inspires new and pleasing hopes concerning the most miserable of our race, and calls into doubt the common doctrine of habits. When such numbers, so long accustomed to idleness and vice, are reclaimed to industry and order, we are led to expect that the Ethiopian will erelong change his skin, and the leopard his spots. But I forbear. Accept the well-meant tribute of my thanks, and permit me to join the poor of Munich and many other cities, and with all the friends of humanity, in fervent supplication to the Author of all good for the preservation of your life, and for the confirmation of your health, and for increased and extensive success to your multiplied labors and Institutions for the good of mankind.

" With these wishes, and with sentiments of unfeigned respect, I am, sir,

  " Your much obliged, and most humble servant,

    " ELIPHALET PEARSON, *Corresponding Secretary.*

"CAMBRIDGE, 14th November, 1796.

    COUNT RUMFORD."

Count Rumford made the following reply to Professor Pearson, which also I copy from the original on file : —

"Munich, 14th February, 1797.

"Sir,—I have received your very obliging letter of the 14th November, 1796. The honor which the worthy President and the Fellows of the American Academy of Arts and Sciences have conferred on me by accepting the proposals I took the liberty of making to them in my letter to the President, of the 12th July, 1796, has given me the highest satisfaction; and I beg, Sir, that you would express to them my warmest thanks, and assure them that it will be the study of my life to deserve this flattering proof of their esteem and regard.

"I am much obliged to you, Sir, for the pains you have taken to make me so completely acquainted with everything I could wish to know respecting the business of transferring American Stock. Enclosed I send you a power authorizing the two Gentlemen you proposed — and two Gentlemen more agreeable to me could not have been found — to transfer 'to the Fellows of the American Academy of Arts and Sciences,' Five Thousand Dollars, assured debt, entered to my credit in the Books of the Treasury of the United States, for which a certificate numbered 2633 was issued in my name on the Fourth day of March, 1796. That this stock actually stands in my name in the Books of the Treasury of the United States, I am assured by a notarial Declaration of Peter Lohra, Notary Public for the Commonwealth of Pennsylvania, residing in the City of Philadelphia, dated the 27th October, 1796, a copy of which is inclosed. But, very unfortunately, the vessel in which the original certificate (with two others of equal amount) was sent to Europe was lost on her passage. How long this accident will delay the completion of the business in question I know not, but nothing in my power shall be left undone to finish it as soon as possible. In the mean time I have taken the most effectual measures I could devise to secure to the Academy the property they have done me the honor to accept, and have given directions that the Interest of the Five Thousand Dollars three *per cent* Stock in question should be paid regularly to the Treasurer of the Academy from the first of January, 1797, till the transfer of the Capital can be made. In short, I consider this Property as being no longer mine, and I have exerted myself to the utmost of my abilities in the enclosed declaration — which I hope may pass for a Deed of gift, however it may be defective in point of form — to put it legally out of my power. In all events, however, even should there be a flaw in this Instrument, and should I die before the transfer of the Stock could be made, as in my last Will and Testament which is lodged in the hands of Sir Joseph Banks, Baronet, of Soho Square, London, President of the Royal Society, I have bequeathed Five Thousand Dollars three *per cent* American Stock to the Academy for the purposes mentioned in my letter to the President of the Academy, of the 12th July last, no accident that can possibly happen can prevent the accomplishment of my wishes with respect to this business.

"Inclosed is a letter from me to the Directors of the Bank of the United States, which I beg you would close with a seal and forward, when you shall have perused it and taken a copy of it for the information of the Academy, who will be pleased to take such measures in regard to the business in question as they may think proper. It will give me great pleasure to learn that Dr. Willard, and my friend, Colonel Baldwin, have found means to complete this business by making the transfer of the Stock, but if anything more should be necessary to be done by me to enable them to finish the transaction, you or they will be pleased to acquaint me with what I can do farther to expedite and facilitate the business.

" Begging you would assure the American Academy of Arts and Sciences of my best respects, and of my unfeigned gratitude for the distinguished honor they have conferred on me, I am, Sir, with great regard and esteem,

"Your most obedient humble Servant,

"RUMFORD.

" Mr. Pearson, Secretary, &c."

The paper, duly signed and witnessed, by which the transfer of stocks was made to the Academy, is preserved in duplicate in our archives. The two bearing the seal

17

of Count Rumford, partially defaced in each, furnish together the means by which the engraver has prepared the copy attached to the autograph signature of our benefactor.

The portion of the instrument presented on the plate upon the opposite page is not a very fair specimen of the handwriting of the author, being coarser and more irregular. The signatures of his friend, the Countess of Nogarola, and of his daughter, witnessing the instrument, are its proper accompaniments.

The inner legend of the seal is *Pro Fide, Rege, et Lege.*
The lower one is *Dulce est meminisse laborum.*

At a meeting of the Academy, Jan. 31, 1798, it was

"*Voted,* That the thanks of the Academy be presented to Count Rumford for his very generous donation for the use of this Institution, and that a committee be now appointed to draught a vote for that purpose, to be reported to the Council, or, according to circumstances, to the Academy at their meeting, as soon as it shall appear that a legal transfer of the property shall have been made, and that it be immediately after transmitted to that liberal benefactor of mankind.

"*Voted,* That the committee for the above purpose be John Davis, Esq., Mr. Professor Pearson, and Dr. Warren.

"*Voted,* That a committee be appointed to take up the subject of Count Rumford's donation, and report at the next meeting of the Academy their opinion of the best method of carrying his generous design into execution, as expressed in his letter to the President of the Academy.

"That the Committee for the above purpose be, President Willard, Hon. Judge Paine, Mr. Professor Pearson, Mr. Gannett, and the Hon. Judge Winthrop.

At a meeting of the Academy, May 29, 1798, the Report of the first Committee, which was as follows, was accepted : —

" Whereas Benjamin, Count of Rumford, of Munich, in
Bavaria, has presented to this Institution the sum of Five
Thousand Dollars in three *per cent* stock of the United States,
the interest of which, by the terms of the donation as expressed
in his letter of July 12, 1796, to the President of the Academy,
is to be 'applied and given . . . . Heat or Light,' which donation has been accepted by the Academy, and by proper certificates, which accident only has delayed, has now become the
property of the Academy.

" *Voted*, That the thanks of the Academy be presented to
Count Rumford for this his very generous donation, and that
they experience the highest satisfaction in receiving this additional and very liberal aid for the encouragement and extension of those branches of science which he has so successfully
cultivated. That they entertain a high sense of the sentiments
and views, so becoming to a Philosopher, which have prompted
him to this distinguished act of liberality; and in the execution
of the grateful office which they have undertaken of awarding
and distributing the premiums which Count Rumford has thus
appropriated they will sacredly comply with the conditions of
the donation, indulging the hope that he will meet his reward
in learning that many in his native country are thereby excited
to emulate his labors and to promote the accomplishment of
his beneficent wishes for the advancement of science and the
augmentation of human happiness.

" *Voted*, That the Corresponding Secretary be requested to
transmit a copy of the preceding vote to Count Rumford by the
earliest opportunity."

At a meeting on May 28, 1799, probably by suggestion of the second committee above appointed, it was

" *Voted*, That the Secretary of the Academy cause the
terms of Count Rumford's donation to be published in the
several capitals of the different States, and in some of the American Islands, and information that the Academy are ready to
adjudge the premium, provided for by Count Rumford, to the
person or persons who shall appear to be entitled to the same."

Among the same files from which the above documents are copied, are papers relating to several applications made by themselves, or by friends in behalf of those who either sought aid from the fund in pursuing their experiments, or advanced a claim for discoveries or improvements of a sort to entitle them to the award of the medal. And here, departing from the order of time as regards events in the life of Count Rumford, it may be allowable, as it is convenient, to trace the history of the administration of the trust for the premium or medal by the Academy. While the Royal Society had the whole Continent and all the Islands of Europe as a field for selecting the recipients of its biennial award of the Rumford medals from among those numerous savans who by their researches and discoveries should reach results entitling them to the honor, the Academy, with larger space, indeed, for its oversight, was at a manifest disadvantage as regarded the likelihood of finding once in each period of two years a subject of the same award. At first thought it may seem to one who has not thoroughly and with broad and full information considered the facts of the case, that the Academy has been too exacting in the conditions which it has set and applied in administering its trust, and that it has had in view a requisition of scientific discoveries in reference to heat and light of such signal and conspicuous character as can but very rarely reveal themselves, even in the steadily progressive course of experimental philosophy. And then, having before us in contrast the eminently practical and economical, we may even say thrifty and homely, nature and utility of Count Rumford's own inventions, methods, and appliances, another suggestion might naturally present itself. We have had to bring him before us as actually engaged with his own hands in constructing chimney-flues, kitchens, and cooking-utensils, and have yet to speak and read of him as introducing improvements in common household lamps. If now any one should have visited and examined the kitchens and the sitting-rooms of New England during the last fifty years, or read the advertisements in the newspapers and the shop-cards so freely distributed, announcing wonderful improvements in stoves, furnaces, and lamps, or gas-burners, and have added to these observations a walk through the departments of the Patent Office at Washington assigned to such apparatus, he would be most likely to infer that the Academy could have been at no loss to find a proper recipient of the Rumford Medal once in each two years. But it has proved to be otherwise. The Academy promised sacredly to discharge its trust. The homeliness or economical character of an invention or a discovery would never have offended its dignity if a just claim had been based upon it. The Academy, as we have seen, took measures to circulate through the public prints the knowledge that it had an honorable award at its disposal for all who were entitled to receive it. The correspondence and applications on its files, and the numerous reports of its investigating committees, prove that there has been no lack of notoriety as to the facts and objects of its trusteeship, nor of a disposition to do full justice to all who sought a hearing from it. But until the year 1839 the Academy, in the exercise of its best discretion and under the guidance of its common conscience, had not once made the award of the Rumford Medal.

Meanwhile the fund had accumulated by its own

interest so as to present in itself a matter of embarrassment. A committee of the Academy chosen for the purpose, consisting of the eminent Dr. Nathaniel Bowditch, President Josiah Quincy of Harvard College, and the Hon. Francis C. Gray, made a Report at the end of December, 1829, which resulted in legislative and judicial measures for relieving this embarassment.

The Academy had given its pledge, while Count Rumford still lived, that it would "sacredly comply with the conditions of the donation." These conditions were mainly two, — one of them, however, being limited by the other. The Academy was to have in view the award of its medal once in two years, but it was to be given only to the author of the most important discovery or useful improvement made in the two preceding years on heat or on light, on the American Continent or any of its Islands. To refuse to award the medal to one who had a right to it, or to bestow it on a claimant who had no sufficient merit, or upon a favored experimenter, for the sake of not allowing the biennial award to fail, would have equally thwarted the intent of the donor. A discovery or an improvement of a sort to satisfy the terms which Count Rumford could define only relatively, because not admitting of an arbitrary or of an absolute measurement, was the requisite fact to engage the attention of the Academy. As such discovery or improvement was to have been made a matter of public notoriety by printing "or otherwise," and as the Academy had taken measures for giving the widest circulation to the terms of the trust which they held, it was not likely that ignorance on the side of either party concerned would deprive any one who might justly be entitled to the premium of the honor which it would confer. The committee above named say in their Report, that the premium had not up to that date been awarded, "none of the discoveries or improvements for which it has been claimed being deemed by the Academy of sufficient importance to deserve it." The Report continues : —

" By constant accumulation the fund has now increased to the sum of nearly $20,000. The history of science in other countries unites with our own experience to convince us that Count Rumford's plan, contemplating the assignment of a biennial premium for important discoveries or useful improvements on light and heat first made public within two years preceding, and interrupted only by ' occasional non-adjudications,' is absolutely impracticable. Such discoveries and improvements are not often made, and many of those which are made require more than two years to test their merit. It is perfectly manifest that the non-adjudication must be the regular and usual course, and that the assignments of the premium must be occasional, and even rare. The very increase of the fund constantly increases the difficulty of bestowing the premium ; for the Academy are expressly directed to award it only to improvements or discoveries of sufficient importance in their opinion to deserve it, and an invention may merit a premium of $300, which is altogether unworthy of one of $2,000. A strict compliance with the incidental request that the fund should increase indefinitely may therefore prevent the assignment of any premium at all, and thus entirely defeat the great object of the foundation, and render it totally useless. To permit such a result is not a faithful fulfilment of the intentions of the donor.

" If it be found, by long experience, that a rigid adherence to particular limitations, not essential to the main object of the Institution, tends to defeat that object, it must be presumed that the founder would wish those limitations modified, and it is the bounden duty of the Academy, and of all who have an interest in his property, to endeavor to have them so modified as to promote the attainment of the end which he proposed."

The committee add, as another important consideration, that in providing that the additional income of the fund accruing from an occasional non-adjudication of the premium should be given to its next recipient, Rumford could hardly have foreseen that the accessory would ever so far exceed the principal. The income of the fund for two years being at the time two thousand dollars, and steadily increasing, it would be extravagant to award it as a premium. "It must lose the character of a prize, and be sought with mercenary views, rather than as an honorable distinction."

The Report closed with "a plan for facilitating the awarding of the premium and applying the surplus income," as the best they could "devise to execute in practice the intent and promote the general object of the donor." The scheme suggested was substantially that which was adopted by the Supreme Judicial Court of the Commonwealth of Massachusetts in its decree in Chancery.

The Academy first applied to this court for legal relief, but the bill was dismissed, as the equitable jurisdiction of the court over trusts was limited to "cases of trust arising under deeds, wills, or in the settlement of estates." The Academy then had recourse to the Legislature of the State, which passed the following special Act, approved by the Governor, March 16, 1831: —

"An Act authorizing the Supreme Judicial Court to hear and determine in equity all matters relating to the donation of Benjamin Count Rumford to the American Academy of Arts and Sciences.

" Be it enacted by the Senate and House of Representatives, in General Court assembled, and by the authority of the same, That the justices of the Supreme Judicial Court be, and they hereby are, authorized and empowered to hear and determine in equity any and all matters relating to the donation of Benjamin Count Rumford to the American Academy of Arts and Sciences, and to make all necessary or proper orders and decrees touching the same."

Count Rumford by his last will, made in Paris, had bequeathed the residue of his estate to Harvard College, for the purpose of founding a Professorship to teach by lectures and experiments the utility of the physical and mathematical sciences for the improvement of the useful arts and the industry and well-being of society. The College, therefore, became a party to the hearing of this case in equity, and as defendants withstood the prayer of the Academy for a legal liberty to depart from the conditions attached to Count Rumford's donation. The College claimed that the objects which he had in view in his fund for a premium intrusted to the Academy were substantially included in and covered by the objects assigned for the Rumford Professorship, and insisted, " that if the said fund and the accumulation thereof, or any part thereof, cannot be appropriated and applied in the hands of the said plaintiffs to the execution of the general intent of said donor in making his said donation to the said plaintiffs, the same, or so much thereof as cannot be so applied, ought to be decreed to be paid over to these defendants, as residuary legatees of said Count Rumford, for the use of the said Rumford Professorship."

The case was fully heard with arguments of counsel, and an application by the court of those principles of equity which allow a modification of the conditions

attached to a trust fund when circumstances prevent
the strict fulfilment of the terms set by the donor, and
which admit of a re-direction of the proceeds of the
fund in a way to approximate towards the ends he had
in view. The matter was then referred to a Master
in Chancery " to report a scheme for carrying into effect
the general charitable intent and purpose of the donor
conformably to the prayer of the plaintiffs' bill." His
scheme having been submitted, it was,

" By the court ordered, adjudged, and decreed, for the
reasons set forth in the bill, that the plaintiffs be, and they are
by the authority of this court, empowered to make from the
income of said fund, as it now exists, at any annual meeting of
the Academy, instead of biennially, as directed by said Benjamin Count Rumford, award of a gold and silver medal, being
together of the intrinsic value of three hundred dollars, as a
premium to the author of any important discovery or useful
improvement on heat or on light which shall have been made
and published by printing, or in any way made known to the
public, in any part of the Continent of America, or any of the
American Islands, preference being always given to such discoveries as shall in the opinion of the Academy, tend most to
promote the good of mankind ; and to add to such medals as a
further reward and premium for such discovery or improvement,
if the plaintiffs see fit so to do, a sum of money not exceeding
three hundred dollars.

" And it is further ordered, adjudged, and decreed, that the
plaintiffs *may* appropriate from time to time, as the same can
advantageously be done, the residue of the income of said fund
hereafter to be received, and not so as aforesaid awarded in
premiums, to the purchase of such books and papers and philosophical apparatus (to be the property of said Academy), and in
making such publications or procuring such lectures, experiments, or investigations, as shall in their opinion best facilitate
and encourage the making of discoveries and improvements
which may merit the premiums so as aforesaid to be by them

awarded. And that the books, papers, and apparatus so purchased shall be used, and such lectures, experiments, and investigations be delivered and made, either in the said Academy or elsewhere, as the plaintiffs shall think best adapted to promote such discoveries and improvements as aforesaid, and either by the Rumford Professor of Harvard University or by any other person or persons, as to the plaintiffs shall from time to time seem best."

The court also authorized the investment of the fund, or any part of it, in other first-class securities than government bonds.[*]

It is easy to express the obvious suggestion, that the enlargement and direction thus allowed by judicial decision to the use of the trust fund committed by Count Rumford to the Academy, for one specified and well-defined object, exceed any possible construction that can be put upon the liberal terms of his deed of gift. But it is just as easy to meet the suggestion by affirming that the judicial decree has in view, and aims, it may even be said, most conscientiously to fulfil, the intent of the donor. Under its decision the Academy may make the munificence of Count Rumford most serviceable at the fountain-head and sources of that scientific development which alone can secure biennially, or at longer or shorter intervals, a signal result marking a point in the flow of the stream. Books and lectures presenting the last discoveries, or methods for discovery, in the Count's favorite subjects of experiment, may be regarded as even something better than an alternative in the improvement of his fund, to the use of it for a medal or premium under the pressure of a supposed obligation to bestow it with chief reference to the lapse of two years.

[*] Gray's Report. Vol. XII. pp. 581 - 602.

In view of all the circumstances and of the difficulties which the case presented, one may reasonably affirm that when the honored and venerated chief-justice gave validity to the decree of the court, he might have felt the full assurance that Count Rumford himself would have dictated its terms.

In the year 1839 the Academy gave, from the interest of the Rumford Fund, the sum of six hundred dollars to Dr. Hare, of Philadelphia, in consideration of his invention of the compound blow-pipe and his improvements in galvauic apparatus.

The Rumford Medal was awarded by the Academy, in 1862, to John B. Ericsson for his caloric engine.[*] In 1865 the Medal was awarded to Daniel Treadwell, former Rumford Professor in Harvard College, for improvements in the management of heat.[†] On February 26, 1867, the Medal was presented to Alvan Clark for improvement in the lens of the refracting telescope.

On January 11, 1870, the Medal was presented to George H. Corliss for improvements in the steam-engine.

The Rumford Fund, in 1870, exceeded thirty-seven thousand dollars.

A committee of the Academy, called the Rumford Committee, is chosen annually, who report upon the fund and recommend appropriations from it for purposes conformed to the decree of the court.

[*] See *Proceedings of the Academy,* Vol. VI. p. 16.
[†] *Ibid.,* Vol. VI. pp. 495, 497, 516.

CHAPTER VI.

IN this chapter, which will cover two more years of
Count Rumford's residence in Germany, I shall
draw largely from the autobiographic sketch of his
daughter, because it is full of interesting information
concerning his domestic and private life, of which we
know but little from any other sources. We must

reconcile as we may the ardent expressions of the father's affection for his daughter in his letters with her own disclosures of the occasional severity of his discipline.

It was in very hot weather, probably in the last of July or early in August, 1796, that they left England, compelled to make a circuitous course to enter Germany.

The daughter describes the leave-taking from friends on the eve of quitting London. The carriage which the Count had brought with him from Munich being too small for the party, he was obliged to procure a second one. This, having belonged to a duke, still bore his arms, and there was no time to allow for re-painting. The party arrived at Hamburg on the third day, after a boisterous passage, being obliged to take that route on account of the war.

The armorial bearings on one of their carriages proved to be a great annoyance to them, as visiting upon them the tax of greatness. The Count wished but five post-horses to be attached to the carriage. The post-master insisted upon his starting with eight; and the same number used in starting would be required at every change and relay along the route. The parties were equally obstinate; the official removed the five horses, and the Count and his valet went to seek others, or redress. Pending the issue, the daughter was left in one of the carriages, and her maid in the other, in one of the most crowded streets of Hamburg. The Continent being then ablaze with war, this bustling city was neutral. The young lady and her maid, wearied, sea-worn, and craving rest and refreshment, which could not easily be found where all houses of entertainment were thronged, would really have suffered had it not been for an adventure, which the daughter relates so naively — with an intimation that it might have resulted in furnishing her with a step-mother — that it must be given in her own words.

" A lady, before whose door stood one of our carriages, took pity on us, coming kindly to invite us in, and, my father being returned at the time, we gladly accepted. We were shown into cool, delightfully clean rooms, a little darkened (it being in the month of August the heat was intense), and where we found sofas, easy-chairs, and plenty of places to lounge in. So great was the change from what we had before experienced, it could be compared to nothing but heaven upon earth. After being somewhat rested and recovered, then came refreshments of everything proper, good, and enough of it. Aichner and my maid had likewise all things of a nature to comfort them, and when nothing else remained to be done we were requested to take repose; but as our horses, to the number of five, contrary to the post-master's wishes, were to be at the door at a certain time we could not comply. My father introduced himself to the lady, and the lady herself to him. She, it seemed, was the widow of a German officer, whom, by reputation, my father knew well, and this leading to conversation, they got on charmingly. Both were well looking, of proper ages, — she the younger, he not old. Any one in the habit of match-making, so called, would have declared them made for each other. Understanding I was my father's daughter, she made much of me; and I, far from having forgotten my poor mother, seeing her kindly affected to me, and drawing myself nearer and nearer to her, seemed to be in her arms before we were either of us aware of it, — both of us shedding tears plentifully. It came out that she, about a year before, had lost an only daughter, whom she thought about my age. She was the perfect mother. My father began to make a motion to go; was, perhaps, not satisfied; would have preferred seeing the lady looking out for a second husband. When we took leave my father told her that should he find himself again in Hamburg, and I to have learned German, I should call and thank her for her kindness in her own language. We were both there again, but had forgotten both the lady's name and address. Truly unfortunate!

" Three weeks' constant travel, circuitous routes to avoid. troops, bad roads, still worse accommodations, passing nights in the carriages for the want of an inn, scantiness of provisions, joined with great fatigue, rendered our journey by no means agreeable. The Fair at Leipsic, as we came along and passed a day there, not being able to proceed for the want of horses on account of it, was amusing. I bought many little objects of curiosity, which I kept a long time in remembrance of it.

" The beautiful, luxuriant fields of rye and wheat in the two Saxonies, then in perfection, a short time before the reaping, to any one accustomed only to enclosed countries, were striking, and gave an idea of great richness. With hardly sufficient room for the wheels of the carriage, not a fence, seldom a tree, still less meeting man or beast, gave a look to the country of real enchantment, resembling more the never-ending waves of the sea than cultivated land. It is true, after a while you come to a mean, dirty-looking village, of a nature to destroy fine illusions, but where, however, are to be seen pretty blue-eyed, light-haired, white-faced women and children. In the Saxonies the German language is said to be the most purely spoken. In the mouth of a Saxon lady it is said to be really soft, — a character in the general way it does not sustain.

" Our arrival at Munich was a joyful event, — an end to the tediousness of the journey, besides being cheered by the handsome, pleasant appearance of the city. My father's habitation merits and must have a particular description, as will from thence be dated, for some time to come, most that relates either to him or myself; and because the building was really magnificent and equally so in its furniture, it may not be amiss to mention by what good fortune he became the occupant, for own it he did not.

" It was an elegant palace, furnished sumptuously some years before for a person of distinction, who dying, it was shut up. Afterwards my father persuaded the then reigning Elector, Charles Theodore, to have it opened and let the Russian Ambassador take the first and my father the second floor. Through the *porte-cochère* passed all vehicles, foot-passengers, &c., by the width, possibly, of two rooms, — those making part of the first floor, — into an open court enclosed by the building. The principal staircase — there being others — commenced between the entrance and the court, wide enough for four abreast, with oak or mahogany stairs waxed and rubbed, looking like plate-glass. As an inhabitant of this place, where my father spent many of the most useful years of his life, I propose to mention it without going into more particulars."

The course of Miss Sally's narrative must here be interrupted, first to introduce another letter from her to her friend, Mrs. Baldwin, and then to recognize her father's valuable service in the responsible work for which the Elector had summoned him back to Munich.

"Munich, October 16, 1796.

"MY DEAR MRS. BALDWIN, — Though this is the third letter that I have written you since I left America, and I have never received a line from you, yet I cannot refuse myself the pleasure of writing you a few lines to tell you I am well and happy, and that I often think of you. I arrived here with my father after a pleasant journey of three weeks and two days from London. My reception here was highly flattering, and I have every reason to be pleased and happy with my new situation. This country is much more like America than England, and the climate is exactly like that I have ever been used to in America, so that I sometimes almost fancy myself there. The town of Munich is large, clean, and well built, and it affords every public amusement that is to be found in any city of Europe. Be so good as to give my respects to your husband, and love to the children. I am, with real esteem and friendship,

"Affectionately yours,
"SARAH RUMFORD."

Had the daughter written the pages which have been copied at the date of the incidents related in them, she would doubtless have had much more to tell us about the distractions and anxieties of the time and place on her arrival in Munich.   Her father was for a few weeks engrossed and heavily burdened by the responsibilities laid upon him in the turmoil which then convulsed the continent of Europe.   Bavaria sought to maintain a rigid neutrality between the contending powers of the great revolutionary upheaval, and was therefore, of course, in imminent risk of being scourged by either or both of them.   The immunity with which, for a time, she escaped was secured to her by the wisdom and skill of Count Rumford, whose services in the emergency were most gratefully appreciated.   His military talent was again called into exercise to meet a threatening emergency.   General Moreau, after having crossed the Rhine, and by a series of successes beaten the various corps which had disputed his passage and his onward march, made an advance towards Bavaria.   Count Rumford arrived at Munich eight days before the Elector was compelled to quit his residence and to take refuge in Saxony.   Rumford remained in the city with full delegated authority, and with instructions from the Elector to watch the course of events, and to act according to the exigency of circumstances.   These were not slow in requiring his intervention.   After the battle of Friedburg the Austrians, repulsed by the French, withdrew to Munich.   The gates of the city were shut against them.   They then made a circuit, passed the Iser by the bridge, and established themselves on the other side of the river on a height which commanded the bridge and the city.   There they planted batteries, and anxiously awaited the coming up of the French forces. In this situation some incautious proceedings which took place in Munich were interpreted by the Austrian general as an insult aimed at himself, and he demanded the reason of the Council of the Regency, at the head of which was Rumford. He also gave the menace of an immediate attack upon the city if a single Frenchman should be allowed to enter it.

At this critical moment Rumford availed himself of the ultimate orders of the Elector to take the chief command of the Bavarian forces. His firmness and presence of mind impressed both parties. Neither the French nor the Austrians entered Munich, and that city, escaping the direful calamities which had been so imminent, was soon after delivered from the presence of the hostile forces. But before, and while the danger lasted, Munich was full of Bavarian troops, and the Count did not forget his philosophical and economical experiments, for which he had new and emergent occasions and opportunities. The care of sheltering and feeding this large body of Electoral forces came upon him, and he turned the task to the account of science. He tells us in his Essays how he plied his ingenuity in the processes of cooking, and in his improvements in boilers and in the saving of fuel, to make the soldiers more comfortable than ever they had been before, and at much less expense.

On the return of the Elector he made the warmest recognition of the value of Rumford's services, which exceeded his ability to reward them. The Count was then placed at the head of the Department of General Police in Bavaria. The services which he rendered in this position, though less brilliant than his military reforms, were neither less valuable nor less signal. While we resume again the light relations given to us by the American girl about her court life, and her frequent misunderstandings with her father, we must think of him as weighed down by many heavy cares which might at times make him irritable and unsympathetic with a country maiden's fancies. The Count also at this period encountered much opposition in the exercise of his office, and began to feel with some severity the force of the jealousy turned against him as a foreigner invested with so many intermeddling functions. The excursions which were to his daughter but the pleasurable incidents and interchanges of an unemployed life were sought for by him as means and intervals of relief from over-work, which, while engaging his zeal and activity, made serious breaches upon his health, and more than once threatened him with fatal disease.

We have a pleasing reference to the intimacy which existed between Count Rumford and that complacent Scotch cosmopolite, Sir John Sinclair, in the published correspondence of the latter. He introduces a letter which he received from Rumford, written just after the temporary subsidence of this war alarm, with the following comment : —

"From similarity of pursuits I had contracted [in London] a cordial friendship with Count Rumford, a well-known native of America. He was a man of an ardent mind, which enabled him to conquer many difficulties ; and by his inquiries regarding the proper application of heat he introduced many useful discoveries which will find their way to many countries, even where the name of the inventor may remain unknown.

"Among a number of communications the following is one of the most important, as it exhibits the distinguished philosopher placed at the head of an army in a foreign country, yet anxious to withdraw from active life, and to resume the more pleasing employment of scientific investigation : —

"Munich, 18th October, 1796.

"I thank you, my dear Sir John, for your friendly letter, which I have just received. I am glad your new kitchen [one of which the Count had had the supervision] answers your expectations, and hope it will be imitated. I ought to have begun my letter by acquainting you that immediately on my arrival here from England I delivered to the Elector the diploma you sent him [of membership of an agricultural society], and that I had it in charge from his most Serene Highness to express to you his thanks for your attentions to him. He appeared to me to be much pleased at being chosen a member of your Board, and will, I am confident, have great satisfaction in contributing as much as possible to the success of your laudable undertakings. I have projected several new experiments, from the results of which I hope to get some new light with respect to vegetation and nutrition; but I am at present so much employed with business of a very different kind (the command of the Bavarian army), that I have no leisure to give to my favourite pursuits. But as the alarms which were the occasion of my being called upon to take the command in chief of the Bavarian troops have subsided since the French armies have left our neighbourhood, I hope soon to be able to put up my sword and resume the more pleasing occupations of science and philosophical experiment.

"Wishing you much success in your endeavours to promote the prosperity of mankind, by the introduction of useful improvements, I am, my dear Sir John, with unfeigned regard and esteem,

"Your affectionate and most obedient Servant,
"RUMFORD.

"P. S.—I am very sorry indeed to hear you have withdrawn yourself from the 'Great Council of the Nation.' Pray don't let yourself be disgusted or discouraged. The cause is good, and perseverance will in the end command success." *

It is probable that if Count Rumford, remaining in

* The Correspondence of the Right Hon. Sir John Sinclair, Bart., &c. London. 1831. Vol. II. pp. 57 - 58.

England, and closing his relations with Bavaria, had sought political position and influence, he might have found a seat in the House of Commons, or even a subordinate office in the Cabinet. His foreign duties and his obligations to the Elector debarred him, however, from many positions of trust and honor in England, while, as we shall soon see, the fact of his being a British-born subject was a constitutional or conventional obstacle in the way of his exercising a very high diplomatic office which the Elector had assigned him.

The following letter of Colonel Baldwin to Josiah Pierce, half-brother of Count Rumford, concerns the latter's kind care for their mother: —

"WOBURN, November 12, 1796.

"DEAR SIR, — I have received several letters from your brother, Count Rumford, and his daughter Sally, all dated at London. As one of the Count's letters relates principally to your mother's concerns, I have transcribed it and enclose a copy thereof for her perusal [referring to the letter dated July, 1796], which you will please to deliver to her. Consult and determine in what mode you would wish to have the business negotiated. If you were coming here on business, you might bring an order from your mother, drawn agreeably to your brother's plan, which you will see in the copy of the letter herewith transmitted. You might also take her power of attorney, which would enable you to conform to any unforeseen circumstances. If you have no business, or it should be inconvenient for you to come up, it may be negotiated without your coming at present. My attention is fully occupied, but I shall not hesitate to devote sufficient time to effect this benevolent design.

"I do not know whether Sally has written to any of your family, but she is very full in her apologies for not writing to more of her friends, and wishes us to communicate her grateful remembrance and love to her relations and friends. There seems an unbounded love and affection between her and her father; they are delighted with each other. I participate in their happiness.

"I wish to inquire whether it would be agreeable to you to close the business in which we have been partners, and what your expectations are, and the proposition you would wish to make for a settlement. And I also wish for your opinion whether I could settle a son in your neighborhood upon a plan that would be flattering; and if it is not too much trouble, that you would state the objects proper to direct our attention to, and any circumstances that might operate against them.

"Mr. Ingals, the bearer, is waiting. I have no time to enlarge. I am pleased to see him so well. Mrs. Baldwin joins with me in respects to your father and mother, and love to Mrs. Pierce, and compliments to Dr. Thompson and lady, and all inquiring friends; and am, with much esteem, dear Sir,

"Your obedient Servant,
"LOAMMI BALDWIN.

"JOSIAH PIERCE, Esq." [Then residing in Flintstown, Me.]

Mr. Baldwin, who was a scrupulously exact man of business, found it necessary to be very careful in the friendly agency which he sustained between the Count and those with whom he had pecuniary transactions. From a copy of a letter addressed by him to Mrs. Ruth Pierce at Flintstown, which I have before me, dated February 2, 1797, I observe that he asked her to request her sons, Josiah and John, to pay her the value of the draft out of some funds of his own in their possession. The reason he gives for the request is, that, having advanced money to Sally when she sailed for London, he had sold the draft on London which she had given him in payment, and that this had come back protested, putting him to charges for that and the loss of interest. The purchaser had proposed to be lenient in his exactions if he could have as a substitute the new draft in favor of the Count's mother, to replace that of her granddaughter.

One of Mrs. Pierce's orders upon Mr. Baldwin is as follows : —

"FLINTTOWN, June 6, 1797.

"SIR, — If you will deliver Mr. Barnard Douglass the bill of exchange which my son, Count Rumford, requested you to draw in my favor for the year 1797, or, if the bill is sold, the proceeds of it, you will greatly oblige her who is, with the greatest esteem and respect,

"Yours,

"RUTH PIERCE."

An indorsement on the above reads : —

"BOSTON, June 17, 1797. Received of Loammi Baldwin a set of bills of exchange, drawn by him in my favor, on Sir Robert Herries & Co., Bankers, St. James Street, London, dated March 26, 1797, for the sum of Thirty Pounds sterling, which bills I promise to sell for the most they will sell for, and deliver the proceeds of sale thereof to Mrs. Ruth Pierce, agreeably to the within order.

"BARNARD DOUGLASS."

"Attest, BENJ. F. BALDWIN."

Here is a letter from the Count to his friend Baldwin, of a most pleasing tenor. It again refers to the wish of the writer at least to make a visit to his native country, and it relates the grateful circumstances under which his daughter received her title as Countess, and her pension, both of which she enjoyed to the close of her life.

"MUNICH, 15th Feb., 1797.

"DEAR SIR, — I have this day sent under cover to Mr. Pearson, Secretary to the American Academy of Arts and Sciences, a power of Attorney, authorising you and Dr. Willard to transfer 5000 Dollars American 3 *per cent* Stock, which now stands in my name in the Books of the Treasury of the United States, to the Fellows of the said Academy. The loss of the original Certificate which was issued for this Stock may perhaps occasion some delay in the completion of this business, but I hope you will find means to finish it without much trouble to yourselves.

"As soon as this is done, I shall request your assistance in transferring an equal sum to my much-loved Mother, to whom I am desirous of giving a small token of my filial affection, and of my sincere gratitude for all her kindness to me in the early part of my life.

"My Daughter, who is with me, and who is the comfort of my life, desires her most particular compliments to you and to your Lady. She often mentions your goodness to her, and looks forward with impatience to the time when she hopes to pay you a visit accompanied by her Father.

"Nothing could afford me so much heartfelt pleasure as to be able to gratify these her most earnest wishes, which are so natural, and which I feel perhaps still stronger than she does. She is a very good Girl, and is much loved here by everybody who knows her.

"The Elector has lately made me very happy by permitting me to resign to her one half of a Pension I enjoyed, which was granted to me several years ago as a reward for my public services. Two Thousand Florins a year (equal to about two hundred pounds sterling) are secured during *her* life to my Daughter (who has been received at Court as a Countess of the Empire). And this grant is accompanied by a circumstance which renders it peculiarly agreeable to her and to me, which is that she may enjoy her Pension in any country in which she may choose to reside.

"She is now above want, and her happiness in life will depend on herself. The best advice I can give her she will not fail to receive.

"I was happy to learn that you are so busily employed in schemes of public utility. Our juvenile pursuits and our amusements were always the same, and we have neither of us any reason to complain of the frowns of fortune.

"I am, my Dear Sir, with unalterable Esteem,
"Yours Affectionately,
v RUMFORD.

"The Honble LOAMMI BALDWIN,
Woburn, near Boston."
("Received at Boston Post-Office, June 10, 1797.")

The above indorsement on this letter, indicating the lapse of nearly four months between its date and its receipt, is an indication of the difficulties and delays attending transatlantic correspondence when the ocean and the land were the scenes of revolutionary struggles.

Under the same date the Count addressed the following letter to President Willard, of Harvard College.

.

"MUNICH, 15th February, 1797.

"Being charged by my daughter to forward to you the enclosed letter, I cannot help adding a line, to return you my sincere thanks for your very friendly letter. I ought, perhaps, at the same time to ask your pardon for the liberty I have taken in sending, under cover to Mr. Pearson [Prof. Pearson was then Corresponding Secretary of the American Academy of Arts and Sciences], a power of attorney to you and my friend Col. Baldwin, authorising you to make a transfer for me of five thousand dollars American three *per cent* Stock to the American Academy of Arts and Sciences.

"I feel myself highly flattered by the approbation you are pleased to express of my Essays. It has ever been my most ardent wish to be of some use to mankind, to be able to flatter myself when I am going out of the world that I have lived to some useful purpose. And I feel very grateful to Providence for the many opportunities I have had of pursuing with effect my favorite object. There are few persons, I believe, who have passed through a greater variety of interesting scenes than myself, and no one surely can feel more deeply, more intensely, everything that is interesting and affecting in the occurrences of life.

"My daughter, who will never forget your kindness to her, desires me to present her best respects. Permit me to join with her in thanks, and to assure you that I shall never cease to be, with unfeigned regard and esteem, my dear Sir,

"Yours, most sincerely,

"RUMFORD." *

The following long letter of the Count to Baldwin will be found referring to many matters of interest, especially to some relating to the private affairs of the writer, and to certain annoying and perplexing transactions with which he seems to have been embarrassed by relatives of his wife and daughter in America.

"Munich, 17th Dec'., 1797

"MY DEAR SIR, — I am still in a state of uncertainty respecting the fate of a number of letters on matters of importance to me, which I wrote to several of my friends in America, and among others to yourself, in February last. I have, however, some reason to think that they arrived safe, and that the answers to them were lost between England and Hamburgh, in their way to Germany, in June last. An English packet-boat on which I know there were letters for me which had come ·from America, addressed to the care of my Banker in London, was taken by the French at that time, and I think it more than probable that these were answers to my letters of February last,

* Memorials of Youth and Manhood. By Sydney Willard.

above mentioned. As soon as I was acquainted with the loss
of these Letters, I immediately wrote to my friends in America
to acquaint them with that accident, and to request them to
send me duplicates of their last letters; but since that time
I have received no news whatever from your side of the
Atlantic.

" My letters of February last related chiefly to arrangements
which were necessary to complete the business relative to my
donation to the American Academy of Arts and Sciences, in
which business I had requested and duly impowered you to take
a principal part. And I trust you will have found means to
complete those arrangements in a manner satisfactory to the
Academy. Should anything more be necessary to be done by
me, you will be so good as to indicate to me what is farther
necessary, and I shall lose no time in doing it.

" I have now, my Dear Sir, to request your friendly assistance in a matter of a more private and confidential nature, and
which I have much at heart to have properly arranged. Many
years ago I wrote to a man in America, whose name I cannot
pronounce without indignation, to desire that he would take the
care, &c., &c.

" There is another affair of a very interesting nature, at least
very interesting to my feelings, in which it is in your power to
render me a very important service. My Daughter (who
charges me with her best compliments for you and your Lady)
never ceases her solicitations to engage me to pay a visit to my
friends in America. And her wishes are so powerfully seconded by my own feelings and longing desires to breathe once
more my native air, that I have come to a resolution to make
the journey as soon as the restoration of Peace and the arrangement of my concerns in this country will permit it. If the
public affairs of Europe and of America take the turn I expect, and if no unforeseen event should happen to prevent my
carrying my Schemes into execution, I think you will see
us in America in 15 or 16 Months from this time. In the
meantime, there are several private family concerns which I
could much wish might be arranged and settled before my

arrival in America; and you will oblige me very much by lend-
ing me your friendly assistance in that business.

"Either myself or my Daughter must have an undoubted
legal claim to the Personal Estate left by my late wife at her
death. But as, since my seperation from my family in the year
1774, I have, by my own exertions, acquired a sufficiency, not
only for my own comfortable support during my life, but also to
enable me to make a handsome provision for my Daughter, and
even to give her something to dispose of by will to any of her
friends to whom she may wish to leave tokens of her affection,
I have no wish to bring forward any claims, either for myself or
for my Daughter, relative to her Mother's fortune, or to call
those to any account who are in possession of it; and for their
quiet and security I am willing to renounce in the most formal
manner all claims on that account, and to engage my Daughter
to do so also: *provided, however*, and this is a condition on
which I shall insist, that receipts and general charges are signed
on both sides.

"This proposition was made, by my direction, by my Daughter soon after my arrival in England, in a letter to her brother,
Mr. Rolfe. But as no answer has yet been made to it, I am
apprehensive that my Daughter's letter miscarried, or (what I
should be very sorry to be forced to believe) that Mr. Rolfe
does not chuse to be satisfied with this proposal. As the final
and irrevocable settlement of this business is a matter I have
much at heart, I wish you would undertake to settle it, and I
hereby authorise you to do so in mine and my Daughter's names,
and to sign in our behalf whatever may be necessary to put
the matter beyond all possibility of farther litigation or dispute.
Should it be necessary for you to take a journey to Concord to
do this, I should be much obliged to you if you would do so,
— on condition, however, that you make the journey entirely
at my expense.

"Should any attempt be made by Mr. Rolfe to bring forward
any demands for *maintenance*, *&c.*, you will, I trust, without
much difficulty, be able to make him feel how very unjust and
improper such pretensions would be under *any imaginable cir-cum-*

stances, but especially after the very generous offers that have been made to him. Should, however, such demands be not only made, but *insisted on*, you will please to declare in my name, not only that *they will never be admitted*, but also that the offer already made will be revoked, and other measures pursued. You may also, *in that case*, give Mr. Rolfe to understand, *at parting*, that I shall take care that his Sister, in the Will I have enabled her to make, shall not forget his usage of her. Should he behave handsomely in this business, you will, of course, avoid saying anything to him that would wound his feelings. I should never have had any suspicions of his behaving otherwise than handsomely, had it not been for a specimen of his manner of making up accounts which I saw among the papers my Daughter brought with her from America, and from the circumstance of his never having answered any of her letters. Though my Daughter is quite willing to renounce all pretensions to her mother's fortune, yet she is naturally desirous to have something that belonged to her to keep in remembrance of her, — a string of beads, a ring, or something of that kind, — and she desires that you and her Brother would select some article of this sort for this purpose.

"There is another concern which my Daughter requests that you would settle for her at Concord. Her Grandfather Walker left her a legacy in his Will which has not yet been paid. She desires you would apply to her Uncle, the Hon. Judge Walker, from whom she is to receive this Legacy, for his note of hand, on interest for the amount of it; and for the interest upon it since it became due, from the 18th October, 1792, when she compleated her eighteenth year. You may at the same time acquaint Judge Walker, that, in case of my Daughter's death, this money will (according to the dispositions of her last Will and Testament) return to the family from which she received it. In the meantime, she very naturally wishes that this property might be properly secured to her, and that it might be on interest.

"There is another pecuniary affair which I should be obliged to you if you would settle for myself with Mr.

Walker. He has, for these last twenty years at least, paid the Taxes, on my behalf, for *four* shares (or perhaps they may be six) which belong to me in a new Township, called Pennicook, lying somewhere near Saco river. Will you be so good as to repay him these advances, with the interest, &c.

" I wish you would also make inquiries respecting the quantity, quality, situation, and value of these lands, and let me know whether it would be most advisable for me to keep them or to part with them.

" There is still one more commission with which we are desirous of troubling you ; and though it is rather of an uncommon nature, and may be attended with some embarrassment, we cannot help flattering ourselves that you will undertake it. I must introduce it by an account of a little event which gave rise to the idea of the undertaking, in the execution of which we shall request your assistance.

" In March last my Daughter, desirous of celebrating my birth-day in a manner which she thought would be pleasing to me, went privately to the House of Industry, and, choosing out half a dozen of the most industrious of the little Boys of 8 and 10 years of age, and as many Girls, dressed them new, from hand to foot, in the uniform of that public Establishment at her own expence, and, dressing herself in white, early in the morning of my birth-day, led them into my room and presented them to me when I was at breakfast.

" I was so much affected by this proof of her affection for me, and by the lively pleasure that she enjoyed in it, that I resolved that it should not be forgotten ; and immediately formed a scheme for perpetuating the remembrance of it, and often renewing the pleasure the recollection of it must afford her. I made her a present of 2000 Dollars American three *per cent* Stock, on the express condition that she should appropriate it *in her Will*, as a capital for clothing every year, *forever*, on *her* birth-day, twelve poor and industrious Children, namely, 6 Girls, and 6 Boys, each of them to be furnished with a complete suit of new clothing, of the value of five Dollars, made

up in the same form and colours as the uniforms of the poor
children she clothed on my birthday.

"To complete this arrangement it was necessary to determine who should be the objects of this charitable foundation,
and it gave me much satisfaction to find that my Daughter did
not hesitate a moment in making her option. She immediately
expressed her wishes that it might be the poor children of the
Town where she was born, — a spot which will ever be very
dear to her, and where she is anxious to be remembered with
kindness and affection.

"Though the inhabitants of the Town of Concord are too
rich, and have, fortunately, too small a number of objects of
charity, to stand in need of such a donation as that which my
Daughter is desirous of their accepting at her hands, yet, as
the object she has principally in view — the encouragement of
Industry among the children of the most indigent classes of
society — must meet the approbation of all good and wise men,
she cannot help flattering herself that the Town of Concord
will do her the favour and the honour to accept of this donation
for the purpose stipulated, and that either the Selectmen of the
Town, or the Overseers of the Poor, for the time being, will
take the trouble *annually*, of seeing that the conditions of it are
fulfilled.

"What I have to request of you, my Dear Sir, is, that you
would mention this matter to some of the principal Inhabitants
of Concord, and endeavour, to obtain their approbation of the
scheme and a promise of their support of it, and their assistance
in carrying it into execution. As soon as I shall be informed
by you that our Plan meets with their approbation, my Daughter will make an application to them in a more direct and formal
manner; and I hereby engage to be her surety for the punctual
performance of all that she may promise in the progress of this
business.

"I shall hasten to conclude this long epistle by requesting
that you would excuse the liberty I take in giving you so much
trouble with my affairs, and that you would rest assured that I
shall not fail to embrace with eagerness every opportunity that

shall offer of giving you the most convincing proofs of my gratitude, as well as of the unfeigned regard and esteem with which
I am, my dear Friend,

"Most affectionately Yours,

"RUMFORD.

"The Honble Col. Loammi Baldwin.
("Received April 21, 1798.")

This "long epistle," as the Count well describes it,
can hardly have failed to engage the attention of the
reader as giving hints and intimations of some of those
traits in the writer which express his real character. He
evidently cherished a serious intention of at least making a visit with his daughter to his native country, if
not also of taking up his permanent residence here.
His fame was now well established in America, and
many friends and correspondents whom he had here
were prepared to welcome him with pride and gratitude.
I have come upon many contemporary evidences that
several of these friends were engaged in selecting for
him a desirable estate, which he might purchase and
improve, and had written to him very freely upon the
subject. It was just at a period when some of the
most extensive private domains were purchased at small
cost by gentlemen rich for those days, who built upon
them substantial mansion-houses, and introduced some
of the earlier improvements of agriculture. Court
Rumford would have been a conspicuous example
among this class, and would surely have signalized
his renewed citizenship in Massachusetts by building a
stately mansion, adorning pleasure-grounds, and managing a farm. It would seem as if the region which
drew the preferences of his friends and advisers was in
the neighborhood lying between what are now known
as North Cambridge and Belmont.

But before finally committing himself even to a temporary visit to the scenes and companions of his early years, Count Rumford, with that deliberate and cautious wisdom of providing conveniences and safeguards for his plans which was habitual with him, determined to have all seeming difficulties and embarrassments removed or disposed of. He was still a proscribed and outlawed exile, alike by the laws of Massachusetts and of New Hampshire; and the general government had no power to remove these disabilities, even had it sought to do so. His return and residence here could only have been by sufferance, but his eminence attained abroad would be expected to secure him immunity from slight or insult. The inhabitants of Woburn, not to be behind the State or any of its municipalities, had voted in town meeting, May 12, 1783, "that the absentees and conspirators, or refugees, ought never to be suffered to return, but be excluded from having lot or portion among us." * Nor could he legally, as an alien, hold real estate within our territory. As we have already seen, he had previously inquired of his friend Baldwin whether he might safely venture to return, and whether "party spirit" was at all abated. He would have found at work here at that time a party spirit of the most intense and virulent character, though it concerned other issues than those in which he had been involved.

The same local legislation which outlawed him had also deprived him of all property rights and claims on this soil. His references to such claims as still valid must be interpreted accordingly. The patriotic position which the members of his family and that of his

* Sewall's History.

wife had taken and maintained when he fled the country secured to them, of course, the property in which he otherwise would have had an interest. At no subsequent period could he have interfered in its management, or disposed of, or advised the disposal of, any part of it, except by the same sufferance from those immediately concerned, who would have winked at his presence in this country. The property of his deceased wife, having come for the most part from her former husband, Colonel Rolfe, would mainly go to her son by him, Paul Rolfe. A portion of the widow's dower, which she had enjoyed as Mrs. Thompson, would legally descend to the Count's daughter by her. But it would seem that while her inheritance of this was in some way impeded, the Count had reason to apprehend that he might be made independently answerable for the charges of his daughter's maintenance and education during the years in which her father had apparently left her to the care of others. The disrepute attached to his own name in Concord till he had won for it eminent distinction, would allow of irregularity and even of injustice in the transactions of administrators and guardians. As to the " man in America " whose name, as the Count wrote to Colonel Baldwin, he "could not pronounce without indignation," it is hardly worth our while to inquire. Yet I think I might name him, though I should be unwilling to justify any charge thus implied against him. It is interesting to note the Count's incidental assertion that he had written to this man " many years ago." The period designated is indefinite, but it must suggest a date of the Count's intercourse by correspondence with some one near his early home previous to any letter which I have been able to obtain. The Count shows his willingness to renounce, even on his daughter's behalf, all claims which she or he might have upon the estate of his deceased wife, and he assumes the whole responsibility of her maintenance henceforward, and of provision for her survival; covenanting, however, as a condition, that no charges for the past should be set up against him or her. This requisition he enforces with a threat concerning last wills and testaments to be insured by a foreign sanction. Miss Sarah's Grandfather Walker had left her a legacy of £140 when she should be married, or be eighteen years of age. On this the Count had computed interest from the completion of her eighteenth year up to the time of his writing. This he required for her, with a generous stipulation that it should revert at her decease to the Walker family. He tenderly demands for her also some keepsake of affection, if it be but "a string of beads," of the lonely mother whom she had loved.

I am inclined to think that the parties concerned made no serious effort in reference to the Count's invalidated rights to the shares in some wild land in Maine.

A lively account will be found further on, from the daughter's pen, of the celebration of her father's birthday which suggested to him the proposition submitted to the selectmen of Concord. The Count did not exercise his usual discretion, and seems to have become wellnigh oblivious of the characteristics of his native land, when he suggested the introduction here of one of the most odious customs of the Old World, in associating a grotesque pauper uniform with a beneficiary institution. Children so disfigured in their array would have been a ridiculous spectacle in a New England country town, and their garb, which would have made them a jeer, would have been a severer infliction than their poverty.

The matters referred to in the long epistle are recognized in the correspondence which follows.

"WOBURN, March 16, 1798.

"MY DEAR COUNT,—I have been waiting in expectation, from time to time, that I should soon have it in my power to announce to you the full and complete negotiation of your most liberal donation to the American Academy of Arts and Sciences, which has been delayed the longer as we did not very readily find the precise mode of making the transfer where the original certificates (as in this case) were lost. However, the business is finally completed, and the Academy is in the full possession of your generous donation of five thousand dollars, three *per cent* Stock of the United States, — a donation the most liberal and important of any that this Society has ever realized. And notwithstanding you may not have heard (as you might justly expect) much from us during the transfer, yet I do assure you that this event has not been marked with silence here.

"There is a committee of the Academy appointed to address you upon this pleasing occasion, and I hope erelong we shall have the renewed pleasure of transmitting to you some fruits of your solicitous endeavors to investigate a subject so difficult, and, at the same time, so important to mankind. It rather seems a mystery that the philosophy of Fire and Light, the most effulgent agents in nature, should be the most difficult to see into and investigate.

"Your much esteemed Essays are now republishing by Mr. David West, of Boston. This book, besides the great utility of the various subjects it treats of, is highly valued for the style in which it is written, and has been recommended by some of our professors in languages as the best sample for imitation of any extant.

"I have now only to add my love to your daughter, the Countess, to whom Mrs. Baldwin has just written, and close at this time with that sentiment I have so often expressed, without which I don't know that I shall ever conclude another letter until the object (which is to see you once more in your native country) is obtained.

"I have the honor to be, with great respect, my dear Count,

"Your obedient and very humble servant,

"LOAMMI BALDWIN.

"Sir Benjamin, Count of Rumford."

"The above letter to be forwarded by Dr. Welsh's son, of Boston, who is going to Berlin, as Secretary to Mr. Adams, the American Minister at that Court.

("Sealed up, July 30, 1798.")

Considering the punctilious character, especially in all business affairs, both of Count Rumford and of Colonel Baldwin, it must have been a grievous vexation to them that, besides the delays connected with the transmission of letters, there should have happened a protest of a note drawn by the Countess for the benefit of his mother, as this letter indicates.

"Munich, 7th January, 1798.

"Dear Sir, — By some unaccountable delay, your letter of the 5th Dec', 1796, did not reach me till a few days ago. My Bankers in London, Sir Robert Herries & Co., of St. James' St., have directed their Correspondent in Boston (whose name you will be made acquainted with) to pay you the amount of the Bill of Exchange drawn by my Daughter on my late Agent in London, Capt. Armstrong, for £30 sterling, dated Boston, October 23ᵈ, 1795, together with the Costs arising from the protest of that Bill, Interest, &c., which altogether amounted to £32. 5. 9. sterling, according to the account you have transmitted to me in your letter above mentioned, of the 5ᵗʰ Dec', 1798, which, together with the interest on the same since that time, you will now receive.

      . " I am, Sir, Your most Obedient Servant,

                                " RUMFORD.

  " The Honᵇˡᵉ Loammi Baldwin,

" Senator, &c.   Woburn, near Boston,

                                     Massachusetts.

  " North America."

It must have been with some misgivings of his own that Colonel Baldwin, in the following letter, communicated to the Selectmen of Concord, N. H., the proposition concerning a charitable institution.

                             " Woburn, 24th September, 1798.

" Gentlemen, — Sir Benjamin Thompson, Count of Rumford, and his daughter, the Countess of Rumford, now at Munich in Bavaria, have made provision for establishing a fund of two thousand dollars, three *per cent* Stock of the United States, the income whereof is to be appropriated to clothe annually in the uniform of the House of Industry at Munich, on the 23d of October, forever, twelve poor and industrious children of the town of Concord, being the place of his daughter's birth, a spot dear to her, and where she is anxious to be remembered with kindness and affection.

" The Count seems well apprised of the flourishing state of your town, that it is above the need of his assistance. Yet, as the encouragement of industry seems a principal object with him, they hope that the scheme will meet your approbation. In a letter which I received from the Count, dated the 17th December, 1797, wherein this plan of the institution was proposed, is a paragraph to the following effect : —

" ' Though the inhabitants . . . . of it are fulfilled.'

" There is also in the same letter a closing paragraph, which is as follows, namely : —

" ' What I have to request . . . . this business.'

"I hope the foregoing sketches will be sufficient to give you the outlines of this plan. I have had conversation with several gentlemen of the town of Concord upon the same business, who will perhaps be able to give further information respecting the matter; particularly I beg leave to refer you to the Hon. Judge Walker, to whom I have communicated the contents of the letter which I have received upon this subject from the Count.

"When I contemplate the many, the very many, important improvements, institutions, and establishments the Count has made, which go directly to meliorate the condition of mankind, I am led, with grateful pleasure, to bless his name, and glory in our country which gave him birth. And I should rest in full confidence that your proceedings and report in this concern will be such as will aid his usefulness and extend his benevolence in the world.

"I have all along intended to wait on you in person with the Count's proposals, but have hitherto been disappointed, and now despair of having that pleasure this season; and so much time has elapsed since I received them that I have now only to request that your consideration and decision in the premises may be as speedy as their nature and your convenience will admit, and shall wait your advice.

"I am, with the greatest consideration and respect, gentlemen,
"Your most obedient servant,
"LOAMMI BALDWIN.
"THE GENTLEMEN, SELECTMEN OF THE TOWN OF CONCORD,
N. Hampshire."

The occasion which prompted this intended provision for some poor children in Concord, and the form which was proposed for it, will be found, as before intimated, to be explained by and by in the daughter's autobiography. The true spirit of New England independence and pride, still with an eye open to worldly thrift, and a consciousness that money received in one way or for one object which would be objectionable may still be made available in another way and for another object, is to be observed in the following reply of the selectmen to Count Rumford, through Colonel Baldwin. They will be very glad to receive the money proffered by him and his daughter, and though they dislike the conditions prescribed for the gift, and freely express their objections, they will manage in some manner to accept them, rather than lose the money, offering, meanwhile, an opportunity for the modification of the terms.

" CONCORD, N. H., Nov. 17, 1798.

" DEAR SIR, — In your obliging letter of the 24th Sept., which we had the honor to receive, we find stated a plan of an Institution, proposed by Sir Benjamin Thompson, Count of Rumford, and his daughter, the Countess of Rumford, for establishing a fund of two thousand dollars, 3 *per cent* stock of the United States, the income of which is to be appropriated to clothe, annually, in the uniform of the House of Industry at Munich, twelve poor, industrious children of the town of Concord, and the same to continue *in perpetuam*.

" Having attentively considered the proposals of the Count and his daughter, we, as a committee, in behalf of the town of Concord, request the favor of you, sir, to communicate to them the following, viz. : —

" That the object under consideration, to wit, the encouragement to industry, appears to us important, and meets the approbation of every good and enlightened citizen; but that the means proposed to be used for the accomplishment of that object will have the desired effect is with us a doubt. Whether the clothing of these twelve children, which to them will be temporary, or minds well informed in useful knowledge, which will be durable, and of which none can deprive them, will be most likely to effectuate so noble and benevolent a design, are questions which we beg leave to submit to their judicious consideration.

" That although a spirit of industry may be excited in children
by holding up to them the idea of clothing, and that from that
clothing a temporary comfort will indeed arise, yet we humbly
conceive that by furnishing them with the means of acquiring
moral and political knowledge they might be equally excited,
and, should their proficiency be good, — which, from observing
the general desire after knowledge among our youth, we do not
doubt, — it would not only afford them present comfort, but will
directly tend to meliorate their several conditions in this life,
will prepare them more fully to enjoy the blessings of civil and
religious liberty, and induce them, as they rise into active life,
more cordially to bless the memory of their munificent benefactress.

" Whichsoever may appear most effectual in bringing about
the object of the Institution, we beg leave of you, sir, to
inform Sir Benjamin Thompson, Count of Rumford, and his
daughter, the Countess of Rumford, that we will, with grateful
hearts, accept the donation for the stipulated design, and that
we shall with the greatest pleasure exert our united influence
to aid them in the accomplishment of so important and benevolent a purpose.

" We are, sir, most respectfully yours,

> "JOHN ODLIN, } Selectmen
> RICHARD AYER, } of
> Concord.

"Hon. Loammi Baldwin, Woburn, Mass."

No further steps were taken during the lifetime of
the Count in reference to this proposition. His daughter cherished through her life the purpose of substantially carrying into effect the original design of her
father, or of establishing some equivalent substitute for
it. She accordingly made a provision in her will, very
generous in its terms, though it still waits for full
realization in a philanthropic institution. Mention
will be made of this in its proper place. I now resume her narrative.

" The amusements were refined, from their being at court. The Elector, at the age of seventy-one, having married an Italian princess of seventeen, it gave rise to a joke that it was only the numbers reversed. Unfortunately it proved more than simply a reversement of numbers. The Electrice, besides being accomplished and handsome, intense in her love for and indefatigable in the pursuit of amusement, contrasted greatly with the Elector's years, his want of rest and quiet. But on account of the beautiful, spirited princess, all was gayety. Balls succeeding balls ; drawing-rooms, concerts, the same. The splendid palace of Nymphenbourg, the summer court residence, became the seat of hilarity, fashion, and elegance. The young Electrice figured at the head of it, singing agreeably, often performing in public, and dancing well, though a little lame. It was amusing to bystanders to be witnesses to the conjugal struggles ; the Elector looking steadfastly to the door, impatient for the moment to arrive to retire, and she, in the supplicating, artful manner of youth, saying, ' One dance more ! One dance more ! '

" The German ladies, in general, are accomplished and charming, vying with Parisieners, yet less celebrated ; possessing the more substantial qualities of the English, those of sincerity. The German gentlemen are profound in knowledge, strict in probity, with not a shadow of conceit or foppery, with perfect high-breeding. Undoubtedly this is why their seminaries of learning are so esteemed and sought after. It is not in these schools that a child would be taught duplicity, or independent rudeness of manners, as in many others. But at this moment the word was *Reform*. The effects of the French Revolution, the great upsetter of everything, were then felt, though now, fortunately, it is at an end, and the scales of justice, wisdom, and good order have resumed their activity.

" I do not wish to cast blame on my father, persuaded that in what he did, it being according to the customs of the times, he considered it doing right. He was besides upheld by the kindness of the Elector, as well as allowed by him the means. He seemed to be a real favorite of the Elector's, and on his side

he was unfeignedly attached to him. Indeed, I presume the
Elector was a really good, excellent character. An anecdote is
related of him in connection with my father, which shows him
to be such, besides indulgent. In some transaction, my father
being blamed, the Elector took his part. My father afterwards,
finding that he had really been to blame, went not only to thank
the Elector, but to own his fault. The Elector replied, 'If
you had been in the wrong ten times, I would have insisted on
the contrary !'

"From a change of times and politics, the poorhouse, with
some other institutions, I presume, have not been kept up.
But the Duke of Deux Ponts, successor to the Elector, — he
who afterwards, much against his inclinations, esteeming much
more the title of Elector, was made King by Bonaparte, —
was so kind as not to suffer my father's English Garden, or,
rather, the one built under his care, to fall into dilapidation.
This garden, about seven and a half miles in circumference, has
two branches of the Iser running through it, over which are
some fancifully constructed bridges. The walks and drives are
serpentine, in the English style. A Chinese tower, a café,
with other edifices, were placed to afford entertainment. At
the entrance a monument was erected to my father, with a
pretty inscription, before his death. English ladies' riding was
to be introduced, — a reform, so-called, of high importance. Not
but what the German method for ladies was infinitely safer.
The two side-saddles brought from England by my father were
now to be put to use, in an exhibition of the English manner of
riding.

"It was the month of September, — as is well known in most
northern latitudes, a fine month. The sun had lost his fiery
hue, was shining with the mild, pale lustre of declining life, or,
in other words, as denotes a change from the brilliant, captivating season of the year, where smiling nature affords pleasure
with utility, instead of calm resignation. There was visible in
the court a clump of horses, with three of General Thompson's
people to tend them, — the groom, the huntsman, and the
ostler ; but the huntsman, possibly, as called in German, the

yager, is an essential personage in all military honors. He
wears a high, upright feather in a three-cornered hat, with
different livery, more distinguished than that of the other servants. There were several horses. Some appeared warm and
fatigued, as if the mounters had just quitted them, which was
the case, they being those of the General's two *aides-de-camp*,
Lieutenant Spreti and Captain Count Taxis, with one or two
others who had come to join their General in a riding-party,
or, as he was generally called, his Excellency. As three of the
horses had principal parts to act, a description of them will here
be given. They bore the names of Tancred, Fawn, and
Lambkin. The last was destined for a lady not used to riding,
requiring a gentle horse, — as was Lambkin particularly so, as
the name bespoke. This lady was the Countess of Nogarola,
a particular friend of the Baron's, familiarly called by him
Mary. Tancred was for another lady, in fact, the Count's
daughter, called die Frau *freilin Sally* (Miss Sally), or die freilin
Gréfin (Miss Countess). The daughter was about sixteen [and
nearly half as much more], and the friend twenty-five or
twenty-six. Tancred was nothing remarkable, but would go
very well with the free use of the whip; but Fawn was the
personage, like the yager, — the General's right-hand man and
favorite. How can such perfect beauty and excellence be described? Nothing short of a jockey could do justice. He was
of proper height and size, round, plump, had a little head, small
features, legs and feet, a sharp, knowing eye, and the color of
the most beautiful fawn. Of course, his hair was made to
shine like satin. He had a way, when standing any time, of
turning his head almost quite round, as if looking for some one
(his master fancied it was for him), and if nothing came of it he
would begin pawing and jumping. His back was hollow and
neck curving."

The young lady introduces at this point in her narrative a spirited drawing of horse and groom, not
saying, however, of which of the three animals it is
a sketch.

"After much bustle all was stillness as the word went forth —the General and his suit descend,—then a rustling on the magnificent looking-glass staircase, nearly multiplying objects into innumerability. And what objects! The Baron, a handsome man, about forty, decorated with honors, star and garter, appeared accompanied by his ladies, one under each arm, beautifully dressed in the English style, excepting more richly, in scarlet with feathers and ermine. One of the ladies was sixteen [better, twenty-two]; the other, twenty-six. Lambkin being brought forward for the elder of the ladies, and it requiring some time to get her mounted, on account of her being no horsewoman, the younger lady became impatient, and very much so, being fond of the amusement, giving one of the grooms a look, had the horse destined for her brought forward, skipped on with trifling assistance, and almost immediately disappeared; not going far, however, for when the party passed the *porte-cochère*, she and her Tancred were found perched at one side of it. This appeared amusing to the company; occasioning a general laugh. But not so to the Baron. He frowned, and particularly so when he perceived the young lady's whip dropped, and the young aid, Count Taxis, dismount to pick it up.

"This accident was followed by a detention from this young

lady's shaking about her saddle, declaring it would turn, desiring it to be fixed differently. This being complied with, the cavalcade began its march, — the Baron on the splendid Fawn, a lady on each side of him, the aids and others behind ; and novel was the sight, the ladies being dressed and seated nearly as the English. The ' English Garden ' was the place destined for the ride ; but to reach it a part of the streets of the town were to be passed through, and many were the curious ones at the windows to see the sight. All things went on well thus far, and would have without doubt continued so, had not the younger of the ladies, without due consideration, giving a whip to her horse, set out, soon losing sight of the company, the timidity of the other lady rendering it impossible for them to follow. The Baron much frightened at seeing this young person go off alone in unknown roads and winding paths, looked to his aid Spreti to tell him to follow her ; but before the words could be got out of his mouth the other one, Taxis, was on the gallop. On arriving home in safety, relieved of our riding-habits, we assembled as usual at the supper-table of my father to take each of us a basin of chocolate. I made bad dinners, not being fond of foreign cookery ; was fond of chocolate, but never had half enough of it. Our respectable, charming guest was the Countess of Nogarola, who will be often mentioned in this narrative.

" The Palace, my father's lodgings, was a building three stories high, sixty or sixty-five feet in front, running back possibly three times that distance, with an open space enclosed, already mentioned, called the court. The second floor, my father's habitation, was composed of two halls, one front and the other back ; the one with windows on the street and also on the court extending the width of the front part of the palace ; the back premises, with windows on the rear ; and on the court were the rooms my father particularly occupied. There were three staircases, a gallery, and eight rooms ; the gallery, uniting the two halls, consequently gave a passage throughout the house, and gave the whole a handsome appearance. The floors were of different-colored marble, or of smooth stone, resembling it, inlaid ; the windows five in number, with five of plate glass opposite ; an arched painted ceiling representing, as large as life, and well executed, heathen gods and goddesses, instructive as well as amusing. The second floor was handsome, conveniently furnished, in fact, might be considered elegant, yet was nothing in comparison with the first floor. That was a display of luxury and elegance fatiguing even to look at, to say nothing of the effect of a daily, hourly occupation. But the Russians are fond of pomp and show.

"The Elector did not in the general way dress with half the elegance and study of the Ambassador, whose household was composed of servants unlike all others, from their extraordinary height, and elegance of dress ; and as to their number, it was so great as never to come within my knowledge. The Ambassador had no lady ; yet, to a great dinner that he gave, my father being invited, I was permitted to go to be a witness to novel scenes, to do justice to which would be long and difficult. I will only mention that it was as magnificent as can be supposed, given by a person of his high calling and his apparent love of show. In short, there was a profusion of everything that could tempt the appetite or delight the eye, joined to company of the first class.

"My father had some peculiarities of character, and also of domestic arrangements, besides having odd things befall him. One of these was his having a monument erected to him, with an inscription, long before he died ! He kept through the year a box at the opera, without going, perhaps, three times himself. A doctor, by the name of Haubenal, he hired by the year! He made me a singular present ; indeed, it may be said five, there being five things. The circumstances were these.

"As I was sitting one day quietly in my room, meditating, not having much to do, my door, being shut, suddenly opened, and in skipped a little white, shaggy dog, as white as snow, excepting black eyes, ears, and nose. This was one of the presents from my father. I was pleased with her and kept her a long time. She was named by my father 'Cora.'* But

* This little dog must have become quite a pet of her mistress, for I find the fol-

while I was caressing her the door opened again, three people
entering, a woman with two men. The woman spoke first,
addressing me in French, saying her name was Veratzy, and that
she was sent by my father to offer her services as a teacher in
French and music. Making a low courtesy, she stood back to
let the others speak. They did so, and it was the same story.
They had come, by my father's desire, as teachers. One, by
the name of Dillis, a Catholic priest, was a professor of drawing. It was not uncommon with that class of people, their
salaries being small, to have professions. This Dillis, for instance, was one of the best men in the world, worthy his calling as a minister, supporting by his industry, joined to his trifling
salary, two aged parents, and bringing up three brothers. These
priests cannot marry. The other professor was for Italian, — Alberté, or Alberty, as I shall call him, sent also by my father to
offer his services as teacher in the Italian language. The
Signor Alberté, as he was called, was most judiciously chosen,
— an antidote, in appearance, to the softer passions supposed to
be so easily inspired by the people of his nation. His portrait
merits a description, particularly as he was sent by my father to
teach me the lovely, harmonious language of Italy. His stature
was under the common size, but to appearance greater, from a
great prominency of back and shoulders, so as nearly to hide all
signs of a neck. His voice was not more fortunate, being
harsh. His head corresponded with the prominency of his
back ; his nose the same, with sharp, fierce-looking eyes. Yet
he was a very good-humored, good kind of a man, and master

lowing reference to Cora in a letter written by Sarah to a female friend, December 16,
1799, while she was on a visit at President Willard's, in Cambridge.

"I arrived here safe the evening I left you, and had the satisfaction of finding the President's family all well, excepting himself. I went to meeting yesterday all day, and I found Cora was likely to be so unhappy to be left at home among
strangers, I carried her with me in my muff. She began to breathe very hard and to
cough a little before meeting was done, but upon the whole she behaved very well."

Whether the excellent pastor of the Cambridge congregation, the Rev. Dr.
Holmes, knew of this arrangement, it would be difficult to decide ; but we may be
sure that some of the College students, who then attended the parish meeting-house,
and whose eyes must have turned with interest to a Countess in the President's
pew, must have been privy to the fact.

of his profession. Ignorant of the different merits of these people at the time, and that I was doomed to similar visits, my surprise was great, and not greater than my disgust at the one just described. But summoning all possible fortitude, I dismissed them with saying I would think of it; well determined to have nothing to do with them. But these making only four of my father's donations, another remains to be mentioned. It was another visitor. I had heard of Dr. Haubenal, but had not seen him. He now entering, as did the others, from my father, it was by his announcing himself and offering his services that I knew him. Of the two I was the more surprised and shocked at a doctor's offering his services before wanted than I had been even at the sight of the Italian. I began immediately to cough before he got out of my room. It seemed as if it was owing to this untimely visit of the doctor, though the fact was, I had been several days threatened with a cough.

"Said I to myself, Surrounded by people who speak French, —and all genteel people speak it at Munich,—and knowing considerable of the language already, where is the use of my fatiguing myself with masters? Music the same. I knew something of it, did not wish to trouble myself any farther, and thought it hard there should be a question of it. As to Italian, I had no wish to know it, being persuaded I should not have occasion to go to Italy, and as to reading, there was surely enough to read in my own language. In the like manner I went on, believing myself in the right and my father in the wrong, till I fell into a copious flood of tears. At this moment precisely my father enters my room, and with a countenance so joyful that necessity compelled me to quit my troubles in contemplation of his apparent self-satisfaction. It appeared it was a question of travelling some way with a very old, beloved friend of his, and who, in short, was no other personage than a princess, — the Princess de L——.

"I was not to be of the party, but to go to the Countess in the mean time. He said, 'You know she is an angel of a woman, and, without doubt, will make you very happy.' Good as she was, however, the first thought struck me, How horrible to be left behind — as I still deemed it — among strangers ; and I inquired very pitifully if my teachers were to accompany me. Nothing of the kind, no question about it, was the reply. Amusement was the object of the day ; so I began to be tolerably reconciled.

"Such was my father's satisfaction at the prospect of taking this journey with his beloved princess, that not till just going out of the door did he remark my troubled looks, and that I had been crying. Mistaking the cause, he said in an affectionate manner, 'Do not grieve, my dear, I shall soon be back.' Of a childish nature as was my grief, so was now my merriment at the mistake. He had almost persuaded me I was glad he was going; thought, at least, I should have my liberty, which I viewed 'not to be the case as I then was. But I was unjust toward my father, while he was as kind as fathers in general. I took everything amiss, — as, for instance, my having these different masters. The fact was, I was unhappy everywhere, viewed Germany a great way off, as I called it. I was what we call homesick, — a disagreeable complaint, for a time incurable.

"The Countess, in her evenings with us previous to this contemplated journey, held out pleasing ideas of things to take place when I should be with her. We were to go to a ball at court (all genteel amusements at Munich being at court). Count Nogarola (husband to the Countess) not keeping his carriage at the time, my father was to lend us his, since he would not need it, as he was to take the journey with the Princess in her carriage. So we had planned many and various amusements. But for all that, when I saw my father make preparations for his journey, I would be crying, but with no one to witness my tears but little Cora.

"My father, being high in military station, could not go away at a minute's warning, as at this moment he was in command of the Bavarian troops, and there was war on all sides. The French and Austrians both attempted to enter the city, but were prevented. The time for the journey having come, the Countess arrived to escort me to her house, and the Princess

L—— was actually in her carriage at the door. My father, in the general way a slave to order, from imperious necessity had been now faulty, not being ready at the time agreed upon between him and the Princess, which was the more distressing as she declined to enter. This occasioned my father great bustle and confusion, so much so that, when he came to go, such was his absence of mind, that, though passing near, he did not seem to see and took no notice of the Countess or myself. I having equipped myself to accompany the Countess, my maid standing by with my packet of things, only waiting to receive my father's last kind look, and to hear his last words of farewell, to have him depart in this strange manner, not having the least idea of the cause, was astonishing. The Countess was surprised, and I broken-hearted. Off went my bonnet, declaring, if I must be miserable, it should be at home. I made sure he was gone to be married, fancying I saw some white round Aichner's hat (the white cockade on a servant's hat denoting marriage). I recited to the Countess the old adage, —

> ' The mother 's a mother all the days of her life ;
> The father 's a father till he gets a new wife.'

The Countess, after reflecting some time on what I said, with seeming difficulty to preserve her seriousness, informed me that at least this time my father had not gone to be married, for that the Princess was a married lady, and the Prince, her husband, was to be of the party. A servant was rung for to know the particulars, when we were informed of what has been already mentioned. 'Oh!' I exclaimed, 'it is put off, that is all; the time will come, I shall sooner or later have it to experience.' 'So long as it is not to be for the present,' replied the Countess, 'put on your things again, and come along. Let us see what rational amusement will be found in my quarter.' I went, and was as happy during the ten days of my father's absence as could be expected; never losing sight of the idea that I was among strangers, — alone in the world!

" Our excellent friend, the Countess, in trying to render me happy, did not forget the Baron, whom, after the Count Nogarola her husband, and two darling children, a girl and a boy, Therese and Andrew, there was no one she so much loved and respected. With regard to myself, as was before mentioned was the intention, I accompanied the Countess to a drawing-room. After this there were parties at home, or going out. A fashionable place of resort was at what was called the Hausmeister's, in the English Garden. After some turns round the Garden we would go there, taking refreshments. In the manner in which my father was travelling he had no need of his aids, which left them at leisure to amuse themselves. In our different excursions it was seldom that Count Taxis did not either go with us or meet us. The Countess seemed intimate with his family, and to have a good opinion of him, and her conversation with me concerning him was of a nature to make me think well of him. This was not the case with my father, which I had remarked, but did not know the cause. Among other things, the Countess informed me that this gentleman, a short time previous, had publicly declared his intention of not marrying a noble young lady of Munich, whom I knew, but whose name I have no call to mention, — a match made up by his and her family. He had taken a sudden fancy to learn English, and often called to speak it with the Countess and myself, — she speaking English uncommonly well. The Countess conducted me one day a few miles out of town to see a beautiful view. After looking at it some time, she, taking paper and pencil, began sketching. She invited me to do the same, saying it was not difficult, and that she would assist me. I accepted, and we finished the sketch together. When we returned home Dillis was sent for and desired to put the sketch in a state that I, with his assistance, could finish it. He did so, and I afterwards became his pupil. In the like manner, enticed on by the Countess, I became accomplished in matters in which my father had failed to help me through rougher measures.

"The next concern was music. I well understood my father's wish for me to cultivate it, and as decidedly so my own not to comply. If I was pleased with the measures taken by the Countess about drawing, in those respecting music I was charmed by a performance of this lady's on the piano, — assembling her two cherubs, Therese, about six, and Andrew, about eight, to assist, as she pretended, in singing. The performance of the children was novel and pleasing, inspiring me with a wish, as was intended, to unite my weak assistance, the Countess knowing I understood music a little. In short, the plan took. I told the Countess, if she would allow me, I would play and sing a little song of which I knew the first verse.

> 'Tell me, babbling echo, why
> You return me sigh for sigh?
> When I of slighted love complain,
> Thou delight'st to mock my pain.'

After which I played 'God save the King' in character, that is to say, in a thumping manner, and attempted 'Washington's March, but failed, — my sum total in music. I was praised beyond measure, and, thus encouraged, decided to take Miss Veratzy as teacher.

"Twenty-four hours had elapsed before either the Countess or myself were informed of the arrival of my father. His travelling companions making a little stop to pay him a visit, we were not sought after. The system of the great world seeming to be 'not to let the right hand know what the left hand doeth,' perhaps that was the reason. In the less cultivated climes of America, in case of visits of the great and respectable the whole neighborhood even would have been summoned to help out in making things agreeable. The Countess and I were, however, invited on the evening of the second day to partake of the usual supper of chocolate. We were both thankful and glad to see my father again, — the Countess, from an angelic temper of forgiveness; and I, from the natural love of a child to a parent. After the most prominent incidents of the journey, such as my father thought proper to communicate, the conversation turned on my consenting to take teachers, on my introduction to Dillis, and my thinking of turning my attention to music, in short, my receiving lessons from the said Miss Veratzy. In order to profit as much as possible from this unusual docility, my father began talking about the beauties of the Italian language, and what a pity it was I should not know something of it for knowing music. In short, it was decided that I should take the Italian master. I looking rather serious, the cause was inquired of it. I answered, that it struck me that a person would make more progress, and for a certainty it would be much more agreeable, to have a master not such a lump of deformity as was this Signor Alberty. My father replied, that the Italians, being considered a very gallant, captivating people, it was not considered prudent to have them as teachers with marked personal attractions. The observation reminded the Countess of an anecdote in circulation of a lady of distinction having fallen violently in love with her music-master, or rather the person who often accompanied her in her music, she being herself a fine musician. My father seemed much surprised and very sorry at the news, for the lady was in high place, and even an heir to the crown might have been derived from her. Still on the subject of teachers, my father asked the Countess how a little girl, about eight, named Sophy Baumgarten, niece to the Countess got on. The mother, the Countess of Baumgarten, was the Countess's only sister. The answer was, that Sophy did not get on so well, owing to the peculiarly light, trifling character of her mother.

"It would be difficult to find two characters less resembling each other than these two sisters, — the Countess of Nogarola, with a first-rate understanding, a model of virtue, not plain, but not handsome; the other, a few years before, a celebrated beauty. She was so much admired and celebrated in the world that even crowned heads confessed her charms. All gentlemen were in love with her. Alas, poor lady! she ended in not sufficiently respecting herself. A few days after this found me established with the whole catalogue of teachers, Alberty at the head of them. My studies went on like clock-work; my father had a great deal of order. A hairdresser came daily to dress my hair. Good Animeetle was exchanged for Cecilia Dumesnil, a French girl, on account of the language. Parents do wrong to push their children. Application is not for all. Better let them remain a little ignorant, than lose, perhaps, their lives.

" The time arrived for me to be plunged in study, surrounded by my teachers, — Signor Alberty, with his four feet in stature, his great nose and tremendous prominency of back, at the head of them. It was, nevertheless, in Italian that I made the most progress. Not that I neglected any of my studies. I succeeded in giving such satisfaction that my father in great affection called me *his own child*, — a little vanity in the expression which must be excused. Alas! frail nature admits of no control. In vain would vanity and ambition take the lead. My health began to decline. My flesh left me as if it had wings to fly away. I became ailing, and this ended in the whooping-cough. As already mentioned, the house, or rather the palace, we occupied was large; my father living at one extremity, and I at the other. All who have had the whooping-cough must know how troublesome it is, and that a person is everything but interesting when in a fit of it. My father had never exactly seen me at one of these moments, till going in haste into his apartment set me out coughing with the whoop. After looking at me with something bordering on a frown, he told me to ring a bell. I did so. He sat writing, and, looking up, said it was not the right one, it must be another. My father had great order in everything. If, for instance, a particular servant was wanted, there would be a particular bell to give him notice. Two servants now came, I having rung two bells; the valet, being one, was kept, and the other sent away. My father said to him, ' Macht der Haubenel hier kommen!' I did not know German, but understood enough of this to conclude that it summoned the doctor, and began retreating. My father called me back, asking me if I was afraid of a doctor; adding, that he understood I had not treated him civilly some time before. I was informed that in all probability the doctor would soon be with me; as it happened, nearly as soon as I had got into my own room. I was to show the doctor politeness. Very well! That was not difficult. But to be dosed, I muttered to myself, for so simple a thing as the whooping-cough, — I never heard of such a thing.

" A word of explanation for this apparent obstinacy may not

be amiss. I think I must have implied more than once that I had a great love and veneration for my mother. It was very natural. She had taken care of me in my infancy and childhood, and brought me up. I recollected often hearing her disapprove the habit many have on the slightest indisposition of seeking medical assistance. Yet, poor woman! I best recollect her as on her sick-bed, with the doctor by her side, for she never had even tolerable health. Children hear and reflect more than is always imagined. I remembered her telling a little story of my father, that, if anything ailed even a finger, the whole house must be put in an uproar about it. So that, in the present instance, if I say the physician arriving left me an emetic, which I put aside and would not take, I only followed the precepts of my mother instead of those of my father. I was perfectly freed of the disorder in a short time without the least medicine.

"In one of our horseback excursions we had the usual party, except that the Countess was kept back by a previous engagement. It proved fortunate, for our horses were restive and troublesome, so much so that, when we arrived at the Garden, — as usual, our destination, — my father told one of his aids — Spreti — to go with him, and the other to stay with me ; and the same to the grooms. He wished to let Fawn have his run out. We were jogging along when Tancred started and like to have thrown me. Count Taxis, frightened, said to me in English (which I did not suppose he knew much of, we never speaking the language, and which, therefore, surprised me) 'Take care, my dear!' From my looking down and making no reply, he thought I was offended. He drew his horse near to mine, and, looking me archly in the face, asked me if I did not think that in learning English he learned pretty things. I told him it depended on the sincerity of them. I spoke without reflection, but think he construed them into more seriousness than I really meant, by his dwelling some time on assurances of the sincerity of his words and thoughts towards me.

" By an unforeseen accident, if these assertions were true, he was called upon to feel and express more forcibly than by simple words. I had been indisposed for several days, but said nothing about it, from the childish, foolish idea that I should be, as I termed it, dosed. From the same childishness, because I was fond of going on horseback, I came out when I ought to have stayed at home; and from being in a restrained posture and among strangers, it naturally made me worse. In short, I grew so bad I thought I was dying, and told the Count I wished to get off the horse. While he was dismounting and making signs to the groom to approach, without his perceiving it I slipped my foot out of the stirrup, and took hold of the saddle to let myself down, but before I could do it my senses had left me; so that when Taxis turned his head, it was not to see me on the seat, but prostrate on the ground. There was the greater cause for alarm from his supposing I had fallen, instead of letting myself down, and that my fainting was owing, most likely, to some hurt. The first thing I realized, on coming to my senses, was Taxis and the groom exceedingly frightened, lifting me about, not knowing what to do with me. It would be difficult to describe the expression of their faces when they found me alive instead of dead, as they owned they much feared; supposing me to have received some great, and perhaps fatal, blow from the fall. They were likewise much rejoiced on my giving particulars, and assuring them I was not in the least hurt. The groom thought he should never dare to see my father again, had anything terrible happened to his daughter while in part under his care. The expressions of Count Taxis were more refined, as may be imagined. He showed such feeling and friendship on the occasion, I own it impressed me with the most lively gratitude and friendship for him. He thought best to let the groom go in search of my father, who soon joined us, when we all returned safely together.

"As under absolute governments distinction of classes is observed, so that between the General and his aids is not forgotten. My father, in coming to the door after our ride, with a familiar nod of the head, without asking them to enter, dismissed his aids. But Taxis, as it appeared, went straight to the Countess, giving her information of the bad success of our party on horseback, for almost as soon as ourselves she had mounted to our apartment. Seeing her reminded me of a ball to take place at the court the following evening, where she was to go, and I to accompany her. She presumed I would not go; and neither my feelings nor propriety could authorize the act. But a foolish, wild thought having crossed my mind, decided me on going, and I went. On entering the spacious, splendid halls, the first duty was to pay court to crowned heads, — those in question, the Elector and Electrice, — which ceremony passed, we seated ourselves. Count Taxis, as one of the young persons generally present at court balls, perceiving us, came up to speak to us. In looking at me with considerable attention, as he inquired after my health, particularly to know how I found myself after the ill turn in the Garden, he suddenly turned away his head with a singular expression, beginning at the same time an animated conversation with the Countess.

" Without exactly hearing what was said, I had reason to think myself not foreign from the subject, they frequently casting on me their eyes. In this supposition I was soon confirmed, the Countess going to take leave of the Electrice, then coming and saying to me that we were to return home, I being too ill to be out. ' Yes,' replied Count Taxis, being still near us, ' you ought not to have come.' ' What,' I said, looking him in the face, ' when I came on purpose to thank you for your kindness of yesterday, are you not glad to see me?' He making me no reply, I consoled myself with fancying he looked affected. We soon found our carriage and reached home.

" The ball-dress quitted, and I a little rested, I was tempted to follow my two friends, my father and the Countess, she being still with us, to the *tête-à-tête* supper-table. I went, but neither partook nor stayed long, quitting them without giving a reason, leaving them to think, if they might, that it was with an intention to return. On the contrary, I went to my room, summoned my maid, desired her to prepare my bed, and assist me in getting into it, I being so violently seized with a fit of ague as to be nearly unable to help myself. The girl, having executed my orders, was for running to inform my father and the Countess, but I stopped her, forbidding it; and not till an equally violent fever fit succeeded, the maid much frightened, contrary to my orders, going to give them notice, all hands arrived soon, followed by the doctor. My father had offended me a few days previous by saying I was always ailing, and I had not forgiven him. So I had two motives in going off in that clandestine manner,—one, because my father had affronted me; and another, the dread of the doctor's prescriptions. And now they began. An emetic was proposed. I refused it, saying that, so far from requiring it, I was then hungry. It was urged, even insisted on. I declared if they approached me I would dash the cup which contained it from their hands. It was given me, without my knowing it, in some herb tea.

"On experiencing the sickness, and presuming from what cause, I cried bitterly, and said they had deceived me. This was the last trouble they had with me of this nature. I was soon so ill as not to know or care what took place. I was confined six weeks to my bed with a fever,—part of the time between life and death.

"My next appearance was in the banqueting-hall, celebrating my father's birthday [in March, 1797], at my expense (my father allowing me pocket-money), but planned and principally executed by the Countess, on the sly, to occasion a surprise. The preparations of this festival were various, requiring three weeks' time to execute. I had little to do in them excepting being enjoined to keep the secret from my father. I was, besides, convalescent only, unable to lend much assistance.

"The first concern was to have a bust made of my father. For the want of the original to copy, a portrait was made use of, which answered, they having got a very tolerable likeness. A short time before the occasion arrived, having procured a profusion of artificial flowers, this bust was ornamented, as likewise some of the rooms, to the number of five, one of which was an immense hall allowed for my use, my father having no use for them. All of these being handsomely, some even elegantly, furnished, and being reached by the splendid staircase of looking-glass, rendered a festival easy to give, and elegant in its effects. Besides which nothing was spared to render ours conformable to the elegance of the apartments.

"Refreshments in great plenty, proper for the occasion; a society as select as it was numerous; the rooms illuminated — to speak largely — to vie with the noonday sun! the music, both vocal and instrumental, the best that Munich afforded, perhaps none better in the world. More attention was paid to this particular, my father being extravagantly fond of music. And from a very pretty manner they had of ornamenting with flowers, that of twisting them into letters and then to words, expressing verse, prose, &c., my father had many pretty compliments paid him, particularly in the ornamenting of the bust. Around this bust was a group which drew upon us all much praise and many compliments, — the Countess, her two children allowed to be present, Sophy Baumgarten, about eight years old, daughter of the Countess Baumgarten, sister to the Countess Nogarola; myself; six children (little girls) from my father's poorhouse, prettily dressed at my expense, in white, as were we all. For the more elderly part of our guests cards were prepared; music for the dance, vocal and instrumental music for the ear, — which made three distinct amusements without counting that of not doing anything at all.

"My father's two aids, Lieutenant Spreti, and Captain Count Taxis, were not forgotten in the number to be invited, and who accepted and were present. Neither of them had I seen during or after my illness. Of course the latter was the only one interesting to me. With Lieutenant Spreti I had barely ever exchanged a word. The festival began, we all at our places, the lights glittering, the company arrived, the music struck up a divine piece, vocal and instrumental, in which all who could sing joined in a chorus, when my father was ushered in. A considerable difficulty had arisen to get him dressed without his knowing for what purpose, and to prevent his seeing the lights of my highly illuminated rooms, some being on the opposite side of the court facing his. All, however, was happily accomplished, and he arrived utterly astonished, as much so as the guests, who were curious to see the effect all this might have on him. I, very naturally, was not one of the least curious to a point, I must say it in justice to myself. I quite forgot myself,—forgot I had a part of no little importance, that of being the ostensible mistress of the house. But I thought nothing of it. My father behaved charmingly. After the first surprise, which was great, he went about bowing and smiling, showing his white teeth, of which he was very proud, thanking people for the trouble, as he termed it, of coming to see him.

"The music was not spared, several fine pieces were performed, but we all of us had something to do. The Countess had a simple song enabling her little children with their juvenile voices and talents to join her, having a pretty effect, as likewise a piece of music of a superior quality on the piano, (she being a fine musician,) accompanied by the other musicians. I had a letter of compliment in Italian to present my father,—he not knowing me so far advanced in the language. The poorhouse children presented written expressions of their gratitude and respect. The little Miss Sophy Baumgarten, above mentioned, had a more dignified part to act than any of us, being signalized out by my father (while the Countess, her children, and myself, were barely noticed) as the object of great attention. So pointed was it as to attract the notice of all present. At all events, such undoubtedly was the intent; for if it was to cross the room this child was led by the hand, and, if seated, placed by his side.

"Contemplating some time this singular sight, I applied to the Countess to know what it meant. She, not giving me a positive answer, smiling, said I was to take notice that her sister, the Countess of Baumgarten, was not present; which, in the crowd, I had not before observed. This adding still to the mystery in which before the matter was enveloped, I returned with eagerness to my business of watching, and in consequence of it the truth was revealed to me, either by my good or bad genius,—I think it was the latter,—as I had better not have known it. The striking resemblance that existed between my father and the said Sophy put it beyond a doubt that I was no longer to consider myself an only child,—which was the case before. Be it from jealousy, or from what other cause, the thought made me miserable. In cases of great trouble and perplexity, often great resolutions, even unnatural energies, come to our aid. My surprise and vexation were great. Had I been alone, most likely vent would have been given by a few tears. But in a mixed, great society like that, how would it be possible? Then a thought struck me, which, as I observed before, either my good or my evil genius pointed out, and this time I will give no opinion as to which I think it was. But the thought was retaliation, or, in other less soft words, revenge."

It will be a satisfaction to the reader to be informed that, so far as is known, the Countess never put her resolve into execution.

"I had been given to understand, that, as head or mistress of the festival, or dancing part of the amusement, I was not to dance; as, since it would be impossible to dance with all, to dance with some would give offence. Consequently I had refused my friend Taxis, who had not only invited me, but who had several times repeated the invitation to dance with him, and who was seldom far from me, and was lavish of kind looks. I now, in return, showed a disposition to be friendly, sought him with my eyes, and, slighting consequences liable to ensue, danced with him. As we disappeared in the dance and the crowd, I took care to look to see if my father perceived us, and fancied he did.

"We all separated at a proper time, apparently well pleased with each other, and the company the same with the entertainment. I, in part forgetting my little or great vexation, as any one may think it, was very happy. All had been kind and civil to me. I having been so ill, some, those with whom I was most acquainted, seemed to express a joy to find me alive again; and all told me they had sent repeatedly, which I already knew, to inquire after me. In short, all this made me very happy, and I began to form dreams of happiness.

"The morning after the party my father sent for me to come and breakfast with him,—a favor seldom allowed. It is true, he had generally at that hour gentlemen around him, rendering it improper. But I was much flattered by this invitation, drawing from it favorable conclusions, that he had been pleased with the fine banquet made in honor of him; in short, that he had no objection, as I was dying to do, to talk over the occurrences, in calling to mind the features of it the most prominent and agreeable. By all those in the habit of frequenting such occasions, this is an absolute want, — the pleasure equalling nearly, if not quite, the first enjoyment. When girls get together for this discussion, it is, 'How pretty he was!' and 'How ugly she was!' While at my toilet, arranging myself, never with more care, what with reflections on the preceding evening and the anticipated pleasure of the breakfast, there became riveted on my countenance a smile, like distorted muscles after an inordinate laugh, difficult to change; so that on arriving at my father's, which had been by a jump and a bounce, that enchanting complacency, so great, seemed for a moment to disconcert him. But a general is not easily turned from his plans. It is for us, poor, weak females, to be overcome by circumstances. Obey! is the order with them; no reasoning.

"Without endeavoring to give a darker coloring to the picture than what is due, or to cast blame illy becoming a child, let us rather attribute things to the casualty of human nature; at the same time, receive them as a warning and check to too elevated ideas of happiness seldom or never realized. This was my situation; this check I had. When quitting my father's apartment, it was with totally different feelings and expectations than when I went. It was now, without doubt, to see life unadorned by youthful imagination. In short, my troubles came from exaggerated or real faults which I had committed. It was thought improper that I should keep a secret from my father, he my best friend, — it being the case in the affair of the banquet; surprises, requiring to be carried on by the sly, led to deception, a vile trait of character, and, if necessary, to falsehoods. In short, my conduct to Count Taxis was alluded to and disapproved. So that here, with one blow, were demolished all my fine castles in the air.

"I was, as in times before, to spend my time in tears and study. I received my admonition in silence, without making a reply, — I will not say from what motive, but fear it was more independent than wise. I did not say, as I could have done, that the Countess, all but an angel, from the purest and best of motives, was the beginner and ender of the banquet; that I, in revealing the secret to my father, must have betrayed her; and, to sum up the whole, if he expected me to be so perfect in my conduct towards Count Taxis, why was he not more so in that with his beautiful illegitimate!"

The young lady goes on to describe her sufferings from continued ill-health, from her sensitiveness, from her father's disapproval of her innocent attentions to Count Taxis, and from the rigidness of the diet to which she was subjected. She grieved also at a prospective separation from the Countess Nogarola, whose husband, obliged to go to Italy on business, thought of taking his family with him. Dr. Haubenel proposed a journey for her health, in which the Countess and her father should be her companions. Accordingly, in a pleasant season, they left Munich, in her father's carriage, with a maid and valet, and, driving a day's journey to a beautiful seat of the Elector's, at Ammerland See, they sent back their vehicle and servants, that they might be more free in their movements. They had the Elector's permission to make a temporary home at this princely residence, where they had attendance, with sumptuous fare, and fine scenery, and mountain views. Miss Sarah writes that she exceedingly enjoyed the change to freedom and nature, after eighteen months of confinement to the artificial life of the city and the lassitude of illness. The lake afforded them fine fish for their table, and in an elegant pleasure-boat manned with able rowers they enjoyed excursions and angling upon it, while at evening, the maid attending Sarah and the Countess, they would bathe in the soft waters.

This repose was to be followed by a journey, the route of which her father kept secret, that mystery might add to the enjoyment. "My father had appeared to try to see how agreeable he could make himself; as if wishing to wear off by it some of the disagreeable impressions of his late conduct, in drawing so many tears from my poor eyes. And he was ingenious in it. He could do one way or the other. And it was invariably the case, that when quiet and happy himself, he was like others, or, in other words, agreeable; but when perplexed with cares or business, or much occupied, there was no living with him."

This sharpness of a daughter's judgment of her father must be regarded as lying rather in the force of its expression than in any real severity of feeling. The amount and variety of work performed by Count Rumford, the multiplicity of the details which engaged his attention, and the large number of agents and subordinates whom he had to direct, as well as his almost mechanical observance of order and system, might naturally engross his mind in his hours of business. That he was affable and genial when he had intervals of leisure and repose might well relieve him from all reproach for austerity at other times. Nor is it to be forgotten, that, having to act in a full parental capacity to a motherless and evidently somewhat volatile and self-willed young woman, he might have had a judgment of his own, had he chosen to express it, to offset that of his daughter on himself.

The " mystery " of the movements of the Count was
not a very deep one. The party set out on foot, taking a guide with them, through fields and by-roads, and
after three or four hours' travel they came to what
seemed to the young lady an immense chateau, so large
that the whole of it could not be seen, and surrounded
by water, so as to be accessible only by a drawbridge.
Her father seemed to be familiar with the spot, and,
pulling at a cord, caused a very heavy-toned bell to
sound its echoes loudly, when two well-dressed men
appeared, with whom he had some secret whispering.
The consequence was that the great doors opened as if
by enchantment. The party were shown into elegant
apartments, were most hospitably entertained, and
yielded to urgent solicitations to pass the night within
its walls. Though Miss Sarah was soon impressed by
the fact that not a female was to be seen about the
establishment, and that their entertainers were all gentlemen "of breeding," it was not till the next morning that she knew the establishment to be what she
calls a convent.

They visited another like institution the next day.
The young lady relates at some length their experiences
in the ascent of a mountain, which they made at night
on account of the heat of the weather. It was a rugged
task for the ladies, especially for the delicately nurtured
and fragile Countess Nogarola. They experienced the
embarrassments arising from the ordinary female costume for such a tramp, and the Count's practical wisdom seems to have suggested to them such an approxi-
mation of the arrangement of their apparel to circumstances as anticipated the style of some of the more
independent of their sex in our times. The poor

Countess, as she went half-way up the mountain, "trying to make herself a little more comfortable, put her stockings (horribly wet, as were mine, with all the rest of our things) on a bush to dry. A mischievous cow ran away with one, champing it to pieces; so that when we came down from the summit we found the poor Countess with but one stocking, mourning the loss of the other. My father's man, taking off one of his, supplied the place of it, but not without difficulty to make it fit in her much smaller, more delicate shoe." The Count himself, who had made the ascent before, did not escape without a fall and a roll over the rocks, which afforded amusement to his daughter. They had a pretty adventure at their resting-place in being entertained by two peasant-girls, who, having two *chalets* half-way up the mountain, were sent there to watch the cows that were pastured there in midsummer.

The party returned pleased and renovated to Munich; the American girl growing more reconciled to her lot, and anticipating with more relish the court routine of another winter. But her trials were not over. Her friend the Countess was accustomed to dine once a week with her mother, the Countess of Lerchenfeld. Miss Sarah being now for the first time invited to join her friend, obtaining the consent of her father, went, and unexpectedly, as she implies, found Count Taxis of the party. She represents her father as habitually afraid or suspicious of the intrigues of ladies, and that he was thus prompted on the next day to make a visit to the Countess of Lerchenfeld, where he learned who had been his daughter's companion at dinner. He chose to regard the affair as a female conspiracy, and the following day brought him to the apartments of his daughter with lowering looks, and even more incensed than he had been at the secrecy with which she had planned the birthday banquet.

"I feeling myself innocent, as I was (it being as much a surprise to me as to my father that the invitation to the dinner was to meet Count Taxis, that being the subject of the difficulty), I at first only stared. After which, on knowing what it meant, like many young people who laugh when there is nothing to laugh at, an irresistible inclination seized me to laugh; which I having for some time suppressed only burst forth with the greater violence, and it ended in my father's boxing my ears. Little expecting such an indignity, I quitted the room without making an observation, or trying to appease him by saying I was innocent. Nor did he ever know, as I believe, but what I had given *rendezvous* to Count Taxis, and met him from a spirit of intrigue. Much the contrary, the Countess knowing very well I should not have gone, had I known for what purpose. Besides, she was too just and delicate to place me in such a situation."

We must infer, therefore, that Count Taxis came in by chance to the dinner. Our sympathies are engaged for the girl in the following like episode.

"I must be allowed here to take a step of retrogression. When I was a little girl of four or five years old, I had two playmates about my own age, by name William and Elenora Green; and we were very fond of each other. We were sent to day-schools together in the neighborhood, and were so much together that we were called the inseparables. We grew up in this manner in real love and friendship. We knew no difference from brother and sisters, excepting I might have been a little more civil than the sister. For William was exceedingly pretty and engaging, and his mother, doatingly fond of him, led him to exact more from us than he otherwise might have done. Mrs. Green, the mother, was rather romantic in her character, and dressed her son fantastically, keeping his hair (beautiful golden locks) always in ringlets, with belts of curious construction round his waist confining beautiful dresses, a jockey cap with feathers on his head; and, more than all the rest, she bought him a fife, and had him instructed to play on it several little tunes. It was this fife particularly which I was obliged to hear, for Elenora would not. As may be supposed, the music of such a child was not the most agreeable. Even while I would be listening to the little Apollo, my eyes would wistfully be turned towards Elenora, much preferring some other amusement. But William was not ungrateful. Taken away, at a later period, to other schools, he never forgot us,—or, in plain words, myself; seeking all the means proper in his power to give me testimonies of his friendship. His mother knowing this, as I have observed, being a little romantic, made proposals to my mother that at a future period we should be married. My mother, thinking well of the lad, liking the family, and having my happiness at heart, gave consent at once. The same thing happened to me here. Count Taxis, through the Countess, asking me of my father, I got my ears boxed, and Count Taxis with his regiment was sent into the country! One actuated by the feelings of a mother, the other by those of an ambitious father!'"

The young lady, drawing a parallel between her condition and that of Job, when the messengers of woe came to him in succession with ill tidings, proceeds thus:—

"The Countess called one morning (thinking, perhaps, I had better know the truth of things) and said: 'The negotiation with your father has not succeeded. To end further importunities, the Captain and his regiment quit Munich this morning, to have their residence in the country. And I only am left to tell you.'

"While she was yet speaking, there came a messenger from Count Nogarola, and said: 'From letters just received, he finds it necessary to set out for Italy to-night or to-morrow morning, and you have only time to return to make preparations.'"

" While the messenger was still speaking, there came also another, and said : ' The Baron sends you a paper.' It being in English, I cast my eyes on an article bearing the date of New York : ' Lost, being killed in a duel, Captain William Green, one of our most promising and beloved naval officers, barely attaining the age of eighteen. A duel said to be undertaken to vindicate the honor of a beloved sister. The sister is said to have had her mind deranged by grief at the death of her brother.' Knowing that the fond mother of William, after his finishing his studies, put him into the navy, there could be no doubt who this officer was, or of the identity of the sister. I had heard, too, that Elenora, when quite a child, had been pushed on, from ambition, to marry one gentleman while she was particularly attached to another. Relating this attachment was the cause of the duel, as I afterwards learned.

" I was not, like Job under accumulated afflictions, all humility and submission ; nor, like his wife, with profligate remonstrances ; but rather listened within myself to the precept of Solomon, that ' all is vanity and vexation of spirit.'

" Having given one parable, I shall give another. A gentleman of my acquaintance, I will say, a friend, having had and lost two beloved wives, in the height of his grief at last declared he would go and live in the burying-ground with them. Being . asked with which of them, he was embarrassed for an answer."

Miss Sarah adds that she cannot say over which of her four lost friends — including Elenora — she grieved the most, but proceeds to describe the sorrows of the day following, which was begun by leave-taking with the Countess. She was wrought almost to madness, and, seated alone on her sofa, her little dog Cora near to her, yielded to such passionate outcries as to lead her maid to summon her father into her room.

" He came in with his stately military march, and seated himself. I rose from my posture, taking Cora in my arms, and considerably abating in my great grief, or, rather, in the expression of it. He said to me, ' You seem very unhappy ! ' For some time I remained quiet, then, thinking I had hit on a good answer, replied, looking at Cora, ' You gave me this little beast. Is it your intention to take her away from me again ? ' My father rose, and, in quitting me, said, ' I am not the cause of your losing the Countess.' "

The Count, to divert the mind of his daughter, arranged another trip with her which showed his real interest in her happiness and improvement, and also afforded her enjoyment. He had invited temporarily into his family, M. Quintin, one of the French nobles driven away from France in the Revolution. " He had resided in England and been naturalized, having there taken the name above given; otherwise he was the Marquis of Chersæna [?], a respectable character; at this time not at his ease in point of property, but some years after, at the Restoration, returning to France, he was made Governor of the Tuileries, as his father had been before him."

M. Quintin was about to go to Vienna. He proposed to descend the Iser as far as Passau on one of the rafts by which the country people carried their wood to market in Vienna. Little huts or shelters were constructed on these rafts and made very convenient for travellers. The daughter was taken by surprise, one morning, by finding herself with her father, M. Quintin, and servants, on one of these rafts, on which a hut had been constructed for her, floating down the river. They carried also a curiously constructed Russian carriage belonging to the Count. They descended the Iser to its confluence with the Inn and the Danube ; and there, bidding adieu to their friend, they took post-horses on their way to Salzburg to see

the famous salt-mines, which her father had never visited.
They entered the mines, and examined the processes of
digging, manufacture, *caving*, or bracing the passages,
and purifying the air. They also visited Berchtes-
garden to see what was then the most famous toy-
manufactory.

On her father's appointment as Minister Plenipotentiary from Bavaria to the Court of Great Britain,
in which office he thought he should be received, he
quitted Munich, taking her with him. She paid her
last respects to the Elector and Electrice, and to her
father's and her own many friends. Of two of her
friends, she says, she had already taken a long farewell
in her heart. The Countess Nogarola she never saw
again, though she continued to correspond with her till
the death of that lady, not many years after. As to
Count Taxis, we must have her own words.

" On our second day's journey, we having stopped at an inn,
as we were getting into the carriage to pursue our way, Count
Taxis came up post-haste on horseback to meet us. Two
minutes later, and we should have been gone. The Count bid
us both farewell, but in different ways. With my father a
respectful bow and shake of the hand; with me, a paper left
in my hand. It was a great event; for never had I before the
honor of receiving a line from him or from any one else, for a
certainty, of that nature. As I already had had my ears boxed on
account of this gentleman, I took care not to expose the letter.
But how to wait till night before reading it? For we were to
make no other stop during the day. I was compelled thus to
do, and had all the time, in consequence, to ruminate on the
subject of the letter.

" Taking leave of friends being of a melancholy nature, I
took it for granted the tenor of this letter would wear that impression. I was several times nearly affected to tears, to think

what must have been the Count's feelings. I only flattered myself that he attributed things to their right causes, and did not blame me. But the moment at length arrived for me to read the letter, and what was my surprise, on reading it, to find only a few gay farewell lines, with neither regrets nor melancholy! Had he not himself given me the letter, I should not have believed he wrote it. The only thing bordering on civility was, that the Countess told him to cherish the hope of my return, and which method he had adopted.

"In order not to make Count Taxis appear unfriendly or deceiving, as I do not think him so, I must observe that several times, through the Countess, with whom I was in constant correspondence, I had little messages to convince me I was not forgotten. As I shall not again have occasion to speak of this gentleman, I will here mention his unfortunate, untimely end. Both he and Lieutenant Spreti, my father's other *aide-de-camp*, lost their lives in Bonaparte's campaigns in Russia. The Bavarians at that time lost thirty thousand men."

Taking the route through Hamburg, for the same reason which had led them to enter Germany by that way, the party had a most disagreeable, and even perilous journey. The distractions of a state of war had demoralized even the quiet and honest peasantry, multiplying freebooters, and exposing travellers on neglected and dangerous highways and byways to great risks of violence. Robberies and murders were frequent on all sides. The inns and public-houses were wretched and unsafe. The Count, his daughter, and servants were often obliged to sleep in their carriages, in which they met with two accidents that caused them much alarm. On one occasion, passing a bridge without a parapet, the horses, seized with a fit of backing, came near precipitating them over a frightful precipice. While the Count put his head out on one side to warn the coachman, Miss Sarah jumped out safely on the other side. She says her father used often to describe the incident to his friends, as proof that she knew how to take care of herself. As the cost of exchange on London would have caused a heavy loss on paper money, the Count was obliged to take with him a bag of coin so heavy as to require aid from others to lift it. This was a source of constant anxiety, whether in the carriage, by day or night, or when taken into a room at an inn.

They passed safely through all their perils, and to the delight of the young lady, who, though she had enjoyed much in Germany, was a dear lover of England, they reached London. The father, on finding that as a born British subject he could not be received in a diplomatic capacity, decided not to return to Bavaria, where war and distraction were so unfavorable to the pursuits which now chiefly engaged him. Not being in good health, he purchased a villa at Brompton Row, Knightsbridge, near London, because of its salubrious situation, and here his daughter lived with him quite happily for a year. While the Count was busying himself with the plan and initiation of the Royal Institution, and in all the intercourse, social and scientific, with the most distinguished men in and around the capital which was so freely open to him, his daughter had her own resources. She describes with great animation her delight in English comforts, refinements, and festivities. Especially is she ardent and eloquent in her tribute to Lady Palmerston as a lovely woman, a faithful mother, and a notable housekeeper. Miss Sarah was cordially received at the three residences of Lord Palmerston, — Hanover Square, Broadlands, and Sheene. At Broadlands, during the Christ-

mas festivities, she says that she " met some of the first
people in the world," and the only language which she
can find adequate for describing the way in which Lady
Palmerston did the honors is by saying "that in all
probability there was nothing else to be found to match
it in the whole world."

But the daughter's troubles in affairs of the heart
seem to have in some degree qualified her enjoyment
in England likewise, as she and her father were not in
accord about any tentative suitors.   The following account has an air of candor, and engages a degree of
sympathy for Miss Sarah, now in her twenty-fifth year.

" When my father was engaged in dining out where he could
not take me, Sir Charles Blagden, one of his most intimate
associates, would be invited to dine with me, *en tête-à-tête*, i. e.
in friendly chat. Sir Charles was a bachelor, not so old as
my father, but not young. After we went to Germany, he
wrote to my father to say that he liked me well enough to make
a wife of me, requesting that favor.

" My father was ingenious. He did not wish it, yet how
affront such a friend ! His proceedings were thus: He would
often turn the conversation on this gentleman, relating anecdotes not of a nature to enchant a young person, without saying
that he had written about me. After which, the truth coming
out, I was desired to give my decision. I, of course, was
shocked that the thing should be mentioned. This did not
prevent all three of us being excellent friends when we met
again. Sir Charles told me one day he liked me better than
he did my father, which I thought a great compliment. My
father was not a bit jealous. He would say we were just alike.
We were all happy, had we but have known it. But we were
to separate, — I returning to America ; my father going to
France, where he married Madame Lavoisier, who did not
wish a daughter-in-law, which kept me in America."

Before she left her father she describes him as suffering much from ill health. He put himself under the care of the celebrated Dr. Ash, and had recourse to the waters of various mineral springs. He altered and fitted up his house at Brompton in such an ingenious way, and with such contrivances and arrangements, as to make it an attraction for many curious persons to visit. The daughter's return to America at this time was not caused, as the last extract would seem to imply, by·her father's second marriage, which did not take place till some years subsequently. He was offered a very honorable position and employment in England, but felt bound, after this residence there of a year, to return to Germany.

The appointment of Envoy Extraordinary and Minister Plenipotentiary from Bavaria to the Court of London, which Count Rumford had received from the Elector, was an honor conferred upon him for several reasons. The zeal and activity with which the Count had devoted himself to so many forms of public service had again seriously overtasked him, and had greatly impaired his health. He had also encountered much and very disagreeable opposition from jealous or interested parties, the effects of which began to tell painfully on his temper and cheerfulness of spirits. It is noticeable, however, as a marked and praiseworthy quality in his character, that he made but infrequent, and then always guarded and dignified, reference to the public or private enmities excited against him by the splendid success of his career and the efficient working of his schemes. When thwarted in one of them, he makes this general reference to such opposition, in speaking of " the malicious insinuations of persons who, from motives too obvious, took great pains to render abortive every public undertaking in which I have been engaged." But the confidence, esteem, and gratitude of the Elector never failed him. While desirous that he should not succumb under such severe work, nor be crossed and irritated by opposition, the Elector was intent upon securing for him the rest and relief of which he had need without depriving himself entirely of the Count's services. The latter, as we have seen, taking his daughter with him, went to England, arriving in London near the end of September, 1798, in the full belief that he would be received in his high diplomatic office. But the fact of his birth as a British subject, which had heretofore been so signal a condition of his advancement, now withstood the gratification of his ambition. Usage did not permit that a native subject of the king of England should be accredited as a foreign minister.

It had proved a severe trial of English magnanimity to accept that arch-rebel John Adams in his diplomatic capacity from the new American people. But the inevitable condition was that the United States could have no representative at the British Court, at least for a generation to come, unless the mother country would receive as such a born subject of the realm.

It would have presented a yet more curious problem for the British government, if Rumford, on a temporary visit to his native country, had been recognized as a citizen, and then sent in a diplomatic capacity to the Court of St. James.

As this diplomatic appointment was of itself a proud distinction, and one of the most interesting incidents in Count Rumford's singularly eminent career; and as the honor of the office, with the prospective social position which it would secure him, was evidently highly prized by him, as also the discomfiture which he experienced in his disappointment was equally great, — I am glad to be able to give an authentic statement of particulars concerning it.*

The Elector of Bavaria had offered the position of Minister at the English court to Count Rumford as the successor of Count Haslang, who had retired after having held the office very many years. The appointment of Rumford being known in England before his arrival, Lord Grenville, on the 14th of September, 1798, sent a despatch to the Hon. Arthur Paget, the English Minister at Munich, as follows : —

[*Copy.*]

" Downing Street, Sept' 14, 1798.

" Honble Arthur Paget.

" Sir, — His Majesty has seen, with some surprise, in the late dispatches from Mr Shepherd, which I have had the honour to lay before him, that the Elector of Bavaria has nominated Count Rumford to succeed Count Haslang as His Electoral Highness's Minister at this Court. It is, I apprehend, a thing if not wholly unprecedented, at least extremely unusual, to appoint a subject of the Country to reside at the Court of his natural Sovereign in the character of Minister from a Foreign Prince. And I am to direct you to lose no time in apprizing the Ministers of his Electoral Highness that such an appointment, in the person of Count Rumford, would be by no means agreeable to His Majesty, and that His Majesty relies, therefore, on the friendship and good understanding which has always hitherto subsisted between Himself and the Elector of Bavaria, that His Highness will have no hesitation in withdrawing it, and

---

* I am indebted to the kindness of Dr. H. Bence Jones in procuring for me from the late Lord Clarendon, but a few days before his decease, copies of papers from the Foreign Office relating to this incident.

nominating as His Minister some Person to whom the objection here stated does not apply.

"There cannot be the least doubt but that the Elector will consent to this request the moment that it is suggested, and that the reasons upon which it is founded are pointed out to his observation. But should there unexpectedly arise any difficulty about a compliance with a Request which His Majesty is so clearly warranted in making, I am to direct you, in the last Resort, to state in distinct terms that His Majesty will by no means consent to receive Count Rumford in the character which has been assigned to him.

"Should anything be said of the Harshness of requiring the recall of a Minister already appointed, and actually set out (as Count Rumford is understood to be) for the place of his destination, you will not fail to answer, that, had the usual notification of an Intention to appoint a new Minister to this Court been previously made here, and the name of the person destined to his Employment mentioned to His Majesty (an attention which might reasonably have been Expected upon an appointment so unusual in its circumstances) His Majesty would then have been able to state his objection without risking any *Eclat*, or appearing to compromise the personal character of the Gentleman whom His Majesty declines receiving.

"Instructions are sent (by the Same Post with this letter) to Sir James Craufurd at Hamburgh to communicate privately to Count Rumford, on his arrival at that place, the nature of the Representation which you are directed to make at Munich, and to dissuade him from prosecuting his journey to England.

"In addition to the general arguments against this appointment, as applying to any Person, a subject of His Majesty, you will observe that the circumstances of Count Rumford's having heretofore filled a confidential Situation (that of Under-Secretary of State in the American Department) under His Majesty's Gov' makes the appointment in his Person peculiarly improper and objectionable."

The next day Lord Grenville addressed to Count

Haslang, late Bavarian Minister, a note in French, of which the following is a translation: —

"DOWNING STREET, 15th September, 1798.

"Lord Grenville presents his compliments to Count Haslang, and has the honour to assure him of the pleasure with which he learns that the matter in question, referred to in the note of the Count, has been disposed of to his satisfaction.

"Lord Grenville desires, likewise, to express to the Count his regrets at having been deprived of the opportunity of communicating with him on affairs of the court. By the note which, on account of the absence of the Count, Lord Grenville sent to his house, he had invited him to call upon him in order that Lord Grenville might impart to him the decision of his Majesty on the subject of the nomination of Count Rumford. But, Count Haslang being absent, the same communication has been made directly to Count Rumford."

[*Copy.*]

[Count Rumford to Lord Grenville.]

"MY LORD, — Notwithstanding the information, and the intimation your Lordship has caused to be communicated to me by Mr. Canning, Under-Secretary of State in the Department of Foreign Affairs, I conceive it to be my duty formally to notify to your Lordship that His most Serene Electoral Highness, the Elector Palatine, Reigning Duke of Bavaria, my most gracious Master, having been pleased to appoint me to be His Envoy Extraordinary and Minister Plenipotentiary at the Court of His Majesty the King of Great Britain, I have come to England in consequence of that appointment, and of the Orders and Instructions of His most Serene Electoral Highness; and am charged with a Letter from His most Serene Electoral Highness to the King; which Letter, agreeably to the Instructions I have received, I ought to endeavour to obtain permission to deliver to His Majesty with my own hands.

"Being thus circumstanced, your Lordship will, no doubt, see

22

the propriety and the necessity of my asking an Audience or personal interview with your Lordship, which I now do, in order that I may have an Opportunity of stating to your Lordship more fully the objects of the Mission with which I am charged, and of receiving from your Lordship such information on that subject as may enable me to give a clear, authentic, and satisfactory account of the success of that Mission to the Sovereign who has deigned to entrust me with the management of his Affairs at this Court.

"Requesting that your Lordship would be pleased to inform me when and where I may have the honour of waiting on you,

"I have the honour, &c.

[Signed]   "RUMFORD.

"London, 19th September, 1798.

[*Copy.*]

[Lord Grenville to Count Rumford.]

"Downing Street, Sep" 21st, 1798.

"Count Rumford.

"Sir, — In conformity to the Communication which Mr. Canning has already made to you, I have now the honour to enclose an extract of the Instruction which, by His Majesty's command, I transmitted to Mr. Paget immediately on His Majesty's receiving the Information of your nomination to succeed Count Haslang.

"You will not fail to observe that the Representation which Mr. Paget was directed to make on this Subject rested wholly on the circumstance of the decisive objection which His Majesty feels against receiving as a public Minister accredited from Another Sovereign, a Person who is not only a subject of His Majesty, but has actually been employed in a Confidential situation under His Majesty's Governm'. His Majesty had graciously been pleased to express His wish that this Intimation should reach you before you set out for England, in order to avoid the Inconvenience to which you might otherwise be exposed. With this View the Instruction sent to Mr. Paget was accompanied by a Despatch transmitted by the same post to Hamburgh, in which

His Majesty's Minister at that place was directed to communicate to you privately, on your arrival there, the nature of the Representation to be made by Mr. Paget.

"As this course has been precluded by your actual arrival in London, and as you have been apprized here of the circumstance in question, I conceive it will be more agreeable to you that the substance of the Representation with which Mr. Paget was charged, should be transmitted by you to the Elector, rather than thro' any other channel. With this view I shall acquaint Mr. Paget, that he may forbear to execute his Instructions, except in so far as relates to the assurances to be given to H. E. H. of His Majesty's constant and Invariable Friendship, & of His Willingness to receive as His Electoral Highness's Minister any Person whose nomination is not liable to objections as strong as those which I have already stated."

[*Copy.*]

"Downing Street, Sept' 21, 1798.

"Honble Arthur Paget.

"Sir, — Count Rumford being arrived in London and having been apprized of the objections which His Majesty had stated to receiving him in the Character of Minister from the Elector of Bavaria; and having undertaken to transmit to His Electoral Highness a statement of the grounds upon which these objections are founded, I have written to him a letter, a copy of which I herewith Inclose, and in conformity to which you will be pleased to regulate your conduct on the subject of the Instructions contained in my Dispatch of the 14th Instant.

Count Rumford was then forty-five years old. A portrait in oil, now in the possession of Joseph B. Walker, of Concord, N. H., had been taken of him at or about that time. It presents a man of fine appearance, with imposing presence and beautiful features. An engraving from it serves as the frontispiece to this volume.

Of course, therefore, the Count never exercised the

diplomatic office, but lived as a private person. He acted, however, as the agent of Charles Theodore, the Elector, and when another minister was appointed was on most intimate terms with him. The Bavarian army, then in the interest of Austria, was in the pay of England. I shall have occasion by and by to quote the statement of the daughter that her father felt deeply chagrined at the foiling of his passion for official distinction experienced in his respectful rejection as the Bavarian ambassador. That he soon found full occupation in an enterprise which, if for the time it attached to him less of personal distinction, was to insure a permanent honor to his name, may have decided him to remain in England and bear his disappointment. Probably he learned even before his arrival that there was an obstacle to his reception in the character in which he came, for, as will appear from a letter of his, soon to be given, he proposed at this time to make another effort to visit America.

The following letters were addressed to him by Colonel Baldwin on dates previous to his leaving Munich.

"WOBURN, July 31, 1798.

"MY DEAR COUNT, — Mr. Welsh, a son of Dr. Welsh of Boston, sets out to-morrow morning for Newburyport, from whence he expects to embark for ——, in order to proceed to Berlin, the capital of the Prussian dominions, where he is to officiate as secretary to the Hon. Mr. Adams, the American Minister at that court.

"The young gentleman is of a very respectable family and sustains an exceedingly good character. He will be the bearer of a number of letters to you and the Countess, your daughter, to whose attention I beg leave to recommend him, and any civility with which you may please to notice him will add to the numerous favors which I have already received. I am, with the greatest respect and esteem,

" Your most obedient and very humble servant,

" LOAMMI BALDWIN.

" Sir Benjamin, Count of Rumford."

" Woburn, July 31, 1798.

" My dear Count, — I have time by Mr. Welsh just to acknowledge the receipt of your favors of the 17th of December and the 7th of January last. Mr. Welsh, whom I have taken the liberty to recommend to your notice, will be the bearer of this and a number of other letters which should have been forwarded long ago, but I must beg you to excuse it. For reasons which I shall give you at another time, they have been delayed.

" I have, agreeably to your desire, attended to the various objects you have mentioned in your letter of the 17th of December last, and have them all in train, and hope soon to effect them agreeably to your wishes. I happened to see Mr. Rolfe as he was on a journey, and had a pretty full conversation with him. He seems desirous of meeting you on the terms proposed, and acknowledged them generous, yet seemed to hesitate a little on account of some administration accounts with Judge Walker. However, he concluded to take a little more time to consider and write me, but has not done it yet.

" I have seen Judge Walker since. He tells me that the accounts referred to above will be closed the beginning of August next. He is very willing to do everything you wish on his part, but thinks your daughter should give him some kind of a discharge when the business is closed.

" I have no doubt, from what I learn from those gentlemen of Concord whom I have conversed with on the subject of the Countess of Rumford's benevolent donation, but that it will be most cordially received. The Mrs. Nowell whom you mention is dead. Your dear mother was with us here last week, in fine health for a lady of her years, and looks just as she used to do. She desires to be remembered to you and your daughter. Friends in general well.

"I shall write you more fully, and I hope more satisfactorily, in a few days. Give my love to the Countess, and tell her that I thank her most sincerely for her successful endeavor in persuading her dear father to make a visit to his native country. We long for the time to come that we may see him here. We rejoice to hear the resolution you have taken, and sincerely hope no event will happen to prevent it.

"I am, with much respect, my dear Count,

"Your most obedient and very humble servant,

"LOAMMI BALDWIN.

"Sir Benjamin, Count Rumford."

Colonel Baldwin, in a business letter, communicated to Count Rumford's mother, now advanced far in years, the prospect of seeing her son in his native country. She was then residing with her husband, in Flintstown, Me.

"Woburn, August 23, 1798.

"Dear Madam, — I have just received instructions from your son, the Count of Rumford, to draw on his agents, Sir Robert Herries & Co., in London, for £30 sterling, it being for the amount of his daughter Sarah's draft on Edward Armstrong, Esq., his former agent, dated October 23, 1795, that was protested, &c. Which bills, or the money therefor, together with another set, dated the 26th day of March last of the same amount, are now ready to be delivered to you or your order, agreeably to the provision your son has made. I hope you will soon have a convenient opportunity to send for it, as I know of none at present by which I can send to you.

"I have lately received communications dated the 17th December, 1797, from the Count, upon various subjects, one of which is respecting a visit to America that he with his daughter proposes to make in about fifteen or sixteen months from the date of his letter, if peace shall be restored and the state of affairs in Europe will admit of it, which he expects to be the case. I pray God to grant it may be so.

" Mrs. Baldwin joins with me in love and respects to you and Mr. Pierce, and all your children.

" I am, dear madam,

" Your obedient, and very humble servant,

"LOAMMI BALDWIN.

" Mrs. Ruth Pierce."

At the time of writing the following letter, it would seem that Count Rumford, though he had been in England but a week, must have been made aware that the objections to his reception as the Bavarian Ambassador could not be removed ; for he could hardly have contemplated even a visit to America, unless he had looked for but a brief tenure of office, if allowed to hold it.

" London, 28th Sept., 1798.

" My Dear Sir, — I arrived in this City last week from Germany, and I expect to be able to remain here several months.   I have, indeed, some hopes of being able to pay you a visit in America in the Spring.   But these hopes, though apparently well founded, may easily be disappointed, for there are several events, none of which are very improbable, that would render it impossible for me to be absent from Europe next year. It is, however, my fixed intention to pay a visit to my friends in America as soon as ever it shall be in my power, which most probably will be in the course of a year or two.   I have even a scheme of forming for myself a little quiet retreat in that country, to which I can retire at some future period, and spend the evening of my life.   Perhaps you may be so good as to assist me in carrying this plan into execution.   As I am not wealthy, and prefer comfort to splendour, I shall not want anything magnificent.   From forty to one hundred Acres of good land, with wood and water belonging to it, if possible in a retired situation, from one to four miles from Cambridge, with or without a neat, comfortable house upon it, would satisfy all my wishes.

"Do you know of anything of this description that is to be bought?   And how much would it cost?   I should want nothing from the land but pleasure-grounds, and grass for my cows and horses, and extensive kitchen garden and fruit garden.   I should wish much for a few acres of wood, and also for a stream of fresh water, or for a large Pond, or the neighbourhood of one, for without shady trees and water there can be no rural beauty. What is land an Acre in the situation above mentioned?   What near the road?   What at the distance of half a mile from it? What are the taxes I should pay in your country?   Could I, as a stranger, purchase and hold an Estate?   I should be much obliged to you, my Dear Sir, if you would give me information and advice on these various subjects.   I need not tell you how much it would tend to increase my enjoyments to live in your neighbourhood.   My Daughter is quite enchanted with the scheme, and never ceases to urge me to execute it as soon as possible, and on her account I am anxious to engage in it.   I wish to leave her *a home*, something immoveable that she may call her own, as well as the means of subsistence, at my death. And I am not surprised nor displeased to find that she prefers her native country to every other.

"To own the truth, I am quite of her opinion on that subject.   She desires her best compliments to you and to your Lady.   She is very grateful to you for all your goodness to her. It is now a great while indeed since I heard from you.   Pray write me soon, and believe me, ever,

"Yours most affectionately,

"RUMFORD.

"To the Honble LOAMMI BALDWIN, Esq.

"When you write to me, please to address your Letters thus : —

"Count Rumford, to the Care of Messrs. Herries, Farquhar, & Co., Bankers, St. James St., London."

("Received at Woburn, by hand of Dr. Walter.")

A letter written by Miss Sarah at this time shows

her keenness of discernment, and her frankness in expressing the results of it.

"London, 24th October, 1798.
Brompton Row.

" MY DEAR Mrs. BALDWIN, — Though I was very sorry and much disappointed at not hearing from you sooner, yet your letter, when it did arrive, gave me much pleasure. I am even disposed to make every apology for your long silence you could wish. Indeed, I think the situation in which you are, and the variety of domestic affairs which you have to take up your time and attention, is a sufficient excuse for not writing sooner. I am glad, however, to hear that your health is good, as likewise the health of that said friend of yours, — who is very naughty to be absent so much, and leave all the cares of the family to you. Oh! those gentlemen of business seem odd things to us who have no further ideas of riches and honor and glory than a decent comfortable living and a good reputation.

" But I should not venture to write in this manner to you did I not perfectly remember that we used to be just of the same opinion upon these subjects. I do not know what you have done, but I have not yet found reason to alter my opinion; and, to let you into a secret, I have since learned to know more about the consequences of living with a man of business. I have found a very good father, but who is likewise prodigiously occupied in public affairs. Had I acquired his fortune and half his renown (for between you and me, let me tell you that neither Colonel Baldwin nor my father is an enemy to a little well-deserved renown), I should think myself happy, and should go and settle down in some little corner of the world, and endeavor to enjoy the fruits of my labor.

" Believe me your most affectionate and sincere friend,
" S. RUMFORD.

" Mrs. BALDWIN, care of LOAMMI BALDWIN, Esq."

The revival and circulation in America of the report that Count Rumford, supposed to have finally left the service of Bavaria, intended to return to his native country, met here a hearty interest with his many friends. He had already begun to receive in America marks of public regard. Judge Tudor, one of the founders of the Massachusetts Historical Society, the oldest in the country, having nominated Count Rumford as a corresponding member, he was elected as such at a meeting of the Society on January 30, 1798. The following cordial letter was received from him in response, and having been read at a meeting of the Society on July 19, 1798, by the Corresponding Secretary, it was voted that it be published in one of the Boston papers, and that a set of the Collections of the Society, handsomely bound in four volumes, be sent to the Count. Of this correspondence the admiring Pictet writes : " The Historical Society of Massachusetts, in choosing the Count to membership, expressed to him, through its President, their unanimous desire to see him return to his own country and settle among them. His answer, which may be read in the American papers of the time, was much admired. I regret that I cannot transcribe it."

I am glad that I can transcribe the letter from the files of the Society as follows : —

" REVEREND SIR, — I have had the pleasure to receive your letter of the 31st January, in which you inform me of my having been elected a Member of the Massachusetts Historical Society. I request, Sir, that you would present my best thanks to that respectable body for the honor they have done me, and at the same time assure them that I feel myself highly flattered by this distinguished mark of their regard and esteem.

" Though my present situation and connections must for the present, and may perhaps for ever, prevent my having the satisfaction of co-operating with the Society in the furtherance of their interesting and useful researches, yet I shall have much pleasure in contemplating, even at this great distance, the fruits of their meritorious exertions; and shall feel no small degree of pride in seeing myself enrolled in the same list with those generous benefactors of future generations whose names will go down to posterity with the treasures they are collecting.

"There are few things that could afford me so much heartfelt satisfaction as to be able to avail myself of the kind invitation of the Society to come and take my place among them. I have ever loved my native country with the fondest affection; and the liberality I have experienced from my Countrymen — their moderation in success, and their consummate prudence in the use of their Independence, have attached me to them by all the ties of Gratitude, Esteem, and Admiration.

"Requesting that you, Sir, would accept my thanks for the flattering manner in which you have conveyed to me the Resolution of the Society, I have the honor to be, with sincere Regard and Esteem,

"Your much obliged and most obedient Servant,

"RUMFORD.

"Munich, 11 April, 1798.

"The Rev. Jeremy Belknap, D.D., Secretary to
the Massachusetts Historical Society."

Another yet more gratifying recognition of the fact that whatever of reproach had rested on his name in his native country was now removed, was received by Count Rumford at this time. The representation generally made in the various biographical sketches of him — following the statement first put in print by Pictet — is that he was solicited by the government of the United States to return here, and that the request was accompanied by the offer of a place in its pay and service. Thus Pictet, whom we must regard as relating the communication made to him by his friend, says : —

"Meanwhile the report was circulated in America that he had finally left Bavaria, and the government of the United States, through the American Envoy at London, addressed to him a formal and official invitation to return to his native country, where an honorable establishment would be provided for him. The offer was accompanied by the most flattering assurances of consideration and confidence."

It is only after considerable inquiry and search given to the investigation of the facts connected with this interesting subject that I have succeeded in reaching an authentic and clear account of them from original, unprinted documents. I had thought it quite unlikely that the initiative step was taken by the government of the United States in inviting the return of Count Rumford to America, and in connecting with the invitation the proffer of a place in the public service. True, the great and well-deserved fame which the Count had attained in Europe, and which was not diminished, however it may have been qualified, as it reached America, might have seemed to justify the general government in overriding State enactments by inviting home a proscribed citizen. But it was none the less a fact that Count Rumford was under a legal disability. He had been proscribed as having been hostile to the American cause when he left the country, and he had added to his original offence the graver one of having guided the counsels and commanded the forces of the enemy. The treaty of peace between Great Britain and America pledged the general government to appeal to the State governments for a degree of leniency toward the outlawed Tories; but this condition fell short of restoring citizenship, or a right to return here to the proscribed. We have seen, too, that the Count, in a letter to Colonel Baldwin, had not forgotten the disability under which he lay. The natural inference, therefore, was that whatever action was had by the government of the United States in the case of the Count was prompted by some expression or proposition of his own.

The Hon. Charles Sumner, Senator of Massachusetts, and Chairman of the Senate Committee on Foreign Affairs, was kind enough, at my request, to institute a search in the records of the State Department at Washington, for the purpose of finding, if there were such, any official documents of the tenor above described. He informs me that no such documents appear. But inquiry in another direction, suggested by the statement of Pictet, that the alleged invitation was made to Rumford through the American Envoy at London, has enabled me to give a full account of the matter.

Count Rumford, as I have said, became, after the close of the war of the Revolution, a most warm and faithful friend of his native country, holding correspondence with many of its citizens, to whom he communicated his plans, and sent his works, and generously dividing among its literary and scientific institutions his benevolent endowments. He also, when in England, and afterwards when in France, maintained the closest social relations with Americans resident in those countries either as officials of our government or in private life. Among his most intimate friends in London at this time were the Hon. Rufus King and the Hon. Christopher Gore. The former was the American Ambassador. Mr. Gore, afterwards Governor of

Massachusetts, had been commissioned in 1796, with Pinckney and Trumbull to represent American claims for British spoliations on our commerce. For this purpose he was abroad eight years, being the confidential friend of Mr. King, who left him as American *Chargé d'Affaires* in London, on his return home in 1803. The Count's intercourse with these two gentlemen led to the results which are stated with substantial correctness by Pictet. No publication has yet been made of the official papers of the Hon. Rufus King, though his son, the late much-honored President of Columbia College, New York, was pledged to the undertaking. To my application to a grandson of the ambassador, Mr. Charles R. King, of Andalusia, Buck's County, Pennsylvania, I received a most satisfactory reply, the tenor of which is indicated by the following extract from his letter to me:—

"The search among my grandfather's papers for correspondence with Count Rumford has proved more successful than at one time I supposed would be the case. Enclosed with this you will find copies of letters referring to the interesting facts respecting which you desired information, and which I think have never been published.

"The letter of Rufus King to Colonel Pickering, of the 8th December, 1798, shows clearly the reasons which moved Count Rumford to desire to leave England and to return to this country ; and the suggestion that he should be cordially welcomed here drew from James McHenry, the Secretary at War, an answer of the 3d July, 1799 (which I am sorry to say, I cannot find), containing, as permitted by President Adams, the offer to the Count of the Superintendence of the Military Academy and of Inspector-General of Artillery. The letters of King and Rumford show clearly the deep regard and friendship they had for each other, and the earnest desire of both to advance the welfare of their native country, &c., &c."

The following correspondence, copied from the originals, is of great interest : —

[*Copy*.]

"London, December 8, 1798.

"Dear Sir, — Count Rumford, late Sir Benjamin Thompson, whose name and history are probably known to you, and whose talents and services have procured the most beneficial Establishments and reforms in Bavaria, was lately named by the Elector to be his Minister at this Court. On his arrival he has been informed, that, being a British Subject, it was contrary to usage to receive him, and that therefore he could not be acknowledged. The intrigues and opposition against which he had for some years made head in Bavaria probably made him desire the mission to England. The refusal that he has here met with has decided him to return and settle himself in America. He proposes to establish himself at or near Cambridge, to live there in the character of a German Count, to renounce all political Expectations, and devote himself to literary pursuits. His connections in this country are strictly literary, and his knowledge, particularly in the Military Department, may be of great use to us. The Count is well acquainted with and has had much experience in the establishment of Cannon Foundries; that which he established in Bavaria is spoken of in very high terms, as well as certain improvements that he has introduced in the mounting of flying Artillery.

He possesses an extensive Military Library, and assures me that he wishes nothing more than to be useful to our Country. I make this Communication by his desire, and my wish is that he may be well received, as I am persuaded that his Principles are good, and his talents and information uncommonly extensive. It is possible that attempts may be made to misrepresent his political opinions ; from the enquiry that I have made on this head, I am convinced that his political sentiments are correct.

" Be good enough to communicate this letter to the President.

" With great respect and esteem, I have the honor to be, dear sir,

" Yours faithfully,

"RUFUS KING.

" COLONEL PICKERING."   (Secretary of State.)

"LONDON, March 10, 1799.

" DEAR SIR, — I annex a copy of a letter from Count Rumford, formerly Sir Benjamin Thompson, to me upon a subject somewhat interesting. I am persuaded that the establishment of an American Military Academy is an object of the first importance to us. Count Rumford has founded one in Bavaria that enjoys a very high reputation, and I have reason to believe that he would receive very great pleasure in communicating to us the results of his Experience on this subject. I have not seen his Military Books, Drawings, &c., but am informed that that they are inestimable. The cannon he proposes to make a present of to the United States is a perfect Model, and will serve to assist us in the casting and mounting of our Field Artillery. I have sent a copy of the Count's letter likewise to Col. Pickering, and must wait for the President's instructions through him or you in what manner I shall answer it. Count Rumford proposes to return with the view of residing part of his time in his native Country. On this subject I take the Liberty to refer you to a letter from me to Col. Pickering, and will only add, that it would undoubtedly be encouraging and grateful to him to receive an assurance from the President through me, or in any other way, that he will be received in a kind and friendly manner. . . . . .

" With sincere esteem and respect,

"RUFUS KING.

"JAMES McHENRY, ESQ."

[*Copy.*]

"Dear Sir, — I send you herewith a small Pamphlet which will explain to you the Causes which have rendered it impossible for me to go to America this Spring as I had intended. I have not, however, given over all ideas of visiting that Country at some future period ; very far from it, I really hope and expect to be able to go there next Spring, and will most certainly do so, if it should be possible, provided you should continue to advise it, and to encourage me with the hopes of a kind reception.

"I beg you would do me the honor to present one of the enclosed Pamphlets to his Excellency the President of the United States, and accompany it with my best Respects and most cordial wishes for his health and happiness and for the prosperity of the United States.

"The Model of a Field-Piece on a new, and I believe on an improved construction, which I have destined as a Present to the United States, I shall pack up and send to you in order to its being shipped for America as soon as I shall get it from His Royal Highness the Duke of York, who has desired to have a copy of it.

"You will recollect that in a conversation we had at your house on the great importance to the United States of the speedy Establishment of a Military School or academy, I took the liberty to say that to assist in the establishment of so useful an Institution I should be happy to be permitted to make a present to the Academy, of my collection of Military Books, Plans, Drawings, and Models. I now repeat this offer, and with a request to you that you would make it known to the Executive Government of the United States, and that you would let me know as soon as may be convenient whether this offer will be accepted.

"I have the honor to be, with the most sincere regard and esteem, Dear Sir,

"Your most obedient and most faithful servant,

"RUMFORD.

"Brompton Row, 13 March, 1799.

"His Excellency Rufus King, Envoy Extraordinary and Minister Plenipotentiary of the United States, &c."

[*Copy.*]

"London, Sept. 8, 1799.

"Dear Sir, — I have more than once expressed to you a wish that you might find leisure, as well as inclination, to revisit your native Country, where, I have been persuaded, you would meet with a friendly and cordial reception, and by your presence and advice might be of great advantage to our public institutions, the establishment of which, upon approved principles, is an object of the highest consequence. I am happy that I have it in my power to assure you that I have not been mistaken in these sentiments, and it affords me peculiar satisfaction to execute the order that I have lately received from my Government to invite you in its name to return and reside among us, and to propose to you to enter into the American Service.

"In the course of the last year we have made provision for the institution of a Military Academy, and we wish to commit its formation to your experience, and its future government to your care. It is not necessary on this occasion to send you a detailed account of our Military establishment, which indeed would be best explained by a reference to the Laws upon which it depends; these are in my possession, and shall be put into your hands if you desire it. In addition to the Superintendence of the Military Academy, I am authorized to offer to you the appointment of Inspector-General of the Artillery of the United States, and we shall, moreover, be disposed to give to you such rank and emoluments, consistent with existing provisions, and with what has already been settled upon the former of these heads, as would be likely to afford you satisfaction, and to secure to us the advantages of your service.

"If your engagements will allow of your entering into our service, which I sincerely hope may be the case, I will ask the favor of you to take an early opportunity of signifying the same to me, in order that we may proceed to further and more particular explanations upon the subject.

"With the greatest consideration and esteem, I have the honor to be, Dear Sir,

　　　　　　"Your obedient and faithful servant,

[Signed]　　　　　　　　　　　　"RUFUS KING.

"Count Rumford, &c., &c., &c."

[Count Rumford's reply.]

"Brompton, 12 Sept 1799.

"DEAR SIR, — I am to acknowledge the receipt of your Excellency's most flattering letter of the 8th inst., the perusal of which has filled my mind with sentiments much more easy to be conceived than expressed.

"I am deeply sensible of the honor that has been conferred upon me by the Government of the United States, by the kind invitation they have sent me to come and reside in my native Country, and also by the other distinguished and most flattering proofs of their confidence and esteem with which that invitation has been accompanied.

"Nothing could have afforded me so much satisfaction as to have had it in my power to have given to my liberal and generous countrymen such proof of my sentiments as would in the most public and ostensible manner have evinced, not only my gratitude for the kind attentions I have received from them, but also the ardent desire I feel to assist in promoting the prosperity of my native Country. But engagements which great obligations have rendered sacred and inviolable put it out of my power to dispose of my time and services with that unreserved freedom which would be necessary in order to enable me to accept of those generous offers which the Executive Government of the United States has been pleased to propose to me. But although it is not in my power to dissolve those ties by which I am bound, yet I have no doubt of being able to obtain permission to visit America, and should that permission (which I shall certainly solicit) be granted, I shall take an early opportunity of crossing the Atlantic in order to pay my personal respects to the President of the United States, and to return him my thanks for the distinguished honor he has been pleased to confer on me.

"I cannot finish this letter without requesting that you, Sir, would accept my best acknowledgments for the many civilities I have received from you, and more especially for the very polite manner in which you have been so good as to communicate to me the favorable sentiments of the Government of the United States with respect to me.

" With the most sincere wishes for the Prosperity of the United States, I have the honor to be, Sir,

" Your Excellency's most obedient Humble Servant,
" RUMFORD.

" His Excellency Rufus King, Envoy Extraordinary and
Minister Plenipotentiary of the United States
at the Court of London."

[*Copy.*]
" London, Sep. 7, 1799.

" Dear Sir, — I have duly received your Letter of the 3d of July, respecting Count Rumford. We have had some conversation upon the subject, which will be resumed. I, however, conclude from what has already passed, that, though much gratified with the offer, he will wisely decline accepting it. I shall hereafter send you a more exact report upon this subject.

" The Count's Letter to you accompanying the Models of the Field-Piece and ammunition-waggon was written and sent to me before he had any knowledge of the subject of your letter of the 3d of July. I hope we shall not be disappointed in sending you the Boxes which contain these Models by the General Washington, a stout ship now ready to sail for Philadelphia.

" With sincere respect and Esteem, I have the honor to be, Dear Sir,
" Your most obedient servant,
[Signed] " RUFUS KING.

" James McHenry, Esq."

[*Copy.*]

" Dear Sir, — *At length* they have returned the Model of my Field-Piece, though not till after I had repeatedly made application for it. I have repacked it and its Ammunition-Waggon in their deal boxes, and if you will give me leave I will send these two boxes to your house, in order to their being sent *by you* to America.

" Enclosed is the draft of a letter which I send to you for

your opinion of it, requesting that you would make such alterations in it as you may judge to be proper.

"If you think my letter ought to be addressed to any other
Person than the Person proposed, you will tell me so. You
will likewise be so kind as to point out the Person or Persons
to whom the models ought to be presented.

"I was yesterday at Gravesend, and saw my Daughter into
the Boat that carried her on board the Minerva. She has left
England deeply impressed with a sense of the kindness she
experienced from you and from your Lady. Her father joins
her in thanks for these kind attentions, and will ever remain,
my dear Sir,

"Your much obliged and most obedient servant,

"RUMFORD.

"Brompton, Monday morning, 26th August, 1799."

"His Excellency Rufus King, &c., &c."

[*Copy.*]

"Brompton, August 28, 1799.

"Dear Sir,—I have duly received your obliging letter of
the 26th, and herewith return the Draft of a letter that you
propose should accompany the models of the field-piece, &c. I
see nothing to add or alter excepting in the address, which
should be to the Secretary at War, instead of the Sec'y of
State. I have taken the liberty, as you will observe, to make
this alteration with a pencil.

"The models should also be addressed to the Secretary at
War. As we are now shipping a number of articles to Philadelphia, I have desired my Secretary to take measures to remove
the boxes directly from your house to our Agent's in the City, as
soon as he learns by a note from you that they are ready.

"I have lately received a Dispatch from my Government,
the contents of which will not fail to increase those favorable
sentiments you so naturally feel concerning your Native Country, and I permit myself to hope will prove an additional motive
to the execution of your intentions soon to revisit it.

"As I shall be in town in the course of the next week, where

I expect the pleasure of meeting you, we will then enter more particularly upon this agreeable subject. In the mean time I have the honor to be, &c., &c.

"RUFUS KING.

"Count Rumford, &c., &c."

On the 9th of March, 1800, Count Rumford having asked of Mr. King "a list of all the Universities, Academies, Colleges, and other scientific bodies of note and respectability in the United States, together with the names of their Presidents," desiring to send them "our Prospectus," that is, of the Royal Institution of Great Britain (and having received from Mr. King a list of eleven), wrote to Mr. King as follows: —

"Dear Sir, — In consequence of the permission you gave me, I send you herewith Eleven packages, containing each a Copy of the Prospectus, Charter, Ordinances, Bye-Laws and Regulations, of the Royal Institution of Great Britain, accompanied by a letter written by myself, at the desire and in the names of the Managers of the Institution, expressing to the different learned Societies in the United States the wish of the Managers to communicate with them in all things that may tend to the advancement of useful Knowledge.

"It will give me great satisfaction to hear of the safe arrival of these packages at the places of their destination, but still greater to hear that the new establishment for diffusing the knowledge and facilitating the general introduction of new and useful improvements which I have been instrumental in founding in this Metropolis should be thought worthy of imitation in my native Country.

"With my best wishes for the Prosperity of that Country, and with much esteem and regard for its worthy Representative in this,

"I am, my dear Sir, yours most faithfully,

"RUMFORD.

"Royal Institution, 1st June, 1800.

"Rufus King, Esq., &c., &c., &c."

It thus appears that the proposition for his return to America originated with Count Rumford himself and was warmly seconded by his friends. No doubt he would have accepted the honorable trusts thus proffered to him had he not found himself most laboriously and hopefully employed in the founding of that now venerable and honored Institution in London whose origin we are soon to trace.

In addition to the letters given above I copy another, which is the only one known to me referring to this matter, already in print. It was the reply of President John Adams to Secretary McHenry.

" Quincy, 24th June, 1799.

"Sir, — I have received your letter of the 18th, and have read Count Rumford's letter to Mr. King.

"For five or six years past I have been attentive to the character of this gentleman, and have read some of his Essays. From these I have formed an esteem for his genius, talents, enterprise, and benevolence, which will secure him from me, in case of his return to his native country, a reception as kind and civil as it may be in my power to give him. But you know the difficulties those gentlemen have who left the country as he did, either to give or receive entire satisfaction. I should not scruple, however, to give him any of the appointments you mention, and leave it with you to make such proposals to him through Mr. King, within the limits you have drawn in your letter, as you should think fit. I return Mr. King's letter, and enclose one from Mr. William Williams, a very respectable personage, recommending Rufus Tyler to be an officer in the army." *

The Count, not having asked for an office, had one in this circuitous way proffered to him, which, of course, he was under no obligation to accept. Pictet

* Works of President John Adams, Vol. VIII. pp. 660, 661.

follows the assertion quoted above, as to the solicitation made to the Count to return to America and accept an "establishment" by adding this : —

"The Count replied, testifying his profound appreciation of this mark of regard, that engagements rendered sacred and inviolable by great obligations would not allow him to dispose of himself in a way to enable him to accept the offer which had been made to him. Certainly there is no trace, of animosity in these communications."

In his Essay on Gunpowder,* the Count says that he had sent to the United States government, as a present, a model field-piece of his own construction. I have sought information from the War Department at Washington as to any record concerning the receipt or acknowledgment of this gift, or of the military library, drawings, &c. which he proposed to send hither. The Inspector-General, in behalf of the Secretary of War, writes me in reply, that a search has shown " that the records of the Department afford no intelligence concerning Count Rumford. If any papers relating to the subject were ever filed in the War Department, they were no doubt involved in the destruction of the War Office by fire, in the year 1800."

The well-authenticated facts which have thus been laid before the reader concerning an incident in Count Rumford's personal history which had heretofore been so positively stated, but yet so vaguely related, and without proper vouchers, are equally honorable to himself and to those who held high trusts under the American government.

The noble undertaking to which Count Rumford

* Academy's Edition, Vol. I. p. 177.

committed himself with such devotion and zeal, to be fully described in the next chapter, is assigned in the following letter as the cause of his postponing his visit to America.

"LONDON, 14th March, 1799

" MY DEAR FRIEND, — I will not attempt to describe the painful disappointment I feel at being obliged to give up all hopes of seeing you, and the rest of my dear friends in America, this year. A small pamphlet which you will receive with this letter [containing the proposals for the Royal Institution] will acquaint you with the reasons that have induced me to postpone my intended voyage ; and you will, I am confident, agree with me in opinion, that I have done right in sacrificing the pleasure that voyage would have afforded me to the most important objects to which my attention has been called.

" I beg you would be so kind as to give my dear Mother the earliest notice of this change in my plans, and that you would at the same time endeavour to give her just ideas of the very great importance of the undertaking in which I have been called upon to give my assistance ; and show her how impossible it was for me to refuse that assistance, especially as it was asked in a manner so honourable to myself. And as the success of the undertaking will be productive of so much good, and will place me in so distinguished a situation in the eyes of the world, and of Posterity, you will, I am persuaded, find little difficulty in persuading her that I have done perfectly right, and in reconciling her to the disappointment she will naturally feel at not seeing me arrive in America at the time appointed.

" You must give me leave to complain of you, my good friend, for your silence. Several vessels have lately arrived from Boston and have brought letters both for myself and for Sally. But there were none among them . from you. Why should you not embrace the opportunity when you will be sure to find me and my Daughter in London, to take a trip across the Atlantic to see Great Britain ? You shall find a home and

a hearty welcome in my house as long as it may be convenient
to you to stay with us.

" By the by, I much wish you could contrive to bring
P——, &c., &c.

"I am, ever, Yours most Sincerely,
"RUMFORD.
" The Honble Colonel Baldwin, Woburn, &c."

("Rec^d Aug. 27, 1799.")

The following letter from the mother of Count Rumford to Colonel Baldwin, like those of her son relating
to herself and her husband, his step-father, gives full
evidence of the affectionate regards of the parties
concerned.

"Fitustrown, July 18, 1799.

" Dear Sir, — I have waited a long time in anxious ex
pectation of seeing my son, but I fear that I shall be disappointed. I have not called for my bill of exchange, for I
thought if my son was coming to America as early in the year
as he was expected, I would wait until his arrival. I am now
in want of some money. When I was at Boston last, Mr.
Samuel Clapp told me that if I would get my bills drawn in his
name, or in his favor, — I have forgot which, but it was to be in
such a way as that it would be proper for him to indorse them,
— that he would take them and indorse them, and sell them,
and forward the money for me to Portland. If you would be so
kind as to draw my bills in such a way as that it will be proper
for Mr. Clapp to indorse them, and put them into his hands, it
will do me a great favor.

" I have had thoughts of coming to Boston this season, but
my health is so poor that I do not feel able to perform the
journey. My husband is very weak and infirm. If you should
get any intelligence of my son, I desire that you would inform
me of it as soon as possible, for I feel a great anxiety to hear
from him. I fear that something extraordinary is the matter,
that I do not hear from him. Please to give my love and

regards to your family and inquiring friends. Your compliance
with my request in this letter will be a great favor that will be
acknowledged with gratitude by

> " Your obliged friend,
>
>   "RUTH PIERCE.

" Hon. Loammi Baldwin, Esq., Woburn."

Pictet says in reference to the daughter's return to
America at this time: "The contrast between the
pleasant and quiet ways of her own country and the
hubbub of the court of Bavaria, where her father resided, was too severe for her to reconcile and conform herself to it. Her health suffered; she could
breathe only the air of America, and she returned thither.
She kept up with her father a constant and most interesting correspondence, to judge of it by the fragments
which he has allowed me to read."

Sarah took with her the following pleasant letter to
Colonel Baldwin: —

> "Brompton, near London, 24th Aug., 1799.

" My Dear Friend, — I cannot permit my Daughter to
return to America without charging her with a few lines for
my *oldest* friend and school-fellow, the companion of my earliest
youth. In straining my recollection as much as possible, in
order to look back into that dark cloud that covers the early
period of life, I can remember no person distinctly longer than
yourself, except it be my mother. I must therefore consider
you as one of my oldest acquaintances, and I have never ceased
to regard you and to love you as one of my best friends. A
few months ago I flattered myself with the hope of soon seeing
you, but events happened to frustrate those hopes. But though
my voyage to America is postponed, it is by no means abandoned.
On the contrary, I really think it very likely that I shall pay
you a visit next Spring.

" My Daughter will explain to you all the various reasons

that conspired to prevent my accompanying her to America this year. She will likewise tell you how happy you will make me if you would embrace the opportunity now, while I am on the spot, of visiting England. I can offer you a comfortable room in a small but neat house in the suburbs of London, and you need not doubt of finding a most hearty welcome. If you come this winter, it is very possible that I may return with you next Spring, for it is my intention to pay a visit to America next year.

"I need not recommend my Daughter to you, for she is already assured of your friendship. I hope you will not find her altered for the worse in consequence of her visit to Europe, — I mean mentally. For, with regard to her looks, it was not to be expected that four years at her time of life should pass away without leaving some traces behind them.

"As to her health, it is, Thank God, now tolerably good, but the climate of Europe certainly has not agreed with her. She was at one time dangerously ill at Munich, and never was quite well during the two years she resided in Germany.

"My Daughter will tell you what I am doing in this country, and will acquaint you with my plans and wishes respecting her establishment in America. If you can further the execution of my schemes, I have no doubt but you will do it. There is nothing I have so much at heart as to make my dear Mother perfectly comfortable and happy during the remainder of her life.

"Pray advise and assist my Daughter in the accomplishment of my wishes in this respect. There is no way in which you can so essentially oblige me. Pray write to me now and then, for it always gives me much pleasure to hear from you.

"Wishing your health and all happiness and prosperity, I am, my Dear Friend,

"Yours most affectionately,

"RUMFORD.

"The Honble Col. Baldwin."

The Countess makes the following record : —

"1799. Brompton Row, No. 45, 25th August. The Count takes his daughter and only child in a coach and four to Gravesend, to embark for America, in ship Minerva, Captain Turner, under protection of a Mr. and Mrs. Cushing."

Near the day upon which the Count parted with his daughter in England, Colonel Baldwin addressed the following letter to her grandmother : —

"Woburn, August 29, 1799.

"DEAR MADAM, — I have received your letter of the 18th ult., but the distressing sickness which has for so long time grievously afflicted my late dear companion in life, and which ended in her dissolution the 8th inst., has prevented my answering it until this time. However, the bills have been ready for your order ever since the period for drawing them commenced. In addition to all my troubles I have to lament with you that we are not to see that man favored above all men, your dear son, and his daughter, in this country, the present season. For by two letters from the Countess to Mrs. Baldwin, one dated the 16th day of March, and the other the 6th April last, which we received a little before Mrs. Baldwin's death, we were first made acquainted with this disappointment. Sally was very well at the date of both these letters, and desired to be remembered to all her relations and friends.

"I have this day received a letter from your son, the Count, dated 14th March last, with a paragraph in it which seems to belong to you as well as to myself, and notwithstanding there is too much in it that will excite our regret, yet there is something also to elevate and add satisfaction to the mind. [The paragraph is as follows : (see letter on page 361.) The portion quoted is 'I will not attempt . . . . . the time appointed.']

"I think, madam, that after this elegant and reasonable apology, nothing that I can say will do any good. The pamphlet which the Count alludes to is the plan of a new institution for founding a society in the capital of the British dominions, the principal management of which, I understand, is intrusted to his care. There is another consolation for us, that although we do not see him this year, his visit is only postponed; for by a paragraph in a letter he wrote to Dr. Walter, I find that he has not given up the design, but means to come out next spring.

"[Sept. 8, 1799.] I have asked Mr. Samuel Clapp if he will be kind enough to take bills and dispose of them, and send you the proceeds, &c., agreeably to your desire, and he says that he will, but advises by all means not to dispose of them just at this time, if you can do without, for bills are now selling at ten *per cent* or more under *par*. He thinks they will be higher in a little time. I wish you would let your son Josiah know that his mother Thompson is very desirous of seeing him at Woburn as soon as possible. Please to remember me to your good husband [he had been a partner in trade with Colonel Baldwin], your sons and daughters, and all inquiring friends. I am, with much esteem and respect,

" Your friend and humble servant,
"LOAMMI BALDWIN.

" Mrs. Ruth Pierce."

The receipts are copied as signed by Mrs. Pierce and her son Josiah, on the sale of bills, with charges for protest and interest.

The young lady, for her homeward passage, was committed, as we have seen, to the care of a gentleman and lady bound for Boston, who faithfully discharged their trust. Her father parted with her at Gravesend, the place of her embarkation. It was then his intention to follow her to America in a few months, for, at least, a visit to this country. But circumstances which he thought imperative prevented him. The separation between father and daughter, though not final, proved a long one. She reached this port on October 10, 1799, being then just twenty-five years of age. Colonel Baldwin went to Boston to receive her and to take her to his own home.

On the New Year's day after her arrival, Colonel Baldwin and others of her own and her father's friends gave a ball in Woburn in honor of her return. "The Countess appeared on the occasion in one of her court dresses, of blue satin."

She goes on with her personal narrative here by saying that it was thought best on her return that she should go to board with her old schoolmistress, Mrs. Snow, who still continued, esteemed and active, in her employment, having a select establishment with heavy charges and consequently but few pupils. She previously made visits to her father's honored friend and correspondent, Colonel Loammi Baldwin, at Woburn, to her aunt Reed's, and to Concord. Colonel Baldwin records taking her from her uncle Reed's to Boston, on December 11, 1799, and also a payment for tickets to the theatre some time after with her, and a payment on· June 14, 1802, to Jephthah Richardson for housekeeping, &c. for himself and "the Countess."

Though I thus anticipate the course of the narrative of Count Rumford's career, it may be as well to follow the brief remainder of the daughter's manuscript to its close as it concerns herself.

She speaks kindly and gratefully of Mrs. Snow, who received her cordially, and says she was as happy in finding herself at her old school "as was consistent with falling from heaven to earth." She proceeds in her narrative as follows : —

"No other term can express it. Going to my father young, my character was formed by him, and I was accustomed to the society he frequented. I presume that of Munich and London, his chief places of residence, may be called the best in the world. To tell the truth, I view my life as pretty much ended, in all that is worth possessing, when I quitted my father at Brompton. Nor was his very different after quitting Munich, particularly after his unfortunate marriage, — for certainly marriages like his cannot be termed otherwise than unfortunate."

The Countess — to give the young lady the title that properly came to her — found her situation in society somewhat embarrassing, even though she was a school pupil. She says she received much attention, not only from her fellow-pupils, but from many prominent people. She was looked to as an oracle, and expected to be very communicative and interesting as to the scenes and experiences of her foreign life. While abroad she had been disciplined to deferential silence and attention; but the tables were now turned upon her, and she was expected to contribute to the entertainment of others. She tried to perfect herself in music, though "thumping and rattling the keys of the piano," was evidently not music to her heart. She made up her mind that this, being the sixth or the seventh, should be the last, of her schools, as she painfully reminded herself that she had been set to the tasks of pupilage in every place of her residence. She resolved to correct her faults and to increase her stock of knowledge. One of these faults was a dislike of her needle. She had actually given away a pretty dress to avoid the trouble of embroidering it. She resolved to retrieve her character in that respect, and in a short time wrought and sent to her father an embroidered waistcoat. She also drew "a picture of a shepherd boy, about half a yard high, with a very beautiful expression of countenance." Remembering her former heart-trials, the Countess adds : —

"This picture I did not send to my father, but only told him about it, not omitting a circumstance which was true, that the picture in which I had succeeded pretty well, as all said, resembled much a young teacher we had in the school. My father did not approve of captivating male teachers for misses' instructors. He was so used to the great world; I suppose in those places it was not thought best. I am sure the good old hump-backed, long-featured, great-nosed Alberti he gave me for Italian must have had great success among mothers for their daughters, under like prudent precautions."

This "handsome teacher," whose name was Gurley, she thinks would have made great havoc in the school if one of the little flock had not got the start of the rest by running away with him to New Orleans, where both of them soon after died. This information the Countess wisely withheld from her father. She also had a Spanish teacher, and seems to have really devoted herself to hard work for self-improvement and culture, alike for the purpose of turning to account the advantages she enjoyed as to please her father. She says that the reason her father alleged for not recalling her to Europe on his marriage to Madame Lavoisier was that his lady did not wish to have with her a daughter-in-law. She herself, however, was persuaded that her father did not think her fitted in manners and acquirements to shine in the circles which he and his millionnaire wife frequented. The refinements of French ways impressed the daughter, but she could not easily assume or conform to them. She says that Madame de Rumford was truly a brilliant character, and it seemed at first as if the Count had renewed his youth. He

24

was very attentive in writing to his daughter, and she
counts one hundred and four letters as received from
him between her leaving him and her rejoining him, —
an interval of eleven years.

She acquiesces in the wisdom of his judgment that
she was better fitted to live in this country, but adds
that the contrast between her situation and his prevented her making the most of herself here.   By invitation of a very rich lady, a friend of hers, whose daughters were all married at a distance, she became to her a
favored companion, and travelled with her to New
York and Philadelphia, and in the British Dominions.
She also made short visits to the few relatives who
offered her their hospitalities; but she acknowledges
that she was discontented everywhere.

The following long letter from Baldwin, though it
unduly lengthens this chapter, may properly close it, as
it belongs to the period before us, and is a reply to the
similar extended letter of the Count.

"Worcester, November 4, 1799.

"MY DEAR COUNT, — I am happy in having an opportunity
of congratulating you on the safe arrival of your amiable daughter in her native country again, where she is most cordially
received by strangers as well as friends.   But one of the number of her dear and most affectionate friends is fled.   [The
writer then gives a very touching account of the death of his
wife on the 8th of August preceding, after a distressing illness
of more than seven months, and proceeds.] I trust that this
sketch will serve to show that I have something whereon to
found an apology for not writing you before.

" I have received your much esteemed favor of 24th August
last by the hand of your daughter. I most sensibly feel the
sentiments you have therein so tenderly expressed, and notwithstanding all the regret and mortification which I suffer in conse-

quence of the disappointment in not seeing you this year, I still anticipate with pleasure the next period which you have fixed upon to make us the visit, — the postponement will seem something like Jacob's second service for Rachel. I recollect with the purity of youthful fondness the many pleasant hours spent when you were here, and seem ready rashly to decide on the visit which you have with so much affection and friendship invited me to make. But when I consider the many important engagements I have on hand, it would certainly be considered the height of imprudence in me at this time to break off and abandon them all. But, however, I can accept your own proposition to postpone and not give over the design. For though I may have passed the meridian of life, I am at present, thank God, in perfect health, and in the enjoyment of a good constitution, which, I trust, has never been impaired by excesses.

"However, I have been recently admonished not to place too much dependence on this. In the instance of Mrs. Baldwin, who (the very evening that she was seized with that distressing, deadly sickness which chained her down to misery for near eight months, and then ended in death), of her own accord, in the most agreeable manner, with seeming caution and modesty, observed to me while alone with her at supper, being Sunday evening, how perfectly she enjoyed her health, her first friend, the family, and life in general, not three hours passed thereafter before she was arrested, and Death seemed to lay his cold hand and summoned her hence. Her physician pretty soon gave her over and resigned her to that king of terrors. Not so her husband, more reluctant still. He supported a ray of hope, that with all that source of youthful strength and vigor which she had before in so high a degree possessed, she might possibly outlive her disorders, and have perhaps just life enough to build a recovery upon; and every means in my power was used to that end. Sometimes I was flattered, at other times discouraged, and thus was agitated until the 8th day of August, when her dissolution happened, and put an end to all exertions and all hope.

" But, notwithstanding this, I feel as great a desire of seeing my best surviving friend, and the companion of my youth and early part of my life, as ever. And when I add to this that long-established desire, that ardent wish, which I feel for seeing England and feasting on the improvements of that country, I will think that I shall visit the seat of science.

" In the arrangement of my pursuits, when the power is in me to choose, I have deviated perhaps from the general run of mankind, for I would wish to apply the last day of my labors to plan and execute a canal, or plant out an orchard, or something that would result in some permanent benefit for posterity.

" We have had the pleasure of your daughter's company a few days, and the inexpressible satisfaction of hearing from her mouth the circumstances of the first interview with her father, and how deeply you are engaged in philanthropic pursuits, also some of the interesting events that have happened during her absence from America, and are exceedingly pleased with the improvement of her mind.

" I have received three letters from you since I wrote you last by Mr. Welsh the 31st of July, 1798. The first of these letters was dated September 28, 1798, another March 14, 1799, and the last by your daughter, of 24th August, 1799, with the plan of your new Institution, for which I beg you to accept of my sincere thanks, and I wish you Divine success in that undertaking. I have a disciple for you now in his last year at Harvard College, reading with love for the arts.

" I am conscious of my neglect in not writing to you as I ought to have done. I was about closing a letter to you last January, to be accompanied by the answer from the inhabitants of the town of Concord to the proposal made by your daughter establishing a fund for clothing twelve industrious children of the poorer class of citizens, &c. But Dr. Walter happened to make me a visit just at that time, and brought me your favor of the 28th September, 1798, and at the same time read me a paragraph of one of your letters to him that expressed so fully your determination to make us a visit in the spring that I proceeded no further in the business, and you cannot readily conceive how much we were disappointed when we came to find out that neither you nor your daughter were coming over this season.

"However, I now enclose you a copy of the answer which the committee of Concord have returned to me on the subject of your daughter's donation; and as they seem to have a disposition to vary the plan, I have also prepared you a copy of the letter which I addressed to them on the subject, that you may see the whole transaction.

"I saw Judge Walker and Mr. Rolfe last winter again, both of them in one day, but not together. I was flattered with their conversation upon the old subject, and was led to believe that a settlement such as you wish would have been effected before this time, and was surprised to find by your letter of the 14th of March last, that Mr. Rolfe had forwarded any such thing as a demand, especially after what had passed between him and myself, which was, in my view of the matter, tantamount to a promise to close with your proposition. However, I cannot say but what there appeared a kind of reserve in him. I have seen him since your daughter has returned, and had a more serious conversation than ever. I urged the matter home. He told me that he believed you misunderstood his meaning in sending you the statement he did. He spoke respectfully of you, and was very sorry if you had misconceived his intention. He expressed himself in terms purporting the strongest friendship for you and his sister.

"I suspect that he does not feel perfectly satisfied with his uncle Walker's statement respecting some debts which have been rendered desperate, and wishes to bring his uncle to compound with him, and give up a balance due his uncle on the settlement of his guardian accounts. However that may be, Sally has set out this day from my house for Concord, with this advice from me, to push with manly firmness the settlement with her uncle and brother as far as her influence will go, and then, if she cannot effect it, to write me word, and I will (sickness or death only excepted) go immediately up and assist her.

"I have already been pretty serious with Rolfe in preparing

the wayward notwithstanding there appears in him a strange kind of evasion, yet I still think that we shall succeed in making the settlement.

"I have with particular pleasure attended to your proposition of forming for yourself a little quiet retreat in America, and made your proposed scheme known to a few of our best friends, who have most cheerfully afforded me their aid in search of a spot worthy your attention. There are several in the neighborhood of Cambridge that have been mentioned; some of the most eligible I fear are not just at present come-at-able. However, we can raise a most powerful influence when it comes to the case in hand. Meantime I shall continue upon the look out.

"Your dear mother is again a widow. Her late husband, Mr. Pierce, died on or about the 18th of August last, at Flints town, on Saco River, where they have lived for a number of years past. Josiah Pierce, Esq., their oldest son, who is now with me here on a visit from Flintstown, informs me that your mother is not in quite so good health as she has been for some years past, but is at Portland with her youngest daughter, Hannah Douglass, who is much out of health at this time, but not considered immediately dangerous.

"I have drawn a set of exchange for your mother on your bankers in London for £30 sterling, dated the 26th of March last, as usual, and delivered them to Josiah Pierce, Esq., agreeably to your mother's request. I suppose that your daughter will draw for her in future. However, in this or in any and every thing else, as far as lies in my power, I shall cheerfully contribute to her comfort, nor shall I fail to assist Sally in carrying her plans for an establishment into effect agreeably to your wishes.

"I have a favor to ask of you, my dear sir, and I feel confident that you will indulge me in the request I am about to make. I have already told you that I have a son at College whose genius inclines him strongly to cultivate the arts, and I think it rather doubtful whether he will apply his studies to either of the three learned professions with that success as to become eminent. I

have, therefore, thought whether it would not be best to endeavor to provide him a place for a year or two with some
gentleman in the mathematical line of business in Europe, who
is actually in the occupation of making and vending mathematical and optical instruments in an eminent degree; perhaps
a character something similar to what the late Mr. George
Adams of London was, might suit. It may be that you know
of some good place. In this I wish for your good assistance so
far as to make inquiry whether he could get admitted, what the
terms would be, what kind of rank he would be considered to
have in such a place, where he might work at some branches of
the business as well as attend on customers; in short, I wish to
know all about it. Perhaps he may settle a profitable correspondence in trade with the same gentleman when he comes to
return to this country again. He is very lively, ready, and
enterprising, and has ever sustained a good character. I have
raised expectations of his usefulness, if I can but hit his prevailing genius.

"I have also one favor more to ask, which is to request your
attention to the little memorandum that I have taken the liberty
to enclose, for a number of articles which I cannot readily procure here, and the amount of the bill I will pay to your mother
or your daughter, or remit it to yourself, as you may please to
order.

"In the cask of fruit which your daughter and Mr. Rolfe
have sent you, there is half a dozen apples of the growth of my
farm, wrapped up in papers with the name of *Baldwin apples*
written upon them. If those apples should continue in a state
of preservation until you receive them, and you happen to be in
company with any good connoisseurs in the distinguishing character of that kind of fruit, it would gratify me much to know
the true English name of it. However, I rather doubt whether
the nice characters of this apple will answer exactly to any particular species of English fruit, as it is (I believe) a spontane-
ous production of this country, that is, it was not originally
engrafted fruit.

"I have made an apology for not writing you so much, and

now I must make one for writing more than I ought.   But I feel confident that your goodness will excuse both.   I entreat of you to write me at all opportunities, and tell me how you progress in your new Institution.

"Judge Blodget of Goffstown, N. H., whom you know, and Dr. Hay, have both desired me to present their respects to you.

"I am, with the most unfeigned affection and esteem, my dear Count,

"Yours sincerely,

"LOAMMI BALDWIN.

"BENJAMIN, Count of Rumford."

"*Memorandum for London, to the care of Count Rumford.*

"4 thermometers exactly corresponding with each other through all the degrees of graduation, plainly mounted in manner suited to endure in experiments where a pretty severe heat is required; the other two a little in the elegant style.

"1 mercurial barometer.

"1 ream of pretty large size lawn paper, thin and light, but of a strong and compact fabric, suitable to make a balloon for experiments in natural electricity.

"Two or three crowns' worth of fine gold or silver wire for to entwine about the flying line of an electrical kite or balloon; perhaps gold thread wire before it be flattened might answer.

"Some of the best transparent liquor varnish for preserving the brightness or polish of brass work, with directions for using it; say, to the amount in value of three or four crowns.

"1 good collar-mandrel for a turning-lathe, provided with spiral threads or screws on the spindle of the whirl, for the purpose of cutting screws in the lathe, of different combs, or threads; also the tools to be used in working the lathe for cutting screws.

"1 boiler of the most improved kind for cooking, of about thirty gallons' capacity.

"1 boiler of about ten or fifteen gallons, upon the Rumford plan.

" 2 nice measuring tapes, of two poles or fifty links of the chain in length; enclosed in cases, &c.

" A magnet, natural or artificial, highly affected, suitable for impregnating the needles of the compass.

" 1 set of glasses for a lucernal microscope.

" I have an 18-inch reflecting telescope, the tube of which is about 2¾ inches' diameter, but the reflector and speculum in both a little sullied or tarnished. I wish to know whether they can be repolished and put in order without the whole instrument being sent with them, and what the expense would be of doing it.

" Yours,

" L. BALDWIN.

" The above letter sent by the Minerva."

There is an interesting story connected with the " Baldwin apples " referred to in the preceding letter. The tree from which came the scions that have now so widely propagated that very popular apple grew on a hillside in Medford near the Woburn line. The trunk of the tree having been drilled by woodpeckers, the fruit was known as the " Woodpecker apple," soon shortened into " Peckers." The tradition is, that Baldwin and Thompson first learned the excellent quality of the fruit on one of their walks to Professor Winthrop's lectures. If this be true, it is strange that Baldwin made no reference to the incident when sending the apples to Rumford. The Colonel had given some scions of the tree to a nursery-gardener, who named the fruit from the donor. The old tree fell in the September gale of 1815.*

* Brooks's History of Medford, pp. 19, 20.

CHAPTER VII.

THE reasons assigned by Count Rumford in the correspondence with his friends in America, given in the last chapter, for not at this time revisiting his native country, were principally two, — his still existing obligations to the Bavarian government, and the absorbing interest with which he was engaging in the establishment of a new Institution in London. The conception and plan of this Institution are to be regarded as exclusively his own. His, too, was the organizing mind, nor can I discover any evidence that he was induced, or felt it desirable, to modify his original idea of it, or to change the details of his plan by suggestions from any of the wise and earnest advisers and helpers whom he engaged in it. While he was himself one of the most zealous and laborious Fellows of the Royal Society, he saw that without trespassing at all upon the range, wide as it was, that was recognized by his associates, there was room for an Institution whose aims should be more practical and popular, coming into direct contact with the agricultural, the mechanical, and the domestic life of the people. To Rumford, then, belongs the signal honor of creating an Institution which has a most creditable history, and which has been the medium for bringing forward, through the opportunities there afforded them, many men who have won the highest distinctions in practical science.

Count Rumford's spirit and activity had at this period of his life become restless, and perhaps slightly morbid. He had been for many years so busily engaged in most exacting labors, in which he had employed a large number of assistants and subordinates, that he, beyond most men even of marked ability and influential position, needed to have some conspicuous and comprehensive scheme to engross his mind and to task his energies. For reasons soon to be mentioned he had grounds for believing that his official position and his high functions in Bavaria would no longer secure him such opportunities for civil and military administration or high influence as he had so long enjoyed. Failing, to his great chagrin, of reception in

his diplomatic functions in England, it would seem
that his disappointment affected his spirits. He did
not relax in any degree his benevolent efforts, and he
resolutely maintained and pursued the leading object
of his whole eminently beneficent career, namely, the
making of all the inquiries and discoveries of science
available for the direct relief, service, and comfort of
the common people. It will be observed that the
Count refers to a publication of his in 1796, as containing a suggestion of his first idea of his Institution.
As we come to read his own account of it, and follow
it out in its details of objects and methods, we shall be
satisfied that it was no extemporized scheme which was
hastily devised, but that it had been long and carefully
elaborated by a patient development of an idea which
he had cherished in his own mind for several years.
We may well share the surprise which he himself expressed, that an Institution answering, in some general
way, at least, to that which he proposed, had not already
been initiated either on the Continent or in England,
and that it had been left to him to set forth the need
and scope for it, and to win the high honor of securing
·for it an existence and full success.

Count Rumford had taken special pains, as indicated
by his letter to Mr. King, to have copies of his Proposals for the Institution reach this country, hoping
that a similar plan would find its advocates here. I
have one of them before me. It is a pamphlet of fifty
pages, bearing the following title: * "Proposals for
forming by Subscription, in the Metropolis of the
British Empire, a Public Institution for diffusing the
Knowledge and facilitating the general Introduction of

* It is in the possession of the Massachusetts Historical Society.

useful Mechanical Inventions and Improvements, and
for teaching, by courses of Philosophical Lectures and
Experiments, the Application of Science to the Common
Purposes of Life." This copy, bearing the autograph
of Count Rumford, was presented by him " To his
Excellency John Adams," as from " one of the Managers of the Institution," and was printed in London
in 1799.* The Introduction, signed by Rumford, is
dated from Brompton Row, 4th March, in that year,
and makes nearly half of the pamphlet, giving a very
admirable account of the origin of the Institution. Dr.
Franklin himself never wrote an essay indicating a more
practical sagacity, or expressed in a more direct and
forcible style of lucid composition, than characterize
this piece of Rumford's. His aim, he says, is to bring
about a cordial embrace between science and art, by
enlightening and removing prejudice against changes,
inventions, and improvements, and by establishing relations of helpful intercourse between philosophers and
practical workmen. He would engage their united
efforts for the improvement of agriculture, manufactures, and commerce, and for the increase of domestic
comfort. He says : " The pre eminence of any people
is, and ought ever to be, estimated by the state of taste,
industry, and mechanical improvement among them."
" The vivifying rays of science, when properly directed,

* Dr. H. Bence Jones, the Secretary of the Royal Institution, has kindly sent
me a copy of the reprint of these " Proposals, &c." which was published in May,
1870.

He introduces this reprint with the following prefatory note : —

" No copy of this Prospectus, printed in 1799, exists in the Library of the Royal
Institution. Happily two copies have been preserved, the one at Althorp, and the
other at the British Museum."

" Through the kindness of Earl Spencer, the Managers have been able to order this
very early Record of the Institution to be reprinted."

tend to excite the activity and increase the energy of an enlightened nation." "It will not escape observation that I have placed the *management of fire* among the very first subjects of useful improvement, and it is possible that I may be accused of partiality in placing the object of my favorite pursuits in that conspicuous situation. But how could I have done otherwise? I have always considered it as being a subject very interesting to mankind; and it was on that account principally, that, at a very early period of my life, I engaged in its investigation; and the more I have examined it and meditated upon it, the more I have been impressed with its importance." One is pleased with the wisdom of his homely earnestness, in the fact that he could then offer as novelties such suggestions as these: that arts and manufactures of every kind depend, directly or indirectly, on operations in which fire is employed; that the comforts and conveniences of human ingenuity are obtained through its assistance; that fuel costs the kingdom more than *ten millions* sterling annually, and that much more than half the fuel that is consumed might be saved.

The writer adds a brief account of the history of these "Proposals," and of the causes which gave rise to them. He avows that he had long been in the habit of regarding all useful improvements as dependent upon mechanical agencies and the perfection of machinery, with skill in the management of it, and of considering that the profit to be thus gained was the chief incitement to industry. The plan which he now offers to the public is the result of his own meditations as to the means that might most wisely be employed to facilitate the general introduction of such improvements.

" In the beginning of the year 1796 I gave a faint
sketch of this plan in my second Essay ; but being
under the necessity of returning soon to Germany, I
had not leisure to pursue it farther at that time ; and I
was obliged to content myself with having merely
thrown out a loose idea, as it were by accident, which
I thought might possibly attract attention. After my
return to Munich, I opened myself more fully on the
subject in my correspondence with my friends in this
country [England], and particularly in my letters to
Thomas Bernard, Esq., who, as is well known, is one
of the founders and most active members of the Society for bettering the Condition and increasing the Comforts of the Poor." *

The Count subjoins, in a note, three letters of his to
Mr. Bernard, dated at Munich, 28th April, 1797, 13th
May, 1798, and 8th June, 1798. The first of these
letters returns the writer's grateful acknowledgments
for the honor done him by his election as a member of
the Society for bettering the condition of the poor. It
closes with a characteristic suggestion that visible examples, "by models," will advance its objects better
than will anything that can be said or written. The
third letter emphasizes a well-pointed hint, that indolent,
selfish, and luxurious persons "must either be allured

* In the Gentleman's Magazine, Vol. LXXXVIII., for 1818, p. 82, there is an
obituary notice of Sir Thomas Bernard, third son of Sir Francis, Royal Governor of
Massachusetts, from which the following is an extract: "In 1799, on the suggestion
of Count Rumford, he set on foot the plan of the Royal Institution; for which the
King's Charter was obtained on the 13th of January, 1800, which has been of eminent service in affording a school for useful knowledge to the young people of the
metropolis, and in bringing forward to public notice many learned and able men in
the capacity of lecturers; and most of all, in its laboratory being the cradle of the
transcendent discoveries of Sir Humphry Davy, which have benefited and enlightened
Europe and the whole world."

or shamed into action," and that it is very desirable "to make benevolence fashionable." The writer also expresses his interest in his correspondent's "plan with regard to Bridewell. A well-arranged House of Industry is much wanted in London." He closes by asking Mr. Bernard "to read once more the Proposals published in my second Essay. I really think that a public establishment like that there described might easily be formed in London, and that it would produce infinite good. I will come to London to assist you in its execution whenever you will in good earnest undertake it."

Returning to England in September, 1798, the Count says he found Mr. Bernard very solicitous for an attempt for the immediate execution of the plan. "After several consultations that were held in Mr. Bernard's apartments in the Foundling Hospital, and at the house of the Lord Bishop of Durham, at which several gentlemen assisted who are well known as zealous promoters of useful improvements, it was agreed that Mr. Bernard should report to the Committee of the Society for bettering the Condition of the Poor the general result of these consultations, and the unanimous desire of the gentlemen who assisted at them that means might be devised for making an attempt to carry the scheme proposed into execution."

As the Count had thus, for convenience' sake, availed himself of the interest which had already drawn together in associated action a body of gentlemen organized into a benevolent society, and as the report on his new project was to be made by a committee of that society, he was at once concerned to secure from the start the independent existence, activity, and membership of the proposed Institution. The committee agreed with him, that the objects of the Institution were too interesting and important to allow of its being made " an *appendix* to any other existing establishment," and, therefore, that it ought to stand alone, on its own proper basis. Eight members of the above-named society were appointed to confer with him on his plan.* Meeting with this committee on the 31st of January, 1799, the Count presented them with an elaborate and complete working plan for an Institution, which they unanimously approved. It was thought, however, that the plan entered too much into details for submission to the public in the existing stage of the enterprise, and therefore the Count revised and modified it, sending a corrected copy of it to each member of the committee, accompanied by a letter as follows : —

" GENTLEMEN, — Inclosed I have the honour to send you a corrected copy of the Proposals I took the liberty of laying before you on Thursday last, for forming in this capital, by private subscription, a Public Institution for diffusing the knowledge and facilitating the general and speedy introduction of new and useful mechanical inventions and improvements ; and also for teaching, by regular courses of Philosophical Lectures and Experiments, the application of the new discoveries in science to the improvement of arts and manufactures, and in facilitating the means of procuring the comforts and conveniences of life.

" The tendency of the proposed Institution to excite a spirit of inquiry and of improvement amongst all ranks of society, and to afford the most effectual assistance to those who are engaged in the various pursuits of useful industry, did not escape your observation ; and it is, I am persuaded, from a conviction

* These gentlemen were, the Earl of Winchilsea, Mr. Wilberforce, the Rev. Dr. Glasse, Mr. Sullivan, Mr. Richard Sullivan, Mr. Colquhoun, Mr. Parry, and Mr. Bernard.

of the utility of the plan, or its tendency to increase the comforts and enjoyments of individuals, and at the same time to promote the public prosperity, that you have been induced to take it into your serious consideration. I shall be much flattered if it should meet with your approbation and with your support.

"Though I am perfectly ready to take any share in the business of carrying the scheme into execution, in case it should be adopted, that can be required, yet there is one preliminary request which I am desirous may be granted me; and that is, that Government may be previously made acquainted with the scheme before any steps are taken towards carrying it into execution; and also that his Majesty's ministers may be informed that it is the contemplation of the Founders of the Institution to accept of my services in the arrangement and management of it.

"The peculiar situation in which I stand in this country, as a subject of his Majesty, and being at the same time, by his Majesty's special permission, granted under his royal sign-manual, engaged in the service of a Foreign Prince,—this circumstance renders it improper for me to engage myself in this important business, notwithstanding that it might, perhaps, be considered merely as a private concern, without the knowledge and the approbation of Government.

"I am quite certain that my engaging in this, or in any other business in which there is any prospect of my being of any public use in this country, will meet with the most cordial approbation of his Most Serene Highness, the Elector Palatine, in whose service I am,—for I know his sentiments on that subject; and although I do not imagine that his Majesty, or his Majesty's ministers, would disapprove of my giving my assistance in carrying this scheme into execution, yet I feel it to be necessary that their approbation should be asked and obtained; and, if I might be allowed to express my sentiments on another matter, which, no doubt, has already occurred to every one of the Gentlemen to whom I now address myself, I should say that, in my opinion, it would not only be proper, but even necessary, to inform Government of the nature of the scheme that is proposed, and of every circumstance relative to it, and at the same time to ask their countenance and support in carrying it into execution; for although it may be allowable in this free country for individuals to unite in forming and executing extensive plans for diffusing useful knowledge, and promoting the public good, yet it appears to me that no such establishment should ever be formed in any country without the knowledge and approbation of the Executive Government.

"Trusting that you will be so good as to excuse the liberty I take in making this observation, and that you will consider my doing it as being intended rather to justify myself by explaining my principles than from any idea of its being necessary on any other account, I have the honour to be, with much respect, Gentlemen,

"Your most obedient and Most humble Servant,
"RUMFORD.

"Brompton Row, 7th February, 1799.

[Addressed] "To the Gentlemen named by the Committee of the Society for bettering the condition of the Poor, to confer with Count Rumford on his scheme for forming a new Establishment in London for diffusing the Knowledge of useful Mechanical Improvements, &c."

The committee above named had in the mean while held a meeting on the 1st of February, the Bishop of Durham in the chair, and, after reporting their conference with the Count, gave their full approbation to the proposed project. In order to provide funds for initiating the society, it was proposed that subscribers of fifty guineas each should be the perpetual proprietors of the Institution, and be entitled to perpetual transferable tickets for the lectures, and for admission to the apartments of the Institution; and that as soon as thirty such subscribers should be obtained a meeting of them should be called for the consideration of a plan, and for the election of managers. The report of the committee was approved, and they were requested to take measures for carrying its suggestions into effect, as well as to draw the outlines of a plan for the Institution.

This preliminary work being accomplished, the committee circulated among their friends and others whom they thought likely to favor the scheme, a paper of proposals soliciting subscriptions, and requested them to reply by letters addressed "To Thomas Bernard, Esq., at the Foundling."

Fifty-eight most respectable names had been sent in before arrangements could be made for a meeting of the subscribers; and this hearty response induced some change in the plan in respect to the first choice of managers, and in regard to an application for a charter before any further organization.

Count Rumford, at this stage of the business, and before a meeting of the subscribers had been held, addressed to them a pamphlet containing all the matters that have been thus summarized. It was dated from Brompton Row, 4th March, 1799, and was intended to prepare them for the meeting soon to follow. He expressed his readiness to take any part that might be desired.

"The Proposals, &c.," evidently from the pen of the Count, are then set forth in the pamphlet, and contain a complete plan for the organization, administration, and support of the Institution, with minute specifications of its objects, when carried into details.

Those objects, first stated comprehensively, are " the speedy and general diffusion of the knowledge of all new and useful improvements, in whatever quarter of the world they may originate; and teaching the application of scientific discoveries to the improvement of arts and manufactures in this country, and to the increase of domestic comfort and convenience." Efforts were to be made to confine the Institution to its proper limits, to give it a solid foundation, and to make it an ornament to the capital and an honor to the nation. Spacious and airy rooms were to be provided for receiving and exhibiting such new mechanical inventions and improvements, especially such contrivances for increasing conveniences and comforts, for promoting domestic economy, for improving taste, and for advancing useful industry, as should be thought worthy of public notice.

Perfect and full-sized models of all such mechanical inventions and improvements as would serve these ends were to be provided and placed in a repository. The following are the specifications: Cottage fireplaces and kitchen utensils for cottagers; a farm-house kitchen, with its furnishings; a complete kitchen, with utensils, for the house of a gentleman of fortune; a laundry, including boilers, washing, ironing, and drying rooms, for a gentleman's house, or for a public hospital; the most approved German, Swedish, and Russian stoves for heating rooms and passages. In order that visitors might receive the utmost practical benefit from seeing these models, the peculiar merit in each of them should, as far as was possible, be exhibited *in action.* Open chimney fireplaces, with ornamental and economical grates, and ornamental stoves, made to represent elegant chimney-pieces, for halls and for drawing and eating rooms, were to be exhibited, with fires in them. It was proposed, likewise, to exhibit " working models, on a reduced scale, of that most curious and

most useful machine, the steam-engine"; also, of
brewers' boilers, with improved fireplaces; of distillers'
coppers, with improved condensers; of large boilers
for the kitchens of hospitals; and of ships' coppers,
with improved fireplaces. Models also were to illustrate and to suggest improvements in ventilating apparatus; in hot-houses, lime-kilns and steam-boilers for
preparing food for stall-fed cattle; in the planning
of cottages, spinning-wheels, and looms "adapted to
the circumstances of the poor"; models of newly invented machines and implements of husbandry; models
of bridges of various constructions; and, comprehensively, "models of all such other machines and useful
instruments as the managers of the Institution shall
deem worthy of the public notice."

In glancing the eye over this summary it seems as if
we were reading backwards the history of human ingenuity in thousands of cases of successful effort, and
in innumerable instances of baffled and disappointed,
though ingenious and devoted, scheming for facilitating,
simplifying, and economizing toil, saving resources,
and multiplying the comforts and conveniences of human life. We have in Rumford's schedule an inventory of the contents of a national patent-office,
and a condensed catalogue, in prospect, of the contrivances of skill and genius displayed in the halls of fairs,
bazaars, and agricultural and mechanical expositions.*
Each article exhibited was to be accompanied by a de-

* In reading the inventory of the truly scientific and useful articles which Count
Rumford proposed to receive into his repository, it is interesting to note the progress
which had been made in England in such matters in less than a century and a quar-
ter by comparison with some of the contents of another collection. In 1681, Dr.
Grew, a Fellow of the Royal Society, published under its patronage, with the aid of
Daniel Colwall, Esq., who was at the charge of the illustrative engravings, a fulso

tailed account or description of it, illustrated by correct drawings, with the name and residence of the maker, and the price at which he would furnish it.

The second great object of the Institution, namely, "teaching the application of science to the useful purposes of life," was to be secured by fitting up a lecture-room for philosophical lectures and experiments with a complete laboratory and philosophical apparatus, and all necessary instruments for chemical and other experiments. This lecture-room is to be used for no other purposes but those of natural philosophy and philosophical chemistry, and it is to be made comfortable and salubrious for subscribers. The most eminent and distinguished expounders of science are to be exclusively engaged, and the managers are to be strictly responsible for their rigid restriction of their discourses to the subjects committed to them. If there is spare room, non-subscribers may be admitted for a small fee.

The subjects proposed for the lectures include the following:— Heat and its application; the economizing of heat from the combustion of inflammable bodies used as fuel; the principles of warmth in clothing; the effects of heat and cold on the human body in sickness and in

<hr>

volume of 415 pages, and 31 engraved sheets, with the following title: "*Musæum Regalis Scientiæ*; or, A Catalogue and Description of the Natural and Artificial Raritys belonging to the Royal Society, and preserved at Gresham College; whereunto is subjoined the Comparative Anatomy of the Stomach and Guts." The next year it was ordered that the Doctor assume the charge of the repository, under the title of *Præfectus Musæi*, &c., and "make a short Catalogue of the Raritys," &c. The Doctor's books are among the curiosities of literature. Here are some of the "Raritys" watched over by the Royal Society:—

"The sceptre of an Indian king, a dog without a mouth, a Pegu hat and organ, a Bird of Paradise, a Jewish phylactery, a model of the Temple of Jerusalem, three landskips and a catcoptrick painting given by Bishop Wilkins, a gun which discharges seven times, a pair of Iceland gloves, a pot of Macassar poison, the tail of an Indian cow worshipped on the Ganges, a tuft of coralline," &c., &c.

health; the effects of breathing bad air; the means for making dwelling-houses comfortable and healthful; the construction of ice-houses and the procuring and preserving ice; means for preserving food in different seasons and climates, and of cooling liquors without the aid of ice; the art of producing, composing, and adapting manures for vegetation for different soils; the changes produced in various substances used as food in the processes of cookery; the changes wrought in food by its digestion; the chemical principles in the process of tanning leather, with improvements in that art; the chemical principles in the arts of making soap, of bleaching and of dyeing, "and, in general, of all the mechanical arts, as they apply to the various branches of manufacture."

It was proposed to raise the funds for the support of the Institution by a subscription of fifty guineas from each of the proprietors and founders, a contribution of ten guineas from each subscriber for life and of two guineas from annual subscribers, by donations and legacies that might reasonably be expected, and by fees from visitors and attendants on the lectures.

The original subscribers, or proprietors, before being called upon for payment, were to be secured against any further demands for contributions, and from all legal obligations for debts that might afterwards be incurred by the managers, through the terms of a charter providing them that security. These proprietors were not to be compelled to serve as managers or visitors against their consent or inclinations. Half of the sums subscribed by them was to be permanently invested in the public funds, or in freehold property, that the income might meet the expenses of the Institution.

Each proprietor was to be "an hereditary governor of the Institution," holding a perpetually transferable share in its property, having a voice in the election of its managers and visitors, and receiving two transferable tickets admitting to every part of the establishment and to all the lectures and experiments. The consent of the managers, though not necessary to the holding and use of the privileges of proprietorship when transferred by inheritance to a new possessor, should nevertheless be requisite when the transfer is made by sale or donation. The recommendations of proprietors should be sufficient for securing admission, when there is room, for all orderly persons who may wish to attend the Institution.

Each subscriber for life should receive one ticket, not transferable, securing free admission to every part of the establishment and to all lectures and experiments. An annual subscriber should have the same privileges for a single year, and might at any time become a subscriber for life by paying eight additional guineas. Proprietors and subscribers of all classes were to be equally entitled to have drawings or copies made at their own expense, for themselves or for their friends, of all models in the repository, and workmen and workshops were to be provided, under the direction of the managers, to execute such orders properly and reasonably; the copies thus made of all machines, models, and plans to be authenticated by the seal or stamp of the Institution. Workmen employed on these orders were to have free access to their models, and, with the approval of the managers, might commit to the repository any specimen article of their own manufacture, with their address, price, &c.

The Institution was to be governed by nine managers, chosen by and from the proprietors by sealed ballots sent in previously to the annual meetings. These managers were to be distributed in three classes of three each, for terms respectively of one, two, and three years, and were to be re-eligible without limitation. Fourteen days before the annual meeting the managers for the time being were to send to each proprietor a printed list, authenticated, of such proprietors as had offered or consented to be candidates for the vacancies to be filled in the management. The proprietor was to designate by marking on the list the names of those whom he approved, and then to seal, without his signature, and send the slip to the managers under an additional cover, which he was to sign with his name; this additional cover being torn off, the lists, still sealed, were to be mixed unopened in an urn. By this arrangement only proprietors could send in ballots, and their individual ballots would be secret. The managers were to serve without pay or any pecuniary advantage, and were to be held solemnly pledged to the faithful discharge of their duties, and to a strict adherence to the principles of the Institution. They were to keep the property insured, to examine all accounts and disbursements, to keep minutes of their doings, and to practise a rigid economy. They were to give no premiums or rewards of any kind from the funds. Ordinary meetings were to be held weekly, and extraordinary ones when necessary, three of the managers making a quorum for business. The presence of six of the managers, however, should be requisite in the making of all rules, regulations, and standing orders, which should have force after having been made known to all the proprietors. There was to be also a committee of visitors, in number the same as that of the managers, and chosen for the same terms of years, who should annually make a thorough examination of every part of the Institution, audit its accounts, criticise its efficiency, and send in a printed report to the proprietors. No one could be eligible as both manager and visitor.

The managers were charged to procure models of all inventions and improvements in mechanical arts made in any country. These were to be the permanent property of the Institution, whose surplus funds were to be used for purchasing them. Special efforts and inquiries were to be made to obtain from over the British Empire and from foreign countries all such new and useful improvements; and a room in the Institution, open only to proprietors and subscribers, should be appropriated for the record of all such information. So deliberately and judiciously were all the arrangements and details for the organization and conduct of the Institution devised in the orderly mind of Rumford, that it seemed as if it were already in working order while still it existed only on paper. It would appear that its originator was guided by his own strong conviction that a well-devised plan, carefully elaborated in its most minute principles, would avert the necessity of that preliminary and incidental discussion which so often checks the enthusiasm needed to secure the first success of such an undertaking. It was well understood from the first that Rumford was the leading and guiding spirit of the Institution. There is no trace of any jealousy or disaffection, or even of any personal variance, excited towards him by his somewhat authoritative leadership. The hearty response and co-operation of all the prominent persons whom he sought to engage, and the pecuniary contributions so readily gathered, are evidences of the confidence reposed in him.

After the first printing and distribution of these " Proposals," and before the Institution had received its charter-title, a general meeting of the proprietors was held at the house of Sir Joseph Banks, in Soho Square, on March 7, 1799, the host occupying the chair. It was then found that fifty-eight persons had made themselves proprietors by the contribution of fifty guineas each. The list contains many distinguished names of scientific men, gentlemen, members of Parliament and of the nobility, including one bishop, some of whom were more than simply Mæcenases.

It was then decided at once to choose the committee of managers, who should be instructed to apply to his Majesty for a charter for the Institution, to lay an outline of its plan before the Right Honorable Mr. Pitt and his. Grace the Duke of Portland, to send it forth to the public, and to publish the proceedings in the newspapers. The thanks of the meeting were given to the presiding officer. The following information is added to the published record: —

" N. B. — Count Rumford's original Proposals for forming the Institution may be had of Messrs. Cadell and Davies in the Strand."

At the first meeting of the managers before the charter was received, held at the house of Sir Joseph Banks, March 9, 1799, "On a motion made by Count Rumford, it was

" *Resolved*, That Sir Joseph Banks be requested to take the chair, and that he do continue to preside at all future meetings of the managers, until a charter shall have been obtained from his Majesty for the Institution."

Other resolutions were passed for effecting a preliminary organization. Thomas Bernard, Esq., was chosen Secretary. The Proposals for forming the Institution, as published by Count Rumford, were approved and adopted by the managers, "subject, however, to such partial modifications as shall be by them found to be necessary or useful." Count Rumford and Mr. Bernard were appointed to prepare a draught of a charter.* Earls Morton and Spencer, Sir Joseph Banks, and Mr. Pelham, were requested to lay the Proposals before his Majesty, the Royal Family, the Ministers, the great officers of State, the members of both Houses of Parliament and of the Privy Council, and before the twelve Judges. Thanks were also voted to the above-named booksellers for their generosity in offering to print gratuitously five hundred copies of the "Proposals."

Count Rumford, with dignified modesty, yet with due urgency, attaches a fly-leaf to his pamphlet, with a printed form for subscriptions and donations.

We turn now to another contemporary publication which presents to us the organized completion of the establishment in the conception and initiation of which Count Rumford had exercised such ingenuity and practical wisdom, and in whose service he had been so zealously engaged. It is a publication in quarto form, of ninety-two pages, bearing the following title: "The Prospectus, Charter, Ordinances, and By-Laws of the Royal Institution of Great Britain. Together with

* Sir John Sinclair, in his "Correspondence, &c.," Vol. 1. p. 28 (London, 1831)," says of the Institution, that it "was placed on a permanent footing by an act which I was the means of carrying through Parliament."

Lists of the Proprietors and Subscribers; and an Appendix. London. Printed for the Royal Institution. 1800." It bears a vignette of the corporate seal of the Institution, which is a flourishing and fruit-bearing tree sprouting out of a mural crown, the circle being surmounted by the royal crown of Britain. The King appears as Patron, the officers of the Institution were appointed by him at its formation, the Earl of Winchilsea and Nottingham being President; the Earls of Morton and of Egremont, and Sir Joseph Banks, Vice-Presidents; the Earls of Bessborough, Egremont, and of Morton, being respectively the first-named on each of the three classes of Managers,—on the first of which, to serve for three years, is Count Rumford. The Duke of Bridgewater, Viscount Palmerston, and Earl Spencer, lead each of the three classes of Visitors. The whole list proves with what a power of patronage, as well as with what popularity and enthusiasm, the enterprise was initiated. Dr. Thomas Garnett was made Professor of Natural Philosophy and Chemistry, and Thomas Bernard, Esq., Treasurer. A Home and Foreign Secretary, Legal Council, a Solicitor, and a Clerk, complete the list.

Then follows the Prospectus, which is evidently from the pen of Count Rumford, as it exhibits his direct and earnest style of presenting and emphasizing, as of the highest practical interest for civilized society, all those multiplied, homely, and economical objects of inquiry and improvement which tend to promote the welfare and increase the conveniences of human life. The word INSTITUTION, the writer says, was chosen after mature deliberation, as having been least appropriated by previous establishments, and as best adapted

to the comprehensive designs of the new society. He
urges, at the start, the forcible truth, that it has been
by the aid of machinery in procuring the necessaries,
the comforts, and the elegances of life that all the
successive improvements have been made in the condition of man, from a state of ignorance and barbarism
up to that of the highest cultivation and refinement,
and that the stage of civilization is relatively to be
judged by the state of industry and mechanical improvements among a people. In illustration of this
truth, he refers to the experience of all ages and places,
and to the differences observable in various nations,
provinces, towns, and even villages, as flourishing and
populous according to the measure of the activity of
their industry. Exertion quickens the spirit of invention, makes science flourish, and increases the moral
and physical powers of man. Thus the printing-press,
the art of navigation, "the astonishing effects of gunpowder," and the steam-engine, have changed the course
of human affairs, and wrought influences the effects of
which are incalculable for the future, though willing
ignorance would have derided these inventions as impossible, or rejected them as unnecessary. In proceeding to point out the causes which impede progress, and
to invite the public to engage in efforts to advance it,
he enlarges upon some of the views already presented in
the Proposals. He refers to the causes of the slowness,
indifference, and jealousy under which improvements
make their way, and specifies the influence of habit,
ignorance, prejudice, suspicion, dislike of change, and
the narrowing effect of the subdivision of work into
many petty occupations. The scorn of improvement,
the greed for wealth, the spirit of monopoly and of

secret intrigue, are exhibited even among manufacturers. Between workmen and merchants comes in a class of men who have a great and essential task to perform.

"These men are Philosophers, who have devoted themselves to the labor of observing, comparing, analyzing, inventing. The movements of the universe, the relations and habitudes of men and of things, causes and effects, motives and consequences, are the powers on which they meditate for the development of truth, by those remote analogies which escape the vulgar mind. It is the business of these Philosophers to examine every operation of nature or of art, and to establish general theories for the direction and conducting of future processes. Invention seems to be peculiarly the province of the man of science; his ardour in the pursuit of truth is unremitted; discovery is his harvest; utility is his reward."

Yet even these philosophers may become merely abstract and contemplative dreamers, detached from the ordinary pursuits of life, and unwilling to descend from the sublimities of science to the details of common occupations. They need the stimulus of interest and of the capital of the manufacturer, who, in his turn, needs the information and the accurate reasoning of the man of science. There are three direct methods for removing these difficulties. One of these is to give premiums or prizes to inventors, which is secured through "The Society for the Encouragement of Arts, Manufactures, and Commerce," instituted in 1753. The second method is by granting temporary monopolies, which is provided for the patent and other laws. The third is that the agency of which is secured by the new Institution, for diffusing the knowledge and facilitating the introduction of useful mechanical inventions and improvements.

"In the execution of their plan the Managers have purchased a commodious house in Albemarle Street for the reception and exhibition of models of all contrivances and improvements worthy of public notice. Instead of *descriptions*, it will furnish a repository of things *visible* and *tangible*. Manufacturers and consumers may here meet for mutual advantage. There will also be a library of all 'the best treatises devoted to the objects of the Institution. A lecture-room will be provided, thoroughly fitted with laboratory and apparatus, for philosophical lectures and experiments by men of the first eminence in science."

Words which include sciences define the specific subjects for attention,—food, clothing, houses, towns, fortresses, roads, canals, carriages, ships, tools, weapons, &c., &c. The science of chemistry will be brought to bear on the nature of soils; on tillage and manures; on the making of bread, beer, wine, spirits, starch, sugar, butter, and cheese; and in the processes of dyeing, calico-printing, bleaching, painting, varnishing, &c.; on the smelting of ores, the compounding of metals, mortar and cements, bricks, pottery, glass, and enamel. The making of roads and of vehicles, canals and vessels and engines; the improvement of rivers, harbors, and coasts, and of the art of war, — will have large attention. Above all, "the phenomena of *light* and *heat* —those great powers which give life and energy to the universe—powers which, by the wonderful process of combustion, are placed under the command of human beings —will engage a profound interest."

Infinite public advantages for the learned and the ignorant, the rich and the poor, may be made sure by the diffusion of the spirit to be promoted by this Institution. Good taste, good morals, rational economy, industry, and ingenuity will be secured by its progress, "and the pursuits of all the various classes of society will then tend to promote the public prosperity." Had Rumford done nothing but write the Prospectus, that alone would prove him the philosopher and philanthropist.

The charter of the Institution passed the royal seals on the 13th of January, 1800. The twenty-fifth day of the coming March was appointed for organization under it. Count Rumford is named among the grantees, and its provisions conform substantially to his own well-wrought plan already described. The ordinances, by-laws, and regulations of the Institution, which are likewise for the most part adjusted to that plan, and provide for carrying it into details of efficiency and practical benefit, indicate the agency of the master-spirit of the whole enterprise. Precautions are taken to guard against the influences of jealousy and favoritism in its membership and administration, and to hold it strictly and generously to its prime purposes of benefiting the public by research, the diffusion of scientific knowledge, and the service of the most homely and economical interests of humanity. The managers are to furnish the laboratory, the workshop, and the repository of the establishment in the most complete manner, and to provide an able chemist as a teaching and demonstrating professor, and also to engage other professors and lecturers in experimental and mechanical philosophy. No political subject is to be even mentioned, and no themes are to be introduced but such as are connected with the objects of the Institution. The payment for proprietorship from May 1, 1800, to May 1, 1801, was fixed at sixty guineas, and ten guineas were to be added each year for all newly elected proprietors, up to the 1st of May, 1804, when the fee, then one hundred guineas, should be the qualification for admission till further order.

Only foreigners were to be eligible as honorary members of the Institution, and they only when distinguished for knowledge in science or in some useful art. This rule was subject to exceptions for members of the Royal Family, foreign sovereign princes, and resident ambassadors. Ladies were admissible as life or as annual subscribers. Any subscriber might, for cause, be ejected, and then should be forever after ineligible. Occasional scientific and experimental lectures might be given through permission of the managers by qualified men of eminence. Any number of committees might be appointed for specific scientific and experimental investigation.

The funds were to be disposed of as provided for in the plan. No presents, or occasional or special rewards or gratuities, were allowed, either to inventors and discoverers or to the salaried employes of the Institution.

The list of proprietors, which steadily lengthened with each progressive step for initiating and organizing the Institution, bears the names of the highest of the nobility, of many of the prelates, members of Parliament, scientific men, and distinguished commoners, — in number, two hundred and eighty-one. There were two hundred and sixty-seven life subscribers, two of whom were ladies; and four hundred and thirteen annual subscribers, one hundred and three of whom were ladies; the fee being raised to three guineas.

At a meeting of the managers, held in the first month of the charter organization, some of the detailed subjects of inquiry and improvements which were specified in Count Rumford's schedule already given, and a few others, were assigned to committees for investigation, beginning with the processes for "making bread," and ending with those "for procuring iron from its ores."

At the same meeting Count Rumford was requested to take measures for, and to superintend, the publication of the journals of the Institution, employing such assistance as he might need. No private advertisements were to be published with the journals, and a printing-press was to be established as soon as possible in the Institution. The first number of the journals appeared April 5, 1800. They were to be published, if possible, at intervals of two weeks, and were to be adapted to a wide circulation, at a cost, when of eight pages, of threepence, and when of sixteen pages sixpence, a part. The preface of the first bound volume, completed in 1802, informs us that the first three sheets of it were published under Count Rumford's direction. They contain reports of the meetings of the managers of the Institution, providing for committees and professors, assigning subjects for scientific investigation, — the art of making bread being the first of them, — an account of the edifice and its arrangements then in progress, and a report made to the managers, May 25, 1801, by Rumford, on the progress and hopeful prospects of the Institution. The arrangements, conveniences, and contrivances described in this report all indicate the ingenious painstaking of the master-hand which was at work upon them, and the beginnings of a rich library of scientific journals and books gathered from Europe and America. Count Rumford also contributed to the pages two essays: On the Means of Increasing the Heat obtained in the Combustion of Fuel, and On the Use of Steam as a Vehicle for Conveying Heat.

Of a list of four hundred and thirty-eight donations of books, articles of furniture, and instruments made in the first year to the Institution, most of them singly, by individuals, no less than one hundred and seventy-five are credited to Count Rumford, including a London edition, in two volumes, of Franklin's Life and Works. He had, at this time, accumulated a very large and valuable collection of apparatus and philosophical instruments, many of them the work of his own hands as well as the contrivances of his own ingenuity, provided in pursuing his varied experiments. These, in large part, the Count most generously gave to the Institution, which he also supplied—according to the general rule that he had been so careful to introduce as of comprehensive application in its plan — with well-constructed models of all his own inventions. The repository very soon became a centre of attraction for visitors as well as for residents in the metropolis.

A contemporaneous account of the opening of the Institution is given in the Gentleman's Magazine for 1800,* as follows: —

"Tuesday, March 11. — A society under the title of 'The Royal Institution of Great Britain,' and under the patronage of his Majesty, commenced its sittings for the first time this day. Its professed object is to

<hr>

* VoL LXX. Part I. p. 382.

direct the public attention to the arts, by an establishment for diffusing the knowledge and facilitating the general introduction of useful mechanical inventions and improvements."

Count Rumford took a most active part in all the meetings of the managers up to that of September 14, 1799, after which he was absent until the 3d of February, 1800; and as there is a record of the unfortunate illness and long confinement of one of the managers whose zeal had been so conspicuous in the formation and success of the Institution, he was probably ill during that interval.

On the 10th of March, 1800, the Count was residing in the house of the Institution, and he was requested, as long as he did so, to superintend all the works, the servants, and the workmen. In August he was at Harrowgate, and on October 20 in Scotland. He continued in the house probably until about the 6th of July, 1801, as it was then

" *Resolved*, That Count Rumford be requested to continue his general superintendence of the works going on at the house of the Institution, agreeably to the several resolutions of the managers in that respect, in the same manner as if he had continued to reside in the house."

Count Rumford reported, that, at the recommendation of Sir Joseph Banks, he had had a conversation with Dr. Young respecting his engagement as Professor of Natural Philosophy at the Royal Institution and editor of the journals, together with a general superintendence of the house. And " it appearing from the report of Count Rumford that Dr. Young is a man of abilities equal to these undertakings, it was

" *Resolved*, That Count Rumford be authorized to

engage Dr. Young in the aforesaid capacities, at a salary of £300 *per annum.*"

The Count's visit to Harrowgate, in Yorkshire, in July, 1800, was with a view to the recovery of his health. References have more than once been made in the previous pages to the prostration and suffering which were visited upon him while performing his most arduous labors, and, as he seems to have thought, in consequence of the exertions and self-sacrifices which they required of him. There are hints dropped in some contemporary notices of him which imply that he practised some unwise or fanciful experiments on himself in the matters of diet and exercise, and that his originality or ingenuity in this direction may have enfeebled him. There are no apparent grounds for these reflections save the facts that he was frequently ill, and that he was somewhat notional as regards his food. He certainly was not a hypochondriac, though he was probably a dyspeptic. His associate, Dr. Young, describes his peculiarities of physical habit, and the regimen to which he had recourse, as being adopted in obedience to his medical advisers, rather than as fancies of his own. The Count's daughter makes many references to her father's frequent weakness and illness, and we have seen that he himself mentions his own troubles of this sort as compelling him to intermit his labors in Munich for the sake of rest and travel, and that he was not able to resume them all on his return.

The more, therefore, must we appreciate his never intermitted industry, and constant devotion of time and thought in efforts and ingenious schemes for the good of others. If many of these labors were devised and carried out, as in all probability they were, while he was

himself often disabled and dispirited, they certainly increase his claims upon our respect and gratitude. He
even tried to make his own experiences as an invalid,
and the methods by which he sought health, the indirect
occasions for furnishing materials for his Essays. Thus
in this visit of two months to the waters at Harrowgate
he contrived by his experiments on himself to gather
information and to enlighten others on the salubrious
effects of warm bathing, which he made the subject
of a publication, his thirteenth Essay. He began by
conforming himself to the advice of his physician, in
accordance with the professional theory at the time, of
taking his warm bath on the evening of each third day,
and going immediately to his bed, which had been
warmed in order that he might not be exposed to a
chill. But he found that, so far from experiencing any
benefit from this practice, the nights after he had taken
his baths were the most restless and feverish, showing
that in his case, at least, the prescription was unsatisfactory. Acting on the advice of a fellow-lodger at the
Ganby Inn, he took his bath at midday, two hours
before dining, employing the interval in his usual work.
He also took his bath on alternate days, and finally, as
he was stronger and had a better appetite, in spite of
the remonstrance of his medical adviser, he bathed daily.
He satisfied himself that in his own case, contrary to
established opinion, a warm bath was not relaxing or
enfeebling, but really had an invigorating effect, while
he believed that a cold bath gave the system a severe
shock which only those of a rugged constitution could
bear. He says that he was restored to better health
than he had enjoyed for seven or eight years, having
never till then recovered from his dangerous illness in

Bavaria. He adds some directions as to the mode in which baths should be constructed, and recommends them further as a means of harmless and useful luxury. To increase the pleasure of a warm bath, he suggests the burning of sweet-scented woods and aromatic gums and resins in small chafing-dishes in the bathing-rooms, by which the air will be perfumed with the most pleasant odors. He adds: —

"Those who are disposed to smile at this display of Eastern luxury would do well to reflect on the sums they expend on what they consider as luxuries, and then compare the real and *harmless* enjoyments derived from them with the rational and innocent pleasures here recommended. I would ask them if a statesman or a soldier going from the refreshing enjoyment of a bath, such as I have described, to the senate or to the field, would, in their opinion, be less likely to do his duty than a person whose head is filled and whose faculties are deranged by the use of wine?

"Effeminacy is no doubt very despicable, especially in a person who aspires to the character and virtues of a man. But I see no cause for calling anything effeminate which has no tendency to diminish either the strength of the body, the dignity of the sentiments, or the energy of the mind. I see no good reason for considering those grateful aromatic perfumes, which in all ages have been held in such high estimation, as a less elegant or less rational luxury than smoking tobacco or stuffing the nose with snuff."

He pleads for the reconstruction in England of the baths which the old Romans once established there, and is enthusiastic in describing and commending the vapor baths of the poor Russian peasants.

Letters of the Count to friends in America, written at this time, give evidence alike of his interest in their personal service and of his desire to keep them informed about himself. The following, to Colonel Baldwin, is in answer to one already given.

" BROMPTON, 1st Febry. 1800.

"MY DEAR SIR,—I arrived here from the country last evening, and as I hear that there is an American Ship just upon the point of sailing from the Downs for Boston, I shall, if possible, get this letter put on board her. Your letter of November last reached me about ten days ago.. But being then at a considerable distance from London, I could do nothing towards executing any of your commissions. I have this day entered on that business by consulting with Mr. Fraser of New Bond St., Mathematical Instrument Maker to his Majesty, and a very old acquaintance of mine, respecting the best means of forwarding your views regarding your son. From Mr. Fraser I learn that the Instrument-making business is divided into two distinct branches in London, namely, working Instrument-Makers and Shopkeepers; and that though some few of the great Shopkeepers — such, for instance, as Ramsden, Dolland, Adams, Fraser & Co. — have workshops in their houses, and employ some workmen, yet that by far the greater part of the articles in which they deal are made by manufacturers who live in their own private houses and keep no open shops. Working Instrument-makers take apprentices who are always bound for seven years, and with them they commonly receive a premium of about £50 or £60 sterling.

"The great dealers in Mathematical Instruments also take apprentices, but they have seldom opportunities of much practice in making instruments. They learn to know the construction of them and to judge of their merit of work, and of the defects and perfection of the instruments in which they deal; and they likewise learn to take Instruments to pieces, to clean them, and to examine their accuracy. But no Instrument-Maker or dealer in Instruments would, without a very large premium, undertake to instruct a young gentleman in the course of two or three years, and make him perfect in both branches of the trade.

"Mr. Fraser thinks that it would not be possible to get your son into one of the shops of London for a term of from two to four years for a less premium than from £60 to £100 sterling: your son to be boarded in the house free of cost to him or to you during that period. I shall make further inquiries, and shall take an early opportunity of acquainting you with the result of them. As I have not a moment to lose, the Ship being on the point of sailing, I shall add nothing more to this letter than merely my best thanks for all your kindness to my Daughter, whose gratitude is equal to my own.

"I am Yours most faithfully,

"RUMFORD.

"I shall, as soon as possible, set about executing your other commissions. I am embarrassed about your Thermometers, as you do not mention the extent of their scales.

"My Daughter writes me that you are very kind to her, and have expressed to her your readiness to afford her assistance in the accomplishment of her schemes. I beg you would always give her your advice on all occasions, and I shall be extremely grateful to you for all the assistance you may afford in making the situation of my dear Mother as comfortable as possible. I long very much indeed to see my beloved Parent.

[*Superscription.*]

"If the Ship Thomas Russel should be gone from the Downs, where she now is, this letter is to be returned to Count Rumford at Brompton.

"The Honble Colonel Baldwin, Woburn.

"To the Care of Mr. Cushing, Merchant, Boston, State of Massachusetts.

"By the American Ship, Thomas Russel,—Capt. Jackson."

The following letter to President John Adams was designed to open a correspondence between the American Academy and the Royal Institution:—

"Sir,—The Managers of the Royal Institution of Great Britain have directed me to transmit to the American Academy of Arts and Sciences the enclosed Prospectus. I have therefore the honour to forward the same to your Excellency, and to request that you would lay it, or cause it to be laid, before that learned and respectable body.

"I have likewise the honour, in conformity to the Instructions I have received, to request that the American Academy of Arts and Sciences may be assured of the sincere desire of the Managers of the Royal Institution of Great Britain to cultivate a friendly Correspondence with them, and to co-operate with them in all things that may contribute to the advancement of Science and to the general Diffusion of the Knowledge of all such new and useful Discoveries and mechanical Improvements as may tend to increase the enjoyments and promote the Industry, Happiness, and Prosperity of Mankind.

"I have the honour to be with great Respect,

"Your Excellency's most Obedient and most Humble Servant,

"RUMFORD.

"Royal Institution, Albemarle St., London, 1ˢᵗ June, 1800.

"His Excellency John Adams, President of the United States and President of the American Academy of Arts and Sciences."

With a similar intent the Count addressed the following letter to the President of Harvard College:—

"Royal Institution, Albemarle St., London, 1ˢᵗ June, 1800.

"Sir,—By direction of the Managers of the Royal Institution of Great Britain, I have the honour to transmit to the President of Harvard University the inclosed publication, in which an account is given of an establishment lately formed in this metropolis for promoting useful knowledge.

"I have likewise the honour, in conformity to the instructions I have received, to request that the heads of the University may be assured of the sincere desire of the Managers of the Royal Institution of Great Britain to cultivate a friendly correspondence with them, and to co-operate with them in all things that may contribute to the advancement of Science, and to the general Diffusion of the Knowledge of all such new and useful Discoveries and mechanical Improvements as may tend to increase the enjoyments and promote the Industry, Happiness, and Prosperity of Mankind.

"I have the honour to be, with much respect, Sir,

"Your most obedient humble servant,

"RUMFORD.

"To the Rev. Dr. WILLARD, President of Harvard University, Massachusetts." [*]

Domestic and scientific concerns are happily combined in the following letter to Colonel Baldwin, written from the Count's lodgings in the Institution in Albemarle Street: —

"ROYAL INSTITUTION, 9th June, 1800.

"My DEAR SIR, — I cannot neglect so good an opportunity of writing to you as the return of Mr. Higginson to America now offers. And I must begin my letter with a subject which is ever uppermost in my mind. My Daughter and my dear Mother will probably be in your neighbourhood when this letter reaches you. I most earnestly recommend them both to your kind attentions. I have one wish, and one only, respecting them, which is, that they may be as happy as possible. As I am at so great a distance from them, I am but ill qualified to judge of their wants and their wishes. Pray assist them in every way in which your friendly assistance can be of use to them or make them comfortable and contented. I once imagined that my Mother might perhaps be disposed to prefer Woburn to every other situation for the place of her residence, and I have long wished to see her and my Daughter comfortably settled under the same roof. What can be done to unite them cordially in the same scheme and mode of life?

"If this can be done, I should prefer it to any other plan.

[*] Memoirs of Youth and Manhood. By Sidney Willard. Vol. I. p. 139.

But if it cannot well be arranged to the *entire* satisfaction and comfort of both, I shall always be perfectly satisfied if I know that they are both pleased and contented. I always was of opinion that people should be left to act freely and make themselves comfortable and happy in their own way. It is very possible that my Mother may have good reasons for preferring a place of residence and mode of life very different from that which I, at this great distance, might think would please her most. I wish I knew what she wishes. I should then have no doubts how to act and what to propose. Perhaps my Daughter may marry (which she has my leave to do whenever she pleases, and with whom she pleases). This may greatly alter her relative situation with me and with my Mother. She may perhaps wish at some future period to make me another visit in Europe, and even in this scheme I shall not oppose her inclinations, if her heart should be set on the gratification of them. I do not mean to be an indulgent father in theory only.

"Pray let me know what you think on these subjects, and tell me how I must act to make two Persons who are very dear to me as happy as possible.

"I ought to take shame to myself for giving you so much trouble, when you may think I have paid little attention to your requests. The enclosed account of Mr. Fraser will acquaint you with the particulars of those articles which you will now receive by Mr. Higginson.

"The Lathe, Mandrel, &c., which are ordered from the very best workman in that line in Great Britain, will be forwarded when finished, as will be also the Lucernal Glasses, which are never found ready made. If you wish to have two equal mercurial Thermometers of the greatest possible Range of Scale, viz. from freezing to boiling mercury, or from 40° below Nothing to about 600° above Nothing of Fahrenheit's Scale, I will order them for you. They will cost about 2½ Guineas each. Give me your orders.

"My Daughter will acquaint you with the brilliant Success of our new Institution. The Subscriptions have amounted this year to above £ 24,000 Sterling. And as little of the Institution has yet been *seen* except upon paper, and in the form of Proposals and descriptions of what it is intended to establish, I consider this unexampled support as a flattering testimony of the public opinion entertained of the talents and probity of the founders of the Institution. You will naturally perceive how strongly these proofs of the public esteem and regard must bind me to the Institution, and render it my duty to watch over it, and do everything in my power to make it perfect and durable. I wish you would come and see it this autumn. I can offer you a very comfortable house while you stay in England, and if you should *want* a travelling companion, I believe you could find one without going very far to look after him. It is highly probable that I should be able to return with you to America in the month of March, or I would wait till May or June, if a wish to examine the Canals in England should render you desirous of staying a few months longer in this country.

"I am ever, my Dear Sir,

"Yours, Most Affectionately,

"RUMFORD.

"Count Rumford, for Colonel Baldwin,

"Bought of Wm Fraser, Mathematical Instrument Maker to his Majesty and Optician to His Royal Highness the Prince of Wales. No. 3 Bond Street.

	£.	s.	d
A Portable Barometer, with Rack work and a packing case	3	13	6
A Pair of 8 inch Magnetic Bars in a Mah^y Box	1	1	0
A Thermometer on a Metal Scale, in a Case	1	5	0
A do. on an Ivory Scale, in a Glass tube and a case	1	1	0
2 Two Pole Tapes in Boxes	0	15	0
A Pint & ½ a Gill of Pure Brass varnish, brushes, &c.	0	10	6
A ream of the best Lawn Paper	0	12	0
½ oz. of Silver wire 4,'9, and 4 oz. of Plated do. 5,'6	0	10	3
	£9	8	9

"Sir,— Not being certain as to what degree of heat the Thermometers were to be used in, I have only sent two Boiling-water Thermometers. If they are required to endure a greater heat they must be made on purpose. The Collar and mandrel, &c is in hand, but there being but one workman in London whose Lathes I could recommend, and his being so much employed, renders it impossible to get it finished in less than three weeks or a month. The set of Glasses for the Lucernal Microscope must also be made on purpose, which will take nearly two weeks. The collar and mandrel, with screw-tools complete, will come to £5. 15. 0, and the set of Glasses for a Lucernal Microscope will be £3. 3. 0.

" P. S. — It will be of no use to send the Speculums of the Reflecting Telescope without the brass work, as the goodness of the Telescope principally depends upon their being properly adjusted.

" The cleaning of the Speculum would cost about 25/s.

" Wm FRASER.

" In Varnishing any Brass-Work, the Brass is first to be warmed just sufficient to evaporate the Spirits and leave the Wax or Gum on the Brass. It is to be put on as lightly as possible, so as to be all covered.

("Received Augt 6, 1800.")

It would have been a most gratifying and delightful incident in the life of Count Rumford, if, in fulfilment of the terms of his own cordial invitation, his friend Colonel Baldwin had had leisure at the time to indulge his own earnest wishes by joining the Count in London, to revive the pleasant memories of their youth, and to enjoy the privilege of such a companionship for introduction to eminent scientific men and for travel in England or on the Continent. But Colonel Baldwin was, in a more limited sphere, serving his native State as faithfully as was the Count in his larger opportunities advancing the interests of practical science for the civilized world. In the mean while Colonel Baldwin was faithful to the highest obligations of respect and admiration for his friend by preparing himself for writing and publishing during the Count's lifetime the best accounts of him and of his great undertakings which had appeared in print. They are found in that series of articles in two volumes of the " Literary Miscellany," published in Cambridge, which have been already referred to and quoted.

Dr. John Davy, in his memoirs of the life of his brother, Sir Humphry, gives a sketch of his connection with the Royal Institution as assistant lecturer on chemistry and director of the laboratory, — this being a temporary arrangement till he should be qualified for the professorship of chemistry. While recognizing very fully and adequately the hopeful and promising inauguration of the new Institution, and the signal services which have been performed through it, this biographer hardly does justice to the claims of Count Rumford as its master-spirit, or to his agency in bringing Sir Humphry upon the scene where he won his first eminent distinctions. Dr. Davy very justly says that the Institution was a new experiment, engaging the zeal and active co-operation of people of rank and fortune, and opening a most auspicious era for general science, especially for chemistry, in the expansion and extension of its relations. The Continent was then closed by war. A large number of influential persons in society were induced to enlist in the high and profitable pursuits which the Institution opened to them, and they found alike amusement, gratification, and practical profit by attendance upon its lectures and experiments and by visiting its repository of models and inventions. Dr. Davy gives an excellent description of the laboratory of the Institution, which was for that time very completely and even lavishly furnished. The founder had from the first resolved that all the apparatus of science which skill and money could then secure should be provided for lecturers and experimenters.

A more full recognition of Count Rumford's agency in securing the services of Davy than that which is given in the memoir by his brother may be found in the earlier biography of him by Dr. John Ayrton Paris.* Dr. Paris quotes a letter addressed to himself (p. 76) by Mr. J. R. Underwood, one of Rumford's most intimate friends and associates in the Institution, to the effect that he and Mr. James Thompson had made known to the Count Davy's talents and eminent qualities for a lecturer. Davy had been pursuing some investigations on heat, probably instigated and guided by Rumford's publication of his own experiments. There will be occasion by and by to make a passing reference to an absurd allegation that Davy had anticipated the discoveries of Rumford on his great subject. The attention of the Count having thus been called to this promising youth, Rumford at once wrote to Davy, who came, at his summons, to London, and after several interviews with him accepted, at Rumford's instance, the invitation of the managers to become Director of the laboratory and Assistant Professor of Chemistry, February 16, 1801. Though Davy in a letter reports that the Count was most liberal and polite in behavior towards him, it is a curious fact that the Count at first received a highly unfavorable impression from Davy's personal appearance (pp. 79, 80). This the Count expressed in a letter to Mr. Underwood, nor would he allow Davy to lecture in the theatre of the

* London, 1831.

Institution till he had himself had trial of him in the smaller room. His first lecture, however, removed the misgiving, and Rumford heartily said, " Let him command any arrangements which the Institution can afford." Davy was uncouth in appearance and address, and he had to bear many mortifications in his first mingling with society in London. Rumford was at one of Davy's lectures as late as May 25, 1802, having in the autumn of the previous year been absent in Paris. Perhaps it was well that these two eminent men of science, with their marked peculiarities of character and temper, were not long kept in intimate intercourse. They would hardly have been personal friends, as they shared some of the same weaknesses of sensitiveness and irritability.

I am indebted to Dr. H. Bence Jones, the Secretary of the Royal Institution, and the author of the admirable memoir of Faraday, for his kindness in copying and transmitting to me the following letter of Count Rumford to Davy : —

" ROYAL INSTITUTION, 16ᵗʰ Feb. 1801.

" DEAR SIR, — In consequence of the conversations I have had with you respecting your engaging in the service of the Royal Institution of Great Britain, I this day laid the matter before the Managers of the Institution, at their Meeting : (Present, Sir Joseph Banks, Earl of Morton, Count Rumford, and Richard Clark, Esq.,) and I have the pleasure to acquaint you that the Proposal I made to them was approved, and the following Resolution unanimously taken by them : ' *Resolved*, That Mr. Humphry Davy be engaged in the service of the Royal Institution in the capacity of Assistant Lecturer in Chemistry, Director of the Chemical Laboratory, and assistant Editor of the Journals of the Institution ; and that he be allowed to occupy a room in the house, and be furnished with coals and candles, and that he be paid a salary of one hundred guineas *per annum*.'

"On this occasion I did not neglect to give an account to the Managers of the whole of what passed between us respecting the situation it was intended you should fill in the Institution on your engaging in its service, and the prospects that could with propriety be held out to you of future advantage; and the Managers agreed with me in thinking that as you had expressed your willingness to devote yourself entirely and permanently to the Institution, it would be right and proper to hold out to you the prospect of becoming in the course of two or three years Professor of Chemistry in the Institution, with a Salary of three hundred pounds *per annum*, provided that within that period you shall have given proofs of your fitness to hold that distinguished situation. Although you must ever consider the duties of the office you may hold under the Institution as the primary objects of your care and attention, yet the Managers are far from being desirous that you should relinquish those private philosophical investigations in which you have hitherto been engaged, and by which you have so honorably distinguished yourself and attracted their attention. It will afford them the sincerest pleasure to encourage and assist you in these laudable pursuits, and give you every facility which the Philosophical apparatus at the Institution can afford to make new and interesting experiments.

" You will naturally consider the Journals of the Institution as the most proper vehicle for communicating to the public, from time to time, short accounts of the progress you may make in your investigations; this will, however, by no means be considered as precluding you in any degree from presenting to the Royal Society of London, or any other learned body, Philosophical papers, or Memoirs on such scientific subjects as may engage your attention, or from publishing in any other manner the results of your researches.

" As you are fully informed with respect to the nature and objects of the Royal Institution, and are acquainted with the respectable characters of those distinguished persons with whom

I have the honour to act in the management of its concerns, you cannot, I think, entertain the smallest doubt of their constant protection, and of their readiness on all occasions to do full justice to the zeal and abilities you may display in the situation in which they have placed you.

" It is with much esteem and a sincere desire that the talents which at so early a period of life you discovered may be cultivated with care and always employed with success, that I am, Dear Sir,

" Your Most Obedient Servant,

" RUMFORD."

I am also indebted to Dr. Jones for his kindness in copying for me the following extracts from the managers' minutes : —

" *March* 16, 1801. — Count Rumford reported that Mr. Davy arrived at the Institution on Wednesday, the 11th of March, 1801, and took possession of his situation.

" In consequence of the verbal directions which Count Rumford had received from the managers to prepare a room in the house of the Institution for Mr. Davy, namely, that adjoining the room now occupied by Dr. Garnett, and to refund to the Doctor the expenses he had been at in furnishing the said room, the Count reported that the committee of expenditure had paid to Dr. Garnett £ 20 2 3 for a new Brussels carpet, and £ 17 6 0 for twelve chairs, making in the whole the sum of £ 37 8 3, and that the said carpet and chairs have been employed in furnishing the room occupied by the managers.

" Count Rumford reported further that he had purchased a cheaper second-hand carpet for Mr. Davy's room, together with such other articles as appeared to him necessary to render the room habitable, and among the rest a new sofa-bed, which, in order that it may serve as a model for imitation, has been made complete in all its parts."

Faraday also was largely indebted to the opportunities and facilities furnished by the Royal Institution

in fostering his early ardor for science. During his
apprenticeship as a newspaper-boy and a bookbinder,
and just as he was reaching manhood, a customer of his
master, who was a member of the Institution, gave him
tickets to four of the lectures which Davy delivered
there early in 1812. Faraday wrote out these lectures
from notes which he made of them, illustrated them by
drawings of his own, and sent his manuscript to Davy
with a letter expressing his desire to escape from trade
and engage in scientific pursuits. Davy promptly responded to his confidence, and though he detected signs
of fitness for such pursuits in his correspondent advised
him not to abandon his trade, as science was a poor
paymaster, while at the same time he promised the
youth his patronage, and offered to secure to him the
bookbinding of the Institution and of his friends.
Davy soon after invited Faraday to an interview, at
which he offered him the place of assistant in the laboratory on a salary of twenty-five shillings a week, with
two attic rooms. This was in the early part of March,
1813. Faraday at once occupied his lodgings in the
building, and engaged with devoted industry and zeal in
chemical manipulation in the laboratory. He lectured
before the Institution for the long period of thirty-
eight years, and having, in 1825, been made its Director, is thought by his biographer to have averted its
decline or secured its continued existence. It furnished
him a home and a sphere for eminent service during
more than half a century.* I am not aware that Faraday ever met with Count Rumford, but think it not at
all unlikely that he did so while spending three months

* Dr. H. Bence Jones, in his "Life and Letters of Faraday" (London, 1870),
gives much interesting information about the Institution.

in Paris in the autumn and winter of 1813 as the companion of Davy.

Considering that there was then in London no other well-furnished laboratory, and indeed no other establishment with an endowment and an organization for securing the best opportunities for experimental research with the facilities and the patronage of an appreciative audience in attendance upon lectures, we may well claim for the Royal Institution the honor of adopting Faraday — perhaps the most distinguished man in the whole of his own field which the world has produced — as its most accomplished alumnus. In those qualities of character which made him so lovable, for magnanimity, simplicity, ingenuousness, and modesty, as well as for his single-hearted devotion to science, he stands without a rival at the head of the roll of fame. The foibles of vanity, self-assertion, and arrogance which we have to lament on his own account in Davy show no traces of their presence or influence in Faraday. It would have been pleasant to trace, if facts would have enabled us to do so, any tokens of an acquaintance, which we may be sure would have been a friendship, between him and Rumford; for we may say of the latter, with full confidence, that he was free from jealousy, and that, whatever foibles he may have exhibited, he would have found in Faraday one whom he would have most cordially appreciated and admired, and one whom he would have delighted to extol.

M. Pictet would appear to have been the most admiring, constant, and enthusiastic among the many devoted friends of Count Rumford. He was himself highly cultivated and passionately fond of scientific pursuits, with strong religious feelings, and of an ardent temperament. In his first letter to his fellow-editors, written in London, June 21, 1801,[*] he says that the principal motive which induced him, in such distracting times of war, to undertake his tour, was his admiration of Count Rumford and his desire to visit the land where he dwelt. The Count had long before proffered him his hospitalities at his own home at Brompton, though until his arrival at the house they had never seen each other. The Count insisted that a friend of Pictet's, who had come with him from Paris, though a perfect stranger, should likewise be his guest. The host took them both, on the day of their arrival, to the Royal Institution. This was the admiration of Pictet, who proceeds to translate for his *Bibliothèque* the report of the Institution published in the second number of its journal. In one of his notes to this report the correspondent describes the lecture-rooms or amphitheatres as disposed and contrived by the Count with wonderful adaptation to their purposes. In another note the Frenchman proves how soon he had learned in England the cant meaning of the word *job*, — which, however, he spells with two b's, and does not attempt to turn into a French equivalent. He says the Count was so determined to exclude all speculation and all chance for private individual thrift or gain from the Institution, that even in the saloon, or restaurant, viands, tea, and coffee were furnished at prime cost to all attending the establishment who needed refreshment, — precluding " what is known so well in England *sous le nom de jobb.*"

Delighted with his inspection of the Institution,

<hr>

[*] *Bibliothèque Britannique, Sciences et Arts*, Vol. XVII.

Pictet expressed to the Count his surprise that in so enlightened and advanced a country as England it had not before occurred to some man of genius to anticipate the plan. He reports the reply of the Count.

"No doubt others before myself had anticipated the benefits which an association of men might draw from uniting their efforts for a common good. But sad experience has generally proved that enterprises designed for this apparent or real end are not slow in degenerating and being perverted to the private interests of a few individuals, so that most of the members have been duped. The result has been such as to warrant distrust grounded on facts very mischievous in their consequences. I have sought to make sure of the good without leaving the door open to abuses. That is the spirit and the whole tendency of our Institution, as our rules manifest. If I succeed, as I am really bound to hope, this auspicious enterprise in winning confidence will increase my means and opportunities, and the Establishment will acquire a consistency proportioned to its real utility."

Pictet witnessed in the Institution the experiments of Dr. Wollaston in galvanism, and the decomposition of water by two processes. It was during this visit of his as an honored guest of Rumford's at his famous model house at Brompton, that Pictet, making use of his fair opportunities, held those confidential interviews with his host, information obtained from which was quoted on an early page of this memoir. It is reasonable to infer that the Count was aware of his friend's purpose to make him so prominent a subject of the contributions made by him during his tour to the excellent Geneva journal, of which he was, as has been said, one of the originators and editors, — the Bibliothèque Britannique. It is here that we find a full description of the Count at home, or, rather, of his home. I translate the following from his ninth letter (Vol.

XIX. *Science et Arts*, January, 1802, v. 1.). It is dated London, August 15, 1801.

"I have been living for the last eight days at the Elyssium, which belongs to Count Rumford, and I lead there the most pleasant life which it is possible to imagine. It is the fitting time for attempting to describe to you this agreeable and ingenious structure. The house forms a part of a long range of edifices, Brompton Row, about a mile from London, which lines the great road that conducts to the bridges of Fulham and Battersea. Between the dwellings and the carriage-road is a space planted with trees and sown with grass, — an arrangement generally adopted in the environs of the capital, and which agreeably combines for the view many advantages. The windows have a double glazing, and the exterior makes a three-sided projection, in which are placed vases of flowers and odorous shrubs, which you may have at your pleasure within or outside of the apartment, according as you open or close the inner sash. The table on which these vases stand is perforated, in order to furnish the plants of a hot-house character on it with the air necessary for vegetation, and the side sashes of the exterior windows open as they are needed.

"The house has five stories, including the offices, which in this country are always set under the level of the earth. The arrangement is the same in all the stories, two apartments and a staircase. On the ground-floor is the parlor, where morning visitors are received, and the dining-room. On the first flight is a bedchamber, and a saloon for company; on the second, the same arrangement; on the third, a bedchamber and a work-room for the occupant of the dwelling. In this room, which has a view of the country, the light comes in through a set of adjoining windows arranged in an arc of a circle, through which even in the middle of the apartment you may see a quarter of the horizon. Their sills are arrayed with flowers and shrubs, and the eye, looking over the trees and the neighboring fields, seeing nothing intervening, the illusion is complete; you suppose yourself to be in the country close to a garden bordered by a park. Back of the main house is a structure of outbuildings a which enclose a stable and coach-house, a chemical laboratory, room for a valet, one for a carpenter, &c. The two buildings are separated by a small garden, but there is a communication between them by a covered gallery, which is warmed in the winter by pipes of hot air.

" The agreeable and the useful have been combined in this abode with much ingenuity and success. You divine at once that everything that concerns the use of fuel, whether for the kitchen or for warmth, has been carried to the highest degree of economy and perfection. The mantel-piece in the rooms makes no projection, and masked as it is in the summer by a border of painted canvas, you confound it with one of the panels of the wainscoting. These panels at the right and the left of the fireplace are hung on sunken hinges, and you raise one or the other of these, in the style of a table, when you wish to write or read near the fire. The same arrangement is adapted to the piers which separate the windows, and you can at your will produce either a table or a simple panel, when you allow it to fall back again. The wainscoting coming out flush with the front of the throat of the chimney, it makes no farther projection, and this arrangement furnishes in depth the necessary place for setting closets, where clothing, books, and everything which you wish to keep safe from dampness and dust, is protected and disposed of invisibly.

" The bedchambers are disguised in the same way, that is to say, the bed is concealed under the form of an elegant sofa, of which the seat is formed by one of the mattresses, and the other is constructed in a way to fold up as with a hinge through the length of the back part, and then contracts the bed by its doubled thickness to the ordinary size of an ottoman. Two cushions ornament the ends. Under the sofa are two large and deep drawers which contain the bedding, coverlet, and nightgear, and which are hidden by a fringed valance. In a few minutes the sofa is converted at night into an excellent bed, and in the morning the bed becomes for the day an ornamental piece of furniture.

"The most elegant simplicity is observable in all the furniture, which is different on each story; and even in the choice of the colors you see that the taste of the owner has been aided by those natural rules for the blending of tints which, as he himself has discovered, always harmonize for the eye when they are respectively the complement of the colors which the whole prismatic spectrum presents. You see that these discoveries of Newton can be applied to the choice of a ribbon as well as to a cosmos.

"I forgot to tell you of the ingenious and convenient arrangement of the dining-room. Its area is changeable by means of a partition of window-sashes with large panes, forming a very large double door, which opens on the side of the casements for the sunlight, and by which also the heat escapes in the winter. When the folding doors are open at right angles they correspond with the windows, and the room is to that extent enlarged ; the same doors form then two side recesses which answer for two sideboards, communicating within and outside the room, by which the service of the table is performed without the servants having to come in. If you wish to contract the room and to preserve its warmth by the effective agency of double windows, you can close the folding doors, and, without depriving yourself of light or of the charming view of the shrubbery with which all the windows are decked, you are completely protected from all chills.

"I occupy by myself half of this charming dwelling. On the ground-floor is my working-room, and on the first story my bedchamber and parlor. The house is equipped with the most perfect simplicity and the most complete order, and a person could not conceive a more pleasant life, nor one more *comfortable* (why do we not adopt that word which we need in our language?) than that which is led here. Perfect freedom is given and enjoyed. Our first *tête-à-tête* takes place at breakfast, and I never leave it without having learned something new, interesting, or useful. I try always to arrange my day's work with reference to engaging my friend in some object of research which is common to us ; and if I do not always succeed in it, I have at least the assurance of rejoining him in the evening,

and then for two hours we chat about matters which interest
us alike, and I cannot describe the charm which I find in these
conversations. I make notes of them immediately afterwards,
for, if possible, I would not lose a word of them. And what a
life is his! His memory retraces faithfully all the principal
facts, and even all the anecdotes, of his early years. I press him
every day to commit these things to writing. He objects, and his
other engrossing occupations, which are excessive, leave him no
time for it. And who knows if he will ever find the time? I
believe it is my duty, as a friend, to profit by the opportunity
which has brought me near to him to try to draw out in our
intercourse all the marked incidents of his life, and to send to
you in confidence these biographical particulars which you may
keep in your portfolio. I am favored by being able to gather as
from the lips of two of his oldest and most intimate friends,
whom I frequently see, Sir Ch. B[lagden] and Mr. De P——,
the Bavarian Envoy, many of those facts which his modesty
conceals. In combining all these means I shall thus have
something more complete and more authentic than we read about
him in the English journals, and which sometimes make him
laugh. And to trust as little as I can to chance in carrying out
this purpose, I will profit by what remains of my letter to copy
what I have already gathered. I will complete it, if I can, in
my next, and will follow, so far as my notes will allow, the order
of time." [Here is added the memoir given on previous pages.]

In this attempt to describe with such minuteness
the novel and convenient devices which Count Rumford had introduced into his house at Brompton, Pictet
was simply endeavoring to convey to readers on the
Continent, by this method, something of the privilege
which residents in and near London enjoyed of satisfy-
ing their curiosity by observation. The ingenious and
tasteful arrangements in that house made it for several
years one of the most attractive objects for curious
sight-seers; and the Count's gratification, and perhaps

his love of appreciation, was ministered to in having the edifice freely exhibited to visitors from all classes of society who thronged to examine it. Of one of the novel contrivances in that edifice, on which the Count greatly prided himself, Pictet was strangely unobservant. It was what the Count called a *concealed kitchen*, recommended and described by him in his Tenth Essay. Two of these, very complete, had been fitted up by him in the Royal Institution as models,—one in the housekeeper's room, the other in the great kitchen. He writes: "There are also two kitchens of this kind in my house at Brompton in two adjoining rooms, which have been fitted up principally with a view to showing that all the different processes of cookery may be carried on in a room which, on entering it, nobody would suspect to be a kitchen."

And he proceeds to describe the contrivance at length, with diagrams.*

In translating for their own pages Count Rumford's Prospectus of the Royal Institution, the editors of the Bibliothèque Britannique † introduce it with the following prefatory remarks, commencing with an extract from Madame de Stael's essay on Literature considered in its Relations to Social Institutions.

"'Nothing so animates and tones the spirit as the hope of rendering useful service to the human race. When the thought proves the immediate precursor of action, when the happy purpose can at once be transformed into a benevolent institution, what interest will a man not find in the development of his intelligence!'

"These reflections of a celebrated woman apply with full justice to all the enterprises of a philanthropist whom we have

---

* Tenth Essay, Chap. XIV.　　　　　† Science et Arts, Vol. XIV.

distinguished among the first, Count Rumford, whose name now resounds through Europe. Yes, without doubt, after the spectacle of a man nobly struggling against adversity, this, of a man of genius incessantly engaged in promoting the welfare of his fellow-men, is the noblest which can be offered to the contemplation of generous souls, and to the imitation of those who, animated by the same spirit, and strong in the same purpose, can be drawn on by the influence of the example to the noble career of benevolence.

"And if one considers that genius recognizes in the sciences and arts its implements of work, its most energetic resources, one is penetrated by a most profound and just regard for objects of pursuit so fertile in grand results. One realizes the whole truth of this reflection, expressed in a sentiment of the writer just quoted: 'In examining,' she says, 'the actual state of our enlightenment, we see at a glance that our true riches are the sciences.' This avowal, dropped in a work consecrated to and inspired by an enthusiasm for literature, says a great deal. But the labors of Count Rumford surpass it. He has succeeded in consummating a magnificent enterprise conceived and executed in less than one year. He has aimed to increase the points of contact between the sciences and the arts, to vivify the one by the other, and to apply them together to the needs of humanity and to the perfecting of social blessings. The value of the paper which presents his Proposals and the description of his Institution is doubled by the fact, that in another point of view it may be regarded as an eloquent discourse upon the advantage and the means of making the sciences and the arts reciprocally helpful to their own perfection. In this point of view it may claim the attention of all those among our readers who are interested in the progress of this class of human attainments. We proceed to translate nearly the whole of it."

Then follows the substance of the Proposals and Prospectus, translated into French.

It would have been exceptional to all human experience, alike in the organization and administration of scientific and benevolent schemes, as well as of institutions which are supposed to be more likely to engage the jealousies or rivalries of men, had no private or public variance arisen in connection with the early history of the Royal Institution. There are traces of some personal alienations as having occurred in the first year of its existence, and the compass or the cumbersomeness of its plans, notwithstanding its seemingly large resources, required some modification.

I will offer as full and intelligible an account of these matters of variance as I have been able to verify from the means within my reach. Dean Peacock, in his Life of Dr. Thomas Young,* contents himself with the following curt narration : —

"In the year 1801, Young accepted the office of Professor of Natural Philosophy at the Royal Institution, which had been established in the year preceding, chiefly by the exertions of the well-known Sir Benjamin Thompson, Count Rumford. It was designed as a great metropolitan school of science, where lectures should be given, models of useful instruments exhibited, and collections of books on science and of chemical and philosophical apparatus formed on the most magnificent scale. Its founder, if such he may be termed, had further views also, of making it subsidiary to the promotion of many useful projects and inquiries which he had recently proposed in his Essays, which enjoyed an extraordinary popularity. After managing the affairs of the Institution for a few months, and commencing the editing of its journal, he quarrelled with some of the directors and abandoned the scheme altogether. The conducting of the journal was thenceforward intrusted to the joint care of Dr. Young and his colleague Mr. Davy, at that time Professor of Chemistry, &c."

Having found no reference made by Count Rumford

* London, John Murray, 1855, p. 134.

himself, In any printed or manuscript papers from his pen which have come to my hands, to any "quarrel" of his with the directors of the Royal Institution, or even to any modification of his original plan found to be necessary in its practical work, I drew upon the kindness of its present Secretary, Dr. H. Bence Jones, for such information as he might be able and disposed to give me, if possible from the records. He has most courteously responded by acquainting me with what he knows or can surmise about the matter. He writes to me that "unluckily no one took any care of the original documents of the Royal Institution. The digested minutes of the business are all that remain. All the living letters that would have told their own history are lost." Being himself engaged at present in writing a sketch of the early history of the Institution, he intends to show—

"How we departed from Count Rumford's scheme, and by the genius of Davy became the place for scientific research. You asked me about the laboratory. Essentially, Davy's and Faraday's laboratory was that which Rumford built. But the room that Rumford built was not the room he originally intended for the laboratory. Workshops and model rooms for physical things for the benefit of the poor and sick were more in accordance with his ideas than a chemical laboratory. Even the kitchen was far more to him than analytical investigation. True, his idea of a laboratory was a kitchen and a chemist. Mr. Hatchett saw that the dark room would not do, and got another room built with four skylights, before the model and lecture rooms over the dark room were finished. In September, 1799, Rumford was authorized to engage Dr. Garnett, the first Professor of Chemistry and Physics. He came on the 23d of December. Before February, 1801, there was war between Garnett and Rumford. It broke out regarding Garnett's lectures. Garnett published two syllabusses, which the managers objected to. On the 16th of February Rumford engaged Davy. On March 11 Davy came. On the 15th of June the resignation of Garnett was accepted. On July 6, Rumford was authorized to engage Dr. Young.

"It is very clear to me that Count Rumford fell out with Mr. Bernard, and with Sir John Hippesley. The fact was that Rumford's idea of workshops and kitchen, industrial school, mechanics' institution, model exhibition, social club-house, and scientific committees to do everything, &c., &c., was much too big and unworkable for a private body, and was fitted only for an absolute wealthy government, and was going rapidly into difficulties which, in 1803, led to the proposal to shut up the affair and sell it off. Rumford, seeing he could not have his way, went to Paris. Mr. Bernard and Sir John Hippesley again took up the Institution, and by Davy's help carried it on, without any workshops, or mechanics' institute, or kitchen, or model exhibition, but with experimental researches, libraries, and a mineralogical collection, which were, according to Rumford's ideas, for the benefit of the rich, and by no means capable of doing any good to the poor, — the object he had in view in his society for the diffusion of useful knowledge."

I shall not venture to question either the facts or the opinions drawn from them in Dr. Jones's letter to me, and shall wait with interest, as will so many others, for his promised volume. Indeed, I have some independent grounds to sustain his views. It may be mentioned here, however, that, as will soon be related, Count Rumford left England, as it proved for the last time, in May, 1802, his purpose and desire to return there having been impeded by obstacles of war and other circumstances. For at least a year, then, previous to the time at which there seems to have been a prospect of the failure of the Institution, his presence and influence had been withdrawn.

Some light — though, it must be confessed, not to the extent of imparting full information, may be thrown upon this incidental but interesting point in the history of the Royal Institution by a contemporaneous publication, reference to which has thus far been deferred in these pages as it contains matter that may most fitly be quoted here.

Just at the close of the last century and the beginning of this there was published in London a series of five volumes of contemporary biography, entitled "Public Characters." In the volume published in October, 1802, appears a short biographical sketch of Count Rumford, which bears date 1801–2, and which must undoubtedly have passed under his own eye, at least in print. I have not ascertained by whom it was written, but the writer of it affirms that he received information from some of Rumford's American countrymen. After a statement, in the main correct, of the more important incidents in his career, the writer proceeds as follows:—

"It was also owing to his exertions that the Royal Institute [*sic*] was first established, and should any beneficial advantages arise from it hereafter, he, and he alone, ought undoubtedly to have the whole and sole merit. But candor will not allow us to conceal that the effects likely to be derived from a new society of this kind are not such as could have been either wished or expected. In the establishment of her National Institute, France exhibited a gigantic superiority in respect to human intellect, and by concentrating in one common focus everything respectable, either in the sciences or *belles lettres*, exhibited such a blaze of genius as had never been beheld before in Europe."

The writer of the biography says here in a note :—

"As a proof of this, the old members of the Academy of

Sciences, esteemed the first in Europe during the monarchy, constitute only Class 1 of the National Institute."

He then proceeds : —

" We appear to be successful in *mimicking* the name alone, for to have rivalled the establishment (if it were possible for us to rival it!) it would have been necessary to have called forth the exertions of every man among us conspicuously eminent in the mathematics, practical astronomy, oratory, natural and civil history, painting, poetry, music, &c., &c. To have rewarded these, Parliament should have provided ample salaries; and to have prevented the whole from dwindling into a *ministerial job*, the members ought to have been elected by ballot. Instead of this a puny imitation was adopted, and one professor only appointed. True it is, there are few men in the kingdom who could have been selected perhaps with greater propriety, or who possess more various powers, than the gentleman in question, — Dr. Garnett, a man of considerable eminence in the philosophical and literary world; it is the inefficacy and nullity of the plan only that is here arraigned, without intending to throw the slightest blame on the original projector, who was perhaps cramped in his views and impeded in his exertions."

In a note to this last paragraph the writer communicates the information, such as it is, which must relate to the "quarrel," previously referred to.

" Since writing the above, the editor has learned that many disputes have taken place relative to the management of the Royal Institution, in consequence of which Dr. Garnett has found himself reduced to the necessity of resigning his situation. He also hears with great sorrow that a breach has taken place in the friendship that subsisted between the Count of Rumford and Dr. Garnett; but, as he is unacquainted with the particulars, he will not presume to censure either of the parties in question." *

* An American editor selected from the five volumes of the London edition of
" Public Characters " materials enough to fill a single volume, the contents of which

As to the matter of alleged variances between Count Rumford and the managers of the Royal Institution, I can say little more than that I have met with no information which would warrant even the inference that he, in any case or to any extent, was at issue with them as a body, or that they as such were upon any subject in opposition to him. With individuals once sharing friendly and very cordial relations with him, Rumford did undoubtedly cease to hold such relations, whether because he alienated them wilfully, or because they found him personally or officially disagreeable to them. In another connection I shall have occasion to quote the repeated assertions of his once very intimate companion and associate, Sir Charles Blagden, that he had parted friendship with the Count and should no longer correspond with him. This variance, however, was strictly personal, having apparently no connection with the affairs or the management of the Royal Institution. Dr. Young would seem to have had no quarrel with Rumford. Of this eminent philosopher, Dr. Jones very justly says, in a letter now before me: " Young was never out of scientific war, and never got the honor he deserved. His is a strange history. He ought to

he thought would be generally interesting to the people of the United States. This volume, published in Baltimore in 1805, is the one from which the above extracts are made (pp. 177, 178).

Though aside from the point now engaging me, I am prompted to quote the next paragraph of this biographical sketch, as follows : —

" Count Rumford is allowed to be a man of profound research, close application, and extensive science. His house at Brompton is well calculated to give an idea of the owner. The uppermost story is converted into a laboratory for chemical experiments. His chimneys are contrived so as to economise fuel, prevent smoke, and produce heat; while his double windows, constructed in imitation of those of Germany, Sweden, Denmark, and Russia, exclude the frost during the winter, and serve as so many conservatories for such plants as are incapable of being inured to bear the rigors of our climate."

have been the great man of England.   He should have
given himself entirely to science.   What an unfortunate
man he was in the number and size of his disputes!
Whatever he touched led to a fight.   And yet he was a
gentleman and a Quaker by birth."

Dr. Young speaks in high terms of the character of
Rumford's Experiments on Heat.*   As Corresponding
Secretary of the Royal Society, it was Young's official
duty to transmit to Malus and Fresnel the Rumford
Medals, as awarded to them.   Writing to the latter in
1827, he accompanies the medals, and a draft for
£55 16s., the accumulated surplus income of the fund,
with a letter containing these sentences: "At last,
then, I trust you will no longer have to complain of
the neglect which your experiments have for a time
undergone in this country.   I should also claim some
right to participate in the compliment which is tacitly
paid to myself in common with you by this adjudication, but, considering that more than a quarter of a
century is past since my principal experiments were
made, I can only feel it a sort of anticipation of *posthu-
mous* fame, which I have never particularly coveted."†

It would seem to be only through the strange chances
by which allotments of honor and glory are dropped or
withheld, that Young himself should never have received the Rumford prize.

The sharp and sweeping assertion of Dean Peacock,
that Rumford "abandoned the scheme of the Institution altogether," is not sustained by facts.   The friends
and coadjutors whom he had drawn in to his design,
and who undertook with him its early management and

* Miscellaneous Works, edited by Dean Peacock.   Vol. I. pp. 83, 168.
† Miscellaneous Works, Vol. I. p. 409.

contributed their services, may have found practical difficulties in its administration. The economical and utilitarian objects of the widest popular interest and activity, which were always so prominent in the schemes of Count Rumford, may have involved a too complicated or diffusive responsibility. Possibly, one or more of the men who were ready to work for the Institution in its higher scientific directions, might have been disposed to subordinate or slight the purposes which the founder regarded as primary and most serviceable. That he had variances with one or many of his associates would by no means prove an error of judgment or a fault of temper on his part, if there were not other indications of a morbid sensitiveness and irritability that had come over him at this period of his life. It is certain, however, that the aim and the work of the Institution were modified some time after the Count was in circumstances either to approve of and help in, or to oppose, the change.

Dr. Jones writes to me as follows:—

"In 1810, March 3, Davy gave a lecture 'on the plan which it is proposed to adopt for improving the Royal Institution, and rendering it permanent.' This gives a general view of the change which took place in Rumford's plan, but it gives no names. . . . . . I have as yet got nothing more definite except a statement, which I cannot find to quote, on the number of enemies that Rumford made before he left in 1802. But of indefinite corroborating facts there are many. The greatest is that his relationship with Mr. Bernard and the other managers, excepting Sir Joseph Banks, ceased entirely. He wrote to the clerk of the Institution that 'he wished to hear how things went on, for he had no one to tell him.' The day almost that he left, his arrangements were changed, regarding the terms of admission. The thing was done hastily. The great object he had in view of a mechanics' school, workshop, &c. was immediately stopped. The favorable report he made of the success of his work — a report read after he had almost started — was discredited by Mr. Bernard, and I am much mistaken if the managers did not suspect the accounts ' had been cooked,' so to say, for they called in an accountant. Mr. Bernard says, ' Upon the whole the visitors have the pleasure of stating to the annual meeting, that they conceive there is nothing that merits censure, and much that deserves approbation.' But not a bit of approbation do they give, that I can see. Count Rumford's name never occurs in the minutes of the managers, and they ought to have given him the highest praise, at least for his ideas in forming ' the Rumford Institution,' as I shall call it. The Bernard Institution, which came after it for seven years, was nothing but giving ' fashion to science,' instead of ' usefulness of science to poor and rich,' which is my motto for Rumford's Institution. But his idea was utterly beyond a private society. It included everything, — the industrial exhibition, the mechanics' school and institute, the association for scientific investigation, the club with a school of cookery, the Society for the Diffusion of Useful Knowledge, lectures and journals, &c. All were to be in one building under Rumford's dictatorship ; and if he had had money and support enough, in three more years he would have done the work. But his lieutenant, Webster, Assistant Professor of Geology at the London University and Assistant Secretary of the Geological Society, was deposed, and fashionable science began in 1803, and has gone on up to this day. The support of the laboratory, and the proud deeds of Davy and Faraday have saved us from being a lecture-shop for ' a number of silly women and dilettanti philosophers,' — which was the character given of us when Thomas Young was lecturing. When Rumford left England, in May, 1802, he certainly intended to return. But he never says a word about coming back to his Institution. He keeps up no relations with the managers, nor corresponded with any one of them that I can find. For in 1804 he sends a sort of message through the clerk to the managers, about a bill. He sends his regards to Davy and

"Young, but little more. I had some hopes of getting some correspondence of Sir J. Hippesley, who, next to Bernard, took the most active part in the Institution, but am disappointed."

The Royal Institution has had an honorable history, and for the most part one singularly free from acrimonious contentions, personal variances, and dividing issues about elections to membership or the choice of officers. In this peaceful and quiet course it has been favorably distinguished above even the Royal Society, which has passed through many severe agitations and many critical periods. The courses of lectures given successively before the Institution by Drs. Young and Dalton, by Sydney Smith, Faraday, and Tyndal, have kept it before the public as acting with fresh vigor among the higher agencies alike for engaging the highest professional talent and for advancing and popularizing science among the masses. Undoubtedly it has yielded to some modifications of the original design and intent of its founder; not more so, however, than to admit of the adaptations which time requires of all organized bodies and of all institutions working by a code of rules which, because they are admirably adapted to the exigencies first served by them, would become antiquated if they did not yield to, and in fact assimilate, the new elements of progress. Yet, as we read over the pamphlet prepared by Count Rumford nearly three quarters of a century ago, and note how comprehensive and elastic was the scheme proposed by him, and how directly and enthusiastically it assumed the office of working in every way for the good of common people, we can hardly apply the terms "modification" or "change" to its adoption of any means which would serve its great end. Perhaps if we could imagine the Count himself as being an unseen auditor of all the lecturers who have occupied the platform in Albemarle Street, we might expect it would have been with a degree of surprise that he would have listened to the wit and humor of Sydney Smith as he there discoursed upon moral philosophy. Was it in compliment to the Count, or as a piece of his raillery, that the jesting divine, in his third lecture, described what Priestley did for Hartley's system as " Rumfordizing" it ?*

Sir James Mackintosh, writing from Bombay in 1806, to his friend Richard Sharp, Esq., London, announces his desire to return to England in 1809, and his wish to lecture in London for eight or nine years on moral philosophy. He adds: "Your account of the London Institution has delighted and tantalized me. I wish I were a professor! But the printed paper is too general to admit of any discussion. You do not say how many and who are to be professors. It may surely be a little more solid than the fashionable nerves of Albemarle Street could endure, without ceasing to be popular." †

Dr. Jones, in the letter of his last quoted, refers to the raillery of which the Institution had been the subject in the attempt to make science fashionable. But the jeers and ridicule which it encountered from this

* Elementary Sketches of Moral Philosophy delivered at the Royal Institution. By the late Rev. Sydney Smith. London, 1850, p. 49.

A very interesting sketch of the origin and history of the Royal Institution is given by Mons. Ed. Mailly, in his " Essai sur les Institutions Scientifiques de la Grande Bretagne et de l'Irlande " (Bruxelles, 1867), though the writer perpetuates some of the common errors in the short biographical account of Rumford which precedes it. A translation of this sketch, the errors just mentioned being left without correction, is given in the collections published by the Smithsonian Institution for 1867.

† Memoirs of the Life of the Right Hon. Sir James Mackintosh. By his Son. London, 1836. Vol. 1. p. 172.

comparatively venial weakness, in turning social caprices to the service of science, was but a slight trial for the dignity of the Institution to bear, in comparison with the flood of sarcasm, contempt, and misrepresentation which had been visited upon the Royal Society. That satirical preacher, Dr. South, in his oration at the opening of the theatre at Oxford, had spoken of the worthies whom the second Charles had endowed with Charter and Mace, as admiring nothing save *pulices, pediculos, et se ipsos.* Butler, in his " Elephant in the Moon,' had made sharp fun of their subjects and methods of investigation. The witty Dr. King thought it worth his while to gather and publish a burlesque collection of " Useful Transactions in Philosophy and other Sorts of Learning," for the purpose of presenting a roguish parallel with the veritable treatises and essays of the Royal Society. The excellent Wotton, in his "Reflections upon Ancient and Modern Learning," seems to have quailed under this bantering spirit as turned against science and philosophy. He seems even to have thought that knowledge had seen its best days for his generation. "The humor of the age," he writes, "is visibly altered from what it had been thirty years ago. Though the Royal Society has weathered the rude attacks of Stubbe, yet the sly insinuations of the *men of wit*, with the public ridiculing of all who spend their time and fortunes in scientific or curious researches, have so taken off the edge of those who have opulent fortunes and a love to learning, that these studies begin to be contracted amongst physicians and mechanics."

In three very caustic articles contributed by Lord Brougham to the Edinburgh Review, exhibiting his flip-

pancy as a writer at that time in its intensest form,* on
Dr. Young's Bakerian Lecture on Light and Colors,
and his paper on "Colors not before described," the
critic, going, as it proved, beyond his depth, exposed
himself, rather than his subject, to ridicule. Dr.
Young, who in the productions thus contemptuously
assailed is said, by his biographer, to have established
the bases of the most important advancement which the
science of physical optics had made since the time of
Newton, published a masterly "Reply," in 1804, of
which, however, the author reports that only a single
copy was sold. Mention is here made of the matter,
simply because in this reply Dr. Young introduced the
following reference to his connection with the Royal
Institution : —

"The reviewer has thought proper to unite, in several instances, with his invectives against me some ridicule of the
objects of the Royal Institution of Great Britain, — an Institution in which its managers have studied to concentrate all that
is useful in science or elegant in literature. This connection
appears to him to add so much weight to his arguments that he
has chosen, without further provocation, to insinuate its existence more than a year after it has been dissolved. I accepted
the appointment of Professor of Natural Philosophy in the
Royal Institution as an occupation which would fill up agreeably and advantageously such leisure hours as a young practitioner of physic must expect to be left free from professional
cares. I was led to hope that I should be able to impress an
audience, formed of the most respectable inhabitants of the
metropolis, with such a partiality as the moderately well-informed are inclined to entertain for those who appear to know
even a little more than themselves of matters of science.
While I held the situation, I wished to make my lectures as

* Edinburgh Review, Nos. II. and IX., 1803, 1804.

intelligible as the nature of the subjects permitted; but I must confess that it was not my ambition to render them a substitute for those of any superficial experimenter that was in the habit of delivering courses of natural philosophy for the amusement of boarding-schools. Whatever may have been the imperfections of my lectures, it cannot be asserted, except perhaps in the Edinburgh Review, that they were fit for audiences of ladies of fashion only. After fulfilling for two years the duties of the Professorship, I found them so incompatible with the pursuits of a practical physician, that, in compliance with the advice of my friends, I gave notice of my wish to resign the office." *

Rumford's original and noble design, frankly avowed, certainly was to make a regard for the welfare of the common people, their relief and thrift and comfort, "fashionable." Nor would he probably have felt the least objection to investing science with the same attraction. Of late years the lectures before the Royal Institution have not been wanting in solidity of substance as dealing with themes which engage the foremost natural philosophers of our times. Sir John Lubbock's lectures on the Origin of Civilization and the Primitive Condition of Man, delivered in 1868; those of Professor Humphrey on the Architecture of the Human Body and those of Professor Odling on the Chemistry of Vegetable Products, delivered in 1870, — are among the latest contributions made by profound investigators to the broadest popular advancement in science. Max Müller's two courses were attractive and instructive.

I will here add the remainder of Pictet's letter, written while he was still in close intercourse with his friend.

" Towards the autumn of 1800, Count Rumford went to

* Miscellaneous Works, Vol. 1. pp. 214, 215.

Scotland. The magistrates of Edinburgh made him a visit of ceremony, gave him a dinner in the City Hall, and added to these marks of distinction the freedom of the city, expressed in the most flattering terms. They consulted him on measures for improving their public charitable institutions and for abolishing mendicity. They put the work into his hands, and this great undertaking was completed in less than a month, with full success. No more beggars are seen in Edinburgh, and all indigent persons there able to work have become industrious.

"The Royal Society of Edinburgh and that of Medicine made the Count an Honorary Member, and the University gave him the diploma of a Doctor of Laws. I regret that I am not able to transcribe this instrument, which was inserted in the Edinburgh Gazette. It is of the most elegant latinity, and expresses laconically and justly the obligations of humanity to my illustrious friend.

"During his stay in this city he was occupied in supervising the introduction in that great establishment, Heriot's Hospital, of the improvements of his own invention in the application of heat to the preparation of food.

"I have before me a recent letter from Mr. Jackson, one of the principal guardians of the hospital, to the author of these improvements. Here is a literal translation [which I translate again from the French].

"EDINBURGH, July 21, 1801.

"MY DEAR SIR, — With a view of procuring the most exact information about the result of the repairs made in Heriot's Hospital, I have preferred to allow a sufficient length of time to pass that their value might be sufficiently tested. To-day I have the satisfaction to inform you that a trial of six months has proved with certainty that the same operations are performed with only *a sixth part* of the fuel which was used before. The saving will nevertheless be only two thirds, because the price of coke is nearly double that of the fuel which we used before. I assure you, with much pleasure, that the food is prepared better than before, and with half the trouble to the servants.

In a word, I cannot express the facility, the convenience, and the economy which attach to the improvements introduced into the hospital under your directions. The kitchen, the laundry, and the drying-room are so perfectly arranged, that, in my humble opinion, it would be impossible to add to their advantages.

" The Lord Provost and the magistrates join me in their thanks, &c.

" JAMES JACKSON.

" The guardians wished to signify their gratitude by a token more durable than that of a simple letter. They therefore sent to the Count a silver casket bearing an inscription very honorable for him, and upon one of its faces is represented in a massive gold relief the principal façade of the building, to the improvement of which he had so efficiently contributed, and the gift is besides a beautiful architectural fancy.

" Finally, he has crowned his work by the superb establishment of the Royal Institution, of which he was the principal promoter, and which I described to you on my arrival. It is one of the most remarkable monuments of his patriotism and of his ingenious activity. This enterprise advances rapidly to perfection, and he devotes to it his most assiduous pains.

" Happy, however, as he might be, and usefully employed in England, he is not permanently fixed here. The same sovereign who, in 1784, had divined what a blessing such a man as the Count might be to his nation, signified a very emphatic intention of calling him back to him. With difficulty could he withstand the appeal of a Prince who sought the good of his country in attaching to himself a man whom he regarded as best able to aid him in his proposed reforms. I think that the next spring, or a little later, he left his quiet residence to resume for some time the high functions in which he had rendered such eminent services in Bavaria.

" Such, my friends, is a *résumé* of my notes. It will but partially satisfy your curiosity, and I am perplexed by my desire to tell you what I think will interest you, and the fear of being indiscreet in my communications."

It is observable that Pictet has no knowledge of, or, at least, makes no reference to, any breach of the most cordial relations between Rumford and his associates. He sent with the letter to his co-editors an engraved portrait of Rumford, which appears with it in the Bibliothèque Britannique, and gives also a list of the Count's papers published in the Philosophical Transactions for 1781, 1786, 1787, 1792, 1795, 1796, 1797, 1798, and 1799. He likewise says that Rumford's Essays have been translated into French, German, and Italian. In the preface to Vol. XXXIV. of the *Bibliothèque* the editors claim that their work has been the medium of making known through France the illustrious career and the philanthropic labors of Rumford.

The embargo still continuing and making intercourse with the Continent from England difficult for travellers, Pictet writes a second letter, dated from Brompton Row, September 1, 1801, in which he expresses himself very warmly as to the enjoyment he is finding as a household guest of Rumford, though he is anxious to return home.

A third letter from Pictet[*] informs his fellow-editors and us, that, notwithstanding the embargo, the Count, disposed to pass some time at Munich, has obtained a passport for himself by way of Dover, and has done him the great favor of procuring for him the privilege of accompanying him. Such indulgence had not been granted for a long time. Their departure is fixed for the 20th of September. The friends are to separate for their different routes at Calais.

Pictet writes that he has been in England three months, and that the visit has been the happiest inci-

---

[*] Bibliothèque Britannique, Vol. XXI.

dent in his life. Besides visiting with the Count the famous brewery of Meux, they had made together a short tour as an excursion to Woburn Abbey, the estate of the Duke of Bedford. They had examined by the way many manufactories and other interesting objects. The writer describes the Duke's estate and farms. The friends spent two days with Sir John Sebright, a warm admirer of Rumford, where a great *fête* was made for them, and where they enjoyed a hunt.

In here parting company with Pictet, to whom I have been so much indebted for confidential information, though it has needed a little revision, I must express my obligations to him for the results of his ardent esteem for Count Rumford, and must claim for the Count the constant regard of one who appears to have been a most excellent man as well as a distinguished philosopher. I have seen a profile drawing of him, with a fine amiable countenance, which he gave to the Countess Sarah, and on the back of the frame of which he has written, " One who is proud to call himself the friend of Count Rumford." *

The Count was abroad from September 20, 1801, to January 19, 1802, when he was at a managers' meeting of the Institution. His last attendance was April 26, 1802. On May 3, 1802, he signed at Brompton a report of his own to the managers. He was at a lecture of Davy's in that month. On May 7 or 8 he went to Paris, where he remained up to July 30. On the 5th of August he writes from Munich. On December 24, he writes from Mannheim, and hopes to be back in the Royal Institution in April or May. Janu-

---

* It is now in the possession of Mr. J. B. Walker, Concord, N. H.

ary 24, 1803, he was at Munich. November 11 he was in Paris, hoping to be in England in the course of the winter. July, 1804, he was in Paris, with the expectation of occupying his house at Brompton in the winter. May 1, 1805, he was at Munich, more than ever uncertain when he should be in England again. He was in Paris in 1807.

But this is anticipating events in his personal experience and in his domestic life the relation of which is to be far from agreeable. Before rehearsing these, I must again make a brief reference to the philanthropic and scientific labors of Count Rumford, as set forth in his Essays.

CHAPTER VIII.

BAVARIA, Great Britain, and the United States of America retain permanent memorials of the philanthropic and the scientific services of Count Rumford. His fame, coupled with strong claims upon the gratitude of large numbers of each successive generation, might be considered as well established in either of those countries. But we must recognize a distinction in the character of his services in each of them, as affecting the renewed or the popular remembrance of him. The severest and the most protracted labors which he performed were those that had employed him in Bavaria, where he had spent the longest period of years successively, after he left his native country. And his work in Bavaria had been mainly that of benevolent activity in instituting, organizing, and overseeing schemes and establishments of a humane and reformatory character. But work of this sort, however effective for the time, and however conspicuous in its beneficence, and however gratefully appreciated, has directly, at least, but a temporary and local influence. The record in the Count's Essays relating to it may indeed, by the help of the press and by commemorative tributes, inspire and guide successive laborers in the fields of practical benevolence, and in dealing with new phases and difficulties of the permanent problems and evils presented by poverty. But as buildings fall to ruin and require renewal, and as cultivated fields and gardens run to waste, and an increasing population multiplies the ranks and intensifies the mischiefs and miseries of pauperism, so there must be a reconstruction, through new adaptations, of the theory and practice of beneficence; while those who labor in this cause for their own generation must consent to be superseded, that others following them may receive their just tributes. Count Rumford is by no means forgotten in Bavaria, nor have the institutions which he so zealously and wisely founded and put into operation passed under complete decay, or fallen into oblivion. Natives and strangers still enjoy their promenades in his English Garden. The Workhouse and the Asylum for the poor still serve their original uses. Three years ago a superb bronze statue of Rumford, cast in the famous foundry of the city, was set up in one of the public squares of Munich. Yet none the less is it true, that, in the changing of generations and under the circumstances of social life in a populous community, while the fame of a philanthropist may be historically assured, the practical fruits of his schemes and plans and labors may not be apparent or seemingly permanent.

In his journeys in the south of Europe, Count Rumford, as has already been related, even while wearied and ill, and seeking relief and rest, incessantly busied himself in the service of the charitable and reformatory institutions of the cities through which he passed. His friend Pictet, whom he had known by correspondence before they personally met, had taken care by his own pen and by the help of his fellow-editors and correspondents, to extend the fame of the Count both for benevolence and for science, through the voluminous pages of the Bibliothèque Britannique. I have translated from those pages the following letter from Dr. Joly, as a happy recognition of the eminent esteem which Count Rumford had secured in both departments of his activity.

"Ornex, near Geneva, November 24, 1797.

"Gentlemen, — Among the very many important services for which we are indebted to your excellent journal, there ought especially to be made known there the works of the Count Rumford. In the midst of a war which has suspended so many enterprises, you have given the results of investigations and experiments which it would seem as if only peace could favor. While warriors have been establishing their fame upon the destruction of men, you have recognized only that which comes from labors to advance their welfare. We have need of this consolation, and of a striking illustration of it. I congratulate myself at having seen a philanthropist *par excellence*. Although you have already given an account of his seventh Essay, you are far from realizing the immense extent of his labors. I hope that he will not delay to give to the public the interesting detail of them.

" The subject with which Count Rumford as a physicist is chiefly engaged is the Nature and Effects of Heat. He is not only indefatigable in his researches, but, ardently desirous of gathering a large co-operation in the investigations directed to that subject, he has made, as you will see in the volume of Philosophical Transactions for 1797, an endowment of £1,000 sterling, the interest of which is to be devoted to rewarding the authors of the best memoirs on this subject, to be adjudged by the Royal Society of London. He has established a similar endowment in the United States, his native country. He requires that all in both countries who desire to co-operate in this study shall have equal privileges in whatever language the memoirs may be written.

" It is not necessary to be a *savant* in order to share in the favors of Count Rumford. Those who have followed his principles in the construction of fireplaces are already enjoying the fruits of his active benevolence. I hope we shall not be slow to appreciate the whole advantage of it in our kitchen furnaces where the fire is shut in. The economy of combustibles is too important for us in our local circumstances for us to fail of giving it all our care.

" Count Rumford has pursued another service with like marked success. He has become the father of the indigent. His establishment for the poor has banished mendicity from Munich, and his House of Industry tends to the absolute prevention of pauperism. The double means used in this undertaking have made me conceive, that, when Benevolence is personified, she ought to wear two visages ; one should express the gaze of pity, with the hand which succors the wretched ; the other should express the pleasing consciousness in imparting a deserved remuneration as a substitute for alms. The Institution once had two thousand poor people in its charge, and now has fourteen hundred. The House of Industry contains from twelve to fifteen hundred persons, of whom several hundreds have there for the first time learned to recognize the honorable employment of labor.

"It is impossible, gentlemen, to tell you all which one finds to admire about this excellent man. If you would judge how an exquisite taste may be combined with a most delicate sensibility to make our fellow-creatures happy in their relaxations after fatigue, you have but to visit the English Garden at Munich. Would you see a productive activity follow a wasteful sterility in a park, you have but to examine the farm of that Garden, or the Military Garden, or the Veterinary School. These establishments are as honorable to the Sovereign who allowed them as to the man who called them into being. Would you conceive the method of reducing to order the most complicated arrangements, and seizing upon the results from such various establishments, and inspecting them with a rapidity which holds you as by enchantment, just take the trouble to look at the pictures of the Military Academy, of the Institute, and of the House of Industry, and at the originals of those pictures. Would you then have the least misgiving of the experiments and the success of Count Rumford, of which you have given an account?

"But one must hurry to go to Munich to do justice, after a thorough inspection, to the candor and the scrupulous exactness of the author of these Essays.

"I have the honor to be, &c.,
"A. JOLY, D. M."

While the Count had been publishing his Essays in England, he had sent copies of the advanced sheets to his friend F. I. Hertuch in Weimar, who with the author's knowledge and approbation, and with help from others, was to translate them into German for as early publication as possible. The translator had previously made a compilation from the writings of Franklin, for which he says he thought those of Rumford "a worthy pendant." The Preface to his first edition was dated at Weimar, where the translation was published, June 16, 1797. The fourth edition of this translation appeared in 1806. The subjects, especially those of reform and benevolence, to which public attention and the enthusiasm of more generous spirits were engaged by those Essays, were then comparatively novel. They were presented by the Count almost equally as pressing obligations of duty and as offering pure and happy satisfactions for those who would labor to advance them. Experience proved that his institutions in Bavaria, however wisely planned, and even however generously supported by government patronage and by money, needed the watchful and zealous oversight of a disinterested and well-sustained superintendent, — needed, in fact, a succession of Count Rumfords. He found on the transient visits which he made to Munich, after. his rejection by the English government as the Minister of Bavaria, that these institutions certainly were not increasingly prosperous. To a moderate extent he might, indeed, take for granted that a few years of their effective working would be corrective or remedial of the gigantic evils of mendicity and pauperism in Bavaria, and therefore that, so far as the decline of the institutions signified that they had answered their purpose, there was really no occasion for regret.

We have seen, too, how largely and earnestly the Count devoted himself in Great Britain to schemes of pure benevolence, in which his scientific interest and

skill were engaged simply to originate or perfect his
most utilitarian practical objects. Of the results of
many of his economical projects and inventions we
must also admit the same qualification. The ingenuity of an inventive and thrifty people would be sure
to introduce a succession of improvements in all the
details and utensils of household economy. Still, besides having done more than any one who preceded
him in drawing general attention to the evils and waste
in connection with the use of fuel and the culinary art,
it is undoubtedly true, that, in so far as the philosophical and utilitarian principles which he advocated and
demonstrated have failed of practical regard since his
own time, Count Rumford's memory and advice might
be profitably revived for the benefit of the third generation after his own. In the pages of a literary periodical
published but a few years ago in London, it was grateful to meet the following sentences : " That untiring
worker, Count Rumford, 'one of the worthiest of
England's sons,' though an American born and bred,
wrought an immense change in the construction of
grates. This was fifty [seventy] years ago; yet the
generality of our fireplaces are as he left them, without
many of the improvements suggested by the Count.
The chief of these is the unsparing use of fire-clay." *

Having attempted, by such a particular narration in
preceding pages, to set forth the documentary history
of the endowments in England and America, and of the
Institution in London by which Count Rumford has
secured a permanent and renewed public fame, and
reserving for subsequent mention the establishment
by him of a scientific professorship in the oldest seat of

* London Reader for 1865, Vol. II. p. 428.

learning in America, I may devote this chapter to a sketch of some of his miscellaneous labors as described in his Essays.

After much time and study, through one whole series of experiments, given to the subject of the best construction of kitchen fireplaces and utensils, the Count instituted a second course of experiments, with a view to contrive closed fireplaces to serve instead of fixed fireplaces for cooking on a small scale. These he knew would be extremely useful to the families of the poor, who cook in the rooms where they live; while even the opulent would be glad to have them in their houses. He had in view another object of great importance, namely, the making of "sauce-pans and other kitchen utensils constructed of porcelain and of earthenware, instead of those now in common use, which are mostly of copper, by which the deleterious effects of that poisonous metal may be avoided."

He had himself set up a large kitchen in the Veterinary College in his English Garden at Munich, in the construction of which not a particle of any kind of metal was employed, earthenware being the substitute. And he caused to be prepared for his own house such utensils "made of white porcelain, very thin, free from all sharp edges, and covered on the outside with thin sheet-iron, to prevent the effects of a too sudden application of heat."

In his Essay upon the Propagation of Heat in Fluids, the Count starts with the admirable caution, — the consequences of the neglect of which he had had to lament in many of his earlier researches, — that "there is nothing more dangerous in philosophical investigations than to take anything for granted, however unquestionable it may appear, till it has been proved by direct and decisive experiment." Thus, he had taken for granted, as apparently everybody had done, "that heat had a free passage in all directions, through all kinds of bodies." But this assumption alike of the learned and the unlearned, and which, to his knowledge, had never been called in question, is erroneous. To this mistaken belief he attributes "the little progress that has been made in the investigation of the science of heat, — a science assuredly of the utmost importance to mankind." He began his own experiments on the subject under that delusion, and only an accidental discovery convinced him of his error, and led him to recognize first that air is a non-conductor of heat; and even then he had been so blinded by his prepossession as not at once to recognize the most evident proof that liquids also would not admit of the free passage of heat in all directions through them. Having in a previous Essay announced his discovery that steam and flame are non-conductors of heat, he proceeds to describe the experiments which proved to him that "although the particles of any fluid *individually* can receive heat from other bodies or communicate it to them, yet among these particles themselves all *interchange* and *communication* of heat is absolutely impossible."

The Count had often burned his own mouth, and seen other persons burn theirs, while eating at dinner of a dish much used in England, namely, apple-pies, or apples and almonds mixed. Apples thus cooked retained their heat for a surprising length of time. Why was it so? There was also a great difference in this respect between several other cooked foods. The philosopher tried to account to himself for the fact which had engaged his attention on his first residence in England. The question came back to him with new force many years afterwards in connection with the following incident. His dinner, a bowl of thick rice soup, having been brought in to him one day when he was very busy, he ordered it set upon the stove, that it might not grow cold. The soup was hot, and the stove was probably cool at the moment, though fresh fuel was soon put in. When the Count was at leisure, feeling very hungry, he turned to his soup and taking a spoonful from near the surface, found it cold and thick. Putting the spoon in deeper the second time, he burned his mouth. Why was this so? Some phenomena which he observed when at Naples, in 1794, he visited the hot springs at Baia, also engaged his interest in the same direction, and even, he says, "astonished" him.

"Standing on the sea-shore, near the baths, where the hot steam was issuing out of every crevice of the rocks, and even rising up out of the ground, I had the curiosity to put my hand into the water. As the waves which came in from the sea followed each other without intermission, and broke over the even surface of the beach, I was not surprised to find the water cold; but I was more than surprised, when, on running the ends of my fingers through the cold water into the sand, I found the heat so intolerable that I was obliged instantly to remove my hand. The sand was perfectly wet, and yet the temperature was so very different at the small distance of two or three inches! I could not reconcile this with the supposed great conducting power of water. I even found that the top of the sand was, to all appearance, quite as cold as the water which flowed over it; and this increased my astonishment still more. I then, for the first time, began to doubt of the conducting power of water, and resolved to set about making experiments to ascertain the facts."

He, however, deferred these experiments till another incident, two years subsequently, freshened his curiosity. While experimenting on the communication of heat, he had prepared several thermometers of an uncommon size, their globular bulbs being above four inches in diameter. These he had filled with various kinds of liquids. One of them containing spirits of wine, poured in as hot as the glass tube would endure, he placed to cool in a window where the sun was shining. The divisions on the tube were marked by a diamond on the glass. The bulb, which was of copper, having been laid aside for two years, and its orifice not being filled with a stopple, some fine particles of dust had found their way into it. These particles, intimately mixed with the spirits of wine, helped to show the whole mass of liquid through the thin, transparent, colorless glass of the tube, in a most rapid motion, running swiftly in two opposite directions, up and down, at the same time. On examining the instrument with a lens, the Count observed that the ascending current occupied the *axis of the tube*, while the descending current followed its *sides*. When the tube was inclined, the rising current moved out of the axis and occupied the uppermost side, the descending current making use of the lower side. When the cooling of the spirits of wine was hastened by wetting the tube with ice-cold water, the velocities of both currents were accelerated; and the motion ceased when the instrument and its contents had acquired nearly the temperature of the air of the room. The motion was prolonged by wrapping the bulb of the thermometer in furs, or any warm covering. The appearances were the same when the experiment was tried with a similar thermometer filled with linseed oil. The observer at once became persuaded that the motion of these liquids was occasioned by their particles going *individually* and *in succession* to give off their heat to the cold side of the tube, and he set himself to contrive experiments to prove beyond all doubt that these and probably all other liquids are, in fact, non-conductors of heat. He inferred that if heat is propagated in liquids only in consequence of the internal motions of their particles, then everything which tends to obstruct those motions ought certainly to retard the operation, and render the propagation of heat slower and more difficult. It was his object to verify this inference. He contrived, therefore, to make a certain quantity of heat pass through a certain quantity, first, of pure water, confined in a certain tube; and then, repeating the experiment with the same apparatus, instead of using pure water, he mixed with it a small quantity of eider-down, which, without altering the chemical properties of the water or impairing its fluidity, served merely to embarrass the motions of the particles of the water in transporting the heat. The Count gives a very minute description of his apparatus, and of the method of his experiments. Remembering his experience in eating hot apple-pies, he determined to test whether apples, which he knew were composed almost entirely of water, really possess a greater power of retaining heat than does pure water. He reduced a quantity of stewed apples, by washing and soaking, to a fibrous remainder, which proved to be less than one fiftieth part of the whole mass, showing that more than forty-nine fiftieths of an apple is little else than pure water. The experiment proved that the conducting power of water, with regard to heat, was impaired when the bulb of his thermometer was surrounded with a quantity of stewed apples. He illustrates his experiments by tables. The results showed that heat is propagated in fluids by the transporting of their particles, which are put in motion by the change produced in their specific gravity by the change of temperature, and that there is no *interchange of their heat* among the particles of *the same fluid.*

Finding that the propagation of heat in fluids might be obstructed both by diminishing their fluidity and by obstructing the motion of their particles, the Count next engaged in experiments to test the *comparative effects* of these two causes, permitting only one of them to act at the time of each trial. To ascertain the effects produced by diminishing the *fluidity* of water, he boiled with it a small quantity of starch ; and to determine the effects produced by merely *embarrassing* the water in its motions, he mixed with it the same proportion of eiderdown as before of starch. The results he compares in tables with his experiments made with pure water, and with water infused with baked apples, to show the different measurements of time consumed by the heat in passing into the thermometer.

The Count concluded that he had thus proved, almost to a demonstration, that heat is propagated in water *in consequence* of its internal motions; that is, that it is transported or *carried* by the particles of that liquid, and that it does not spread or expand in it as had generally been imagined. He had thus proved concerning water the same scientific fact which he had announced in a paper published in the Philosophical Transactions, in 1792, concerning the propagation of heat in air. "The conducting power of water was found to be nearly, if not quite, as much impaired by the mixture of eider-down as was that of air, though the mixture does not affect the specific qualities of either of the fluids, and merely embarrasses their internal motions." He then proceeded to connect these experiments with those which he had made on the various substances used in forming artificial clothing for confining heat. The Count follows the results he had obtained as guides in tracing out the tokens " of the wisdom of the Creator of the world" in the provisions made in the animal and vegetable kingdoms for preserving the life of plants and living creatures, according to the proportion of fluids and solids in them, and the risk of congelation. An illustration of these provisions he finds in the fact that the sap of all trees which are capable of supporting a long continuance of frost grows thick and viscous on the approach of the winter. To this increased viscosity of the sap in winter are to be added the extreme smallness of the vessels through which the sap moves in vegetables and in large trees, the fact that the substance of these small tubes is one of the best nonconductors of heat, and also the protection furnished by a thick covering of bark. He thus accounts for the preservation of the life of trees through a long and hard winter. The Count had observed the extreme difficulty with which heat passes into wood, when he noticed in his foundry, at Munich, that the fireman stirred the melted metal with a wooden instrument, which was found not to be affected through even one twentieth of an inch within its surface by the glowing. fire. The less watery fruits are, the longer will they bear the cold without freezing.

The Count next devised a more elaborate mechanical contrivance for investigating the internal motions among the particles of liquids as they are heated or cooled. He demonstrated that heat cannot be propagated *downwards* in liquids as long as they continue to be condensed by cold, — "that ice would take more than eighty times as long to melt when boiling water stood on its surface as it would take if allowed to swim on the top of the hot water; and that water at the temperature of 41° would melt even more ice, when standing on its surface, than boiling water." The proof was thus complete that water is almost a perfect non-conductor of heat. The experiments with these results were chiefly made in March, 1797. The Count adds to his conclusion, at this point, the following observation : —

"The insight which this discovery gives us in regard to the nature of the mechanical process which takes place in chemical solutions is too evident to require illustration; and it appears to me that it will enable us to account in a satisfactory manner for all the various phenomena of chemical affinities and vegetation. Perhaps all the motions among inanimate bodies on the surface of the globe may be traced to the same cause, namely, to the non-conducting power of Fluids, with regard to Heat."

Pursuing his investigations, the Count recognizes the fact that as the motions in a liquid, when undergoing a change of temperature, are caused by a change in the specific gravity of those particles of the liquid which become either hotter or colder than the rest of the mass, there will be a difference in the conducting power of the liquids, according as their respective specific gravities are more or less changed by any given change of temperature. The less, then, that the specific gravity of a liquid is changed by any given change of temperature, the

more sluggish will be the communication of heat through
its particles.

"Let us stop here," adds the Count, "for one moment, just
to ask ourselves a very interesting question. Suppose that in
the general arrangement of things it had been necessary to contrive matters so that water should not freeze in winter, or that
it should not freeze *but with the greatest* difficulty, very slowly,
and in the smallest quantity possible. How could this have been
most readily effected?

"Those who are acquainted with the law of the condensation of water on parting with its Heat have already anticipated
me in these speculations; and it does not appear to me that
there is anything which human sagacity can fathom, within the
wide-extended bounds of the visible creation, which affords a
more striking or more palpable proof of the wisdom of the
Creator, and of the special care he has taken in the general
arrangement of the universe to preserve animal life, than this
wonderful contrivance; for though the extensiveness and im-
mutability of the general laws of Nature impress our minds
with awe and reverence for the Creator of the universe, yet
exceptions to these laws, or particular modifications of them, from
which we are able to trace effects evidently *salutary* or advantageous to ourselves and our fellow-creatures, afford still more
striking proofs of contrivance, and ought certainly to awaken in
us the most lively sentiments of admiration, love, and gratitude.
. "Though in temperatures above blood heat the expansion of
water with Heat is very considerable, yet in the neighborhood
of the freezing point it is almost nothing. And what is still
more remarkable, as it is an exception to one of the most general laws of Nature with which we are acquainted, when in
cooling it comes within eight or nine degrees, on Fahrenheit's
scale, of the freezing point, instead of going on to be farther
condensed as it loses more of its Heat, it *actually expands* as it
grows colder, and continues to expand more and more as it is
more cooled. . . . . The difference between the laws of the
condensation of pure water, and of the same fluid when it holds

in solution a portion of salt, is striking. But when we trace *the effects* which are produced in the world by that arrangement, we shall be lost in wonder and admiration."

The Count then begs the indulgence and candor of his readers as he pursues the investigation of this subject, and risks the danger "to which a mortal exposes himself who has the temerity to undertake to explain the designs of Infinite Wisdom." He says, that in contemplating the simplicity of the means employed by the Creator to produce the changes of the seasons, with all the blessings accruing from them, and the effects produced by the various modifications of the active powers which we perceive, "we shall be disposed to admire, adore, and love that great First Cause which brought all things into existence." Besides that mechanical contrivance, the inclination of the axis of the earth to the plane of the ecliptic, — the simple but stupendous means which causes the changes of the seasons, — other agencies are engaged in producing the gradual changes of temperature necessary to the growth and perfection of most vegetables. These agencies are required to moderate and equalize the heat of the sun in the extremes of the seasons. Among these agencies the principal is water, acted upon by the remarkable law which causes its condensation by cold.

" Had not Providence interfered in a manner which may well be considered as *miraculous*, all the fresh water within the polar circle must inevitably have been frozen to a very great depth in one winter, and every plant and tree destroyed ; and it is more than probable that the regions of eternal frost would have spread on every side from the poles, and, advancing towards the equator, would have extended its dreary and solitary reign over a great part of what are now the most fertile and most inhabited

climates of the world. . . . . Let us with becoming diffidence
and awe endeavour to see what the means are which have been
employed by an almighty and benevolent God to protect his fair
creation."

It was absolutely necessary that a great quantity of
living water should be preserved in a fluid state in
winter as well as in summer. Water must therefore
be prevented from parting with its heat in a cold atmosphere. Liquids part with their heat only in consequence of their internal motions, and proportionately to
the rapidity of those motions, which are produced by
changes in the specific gravity of a liquid, induced by
a change of temperature. Now it has been proved that
the peculiarity of water is that the change in its specific
gravity induced by any given change in temperature is
very small ; and, when water is cooled to within seven
or eight degrees of the freezing point, it not only ceases
to be further condensed, but actually begins to expand,
and continues increasingly to do so as long as it can
be kept fluid. And when water is changed to ice it
expands even still more, and the ice floats on the surface
of the uncongealed part of the fluid. The consequence
is that the tendency of water to cooling by mere con-
duction when exposed to a cold atmosphere is thus
retarded. The Count then proceeds to trace the operation of the principle which he has thus described, in
effecting, as a result, that when the upper surface of a
lake, for instance, is covered with ice and snow, the
mass of water below loses no part of its heat, but
rather increases it. He then passes to a very lucid
and eloquent exposition of the beneficent agency of
the oceans of salt water under the operation of the laws
he has investigated. It is but just that the "devout

philosopher's " conclusion should be given in his own words.

" If, among barbarous nations, *the fear of a God* and the practice of religious duties tend to soften savage dispositions and to prepare the mind for all those sweet enjoyments which result from peace, order, industry, and friendly intercourse, *a belief in the existence of a Supreme Intelligence*, who rules and governs the universe with wisdom and goodness, is not less essential to the happiness of those who, by cultivating their mental powers, HAVE LEARNED TO KNOW HOW LITTLE CAN BE KNOWN."

In continuing the subject of this Essay in a second part, Count Rumford gives " An Account of several New Experiments, with occasional Remarks and Observations, and Conjectures respecting Chemical Affinity and Solution, and the Mechanical Principle of Animal Life."

The Count had sent a manuscript copy of the first part of this Essay to his friend Pictet at Geneva, who translated and published it. To a letter of acknowledgment from Pictet, the Count had replied in a letter dated June 9, 1797, which he designed simply as a private one, and which Pictet inadvertently put in print. It contained the following sentences: " I should have been much surprised if my Seventh Essay had not interested you, for in my life I never felt pleasure equal to that I enjoyed in making the experiments of which I have given an account in that performance. You will perhaps be surprised when I tell you that I have suppressed a whole chapter of interesting speculation, merely with a view of leaving to others a tempting field of curious investigation *untouched*."

The Count, being apprehensive that these assertions,

which admitted of many interpretations, coming before the public contrary to his intentions, might be perverted, felt called upon to guard himself against misconstruction. He might be charged with giving out obscure hints of important information which he held back, and thus with keeping others in doubt about the originality of the discoveries made by their own investigations. This, he says, would tend to damp instead of exciting the spirit of inquiry. He might also be suspected of "lying in wait to seize on the fair fruits of the labours of others." He therefore justifies himself by affirming that the assertions he had privately made to Pictet were perfectly true. He suppressed some of his speculations on the enticing subject which he had presented to those fond of philosophical pursuits, in order to prompt others to strike out roads for themselves, instead of following in his footsteps. He adds:—

"And with regard to the reputation of being a *discoverer*, though I rejoice, I might say exult and triumph, in the progress of human knowledge, and enjoy the sweetest delight in contemplating the advantages to mankind which are derived from the introduction of useful improvements, yet I can truly say that I set no very high value on the honour of being the first to stumble on those treasures which everywhere lie so slightly covered."

In reference to the religious sentiment with which he had concluded the first part of his Essay, the Count says: "Though some may smile in pity, and others frown at it, I am neither ashamed nor afraid to own that I consider the subject as being of the *utmost importance* to the peace, order, and happiness of mankind *in our present advanced state of society.*"

With these preliminary avowals the Count continues the rehearsal of his experiments to prove of other fluids what he had proved of water as a *non-conductor* of heat. He describes the instruments and the processes by which he verified the fact as regards *oil*, and even *mercury*, which is a metal in fusion, and, inferring the same of all fluids, he concludes " that the property of a *non-conductor* is even *essential to fluidity*." The discovery of so important a truth, he argues, must necessarily change some of our ideas in respect to the mechanical operations in many of the great phenomena of nature, as well as in many still more interesting chemical operations, "which we are able to direct, but which we find, alas! very difficult to explain."

In his paper on Heat, published in the Philosophical Transactions before referred to, he had turned his discovery of the non-conducting power of *air* to accounting for the warmth of the hair of beasts, of the feathers of birds, of artificial clothing, and of snow, the winter garment of the earth, and also to explaining the causes of the coldness and the directions of the winds. Also in his Essay on the Management of Heat and the Economy of Fuel, he had turned the non-conducting power of *steam* and of *flame* to the explanation of the action of the blow-pipe, and to improvements in the construction of boilers. He now proceeds to apply his discoveries to *chemistry*, *vegetation*, and the *animal economy*. " Perhaps," he says, " it will be found that every change of form in every kind of substance is owing to Heat." We must refer the reader to the Essay itself if he would be informed of the interesting facts, and the curious and often bold speculations, sometimes a little beyond his province, which the

Count sets forth.   He reminds us that there are but three forms under which all sensible bodies are found to exist, — that of a *solid*, that of a *fluid*, and that of *gas*; and that every substance with which we are acquainted may exist under all those three forms alternately, the condition for either form being dependent upon *temperature*.   He works out elaborately his hypothesis of the existence of *intense heat* in the midst of cold liquids. He recognizes two ways in which philosophers, like other men, may be excited to action and induced to engage zealously in the investigation of any curious subject of inquiry, — "they may be *enticed*, and they may be *provoked*.   It will probably not escape the penetration of my reader that I have endeavored to use both these methods.   I am well aware of the danger that attends the latter of them ; but the passionate fondness that I feel for the favorite objects of my pursuits frequently hurries me on far beyond the bounds which prudence would mark to circumscribe my adventurous excursions."

Count Rumford made an eighth Essay on the Propagation of Heat in various Substances, by a reprint of two papers, which first appeared in the Philosophical Transactions, — the one having been read before the Royal Society in 1786, and the other, for which he received the Copley Medal of the Society, in 1792.   He gives in it an account of the beginning of his experiments on the conducting power of the *Torricellian vacuum*.   These he had made while on a journey with the Elector, at Mannheim, in July, 1785, in presence of Professor Hemmer, of the Electoral Academy of Sciences, of that city, and of Charles Artaria, meteorological instrument maker, who assisted him.   His experiments led him to a philosophical view of the well-known facts as to the way in which we "catch cold" or become afflicted with catarrhs; why these disorders prevail most in the cold autumnal rains and upon the breaking up of the frost in the spring; whence it is that sleeping in damp beds and inhabiting damp houses is so very dangerous; and why the evening air is so pernicious in summer and in autumn, and why it is not so during the hard frosts of winter.

Finding a great difference between the conducting powers of common air and of the Torricellian vacuum, the Count continued his experiments by testing the conducting powers of common air of different degrees of density. He was surprised at the result of his experiments, though he could not discover the cause of the fact, nor account for it that there is so little difference in the conducting powers of air of such very different degrees of rarity, while there is so great a difference in the conducting powers of air and of the Torricellian vacuum. Obliged by the return of the Elector to Munich to suspend the experiments which he had been pursuing at Mannheim, he was privileged by his patron in being allowed to take M. Artaria back with him to the capital, to aid him in the construction of costly apparatus for pursuing his investigations.

In the second part of this Essay, which is substantially the paper read, as sent by him, before the Royal Society, January 19, 1792, he extends the inquiries he had been making concerning the conducting powers of fluids to those of solids, particularly such bodies as are used for clothing. The especial object of his researches was to ascertain the laws relative to the confining and directing of heat. He constructed what he calls a passage thermometer, the tube of which was suspended in a cylindrical glass tube terminating in a glass globe around the bulb of the thermometer. The space between the inner surface of the globe and the outer surface of the bulb was then filled successively by various substances whose conducting powers he wished to test. The instrument, when filled, was heated in boiling water, and afterwards plunged into a freezing mixture of pounded ice and water, or *vice versa*. The times of cooling or heating were carefully observed by the scale of the thermometer and a watch which beat half-seconds. He subjected to this test raw silk, sheep's wool, cotton-wool, linen lint, the fur of the beaver, the fur of a white Russian hare, and eider-down. The relative *warmth* of these substances proved to be as follows: hare's fur and eider-down were the warmest ; then came in order beaver's fur, raw silk, sheep's wool, cotton-wool, and lastly lint. Rectifying his tests by others which allowed for the respective density and the internal structure of these various substances, he proceeded with his experiments on other solids. In revising the matter of this Essay he was enabled to correct his own error, when he first wrote the paper, as to the conducting power of air.

The Count's ninth Essay is " An Inquiry concerning the Source of the Heat which is excited by Friction." The substance of it was read before the Royal Society, January 25, 1798. It was after he had been summoned back to Munich in 1796, and in the two years following, while war, with the dread of new campaigns and preparation for them, were engrossing the anxieties of every European sovereign and people, that Rumford made the experiments which he here described.

In the scientific results which he obtained from them,
in the theory which he deduced, and in the large philosophical generalizations which he announced as warranted by them, he is fairly to be regarded as the discoverer and first promulgator of the facts and principles
which are grouped under the now familiar designation
of the Conservation and Correlation of Forces. As Lavoisier — with whose widow Rumford was soon to form
what promised to be a felicitous, though it proved to
be an uncongenial marriage, — had illustrated a new era
in chemical science by establishing the truth that in the
processes of analysis no atom or element of matter is
annihilated or irrecoverably lost, so the American philosopher illustrated the corresponding truth as to Heat
and Force once generated.

Count Rumford introduces this, as he does each of
his Essays, with one of those general and comprehensive observations which, as stated in his lucid and
forcible way, convey such obvious truths, that, as we
read them, we almost wonder that they need to be
set forth. He reminds us that the habit of keeping
the eyes open, and the mind attent, in the ordinary
affairs of life, while contemplating some curious operation of nature, or pursuing any mere mechanical process
in art or manufacture, may, as it were by accident, lead
to discoveries such as will not reward the intensest
meditations of philosophers in their hours of study. It
was by accident, he says, that he was led to pursue the
experiments the rewarding results of which he proceeds
to describe. He was engaged in superintending the
boring of cannon in the workshops of the Elector's
arsenal and foundry in Munich, when his attention was
arrested by observing the considerable degree of heat

which a brass gun so soon acquires in being bored. He
found, by experiment, that the metallic chips separated
by the borer had an intensity of heat exceeding that of
boiling water. He was persuaded that a thorough investigation of these phenomena would afford an insight
into the hidden nature of heat, and help to decide the existence or the non-existence of an *igneous fluid*, — a point
on which the opinions of philosophers of all ages have
been divided. He put to himself the question, Whence
comes the heat actually produced in the mechanical
operation above mentioned? Is it furnished by the metallic chips which are separated from the solid mass of the
metal? If so, then, according to the doctrines about
latent heat and caloric, the *capacity for heat* of the parts
of the metal so reduced to chips ought not only to be
changed, but the change undergone by them should be
sufficiently great to account for all the heat produced.
But the test which compared some of these chips with
the same quantity of thin slips separated by a fine saw
from the same block of metal, proved that the capacity
of heat of the former had not been changed. It was
evident, then, that the heat produced by boring was not
furnished at the expense of the latent heat of the metallic chips. Being assured of this fact for a starting-
point, the philosopher proceeded with a series of experiments in the succession of which the elements of his
inquiry and the conditions for investigating them led
him to contrive apparatus, and to advance gradually to
his great discovery. Reminding his readers that he was
not chargeable with prodigality or waste of material in
these experiments, he informs us of an interesting fact
in the process of constructing a cannon of which he
availed himself. In the casting of a gun, he says, the

cylinder is made longer than the intended cannon, a projection nearly ten inches beyond what will be the muzzle of the completed weapon forming part of the contents of the mould. The object of this additional material is, that by the pressure of its weight on the metal below it in the mould, while it is cooling, the gun may be more compact in the neighborhood of the muzzle, when, without this precaution, the metal there would be likely to be porous or honeycombed. Taking a brass six-pounder cast solid, and rough from the foundry, he had it finished by the usual process of turning. He then cut round the projection beyond the muzzle, leaving it attached only by a small cylindrical neck to the intended muzzle. This short cylinder, supported horizontally, and still united to the cannon, was bored, in the usual way, to a depth which left to it a solid bottom two and six tenths inches in thickness. Intending to use this cylinder for the purpose of generating heat *by friction*, a blunt borer of hardened steel was pressed against the bottom of the cavity in it by a force of ten thousand pounds, while the cannon to which the cylinder was attached was made to revolve by horse-power at the rate of thirty-two times a minute. In order that he might measure the heat that accumulated in the cylinder, he introduced into it a small cylindrical mercurial thermometer, through a round hole, drilled perpendicularly to the axis of the cylinder, thirty-seven hundredths of an inch in diameter, and four and two tenths inches in depth. This hole ended in the middle of the solid part of the metal which formed the bottom of its bore. The object of this first experiment was to ascertain how much heat was actually generated by friction under these given conditions, — the pressure of a blunt steel borer, by means of a strong screw with the force of ten thousand pounds, against the bottom of the bore of the cylinder while that cylinder was made to revolve by horse-power thirty-two times in a minute. To diminish as much as possible the loss of any part of the heat that might be generated, the cylinder was carefully wrapped in thick and warm flannel, and defended from the cold air of the atmosphere. The area of the surface at which the rounded end of the steel borer was in contact with the cavity at the bottom of the bore in the cylinder was nearly two and one third inches. The temperature of the air and of the cylinder at the beginning of the experiment was 60° F. At the end of thirty minutes, when the cylinder had made 960 revolutions, the mercury, as indicated by the thermometer introduced into the cavity above described, rose almost instantly to 130°.

In order to approximate to the amount of the heat which had been given off during the time in which the heat generated by the friction had been accumulating, the experimenter took note of the rapidity with which the heat escaped out of the cylinder. To this end, while the machinery was stopped, he left the thermometer in the cavity, observing at short intervals of time the temperature which it indicated. This fell 110° in forty-one minutes.

The weight of the metallic dust which had been detached by the borer from the bottom of the cylinder was found to be 837 grains Troy. The Count asks, "Is it possible that the very considerable quantity of heat that was produced in this experiment (a quantity which actually raised the temperature of above 111 pounds of gun-metal at least 70 degrees of Fahrenheit's thermometer, and which of course would have been capable of melting six and a half pounds of ice, or of causing near five pounds of ice-cold water to boil) could have been furnished by so inconsiderable a quantity of metallic dust, and this merely in consequence of *a change* of its capacity for Heat?" The weight of the metallic dust was no more than $\frac{1}{70}$ part of that of the cylinder. The dust, then, would need to have parted with 948 degrees of heat to have raised the temperature of the cylinder by a single degree. Consequently the dust must have yielded 66,360 degrees of the virtue called *latent heat*, in order to have produced the effects which were reached by the experiment!

This experiment having been repeated with the utmost care several times, the Count satisfied himself that the heat which, as he prefers to say, had been *excited*, rather than *generated*, by them, was not furnished *at the expense of the latent heat* or *combined caloric* of the metal.

The Count's second experiment was for the purpose of ascertaining whether the air, which had free access to the inside and bottom of the bore in the cylinder, did or did not contribute to the generation of the heat. He therefore excluded the external air by means of a piston fitted to the mouth of the bore. The test proved that there was no diminution of the quantity of the heat excited.

A slight doubt suggesting itself whether some part of the heat produced might not be occasioned by the friction of the piston, fitted as it was, air tight, by means of leather collars, the Count had recourse to a third experiment. His apparatus was enclosed in a strong deal box, which was filled with cold water, and suspended between the muzzle of the cannon as it revolved and the borer with the piston that was turned against the bore of the cylinder. Soon the water which surrounded the cylinder began to be warm. In two hours and a half " IT ACTUALLY BOILED !"

The philosopher shall speak for himself: —

"It would be difficult to describe the surprise and astonishment expressed in the countenances of the bystanders on seeing so large a quantity of cold water heated and actually made to boil without any fire. Though there was, in fact, nothing that could justly be considered as surprising in this event, yet I acknowledge fairly that it afforded me a degree of childish pleasure which, were I ambitious of the reputation of a *grave philosopher*, I ought most certainly to hide rather than discover."

He then proceeds to estimate the total quantity of heat generated, accumulated, and dispersed by the experiment in the water and in the apparatus.

From the *quantity* of heat generated in the last experiment, and from the *time* required for its production, Rumford next sought to ascertain the *velocity of its production*. He wished also to determine how large a fire must have been, or how much fuel must have been consumed, in order that in burning equably it should have produced by combustion the same quantity of heat in the same time. He found that nine wax candles of three quarters of an inch in diameter, all burning together with clear bright flames, would not produce so great a quantity of heat as had been excited in the above-described experiment. His computations showed, further, how much heat might be produced through mechanical contrivances, employing the strength of a horse, without either fire, light, combustion, or chemical decomposition, — to be had recourse to in case of necessity in cooking victuals. Having ventured on this suggestion, he is careful to anticipate by his own good sense the ridicule that might be turned upon him, by confessing that no advantageous circumstances can be imagined for thus generating heat by horse-power, inasmuch as more heat might be got by using the horse-fodder as fuel.

In the last experiment the water in the box, though it surrounded the metallic cylinder, was not allowed to enter the cavity of its bore, being prevented by the piston, and so did not come in contact with the metallic surfaces where the heat was generated. No essential difference followed in the trial of another experiment in which this free contact of the water with the inside of the bore was allowed. Rumford was, however, surprised by his incidental observation that the almost insupportable grating noise made by the borer in rubbing against the bottom of the cylinder when only in contact with air was not diminished when they were wet by water.

These experiments having been thus pursued to results furnishing new materials for thought and scientific deduction, the Count says he was naturally brought to that great question which has so long engaged the speculations of philosophers, namely, What is heat? Is there any such thing as an *igneous fluid?* Is there anything that can with propriety be called *caloric?* Whence came the heat given off in the foregoing experiments in a constant stream, in all directions, without diminution or exhaustion, as excited in the friction of two metallic surfaces? It was found that this heat was not furnished by the small particles of metal detached by rubbing from the larger mass. Nor was it furnished by the air, — for in one set of the experiments, the apparatus being immersed in water, the atmospheric air was excluded. Nor yet was the heat furnished by the water, because, first, the water was receiving heat from the machinery, and therefore could not at the same time be giving heat to it; and, second, because there was no chemical decomposition of the water. So considerate and cautious had the Count's method been, that, allowing for the possibility of this latter contingency, he had been on the watch for any sign of the decomposition of the water by the escape of either of its component elastic fluids, and had even made preparations for seizing and examining any air-bubbles which might rise through it. It being evident that the heat was not to be referred to either of these sources, and that the source of it, as generated by friction, was inexhaustible, the conclusion reached by Rumford is thus expressed in his own clear language.

"It is hardly necessary to add that anything which any *insulated* body or system of bodies can continue to furnish without limitation cannot possibly be *a material substance*; and it appears to me to be extremely difficult, if not quite impossible, to form any distinct idea of anything capable of being excited and communicated in the manner the Heat was excited and communicated in these Experiments, except it be MOTION.

"I am very far from pretending to know how, or by what means or mechanical contrivance, that particular kind of motion in bodies which has been supposed to constitute Heat is excited, continued, and propagated, and I shall not presume to trouble the Society with mere conjectures; particularly on a subject which, during so many thousand years, the most enlightened philosophers have endeavored, but in vain, to comprehend.

" But, although the mechanism of Heat should, in fact, be

one of those mysteries of nature which are beyond the reach of human intelligence, this ought by no means to discourage us, or even lessen our ardour in our attempts to investigate the laws of its operations. How far can we advance in any of the paths which Science has opened to us before we find ourselves enveloped in those thick mists which on every side bound the horizon of the human intellect? But how ample and how interesting is the field that is given us to explore!

"Nobody, surely, in his sober senses, has ever pretended to understand the mechanism of gravitation; and yet what sublime discoveries was our immortal Newton enabled to make, merely by the investigation of the laws of its action!

"The effects produced in the world by the agency of Heat are probably *just as extensive*, and quite as important, as those which are owing to the tendency of the particles of matter towards each other; and there is no doubt but its operations are in all cases determined by laws equally immutable.

"Before I finish this Essay, I would beg leave to observe, that, although in treating the subject I have endeavored to investigate I have made no mention of the names of those who have gone over the same ground before me, nor of the success of their labours, this omission has not been owing to any want of respect for my predecessors, but was merely to avoid prolixity, and to be more at liberty to pursue without interruption the natural train of my own ideas."

In reference to the frank avowal made in this last paragraph, a passing notice may not be out of place here, of two depreciatory articles upon Count Rumford's scientific merits in the Edinburgh Review, Vol. IV. p. 399, etc. The articles which are ostensibly critical notices of Rumford's papers concerning the Nature of Heat, and concerning a "Curious Phenomenon in the Glaciers of Chamouny," which he had observed with his friend Pictet, are evidently strongly imbued with jealousy and personal malignity. They sharply charge upon Rumford that he has assumed an original discovery which does not belong to him, and that he plagiarized from Leslie. Rumford had at the time a bitter controversy with Leslie, and it is altogether probable that the latter was the source of the imputation against Rumford of making an unacknowledged use of his thoughts and apparatus.

The records of scientific research, experiment, and discovery do not contain any more lucid or creditable communication in the higher interests of philosophy than that which is so admirably set forth in this last-mentioned essay of Count Rumford. It secures to him an honorable distinction and fame as a prime and eminently successful guide in that new path of experimental philosophy which has developed the principles of the mutual relation and the indestructibility of forces. Professor Tyndall, in his work on Heat, has but moderately recognized the claims and merit of Rumford when, after largely quoting from his Essay, he adds: "When the history of the dynamical theory of heat is written, the man who in opposition to the scientific belief of his time could experiment and reason upon experiment, as did Rumford in the investigation here referred to, cannot be lightly passed over."

The most appreciative recent estimate of Count Rumford's actual experimental discoveries and philosophical genius is that made by Edward L. Youmans, M. D., in his compilation of essays on The Correlation and Conservation of Forces: A Series of Expositions, by Professor Grove, Professor Helmholtz, Dr. Mayer, Dr. Faraday, Professor Liebig, and Dr. Carpenter.* The editor and commentator upon some of the essays

* New York: D. Appleton & Co. 1865

of this series of writers endeavors with marked candor
to recognize their respective services and merits in dealing with the great subject of investigation common to
them and to other philosophic inquirers of the last and
the present age.   He endeavors, indeed, to go farther,
and to trace and distribute among them the portion or
degree of honor which belongs to each of them for his
measure of success in working upon the new vein of
truth.   This distribution, however, he finds to be
difficult.   When many well-informed and acute minds
furnished alike with the stores and results already attained in a special science, and starting from a position
already reached, look out with their unpatented instruments and with their approved methods upon the opening way of investigation for the future, with the themes
which instruct as well as tease their curiosity, it is not
easy always to assign to any one a discovery or an
advance which may be simultaneously made by many.
"Great discoveries belong not so much to individuals
as to humanity; they are less inspirations of genius
than births of eras."   The history of science is full of
the records of these simultaneous discoveries, and the
biographies of philosophers too often are painful plead-
ings for rival claims.

Dr. Youmans, in his introduction to his compilation,
gives a brief sketch of the life and career of Count
Rumford, substantially correct.   After quoting the
sentence given above from Professor Tyndall, he adds
that, —

"If other English writers had been equally just, there would be
less necessity for the exposition of Rumford's labors and claims.
But," he continues, "there has been a manifest disposition in
various quarters to obscure and depreciate them.   Dr. Whewell,

in his History of the Inductive Sciences, treats the subject of thermotics without mentioning him. An eminent Edinburgh professor, writing recently in the Philosophical Magazine, under the confessed influence of ' patriotism ' undertakes to make the dynamical theory of heat an English monopoly, due to Sir Isaac Newton, Sir Humphry Davy, and Dr. J. P. Joule ; while an able writer in a late number of the North British Review, in sketching the historic progress of the new views, puts Davy forward as their founder, and assigns to Rumford a minor and subsequent place."

How unwarranted is the claim for priority thus advanced for Davy will be evident from the simple statement of the facts in the case. In 1799, the year after Rumford's full publication of his experiments with their results, Davy, at the age of twenty-one, published a tract at Bristol relating some of his own experiments, and proving that he rejected the common theory of caloric or latent heat. The notice of Rumford was drawn to Davy through this tract, in which he recognized a partial accordance with his own views, and an interesting and promising, though as yet but very imperfect perception, recognition, and treatment of the elements of the great subject of investigation. Rumford was induced, mainly by his appreciation of the ability manifested by Davy in dealing with that subject which had so long and so successfully engaged his own laborious and ingenious efforts, to entertain favorably the suggestion of giving the writer of the tract a situation in the Royal Institution, as already related. Davy, however, does not appear to have directed his inquiries upon the quantitative relation between mechanical force and heat. It was as long after as the year 1812 that, in his Chemical Philosophy, he for the first time clearly stated the conclusion that " the immediate cause of the phenomena of heat is motion, and the laws of its communication are precisely the same as those of the communication of motion."

Dr. Youmans, with admirable distinctness of statement and with the full warrant of truth, distributes, under the following specifications, a summary of the claims of the American philosopher : —

• " 1. He was the man who first took the question of the nature of heat out of the domain of metaphysics, where it had been speculated upon since the time of Aristotle, and placed it upon the true basis of physical experiment.

" 2. He first proved the insufficiency of the current explanations of the sources of heat, and demonstrated the falsity of the prevailing view of its materiality.

" 3. He first estimated the quantitative relation between the heat produced by friction and that by combustion.

" 4. He first showed the quantity of heat produced by a definite amount of mechanical work, and arrived at a result remarkably near the finally established law.

" 5. He pointed out other methods to be employed in determining the amount of heat produced by the expenditure of mechanical power, instancing particularly the agitation of water or other liquids, as in churning.

" 6. He regarded the power of animals as due to their food, therefore as having a definite source and not created, and thus applied his views of force to the organic world.

" 7. Rumford was the first to demonstrate the quantitative convertibility of force in an important case, and the first to reach, experimentally, the fundamental conclusion that heat is but a mode of motion."

Nor did Rumford immediately find himself to be followed, as he had so plainly intimated his expectations and desire that he should be, by many inquirers pursuing the path and method which he had opened. The distinguished Dr. Thomas Young, at one time the grateful admirer and friend of Rumford, — pronounced by Dr. Youmans "perhaps the greatest mind in science since Newton," — failed to give currency to the novel conclusion which the Count had so sufficiently verified. Yet the publication of Rumford's experiments, and of the views which they led him to adopt, was certainly not among the least of the agencies and guides which have induced so many *savans* of Europe, during the last twenty-five years, to make a profound study of the relations of forces, — a study the signal results of which now enrich so many learned essays. Indeed, so numerous have been the inquirers in this field, and so mutually helpful and suggestive have been the contributions made by each of them to the common stock of the philosophy of forces, that it is impossible to distribute among them the respective shares of award for their individual help in assuring the now accepted theories. The names of Englishmen, Danes, Germans, Frenchmen, and Americans are gathered on the list of those who by speculation, theory, or experiment have followed in the track of Rumford without finding reason to leave it. Seguin of France, Grove and Joule of England, Mayer of Germany, and Colding of Denmark, the earlier disciples of the new theory, have found successors in Helmholtz, Holtzman, Clausius, Faraday, Thompson, Rankine, Tyndall, Carpenter, and others. Professor Henry and Leconte, in the United States, have also made contributions to the theory and literature of the subject.

Dr. Huxley does not fail to assign to Rumford the high place belonging to him for his leadership in "the theory of the persistence or indestructibility of force."[*]

* Lecture on the Advisableness of improving Natural Knowledge.

Count Rumford's papers on Heat, either as communicated to Sir Joseph Banks, as read before the Royal Society and the French Institute, or as put into print under his own eye, will be found to be so continuous and numerous, and to extend over so long a series of years, as to justify the assertion that of all the subjects of his investigation this was his favorite and engrossing theme. His first communication on the subject dates in 1786; his last, in 1812.

If we turn from the strictly scientific to consider briefly the experimental results of the practical projects and improvements introduced by Count Rumford into household economy and the administration of public charity, we can trace these results as he himself saw them during the last years of his residence in England. In Germany the people had been used to closed stoves for obtaining warmth and for cooking food. In England open fireplaces for wood, or open grates for coal, were identified with the habits and the requisitions for comfort and cheer in all houses. English travellers in America to this day — Dickens having been among the most emphatic in his expressions — regard our stoves and hot-air furnaces as abominations. Count Rumford, in the home of his childhood, and in the houses of his neighbors, had seen the enormous square mass of stone and brick rising from the cellar on an arch, and passing through the centre of the structure, which seemed to be built to surround it, till it pierced the roof, without any division of flues through at least a part of its course. There was probably not a stove in New England when he left it, save only, it may have been, the little tin boxes arranged for warming the feet, which some delicate matrons carried with them, on

Sundays, into the barn-like and teeth-chattering meet-
ing-houses.   Franklin had preceded him by a few years
in devising those iron jambs, united by a narrow mantel
at the top, which were inserted nearly on the front of an
old deep fireplace, that had in the mean while been par-
titioned by an apron of brick-work or an iron back like
a gravestone, through an orifice between the top of
which and the throat of the chimney the smoke could
pass off.   As a boy, most probably, Benjamin Thompson had helped his mother to bring in one of the old-
fashioned New-England "back-logs," four feet in
length, from the trunk of a hard-wood tree, for her
kitchen fire, — the only fire kept in such a home, except
on gala-days.   Rumford had seen the Franklin fireplaces in use, and he introduced substantially the really
excellent qualities of them in his own plans.   But very
soon after the Franklin models had become common,
the original provision made by Franklin for the circulation of air through them was neglected.   Rumford
found that if he would meet the demands of the English people, he must gratify the national preference for
meats roasted, fried, and broiled, above those prepared
by boiling or stewing.   He had also to provide, if possible, for apparatus which in the summer season would
allow for the preparation of food without heating the
apartment, while the apparatus would answer in the
winter alike for cooking and warming.   The rigidly
practical and experimental way in which he tested every
scheme and method that he put on trial, and the
conscientious scrupulousness with which he proved all
his processes before he made them public, together with
the admirable candor with which he would recognize
and announce his own mistakes, insured a practical

improvement on every subject of the kind that engaged his attention. He knew very well that as there is no panacea in medicine, so there is no faultless piece of mechanism which will answer ends so unlike as were some of the objects which he tried to attain at the same time.· His desire and pains to secure testimonials, from private persons and from the managers of public institutions, of the utility of his improvements indicate that he had to urge them into notice. They failed in use sometimes, because of the neglect of some of the prime conditions frankly and emphatically declared by him as essential to their success.

The Count's tenth Essay relates mainly to the construction of kitchen fireplaces and utensils. It is the longest of his essays, and was published at intervals, four years after it was announced, in three parts, — the third of which appeared only just before, if not even after, his leaving England for the last time. It is of an exceedingly homely, economical, and thrifty tenor, exhibiting many tokens and expressions of the writer's earnest and practical benevolence, especially of his pure and generous sympathies with, and his desire to promote the comfort of, the poor, as also of his horror of waste of anything good, and of his deep conviction that the means of life may be made to afford far more of pleasure and satisfaction than men ordinarily obtain from them. There are evidences, likewise, in the Essay, that the Count was aware of the jeers and ridicule occasionally visited upon him in the ephemeral journals for his very sublunary theorizings and experiments. We are glad to have had Pictet's testimony, as given on a previous page, that the Count was only amused by some of the references to him in the newspapers.

This Essay treats of the more common imperfections in the plan, construction, and machinery of kitchen fireplaces, and of the means for remedying them; gives descriptions of many kitchens, public and private, then in operation, made under his own oversight and directions, — that on which he prided himself most being in the house of Baron de Lerchenfield, at Munich, — and suggests the necessary alterations and improvements that may be made in open fireplaces, for cooking, and the superiority of closed ones, and of nests of ovens, with a condemnation of smoke-jacks as fearfully wasteful. Then we have a full description of his famous roasters, with improvements. He had found, on his return to England, that this invention of his had in some places fallen into discredit on trial, and that its use had not in all cases vindicated its advantages for promised convenience and economy. These failures he ascribed to a neglect of the rules which he had so carefully given for its construction, and to the heedlessness or prejudices of cooks. He sets himself resolutely to maintain its value, and to expose the errors of its construction or use. He took pains to instruct an ironmonger, Mr. Summers, of New Bond Street, and his cook, how to set a roaster, and to make daily use of it in his kitchen, to show to his customers in the presence of other cooks. He also prevailed on an intelligent bricklayer to be taught how to set roasters properly, and to follow directions without *deviation*; everything depending upon accuracy in this matter. Nearly a thousand of these roasters appear, as the result of the Count's efforts, to have been set up in the next two years. As he always positively refused to take out a patent, or in any way to restrict the freest use of any of his inventions and improvements, and, indeed, exposed models of them in the repository of the Institution for workmen to examine and copy, his sole desire was that the public should be furnished with them at the lowest price for which competing mechanics could afford them. He also added an invention of small iron ovens, to be used for all the processes of cookery, including boiling. Next he turned to the materials for, and the mode of constructing, all kitchen utensils, boilers, sauce-pans, stew-pans and their handles, register stoves, steam dishes and stoves, and portable furnaces, with references to the effects of different kinds of lining and glazing on the taste of food and its healthfulness; and he commends the newly introduced Wedgewood and other kinds of earthenware.

In reading these pages, one can hardly repress a smile to find a philosopher going into such details as does the writer on matters relating wholly to the appetite, the flavor of food, the ways in which it is made palatable, — how meat can be cooked so as to retain its rich juices; how it can be roasted in an oven so as even to taste better than when done before an open fire; how to prevent its becoming sodden; and the reader may even be made conscious of a rising desire within him to get within reach of the hot viands, as the pages tell him how the meat is at one stage of the process to be delicately browned, and how savory the fat of mutton and beef, and even venison, may become in one of these wonderful Roasters. The surprise of the reader, too, is enhanced when he calls to mind that the writer, instead of being an Apician epicure, or a gormand, or a critical discriminator in the pleasures of the table, for himself was remarkably abstemious, most simple in his tastes, self-denying in, or rather unconscious of, such appetites, and more easily satisfied with frugal, plain diet than most men, while he was also positively hostile to all banqueting. The reader will naturally feel that his author can hardly deal so minutely as he does with these provocatives of sense without putting in some disclaimer for himself. And he will find such a disclaimer at the close of the eighth chapter of the Essay, where the Count, after having described an appetizing process for a steak or cutlet, adds : —

"I imagine it would be an excellent dish, and very wholesome; but it must be left to cooks and to professed judges of good eating to determine whether these hints (which are thrown out with all becoming humility and deference) are deserving of attention. For although I have written a whole chapter on the pleasure of eating, I must acknowledge, what all my acquaintances will certify, that few persons are less attached to the pleasures of the table than myself. If, in treating this subject, I sometimes appear to do it *con amore*, this warmth of expression ought, in justice, to be ascribed solely to the sense I entertain of its infinite importance to the health, happiness, and innocent enjoyments of mankind."

An interesting reference is made to the habits of the Chinese, for the sake of an example which the Count thinks his own countrymen might imitate.

"The portable kitchen-furnaces in China are all constructed of earthenware; and no people ever carried those inventions which are most generally useful in common life to higher perfection than the Chinese. They, and they only, of all the nations of whom we have any authentic accounts, seem to have had a just idea of the infinite importance of those improvements which are calculated to promote the comforts of the lowest classes of society.

"What immortal glory might any European nation obtain by following this wise example!

" 'The Emperor of China, the greatest monarch in the world, who rules over full one *third part* of the inhabitants of this globe, condescends *to hold the plough* himself one day in every year. This he does, no doubt, to show to those, whose example never can fail to influence the great bulk of mankind, how important that art is by means of which food is provided.

" Let those reflect seriously on this illustrious example of provident and benevolent attention to the wants of mankind, who are disposed to consider the domestic arrangements of the labouring classes as a subject too low and vulgar for their notice.

" If attention to the art by which food is provided be not beneath the dignity of a Great Monarch, that art by which food is prepared for use, and by which it may be greatly *œconomised*, cannot possibly be unworthy of the attention of those who take pleasure in promoting the happiness of mankind."

Not wholly insensible to the flippant *badinage* with which portions of his economical projects were treated in some quarters, nor to the impatience with which his prolixity and minuteness of detail in very homely counsels were received by many, the Count remonstrates with dignity, while he still keeps to his own chosen method. He says he is willing to be judged by the more intelligent of his readers, and feels that they will appreciate his motive in mingling abstruse philosophical researches and the results of profound meditation with the explanation of most humble and ordinary subjects. He says : —

" I am not unacquainted with the manners of the age. I have lived much in the world, and have studied mankind attentively ; I am fully aware of all the difficulties I have to encounter in the pursuit of the great object to which I have devoted myself. I am even sensible, fully sensible, of the dangers to which I expose myself. In this selfish and suspicious age it is hardly possible that justice should be done to the purity of my motives; and in the present state of society, when so few who have leisure can bring themselves to take the trouble to read anything except it be for mere amusement, I can hardly expect to engage attention. I may write, but what will writing avail if nobody will read? My bookseller, indeed, will not be ruined as long as it shall continue to be *fashionable* to have *fine libraries*. But my object will not be attained unless my writings are read, and the importance of the subjects of my investigations is felt.

"Persons who have been satiated with indulgences and luxuries of every kind are sometimes tempted by the novelty of an untried pursuit. My best endeavours shall not be wanting to give to the objects I recommend, not only all the alluring charms of novelty, but also the power of procuring a pleasure as new, perhaps, as it is pure and lasting.

"How might I exult could I but succeed so far as to make it *fashionable* for the rich to take the trouble to choose for themselves those enjoyments which their money can command, instead of being the dupes of those tyrants who, in the garb of submissive, fawning slaves, not only plunder them in the most disgraceful manner, but render them at the same time perfectly ridiculous, and fit for that destruction which is always near at hand, when good taste has been driven quite off the stage.

"When I see, in the capital of a great country, in the midst of summer, a coachman sitting on a coach-box dressed in a thick, heavy great-coat with sixteen capes, I am not surprised to find the coach-door surrounded by a group of naked beggars.

"We should tremble at such appearances, did not the shortness of life and the extreme infirmity of the human character render us insensible to dangers while at any distance, however great and impending and inevitable they may be."

Again he writes: —

"In justice it ought always to be remembered that my object in writing is, professedly, to be useful, and that I lay no claim to the applause of those delicate and severe judges of literary composition who read more with a view to being pleased by fine writing than to acquire information. If those who are quick of apprehension are sometimes tempted to find fault with me for being too particular, they must remember that it is not given to all to be quick of apprehension, and that it is amiable to have patience, and to be indulgent."

When Lord Brougham, as quoted on a previous page, satirized the Count for giving such particular directions about the proper way of eating Indian pudding, his Lordship must have overlooked a passage in this Essay even more to his purpose as an illustration. After the Count has described most elaborately how stewpans and saucepans should be shaped, how their rims should be turned and their handles riveted, he adds: "There should be a round hole about a quarter of an inch in diameter, near the end of the handle, by which the saucepan may occasionally be hung upon a nail or peg, when it is not in use. The cover belonging to the saucepan may be hung up on the same nail, or peg, by means of the projection of its rim." .

The Count, of course, realized that one of the effects of the introduction of his improvements in household and kitchen utensils would be to render unsalable many manufactured articles then in the market, and to excite the opposition of self-interest among many artisans. So he writes : —

"However anxious I am to promote useful improvements, and especially such as tend to the preservation of health and the increase of rational enjoyments, it always gives me pain when I recollect how impossible it is to introduce anything new, however useful it may be to society at large, without occasioning a temporary loss or inconvenience to some certain individuals whose interest it is to preserve the state of things actually existing.

"It certainly requires some courage, and perhaps no small share of enthusiasm, to stand forth the voluntary champion of the public good. But this is a melancholy reflection on which I never suffer my mind to dwell. There is no saying what the consequences might be were we always to sit down before we engage in a laudable undertaking and meditate profoundly upon all the dangers and difficulties that are inseparably connected with it. The most ardent zeal might perhaps be damped, and the warmest benevolence discouraged. But the enterprising seldom regard dangers, and are never dismayed by them; and they consider difficulties but to see how they are to be overcome. To them *activity* alone is life, and their glorious reward the consciousness of having done well. *Their* sleep is sweet when the labours of the day are over, and they await with placid composure that rest which is to put a final end to all their labours and to all their sufferings."

There is also a fine passage in the beginning of the thirteenth chapter of this Essay.

"Amongst the great variety of enjoyments which riches put within the reach of persons of fortune and education, there is none more delightful than that which results from doing good to those from whom no return can be expected, or none but gratitude, respect, and attachment. What exquisite pleasure, then, must it afford, to collect the scattered rays of useful science and direct them, *united*, to objects of general utility! to throw them in a broad beam on the cold and dreary habitations of the poor, spreading cheerfulness and comfort all around!

"Is it not possible to draw off the attention of the rich from trifling and unprofitable amusements and engage them in pursuits in which their own happiness and reputation and the public prosperity are so intimately connected? What a wonderful change in the state of society might in a short time be effected by their *united efforts!*

"It is hardly possible for the condition of the lower classes of society to be essentially improved without that kind and friendly assistance which none can afford them but the rich and the benevolent. They must be *taught*, and who is there in whom they have confidence that will take the trouble to instruct them? They cannot learn from books, for they have not time to read; and if they had, how few of them would be able, from a written description, to comprehend what they ought to know! If I write for their instruction, it is to the rich that I must address myself, and if I am not able to engage *them* to assist me all my labours will be in vain."

Again he writes: —

"Whenever I sit down to write, I feel my mind deeply impressed with a sense of the respect which I owe, as an individual, to the public, to whom I presume to address myself, and often consider how blameable it would be in me, especially when I am endeavouring to recommend economy, to trifle with the time of thousands.

"Too much pains cannot be taken by those who write books to render their ideas clear, and their language concise and easy to be understood.

"*Hours* spent by an author in saving *minutes*, or even *seconds*, to his readers, is time well employed."

The Count had bestowed great pains and much time in planning, constructing, and improving a *gridiron grate*, with its appurtenances, for the use of those in narrow circumstances. When, by many experiments, he had satisfied himself with the exactness of his patterns, he had castings taken from them by the best London founders. Of these he made a present to the Carron Company, at their works in Scotland, on his journey there in the autumn of 1800. At the same time he made a contract with the company to furnish the articles at their warehouse in London at the lowest reasonable price, that gentlemen might buy them by the dozen for distribution to the poor.

I have made these large extracts from the Count's

tenth Essay, as a substitute for any extended comments or suggestions of my own, that I may give the reader the means of forming an instructed opinion of the chief motives, the sagacious methods, the benevolent spirit, and the actual practical work of its author. We have in these extracts as candid expositions of himself as it is possible for a man to make. If there is discernible in them some traces of human infirmity in the betrayal of a consciousness of good desert, or in the falling back upon a self-appreciation in amends for the lack of expected commendation from others, such weakness will be sufficiently allowed for by the mere recognition of it. The following sentences will properly give us a summing up of the matter: " Whether the reader agrees with me or not, I hope and trust that he will do me the justice to believe that I have no wish so much at my heart as to render my labours of some real and lasting utility to mankind. How happy shall I be, when I come to die, if I can *then* think that I have lived to some useful purpose ! "

Professor Renwick, in his Life of Count Rumford, prepared for Sparks's American Biography, records a fact which ought to find mention here. After referring to the Count's efforts and plans for the improvement of the grates used in England for burning coal, the Professor says that his principles, soon after they were published, reached a degree of development in the United States beyond that to which they were carried by the Count himself, or had attained half a century subsequently in the mother country. When the Count's Essay reached New York, owing to the exhaustion of the neighboring forests and the high price of firewood, bituminous coal from Liverpool had come into general use, the vapor and soot from which, as then burned, were a great annoyance. The Professor adds : —

" It is due to the persons concerned in the introduction of the use of this description of fuel into the United States, and of Rumford's plans and principles for its cleanly and economic use, that they should be commemorated while those who witnessed their experiments and efforts still live to record them. To fulfil this grateful task, we may therefore state that the first range for cooking with coal was imported and set up by William Renwick, in 1796; and that in 1798 it was lined with fire-brick, in conformity with Rumford's principles, under the direction of Professor John Kemp, of Columbia College ; that a Rumford kitchen was put up by Isaac Gouverneur in 1798; and that parlor grates were planned and the details of their setting pointed out to the mechanics who executed them, by David Gordon, — afterwards, on his return to England in 1808, distinguished as an engineer, and for his mode of rendering gas portable for the purposes of illumination." *

In a very short Essay, numbered as the eleventh, the Count offers " Observations concerning Open Chimney Fireplaces." He found that his own reputation and the improvements which he had proposed in these constructions — as in the use of his roasters — had suffered, during his two years' absence in Germany, by the carelessness and other faults of the workmen who had been employed in altering old fireplaces or fitting up new ones. He designates the mistakes and the consequences which have resulted from them, and he insists upon the absolute necessity of strict adherence, without deviation, to the directions, measurements, and proportions which he had prescribed.

More annoying still was another experience which

* Sparks's Library of American Biography, Second Series, Vol. V. p. 114.

the Count endured as he walked the streets of London and read the placards and advertisements in the journals. He found his own name attached to many boasted improvements announced to the public, in connection with certain stoves, grates, etc., that were exposed for sale. The name of Rumford had become a synonyme of Reform. He wished to preserve it from contact with quackery or fraud. He adverts, but very mildly, to this annoyance in this Essay, as follows : —

" As I am extremely anxious not to injure any man, either in his reputation for ingenuity, or in his trade, or in any other way, I shall not say one word more on this subject than what I feel it to be my duty to the public to declare, namely, that I am not the inventor of any of those stoves or grates that have been offered to the public for sale, under my name."

The twelfth Essay, which also is very brief, is entitled "Of the Salubrity of Warm Rooms," of which the Count shows himself a most earnest champion. He draws the distinction between fresh or cold air, and pure or wholesome air. He exposes the folly of sitting in a room which has a large blazing open fire roasting one side of the body, while blasts of cold air are coursing the apartment ; and he explains the remarkable fact that we are not capable of feeling, or rather are not conscious of feeling, both heat and cold at the same time, though we are really subject to them. He shows how streams of cold air are always pernicious, and that the danger from them is greatest when we are least sensible of it. He insists that sudden changes from hot rooms to the cold air, so far from being dangerous to health, are harmless, as well as often pleasurable, — confirming his position by the examples of the Swedes and Russians, who, while living in the coldest climates, keep their apartments very warm. He says that a warm room, by promoting a free circulation of the blood, gives the health and vigor which are necessary in order to support without injury occasional exposure to intense cold. The philosopher speaks in the following paragraph : —

"There is a simple experiment, easily made and no wise dangerous, which shows, in a sensible and convincing manner, that warmth prepares the body to bear occasional cold without pain and without injury. Let a person in health, rising from a warm bed, after a good night's rest, in cold weather, put on a dry warm shirt, and, dressing himself merely in his drawers, stockings, and slippers, let him go into a room in which there is no fire, and walk leisurely about the room for half an hour ; or let him sit down and write or read during that time. He will find himself able to support this trial without the smallest inconvenience. The cold to which he exposes himself will hardly be felt, and no bad consequences to his health will result from the experiment. Let him now repeat this experiment under different circumstances. In the evening of a chilly day, and when he is shivering with cold, let him undress himself to his shirt, and see how long he will be able to support exposure to the air in a cold room in that light dress."

The Count likewise repeats the assertion made to him by Dr. Blane, an eminent London physician, that persons who had lived for years in the hot climates of India, returning to reside in England, did not feel inconvenience from the cold of its climate nearly so much in the first year as they did in the second, after their return. If they could be persuaded to have warm rooms and freely use the warm bath, they would never out of doors suffer any inconvenience, and might exercise much more freely.

The Count's thirteenth Essay, "On the Salubrity of

Warm Bathing," has already been noticed in another connection.

The fourteenth and fifteenth Essays, respectively "Of the Management of Fires in Closed Fireplaces" and "Of the Use of Steam as a Vehicle for Transporting Heat," are substantially additions to the matter of the tenth Essay. They give practical information of high value in all culinary and in many mechanical processes. In the former of the two will be found one of those very candid confessions which the writer, on occasions for them, was always ready to give, of mistakes which he had himself made in some previous conclusions. He renders honorable amends to a cook who was the medium of teaching him his error and the way to truth.

The use of steam, according to the method which the Count suggested, is now almost universally adopted in the kitchens and wash-houses of public institutions, and in dye-houses and breweries, where pipes are made to convey heat to large wooden vats or tubs at a vast saving of time, fuel, and labor.

Mention has already been made, on a previous page, that Count Rumford's efforts, publications, and schemes to provide nutritious food, and to secure an economical use of its materials, were all brought to public notice in England at a period of general scarcity, and when there were even well-founded apprehensions of famine. In the very important and exciting debate on the Corn and Bread Bill before Parliament in 1800, I find that the Count was most honorably and gratefully named for his valuable labors and counsels. Both Lord Hawkesbury and Mr. Wilberforce passed upon him the highest encomiums as a public benefactor. In connection with his name, they mention another eminent philanthropist, Arthur Young.[*]

On a subsequent page I shall have occasion to quote the words of a most eminent scientific man, an associate of Rumford, to whom he was at first indebted for favors, but against whom he afterwards seems to have conceived a dislike, to the effect that at this time the Count was much mortified at being "the object of the impertinent attacks of a popular satirist." The reference, undoubtedly, is to that most sharp-spoken and virulent of political, literary, and social Ishmaelites, William Cobbett, whose voluminous Register was in alternate volumes the vehicle of laudation and of objurgation directed towards the same persons, according to the mood and temporary objects of the satirist. Cobbett spent all the force of his ridicule and invective against Rumford's project of soup-houses for the poor. Doubtless the Count was, on this subject, somewhat oblivious or disregardful of a characteristic distinction between the habits and tastes of the Germans and the French on the one side, and the English on the other, touching the composition, quality, and preparation of their food. The distinction continues to this day, and is observable, if not sometimes more than observable, by every traveller between England and the Continent. In France and Germany it would seem as if the more of a *mess,* and of a compound in which the several ingredients of the mixture do not appear, was set before the natives as food, in the shape of a soup or stew, the more acceptable the contents of the dish would be. In England, on the other hand, the hungry man, even when not dainty, loves to know what he is eating, is

* Annual Register, Vol. XLII. pp. 130, 133.

suspicious of composite fabrics, and prefers to see a whole joint or a cut, which will indicate from what source it was derived. *Soup-maigre*, the solace and sustenance of many a French peasant and household, is an especial horror to an Englishman. Now it is not to be denied that Rumford depended very largely upon, and wrote very largely in the interest of, these lymphatic and often bilious compounds; even that word, " compound," seems rather too substantial to be applied to the products of some of his recipes. He did, however, recommend, with great success, the establishment of public soup-houses, where his cheap, but as he contended nutritive, if not always palatable, concoctions could be dispensed to the poor. He also sought to induce those who were not needy, and even some of his rich friends, to avail themselves of such public dispensations, with the aim and to the extent of giving them their patronage and approval, so as to be induced afterwards in their own families to practise an economy in the use of what was often thrown away.

Cobbett chose to represent the Count's devices of this sort as an aggravation of the indifference and heartlessness sometimes disguised under the schemes and measures for relieving the poor. Dr. Johnson's famous definition of *oats*, as expressing on the English side of the border the food of horses, and on the Scotch side the food of human beings, was not so sharp as were Cobbett's sarcasms cast upon Rumford's thin soups. He insisted on representing it as an outrage upon Englishmen that whatever the degree of their poverty, and however nearly they approached starvation, they should have offered to them, in the name of science and charity, the insipid and flatulent compounds which he chose to ridicule as actually the products of the philosophic philanthropist's recipes. "Dirt and bones" were the terms which he applied to the proffered soups. He was willing that Irishmen should eat potatoes, but Englishmen were worthy of something better. He, however, displayed his own ignorance when he represented even an insipid compound as necessarily without nutrition, or failed to recognize the fact that a bone may contain more invigorating matter than a piece of solid muscular meat of the same weight. The satirist was successful to a great degree in bringing reproach upon a well-intended and beneficent scheme. The soup-houses fell into disrepute, and the result was, to an unfortunate degree, somewhat unfavorable to the whole scheme and method by which Count Rumford had endeavored to reorganize and administer public charity.

More recently a writer in Blackwood's Magazine,[*] in a satirical article on "Panaceas for Poverty," has found matter for raillery and jesting in the purely humane and benevolent methods proposed by Count Rumford for the relief of stern suffering in a time of prevailing scarcity. It is well to keep in mind the fact, that all bantering and trifling, on the part of those who enjoy the comforts or revel in the easy luxuries of life, with the appliances brought to bear, however inadequately, for the relief of destitution, are apt to be regarded by the poor as a heartless mockery of their condition.

In connection with Count Rumford's philanthropic labors, especially those referred to in preceding pages, which led him, from the combined results of his own

[*] Vol. XIV. p. 637.

practical experiments and the theories suggested to him as to the organizing of a wisely benevolent plan, to present a new method for the systematic relief of the poor, I have to mention a fact of much interest. I can well conceive that the Count himself would regard this fact as perhaps the most grateful of all the tributes that have been paid to the labors of his life or to his memory.

In a note which is a part of a correspondence on another subject, my friend, Mr. Thomas C. Amory, lately an alderman of the city of Boston, and one of the most discreet and earnest among those who have administered the municipal charities, writes to me the following sentences, just as I have before me the closing page of this chapter.

"Pardon me if I venture to call to your attention the fact, that those of us, including the Hon. R. C. Winthrop, who took part in organizing the present system of relief of the poor in Boston with the Industrial Aid Society and Provident Association under the same roof, did not lose sight of the example of Count Rumford at Munich. By permission of the Board, I purchased for its use a copy of his works. It might be worth your while, before completing your work, to take a look at the books and pigeon-holes of the Chardon Street building [the magnificent and commodious structure recently prepared by the city for the administration of many of its charities]. The system, of course, is still in its infancy, and has much progress to make before it approximates perfection. But its aim is the same as Rumford's, — to render the poor self-sustaining by finding them work.

"It sometimes occurs to me, that, as Rumford was of our neighborhood, his statue or bust would be a fitting decoration for the blank-wall space of the building over the entrance. He was pre-eminently a philanthropist, and of the best sort, seeking practical ends in improving the condition of his fellow-men.

And though his efforts to reform pauperism and mendicity found their principal field abroad, and this was but one of many ways in which he sought to be of use, the results by example belong to the world, and our Chardon Street building, the first of its kind, would not seem an inappropriate place to do honor to one whose fame belongs especially to Massachusetts, and to Boston as its capital."

CHAPTER IX.

IN giving as full and accurate an account as is possible of the events and the labors of Count Rumford's life, from his leaving England for the last time till his death, I shall be indebted chiefly for my materials to papers left by his daughter. These will be found to have a curious, and in many respects a painful interest, as they give in such detail the particulars of a new domestic relation formed by him, which promised him much happiness, but which resulted in alienation and disappointment, and, it would seem, in clouding and imbittering the last years of the Count's existence. I shall follow the daughter's rehearsal of these experiences, and then gather from other sources such illustrative information as is within my reach.

As regards the daughter herself, in the interval that 'elapsed after her return to America, and before she joined her father again in Europe, I have several interesting matters to communicate. The Count's mother had removed with her husband to Maine before Sarah's return. This led the granddaughter to make frequent visits to that State, in which, while visiting aunts and cousins, she made many acquaintances and friends in Portland, Brunswick, Flintstown, etc. Indeed, it would seem as if she had no settled abiding-place, and became quite reconciled to, if not fond of, a roaming life, which made her the guest of many hospitable homes. I have before me many letters of hers to female friends, and they are largely occupied with affairs of the heart. Her father's distinctions and reputation would have secured her attentions, even apart from her own recommendation of herself by her natural or acquired attractions. We have seen that she considered herself unfitted for a quiet and simple life in a country village, or even in a populous town in her native land, and that her foreign adventures made her crave a renewal of their excitements.

Here is a pleasant note of hers to her father's friend, Colonel Baldwin.

" BOSTON, October 15, 1799.

" DEAR SIR, — " You were so good as to say that you would carry me to Woburn any time. I should like to go. If you could conveniently call or send for me on Wednesday next, I think upon the whole I should like to go. If you can call to see me before that time, and can bring Miss Clarissa [Miss Baldwin], I should be gratified, for I want to see her very much. I never knew till I read the letter you was so kind as to leave me yesterday, that you had a little son.* I feel quite impatient to see him, and if you could contrive to bring him with Clarissa I should be very glad.

" Believe me with much respect,

" Your much obliged

"SARAH RUMFORD."

Count Rumford's stepfather, Mr. Josiah Pierce, had died in August, 1798.

The letter that follows from Colonel Baldwin to the Countess was probably addressed to her while she was residing in apartments in Boston : —

" Woburn, September 27, 1800.

" MY DEAR COUNTESS, — Yours by the stage, I received yesterday. Your grandmamma arrived at my house last Saturday in good health, and tarried with us until Monday, when she went to her sister Simonds, perhaps to visit her relations in Woburn, and then to go to Boston. Perhaps you may see her the beginning of next week. Miss Clarissa skipped upon reading your kind invitation to make a visit just as her brother Cyrus was setting out for Boston this morning in a sulky. The scheme was started for her to go with him, and the experiment to see if she could ride in that way was made. The result was

---

* This, now the only surviving son of Colonel Baldwin, is George Rumford Baldwin, Esq., of Woburn, Massachusetts, who, with the genius and skill characteristic of his family, is one of the most eminent engineers in the United States ; his father having planned and engineered the Middlesex Canal ; his brother Loammi having constructed the United States naval dry docks at Charlestown, Massachusetts, and Norfolk, Virginia ; and his brother James F. having given his science to the Cochituate Water-Works of Boston. The present representative of the family was the engineer of the water-works of Quebec, Canada, and of Charlestown, Massachusetts.

favorable to her wishes, and she was ready before I could scribble this line. They are now both waiting, and the morning lowering. I must defer my observations on the feeling you express in inhabiting your new mansion. I hope, and still think you will prefer Woburn, for to spend half the year at least.

"I am, my dear Countess,
"Yours sincerely,
"LOAMMI BALDWIN."

In a letter from Concord, to a female friend in Boston, dated November 5, 1801, referring to her good purposes of industrious occupation for that winter, Sarah writes: "I should not so much mind spending my time idly, if I had no one to please but myself. My father is very active himself, and usefully active; and he highly disapproves of the manner in which I pass my time. He has proved a kind, good father to me, and in return for his kindness I ought to do everything in my power to please him. He is extravagantly fond of drawing, and thinks if I have a talent for anything it is for that; and often reproaches me for not attending to it more than what I do."

Readers, I feel sure, will not expect or desire from me any apology for the use which I am now to make of some very miscellaneous papers that have fortunately come to my hand, from various sources, filled with details of more or less interest as contributions to a biography. In one point of view some of the contents of these papers are trivial, and may seem in their rehearsal to be below the dignity that should invest our subject. But in another aspect they will engage the reader as really instructive in themselves, and, in fact, as specially essential to our knowledge of Count Rumford in the more private relations of his life, and particularly in those with his daughter. The papers are of the highest authenticity, and have a charming naturalness as well as variety in their details. So far as they divulge matters of a disagreeable and discreditable character, it is to be remembered that public notoriety and scandal once gave a far more extended and sharpened relation of them than they will find in these pages.

It is necessary to anticipate in the order of narration to introduce the materials now to be used.

On returning to his house at Brompton, after the embarkation of his daughter, the Count expressed his feelings on parting with her in a letter which immediately followed her over the seas.

"Brompton Row, 30th Aug., 1799.

"Dear Sally,—After giving myself much trouble, I obtained the information that your vessel sailed from Gravesend the day after I left you there, with a good wind; that you were well and in fine spirits,—as expressed to me, like a bird let out of a cage. While I was very dull and not well, I could not but be struck with the contrast. But no matter, my dear. I should be sorry to have you unhappy because I am. I dare say you will be glad to see me when I join you in America next year, as I hope to do. Or, if I come not there, you will return here. So I shall make no further comments on the subject; only repeat my fervent prayer and wishes for your having a prosperous voyage and finding friends well."

In the interval between the Countess's return to her native country in 1799 and her second visit to her father in 1811, she received from him, as she enumerates them, one hundred and four letters. Remaining in France and England many years after her father's death, she led an unsettled life from that time. In the year

1818, while living at her father's house in Brompton, she had taken under her care an English child two years of age, named Emma Gammell, who ever afterwards lived with her in the closest and most affectionate relations, addressing the Countess as "aunt," being at home with her, and sharing her confidence in all things. A short time before the Countess's death, her "niece" was married to Mr. John Burgom, of Concord, New Hampshire, also of English birth, and continued, with her husband, to live in the Countess's house. In the infirmities of advanced age, some of the peculiarities and eccentricities with which nature and the circumstances of her life had marked Miss Sarah were much intensified. She had divided the hundred and four letters from her father, which she often pored over, into two parcels. One of these, about twenty in number, concerned the Count's efforts and experiences in connection with the Royal Institution. The other parcel, which she was wont to speak of as "the scolding letters," contained either advice and reprimand for herself, or references to his own domestic unhappiness and grievous disappointment in his second marriage. Of this parcel the Countess had made abstracts, sometimes selecting sentences and mixing her own comments with them, sometimes copying the whole of the letter in her father's words. She was, however, very careless about dates, being as likely to attach wrong as right ones, and thus causing some perplexity for a reader who uses these materials in connection with other correctly dated papers. Indeed, the Countess was so habitually negligent in this matter of dates, that Sir Charles Blagden, who, as we shall soon have occasion to note, was one of her warmest friends and most faithful correspondents, among other rebukes which he had the fidelity and courage to administer, asks her pointedly if she had "no almanac."

Shortly before her death, while confined to her bed and chair, and at times not wholly herself, she required her "niece" to bring to her the two parcels of the Count's letters and commit them to the fire. Mrs. Burgom informs me, that, under the persuasion that the letters which related to the Royal Institution might at some time have an historical value, she tried by a little artifice of concealment to avert the fate designed for that package. But the Countess, being at the moment especially persistent and watchful, discovered the intent and peremptorily required their destruction. In view of what has been so imperfectly explained in a previous chapter relating to the Count's breach with his friends and a quarrel about the management of the Institution, there is occasion to regret the destruction of that set of the Count's letters, for they may have contained what we have no trace or hint of in any other paper from his pen, — his own account of the nature and occasion of the variance. The Countess's abstract of the larger package, classed as "the scolding letters," is in my hands, and its use, in the proper place, will afford instruction, though not pleasure.

I have also before me a bundle of some forty or more letters to the Countess, from her friend Sir Charles Blagden. He was her *friend*, faithful, discreet, and so sure of his right and duty in the case as to allow himself great frankness, and even a degree of severity, in some of his communications to her. These letters begin on her return to America, in 1793, and continue at intervals till her second visit to Europe to join her father, when a new series of them commences and continues up to the death of the writer.

Those of Sir Charles's letters which were addressed to the Countess while she was in America, between the dates of her first two visits abroad, are especially valuable from the notices which they contain of her father's course and doings in that interval. Though Sir Charles was mistaken in his surmises as to the probable failure of the Count's matrimonial scheme, it would, perhaps, have been better for the parties if he had been a true prophet. He appears to have been a fair-minded man, and his reference to his own breach of confidential relations with the Count, while not definite enough to acquaint us with the subject-matter of the unkindness, must lead us to recognize in it a token of those qualities in the character or temperament of Count Rumford which alienated from him several who were once his friends.

For another, and though comparatively a trivial, yet by no means an uninteresting, matter of human concern, presenting itself in a very inartificial way in these letters, they are of service to biographer and readers. Sir Charles, as the Countess herself informs us, and as possibly may be fairly inferred from his own expressions, was once willing, perhaps desirous, to marry her. Her account of his application to her father for that purpose, and of the Count's way of dealing with the case, has been given on a previous page. Sir Charles seems not only to have acquiesced in the necessity of laying aside the character of a lover, but also to have willingly assumed the office of a guardian toward the Countess. She was in her twenty-sixth year when the correspondence from which extracts are to be given began. From the tenor of his letters we are to infer some of the contents of hers to him. From this it would appear, that, after he had yielded any expectations or wishes of his own to make her his wife, she required of him the somewhat exacting and embarrassing responsibility of advising her as between various suitors and available gentlemen, whose qualities and pretensions she made known to her former admirer.

Sir Charles being a near neighbor of the Count, as he had lodgings at No. 51 Brompton Row, writes to the Countess under date of June 9, 1800, to congratulate her on her safe arrival in America. He begins in this letter to assume the character of an adviser and counsellor, — sometimes a very frank and even severely rebuking one, — which, as we shall see, led him gradually to take upon himself, apparently with the full tolerance of the Countess, the authority of a father, strangely qualifying the tone of a lover. It seems that Sir Charles had investments in the American funds, and wished to purchase more. He proposes to the Countess that she shall collect his dividends for him, and intimates his intention to go to the United States, at least as a visitor, as he had once already been. The following is an extract.

"From a conviction that your natural discernment and the openness with which I always spoke and acted before you and the Count had made you exactly acquainted with my character and turn of mind, I was induced to request that you would frankly tell me, after you had resided a little time in America, whether my removal from this country to that would, in your opinion, contribute to my happiness. Would you advise me, as a friend, to settle in America? or to make a tour in that country? or not to go thither at all? You have often heard me mention Rhode Island as by far the healthiest and pleasantest spot I had any opportunity of seeing on the west side of the Atlantic."

Then follow specific inquiries as to expenses, privileges, neighbors, etc.

"It will give me very great pleasure to see you again, either here or in America. Do not depend upon the Count's going to visit you there. It is indeed possible that the fancy may suddenly strike him, and then he will set off in an instant, almost without giving notice. But his favorite child, the Institution, cannot yet walk alone, and, if he quits it at the time he talks of, will be a helpless cripple, even if it should continue to exist at all. I still see, with regret, his time and powers wasted on an object so inferior, in my opinion, to those which presented themselves to him in America. But he views the thing in a different light, and I suspect will be led on to stay here one year after another, till you are worn out with expecting him, and the opportunity of distinguishing himself in a rising country will be past."

Sir Charles subscribes himself, "With true esteem and affectionate regard, Dear Madam, your faithful friend and servant."

Under date of September 10, 1801, he responds to a letter from the Countess of the 13th of July, and writes that the Count had read to him "the very handsome letter which he had received from General Knox," concerning the agreeable arrangement she had made for passing the summer at the General's residence in Thomaston, Maine, and he adds : —

"It is with great pleasure that I learn, both from the Count and yourself, the great proficiency you make in drawing. He says that you have naturally a talent for that art, and could with pains arrive to great perfection in it ; that he had advised you whilst you were in Europe to cultivate this talent, but that you did not then take to it as kindly as he wished. I believe it would sensibly add to his pleasure on seeing you again if he

found that you had made the progress in it of which he thinks
you capable. Your father is indeed going to Munich, and talks
of setting out in a fortnight. I had at one time almost settled
to go with him, but he then proposed to stay there all this
winter and next summer. Two or three weeks ago, however,
he changed his plan, and determined to make this only a preparatory visit, and to return hither within three months. This
was more hurry of travelling than I could venture to undertake,
especially as the journey back would be in the bad months of
November and December. So that I now propose to spend the
winter in England. For my own part I sincerely wish that he
had found it expedient to make a voyage to America instead of
this journey on the Continent. I would then certainly have
accompanied him across the Atlantic, notwithstanding the unsettled state of affairs here. He every day talks more and more
coolly about going to America, and though I really think that
he means to make *you* a visit there some time or other, yet it
does not seem as if he promised himself much satisfaction besides. I am persuaded that I should like it much more than he
would, but whether I shall ever have the resolution to set out
unless some particular inducement of company or objects presents itself, remains uncertain even to myself. There is a hint
in your letter about ' seeing your European friends again, before
a great length of time.' To me, and I believe to all your
friends, the visit would afford very sincere pleasure. But before
you undertake it, I would advise you to be sure that the Count
approves of it. I have no reason to think that his regard for you
is lessened, but he seems to me rather more difficult to deal
with than formerly, and particularly more impatient if everything be not said and done exactly according to his liking. I
mentioned that you thought he did not write to you so frequently as he used to do, and he immediately took fire ; but at
the same time showed me a list of thirteen or fourteen letters
which he had sent you in the course of this year, 1801. No
one could deny that it was a sufficient correspondence. As to
his health, it is nearly the same as usual, except that he is
rather thinner, having lived long upon a very spare diet. The

constant agitation of his mind and the irritable constitution with which it is connected will necessarily prevent him from enjoying a regular state of good health; but his life seems to be in no danger. At his desire I always considered myself as your guardian, in case you should want one. And since I knew you, my own inclination prompts me to do everything which I had before undertaken out of friendship for him. The Count assures me that he will write to you before he sets out for Germany. I thank you for your kind remembrance, whether kept within your own breast, or expressed on the bark of trees, or in the naming of places. Be assured of the constant regard and friendship with which I am affectionately yours."

Under date of August 8, 1803, the Knight writes to the Countess from London: —

"When my letter of last June was written, I thought your father pretty much fixed at Munich, and therefore ventured to suggest to you that it might contribute to your happiness if you were to be established at that court. But I learn since that the Elector has set him more at his liberty, and that in consequence he intends to return to England this autumn. Political difficulties may possibly stand in the way of this journey, but he hopes to avoid them. I am still as much at a loss as I was in June, to answer your question whether your father be going to marry. He is now, as I told you in that letter, making the tour of Switzerland with a very amiable French lady. But I have no reason to think that they have any idea of a matrimonial connection. When the Count comes to England, she is to return to Paris; at least, so he writes me word.

"Your present situation, I believe, is approved by your father, for in one of his letters last winter he mentioned that he was better satisfied with your conduct than ever. I wish it made you happier, but am not surprised at the kind of listlessness which your letter so strongly expresses without removing it. Such good affections as yours ought to be placed. On this subject, however, I will not repeat what I expressed so fully in my letter of last June.

" We are here in a great bustle, preparing to repel the invasion with which we are threatened. It is an unpleasant time, and I sincerely lament the renewal of war. It was my intention to have gone into Germany this summer, if the enemy had not so much obstructed the passages.

" My health continues good, but I am not in very high spirits any more than yourself. We have both nearly the same cause for our complaint, namely, the want of objects sufficiently interesting."

Under date of London, December 5, 1803, Sir Charles writes : —

" All I can tell you about your father is this : he continued travelling with the French lady till about the middle of September, when she left him at Mannheim, and returned to Paris. Your father had applied to the French government for leave to come to England through France, but was refused. In consequence he remained at Mannheim till the middle of October, when, having by some means, I do not know how, induced the French government to change their resolution, and allow him to travel in France, he set out for Paris ; and I know that he was in that city on the 1st of November. In the last letter I received from him, which was written the day before he set out from Mannheim, he said that he had great hopes of being in England before the end of this year. Since that time I have heard nothing from him. He continues very intimate with the lady, but whether it will end in a marriage, I cannot say. My own opinion is rather inclined to the negative, yet I have no good foundation for it. However, should they marry, I do not think it would be an unfortunate event for you. The lady is rich, and most probably will have no children. If you should have no other home you would naturally live with them, and in that situation would enjoy every kind of comfort belonging to a single state. Whether that would make you amends for the want of conjugal felicity, you can best judge from your own feelings. And this leads me to the part of your letter which refers to your idea of settling at Northampton [Massachusetts].

My advice on that subject is, that you should by no means enter into such an engagement without your father's express approbation. Acquaint him with all the circumstances, and with your own feelings, as exactly as you can; and then say that you will accept or refuse the offer, according to the advice that he shall give. It is probable that he will not be able to make up his mind till his own affair with the French lady shall be decided; and your suitor, if he is reasonable, will have patience till that time, on your fairly stating to him the causes of your own indecision. Before you make an engagement with this gentleman be sure of yourself in one respect, namely, that you shall not regret the giving up the splendid society in which your father will live in Paris, if he marries the lady in question, for that sort of existence which you will have at Northampton.

" A letter which I sent you the latter end of last July (by the favor of Mr. Gore, who promised to forward it by the first ship for Boston) will have informed you that your father seemed not likely to have any permanent settlement at the court of Bavaria, in which case your establishment there would not be so pleasant as I hoped when I wrote to you in June. Where he will ultimately fix it is impossible to foresee. I do not think it will be in this country, nor probably in France, unless he should marry the lady with whom he travelled. As to America, he seems less inclined to go thither than ever.

" I thank you very much for remembering my dear sister. She died two years ago.

" My own situation is too uncertain to indulge any speculation about going to America. But I am truly obliged by your friendly offer of taking up my final abode with you at Northampton, in case you should settle there.

" Since this was written I have received a letter from your father, dated at Paris, November 11. By this it is evident that he expects to marry the French lady, though nothing is yet finally determined. I again particularly advise you not to enter into any engagement till you know the result of this affair, and the plan that your father shall adopt respecting you, in case it should end according to his wishes, of which, however, I have still some little doubt, because he is, as you know, of a very sanguine temper. He does not seem likely to come to England very soon."

Under date of March 12, 1804, Sir Charles writes to the Countess from Liverpool : —

" The last account I received of your father was dated the 19th of January. He was then at Paris, very assiduous in his attentions to the French lady, with whom, indeed, he spent most of his time. But I believe she had not then determined to marry him, and I am still inclined to think she never will. In the mean time he is entirely losing his interest in this country. His residence at Paris this winter, whilst we were threatened with an invasion, is considered by every one as very improper conduct, and his numerous enemies do not fail to make the most of it. He has quarrelled with Mr. Bernard and others of his old friends at the Royal Institution, and they do all they can to render him unpopular. Probably he has written to you more than once by American ships since his residence at Paris. To me he wrote on the 12th of November, about a fortnight after his arrival there. But I expect no other letter from him, as it would certainly be imprudent in him to keep up a correspondence with this country during his residence in France. I believe there are still letters from America lying for him at Herries the banker's, for, as the Count had not given him directions to forward them to Paris, he did not think himself authorized to do so. Perhaps some of your letters are among them.

" It is a long time since I have seen Lady Palmerston, but I know that she is in tolerably good health. Her eldest son, the present Lord Palmerston, is grown a fine young man.

" I am anxious to know what you have determined relative to a certain affair at Northampton."

Under date of London, July 27, 1804, Sir Charles writes : —

" The last letter I received from your father was dated the

4th of this month. It appears that he was not married then, but that he expected to be soon. He writes on this subject with such confidence to all his friends, that I can scarcely venture to call in question any longer the favorable issue of his suit. Yet, from my knowledge of the lady in question, her sentiments and ideas, I shall not cease to entertain some doubts till the event actually takes place. With respect to you he writes to me thus: 'I have no very late news of my Daughter, but report says that she is about to take a husband. Her fortune, or, rather, *inheritance*, is settled. She will have 6,000 livres a year in the French funds, with the capital, in addition to her pension of 2,000 Florins a year from Bavaria.' Probably he will acquaint you with this himself; if not, I beg you neither to let him nor any person know that I have communicated it to you. I am very much dissatisfied with his conduct toward me in certain points, since he has been in France, and for that reason have not written to him since last December. It is at present my intention to drop his correspondence entirely, and perhaps this is the last letter that you will receive from me for a considerable time."

Reference is made in the letter to the death of Lord Palmerston, and the illness of Lady Palmerston, of whom Blagden writes : —

"A letter from you, I am sure, would give her pleasure. She retains the same regard for your father as formerly. Having thus answered your questions, allow me to add that your account of yourself gives me pain. That you are a tolerable adept at the different games of which you are extravagantly fond ; that you could play at billiards and whist forever, are confessions which I hope you do not make to your father, and particularly not to your lover. If the latter be really a man of sense, and were to judge that such is unalterably your character, he would avoid you as the most dangerous person with whom he could form a connection. But no doubt he believes, as I do, that your dissipation is not natural, and that if your affections were once properly fixed, if you were fulfilling the duties of your sex as the mother of a family, you would feel much more real pleasure in the occupations which would result from that situation than play, or company, or any kind of dissipation ever afforded you. The latter always end with the feeling of which you so justly complain, that 'nothing delights.' With respect to the Northampton gentleman, you seem to me to like him quite well enough to marry him. If, therefore, your father makes no objection, I should think you would do right to give him a favorable answer at once. I have now some doubts whether your father, even if he should succeed in marrying the French lady, would wish to have you reside with him. But do not marry till he gives his consent, or at least till he tells you that he has no objection. How happens it that he had not to the 4th of July received a letter from you on this subject? I should not wonder if his late kindness to you was chiefly at the instigation of the French lady, nor indeed if she contributed to it herself.* She is, in many respects, a very extraordinary woman. Adieu, my dear Countess. Be assured of my sincere wishes for your happiness, whether I write to you or not."

"LONDON, August 12, 1805.

"MY DEAR COUNTESS,— It is now more than a year ago that I wrote to you in answer to your letter of the preceding spring, which is the last that I have received from you. Be assured that I always entertain the same sentiments of regard for you; that I am anxious to know whether your health continues good, and particularly whether you are happy. Has the marriage you had then in contemplation taken place? It would

---

* Sir Charles was right in his surmise that the "French lady" had contributed to certain valuable gifts sent at this time by the Count to his daughter, in anticipation of his marriage. The Countess makes mention in her journals of having received at this time some rich presents of lace, jewels, and trinkets from Madame Lavohier. These, which she highly valued, we shall find she was in danger of losing when the vessel in which she was going to join her father was captured. She recovered them, and had the opportunity of wearing them on fit occasions, and of bestowing them on particular friends and relatives before her death. I have seen many of them, and they are exceedingly beautiful, exhibiting fine taste in their selection, intrinsic value, and the thoroughness and costliness of the workmanship of former days.

give me great pleasure to learn that you are settled to your satisfaction.

"In my last letter I hinted to you that I thought your father had not acted toward me in Paris exactly as a friend ought to have done. He assures me that I am mistaken; but several circumstances, and particularly his withholding from me information of great consequence to me, and which he had the best opportunity of sending, have raised in my mind such a distrust of his friendship that we can never be on the same terms of confidence as before. He is now at Munich, but still professing that he expects an union with the lady whom he has so long attended. You know that I have always doubted of his success in this point, and my doubts are not lessened. Our good friend Lady Palmerston died last January. To the last she retained her affectionate character, and more than once she inquired for you.

"If you see Mr. and Mrs. Gore, remember me kindly to them. I hear that they are building a fine house ten or twelve miles from Boston.

"On whatever terms I may be with your father, depend upon the sincerity of my friendship for you, and my fervent wishes for your happiness.

"I remain, my dear Countess, your faithful servant,

"C. BLAGDEN."

Dating from the "Royal Society, Somerset Place, London, October 25, 1805, Sir Charles writes: —

"MY DEAR COUNTESS, — I send you this short letter to fulfil a promise I formerly made you, namely, that whenever I should learn anything decisive on the subject of your father's expected marriage, I would immediately let you know it. A letter is just come to my hands from a well-informed person, which contains the following passage : —

"'Je puis vous annoncer actuellement d'une manière positive, que le mariage entre M. de Rumford et Madame Lavoisier est définitivement arrêté.'

" This letter is dated at Paris, the 21st of October, and from a direction in it I conclude that the marriage has taken place before this time.

" On the 12th of last August I put a letter for you into the hands of the American Minister here. In it I inquired if *your* treaty of marriage had been concluded. But since that time a gentleman from Boston has told me that it was broken off some time ago. Perhaps this may prove a fortunate circumstance now, as your father has effected *his* marriage. I have not, however, the remotest idea how he intends to act respecting you, and particularly whether he thinks of bringing you to Paris or not. Most likely he has himself written to you all the details. With sincere wishes for your happiness, I remain, my dear Countess,

" Your faithful friend,

" C. BLAGDEN."

At this point we may defer further extracts from the letters of this faithful correspondent, and avail ourselves of the abstract made by the Countess, with her own comments from the papers which have been above described.

The Countess precedes her extracts, copied from her father's letters, with a few reminiscences and frank remarks, giving her own opinion of him and the opinions of others. She herself shared the general admiration of his personal beauty, fine figure, and elegant manners. She thinks he derived his talents from his mother, who was herself noted for her ingenuity, her soft, pleasing ways, and for moderately good looks. She admits that he was naturally aristocratic, and says that he was " a great lover of perfection of every shade and quality." The Rev. Dr. Lathrop, a distinguished minister in Boston, who knew the Count in his youth, is quoted by her as having said that " he was born a nobleman." She says he was a great favorite with the ladies, though some of them sharply censured him for the four following faults: " First, for living so short a time with his wives, considering him from it a bad husband; second, for taking sides against his country; third, letting his daughter get on as she could, he reveling at the time in the city of Paris; fourth, that he should pitch on Paris as a permanent residence, when both in Munich and in London he had made himself so useful, had won such honors, and had such distinguished associates and friends." One of these female critics, the Countess adds, repeated against him, "for leaving his ladies in so easy a manner," the lines of Cowper, —

> " Shows love to be a mere profession ;
> Proves that the heart is none of his,
> Or soon expels him if it is."

Another of the sex, on being told of his dereliction towards his native country, repeated with a sigh, —

> " O ye winds ! breathe not my faults ! "

Sarah writes as if several of these " female critics" had once freely discussed her father's faults and merits in her own hearing, and she appears to have made an impartial report of them. One of these women intimated that the Count in his early manhood had been enticed from the service of his native country by the contrast between the appearance of the British officers, with their fine accoutrements and splendid discipline, and the raw and uncouth American volunteers, — " possibly with tattered garments, giving a shot, and then running behind a tree." " Yes," interrupted another woman, "you know the Count is fond of external show. But you would not have caught your glorious Washington taking up arms against his native country." Some kindly participant in the discussion called attention to the Count's noble qualities, and to his devotion of himself so laboriously to the service of his fellow-men.

The daughter affirms that her father was deeply disappointed at not being received as Minister of Bavaria in England, as he would have greatly valued and enjoyed the consideration which such an office would have added to all his other distinctions. His chagrin was very evident, though he exhibited no bitterness for his discomfiture. She thinks that he was induced to plan and promote the Royal Institution as a substitute for occupation, and for claims to honor. In this latter inference she may have been mistaken, for, as we have seen, the Count was in correspondence with reference to such an Institution with Mr. Bernard before his appointment as ambassador. She is willing, however, to recognize in the engrossing occupation which kept him in England a providential favor to him, as the change of administration in Bavaria, though not depriving him of honor and influence, had qualified his opportunities for devising and effecting his favorite measures. She thinks also that, as Bavaria had become involved in Bonaparte's wars, the fate which befell her father's two aides-de-camp might have involved him, had he returned.

The Count's German valet, Aichner, having been in his service many years and proved himself capable and faithful, had become very essential to his master, and was generally his attendant on all his travels. The Count had allowed him to marry, and the wife was of use to him as a housekeeper. But when these servants became the parents of six children, the Count's com-

placency was somewhat tried. For five of these children
he found situations in Germany. He took the parents
and one of the children, a pretty little girl, with him to
England, in 1798, but found it necessary soon to send
them back to Germany. He engaged, in Aichner's
place, a capable young Englishman, named Roice, who,
being a carpenter, proved quite useful to him in improving the house which he purchased at Brompton.
The German servants returned to Bavaria before the
daughter came to America. She thought they suffered
from homesickness, and, with an indirect reference to
her own feelings, she asked her father to read Cowper's
verses, —

"O solitude! where are the charms," etc.

Sarah adds that though her father was not received as
the Bavarian ambassador, he was honorably and heartily
welcomed by all classes of people. The Palmerstons
were his most intimate friends, and he was on terms of
the freest and most cordial relations with them. The
Count would seldom pass his Lordship's house, in
Hanover Square, without going in, and in the season
for it he made constant visits to the superb estate at
Broadlands. Lady Palmerston, as woman and housekeeper, was the ideal of Miss Sarah's admiration. She
made her home so attractive to her guests that they did
not know how to leave it. "It was a kind of an enchanted castle, where there were regular reunions of the
first society, entertained with amusements and splendid
hospitality." Still, the daughter says, her father's position in England was a "let-down" from what it had
been in Bavaria, and he felt the change in the consideration practised towards him. His house, at Brompton,
a few minutes' walk from Piccadilly, was "pretty," and

on account of its peculiar arrangements it was visited as an object of curiosity by people of the middle and higher classes. But it was not the palace which he had occupied at Munich. He missed the warm and devoted personal friends whom he had attracted to him in that city. So he became restless, going to the Continent and returning after short visits, till he settled in France, and then continuing the same visits to Munich, when he painfully realized the change in his circle there. Next to Lady Palmerston, his best female friend was the Countess Nogarola, and she died from a broken heart at the loss of her only son.

The new Elector and his advisers and confidants were either deficient in sympathy with the Count or directly hostile to him, and there had been an important change in the political relations of the Electorate. The policy of Charles Theodore in endeavoring, as a member of the Germanic Empire, to preserve a neutrality between France and Austria in their wars, had been changed by him before his death, and he had become the ally of Austria. Rumford is supposed to have approved, if he did not suggest, this change of policy, which the succeeding Elector had reason to regard as calamitous. The battle at Hohenlinden in December, 1800, resulting in the defeat of the allies, put the Electorate in the possession of France, of which the Elector consequently became a vassal till the whirlwind of the Revolution again delivered him.

The following note of the Countess referred to her again widowed grandmother.

"Borron, September 15, 1800.

"Dear Sir,—I heard by accident something as if grandmamma was at Woburn. If she is there, it would be a great satisfaction to me to know it. Would you be so obliging as to let me know, by a line, if she be there?

> " I remain your much obliged friend,
>
> "S. RUMFORD.

" Hon. Loammi Baldwin."

The following letter was written by the Countess while she was on a visit to the house of General Knox, Washington's Secretary of War, at Thomaston, Maine.

> "Thomaston, St. George's River, July 12, 1802.

" Dear Sir, — I hope you will write to my father this summer. Before I left Boston I received a very charming letter from him. He was then in London, but expected in May to set out again for Germany. You may recollect that he has already been once to Germany since I saw him. Adieu, my dear sir ; remember me kindly to all friends at Woburn, and believe me to be your very much obliged and sincere friend,

> "S. RUMFORD.

" Colonel Loammi Baldwin."

It may interest some readers to have the daughter's account and views of her father's second marriage and its unhappy consequences, as she presents them in extracts from his letters to her, and from her own observation after she had joined him in France. She says that after his rejection as Minister, " his first bold, imprudent step, completing his many vexations," was this marriage. Though the lady herself was truly respectable, and worth more than three millions of francs, the union proved so little to the Count's honor or happiness, that Baron Cuvier in his Éloge made no mention of it. The causes of their disagreements, she says, were many and various, yet the marriage was entered into under such favorable auspices, it was surprising that it should have resulted so unhappily. Every friend

of the parties said that what begun in friendship between them grew into such a strong affection that they
were really in love with each other, or at least fancied
themselves so for some time. Though the Count was
by no means destitute, yet the lady was so much richer
and so much in love that she settled upon him a large
sum in the marriage contract. This became a subject of
controversy in their subsequent separation, but the
friends who arbitrated in the matter decided in his favor,
because he had expended considerable sums upon the
house and premises which were provided for himself
and his wife.

The daughter urges that if her father "had shown himself mercenary or avaricious on this occasion, it would
have been for the first time. For, excepting a pension,
he left Germany a poor man, much to his credit, considering the honor and kindness that had been heaped
upon him. Such was his poverty, indeed, that he
would have had nothing to leave to her, had not the
Elector, in great kindness, settled the reversion of half
the pension on herself." This, she adds, was paid with
the utmost punctuality. The money which had been
settled upon him by Madame Lavoisier, or the remainder of it, he left, by will, to different institutions.
The daughter, however, with the illustrative example
then fresh in her mind, feels bound to admit that
the Count, like Bonaparte, having reached conspicuous
eminence, had a downfall. With these prefatory remarks, the Countess proceeds to give extracts from,
or the substance of, "one hundred and four letters,"
which she received from her father between 1800 and
1810. Of the first we seem to have the whole, as
follows : —

" London, Royal Institution, March 2, 1801.

" MY DEAR CHILD, — I am still established at the Institution. I have been exceedingly busy, but desire to be thankful that all is now nearly completed, when I shall be at liberty. We have found a nice able man for his place as lecturer, Humphry Davy. Lectures are given, frequented by crowds of the first people. Lady Palmerston and her two daughters, Frances and Elizabeth, are pretty constant attendants.

" They would not receive me as Minister here, but seem disposed now to make it up to me by the respect they show the Institution, — originally and chiefly my work. Bernard says they are crazy about it. It was certainly gratifying to me to see the honorable list of Lords, Dukes, &c. as fifty-guinea subscribers. It is a very extensive establishment, and will cost a great deal of money ; but I hope it will be an equal advantage to the world, as the expense and labor of forming it have been great. To strive for good things I view as a laudable ambition, as I hope you do, my dear Sally. But I hope, above all, to hear of your being well and happy, not doubting the rest.

" I hope to be undisturbed by visitors this morning, or workmen, from my being thought to be at Harrowgate, and to be allowed quietly to fill this sheet. You can form no idea of the bustle in which I live since I have taken up my residence in this place. In short, the Royal Institution is not only the fashion, but the rage. I am very busy indeed in striving to turn the disposition of the moment to a good account for the permanent benefit of society.

" I have the unspeakable satisfaction to find that my labors have not been in vain. In this moment of scarcity and general alarm the measures I have recommended in my writings for relieving the distresses of the poor are very generally adopted, and public kitchens have been erected in all the great towns in England and Scotland. Upwards of sixty thousand persons are fed daily from the different public kitchens in London.

" The plan has lately been adopted in France, and a very large public kitchen for feeding the poor was opened in Paris three weeks since. A gentleman present tells me that the founders of the Institution did me the honor to put my name at the head of the Tickets given to the poor authorizing them to receive soup at the public kitchens. At Geneva they have done still more to show me respect. They have marked their tickets with a stamp on which my portrait and my name are engraved.

"I am not vain, my dear Sally, but it is utterly impossible not to feel deeply affected at these distinguished marks of honor conferred on me by nations at war with Great Britain, and in countries where I have never been, or know little of the inhabitants. But my greatest delight arises from the silent contemplation of having succeeded in schemes and labors for the benefit of mankind."

The Count adds an expression of his hope that his daughter shares with him that pleasure, and announces an improvement of his health from his visit to Harrowgate.

A series of twenty-two letters is passed over without extracts, as their contents relate principally to the domestic concerns of his daughter and to his American friends. The Count writes often about the progress of his house at Brompton, and the Royal Institution, and he refers to the unpleasant intelligence he had received of the French being in Munich. His excellent friend, the Countess Nogarola, "whom he generally, for shortness, calls Mary," writes him word that the people of Munich thought and spoke of him often under the calamity of having an enemy among them. The experience called to mind the occasion when, a few years before, the Count having had the address to keep both an Austrian and a French army out of the city, the people had been profoundly grateful to him, expressing their feeling in various ways and by presents, many ladies having painted pictures for him.*

---

* Some of these, being views in water-color of scenes in the English Garden at Munich, are now in the possession of Mr. Joseph B. Walker, of Concord, N. H.

He writes from the

"ROYAL INSTITUTION, 19th March, 1801.

" Bavaria has made an advantageous peace with France, but has been in danger of being given to the Emperor of Germany. Professor Pictet of Geneva, a great friend of mine, has paid me a visit off and on for some time, and I am now about going into my own house at Brompton to receive him."

The Count describes this house to his daughter in rapturous terms, and regrets that she is not there to see it. In September following, he proposes to set out for Bavaria, the Elector having kindly invited him to return, with assurances of his warm friendship, and that, though many salaries and pensions have been suspended through the war, his shall be paid.

Accordingly he sets out in that month, taking but little clothing and few effects with him, as, if the Elector will excuse him, he does not intend to stay long, the Royal Institution still requiring his oversight. Accompanied by Professor Pictet as far as Calais, who there left him to go to Geneva by way of Paris, the Count, having travelled some fifteen hundred miles, reaches Munich by way of Mannheim, where he writes as follows : —

"MUNICH, 2d October, 1801.

" MY DEAR SALLY, — I arrived here late last evening, and even this morning went to pay my respects to the Elector, who received me with all imaginable kindness. He appears to have plenty of business for me in an Academy he is about building, but as things are not yet in readiness to begin I am excused from remaining ; instead of which I return to England to put an end to the work begun there, that of the Royal Institution. I owe so much to the Elector, it is my duty to do all in my power to give him satisfaction. Besides, he says I shall be President of the Academy when done."

The letter continues in a cheerful strain, as if the Count felt very happy, and found himself at home again. He speaks of numbers of his acquaintance of the highest class, all of whom received him kindly, as if they were as glad to see him as he was to find himself once more surrounded by the friends he loved and respected, amid scenes where he had enjoyed great privileges in the vigor of his life for so many years. Again he writes: "I leave Munich to-morrow, 13th October, 1801. I have the honor to accompany Prince George of Mecklenburg Strelitz, brother to the Queen of Prussia, as likewise the Princess of Taxis, a friend of mine, who lives at Dillingen, where we go first, spending two or three days, then to Mannheim, on a visit of two or three days there."

At Mannheim resided the Baroness de Kalbe, a very particular friend of the Count, and of whom a fine portrait was left among the effects of the Countess.

There was a great *fête* made for the party at Dillingen. Five princes and six princesses sat down to the banquet, and there was a masked ball in the evening. The Count writes: "I had slept but little for some previous nights, and went to bed about twelve; of course, considered early for such entertainments. I found Laura (the Baroness of Kalbe) in perfect health, and as enchanting as ever. She sends you a thousand compliments."

The Count writes from Paris, 25th October, 1801; "I arrived here to-day at three o'clock, and propose staying ten or twelve days. Shall set about seeing the sights, but am somewhat fatigued, having travelled in five days three hundred and ninety miles."

The daughter says this was her father's first visit to

Paris. The reception which he met was "simply enchantment." It appeared to him then as if there were no other spot in the world worth looking at, no other acquaintance worth cultivating. His inventions were in common use; his name was known throughout the whole country: he was making a world of acquaintances, "particularly that of a lady the daughter was to hear more about in the end." Parties were made for him every day. "The Count was put into such good humor that he even sends compliments from some Munich gentlemen whom he finds there, that the daughter had forgotten or never knew. Ladies at Munich, forgotten till now, in these moments of joy desired to be remembered to the daughter. Luckily some of the inhabitants of the earth have remembrance of the daughter, for soon this heaven on earth was to make her father forget her."

In a letter dated at Brompton, January 15, 1802, the Count writes of having returned on the 20th of the preceding month. He had been three months on the Continent, spending seven weeks of the time in Paris. He intended to enjoy again the delights of the French capital on his way, in the course of the summer, to Munich. It was his full intention to get excused from any longer residence at Munich, though the Elector continued friendly to him. The Count mentions having just received from him a very gracious letter, in which the Elector expresses his pleasure at the cordiality extended towards Rumford in France, and advises him to cultivate an acquaintance with a certain lady there, whom he knew by reputation as, among other attractions, having great wealth. When he made this second visit to Paris, the Count accepted an invitation which he had received to lodge with the Bavarian ambassador.

Before he left England again, Rumford published more of his Philosophical Papers and new editions of his Essays, which brought him some hundreds of pounds. He also continued to work very diligently for his Institution.

Dating from Brompton, May 6, 1802, he writes: " In three days I shall set out for Dover, on my way to Paris, where I expect to stay four or five weeks, and then to proceed to Munich." He purposes to take with him two carriages and much baggage. On quitting England the Count makes mention of the melancholy of his friend, Lady Palmerston, at the loss of Lord Palmerston.

Writing from Paris, June 25, 1802, the Count says: " I did not propose to stay here long, but the Elector has written commissioning me to transact some business for him of a political nature, in which he is much interested." Sir Charles Blagden was with him in Paris, and accompanied him to Munich. From this latter place the Count dates a letter September 1, 1802, mentioning his arrival there from Paris on the previous week. He found the Elector living with his family at his palace at Nymphenberg, very quietly. Here the Count met with a hearty reception, and had a general invitation to visit at his pleasure. He found his English Garden grown more beautiful than ever, the Elector sparing no expense upon it. But his House for the Poor had not been well attended to, though there were few or no beggars to be met with in the streets. The Count says that he was received by the public with the most flattering marks of esteem and respect. The Emperor of Russia sent him an invitation to make a visit to St. Petersburg. This invitation was reinforced by the Elector, whose oldest son was to marry the Emperor's sister. But the Count could not make up his mind to the undertaking. He writes: "My health requires that I should keep more quiet. It is all I ask here. I have and ask no augmentation of appointments. Many cannot understand why I am not more anxious for places and money. People even pretend I am going to be Minister of State; but for a certainty I am not, neither do I desire to be. I want only quiet."

In her summary of a letter from her father, dated at Mannheim, November 30, 1802, Sarah says that "he alludes to his love concern; says he has got into full employment at Munich, but would rather be in Paris; and the *certain lady* would rather have him there, — meaning the widow Lavoisier. Oh! in Paris were centred all charms. He did not know the fate that awaited him in that country."

Writing again from Munich, January 22, 1803, Rumford, evidently not meaning to remain, says he is unsettled there, and therefore could not conveniently have his daughter with him, but that at a future time, not far distant, he would attempt it. He was living in considerable style, having his servants, the Aichners, with him, with his equipages. While he was at Munich, he was joined by Madame Lavoisier, and with her he made the tour to Switzerland, as already mentioned.

The Count writes to his daughter from Paris, Rue St. Lazare, November 30, 1803, and describes himself as most happy, seeing interesting sights and receiving the most flattering attentions. He appears to have entered with much zest into the pleasures and amusements of the place. The daughter, in her frank comments, does not keep the secrets which a filial heart generally protects. She says, —

"Without being entirely free from a sense of self-consequence, — more generally known by the name of vanity, — he must have thought himself superior to anything he was before. In Germany he was naturally smiled upon for his ingenuity and his good works. But here he was always addressed with a very peculiar grace, that was flattering, while he had nothing to do but to listen to sweet tones. His method of feeding the poor, that for providing for the army, in short, all his plans, seemed to be put into execution throughout the country, as if all benevolent genius had been asleep, or none had ever before existed. Who, without being different from every one else, could stand all this ! The Count was frail, like others. Parties out of number were made for him."

The letter of the Count to his daughter, relating to his intended marriage, given on a subsequent page, asking for certain certificates from Woburn and Concord, will be found to be devoted to matters of fact. The following extract is from one written about the same time, which was dictated by sentiment : —

"I shall withhold this information from you no longer. I really do think of marrying, though I am not yet absolutely determined on matrimony. I made the acquaintance of this very amiable woman in Paris, who, I believe, would have no objection to having me for a husband, and who in all respects would be a proper match for me. She is a widow, without children, never having had any ; is about my own age, enjoys good health, is very pleasant in society, has a handsome fortune at her own disposal, enjoys a most respectable reputation, keeps a good house, which is frequented by all the first Philosophers and men of eminence in the science and literature of the age, or rather of Paris. And what is more than all the rest, is goodness itself. . . . . She is very clever (according to the

English signification of the word); in short, she is another Lady Palmerston. She has been very handsome in her day, and even now, at forty-six or forty-eight, is not bad-looking; of a middling size, but rather *en bon point* than thin. She has a great deal of vivacity, and writes incomparably well."

The Count had left Paris on the 10th of August, and in the above letter, written on the 22d of January following, he speaks of having received the ninety-second letter from the lady. Sarah gives as a proof that her father was at this time in extreme good-humor the fact that he pays her a most flourishing compliment on her letter-writing, — the daughter "being then in the simple wilds of America, instead of amid the brilliancy and refinement of the Court of Munich."

The Count soon after writes of the lady: "She is fond of travelling, and wishes to make the tour of Italy with me. She appears to be most sincerely attached to me, and I esteem and love her very much."

The daughter adds: "The Elector, as if in true parental kindness to the Count, from a motive of putting him more in competition with the rich lady of Paris, settles upon him at this time four thousand florins a year, in addition to former appointments. The Elector, formerly Duke of Deux Ponts, must have been very good."

On the 7th of February, 1804, the Count writes again from Paris. He and Madame Lavoisier were then making preparations for their marriage. She deposited in his name one hundred and twenty thousand *livres* in the five-per-cent French funds, which was to go to the survivor of the three, — herself, himself, or his daughter. An income of six thousand a year out of her own property was secured to Madame Lavoisier. Her house in Paris, as well as the Count's at Brompton, was to revert to the survivor of the two. A further agreement, to which reference will by and by be made, appears to have been entered into between the parties, as to the retaining by the lady of the name of her former husband.

At this stage of the arrangements, the Count ascertained that requirements of law in France made it necessary for him to obtain certain documents from America. The following is a letter from him to his daughter : —

"Paris, 3 July, 1804.

" My Dear Sally, — This letter, which will be entirely devoted to very serious and important business, will, no doubt, obtain your serious attention.

" In order to be able to complete in a *legal manner* some domestic arrangements of great importance to me and to you, I have lately found, to my no small surprise, that certificates of my birth and of the death of my former wife are indispensably necessary. You can, no doubt, very easily procure them, — the one from the Town Clerk of Woburn, the other from the Town Clerk of Concord. And I request that you would do it without loss of time, and send them to me under cover, or rather in a letter addressed to me, and sent to the care of my Bankers in London. As an accident may possibly happen to that letter, I beg you would at the same time send another set of these certificates directly to Paris, addressed to me, Rue de Clichy, No. 356.

" I should imagine that the Certificate of my Birth might be drawn up in the following form : —

" This is to Certify that Benjamin Thompson, now Count of Rumford of the Holy Roman Empire, the Son of the late Mr. Benjamin Thompson, of Woburn, in the County of Middlesex, in the State of Massachusetts, Yeoman, and Ruth his wife, was born at Woburn, on the 26ᵗʰ day of March, in the year 1753. In witness whereof, I, the Town Clerk of the said Woburn, have hereunto put my name, &c.

" The other Certificate might, I should suppose, read thus: —

" I, N. N., Town Clerk of Concord, in the State of New Hampshire, do hereby certify that it appears by the public records of this Town, that Sarah, the late wife of Benjamin Thompson, Esq., formerly of this place, now a Count of the Holy Roman Empire, died at this place on the —— day of the month of —— in the year ——. In witness whereof, &c.

" If these forms should be objected to, you will send me such as you can procure.

" To the above two Certificates, which are indispensably necessary, you may as well add a third, which may be useful. That is to say, a Certificate from the Town Clerk of Woburn of the death of my Father, and the time when it happened.

" The new French Civil Code renders these formalities necessary.

" As by that Code the consent of Parents is necessary in order to a marriage being legal, I desire you would procure for me the consent of my Mother, expressed in the form hereunto annexed, neatly drawn up, and neatly and properly signed. You can give your personal assistance in that business.

" Two like copies of that consent must be sent with the two copies of the Certificates, and no time must be lost in procuring and sending them.

" I recommend the enclosed letter to your particular care, and I desire that you would deliver it with your own hands, and as soon as possible.

" As I have long since authorized you to settle my affairs with your brother, I request that they may be finally settled immediately, and receipts passed. You will send me his receipt, or a copy of it.

" With regard to the lands at Amariscoggin, I give up all claim to them, and you may dispose of them just as you shall think proper, either to your Uncle Walker or to your brother.

" What I insist on is a final settlement, and complete and legal discharge both from your brother and your uncle.

"Give my best compliments to Colonel Baldwin and to all my old friends. I do not yet despair of seeing America once more. Adieu, my dear Sally.

"Ever Yours most affectionately,

"R."

The Countess, of course, asks aid from Colonel Baldwin.

"Boston, September 13, 1804.

"Dear Sir, — My father has written to me to desire me to get of the town clerk of Woburn certificates of his birth and the death of his father, and has sent a form by which he would wish to have them drawn up. I should take it as a particular favor if you will procure for me two certificates of each from the town clerk, couched in the same terms, or as nearly as possible in the same terms, and properly signed. I wish two, as I am to send duplicates, for fear one set might be lost.

"It seems there is now a regulation in France which makes certificates of a like nature necessary, as likewise the consent of parents, if living, in order to render a marriage legal. A vessel is shortly expected to sail for France, and, if possible, I should be very glad to procure these certificates and forward them to my father by this conveyance.

"Yours, &c. in haste,

"S. RUMFORD.

"Please to obtain a certificate of my paternal grandfather's death, in the following form : —

"I, ——, Town Clerk of Woburn, in the State of Massachusetts, do hereby certify that —— Thompson, of this place, Father of Benjamin Thompson, Esq., formerly of this place, now Count of the Holy Roman Empire, was buried ——, as appears by the public records."

The certificates undoubtedly were duly sent as desired. The acquaintance between the Count and the lady had been long and intimate enough — including that severe trial of the disposition, whether of man or woman, the experiences of travel — to have made their union a propitious one.

In view of his marriage, and when he sent to his daughter for the necessary certificates, the Count had written to his mother: "The lady I am to espouse is four years younger than myself, and is of a most amiable and respectable character."

The parties had been in treaty for a house in Passy, but upon examination they found the title defective. They then made purchase of one in the midst of a garden of near two acres, in the Rue d'Anjou, and in the finest part of Paris. The price paid for this was six thousand guineas, but very much more was laid out under the Count's directions and orders, for alterations, additions, and improvements.

Sarah mentions that Captain and Mrs. Barnard of Boston, who had taken charge of her on her voyage to join her father, were in Paris at this time, and went often to see the Count. They brought her from him, on their return, some rich jewelry and lace as presents.

Many letters, she says, failed to reach her on account of the casualties of war. Her father's marriage meanwhile was delayed, partly, no doubt, by the necessity of obtaining the certificates from America, and partly by another visit to Bavaria, which the Count, it seems, against his will, was constrained to make at the call of the Elector, for his aid in organizing the Academy of Arts and Sciences. The Count felt that this delay might be unfavorable to his prospects, but his sense of obligation to the Elector compelled him to go. He writes as follows from Munich, June 18, 1805 : —

"I left Paris the 9th of June, and arrived here the 16th. My stay here is uncertain, for many things are yet wanting that are indispensably necessary for the success of such an establishment as the Academy of Arts and Sciences. I continue to pursue my Philosophical researches, and that will ever be the most pleasing occupation I can have. I am in the same lodgings I occupied when I was here two years ago, and Aichner and his whole family serve me. But I fancy I shall soon return to the house I was in when you were with me, and to the same apartments, which I shall like better than any others. The Countess of Nogarola sends you a thousand compliments."

His stay in Munich was short, as the troubles of the time compelled even the Elector to leave the city. On September 17 the Count is again in Paris.

The following very interesting letter bears date —

"PARIS, 25th October, 1805, Rue d'Anjou, No. 39.

"You will have intelligence by the papers of events that have lately taken place in Germany. Foreseeing the Storm, I left Munich the day before the Elector left it. I have brought Aichner and his whole family, not being willing to leave them behind. I succeeded in so winding up my affairs in Bavaria as in the future to be able to live where I please. I shall, of course, go from time to time to pay my respects to the Elector, for he has ever treated me with too much respect for me to be negligent on that account towards him.

"I have informed you before of the arrangements Madame Lavoisier and I had made in case of our marriage, and which in fact took place yesterday.

"I have the best-founded hopes of passing my days in peace and quiet in this paradise of a place, made what it is by me, — my money, skill, and directions. In short, it is all but a paradise. Removed from the noise and bustle of the street, facing full to the South, in the midst of a beautiful garden of more than two acres, well planted with trees and shrubbery. The entrance from the street is through an iron gate, by a beautiful winding avenue, well planted, and the porter's lodge is by the side of this gate; a great bell to be rung in case of ceremonious visits."

The daughter's comment on this letter is: " It seems there had been an acquaintance between these parties of four years before marriage. It might be thought a long space of time enough for perfect acquaintance. But, ah Providence! thy ways are past finding out."

An interval, though a very brief one, of cheerfulness and satisfaction was enjoyed by the Count after his marriage. There are but two letters to his daughter recognizing this state of content and pleasant anticipation. He informs her that he left Munich under the pleasantest relations with the Bavarian sovereign and his friends at that court. He had received a letter from Maximilian, congratulating him on his marriage, and approving of his settling himself in France, and at the same time adding four thousand florins a year to his pay, that he might feel on easier circumstances with his lady. The Count's letter, dated Paris, Rue d'Anjou, December 20, 1805, two months after his marriage, is as follows : —

" My Dear Sally, — I gave up my lodgings on quitting Munich, and managed so as to settle all concerns of business. I flatter myself I am settled down here for life, far removed from wars and all arduous duties, as a recompense for past services, with plenty to live upon, and at liberty to pursue my own natural propensities, such as have occupied me through life, — a life, as I try to fancy, that may come under the denomination of a benefit to mankind.

" I brought all the Aichners with me, two of their boys excepted, who are placed in the army, — one as corporal; the youngest, George, about sixteen, as a drummer. The little girl named for you and the Countess [Nogarola], Mary Sarah, —

you two being considered God-Mothers to her, — is very small of her age, considered a dwarf. But she is very clever and interesting, and excites universal attention. Madame seems to take quite a fancy to her, allowing her to dine with us at a side-board when we have no company. The whole family of Aichners, consisting of six, with Father and Mother, are so good, and those of an age to work so industrious, they cannot be considered a burden, and will ever be a comfort to me, being, as it were, my family. And next, my dear, I hope to get you. But next spring we are going to travel into Italy and the South of France, to be gone two years, so you must patiently stay where you are for the present.

" You will wish to know what sort of a place we live in. The house is rather an old-fashioned concern, but in a plot of over two acres of land, in the very centre and finest part of Paris, near the Champs Elyssees and the Tuilleries and principal boulevards. I have already made great alterations in our place, and shall do a vast deal more. When these are done, I think Madame de Rumford will find it in a very different condition from that in which it was, — that being very pitiful, with all her riches.

" Our style of living is really magnificent. Madame is exceedingly fond of company, and makes a splendid figure in it herself. But she seldom goes out, keeping open doors, — that is to say, to all the great and worthy, such as the philosophers, members of the Institute, ladies of celebrity, &c.

" On Mondays we have eight or ten of the most noted of our associates at dinner. (Then we live on bits the rest of the week.) Thursdays are devoted to evening company, of ladies and gentlemen, without regard to numbers. Tea and fruits are given, the guests continuing till twelve or after. Often superb concerts are given, with the finest vocal and instrumental performers."

In spite of the hopefulness in some of the above sentences, the Count seems already to have felt some misgivings during this moderate honeymoon. He was passionately fond of music, though his lady had no predilection for it. Perhaps, as the daughter suggests, if her father had gone on his intended tour with his wife, which the war prevented, changes of scene and companionship might have averted the result which was to follow.

Some interesting particulars relating to political affairs are given in the other of these two letters, dated Paris, January 15, 1806. The Count tells his daughter that the Elector was crowned King on the first of the month, and that the nuptials of the Princess Augusta with Prince Eugene, Viceroy of Italy, will be celebrated on this, the fifteenth day. The Emperor and Empress of France are still at Munich, but are shortly expected at Paris.

After specifying some of the new partitions of territory resulting from the treaty of peace with Austria, proclaimed at Paris on the date of his writing, the Count proceeds : —

"The newspapers will acquaint you with the other particulars of this Peace, which will occasion a great change in the political state of Germany, as, in fact, of all Europe. I hope that I shall not, and I do not think that I shall, lose by any of these changes. At all events, the Elector, or rather the new King, has just written me a very kind letter, giving me hopes, rather than suggesting fears of anything of a disagreeable nature. But dependencies like mine can never be otherwise than uncertain, as I feel it, notwithstanding my marriage. I may make a change, after all, but never certainly to the disadvantage of any one. Between you and myself, as a family secret, I am not at all sure that two certain persons were not wholly mistaken, in their marriage, as to each other's characters. Time will show. But two months barely expired, I forebode difficulties. Already I am obliged to send my good Germans home, — a great discomfort to me and wrong to them."

The following letters from Colonel Baldwin, in one of which he offers his congratulations to the Count, come in their place here.

" Barron, June 10, 1804.

" My dear Count, — Permit me to introduce to you my particular friend John Sullivan, Esq., son of the Honorable and much respected James Sullivan, of Boston, who ranks with the first characters in this country.

" Mr. Sullivan proposes to visit England and France, and perhaps he may make the tour of Europe. His object in travelling is to obtain a greater knowledge of the world, and gratify a curious and philosophic mind. His education, disposition, and manners render him highly esteemed and beloved by his numerous acquaintances. His connections are the most respectable. He married a daughter of your good friend and correspondent, the late Hon. Thomas Russell, Esq., who died some years since, universally lamented.

" I flatter myself that you will find Mr. Sullivan a gentleman worthy your attention. Any civilities you may please to confer on him will add to the many favors already received.

" It is a long time since I wrote last, and I believe it is nearly as long since I received any communication from you. Perhaps I may be one in your debt. But be assured, my dear Count, that I remember you with as much esteem and affection as ever. I have had the pleasure frequently to hear of your welfare through the channel of your letters to the Countess, who (by the way) is often lamenting your long silence of late, and tells me that she has received no answer to a dozen letters she wrote you last year.

" I made a visit to Windham, near Portland, on the 21st of May last, to see your good mother. I found her in a comfortable state of health. She had been afflicted some time before with rheumatic complaints, and was not then entirely free from them. She asked me, with an inexpressible degree of anxiety, whether I thought we should ever see you again in this country, to which I could only make but a silent reply.

" Your daughter, the Countess, who had been there for

some months on a visit, returned with me to Boston the 24th
ult., where she remains at board in Mrs. Snow's family.   Your
daughter enjoys good health and spirits, and possesses the love
and esteem of her numerous and respectable acquaintance.

"Mr. Sullivan will acquaint you how wonderfully the spirit
of enterprise prevails for useful improvements in this country,
in projecting and effectuating bridges, canals, turnpike roads,
and schemes for the enlargement of the capital.

"Pray, write me by the first opportunity, and mention the
very day you propose to embark for America, that I may not be
out of the way on your arrival.

"I am, with the highest respect and esteem, my dear Count,
            "Your affectionate friend and servant,
                        "LOAMMI BALDWIN.
"Benjamin, Count of Rumford."

                              "Worcester, May 9, 1805.

"My dear Count, — Permit me to introduce to your
notice Mr. Nathaniel Bond of Boston, son of my particular
friend, Colonel Bond of Watertown.

"This young gentleman sustains a good reputation, and possesses a mind eagerly bent on improvement, in pursuit of which
he will embark to-morrow for Europe, and contemplates making
the tour of that country.   He proposes to visit Paris some time
about October next.   I have taken the liberty to recommend
him to your attention and favorable notice, and any civilities
you may please to confer on him I shall consider as done to
myself, and will add to the great amount of favors received.

"The consummation [of the purpose] of your marriage with
Lady Lavoisier has lately been announced here.   I sincerely
invoke Heaven for your happiness, and that your days may be
long upon the land, and wish that a few of them which remain
may be spent in your native country.

"I am, with the highest consideration of friendship and
respect,

            "My dear Count, your most obedient servant,
                        "LOAMMI BALDWIN.
"Benjamin, Count of Rumford."

" Woborn, May 19, 1807.

" MY DEAR COUNT, — Permit me once more, and I feel as if it would be the last time, to address you, not in behalf of a friend only, as heretofore, but of a son, dear and beloved, one who has rendered himself eminently so by his own merit. You will naturally consider the emotions which agitate the breast of a lone parent at the departure of a son destined to traverse foreign lands. He will be deeply interested in the temper of the winds and the seas, the physical causes of disease, and all the incidents inseparable from active life. I pray God that he may be preserved from errors on his part, and have but the advice and assistance of his friends if he should happen to stand in need of them.

" I pray you, my most respectful and respected friend, to condescend to notice him. Give him one smile on his way. It will revive and cheer his heart. Give him some anecdote of former times as evidence of your old acquaintance and his home. If my son should be sick, or in trouble, pray visit and advise him."

Another letter from Sir Charles Blagden to the Countess proves him watchful over both father and daughter.

In a letter written to the Countess from London, March 8, 1806, Sir Charles, referring to her father and Madame Lavoisier, after their marriage, says : —

" They are now living together at Paris, and, as far as I can learn, very happily. I know nothing of it from your father himself, which is not surprising, as I some time since intimated to him my wish that our correspondence should cease. We are not, to the best of my knowledge, on terms of enmity, but it is not likely that any kind of confidence or friendship should subsist between us again. This circumstance alone would make me cautious of giving you advice, lest, if it were such as he did not approve, he should impute it to an improper motive. But besides, I really know too little of the people with whom you live, and of the gentlemen who address you, to judge what it would be best for you to do. After the adventure of the gentleman who married so unexpectedly had drawn upon you the public attention, I am sorry that you were placed in so conspicuous a situation at Middletown, and that you appeared to take so much delight in the attentions of another gentleman, whom you own you had no intention to marry. That conduct which is attributed only to exuberance of spirits and want of experience under twenty years of age is thought after that period to indicate levity ; and your character ought *now* to be remarked for steadiness, prudence, and good sense. No well-judging friend would advise you to marry a man whom you cannot love. But it is equally dangerous to take a man who is otherwise unsuitable, merely because he happens under particular circumstances to have flattered your imagination. I am aware how awkward your situation is, and sincerely wish it were changed, either by marriage or by a call from your father to live with him. Whether he has given or ever will give you such a call, I neither know nor can guess ; but I particularly recommend it to you never to take any decisive step without his previous approbation."

The variety of matters touched upon by Sarah, interspersed with fragments of what she saw fit to copy from her father's letters, will relieve the rehearsal from the character of a mere repetition of the same details.

We must call her before us, during the interval between her first two visits to Europe, as a person attracting considerable notice and regard. On her father's account, independently of any attractions of her own, — which were in no degree remarkable, — she would be sure to receive attention and cordial hospitality from his many friends in America. She appears not to have remained long in any one place, but to have led rather an unsettled and aimless life, which evidently called forth from her father frequent remonstrances, with good advice and hearty commendation when he learned anything about her which he could approve.

The most important information given by the Count in a letter dated from his new home is that he had been presented to Bonaparte as consul, and had received from him permission to reside in France and also to take his pension from Bavaria. Ever happy to send his daughter pleasing tidings about the place where he had spent so many useful and happy years, and had received so many gratifying honors from the former and the present potentate, the Count gives some account of the then recent political changes there. The King of Bavaria had acquired a great increase of territory and power from a treaty of peace with Austria. He had received the Tyrol, with the Bishoprics of Brixen and Trent, and all the countries bordering on the Grisons, between the Lake of Constance and the Lake of Guarda, near Verona. But he ceded Salzburg to his brother, the Emperor of Germany. The Count expresses the hope that he shall not himself experience anything unfavorable in his appointments in these changes. He had had the satisfaction of a kind letter from the King, congratulating him on his marriage.

Before the close of the year the Count begins to complain of a confined and uncomfortable situation in his domestic experiences. " He was withstood in his plans, and met with continual contradictions." Notwithstanding the little jarrings that had arisen, Madame de Rumford this year sent the daughter a box of choice millinery by some Boston ladies returning to their country.

The Count had at this time many visitors from abroad, though none from England, free communication with that country being impeded by the war. This was a great discomfort to Rumford, and was doubtless one cause of his restlessness, as he depended much on constant friendly intercourse by scientific . communications with a large number of correspondents.

Another annoyance is indicated in the following extract from a letter: " Aichner and his family have returned to Munich. I was obliged to hire a place for them some time before they went away. They did not agree with Madame de Rumford's servants, though mine were not in the least to blame, for never were there more honest people than Aichner and his wife. It would have been a great comfort to me to have kept them to the end of my life."

One of Aichner's children, as before mentioned, bore the names of the Count's daughter and of the Countess Nogarola, Mary Sarah. This little girl Madame de Rumford kept back, promising to provide for her. She made good her promise, and in due time the girl was married to a young French *marchand*, receiving from her benefactress a marriage-portion of twenty thousand francs.

Indications of the grounds of variance between the Count and his lady appear in a letter dated early in 1806. He writes that Madame is very fond of society, especially that of agreeable, well-informed persons. Her house, he says, " is frequented by several of the cleverest people in Paris. She seldom goes out of an evening, but her house is always open to her acquaintance, and we pass few evenings without company. [Sarah interpolates, " Just what the Count hated."] On Mondays we have dinners of eight or nine, — philosophers, members of the National Institute; on Tuesday evenings a tea-party of eighteen or twenty gentlemen and ladies, staying till about midnight. Conversation their amusement,—a new method of spending time."

Sarah adds that her father had no objection to these dinners of philosophers, except that he "had not a shadow of attachment for the pleasures of the table, being neither an eater nor a drinker." But as to the tea-parties, "these were enough to kill the poor Count in some few weeks, as a restraint upon his former habits."

There is unmistakable sadness in the following extract from a letter written at this time. It brought also a grievous disappointment to the daughter, who had become very earnestly desirous of rejoining her father in Paris, as he had promised that she should, and of sharing with him the place which was "a paradise,' and the companionship of the lady who was "perfection" and "goodness itself."

"In answer to your inquiries respecting myself, I can only tell you that my health continues good. But while making a paradise of our situation, affluence, and all the advantages of a good reputation well earned, the esteem and even united applause of mankind, cannot make amends for disappointments. If I have earnestly wished to hear of your being comfortably settled in America, it is because I have no hope of seeing you happy with me in my present situation. It is not always in my power to render my house agreeable to my particular friends, a disagreeable restraint upon me."

The daughter's comment on the above is as follows: —

"And this for the Count too! He had led absolutely a bachelor's life, no one leaning on him or controlling him during his whole days. Of course, to conform to others or yield on his own part after this liberty enjoyed by him was naturally trying.

And when it is considered, too, that his partner had had no less
liberty of action than himself, it would have been only wonderful had the marriage proved as harmonious as under other circumstances it might have been."

The Count writes under date of —

" Paris, 24th October, 1806.

" My Dear Child, — This being the first year's anniversary of my marriage, from what I wrote two months after it
you will be curious to know how things stand at present. I am
sorry to say that experience only serves to confirm me in the
belief that in character and natural propensities Madame de
Rumford and myself are totally unlike, and never ought to have
thought of marrying. We are, besides, both too independent,
both in our sentiments and habits of life, to live peaceably
together, — she having been mistress all her days of her actions,
and I, with no less liberty, leading for the most part the life of
a bachelor. Very likely she is as much disaffected towards me
as I am towards her. Little it matters with me, but I call her
a female Dragon, — simply by that gentle name ! We have
got to the pitch of my insisting on one thing and she on
another.

" It is possible that, had the war ceased raging, and had we
gone into Italy, where she is dying to go, and with me too, she
having heard me speak much of the delights of that country, —
she having been very happy, too, in travelling with me in
Switzerland, — it might have suspended difficulties, but never have
effected a cure. That is out of the question. Indeed, I have
not the least idea of continuing here, and, if possible, still less
the wish, and am only planning in my mind what step I shall
take next, — to be hoped more to my advantage. Communication with England is prohibited, and it makes me sad."

Again he writes, a year later : —

" Paris, Rue d'Anjou, 24th Octob. 1807.

" I can do no more, my Dear Sally, than simply give you the
anniversary of my marriage, for I am still here, and so far from

things getting better they become worse every day. We are
more violent and more open, and more public, as may really be
said, in our quarrels. If she does not mind publicity, for a certainty I shall not. As I write the uncouth word *quarrels*, I will
give you an idea of one of them.

"In the first place, be it known that this estate is a joint
concern. I have as good a right to it as Madame,—she
having paid rather more in the beginning, but I an immen-
sity of money in repairs and alterations, &c., &c., besides a
great deal of my own time and care spent while we have been
here.

"I am almost afraid to tell you the story, my good child, lest
in future you should not be good ; lest what I am about relating
should set you a bad example, make you passionate, and so on.
But I had been made very angry. A large party had been
invited I neither liked nor approved of, and invited for the sole
purpose of vexing me. Our house being in the centre of the
garden, walled around, with iron gates, I put on my hat, walked
down to the porter's lodge and gave him orders, on his peril,
not to let any one in. Besides, I took away the keys. Madame
went down, and when the company arrived she talked with
them,—she on one side, they on the other, of the high brick
wall. After that she goes and pours boiling water on some of
my beautiful flowers."

Six months more of this infelicitous experience is
summed up in the following extract :—

"Paris, Rue d'Anjou, St. Honoré, No. 39, April 12th, 1808.

"After what you know, my Dear Sally, of my domestic
troubles, you will naturally be anxious to learn the present state
of things. There are no alterations for the better. On the
contrary, much worse. I have suffered more than you can
imagine for the last four weeks ; but my rights are incontestible,
and I am determined to maintain them. I have the misfortune to be married to one of the most imperious, tyrannical,
unfeeling women that ever existed, and whose perseverance

in pursuing an object is equal to her profound cunning and wickedness in framing it.

It is impossible to continue in this way, and we shall separate. I only wish it was well over. It is probable I shall take a house at Auteuil, a very pleasant place, with the Seine on one side and the Bois de Boulogne on the other, about a league from Paris. I have seen a very handsome house there which I can have, — rather dear, but that matters little can I but find quiet. It would be truly unfortunate, after the King of Bavaria's late bounties joined to former ones, if I could not live more independently than with this unfeeling, cunning, tyrannical woman.

"Little do we know people at first sight! Do you preserve my letters? You will perceive that I have given very different accounts of this woman, for *lady* I cannot call her.

"Now, my Dear Sally, as soon as I get settled, enjoying again independence, I shall wish you to join me.

"In the mean time believe me Your Affectionate Father."

The Count bought the lease of his villa at Auteuil in April, 1808.

In a letter to which the Countess assigns the date of Paris, November 29, 1808, her father describes in some detail what will be her situation if she comes to live with him. He says he dines in his own room, with only the little German girl at the sideboard, eating her dinner. Yet he says habit has made supportable what he would have thought never could be. But few visitors came into his apartments, and only two or three were friends to him.

"But," he writes, "alas! they can be of little assistance to me. Peace dwells no longer in my habitation. I breakfast quite alone in my apartment. Most of our visitors are my wife's most determined adherents. Three evenings in the week she has small tea-parties in her apartment, at which I am sometimes present, but where I find little to amuse me. This strange manner of living has not been adopted or continued by my choice, but much against my inclinations. I have waited with great, I may say unexampled, patience· for a return of reason and a change of conduct. But I am firmly resolved not to be driven from my ground, not even by disgust.

"A separation is unavoidable, for it would be highly improper for me to continue with a person who has given me so many proofs of her implacable hatred and malice."

For two or three months during the latter part of the Count's occupancy of the same house with his wife, he was seriously ill.

He informs his daughter that the King of Bavaria, having knowledge of his domestic discomforts, had recently written him a letter that had done him much good. "He speaks most kindly to me, and encourages me to bear my misfortunes like a man of firmness who has nothing to reproach himself with."

The daughter at this stage of the rupture gives, in her comments, such light as she can throw upon the causes and manifestations of this domestic unhappiness. She says that her father and his wife disagreed about most things, if not in everything, and their alienation began after the first flush of friendship had brought them together.

"One wanted this, the other wanted that. Madame loved company, the Count loved quiet. One was lavish in money for entertainments; the other had no objection to spending money, but wished to see something come of it, in short, *improvements*. The lady said, calling him still by tender names, ' My Rumford would make me very happy could he but keep quiet.' The Count, on his side, says, ' I should not mind entertainments, but I hate to live on the scraps of them ever after.' With occasional grumblings they got on for a while. The Count, still engaged on his favorite subjects, — light and heat, — invented a lamp. The French are fond of jokes, and, as the story goes, the light issuing from one of the lamps of his invention was so vivid that the workman, in taking it home to show it, got his eyes so injured and became so blinded that he could not see his way home, and had to stay out all night in the Bois de Boulogne. Even Cuvier relates the joke.

"The *bon-mot*, at the Count's expense, likewise originated in Paris at this time, making fun of his ways for securing an economical feeding of the poor and the troops. The soldiers, when partaking of an indifferent meal, called it '*à la* Rumford!'

"People in society have a part to act, in giving and accepting from others entertainments. The Count in either case could not set himself down in a corner pursuing his investigations into things as he wished to do. He must make himself agreeable, and could do so. He was one of the smallest eaters, and one who drinks less than he did is seldom met with. Thus at banquets, while others would be sipping their fine nectar, smacking their lips at choice viands, cutting their eyes to see what was coming next, discussing eatables, or praising them by eating enormously of what was presented to them, — the Count would set down his glass brimming full, from its not having once approached his lips, or he would move away his plate after it had the tiniest piece of some simple food upon it. But upon him would devolve most of the mental honors of the feast. The writer remembers an occasion of this kind, when, as all the guests were eating, he discoursed upon the bread-fruit."

The Count had prepared his daughter in his last quoted letter to hear of his separation from his wife. In another, soon succeeding it, he told her that the separation was to be brought about by the arbitration of friends. He intimates, however, that he did not expect to remain permanently in the house which he proposed to take at Auteuil, and that he did not look to find perfect peace by himself there, for he should there be surrounded by Madame's friends and adherents, and, of course, she had hundreds where he had one.

M. Guizot, a very intimate friend, in her later years, of the lady thus repudiated, writes in his admiring tribute, soon to be quoted, that the separation took place amicably, on the 30th of June, 1809. The terms of the marriage-contract were respected as regards the joint property of the parties. The Count had at the time a hundred thousand francs in the French funds, mostly from a gift made to him by Madame Lavoisier; and a great part of what he had received from her he retained, in consideration of the large outlay he had made upon the house in the Rue d'Anjou.

If an inference may be drawn from the tone of the Count's letters immediately following his separation from his wife, the sense of relief which he experienced would indicate that his previous situation had been exceedingly irksome.

Thus he writes to his daughter : —

"I find myself relieved from an almost insupportable burden. I cannot repeat too much how happy I am, —gaining every day in health, which from vexations had become seriously deranged. I am persuaded it is all for the best. After the scenes which I have recently passed through, I realize, as never before, the sweets of quiet, liberty, and independence. My household consists of the most faithful, honest people, attached to me, without dissension, bribery, or malice. And, above all, that eternal contradiction. Oh! happy, thrice happy, am I, to be my own man again!"

He says he intends to spend the rest of his days in retirement and in philosophical pursuits. Yet he cannot repress in any of his letters resentful expressions against his late partner. He now became very anxious to have his daughter come to him, but the obstacles of war deferred and impeded her attempt to join him. He had sent for one of Aichner's daughters to wait upon her. To all his other troubles was added an increased fear that his Bavarian pension might be suspended. The Count intimates that his French acquaintances thought he would not be able to continue his style of living without the assistance of his late partner. But he intended they should be disappointed. He had hired his house for life, and had spent upon it nearly a thousand guineas, making it very elegant. His regular expenses would be much less than his annual income. His health improved every day. He was surrounded by good and faithful servants, instead of being in the midst of spies and liars. He had paid his servants well when living with Madame de Rumford, yet they were all of them bribed as soon as they came into the house. He adds: " Madame de Rumford is well. I see her sometimes, though very seldom. After what is past, a reconciliation is impossible. She now repents of her conduct, but it is too late. The less I see her, the better. I now enjoy peace and tranquillity, and my health improves every day."

The daughter very considerately writes : —

" It did not appear that his lady harbored animosity towards the Count, nor even that he did towards her. His first impressions of her were by no means incorrect, for she was in every respect a very superior person. Certain traits in their characters made it impossible that they should live together. Neither was willing to give up a favorite plan. Small disagreements, one by one, led on to a great one. Advantages, however, remained on the side of the lady, as she retained the house which the Count had taken such pains and pleasure to make what it was, very delightful as he considered it. He had looked forward to it as a permanent home, to be shared with an agreeable, rich, and accomplished lady as a companion. His disappointment was certainly great, and no doubt suggested the melancholy purpose, which for a certainty he cherished, of secluding himself wholly from the world. All his later letters to me tended to that point. He invites me to come to him if I can consent to be his companion in perfect solitude, even obscurity. Otherwise I was not to come. The Count's not having been provident in laying up a part, ever so little, of his different pays through life, left him dependent on courts and kings."

The following abstracts from others of the Count's letters will have an interest from their incidental contents. It will be seen that the Count occupies his new home. He received occasional visits from his lady, and this is consistent with an authoritative statement already noted, that the separation between them was an "amicable" one.

"AUTEUIL, 14ᵗʰ October, 1809.

"DEAR SALLY,—The Mentor arrived some weeks since, when I was expecting you. Without doubt the reason you did not come was owing to your not finding proper protection, and in these terrible times of war you cannot be too particular. This unfortunate war chains me to the spot, for I am so situated between three governments that I am obliged almost to turn into a cypher. It is England where I want to go, but dare not risk it. And it is there I should much prefer receiving you than here.

"By the date of this letter you will perceive it to be the anniversary of my wedding-day with Madame Lavoisier, to-day four years. I own I make choice of this day to write to you, in reality to testify joy; but joy that I am away from her, as has been the case for the last six months. It would be difficult to describe what I suffered there for the last year. I often wished you, but am now exceedingly glad you did not come, as it would have made you unhappy and perhaps done me no good. I was made quite ill at last, but now, thank Heaven, I am recovering my health and spirits fast. I am like one risen from the dead. Adieu, my dear child. You will hear from me soon again, and I hope to see you soon. I have some pretty rooms prepared for you. I had one of the Aichners to come and wait upon you, but she did not exactly please me, and I sent her back again. My old servants, her father and mother, are nicely established, owing to mine and the Elector's kindness, at Munich, and are very happy."

"ARTICEL, 12ᵗʰ Nov., 1809.

" MY DEAR DAUGHTER, — Here is another month past, and you do not come. I know all the difficulties of travelling either by sea or by land, so do not blame you; am only sorry. Sorry on several accounts, — on one account, that I want to see you. For do you recollect, my dear, that it is many years since we saw each other? We will not say how many, lest the time should seem longer. And little did I think, when you quitted me at Brompton, it would have been for such a length of time, nor would it have been but for this unfortunate marriage. Never were there two more distinct beings than this woman (for I cannot call her a lady) before and after marriage. But undoubtedly she was pushed on by those looking forward to her fortune, fearing some of it would light on me. She is the most avaricious woman I ever saw, and the most cunning, — things which I could not possibly know before marriage.

" I suffered more for the last fourteen months, indeed, the whole three years and a half that I lived with her, than I had an idea I could have gone through. Luckily I have money enough of my own, but war and these terrible times prevent me from receiving money from Bavaria, or my half-pay from England. Yet I am obliged to keep up a certain consequence, besides being disgusted with everything. I am afraid you will have to quit the world if you stay with me."

"Auteuil, 10th January, 1810.

"Here month after month arrives, but you do not come. I am very impatient to see you, but I am more anxious lest something should happen to you on the way, for discord reigns everywhere. Americans, while at peace with the whole world, have their vessels taken by both the French and English, by their disliking to have them favor one or the other of the nations; which it must be owned the Americans are fond of doing, by being the carriers to both nations, — of great advantage to them.

"I flattered myself on quitting that hornet's nest of a place, the Rue d'Anjou, and having relinquished all my rights and titles there, avoiding scrupulously political cabals, frequenting neither Ministers nor Courts, leading the most harmless life, besides having been of an advantage to mankind thus far, I might be allowed harmless repose. But it is not the case. In some situations a person cannot be allowed to escape difficulty.

"That is precisely my case. I must take sides with one or the other, and because I do not I experience calumny and persecution. The way I reason is, that, having done a pretty good share of good, I think I am entitled to safety and repose; while those still involved in danger and difficulties think that I, having shared honors and kindness, ought to be involved in the common troubles.

"In short, I have no other resource left me but to rush into difficulty and danger, or to quit the world. Bound as I am to a certain power [Bavaria], I can do nothing by halves. The quitting the world occupies much of my thoughts. Will you, my dear, quit it with me, if you come? I cannot retire publicly, and cannot stay."

I am uncertain as to the date of the following letter, but it must have been written soon after the preceding, and was probably left at Auteuil in case the daughter should arrive during her father's absence.

"My Dear Child, — From Mr. Armstrong, our Minister at Paris, I gained information that you have already sailed from

America, in all probability, but that unfortunately the said ship has been taken and carried into Plymouth. My first impression was to be much alarmed, but he assures me that passengers, in his opinion, have nothing to fear, if not detention, extra expence, and a little trouble.

" I am absolutely obliged to set out for Munich, so if you come in the time you must make yourself comfortable. I shall leave people enough to do anything you may wish, and my coachman, whom I do not take with me, is to go often to inquire for you in Paris at the coming in of the diligences. Besides which, should you arrive, you will take the carriage conveying you and your baggage to my, which will then be your, home. So if I find you here on my return, it will give me much pleasure.

" The King had been in Paris and invited me so kindly I thought it my duty to go, but he assures me I shall not be detained there on any business of importance. I go with a heavy heart on account of the poor Countess. She is surely not living at this moment. I have the melancholy tidings from a friend of mine at Vienna, where she has been some months past with her daughter, married to Count d'Apponi, a Hungarian."

I introduce the two following letters, addressed to his daughter by the Count from Munich, in some perplexity as to the date which she assigns to them. In her comments she implies that she arrived at Auteuil during his absence on this visit at Munich, which was not the case.

" I arrived here [Munich] after a pleasant, prosperous journey of eight days. I had foreseen this journey a long time, and delayed setting out in hopes you would come. Had that been the case, I think I should have taken you with me, for you have many friends here who all desire to be kindly remembered to you. Still it would have struck you very dull, as it did me, not to find our good friend, the Countess. Poor Sophy, now

Madame de Miltez, has been very sick, indeed is still. Theresa Nogarola, now Countess d'Apponi, will follow her husband, I think, in the end, to Paris, who has expectations of going there as Minister.

"My reception here has been most kind and flattering. The whole town is in expectation of seeing me again fixed here and employed in the public affairs of the country. But I know positively, and it is my greatest consolation, that I shall be permitted to return quietly to my retreat at Auteuil.

"Adieu, my dear Sally. I shall write to you again, I think, before leaving Munich, but you had better not write me, lest I should be already set out on my return. You must tell the coachman to take you about, and go and call on your countryman, Mr. Parker, and Madame Preble. If you want money, apply to Messrs. Delesserts; and let the Baron know of your arrival at Auteuil, as likewise the Marquis of Chansener, — they are both particular friends of mine. Give no intelligence of your arrival to a certain person. I do not wish it.

"Farewell, my dear child, &c., &c."

"MUNICH, 25th Sept., 1810

"MY DEAR SALLY, — I am still detained, and fear I shall be for a month to come, for the King has an Academy of Arts and Sciences forming, and wishes my assistance, and he has ever been so kind to me in promoting my happiness and prosperity I cannot do too much to serve him, if enough.

"I had one of the King of Bavaria's letters before leaving Paris, and another from the Prince Royal of Bavaria, who is just married to a Princess of Sax-Hilsburghausen, and who will keep his Court at Saltzbourg, where I intend to pay him a visit, and where I am sure of finding a kind reception. His Royal Highness wrote me a most gracious letter of four pages, which he finished by subscribing himself '*Votre dévoué Louis, Prince Royale.*' The subject and every expression of his letter manifested his esteem and regard for me. He is a very promising Prince, and will, I am persuaded, be a good King. All his actions discover an ardent zeal for the prosperity of the nation he is born to govern. His Father loves him very much, encourages me to give full answers to all his questions, and you may suppose I did so when I tell you that in a letter in reply to his there were thirty-three pages of close writing. It is flattering to me to have acquired the confidence of the Princes of Bavaria to the third generation.'

" By what a strange series of events have I been torn by Providence from a situation in which I most unfortunately fixed myself, as I thought, for life ! "   .

" Munich, 24th October, 1810.

" My Dear Sally, — You will perceive that this is the anniversary of my marriage. I am happy to call it to mind, that I may compare my present situation with the three and a half horrible years I was living with that tyrannical, avaricious, unfeeling woman. You can have no idea, my dear Sally, what I had to suffer during the last fourteen months, indeed during the whole three years and a half I lived in that house ; but the closing six months was a purgatory sufficiently painful to do away the sins of a thousand years.

" The Prince Royal was married on the 12th, and we have had continued *fêtes* and rejoicings. The English Garden is in high beauty ; no expence is spared upon it. I am allowed to dine with the King pretty much as often as I wish, but to-morrow I take leave of him, of Munich, and the rest of my friends ; so you will soon, my dear Sally, see me at Auteuil. My plan was to have made quite a *détour*, in search of a fine climate. I meant to go from hence to Milan through the Tyrol, and after paying my respects there to the Vice-Queen, the King of Bavaria's daughter, to go to Turin, and from thence across the mountains directly to Nice. From thence by Toulon, Marseilles, Montpelier, Avignon, and Lyons. I will take you some time, perhaps, by that route.

" But adieu, my dear Sally, I shall soon be with you.

" RUMFORD."

Miss Sarah notes that this was the only one of all her father's letters to her which he signed otherwise than by a simple " R."

The following extract is from another letter written by the Count, at Munich, to his daughter.

" Everybody here of your old acquaintance enquires after you. The three aides-de-camp I had when you were with me, Taxis, Spreti, and Verger, have all been killed in the late wars. The Bavarian troops, who have distinguished themselves by their bravery on all occasions, have suffered greatly. Munich grows larger every day. The English Garden is in the highest beauty.

" My health is perfectly good, and I am very happy. All my late sufferings are forgotten. I feel as if just relieved from an insupportable weight. God be thanked for my delivery! All your friends here have desired to be remembered to you. Adieu, my dear Sally, make yourself as comfortable and happy as you can, and be assured that I have at length quite recovered my reason, and that I am now persuaded that all that has happened to me has been most fortunate for me. I am now a free man."

The Countess says that the above letters from Munich, written while her father was expecting her arrival in Europe, were the most cheerful and healthful ones which she had received from him since his disappointment at not being accepted as the Bavarian Ambassador.

I defer to another chapter an account of the daughter's eventful experiences in her efforts to rejoin her father. The lady concerning whom so many severe and reproachful epithets have been used in the preceding pages is entitled now to a more considerate notice.

For the sake of following without interruption the order of the letters of Sir Charles Blagden and of Count Rumford, no comments or information drawn from

other sources have been introduced, for the purpose
of presenting a more complete narrative of the circumstances perhaps all too minutely reported in them. To
whatever degree the reader of the above letters and
extracts may have given his sympathy and commisera-
tion to the Count, it is impossible to suppress the confession that these relations sadly detract from the dignity with which we should always be glad to invest the
life of a philosopher and a philanthropist. The narrative, painful and humiliating as it is in some of its
details, is not, however, without precedents in the experience alike of sages and of saints. It would be hardly
worth the while for us to make these painful incidents
in the life of Count Rumford the subject of any critical
or judicial examination. The narrative is in the main
self-explanatory. He evidently was not in a healthful
state of mind or of body when he formed the intimate
acquaintance of Madame Lavoisier, and then committed
himself and all his peculiar views and ways of life to
the risks of a matrimonial connection with her. Allowing all that is said in praise of Madame Lavoisier, —
and I have yet more fully to repeat the lofty and hearty
commendations of two of her most near friends, themselves highly distinguished and esteemed, — we may find
a hint not without significance for us in the epithet which
Sir Charles Blagden used, instead of a name, in his letters to the Countess. It was a " *French* lady " to whom
this practical and not at all enthusiastic or sentimental
English philosopher "sacrificed his former independence." She was a lady of the *salon*, — the brilliant
centre, admiration, and idol of a large circle of *savans*
and men of wit, and as such she has found a competent
biographer.

That venerable French statesman and man of letters, Monsieur Guizot, was one of the warmest and most intimate friends of Madame de Rumford, and clung to her society in the last years of her protracted life as to one of his fondest ties to a long-vanished past. The beautiful and affectionate tribute which he has paid to her will doubtless afford a grateful relief to the reader.*

M. Guizot writes: "When I search among my reminiscences of the year 1831, I find there only three persons around whom society still gathered with no other object but that of enjoyment. Imperturbable in her habits of life as in her sentiments, through these revolutionary times, Madame de Rumford always assembled in her saloon Frenchmen and foreigners, *savans*, men of letters and men of the world, and always assured for them alike around her table the interest of excellent conversation, as in her more numerous reunions the delight of the choicest music."

The other two distinguished ladies whom Guizot mentions were the Countess de Boigne, daughter of the Marquis d'Osmond, and the mistress of his hospitalities, and Madame Récamier. He adds: "Of these three persons, justly esteemed and courted, Madame de Rumford was, in 1831, the only one whom I constantly visited." In a note he says, "Five years after her death, by the desire of her family, I gathered my remembrances of this lady, her life and her saloon, in a little memoir, some extracts from which were in-

* It is found in "Mémoires pour servir à l'Histoire de mon Temps. Par M. Guizot. Tome deuxième. Paris, 1859." My references are to pp. 241 and 242 in the body of the volume, and more particularly to No. VII., Pièces Historiques, — "Notice sur Madame de Rumford. Écrite en 1841," in the Appendix to the volume.

serted in the *Biographie Universelle** of Messrs. Michaud, but which had been printed only for her friends, and was known in its completeness only to them."

This charming memoir the author reproduces as one of the "historical pieces" in his Appendix. It presents the house in the Rue d'Anjou, which Count Rumford had done so much to beautify, and the lady, with whom he was so unfortunately at variance, under very different aspects than those which they have had for us in the preceding pages. Writing in 1841, Guizot says : —

"It is now five years since in a beautiful and delightful house, which no longer exists, situated in the midst of a lovely garden, now coursed by a street, was gathered twice or thrice a week a choice and varied company, — men of the world and of letters, *savans*, Frenchmen and foreigners, men of the past time and of the present, old and young, men of the government and of the opposition. Many of those who met there met nowhere else ; and others of them, if they did meet elsewhere, probably met in coldness, or scarcely tolerated each other. But there they treated each other with extreme politeness, and almost with cordiality. It was not that any one was attracted there by any private interest, or for an object which compelled him to disguise his own sentiments ; it was not a house for political or literary patronage, where one might push his fortunes or secure success. The attraction of good company, the pleasures of the intellect and of conversation, the desire to share in the daily incidents of social life, which make the amusement of the polite world and the relaxation of the toiling world, were the sole motives and the charms which collected at Madame de Rumford's such an eager circle, and in it so many men of such varied distinctions.

"Fontenelle, Montesquieu, Voltaire, Turgot, D'Alembert, if they could revisit us, would be surprised at seeing that we

* In the Supplement to that work, Vol. LXXX., 1847.

regarded such a house and its usages as something rare or strange. It was conformed to the spirit, the habitual tone, of life in their time, — a time of a noble and liberal sociability which was engaged in stirring great questions and great interests, extracting from them only their agreeable elements, the movement of thought and hope, leaving to their inheritors the struggle of practical trial and experiment."

M. Guizot then indulges in a long digression, written in a mingled spirit of regret and hopefulness, as he recalls the generation that passed from the stage at the era of the Revolution, and as he tries to bridge the abyss between that fearful epoch and our own. He calls back the glory of that olden time, — the brilliant social circles devoted to the pleasures of the intellect ; the harmonious fellowships of men of various accomplishments and activities, — the nobles, the clergy, the lawyers, men of affairs and of letters, and the highly cultivated women, who mingled on equal terms in all the *coteries* ; and then he reproduces the attractions and engagements of the saloons of those days, with the selecter groups which composed them. His brilliant, but pensive, historical and philosophical review of the revolutionary and transition epoch, is preliminary to his fond memorial of the lady whom he describes as educated under the most delightful influences of the society of which she was among the very last survivors.

.Marie Anne Pierrete Paulze was born at Montbrison, January 20, 1758, and died as Madame de Rumford, in Paris, February 10, 1836; having outlived her last husband nearly twenty-two years. She was the daughter of M. Paulze, receiver and farmer general of the revenues, and a niece of the Abbé Terrai, comptroller-general. From her earliest years she enjoyed at her father's house the society of eminent and cultivated men who were devoted to the highest studies and to reformatory enterprises. There she listened to Turgot, Malesherbes, Trudaine, Condorcet, Dupont de Nemours, and the Abbe Raynal. Her uncle, the Abbé Terrai, wished her to form a marriage at court; but her father, a man of high distinction in science and affairs of state, and possessed of great wealth, preferred one of his own colleagues in the revenue service, Monsieur Lavoisier. To him she was married on December 16, 1771, being then not quite fourteen years of age. Having appreciated and improved upon the brilliant advantages which she had enjoyed at her father's house in the society of wits and *savans*, and receiving a large fortune, she took to her new home for her husband, with youth, beauty, and all accomplishments, a passionate interest in his own studies and scientific pursuits. She became his companion, pupil, and assistant, living in his laboratory, aiding in his experiments, writing at his dictation, and translating and drawing for him. She made with her own hand the beautiful illustrations of his Treatise on Chemistry, and translated, at his request, Kirwan's work on Phlogiston and the Constitution of Acids. (Paris, 1787.)

Though her husband's principles were in favor of reform, he had at the very outbreak of the Revolution contemplated the future with dismay, and had refused the invitation of the King to become one of his ministers. The class to which he and his father-in-law belonged, as speculators in the revenues, constituted the most conspicuous and odious of the victims of the sanguinary passions which were about to have their riot.

37

Robespierre made short shrift with those who were pronounced guilty of having drawn large profits from the old government. Madame Lavoisier's husband and father, with one hundred and twenty-two others of the condemned before the revolutionary tribunal, perished under the guillotine, on the same scaffold, May 8, 1794. The charge against Lavoisier was that he had adulterated tobacco, one of the articles the revenue of which he farmed, with water and harmful ingredients. After being sentenced, he asked for a few days' respite, that he might be informed of the results of some of the experiments which he had instituted, and which were in progress during his confinement. Coffinhal, the coarse jester of the tribunal, cried out, " The republic has no need of philosophers."

These direful times and events dashed all the happy circumstances of the life and home of Madame Lavoisier. She herself narrowly escaped violence by hiding in obscurity. Her husband had devised to her all his fortune, as she was childless, and it was saved from wreck by the fidelity of a servant who managed to secure it by a letter of credit on London, through M. de Marbois. Under the Directory she resumed her place in society, and when order and tranquillity succeeded to the horrors of the proscription she drew around her, besides the surviving friends of her husband and father, another circle of the disciples and successors of the old philosophers, including Lagrange, Laplace, Berthollet, Cuvier, Prony, Humboldt, and Arago. Her attractive home at the Arsenal was a place where all distinguished persons were entertained with grace and amenity. She collected, edited, and published, with an Introduction every way appropriate, the scientific works of her eminent husband. (Paris, 1805.)

I translate again the words of Guizot.

"Among the guests of this home, the sharers in its elegant hospitality, came M. de Rumford. He was then in the service of the King of Bavaria, and enjoyed in public a splendid scientific popularity. His spirit was lofty, his conversation was full of interest, and his manners were marked by gentle kindness. He made himself agreeable to Madame Lavoisier. He accorded with her habits, her tastes, one might almost say with her reminiscences. She hoped to renew, to a degree, her state of happiness. She was married to him on the 22d [a discrepancy of date] of October, 1805, happy to offer to a distinguished man a great fortune and the most agreeable existence.

"Their characters and temperaments were incompatible. Youth alone finds it easy to forget the loss of independence in the bosom of a tender affection. Delicate questions started up between them Their keen sensibilities were tried. Madame de Rumford, on her remarriage, had formally stipulated, in the contract which she had made, that she should be called Madame Lavoisier de Rumford. M. de Rumford, who had consented to this, found it to be disagreeable to him. She persisted, as she wrote in 1808: 'I have regarded it as an obligation, as a point of religion, not to drop the name of Lavoisier. Trusting the pledge of M. de Rumford, I should have been satisfied with that, and should not have made it one of the articles of my civil contract with him, had I not wished to put on record a token of my respect for M. Lavoisier, and a proof of the generosity of M. de Rumford. It is my duty to hold to a determination which has always been one of the conditions of our union; and I have at the bottom of my heart a profound conviction that M. de Rumford will not disapprove of me for it, and that on taking time for reflection he will permit me to continue to fulfil a duty which I regard as sacred.'

"This hope, however, was deceptive. After some domestic

agitations, which M. de Rumford with more of tact might have kept from becoming so notorious, a separation became necessary, and it took place, amicably, on the 30th of June, 1809.

" From that date, and during twenty-seven years, no event, we might even say no incident, disturbed Madame de Rumford in her noble and agreeable way of living. She gave herself up equally to her friends and to society in its limited or restricted circle, which she received at her home with a strange mixture of rudeness and politeness, always showing most companionable qualities and full knowledge of the world, notwithstanding her roughness of speech and her caprices of assumption. Every Monday she gave a dinner to rarely more than ten or twelve persons, and that was the occasion on which distinguished men, Frenchmen or foreigners, *habitués* of the dwelling or casually invited guests, gathered around her and at once established an extemporized intimacy with each other between intellects so cultivated, by the delights of a conversation either serious or piquant, always comprehensive and refined, which Madame de Rumford herself enjoyed more than she participated in. On Tuesdays she received all who might visit her. For Fridays there were large assemblies, composed of very different persons, but all belonging to the best society of their class, and all pleasantly drawn by the attractions of the excellent music which the most celebrated artists and the most accomplished amateurs combined to furnish.

" Under the Empire, added to its general attractiveness, Madame de Rumford's house had a special charm. Thought and speech had there no official character. A certain freedom of mind and tongue ruled in it, without personal antagonism or political biases, emphatically a freedom of mind, a license of thought and speech, without any distrust or disquiet as to what authority might judge or say, — a precious privilege then, more precious than any one to-day imagines. After one has breathed under an air-pump he can appreciate the charms of free respiration."

M. Guizot goes on to relate how, after the Restoration, amid the raging animosities and the imbittering alienations of party spirit, Madame de Rumford's dwelling, if it could not wholly exclude this social bane, admitted but very little of it.

"As formerly the spirit of freedom, so now of equity, was not allowed to be banished from it. Not only did men of the most different parties continue to meet there, but perfect urbanity reigned among them. It seemed as if by a tacit understanding they parted with their differences, antipathies, and rancors at the door of the saloon, and agreed to abstain from those subjects of conversation which had gathered animosities about them, and, instead, yielded to the promptings of a spirit as free and of a heart as tolerant as if they had never been drawn under the yoke of parties. Thus was continued in the home of Madame de Rumford, and through her sway, the social spirit of her time and of the circle in which she had been trained. I do not know whether our posterity will ever see such a grouped society, with manners so noble and gracious, such activity in the ideas and the intercourse of life, a spirit so ardently engaged in the progress of civilization and in the exercise of intelligence, without any of those bitter passions, those inelegant and rough manners, which often accompany, and make unendurable or impossible, the most desirable relations. . . . . This is the rare and charming reality which I have witnessed as continuing and then passing away in the latest of the saloons of the eighteenth century. That of Madame de Rumford was the last of them all. It closed in perfect consistency with itself, without the entrance of any derangement, without passing through any change unlike the tenor of its course. Madame de Rumford had passed her life in the world, in seeking for herself and in offering to others the pleasures of society. Not that the world wholly absorbed her, or that she had not, on fit occasions, more substantial and serious counsels to give to her friends, and an abounding and continued benevolence scattered without ostentation among the unfortunate. But, in truth, the world, society, made for her existence. She lived wholly in her drawing-room. Indeed, she almost died there on the 10th of February, 1836, having been surrounded on the evening before by those whom she delighted to draw around her, and who will never forget the charms of her dwelling nor the constancy of her friendships."

This affectionate and appreciative tribute of M. Guizot must be the compensation for any aspersions or rude epithets which the papers that have been quoted in these pages have cast upon the fair repute of the lady who so engaged his admiration as the representative of an age, a tone of manners, and a form of social delights, which were for him the glory of his own prime and of his past. One can hardly, however, fail of reflecting that some of the qualities and habits which the memorialist himself commended in Madame de Rumford would have no such charms for her husband. Brusque and rough manners in herself, or in any class of her guests, would offer more offence to his refined sensibility than vivacity of spirit or compass of varied knowledge would impart of social pleasure.

It is observable that in no other references to the alienations between Count Rumford and his wife do we find mention of that matter of variance which Guizot makes so prominent. The Count, it seems, had agreed, and had allowed the agreement to form part of a formal legal contract, that his wife should continue to bear the name of Lavoisier as a part of her title. Whatever may be thought of the taste or the propriety of the lady's thus constituting herself a monument of her former husband, it was unpardonable in Count Rumford that he should require of her the annulling of, or even the keeping in abeyance, that condition of their union. It was one which, having exacted, the lady would be likely to insist upon with a spirit measured in its resoluteness by the manifestation, on the part of the Count, of an increasing disgust or opposition. In this case, as generally under similar experiences, the interference of others — alike interested and indifferent parties — tended to widen the breach and to foment strifes between wife and husband. There were relatives of Madame de Rumford who were concerned as to the reversion of her large fortune. Some of the *savans* whom she entertained did not secure, and some were not worthy of, the regard of the Count. The very routine of social *salooning*, such as is described by Guizot, of these miscellaneous groupings of men and women, — many of them, of course, excessively disagreeable, — was odious to Rumford. The wonder is that like a philosopher, balancing privileges against annoyances, he did not avail himself of the ample size of the house in the Rue d'Anjou, and, as he might have done without any eccentric variance with French manners, keep by himself when he was not attracted by his wife's guests, and even seek her company only a part of the time.

I have met with another literary reminiscence of Madame de Rumford, similar in its tone and tenor to M. Guizot's tribute.

The Countess de Bassanville was herself one of the circle composing the society which Guizot has so fondly described. She has also given to the world her reminiscences, in a strain similar to his. Her recollections and her intimacies cover several of those places and scenes which she groups in the title of four small volumes, in French, bearing the title of "The Saloons of the Olden Time." Among these the saloon of the

Countess of Rumford has a conspicuous position, and is described with much vivacity and piquancy.*

The Countess de Bassanville says that Madame de Rumford

"Had the happiness of gathering around her men of all ranks and of all kinds. The Count, her husband, a philanthropic gentleman, was devoted to the culture of the sciences. He had been natural philosopher, soldier, and ambassador, had traversed the world for pleasure and enterprise, and thus knew a multitude of things and a multitude of people. His conversation was largely made up of his own experiences. His lady said he ‘was a veritable sample-card.’ But she uttered this in an undertone, for the Count, who had fought for the independence of America (!), had brought home with him the most absolute despotism. This theoretical liberal was in practice a domestic tyrant. It happened that she was gracious to all, and so to one living with her this cost little ; for she was the most amiable woman in the world."

The Count had once entertained the same opinion of his lady.

The authoress says that among the *habitués* of Madame de Rumford's saloon was a certain Colonel Leroy, who had been in the American war under Lafayette, "and who was admitted solely on the ground of the happy misfortune of being a widower. When the champagne reached his head, he told great stories, though he was held a little in check by Count Rumford's particular and tenacious memory. After the Count's death the Colonel had free scope alike for what he remembered and what he invented."

* Les Salons d'Autrefois. Souvenirs Intimes. Par Madame la Comtesse de Bassanville. Préface de M. Louis Enault. Troisième Edition. Paris, 1869. Some of the other saloons described in this gossipy book are those of Madame la Princesse de Vaudemont ; Aubry ; M. de Bourrienne ; Madame Campan ; Casimir Delavigne, &c.

These few but strong strokes make real to us some of the scenes amid which Count Rumford found anything but pleasure and comfort while he was occupying a home with his wife. If Madame de Bassanville had portrayed a few more of the guests as she has Colonel Leroy, perhaps our sympathy with Count Rumford might be strengthened. The authoress of this book of reminiscences has also written at least two other works, — one on the " Education of Women," and another describing a " Voyage to Naples."

We must now follow Count Rumford to another home, to which he betook himself for relief, and with revived expectations of quiet happiness.

CHAPTER X.

COUNT RUMFORD, recovering, as he said, his independence, sought to enjoy it under such conditions and circumstances of private life as his means and taste dictated. He hired an estate at Auteuil, about four miles from Paris, which was accessible either by a pleasant walk or by a drive, and by the river. He laid out several thousand francs in arranging, improving, and beautifying the house and grounds. As he was passionately fond of flowers, his garden was enriched by the choicest that he could obtain, and was kept in perfect order. He spent much time in walking and working in it.

A very interesting history attaches to this dwelling of his, alike before and after his occupancy of it. From 1772 to 1800 it was the abode of that celebrated woman, Catherine de Lignville, the wife and widow of Helvetius, where Dr. Franklin was a favored visitor. It was there that the lady, in presence of her circle of *savans,* is reported to have said to Napoleon Bonaparte, who was among the guests, " Ah, General, if you only knew how to be happy within the bounds of two acres of earth ! " — a remark which it is supposed may have been recalled to his mind amid his meditations at St. Helena. The eminent physician, Cabanis, was the next tenant of the house.

A tragical event has recently made even more famous the house numbered " 59 Rue d'Auteuil," near the Bois de Boulogne. It was the abode of Prince Pierre Bonaparte, cousin of the Emperor Louis Napoleon. On Monday, January 10, 1870, Victor Noir (whose real name was Salmon, or Saloman, a Jew) with a companion, both of them acting as seconds for Grousset, editor of the *Marseillaise,* called upon the Prince, in behalf of their principal. An altercation ensued, of the particulars of which there are irreconcilable statements. Victor Noir was instantly killed by a shot from the pistol of the Prince, in the main apartment which had witnessed the scientific labors of Rumford.*

In 1838 two streets were opened in the quarter of Paris which takes in the former suburb; one of them received the name of Rumford, the other the name of Lavoisier, in order, as a French friend writes to me, "pour consacrer la mémoire de deux savans, qui s'étaient unis à la même épouse." The Boulevard Malesherbes now traverses the Rue Lavoisier, and has supplanted the Rue de Rumford.

Deferring any reference to the Count's mode of life at Auteuil till I can quote his daughter's account of it, when, after considerable difficulty, she joined him there, I am glad again to avail myself of the letters of Sir Charles Blagden for information of interest. The earnest desire of the Count for his daughter's companionship in his loneliness, and his anxiety and disappointment at the protracted delay of her arrival, have already been fully related.

The Countess had welcomed her father's summons, and her longing to exchange the weariness of her vacant mode of life for foreign scenes overcame any dread she might have of an ocean voyage, amid the alarms and annoyances of war. She left her home early in the summer of 1811,† and, after a visit at Philadelphia,

---

* Engravings of the house and of the room are given in the Illustrated London News of January 22, 1870.

† I have before me in manuscript a poetical piece which has never been published, written by Miss Elizabeth Townsend, of Boston, a friend of the Countess, on the occasion of her voyage. The Rev. Dr. Cheever, in his collection of American poems, publishes some of Miss Townsend's pieces, and in a note to one of them says, "It is equal in grandeur to the Thanatopsis of Bryant, and it will not suffer by comparison with the most sublime pieces of Wordsworth or of Coleridge." I copy a few

sailed from New York on July 24 in the ship Drummond, which was captured, as a suspected blockade-runner, by the brig of war Cadmus, off Bordeaux, and carried into Plymouth September 7, her jewels and other personal property being taken from her.

The Countess wrote to Sir Charles Blagden from Plymouth on September 9, informing him of the annoying circumstances under which she had arrived. He replied, from Maidenhead, on September 13. He refers to several previous letters to her, which she seems not to have received, and informs her that, being ill at the house of a friend, he shall not be able to visit her. Through the help of that friend, Admiral Sir Charles Pole, he puts her in the way of recovering her effects, by advising a simple memorial from herself, addressed to the Lords of the Treasury, stating that she was on her route to join her father in France, and asking that her goods be restored to her on her embarking in a cartel for that country. "If their lordships take no notice of it, you have no remedy, but must pay the duty on what you do not choose to lose, and leave in possession of the officers of the customs what you do not think worth the duty."

lines from the poem in my hands, for the sake of the tribute which it pays to the Countess's father.

> "Cheer him who cheers a grateful age ;
> And, winged by duty, fly to hail
> At once the father and the sage !
> Oft the false lights that learning shows
> But lead the 'wildered wretch astray ;
> The Meteor, Genius, often glows
> Only to dazzle and dismay.
> A nobler image pictures him ;—
> No baleful star in vengeance hurled,
> The central orb, whose blessed beam
> Not only lights, but warms, the world."

So thoughtful was Sir Charles for her proper protection, that, as he writes, on seeing with regret the report of her capture and arrival in the newspaper,* he at once wrote to the husband of a New York lady then in London, whose address, with advice to call on her, he gives to the Countess, naming other persons on whose care she could rely as safe friends.

This friendly anxiety of Sir Charles exhibits itself in a rather more serious way in other replies of his to the Countess, dated from Cheltenham, September 19 and 22. He writes : —

"By the false step of quitting Plymouth before you knew whether there was any one in London on whose protection you could properly rely, you have certainly brought yourself into a disagreeable situation. Perhaps the best thing for you to do would be to return thither and place yourself under the protection of the American Consul, Mr. Hawker, who is a most respectable gentleman, with a wife and family, well known to me. But if you think it best to remain in London, by all means quit your hotel [the Bedford] and go to your father's house at Brompton Row, which is now empty, and taken care of by the Mason family, as when he left it. Possibly you may find little or no furniture in it ; but enough for your use can easily be hired, and in this you would be much assisted by the mistress of my lodgings, at No. 5 High Row, Knightsbridge, to whom I will give you a note on the last page of this letter."

He also advises her in reference to some acquaintances which she had formed, which he would have her civilly discontinue, and to depend chiefly upon "the

* Sir Charles doubtless read the following letter from Plymouth, dated September 7, in the London Morning Chronicle of September 10, 1811 : "The American ship Drummond, Captain Woodbury Langdon, which has been detained and sent in here for breach of blockade by the Cadmus, brig of war, was fallen in with off Bordeaux, on her passage from New York. She has on board seventeen passengers, among whom are Sir James Joy and Countess Sarah Rumford."

Higginsons, who were your father's friends as well as yours, and, I have no doubt, are people of good character." He emphatically enforces upon her the counsel that she should not delay a moment in proceeding to join her father in France.

Sir Charles writes again, October 1, 1811, thus: —

"Your letter of the 29th arrived this day, and I write immediately, lest you should be set off, as you expect that Mr. Langdon has procured your passport. I think you had better have stayed at your father's house than have gone to board with Mrs. Eddy, or any one else. But this must partly be determined by your own feelings. You did right not to go to the play with Mrs. Langdon alone. By all means put yourself under the care and protection of Sir James Joy for your voyage to France. You have done well in taking care of your father's things at Brompton. It will be something to tell him when you arrive in France. The house was let to people who, I fear, did not treat it well. Sir Joseph Banks told me that Lady Banks would receive you kindly whenever you should come to England. Your father consulted Dr. Blane formerly as a physician, chiefly, I believe, by the recommendation of Lady Palmerston, and he was well satisfied with the Doctor. Take care how or with whom you go to the play. It is very possible that much of the happiness of your future life may depend on the prudence of your conduct here, before you go to France. Though your father be parted from his wife, yet I advise you to seek her friendship as far as you can do it without offending him. I have often talked with her about you. As far as I can recollect, there is nothing of mine at the house in Brompton Row but a large trunk of books in the strong room where the chief part of the Count's things are kept," &c., &c.

There is certainly more of the guardian than of the lover in the next letter of Sir Charles to the Countess, dated at Cheltenham, October 7, 1811, as follows: —

" MY DEAR COUNTESS, — As 1 have your real welfare
sincerely at heart, it would give me much greater satisfaction
to hear that you were safe in France under your father's protection than to *see* you in London, or elsewhere. It is not reasonable for you to expect that I should give up the necessary
attentions to my own relatives, or risk a relapse, by hurrying
hundreds of miles about the country, merely for the sake of
passing a few hours with you this year. You might expect it
from a lover, but not from a friend. And as you are now come
to settle in Europe, 1 may hope to have many other opportunities of enjoying your society. Allow me to add that I do not
well comprehend what you are doing, but I begin to doubt from
your letters whether your experience of the world has yet given
you that coolness of head and discreet judgment which your
father was so desirous of your acquiring. Among the persons
you mention the only one whose character I know well is Dr.
Blane, and I believe you will find him of more use than all the
rest put together. So take care not to disgust him. How you
can attach so much consequence to seeing a play, when you
have such great interests at stake, is to me incomprehensible.
You now see that it will be necessary for you to return to
Plymouth, whence you ought never to have gone. You must
judge from what you learn about your passport what is the
proper time for quitting London."

He adds some advice about the house at Brompton,
and he tells her, when she shall see her father, to say to
him " that it will undoubtedly be for his interest to let
it, as no good can attend the keeping it, as at present,
to perish."

It would seem as if the Countess, however impatient
she might be to reach her destination at her father's
home, was inclined to improve her opportunities while
detained on her way. The tone in which her evidently
discreet and faithful friend, Sir Charles, indulges in his
letters to her plainly implies that, while he had be-

come quite reconciled to give over any wish that he might previously have entertained to hold toward her the protective authority of a husband, he regarded her as needing some influence to overrule her own volatile inclinations. He was himself at the time very ill, and also engrossed in his sympathies by the illness of relatives very dear to him. His magnanimity and generosity of spirit are quite observable in that, while alienated from the father and a rejected suitor of the daughter, he exhibits such a sincere anxiety and interest in her behalf amid the risks of the metropolis. I have been informed by an intimate friend of the Countess, that she herself in confidence avowed that, before she returned to America from her first European visit, she would willingly have married Sir Charles, but as he was poor, and her father was unable to give her an establishment suited to her rank and his wishes, he withstood her inclinations.

I have found among the papers of the late Mr. James F. Baldwin the following interesting letters, in the first of which the Countess informs him of her voyage and of her having reached her father's house.

" Auteuil, December 7, 1811.

"MY FRIEND, — I arrived here about a week ago in perfect health, after a journey of six months and some days. It was very long, to be sure, but very fortunate. I must say I found friends everywhere, and not half so many difficulties as I was led to expect from the difficulty of the times.

"We sailed from New York the 24th July, and had a very agreeable, fine passage; but the 24th August were taken just off Bordeaux, and the 5th of September we arrived in Plymouth, where I stayed till the 14th, then went up to London. I was not at all sorry to be taken, for I had a charming visit in Lon-

don, and at my father's house at Brompton Row, and it only
retarded my progress a little.   The 21st October I left London
and returned to Plymouth, but did not leave Plymouth till the
11th November; and that was the only tedious part of my
journey, we being obliged to wait so long at Plymouth for a
wind, and the season being so far advanced it was very unpleasant weather.   However, after being once embarked, we arrived
in about twenty-four hours at Morlaix, where I remained from
the 13th to the 25th, waiting for a gentleman, who was to come
with me, to procure his passport, — my father having already
sent me mine, he having received the intelligence of my being
taken, and taken his measures accordingly.   It is nearly five
hundred miles from Morlaix to Paris, and we were nearly a
week coming, but we had a delightful journey.   Indeed, all my
journeys were prosperous and pleasant.   I think I never had so
pleasant a one in my life as from Plymouth to London, and
from Boston to the southward it was by no means unpleasant.
I made a little tour with Mr. and Mrs. Barnard to Philadelphia,
likewise; so that I have really been in a number of fine cities
since I saw you, — Philadelphia, New York, London, and now
Paris.   It is quite amusing to me to be able to compare all the
places one with another.

" I have mentioned to my father what you said about transacting business for him [in place of the Count's late friend, the
father of her correspondent], and he was very much pleased,
with what I was able to inform him of you, to intrust it in your
hands.   He has gone to Paris to-day, almost for the sole purpose of getting a power of attorney drawn up to send to you to
receive the property he has in the American funds, out of which
he wishes you to pay grandmamma every 26th of March two
hundred dollars, and the residue to place at interest, or do the
best you can with it ; but he will give you more particular directions, without doubt, with the power of attorney.   He,
however, desired me to mention to you, in case he should not be
able to get the power of attorney to send by this opportunity,
and in case there should be some little delay in transacting the
business, that he would take it as a favor if you would advance

grandmamma her two hundred dollars for this time, that she may not want for money, — for which, of course, he will pay you interest. And when you get the money concerns into your own hands, you know you can pay yourself. But this is in case he is not able to procure the power of attorney immediately. He did not foresee the least difficulty, and I hope all arrangements will be made now, for this is an excellent opportunity by Captain Hull, in the Constitution.

" As to my concerns of money with you, if I was sure you had been able to pay it to Mr. Hancock, I should draw upon him for it, I wishing it here. And I had rather draw on him than you, as he had already some money of mine from the old stock, and I wish it all together. I will thank you to write to me as soon as you have an opportunity, and let me know how I stand, and speak to Mr. Hancock, if you please, and tell him I shall be glad of the money, and shall draw upon him for it by the first good opportunity.

" You must not fail to let me hear from you from time to time. I shall always be happy to hear of your welfare and happiness, as likewise that of your family. I will thank you to remember me kindly to all. I have seen little of Paris as yet, therefore cannot say much about it. But my father's situation at this place, which is about four miles from Paris, I find very pleasant, and I see nothing to prevent me from being very happy here. My father is in excellent health. I never knew him better.

" Believe me your sincere friend,

" S. RUMFORD.

" Mr. James F. Baldwin, Merchant, Boston."

The life-long friend and the faithful correspondent and American agent of Count Rumford, Colonel Loammi Baldwin, having died, as before stated, October 20, 1807, the daughter had recommended to her father to find a substitute in that one of his sons with whom she had formed a strong friendship, and who to the close of her long life was her adviser and then her executor. I am able to give from his papers the following letters addressed to him by Rumford.

"AUTEUIL, near Paris, 1ᵗʰ Decʳ. 1811.

"DEAR SIR, — The friendship which subsisted between your late worthy father and myself would alone have been sufficient to have induced me to apply to you on the present occasion; but the excellent character that has been given of you by my Daughter, who is just arrived here, has not allowed me to hesitate one moment in the choice of a friend to assist me in fulfilling the most sacred of duties, that of taking care of an aged parent.

"I shall send you herewith a power of attorney authorising you to receive the dividends that are or may become due to me for stock in the funds of the United States. This stock, amounting to Ten Thousand Dollars, is in the 3 *per cents*; consequently the interest which you will have to receive on account of it will amount to 300 dollars a year: and of that sum I request that you would pay to my Mother, Mrs. Ruth Pierce, Widow, Two Hundred and forty dollars a year, in two payments of 120 dollars every six months, at such periods as she may prefer. The remainder of the annual income of 300 dollars, amounting to 60 dollars a year, you will be so good as to place from time to time, at interest, and in my name, in order to accumulate and form a small capital, that may be ready to be disposed of to answer any sudden demand, in case of any unforeseen accident. As all correspondence between this country and England is forbidden, I shall not venture to write to my Bankers in London, Messrs. Herries, Farquhar, & Co., of St. James' St., who have hitherto been my agents for receiving my dividends on my American stock. But I beg you would take the earliest opportunity of writing to them on my behalf, to acquaint them with my having given you a power of attorney for receiving those dividends in future, and that they will in future receive no drafts on them for my account.

"I request that you would forward the enclosed letter by a

safe conveyance. When you write to me you will be so good
as to address your letters to Count Rumford, *aux soins de
Messrs.* Delessert & Co., *Rue Cambon*, à Paris. Begging you
would remember me kindly to all those persons of your family
who remember me, I am, Dear Sir, with much esteem and
regard,

   "Your Obedient Servant,

      · "RUMFORD.

"To Mr. JAMES F. BALDWIN, Merchant in Boston."

       "AUTEUIL, near Paris, 15th Feb. 1811.

"DEAR SIR, — I took the liberty some weeks ago to write
to you and to transmit to you a Power of Attorney, authorising
you to receive the dividends on Ten Thousand dollars Three
per cent stock in the public funds of the United States. Having
since transferred by a deed of gift the whole of that stock to my
Dear Mother, for whose use I purchased it originally, your
power will of course cease to have effect, and you will give
yourself no further trouble in this business. It remains for me
to ask your pardon for the trouble I have already given you,
and to assure you of the sincere regard with which I remain

   "Your Obedient Servant,

      "RUMFORD."

This final arrangement of the Count in a provision
for his mother, which at the time was most generous
and ample, was the completion of his long-continued
care for her comfort. He had written to her soon after
his arrival in London, by date November 1, 1795,
having, while in Bavaria, sent her annually the interest
of five hundred pounds sterling, that the principal
belonged to her. So he adds, " I have now come to
a resolution to transfer the property I have destined
for you into the American funds, and to send you
a power of attorney for receiving the interest regularly
at Boston. Or, if you please, I will transfer the capi-

tal at once to you, and have it entered in your name in the books of the United States. It will then be yours, to all intents and purposes, and you may dispose of it as you think proper."

For some reason satisfactory to the parties concerned, the mother did not at that time dispense with an agent in the collection of her dividends.

The Count had written to his mother in 1804, from Paris, as follows : —

"I know how much you interest yourself for all your children, and especially for those of them who have been unfortunate in the world, and who stand most in need of your assistance. Of the five thousand dollars in the American funds, which I desired you to dispose of among your children by will, you were so kind to my daughter Sally as to bequeath to her one Thousand. As I have made ample provision for Sally myself, I desire you would make a new will, and give to my sister Ruth, who, I hear, has been unfortunate in life, the thousand dollars in addition which you had destined for Sally. My Dear Mother, I cannot refuse myself the pleasure of giving you a larger sum to dispose of among those you love. I have Five Thousand Dollars more in the American stocks, which I request you would dispose of among your children and grandchildren, by your will.

"It will give you pleasure to know that I enjoy very good health. The air of France agrees with me better than the air of Germany, or that of England, and I am very happy here. I shall go to England and Germany occasionally, but my principal residence will, in future, be in Paris. It is not, however, my intention to become a French citizen.

Again the Count writes from Paris, July 22, 1806 : —

"I should be much less anxious, on your account, my Dear Mother, if I knew that Sally was with you to assist and take care of you. If more money should be wanted to make you both comfortable than what I have hitherto furnished, I have written to Sally to say, that instead of eight hundred dollars I am ready and willing to furnish one thousand dollars a year. It is my most earnest desire to make you as comfortable as possible, and that everything should be arranged as you like best."

In a letter to his mother, dated Paris, December 1, 1808, the Count requests her to have her picture taken "by one of the best limners in Boston," and to send it to him. He writes: "You can hardly conceive how much I have your happiness and comfort at heart. Give my kind love to all my relations and friends. They will, no doubt, have nearly forgotten me; but I never can forget the place of my birth, and the companions of my early years. My life appears to me like a dream. I have been very successful; but, on the other hand, I have been uncommonly active and enterprising. It affords me the greatest satisfaction to think you are satisfied with the conduct of your son."

When the Count made the direct deed of gift to his mother referred to in his letter of February, 1812,* to Mr. J. F. Baldwin, he accompanied it with these kind words : —

"I desire that you will accept of it as a token of my dutiful affection for you, and of my gratitude for the kind care you took of me in the early part of my life. I have the greatest satisfaction in being able to show my gratitude for all your goodness to me, and to contribute to your ease and comfort. I request that you will consider this donation as being perfectly free and unconditional, and that you would enjoy and dispose of what is now your property just as you shall think best and

* In a note to page 11, I have quoted the statement of a grandson of Count Rumford's mother, that she died June 11, 1811. The grandson or the printer is in error as to the date.

most conducive to your happiness and to your satisfaction, without any regard to any former arrangements you may have made at my request.

"My health continues to be good, and I yet feel none of those infirmities of age which sometimes render the evening of life painful. I have the satisfaction to think that I have done my duty through life, and that is a great consolation to me as I approach the end of my course. I shall never cease to be, my Dear Mother, your dutiful and affectionate child,

"BENJAMIN."

When the Count wrote that letter, it was long since he had been addressed by the name of his childhood, which brought him so near to his mother. It would not have pleased us to have had that letter closed with his noble title, even had it been nobler still.

How should we have valued a letter from the mother to her son, addressed to him by either of his names!

Sarah says that she quite delighted her father on her arrival, and he thought she looked remarkably well. She adds that she of course "was happy to meet him, and to partake once more of his society and that of his numerous agreeable acquaintances, and above all to enjoy the quiet security of his paternal love and protection, of which she had been deprived for so many years. For a time, as things went on, nothing could be better." The Count gave her a sad rehearsal of the melancholy and the annoyances which he had suffered at intervals before her coming. He said: "I have not deserved to have so many enemies as I find around me. But it is all from coming into France and forming this horrible connection. I believe that woman was born to be the torment of my life. I would forgive her for what is past, if I could be left in quiet now. But I cannot, nor shall I be, this side the grave. I am obliged to avoid with the utmost care an appearance of being concerned in the public transactions of the day."

The daughter writes : —

" My father's establishment was not, of course, what it used to be at Munich, he being there at home, useful in his way, beloved and respected. Here, there being nothing of the kind, made a great difference. I found him much changed since I parted from him. He had been very ill, but was getting better. The first salutations over, his hat being called for, we took a walk in the extensive garden which he had laid out with great care, and made very beautiful. He had written to me about it, but I found it much finer than I had expected. It covered over two acres, with tufted woods and winding paths, with grapes in abundance, and fifty kinds of roses. A gardener was constantly employed, with a laborer under him. My father was exceedingly fond of flowers, and, in order to gratify him in making things as agreeable as possible to him, a young person — either housekeeper, companion, or both — put them in every place where he was likely to set his foot or turn his eye. We dined late, when candle-light was required. Luckily my eyesight was strong, as appeared to be the case with my father, or it must have been essentially injured by the glare of the lamps. The singing birds which greeted our entrance to the dinner-table made it a perfect enchantment. I used to think I would count the number of the warblers the scene boasted of, but I never came to the end of it.

" The Count would often say that his home seemed to him as it used to do. His daughter, not being at all of a melancholy cast, would hit upon little ways to amuse him, and spend much of her time in running about the garden with him. His horses were so gay and fiery as to require an assistant to the coachman in taking care of them. The coachman not being equal in skill to the one he had left at the house of his separated lady in the Rue d'Anjon, the Count sent a proposition to Madame to buy of him his span of fine horses. She consented to do so. The Count often told laughingly of the sale of these horses to

her. When he made to her the proposal of sale she replied,
'O yes, I will buy them; but, pray, don't cheat me, for I am
told that father and mother will cheat each other in horses.'

"I had not been many days at Auteuil before we had a visit
from his separated lady, for they seemed to be on good terms,
at least, on visiting terms. The lady was gracious to me, and I
was charmed with her, nor did I ever after find reason to be
otherwise, for she was truly an admirable character. Their
disagreements must have arisen from their independence of
character and means, being used always to having their own
ways. Their pursuits in some particulars were different. He
was fond of his experiments, and she of company. Their circles,
too, were naturally more attached to her (they being her old
associates) than to my father. Possibly, too, he might not be
so well viewed by some of the *convives*, fearing the three millions of francs might be in more or less danger. All this made
my father enemies, and when once there was a breach, ever so
trifling, nothing was easier than to widen it.

"It was a fine match, could they but have agreed. It was
said by everybody, both friends and foes, that though the first
flush of youth was past, it was decidedly a love-match. I can
easily believe it, for my father was very playful in his character,
even lovely at times, and much handsomer for a man than she
was for a woman, and certainly of quite as much celebrity in
the world."

It is pleasant to read this kindly estimate of the
"separated lady," from the actual observation and intercourse of the Countess. The latter drops a hint in a
fragment of her gossip, that two nieces of the lady, from
interested motives, did all they could to widen the
breach with the Count, and to keep him in a state of
irritation. She writes that once on a drive with her
father, as they passed near the lady's house, and the
conversation turned upon her, she said, "in an artless
manner that was natural to her, 'How odd it is, my

dear father, that you and Madame de Rumford cannot make it out to live together, when you seem so friendly to each other! Here it is three or four times only since I have been here that she has been out to see us, and even teazing us to go oftener to visit her. It strikes me she cannot be in her right mind.'

"'Her mind is as it ever has been,' replied the Count, 'to act differently from what she appears.'"

The Countess intimates that the lady was very penurious, while the Count was lavish; "money fading away in his hands like water when any of his plans were concerned."

Of the mode of life and of the occupations of Count Rumford in the interval between his daughter's return to him and his death, some of the most interesting information is here deferred, because it will be found in a most authentic form as given by a friend, whose commemorative tribute after his decease will be copied into these pages. The Countess says that he kept himself busily occupied with his scientific and literary pursuits, though he became more and more disposed to seclude himself from the world. He narrowed his circle of intimacies, but found much satisfaction in the companionship of the few friends who came closest to him. He was devoting his mind and pen with much zeal and interest to the composition of a work on "The Nature and Effects of *Order*," that almost deified object of his regard, already mentioned as offering to him the guiding rule and method of life. It is to be regretted that he left only fragments of that intended treatise, which, as found among his papers, did not appear to his friends to admit of publication, and which I infer were destroyed by his daughter when his effects came into her hands.

As one of the eight Foreign Associates of the Institute of France, elected in 1803, we can trace some of his labors and investigations and the results of them while he resided in Paris, in the journals of that body, and in the republication or sketches of some of his papers in the Bibliothèque Britannique. Either a translation or the original English of some of these papers was transmitted to be read before the Royal Society. On March 9, 1807, he read before the Institute a paper on The Adhesion of Molecules in Liquids. He says he had begun to experiment on oxygen in 1786. He had read a paper to his class, June 16, 1806, founded upon a memoir on it which he had composed in 1800, which he had shown the next year to Pictet on his visit to England, and which he had brought before the *savans* in Paris in 1802. In Vol. XXXV. of the Bibliothèque Britannique is a description of a new boiler for economizing heat and fuel, which Rumford had read before the Institute, October 6, 1806, and which was published in Nicholson's Journal in June, 1807.

The Count devoted much time to experimenting upon the draught of carts and carriages with broad or narrow rims to their wheels. It had been supposed that broad wheels, by presenting a greater surface for friction, required a greater draught. But in the vast amount of heavy transportation over the roads of France during the war, it was found that those roads were so cut up, and in such constant need of costly repair, that a great saving was effected by making the rims of wheels broader. Rumford experimented with a view to prove that the change also very much lessened the draught. He read a paper before the first class of the Institute, April

15, 1811,* on his Experiments and Observations on the Advantage of Wheels with Broad Rims for Carriages, etc. He speaks of his trip in the previous autumn in which he had consulted wheelwrights on the subject. He had a carriage constructed for himself on the plan which he advocated, as soon as he returned to Paris, and he braved the ridicule which was sometimes drawn upon him as he drove in it through the streets. He also contrived an instrument, to be attached to the front of his vehicle, for measuring the force required to draw it with three different sets of wheels, and he gives the results of his trial on different kinds of roads, to determine the difference of draught as depending either upon the velocity of the motion or the nature of the road.

On June 24, 1811, he read a paper of his Experiments on the Means of perfecting Lamps, and he exhibited on the occasion fourteen lamps of his own construction.† He had read an earlier paper on the subject on March 24, 1806, and made a previous publication upon it in the Philosophical Transactions for 1793.

On February 24, 1812, he brought before his class in the Institute some further inquiries concerning Heat, with a description of his calorimeter.‡ He said he had been engaged in attempts to devise and construct such an instrument for twenty years, and thought he had at last succeeded. He compares his own experiments with those of Lavoisier.

Before sessions of his class, on December 30, 1811, and continued September 28 and October 5, 1812, he

* Bibliothèque Britannique, Vol. XLVII. p. 81, etc.
† Bibliothèque Britannique, Vol. XLVIII.
‡ Bibliothèque Britannique, Vol. LI., and Nicholson's Journal, June, 1812.

brought the results of series of experiments on the combustion of wood and charcoal, and on the heat developed in the combustion of different kinds of wood.*

There was read before the Royal Society, on January 13, 1812, a paper of Rumford's, being An Inquiry concerning the Source of the Light manifested in the Combustion of Inflammable Bodies.

Three more of the productions of Count Rumford are numbered as Essays in the London edition of his works. Essay sixteenth is On the Management of Light in Illumination, etc.

Essay seventeenth is On the Source of the Light manifest in Combustion.

Essay eighteenth treats Of the Excellent Qualities of Coffee, and the Art of making it to Perfection.

Sarah says that her father resumed for the most part, while she was with him, his former habits of life. He took her with him on his occasional visits to friends, and was glad to have her help in entertaining the few intimates at his own house. She took daily drives with him on pleasant days, and visited all the interesting sights and objects of Paris and its environs. It would appear that the construction of the carriage and the peculiar garb, yet to be mentioned, in which the Count arrayed himself, to say nothing of any quality or interest that might attach to the daughter, attracted the notice of passers-by, even in that cosmopolitan city. Sarah says that, as they were driving, her father would often go in to the meetings of the Institute, and stay a short time, leaving her in the carriage.

The few intimate friends of the Count to whom refer-

* Bibliothèque Britannique, Vol. LII., and Nicholson's Journal, June, 1812.

ence has been made were themselves conspicuous and attractive characters, and held him in high regard. Baron Delessert, his banker and confidential adviser, was always near him. As we shall see, he performed some of the last offices for the Count, and was the medium for carrying into effect the provisions of his last will, and for taking care of some of the property and transmitting the pension of his daughter. The " illustrious " Lagrange was a frequent visitor at Auteuil. The Senator Leçonteux Caneleux was the Count's next neighbor. Mr. Underwood, who had been interested with him in the origin of the Royal Institution, and who remained in France as one of the *détenus* during the war, kept up his acquaintance with Rumford in Paris, and was probably the writer of the account yet to be given, which reports to us some particulars, found nowhere else, of his closing years. Rumford also, growing into a strongly patriotic feeling, was always glad to perform any kindly service for Americans visiting Paris, and he sought to be on intimate terms with such of them as could appreciate his society. Daniel Parker, Esq., a native of America, a gentleman of high culture, and possessed of great wealth, was one of these cherished friends. He lived for forty years in France. He had an extensive, costly, and luxurious estate at Draveil, about fifteen miles from Paris, where he dwelt with princely elegance, and exercised a lavish hospitality. His château, his farms, his gardens and flocks, made his grounds and his family objects of interest, while he offered a welcome to strangers as well as to guests, — Lafayette being among the honored visitors. Henry Preble, the youngest son of the American Brigadier-General Preble, with his wife, an English lady, and his family were guests of Mr. Parker, and through him acquainted with Rumford.*

The Count's Bavarian pension was £1200, which Bonaparte, as already stated, allowed him to receive, with the privilege of remaining in France, on condition of his living in retirement and taking no part in public transactions.

Davy had also obtained from Bonaparte, as a great and especial favor granted to him as a man of science, the privilege of coming into France. While in Paris, Davy went with Underwood to visit and to dine with the Count at Auteuil, on November 10, 1813. Of this visit, Davy's biographer, Dr. Paris,† writes: "Rumford showed his laboratory to Davy. This was exactly eight months before the poor, broken-hearted Count sank into the grave, the victim of domestic torment and of the persecutions of the French *savans*, instigated by his wife, the widow of the celebrated Lavoisier."

That sad sentence must prepare us for such an account — imperfect as it is — as informs us of all that we know of the last days and of the death of Rumford.

The Countess has left among her private papers several allusions to a notion or fancy of her own, which she expressed freely in later years to her intimate friends, to the effect that her father did not die when and where it was represented to her and to others that his life closed. This fancy of hers, whether suggested by any mysterious and unexplained circumstances or management, or springing wholly from her own morbid imaginings, seems almost to have brought her to be-

* There is a fine description of Mr. Parker's estate at Draveil, written by the late Mr. George R. Russell, of Boston, in the Memoirs of Harriet Preble, copied also in the Genealogical Sketch of the Preble Family, p. 287, etc.

† Life of Davy, p. 271.

lieve that her father, disgusted with the world and seeking for absolute privacy or a chance to wander away among strangers, had, with one or two sympathizing or helping confidants, enacted a farce on this occasion. She affirmed that she had reasons for thinking that a trick had been played upon his friends by bringing into his house a corpse to represent him, and that this was the subject of the burial rites supposed to have been performed for Count Rumford. The Countess further alleged that Madame de Rumford shared this opinion of hers, and that she even made, subsequently, three visits to England, where she had never been before, with a hope of tracing her late husband. A reference to this fancy, and to the presumed grounds of it, can be indulged here only as it illustrates the vagaries of human nature, for it would seem as if the occupation of mind which the Countess found in dwelling upon this strange delusion was to some extent a relief from the brooding sorrow of realizing her own loneliness.

The Countess had been for more than a year absent from Auteuil at the time of her father's death. She gives a circumstantial account, the details of which would be unedifying here, of her occasional encounters in his house with a woman who was not a servant, but who seemed to take charge of the flowers, the illuminations, and the singing birds of the dining-room. Her curiosity was roused, and her feelings were alternately excited and quieted as she asked one or another of the domestics about this additional member of the family. At times she seems to have acquiesced in the arrangement as an excusable one, considering the circumstances of her father and the usages of the country where she was. At other times she felt as if she had a right to interfere and remonstrate so as to assert her own dignity. She describes two stratagems, in which she had an accomplice in one of the servants, amounting to practical jokes played upon her father, to let him know that her eyes were opened. The Countess says she was decoyed into Switzerland to get her out of the way, her father promising to join her. Then she was sent on a visit to some friends in Havre, where she was informed by the contents of a letter both of her father's sickness and his death. The woman who occupied the porter's lodge of the mansion at Auteuil, she says, freely expressed to her, on her arrival, a belief that the Count was not really dead. She adds that no human being was invited to the funeral, though Count Leconteux lived within a stone's-throw. She also reports as coming from one of her father's most intimate friends, the Marquis Chansener (?), almost a daily visitor at Auteuil, the following narrative: —

"I went out one day to see the Count. I was not myself very well, but found him never in better health, running about, giving orders to workmen, apparently in a great hurry, as if to finish something. Being on the most intimate terms with him, I asked him if he expected an addition to his family. The Count said, 'No, I only expect to go away myself.' Two or three days after I received a note from Baron Delessert, the only confidential friend of the Count, saying that he was indisposed. I got into my carriage to go and pay another visit, when lo! I met the funeral coming into town."

Madame de Rumford also, it would seem, was absent at the time, but was at once notified, and appeared soon after the funeral. She soon invited the Countess to dine with her. "When the dessert was on the table, and the servants had been sent away, Madame remarked,

'Your father died young, and in a very sudden manner.' 'Died!' replied the daughter, 'I do not believe
him to be dead, any more than I am at this moment.'
Madame instantly dropped what was in her hand, and
retired, desiring the daughter to do the same."

The reader will doubtless observe in this narrative,
the material of which was evidently wrought in the
broodings of a morbid imagination, a token of what
we call an eccentricity of character in the writer of it.
Sarah Thompson was at that time forty years of age.
The only near relative which she had living was Paul
Rolfe, her half-brother, then at his home in Concord,
New Hampshire. Between the two there was no strong
affection, nor was he worthy of much regard. The
strange experiences and vicissitudes of her wandering
life, alternating between the simple and uneventful incidents of American country towns and the excitements
and enjoyments of three foreign capitals, had, of course,
their naturally bewildering effect upon a character which
of itself exhibited no substantial qualities of discretion,
vigor, or genius. Her splendid opportunities may be
regarded as at least fairly balancing the infelicities and
misfortunes which shadowed one half of her lifetime.
She felt that she had really been an orphan through
the whole of her life. Her father in his intercourse
with her was inconstant and unequal; at times seemingly proud of her, and at other times ashamed of her.
Some of his own tastes, habits, and ways of life were
reasonable causes of annoyance to her. It must be
claimed also as an evidence of some filial consideration
and even magnanimity in her, that, after-feeling the
irritation naturally consequent upon her coming to the
knowledge of certain disagreeable facts, she reconciled

herself to the conditions which they compelled her to accept. She had had to see at the court at Munich, and to hold playful relations with, little "Sophy," a child of the Countess Baumgarten by her father; and, seeing his affection evidently divided between his two children, she acceded even gracefully to the sisterly relation. Sophy died in childhood; but Sarah had her portrait, which always hung in her private apartment in all her subsequent places of abode, and it was on the wall of the chamber in which she died. Another irregular connection of the Count's resulted in the birth of an infant, at his house at Auteuil, in the year of his own death. This infant became a man of great excellence of character, and as an officer of the French army was killed at Sebastopol. To a son of this officer, still living in Paris, the Countess left in her will a large legacy.

It was not strange that the Countess, while proud of her father and sincerely lamenting his death, — which left her alone among strangers in a foreign land, though by no means destitute of friends, — should also indulge in some critical freedom when speaking of him after he was gone, not only to those who had known him, but to her own intimate acquaintances in America. Had she herself been of a more substantial, self-disciplined, and at the same time more thoroughly delicate and refined nature, she would doubtless have had over her father a gentle but a powerful influence for good. The Countess thought that he would have been a happier and a better man if he could have had a legal relation with the excellent and lovely Countess Nogarola, whom he greatly admired, instead of an illegal relation with her sister. The portraits of both these ladies were also among the ornaments of Sarah's private apartments, — the treasured memorials, in her later years, of scenes over which time's changes had sadly passed. These two paintings, the work of an eminent German artist, verify the description and the delineation of the greatly diverse characters which she assigns to the two ladies. The Countess Baumgarten's portrait is not attractive to eye or thought. The Countess Nogarola, with her sweet and pensive face and her garb of mourning, fondly holds the gaze of one who looks upon the canvas. I have before me nearly fifty letters written in French by her to Sarah, which have afforded me entertainment and instruction in the perusal, though I must deny myself the space which they would fill here.

Returning from this digression, it is hardly necessary to say that there was no ground whatever for the morbid fancy which the Countess connected with the loss of her father, nor was there any extraordinary circumstance attending his death. He was a lonely, and he was not a happy, man. Having spent years of most thoughtful, wise, and arduous labor for his fellow-men, and having advanced the welfare and comfort and happiness of millions of his race, — especially of the poor, the abject, and the forlorn among them, — he did not himself find serenity of heart, or satisfaction in society, or peace in his own fragment of a home. A fever came upon him which, after a rapid course of three days, ended fatally. We shall see, in a subsequent notice of his character and decease, a suggestion that his death was the result of some whimsical notion of his own about diet or medicine in his illness. But the surmise was one that might naturally be ventured without any positive reason or ground for it.

In *Le Moniteur Universel*, Paris, of August 25, 1814, appeared a notice, dated the 24th, of the Count's death and burial, of which the following is a translation : —

"Monsieur the Count of Rumford, Associate Member of the Institute of France, Fellow of the Royal Society of London, etc., etc., died in the night between Sunday and Monday, at his country-house at Auteuil, of a nervous fever [des suites d'une fièvre nerveuse]. This celebrated man has consecrated his life to the study of the sciences, and always in the service of humanity. He leaves many works which cannot fail to insure that his memory shall be cherished. He was but sixty years of age [in his sixty-second year]. He was interred this morning at Auteuil."

Among the daughter's papers I have found a sheet of manuscript in French, containing the " Address pronounced over the grave of Count Rumford by M. Benjamin Delessert, on the 24th of August, 1814." This also I translate : —

" It is permitted to me, my friends, as a member of the Administration of Hospitals, to be the medium of expressing our sorrow at the loss of the distinguished man who was pleased to honor me with his friendship. I leave it to more eloquent voices to speak of the productions of his rare genius ; to boast of his numerous discoveries in the sciences, and his ingenious methods of penetrating to the secrets of nature ; to describe his theory of heat, his experiments upon light, his observations upon combustion, upon steam, upon gunpowder ; and to commemorate him as the founder of the Royal Institution of London.

" I wish here and now only to recall to your minds those of his most directly useful and beneficent works which have made his name known in every part of Europe. Who is ignorant of what he has done for relieving the scarcity in food ; of his multiplied efforts for making food more healthful, more agreeable, and, above all, more economical; what service he has rendered to humanity in introducing the general use of the soups which go by his own name, and which have been so invaluable to so many thousands of persons exposed to the horrors of the prevailing scarcity! Who has not been made acquainted with his effective methods for suppressing mendicity; with his Houses of Industry, for work and instruction; with his means for improving the construction of chimneys, of lamps, of furnaces, of baths, of heating by steam; and, in fine, with his varied undertakings in the cause of domestic economy!

"In England, in France, in Germany, in all parts of the continent, the people are enjoying the blessings of his discoveries; and, from the humble dwelling of the poor even to the palaces of sovereigns, all will remember that his sole aim was to be always useful to his fellow-men.

"Alas! death has snatched him away in the midst of his labors. Pitiless death has removed him from those to whom he consecrated his existence. But his spirit survives on this terrestrial orb. His genius, smiling over us, lifts itself heavenward, and he goes to take one of the high places prepared for the benefactors of humanity."

The Countess has copied on the manuscript containing the above tribute a stanza which, she says, was written by a noble lady, almost an octogenarian, of high spirit and sensibility, to express her admiring homage to Rumford. I copy this in the original.

> "Bienfaiteur de l'humanité
> Grand sans effort et sans envie,
> Il n'a déployé son génie
> Que pour signaler sa bonté."

Baron Cuvier, Perpetual Secretary of the French Institute, and a very intimate friend of Count Rumford, performed the customary service by delivering an *éloge* upon the deceased before his associates, on the

9th of January, 1815.* This tribute is introduced by a similar commemoration of Mons. A. A. Parmentier, who had died less than a year before Rumford. The key-note to the *Éloge* is given in the opening sentence. Cuvier reminds his audience that the sciences had reached a point at which they excited less amazement by the great enterprises they engage and the shining truths they disclose, than by the immense advantages which their applied uses daily insure to society. Hunger and cold are the two great foes of our race, and, to meet them, all our skill and art are most resolutely directed, in palaces and in hovels. Chemistry has here its realm of power, and the dispensation of blessings. Its conquests cost not a drop of blood, and repair the waste of all other conquests.

After an interesting and eloquent sketch of the life and beneficent labors of M. Parmentier, especially in the field of agricultural chemistry, and in the introduction of the common use of the potato into France, Cuvier devotes a more elaborate and extended treatment to his friend Rumford. The errors — the same that are found in most of the biographical sketches — which Cuvier connects with the early years of his subject, have been referred to on previous pages. His career in Bavaria, with its noble services and its high honors, is admirably presented, while the eulogist vindicates the Count from the charge of being dazzled by, or too fond of, titles and distinctions. Cuvier does justice to Rumford's genius in science, and traces his devoted and eminently successful labors for ends of public utility and benevolence. Especial reference is then made to

* Recueil des Éloges Historiques lus dans les Séances Publiques de l'Institut de France. Par G. Cuvier. Tome deuxième. Paris, 1861.

the scientific occupations of the Count after he had taken up his residence in France. His various lamps became as popular as were his fireplaces and soups. His curious experiments and information on agreeable harmonies and contrasts in colors proved equally instructive for helping ladies about their ribbons and apparel, and for decorators and furnishers of household apartments.

I now translate the words of the *Éloge :* —

" He has constructed two singularly ingenious instruments of his own contrivance. One is a new calorimeter for measuring the amount of heat produced by the combustion of any body. It is a receptacle containing a given quantity of water, through which passes, by a serpentine tube, the product of the combustion ; and the heat that is generated is transmitted through the water, which, being raised by a fixed number of degrees, serves as the basis of the calculations. The manner in which the exterior heat is prevented from affecting the experiment is very simple and very ingenious : he begins the operation at a certain number of degrees below this outside heat, and terminates it at the same number of degrees above it. The external air takes back during the second half of the experiment exactly what it gave up during the first. The other instrument serves for noting the most trifling differences in the temperature of bodies, or in the rapidity of its changes. It consists of two glass bulbs filled with air, united by a tube, in the middle of which is a bell of colored spirits of wine : the slightest increase of heat in one of the bulbs drives the bell towards the other. This instrument, which he called a thermoscope, was of especial service in making known to him the varied and powerful influence of different surfaces on the transmission of heat, and also for indicating a variety of methods for retarding or hastening at will the processes of heating and freezing.

" The last two classes of researches, and those which relate to illumination, ought more especially to interest us [the members of the Institute], because they were made after Rumford had established himself in Paris, and took an active part in our occupations. He regarded them as his contributions as a member of the Institute.

"These are the principal scientific achievements of M. Rumford, but they are by no means all the services which he has rendered to the sciences. He knew that in discoveries, as in good deeds, the work of a man is transient and limited, and that in both of these directions it is necessary to propose and foster durable institutions. So he has founded two prizes, which are to be annually assigned by the Royal Society of London and by the Philosophical Society of Philadelphia [Cuvier's mistake], for the most important experiments of which light and heat shall be the objects, — a foundation in which, while exhibiting his passion as a physicist, he testified also his regard for his native and for his adopted country, and proved that, in having served the latter, he had no ill feeling against the former.

"He was the principal founder of the Royal Institution of London, one of those establishments best adapted to advance the progress of the sciences and their applications to public utility. In a country in which each individual glories in encouraging anything which benefits a large number, the mere distribution of his prospectus procured him considerable funds, and his own active efforts secured his object. The prospectus itself was a sort of description of the result, for it spoke of an enterprise already in great part realized. A large edifice exhibited all sorts of models and machines in working order ; he gathered there a library, and he constructed a fine amphitheatre where courses of lectures are given on chemistry, on mechanics, and on political economy. Light and heat, the two favorite studies of Count Rumford, and the mysteries wrought by combustion which these subject to the service of men, ought to be there constantly under examination. This establishment was the work of only five months, which Rumford had passed in England without a purpose of remaining there."

Cuvier then refers to the Count's military services in Bavaria in the campaign of 1796, to his appointment and rejection as ambassador, to the death of his friend the Elector, and to the circumstances, already related, which induced Rumford to withdraw from Bavaria. The eulogist proceeds : —

" The time at last arrived when a decisive retreat became almost a necessity to him; and it was no slight honor for France that a man who was held in such consideration in the most civilized countries of two worlds should prefer this for a final sojourn. It was because he had promptly apprehended that this is the country where full celebrity is most surely awarded to whatever is worthy of true distinction, independently of the transient favor of courts and all the freaks of fortune.

" We have seen him here, in fact, for ten years honored by Frenchmen and foreigners, held in high regard by the lovers of science, sharing their labors, aiding with his advice the humblest artisans, and nobly serving the public by a constant succession of useful inventions. Nothing would have been lacking to the perfect enjoyment of his life, if the amenity of his manners had equalled his ardor in promoting the public welfare.

" But it must be confessed that he exhibited in conversation and intercourse, and in all his demeanor, a feeling which would seem most extraordinary in a man who was always so well treated by others, and who had himself done so much good to others. It was as if while he had been rendering all these services to his fellow-men he had no real love or regard for them. It would appear as if the vile passions which he had observed in the miserable objects committed to his care, or those other passions, not less vile, which his success and fame had excited among his rivals, had imbittered him towards human nature. So he thought it was not wise or good to intrust to men in the mass the care of their own well-being. The right, which seems so natural to them, of judging whether they are wisely governed, appeared to him to be a fictitious fancy born of false notions of en- enlightenment. His views of slavery were nearly the same as those of a plantation-owner. He regarded the government of

China as coming nearest to perfection, because in giving over the people to the absolute control of their only intelligent men, and in lifting each of those who belonged to this hierarchy on the scale according to the degree of his intelligence, it made, so to speak, so many millions of arms the passive organs of the will of a few sound heads, — a notion which I state without pretending in the slightest degree to approve it, and which, as we know, would be poorly calculated to find prevalence among European nations.

" M. de Rumford had cause for learning by his own experience that it is not so easy in the West as it is in China to induce other people to consent to be only arms ; and that no one is so well prepared to turn these arms of others to his own service as is one who has reduced them in subjection to himself. An empire such as he conceived would not have been more difficult for him to manage than were his barracks and poorhouses. He relied wholly on the principle of rigid system and order. He called order the necessary auxiliary of genius, the only possible instrument for securing any substantial good, and, in fact, almost a subordinate deity, for the government of this lower world. He intended to make Order the subject of a book which he thought would be the most important of all that he had written ; but we find among his papers only imperfect parts of it. As for himself, he was in his own person, at all points and in all imaginable respects, the model of order. His wants, his pleasures, his toils, were as exactly arranged as were his experiments. He drank nothing but water ; he ate only broiled or roast meat, because boiled meats yielded a less amount of aliment. He indulged himself in no superfluity, not even in a step or a word, and it was in the strictest sense that he used the word *superfluity.*

" This was without doubt a means of helping him to devote all his energies most directly to good works ; but it was not a method likely to make him agreeable in the society of his equals. Society likes a little more *abandon.* And so it happens that a certain *hauteur* of perfection seems often a defect, when as great efforts are not made to dissemble it as to exercise it.

"As for the rest, whatever were the sentiments of M. Rumford for men, they in no way lessened his reverence for God. He never omitted any opportunity, in his works, of expressing his religious admiration of Providence, and of proposing for that admiration by others the innumerable and varied provisions which are made for the preservation of all creatures; indeed, even his political views came from his firm persuasion that princes ought to imitate Providence in this respect by taking charge of us without being amenable to us.

"This rigorous observance of order, which probably was prejudicial to the comfort of his life, certainly did not contribute to prolong it. A sudden and violent fever removed him from us in his full vigor, at the age of sixty-one. He died on the 21st of August, 1814, in his country-house at Auteuil, where he was passing the summer.

"The news of his obsequies reached us at the same time with that of his sickness, so as not to allow his associates to offer at his burial the accustomed tribute. But if such honors and such efforts to extend fame and to make it lasting are ever needless, they are so for a man who, by the happy choice of the subjects of his labors, has known how to secure to himself alike the esteem of the wise and the remembrance of the unfortunate."

It is observable that Cuvier, though he was the intimate and confidential friend of both parties, makes no allusion to the unhappy relations between Count Rumford and his wife. The reflection which he casts upon the Count's ungracious manners does but balance the similar allowance which Guizot admitted on the part of Madame Lavoisier.

The newspapers, journals, and magazines of England made the usual recognition in their obituaries of Count Rumford's decease, and paid him, on the whole, just tributes for the benevolent services and the scientific discoveries which had divided between them his thirty-eight years of life in Europe. In the Monthly

Magazine, or British Register (London), for September, 1814, appeared the following: —

"At his seat near Paris, 60, died, August 21, that illustrious philosopher, Benjamin Thompson, Count Rumford, F. R. S., Member of the Institute, &c., an American by birth, but the friend of man, and an honor to the whole human race."

The editors promised a memoir of the Count in their pages, and redeemed the promise by publishing, in the number for May, 1815 (p. 328, etc.), a translation of a large part of Cuvier's *Éloge*. In connection with Cuvier's reference to the Count's agency in establishing the Royal Institution, the editors introduce in a note a very sharp allusion to the variance alleged to have been excited by him among his associates there. The terms of the censure are somewhat severe as directed against one pronounced in the same pages to be "an honor to the whole human race." "We feel it proper to state, that the Count assumed the character of absolute controller, as well as projector, of this establishment, and conducted himself with a degree of *hauteur* which disgusted its patrons, and almost broke the heart of our amiable friend and its first professor, Dr. Garnett."

The other contemporary references and obituary notices which I have seen were, however brief, eulogistic, and not qualified by any abating terms.

The Gentleman's Magazine (London), in the number for September, 1814, announced Count Rumford's death, and promised some memoirs of him in its next number. Accordingly the promised communication appeared in October.* I suppose the original part of

* The Gentleman's Magazine and Historical Chronicle, Vol. LXXXIV., Part Second, p. 394. London, 1814.

the sketch there given to be from the pen of Mr. Underwood, previously mentioned as an intimate friend of Rumford. It contains some very interesting particulars, which, as coming from one who evidently was in close relations with the Count during his last years, have a character of authenticity. The portion of this memoir which is biographical, and relates to Rumford's life before his residence in France, is credited, " with slight alterations, to a contemporary publication." The source of it would seem to be Pictet's contribution to the Bibliothèque Britannique, as it repeats his errors, though it adds some new ones, — as, for instance, in the statement that " Rumford lost his wife before he quitted America." We are glad, therefore, to have the editor's voucher when he adds : " We subjoin some interesting memorials of his character and pursuits, communicated by an intimate friend of the Count's, resident in Paris." I extract largely from these.

" In the summer of 1803 he made a tour of a part of Switzerland and Bavaria with the widow of the celebrated Lavoisier, a woman of highly cultivated mind and capacious understanding, whom shortly after their return to Paris he married. She possesses a portrait of Count Rumford, which was painted by Girodet, the best painter in France, in 1802. But their union proved unhappy, and they at length separated, — the Count retiring to a house at Auteuil, about four miles from Paris (formerly the residence of the celebrated Helvetius, and afterwards of the physician Cabanis), where he passed the rest of his days in philosophical pursuits and experiments, almost secluded from the world. For after the death of his worthy friend, the illustrious Lagrange, he saw only his next-door neighbour, the Senator Lecomeux Caneleux ; Mr. Underwood, a member of the Royal Institution, who assisted him in the experiments ; and an old friend, Mr. Parker, a learned American, who possesses a splendid mansion in Paris, and a very fine landed estate and agricultural establishment in its environs. He ceased to attend the sittings of the National Institute; but for the Perpetual Secretary, Cuvier, a man as morally estimable as his talents are superior to his French fellow-members, he always preserved the highest admiration and esteem.

"One object of his later occupations was a work — not yet finished, though it has been constantly going on for more than twenty years — On the Nature and Effects of Order, which, had he been spared to finish it, would probably have been one of the most valuable presents ever made to domestic society. No man in all his habits had more the spirit of order; everything was classed; no object was ever allowed to remain an instant out of its place the moment he had done with it, and he was never behind his time in an appointment a single instant.

"He was also latterly employed on a series of experiments on the propagation of heat in solids. He had by him several unpublished works, particularly one of considerable interest on Meteorolites, in which he demonstrated that they came from regions beyond the atmosphere of the earth. He has left several memoirs in French (of which he had a few copies printed for the use of his friends) on the quantity of heat obtained by the combustion of various substances and the relative quantity of light from others, with a description of different improvements in the construction of lamps, which he had the satisfaction of seeing very generally adopted in Paris. His admirable paper On the Advantages of Broad Wheels to Carriages is well known. He put this in practice in his own chariot; but, though there could be no doubt of their advantages, they were not used by others, the Count's being the only carriage in Paris that had them. Nor did any one follow (which is not to be wondered at) his whimsical winter dress, which was entirely white, even his hat. This he adopted agreeably to the law of nature, that more heated rays are thrown from a dark body than from a light one. I do not know whether his very simple, and I may add perfect, calorimeter is known in England. The apparatus with which he was making a series of experiments on the relative conducting powers of different solid bodies for heat, and which death prevented his completing, is of the greatest beauty. It consists of a cylindrical vessel of cork (which is a perfect non-conductor of heat), in the centre of the bottom of which the small solid cylinder of the substance to be experimented upon is fitted into an aperture of exactly the same diameter as the cylindrical vessel, which is then filled with water, and heat from the flame of a spirit-lamp is applied to the lower extremity of the substance; the time the heat takes to pass through and raise the temperature of the water indicates the relative conducting powers of the different substances through which it is made to pass. He has repeatedly declared to me it was his decided opinion that heat and light were the result of vibrations in bodies, and were not bodies themselves. He had lately brought to the greatest perfection a lamp for burning spirits of wine, and by which all explosion was rendered impossible. This in France is of the greatest convenience, where, from the low price of alcohol, it is nearly as economical as any other fuel for heating water.

"The Count met with considerable plague in his pursuits from the malignant disposition and jealousies of his fellow-members of the National Institute, in consequence of having differed in opinion on capillary attraction from their despotic leader, Laplace. He often used to exclaim that no one who had not lived a considerable time in France could imagine how contemptible a nation they are, and how void of honor and even honesty. Whenever he ordered any instrument at a mathematical instrument-maker's, a similar one was instantly made for some one of the Great Nation, though of the intended use they were at the moment ignorant; but the hope of supplanting a foreigner and of arrogating to themselves a discovery (a common practice with them) incited them to adopt this dishonorable practice. This forced him to send for a workman from Germany, whom he constantly employed, and who lived in his house. I was one day with the Count at a sitting of the first class of the Institute, when we heard one of the leading members declare that they would set their faces against any discovery which did not originate among themselves.

" The Count displayed extraordinarily spirited conduct and firmness in refusing the French the passage of the city of Munich. He used often to dwell with much pleasure on having been the means of bringing forward two celebrated characters, the Bavarian general Wreden and Sir Humphry Davy,— the former originally a lawyer, or a land steward, and possessing great military dispositions; Count Rumford, then Minister of War to the Elector of Bavaria, gave him a commission: and the latter was recommended to him when he had the direction of the Royal Institution, by Mr. Underwood, and was made lecturer on Chemistry.

" The climate of France agreeing with him far better than that of Bavaria, he received permission of the King of Bavaria to reside there; and his half-pay as lieutenant-general in his service, and pension of retreat as minister of his late father [uncle], were regularly paid him, amounting to about twelve hundred pounds sterling *per annum*. It was this which prevented his return to England, as Bonaparte would not, in that case, have allowed his vassal, the King of Bavaria, to have paid the Count.

" When Bavaria joined in the coalition for the emancipation of Europe, it was agitated in Bonaparte's council to send the Count away. However, as it was proved that he scarcely ever stirred out of his house, he was allowed to remain.

" The German, French, Spanish, and Italian languages were as familiar to the Count as the English, both in speaking and writing. His only recreations were playing at billiards against himself for want of one to play with, and walking in his garden, of which he was very fond, though ignorant of botany, and even of the common names of the commonest plants. He was very fond of chess, at which he played well, but rarely enjoyed this pleasure, as he said that after a few minutes' play his feet became like ice and his head like fire. He drew with great skill the designs of his own inventions, but of painting and sculpture he had no knowledge and little feeling; nor had he any taste for poetry. He had, however, great taste for landscape-gardening.

"His hab'ts of life were latterly most abstemious, so much so that he had not sufficient vital strength to resist a nervous fever, which carried him off on the 21st of August, when he was on the eve of returning to England, to which, as long as he lived, he retained the most devoted attachment."

The French *savans*, with the brilliant exception of Cuvier, have not been lavish in their encomiums on Count Rumford. Those of his associates in the Institute who had read the severe reflections cast upon them in some of the sentences of the above memoir might be released from any obligation to swell his praise, especially if, as there is reason to believe, Count Rumford had treated them in a manner conformed to his opinion of them. I do not know who was the writer of the following complimentary tribute to Rumford, which appeared in a periodical in Paris, just before his death : "His conversation is animated, interesting, and solid : it is that of a man who has seen very much, and who has cast an observing eye upon everything. He devotes himself to doing good to his fellow-men, and cares but little for their gratitude. He gratifies his own fancies, and is not indifferent to fame." *

Dr. Thomas Young, already mentioned in another connection with Count Rumford, was among those who paid to him a qualified tribute after his death. In his Miscellaneous Works, edited by Dr. Peacock, we find from his pen a series of "Biographies of Men of Science," Rumford being included among them.† The

---

* "Sa conversation est animée, intéressante, substantielle : c'est elle d'un homme qui a beaucoup vu et qui a porté sur chaque chose un œil d'observateur. Il s'occupe de bien des hommes et compte peu sur leur reconnaissance. Il suit son goût et n'est pas indifférent à la gloire." — La Décade Philosophique, Littéraire, et Politique, No. XX.

† Vol. II. pp. 474–484. London, 1855.

errors common to most of the memoirs of the Count
appear in this sketch; but Dr. Young, when writing
as from his personal observation, in reference to Rumford's leaving England, says : —

"After so active and diversified a career, it was not to be
expected that he would be satisfied with the monotony of a permanent residence in London.   He was so accustomed to labor
for the attainment of some object, that when the object itself
was completely within his reach, and the labor was ended, the
prospect, which ought to have been uniformly bright, became
spontaneously clouded, or even the serenity became unenjoyable
for want of some clouds to afford a contrast.

"The enthusiasm excited by the novelty of some of his inventions had subsided, and he was even mortified by becoming,
in common with the most elevated personages of the country,
the object of the impertinent attacks of a popular satirist
[Cobbett]."

Dr. Young says that though the Count had devoted
such skill and pains to the arrangement of his house at
Brompton, he was never known to give a single entertainment in it.   He also mentions the Count's appearance in his broad-wheeled carriage, with his white hat
and clothing, and adds: "These peculiarities and a
peremptory, unyielding disposition were the causes
that set him apart from social intercourse, and in all his
connections in life seem to have rendered him less the
object of personal attachment than of esteem for his
talents and activity.   He was mild in his manners and
tone of voice, but authoritative and dictatorial in spirit."

The same writer tells us that Rumford's abstemious-
ness and temperance were the regimen prescribed by his
medical advisers, and were not of his own preference.

Thomas   Thomson,   M. D., F. R. S., etc., editor of
the "Annals of Philosophy," a monthly magazine,

wrote and published in the number of his own Journal for April, 1815, "A Biographical Account of Sir Benjamin Thompson, Knt., Count Rumford." This account contains several errors, and besides exhibits some tokens of ill-nature and personal jealousy. Speaking of Rumford's zeal and schemes for the public relief in the two years of scarcity, 1799 and 1800, Dr. Thomson says : —

"Such was his popularity at that time, that numbers of people adopted his ideas, and fitted up their kitchens according to his models; but I have not heard that his scheme was found to answer in a single instance. I remember going in 1802 to see the Count's own kitchen, which was fitted up according to his own plan. I was very much surprised to observe that not one of the utensils had ever been put to use. Hence it was likely that his notions of cooking were rather theoretical than practical. . . . . The uncommon popularity which the Count enjoyed for some years seems to have produced a bad effect upon his disposition, or perhaps rather induced him to display without reserve those dispositions which he had hitherto been at some pains to conceal. Pomposity, and a species of literary arrogance quite unsuitable to the nature of experimental philosophy, for some years characterized his writings and injured their value. But in some of the last Essays with which he favored the world we find much valuable and curious information respecting the heat evolved by different combustibles while burning, — a subject of great interest, which he prosecuted for many years, and at last elucidated with considerable success.

"I pass over his quarrel with the managers of the Royal Institution, about the nature of which I am not fully informed, though I suppose it was an attempt on the part of the Count to retain in his own hands the entire management of that Institution. Be that as it may, the result of the dispute induced him to leave London, to which he never again returned."

In the sketch which Dr. Thomson proceeds to give

of the scientific writings and experiments of Count Rumford, he connects with each of them some abatement of the consideration due him, or some depreciatory remark. He says that the Count's conclusion " that heat is not a substance, but mere motion," " is going rather farther than the experiments warrant. There is nothing absurd in supposing that friction has the property of drawing heat continually from the surrounding bodies, just as it does electricity, though it is not in our power to explain how it produces this effect."

After this specimen of Dr. Thomson's scientific appreciation, we are hardly surprised at reading the following sentences : —

" The seventh Essay, in which the Count endeavored to prove that fluids are non-conductors of heat, has been sufficiently refuted by the more decisive experiments of subsequent chemists. Indeed, the Count himself, though abundantly obstinate, appears at last to have given up his opinion.

" The publication of Mr. Leslie's book on Heat, in which this subject is treated of at much greater length and much more completely, has deprived his inquiry concerning the nature of heat and the modes of its communication [in Philosophical Transactions for 1804] of most of its interest." *

Of all those who personally knew Count Rumford, his early friend and life-long admirer, Colonel Baldwin, would doubtless have been his wisest and most considerate biographer. The Count was in manhood precisely what he had been in youth, with the development of nature and the field of opportunities to call out his real self. But this friend, who was not spared to write about his playmate and school-fellow after his eventful and eminent career had closed, had already published

* Annals of Philosophy, Vol. V. pp. 241 – 250. London, 1815.

about him some kindly and discriminating judgments, which may not inappropriately be quoted here.

Colonel Baldwin, writing of his friend after he had become distinguished in Europe, and while he was still living, said, reverting to his own acquaintance with the young Benjamin Thompson: —

"The pleasant and happy days which he passed at Concord were insufficient to lull his natural passion to engage in the active scenes of useful life. Although he enjoyed as much as any man the amusements of a country town; although he was susceptible of the comforts of retirement and a peaceful fireside; and although with his wife, who was affectionately attached to him, he might live as an honorable and independent gentleman, he laudably resolved not to sacrifice his bright talents to the monotonous occupations of domestic life. The world had higher charms for him, which led him to relinquish the idea of enjoying them. This ambition was not at all to engage in brilliant scenes of dissipation, but to rise in the estimation of mankind by his usefulness, and call forth that applause which springs from public love.

"Mr. Thompson was, perhaps, for so young a man, too much attached to greatness and splendor; and with a genius which never suffered him to stop short of the object of his pursuit, and with a mind susceptible to impressions from every quarter, he could not fix his attention, according to the cool dictates of common prudence, upon any uniform line of conduct. From this cause alone, a want of regularity in his behavior, impressions unfavorable to his character as a patriot were made upon the minds of his acquaintance at Concord. The Whig party, as it was then called, in the midst of their zeal for the American cause, were too apt to construe indifference into a determined attachment to the British interest, and therefore we need not wonder that Major Thompson had enemies, as indeed he had many. These suspicions were at first cautiously concealed, but finally burst upon his peaceful retirement, and imbittered his domestic happiness."

Colonel Baldwin, after relating the circumstances which induced his young friend to take refuge with his mother in Woburn, and giving the account, repeated in an earlier page, of his trial and acquittal, proceeds to offer such a plea for him that we ought to allow to him its benefit : —

"Supposing that from the probable effect his past conduct had produced upon those who would make appointments, he should never be able to participate in the exquisite enjoyments of patriotism struggling with oppression, and when it was uncertain on which side victory would remain, he left the Americans to seek that patronage and shelter in another country which were refused him here. This step he made for pursuits very different from those which have been imputed to him.

" From this general view of the conduct of Major Thompson and his manner of leaving America, some may have received unfavorable impressions of his character. But he had never made politics his study, and never perhaps seriously considered the origin and progress of the contest; and if he had sought for employment against his countrymen, he had sufficient opportunities of being gratified. But he wished not to build his fame upon his exploits and dexterity in warlike achievements. He wished not to sacrifice his countrymen, that he might thereby become the hero of the British arms. But, believing that the benevolent plans which he has since adopted could never be executed but under the fostering hand of well-directed power, he sought a field for the exercise of his goodness and ingenuity where they could be executed, and where there was the most obvious demand. In doing this, success has attended his steps, and he has erected in the bosom of every poor man a temple to gratitude which will endure as long as benevolence and charity shall be considered Christian virtues." *

It is to be remembered that the foregoing hearty defence of his friend by Colonel Baldwin was likely,

* Literary Miscellany, Vol. I. Cambridge, 1805.

GRAVE OF COUNT RUMFORD AT AUTEUIL

together with the series of biographical sketches and encomiums in one of which it is found, to come under the eyes of Rumford himself. Indeed, it is probable that he received a copy of them, transmitted by the writer.

The cemetery in which the remains of Count Rumford rest is very small in area, and since the commune has been annexed to Paris it has been disused for interments. It is very much crowded with memorial stones, so that they almost touch each other.

The grave of Rumford is marked by a horizontal stone — *pierre tumulaire* — and by a perpendicular monument six feet high, six feet in breadth, and three and a half feet in thickness; both are of marble, and bear inscriptions as follows.

That on the monument is —

À la Mémoire

de

Benjamin Thompson,

Comte de Rumford,

né en 1753, à Concord [?] près Boston,

en Amérique,

mort le 21 Aout, 1814, à Auteuil,

Physicien célébré,

Philantrope éclairé,

ses découvertes sur la lumière

et la chaleur

ont illustré son nom.

Ses travaux pour améliorer

le sort des pauvres

le feront toujours chérir

des amis de l'humanité.

The flat stone is thus inscribed : —

En Bavière
Lieutenant-Général,
Chef de l'État — Major-Général,
Conseiller d'État,
Ministre de la Guerre.
En France
Membre de l'Institut
Académie des Sciences.

Americans who have occasionally visited the cemetery have cleansed and kept fresh these monumental tablets.

Count Rumford executed his last will and testament while he was on a visit at the château of his friend, Daniel Parker, Esq., at Draveil, September 28, 1812.[*] The testator describes himself as "Benjamin Thompson, Count of Rumford, Knight of the illustrious orders of the White Eagle and of St. Stanislaus, Lieutenant-General in the service of his Majesty the King of Bavaria, residing now at Auteuil, Department of Paris." He appoints Benjamin, Baron Delessert and Mr. Parker his executors. Lafayette is one of the three witnesses to the will.

The Count bequeaths to his daughter an annuity of four hundred dollars, which, in addition to her pension of two thousand florins (eight hundred dollars) from the King of Bavaria, he says, "will be, I think, amply sufficient to assure her a respectable and comfortable maintenance in her native country and among her relations and first friends, where I am very desirous that she should establish her residence, being persuaded that this situation will be most suitable for her, and will contribute most to her well-being and happiness."

[*] An attested copy of the will is in the Donation Book of Harvard College, in the keeping of the Treasurer.

The testator puts other funds in trust with his executors to provide for his daughter in case, owing to political disturbances or any other cause, her pension should fail her.

To Harvard College, in Cambridge, Massachusetts, he bequeathed an annuity of one thousand dollars, with the reversion of the annuity of four hundred to his daughter, and also the reversion of his whole estate, certain specified annuities being reserved : —

" For the purpose of founding, under the direction and government of the Corporation, Overseers, and governors of that University, a new institution and professorship, in order to teach by regular courses of academical and public Lectures, accompanied with proper experiments, the utility of the physical and mathematical sciences for the improvement of the useful arts, and for the extension of the industry, prosperity, happiness, and well-being of Society.

" I give and bequeath to the Government of the United States of North America, all my Books, Plans, and Designs relating to Military affairs, to be deposited in the Library, or in the Museum of the Military Academy of the United States, as soon as an Academy of this nature shall have been established in the United States.

" I give to my friend Benjamin, Baron Delessert, my gold enamelled snuff-box, set round with diamonds ; being the same which was given me by his Majesty Francis II., Emperor of Austria.

" I give to my friend, Daniel Parker, Esq., my gold enamelled watch, with the gold chain and seals attached to it, also my gold-headed cane.

" I give to Sir Humphry Davy, Knight, Professor of Chemistry in the Royal Institution of Great Britain, my plain gold watch, as a token of my esteem."

In a sealed letter to his executors the Count commits to them, in trust, certain funds assigned for the benefit of persons having "sacred claims" upon him. As it was his declared wish that his directions in this matter should not be made public, I, of course, withhold them.

In a year after the Count's death, that is, in September, 1815, his executors communicated to the Corporation of Harvard College the generous provisions of the testator. President Quincy, in his History of the College, says : —

"The Corporation took immediate measures to obtain the property and provide for the annuities, in which they received the most effective and earnest co-operation of the executors; and that board directed the President of the University to transmit to them ' an expression of their thanks, and of the full and entire approbation of their conduct, particularly noticing the promptitude with which the estate has been adjusted, the correctness of the principles adopted by the executors, and the perspicuous and satisfactory manner in which the whole has been explained. Accept, then, gentlemen,' the Corporation add, ' this acknowledgment of our sense of your services, and of our gratification at perceiving that Count Rumford's sound and enlightened mind extended beyond his life, in the selection of friends so able and willing to forward his honorable purposes.' " *

The Rumford Professorship was established in the College by the Corporation in October, 1816, and statutes provided for it were approved by the Overseers. Jacob Bigelow, M. D., a highly distinguished physician of Boston, and a gentleman of large culture in art and science, was elected and confirmed as the first Rumford Professor, and was inaugurated on the 11th of the following December. On this occasion Dr. Bigelow delivered a most appropriate, admirable, and instructive address on the life and works of Count Rumford. In it he gave a comprehensive sketch of the steady progress and the permanent acquisitions of philosophy, and illustrated its uniform and constant influence in ameliorating the condition and promoting the happiness of mankind. The love of distinction, says the Professor, may prompt, but only philanthropy and patriotism can inspire and guide, those who give themselves to the arduous and exacting service of science and philosophy. This is a fitting introduction to a concise and animated exhibition of the career of Benjamin Thompson, from his humble origin and his frugal surroundings, through the devoted labors of his life and his benevolent efforts and schemes, to the splendid distinctions which he reached through his own industry, skill, and genius.

I must quote the concluding paragraph of the Professor's address : —

"To the country of his birth Count Rumford has bequeathed his fortune and his fame. The lessons of patriotism which we [officers and students of the College] should learn from his memorable life are important and convincing. It should teach us to respect ourselves, to value our resources, to cultivate our talents. Let those who would depreciate our native genius recollect that he was an American. Let those who would make us the dependants and tributaries of the Old World recollect that he has instructed mankind. Let those who would despond as to our future destinies remember that his eye, which had wandered over the continent and capitals of Europe, settled at last upon the rising prospects of this Western world. For one who is destined to labor in the path that he has marked out, and to follow with his eyes, though not with his steps, the brilliancy of such a career, it may suffice to acknowledge that he is not indifferent to the honor that has befallen him ; that he is sensible of the magnitude of the example before him; that he believes that the true end of philosophy is to be useful to mankind; and that he will cheerfully and anxiously enter upon the duties that await him; happy if by his efforts he can hope to add even a nameless stone to the monument of philanthropy and science that commemorates the name of *him* of whom it may in truth be said that he lived for the world, and that he died for his country."

Dr. Bigelow discharged the duties of Rumford Professor of the Physical and Mathematical Sciences as applied to the Useful Arts until 1827, when he resigned the office. Having repeated for ten successive years his course of lectures, which he made exceedingly interesting to the students by illustrative models, apparatus, and other helps, he published them in a substantial volume, entitled the " Elements of Technology " (Boston, 1829), — thus introducing, if I am not mistaken, the use of a word among us which now serves to express an entire system of education, by new methods, to new uses.*

---

* Almost fifty years after the delivery of his Inaugural at Cambridge, Dr. Bigelow had the extraordinarily happy privilege of pronouncing the opening address at the inauguration of the Massachusetts Institute of Technology, in Boston, November 16, 1865. This address, as a plea for " the new education," excited profound interest and raised an animated discussion between scholars and philosophers in this community. Coming, as it did, from a devoted pupil and lover of the ancient classics, and from a scholar who, in the lure of the past, has few peers, it was unfairly represented in some quarters as a depreciation of thorough learning in the old humanities. But the author nobly and in admirable temper vindicated his position.

Still happily welcomed in street, in social meeting, and in the literary assemblies, the venerable author, the honored Nestor of his profession, having for seventeen years before he resigned the office presided over the American Academy of Arts and Sciences, Dr. Bigelow has gathered many of his previously published productions into a volume entitled "Modern Inquiries: Classical, Professional, and Miscellaneous." (Boston, 1867.) The volume contains the two addresses to which reference has been made. Not feeling the burden of his more than fourscore years, Dr. Bigelow was one of the most active and zealous of the party who, on the first year of the opening of the great roadway to the Pacific, took their route across the continent to California.

The Rumford Professorship at the College remained without an incumbent after Dr. Bigelow's resignation until 1834, when Mr. Daniel Treadwell was elected to it, discharging its duties until he resigned it in 1845.

Professor Treadwell also as an incumbent of this office, and in his genius and scientific attainments, and likewise in the many improvements and inventions which have distinguished his name, was singularly well qualified to represent the objects and purposes recognized by Count Rumford in his foundation. As a lecturer, clear, concise, and effective, the Professor greatly interested the undergraduates of the College, and he was an excellent experimenter. He ranks among remarkable men for the additions which he has made to the industrial arts. Without a liberal education, starting in early life as a silversmith, he added many ingenious tools to the implements of his trade. He invented a machine for cutting wood-screws, — before made by hand, — by which a hank of wire was converted into screws at the rate of a dozen a minute. He first proposed the supplying of Boston with pure water, pointing out the sources; and he showed the importance and economy of reservoirs within the city. The practicability of conducting transportation on a single set of tracks, with proper sidings, he first suggested in a publication in the Journal of the Franklin Institute, in August, 1827. He constructed a power printing-press, from which came the first sheet ever printed by other than hand-power on this continent. He contrived the first machinery for spinning cordage, which is now, in its original form or with slight modifications, used in France, England, Russia, and America. This machinery enabled America for the first time to export cordage. Professor Treadwell first made cannon of steel and wrought iron, of large calibre, in a manner since repeated by Armstrong, and now in common use. For this he received the Rumford Medals from the American Academy. He has made valuable experiments on the force of fired gunpowder, which, together with some valuable papers on Force, have been printed in the Proceedings of the Academy. He collected in Europe nearly all the valuable apparatus now belonging to the Rumford cabinets at the College.

The Rumford Professorship was filled by Eben Norton Horsford from 1847 to 1863, when, on his resigning it, the present incumbent, Professor Wolcott Gibbs, was appointed in the year last named.

"The Rumford Fund" for this Professorship was credited on the books of the College Treasurer, in 1870, at $52,848.00. It will ever be a pleasing and grateful memorial of Count Rumford that his name stands thus so honorably associated, through the beneficent agencies of practical philosophy, with our venerable University; and that his Professorship has been served by a succession of distinguished men marked by his own best characteristics of mind and genius. We recall the time of his own boyhood, when with young Baldwin as his guide and patron, after long walks, he reached the halls of the College, and there nourished the ardor which gave the impulse to his mature life. We recall also another scene in which he appears, a few years after, on the same spot. When in early manhood, amid the passions and alarms of war, he was brooding over the calumny and injustice of which he felt himself to be the subject, he hastened to Cambridge, then a camp, that he might help in removing from the College shelves and cabinets the books and the humble apparatus of those days. He must have remembered these scenes when he so magnanimously made the College his residuary legatee, that through it he might forever be of service to science.

The American Academy has five sheets of manuscript drawings believed to have been made by Count Rumford. They were pasted upon a bandbox belonging to his daughter, and were for many years in Boston at the house of Mr. James F. Baldwin. This box was presented to the Academy by Mrs. Baldwin. The drawings have been carefully removed and preserved. They were probably brought home by the Countess among her father's effects, and put to a womanly use. They are as follows : —

1. A military drawing representing field-works and a village, with streams of water and various eminences.

2. Two drawings, — an elevation and section of a mortar and its bed with an elevating screw.

3. Four drawings of muskets and bayonets.

4. Architectural drawings, marked in pencil " Plan and section of the kitchen in the House of Industry." It represents also two large boilers with their brickwork settings and smoke-flues.

5. " Third floor House of Industry."

With these, from the same box, there is a blank form in manuscript of a " Table of Returns and Delivery of Unprepared Yarn," dated July, 1795.

The drawings of the mortar and muskets are done with great skill, and are carefully shaded.

His daughter's experiences and movements for several years after the death of her father are to be traced chiefly in another set of letters, which she preserved,

from Sir Charles Blagden. It was fortunate for her
that she had so discreet and constant a friend. His
fidelity to her and his authority over her, by the proffer
of advice in the form of positive dictation, prove that
he really intended to act, in place of her father, as her
guardian. He is very frank in telling her of her faults,
and on occasions which called for it he administered
severe rebukes, though he seemed always willing to allow
that her intentions were good. He tells her that she is
"quite a child in character, however well meaning."
This was free utterance to a woman forty-one years of age.

Sarah remained at Auteuil until May, 1815, when
she went to England to reside. By the Count's marriage-contract, his house at Brompton was to be the
property of his wife if she survived him. It was built
on a leasehold, which was to expire in 1863, so that
neither party had an absolute ownership in it. Madame
de Rumford very generously gave the Count's daughter
all her rights in the lease. But the house proved to be
a most troublesome charge to the Countess, and her
vexations fill a large part of her correspondence with
Sir Charles. He was far from regarding the house as
the wonderful and convenient dwelling which Pictet had
represented it. Finding that the Countess was always
spending money on repairs, and was frequently cheated
by tenants whom she allowed to occupy it, he was constantly urging her to dispose of the lease, and, with her
maid, to take lodgings. She was very unstable in her
plans, at times seeming to prefer England as her residence, and then longing to go to Paris, and informing
her friends there of a purpose of visiting them; her
excuse, when she changed her mind, always being some
worrying difficulty about her house.

The following letter was written by her to Mr. James F. Baldwin: —

"BROMPTON ROW, January 23, 1816.

"DEAR FRIEND, — Having heard of a vessel which sails from this port for Philadelphia, I improve the opportunity to acknowledge the reception of yours of December 9, which arrived safe. I am exceedingly obliged to you for the attention of writing, and shall learn with much interest all particulars of my country and friends you may have to communicate. I am ignorant of almost all events; have seen very few Americans since I came away, and have seldom received any letters. I, however, received your first, which I answered, and found two more among some papers I left at Auteuil, on having them restored to me after my father's death. I was from August till the following May at Auteuil at that time, when I came here, where I have remained ever since.

"My object in coming was principally to look after this house and have it repaired, which I have now accomplished. The last of the workmen went away about a week ago, and having commenced immediately on my arrival, you will perceive it was several months I have been engaged in these repairs. I propose to let the house as soon as a convenient opportunity offers, and most likely shall return to France and establish myself there. I like well enough to live in England, and might perhaps prefer it, but do not view it as so much to my interest. It is much dearer living here than it is in France, nor have I so many friends here as I have there. Mons. Delessert and Mr. Parker were very particular friends of my father's, and are very friendly to me. It is through Mons. Delessert I receive my Bavarian pension, and indeed my other little annuity left me by my father; so that it is better to be at hand.

"I will thank you to make inquiries about my brother at Concord [Mr. Paul Rolfe] and let me know, for I wrote to him since I came away, and not receiving any answer led me to fear he might be ill, or that some difficulty had befallen him. I have not received any intelligence either from my friends at Baldwin [Maine], and should like to know how they all do.

"I perceive by one of the letters I mentioned to have found at Auteuil that your sister Clarissa is married. You will give my love to her, if you please, and tell her I hope she is well and happy. And with desiring my compliments to all your friends and connections, believe me, with sincere friendship,

"Yours truly,

"S. RUMFORD.

"P. S. — I forgot to ask you if the money left with Mr. Hancock be safe, and going on well. You will continue to direct to the care of Messrs. Herries, Farquhar, & Co., if you please."

After having fixed upon many successive dates for going to Paris, and finding herself unable to leave Brompton, she at last went to Paris in 1820, and remained there three years under the protection of Baron Delessert and Sir Charles. The latter was himself almost all the time from the Count's death to his own away from England, and generally resident in Paris, — making, however, two visits there, in 1817 and 1819, when he was the guest of the Countess. He had become infirm and gouty, but he seems to have been made welcome. The package of his letters which the Countess left inscribed "From my much lamented and respected friend, Sir Charles Blagden," includes the summons which she received to attend his funeral rites in the Church of the Oratoire in Paris, he having died in that city, March 26, 1820.

The letters begin with one dated in Paris, August 15, 1815, and through the whole series their contents are divided between references to her troubles about her house and particulars concerning Madame de Rumford.

That lady had made a visit to England in 1817, and had returned to Paris in September, in company with Sir Charles. Lady Davy had invited her to partake of her hospitalities, but Madame preferred to have more freedom.

Another subject on which Sir Charles found it necessary continually to prompt the Countess — administering sharp rebukes for her dilatoriness and carelessness — was her disregard of order and courtesy in neglecting, at the right time, the steps requisite for the regular transmission of her pension from Bavaria. She did not attend properly to the obtaining periodically the certificate that she was living, so that the representatives of Bavaria in England and France might follow the rule in the case. The ambassador in London, M. Pfeffel, needed to exercise some forbearance with her.

The Countess was under the impression that Madame de Rumford did not much desire to have her come to Paris, as her presence and the relation between them might possibly be embarrassing to the widow of her father. But it would seem that the latter lady was considerate and reasonably friendly. After her return from the visit to England just mentioned, Sir Charles writes to the Countess, from Paris, September 22, 1817 : —

"Madame de Rumford is in excellent health. She desires me to give you her compliments, and to tell you that she will write at the same time as your god-daughter, Sarah [Aichner]. She has placed the latter with a milliner, that by learning a trade she may have the means of rendering herself independent. Whenever you were mentioned she [Madame] spoke of you with some interest, and even expressed a wish, that, if I should establish myself at the Baths of Tivoli [a hotel in Paris] this winter, you might be there too. And she gave stronger hints than I ever heard from her before, that she greatly disapproved your father's conduct towards you. [Probably in dictating that the Countess should return to America.] This seems to me a happy disposition, which it will depend upon your good conduct to improve."

Dating from Paris, October 24, 1817, Sir Charles writes : —

"This will be brought to England by Monsieur Arago, a distinguished gentleman of science in France, and my good friend. He will be accompanied by Baron Humboldt, whom I believe you have met at Madame de Rumford's or at your father's. These gentlemen mean to stay in London about three weeks, and if you determine to come hither, it will be an excellent opportunity for you to make the journey with them. M. Arago has kindly promised me to give you notice when they set out on their return, which will probably be about the 20th of November. He will let you know a few days before where you can communicate with him, and I trust that you will be exact in making your arrangements to travel with him and the Baron, in case you finally resolve to come. When I consider Madame de Rumford's way of life, it does not seem to me likely that she will find it convenient to be of much use to you, so that your coming hither or remaining in England should be determined chiefly by other considerations."

The Countess could not avail herself of the privilege of having such fellow-travellers, because of the annoyance which her house at Brompton was giving her. She afterwards wrote to Sir Charles that it was her intention to be in Paris on Christmas, 1818. But as she did not arrive, Sir Charles, in a letter to her of that date, writes : "I delivered your message to Madame de Rumford. She seemed glad to hear that you thought of coming ; but expressed a strange fancy, that your object is to take care of me, in case I should be sick. I have no reason to think I shall be sick, and if I should be so, I can be better nursed by the people belonging to this house than it would be decorous for you to do. Madame de Rumford sometimes talks a little at random."

This frank correspondent informs the Countess: "My opinion is, that Madame would be ready to do you any little services, but that you have not to expect great ones from her."

After her stay in Paris from 1820 to 1823, during which interval, as before stated, her wise friend Sir Charles Blagden had died, the Countess returned to England, where she lived, principally at Brompton, till August, 1835, when she came to America. Here she remained till the last of July, 1838, when she again went abroad. She lived mostly at Paris, till July, 1844, when she came back to her native place, occupying the house and the chamber in which she was born, where also she died, on December 2, 1852, in her seventy-ninth year. It appears by her correspondence with her friend, Mrs. James F. Baldwin, of Boston, that the Countess two months before her decease had been packing and storing her effects, and proposing to lease her house in Concord, with a view again to visit Paris.

That house in Concord has interest for us as the one in which the Count lived after his first marriage, and whence he had to hurry secretly away from the visit of an angry mob of village patriots. The use to which his daughter bequeathed the estate — in fulfilment of the charitable design which she and her father had more than fifty years before planned in Munich, on the occasion of the celebration of his birthday — enhances its interest. Her half-brother, Paul Rolfe, died in

Concord, married, but childless, on July 18, 1819, the Countess being the heiress to his and to the maternal property. The estate is finely situated on a bend of the Merrimack River, from which it is separated only by a county road running behind it, — spring freshets having already made threatening inroad in its rear. It consists of ten or twelve acres, and has upon it two cottages besides the mansion-house built by Colonel Benjamin Rolfe, the first husband of the Count's first wife. This mansion of wood, which was stately and costly for its day, with panelling and carving and wrought cornices, has not been improved by alterations and additions made to it by the Countess. Mr. Joseph B. Walker of Concord, the great-grandson of the Countess's grandfather, has in his possession an admirably drawn " Plan of the Homestead belonging to the Estate of Colonel Rolfe," which was made from actual survey by young Benjamin Thompson, and which is inscribed with his name. In Rev. Timothy Walker's diary are references to the building of this mansion by his future son-in-law. Thus, " Monday, 16th April, 1764, visited Colonel Rolfe, and pitched the place for his house." " Monday, 14th May, teams went to Rattlesnake Hill for rocks for Colonel Rolfe." He obtained his granite underpinning from a famous quarry. Three hundred men are at this time constantly employed there, and some of the noblest structures in Boston, like the Merchants' Bank and Horticultural Hall, have been built from it.

By her last will the Countess devised this estate, and the sum of fifteen thousand dollars in money, to trustees, for the establishment and support of an institution to be known as " The Rolfe and Rumford

SARAH COUNTESS OF RUMFORD

The Rolfe — Rumford House, Concord, N. H.

(PAGE 688.)

Asylum," "for the poor and needy, particularly young females without mothers." The testator enjoined that the children to be received into it should be exclusively natives of Concord. The money bequest has ever since been at interest, and in the year 1871 amounted to about forty-nine thousand dollars. The Institution, probably, will not be established and opened for some five or six years, when it is hoped that the fund will have so far increased as to support it. In case the town of Concord should decline to receive, or should fail to undertake and faithfully administer this trust, the bequest was to revert "to Joseph Amedie Lefevre, hereafter to be called Joseph Amedie Rumford, of Paris, France, his heirs and assigns forever." To this gentleman the Countess also bequeathed the sum of ten thousand dollars. She also left a bequest of fifteen thousand dollars, as a "Rumford Fund," to the New Hampshire Asylum for the Insane.

The Countess gave an oil portrait of her father, taken with his insignia and decorations as a Knight and a Count of the Empire, to Harvard College; in one of the halls of which it has since hung, among the portraits of the benefactors of that Institution. Besides distributing her jewels and money legacies among many friends, she left to Mr. Joseph B. Walker and his family the following pictures : —

A portrait, in oil, of the Count, in the uniform of a British officer, taken at the age of thirty in London.

A portrait, in oil, by Kellerhofer, of the Count at the time when he was sent as the Bavarian Ambassador to London.

A portrait, in oil, of the Countess Sarah.

A portrait, in oil, cabinet size, of Captain Lefevre.

A superb portrait in oil of the Elector Charles Theodore, by Kellerhofer, with a stately frame.

Portraits, in oil, of the Countesses Nogarola and Baumgarten.

A colored chalk portrait, cabinet size, of the Baroness de Kalbe.

Original portrait of Count Rumford, in colored chalk, cabinet size, by Lane, taken in 1809, — the one most cherished by the daughter.

There are also German landscapes, painted in water-colors, by ladies of Munich, and presented to Rumford for his signal services in keeping the French and Austrian troops out of the city; views in the English Garden at Munich; a pencil sketch of M. Pictet; and an engraved portrait of Baron Hompesch.

A marble monument, with an appropriate inscription, marks the grave of the Countess in the old burial-ground at Concord.   .

A hall prepared for social purposes and for the delivery of lectures was opened in Concord, in January, 1851, on which occasion an address was made by Mr. C. F. Low of that city, embracing an interesting sketch of the Count's career, taken chiefly from Cuvier's *Éloge.*

It is affirmed that the oldest organized institution in this country offering lectures to the community at large, for the purposes of a lyceum, and as a repository of illustrative apparatus, is that which is still in active operation in the town of Waltham, Massachusetts, and which bears the name of "The Rumford Institute."

The house at Brompton, described so admiringly by Pictet, was, during the Count's occupancy of it, No. 45 Brompton Row. It is now numbered 168 Brompton

Road. It remains very much in the same state as in the Count's time, though a stucco front seems to have been added. The house had been leased by the owner to the Rev. Mr. Beloe, the translator of Herodotus, who gave it up in 1810. The Countess occupied it and leased it, as we have seen, alternately, and in 1837 she sold the lease to the present proprietors. While it was still in her possession it was occupied successively by Sir Richard Phillips and Mr. Wilberforce.

I am under obligations to Mr. G. Henry Horstmann, United States Consul at Munich, for the following interesting letter, describing the recently erected statue of Count Rumford, and the present condition of his English Garden. The letter is dated Munich, October 12, 1870:—

"The bronze statue of Count Rumford stands in the Maximillian Strasse, the finest street of Munich, perhaps of any city of Europe. It is at this part four hundred feet wide, planted with quadruple rows of trees, the crimson-blossomed wild chestnut, and the American sycamore, with wide *parterres* of flowers and grass-plots on either side the pavement, and shady walks between, furnished with garden sofas for pedestrians. The monument stands in front of the new government offices, an imposing building in Italian Gothic, with some seven hundred feet front. To the right of this statue stands one to General Deroy. On the opposite side of the street, and in front of the National Museum, — a large edifice of the same dimensions as the before-mentioned building, — stand in symmetrical positions, Frauenhofer, the astronomer and inventor, and Schelling, the philosopher, the tutor of King Maximillian, erected, as the inscription says, by his 'grateful scholar.' These four memorials are all of uniform size, the figures being ten feet, English, standing on granite pedestals of eleven feet in height. The statue of Count Rumford was modelled by Professor Caspar Zumbusch, of Munich, was cast at the Royal

Bronze Foundry here, by Ferdinand von Müller, and was erected in 1867.   The inscription on the front of the pedestal is : —

. BENJAMIN THOMPSON
Graf
von Rumford.

and on the reverse : —

Errichtet von
MAXIMILLIAN II., Koenig
von Bayen.

"On a scroll in the hand of Rumford is inscribed, —

' Englische Garten
Architecte.'

"It was made at the King's private expense, he following the example of his father, King Ludwig, in thus perpetuating the memory of those men who made themselves deserving in the annals of Bavaria. Bronze statues of Orlando di Lasso and Gluck, composers and musicians, Westenrieder and Kreitmayer, historians and jurisprudents, Gaertner and Kleuze, architects, etc., adorn other parts of the town.

"Scarcely a city of the world can boast of a finer park than that which owes its existence to the creative mind of the subject of your biography ; and every citizen of Munich feels grateful to the man through whose labor a dreary waste of pebbly strand and marshy ground has been converted into a garden, bearing on its broad breast the stateliest forest-trees, groves of shady elms and beeches, with wide stretches of undulating lawns between, and enlivened with streams of water, now meandering under the wide-spreading branches of over-arching bushes, and at the foot of towering hemlocks, now stretching out into a wide lake with green islands in its centre, and now dashing over rocks in roaring cascades, and all supplied by arms of the rushing Isar, which have been led here to beautify the spot.

"The English Garden, as it is called, is a park of six hun-

STATUE OF COUNT RUMFORD IN MUNICH

dred acres. Its length is three and a half English miles, its breadth about one and a half miles. It was planned and carried out in 1789, by Count Rumford, at that time one of the Ministers of the Elector Carl Theodore. It was subsequently enlarged and improved by Maximillian Joseph, the first King of Bavaria, and was further embellished with monuments by his son, Ludwig the First. Scarcely more than a hundred paces from the Ludwig Strasse, one of the handsomest avenues of the city, it commences, so that a few steps bring one from the bustle and noise of a crowded street into the midst of quiet rural scenery. At the entrance from this point stands a marble statue of Youth, by Schwanthaler the elder, its inscription intimating that communion with nature freshly strengthens one for every duty. Farther on, following the carriage road to the right, is the monument to the memory of Rumford. It is of sandstone, with allegorical figures of Plenty and Peace upon its face, and on the opposite side a medallion portrait of Rumford."

In copying for me the German inscriptions on this memorial, — which have been inserted on previous pages, — Consul Horstmann draws my attention to that almost untranslatable word *lustwandler*, which I had rendered "saunterer," and which he renders "pedestrian." He remarks that the German word means a person who is walking for the enjoyment of walking; but is not represented either by the words "pleasure-seeker" or "pedestrian" (which would be *fussgaänger*) as opposed to one who rides, or "promenader," or "saunterer."

The writer goes on to describe the Garden as it now is.

"Still further on, but more towards the centre of the park, upon a hillock, is the 'Monopteros,' a Grecian temple, built by Ludwig, and dedicated to his father, Maximillian Joseph, who did so much in sustaining and extending what Rumford had so well commenced. From here is a pleasing view. Other monuments, bridges, and pavilions adorn the grounds, which are always kept in the most perfect order.

" The English Garden is the great resort of the citizens, who fully appreciate this beautiful spot, and who, in common with all Germans, are so fond of living in the open air. At all seasons of the year are people to be seen both walking and driving along its winding paths, enjoying nature to the full. In the spring of the year it is musical with the notes of the nightingale, the lark, and other song-birds, which are here so numerous. In winter the lake is the favorite skating-ground, and is merry with the sports of thousands of people of all classes and of both sexes. In summer the military and other bands perform here.

" The thanks of the people are due to Count Rumford, not only for the creation of the English Garden, but for the impetus which through this has been given to further improvements. On the opposite bank of the Isar, and connected with it by a bridge, is the new park, extending up the river for over a mile and a half, joined to the city by two bridges. This is to be further extended, and is already in progress, so that ultimately this belt of park-land will fully encircle more than half the city, and will furnish a drive in one direction of ten English miles.

"When I first came to Munich, fourteen years ago, the whole of the right bank of the Isar overlooking the city was a dreary waste of stunted meadow-land without a single bush upon it to relieve its monotony. It is now closely planted with fine trees of large size laid out in groups, the paths winding along in accordance with the natural undulations of the ground ; and this New Park, as it is called, is a worthy continuation of the English Garden.

" The improvements which have been made in the science of arboriculture have made possible the transplanting of very large and old trees, which are often brought from a great distance, so that although only ten years have elapsed since the commencement of these grounds, they have no longer the look of a new plantation. All the trees and shrubs flourish remarkably well. Perhaps this is due in a great measure to the protective spirit of the people, any depredations or injury to the plants being entirely unknown here; neither is there any defacing of the walks, monuments, benches, or other accessories of the grounds.

" A street of Munich bears the name of Rumford."

APPENDIX.

(See page 13.)

THE following document has reference to the provision made for Benjamin Thompson after the death of his father : —

"Articles of Agreement made and fully concluded on this Sixteenth day of October, A. D. 1755, in the Twenty-Ninth year of His Majesty's Reign, between Isaac Snow, Gentleman, as Guardian to Hiram Thompson, Son of Capt. Ebenezer Thompson, late of Woburn, deceased; Benjamin Flagg and Hannah Flagg his Wife; Ruth Thompson, widow of Benjamin Thompson, late of said Woburn, deceased, all of Woburn in the County of Middlesex; and Joshua Simonds of Medford, in the County aforesaid, Yeoman, as Guardian to Benjamin Thompson, Grandson to said Ebenezer, deceased, — Heirs and Guardians to the Heirs of said Ebenezer Thompson, deceased: Having a mind amicably to settle some things that seem to be left disputable in the last Will and Testament of the said Ebenezer Thompson aforesaid, deceased, — Have mutually agreed as followeth, viz. : First, That the said Ruth Thompson shall have free liberty to improve one half of the Garden at the west end of said Deceased's Mansion, and a privilege of land to raise beans for sauce for her own use, near said house, during her being said Benjamin's widow ; and the keeping of the Cow mentioned in said Ebenezer's last Will for said widow is to be kept on the produce of the land and on the place belonging to Hiram. Further, the said widow is to have her wood mentioned in said Will out of the land devised to said Benjamin, and the said Snow doth hereby oblige himself to give to said

widow Eighty weight of beef out of Hiram's part, also Eight
bushels of rye, Two bushels of malt, and Two barrels of Cider,
for the present year. Further, the said widow is to have liberty
of gathering apples to bake, &c., and three bushels of apples for
winter yearly, and every year during her widowhood, off of said
place. Further, Benjamin is to have the improvement of the
land his Grandfather gave him in his Will. Further, Whereas
the said Benjamin Thompson was ordered by his Grandfather,
in his last Will and Testament, to pay to Hannah Flagg, &c.
the sum of £26 13 4, Lawful money, we, the said Benjamin
Flagg and Hannah Flagg his wife, do hereby covenant for ourselves and heirs, that we, nor they, nor any of them, shall sue
the said Benjamin nor his Guardian, by reason of said Legacy,
until he arrives to the age of twenty-one years. Further,
whereas the said Ebenezer left a pew in the new meeting-
house in said Woburn, that was not disposed of in his Will, we
do hereby agree that the said pew shall be for the use of the
heirs of said deceased, and Benjamin's widow, until Hiram
arrive to the age of twenty-one years.

"Furthermore, the said Isaac Snow doth hereby oblige himself (in his capacity) to pay, or cause to be paid, unto Benjamin
aforesaid, or to his Guardian, the sum of Sixteen shillings, L.
M. yearly, and every year, until the said Benjamin arrives to
the age of fourteen years, out of the estate of said Hiram. It
is further agreed that those Books which are in a chest in
said house shall be equally divided between the three heirs to
said estate. It is further agreed that the watch, and provisions
in the house and grain in the barn (over and above what is disposed of to the widow), in case the Bonds, Notes, and Book-
debts fall short, are to be sold to pay debts. Also the clothing
that remains of Ebenezer Thompson, Jr., deceased, is to be
sold to pay debts. If what is heretofore assigned to pay debts
fall short, it is further agreed by the parties that Hiram's Guardian shall reimburse the one half that is wanting out of Hiram's
part, Benjamin Flagg one third part, and Benjamin Thompson's
Guardian one sixth part. It is agreed further, if what is assigned
to pay debts should be more than enough to discharge them,

that the overplus shall be equally divided between the three heirs. It is further agreed, that whereas the said deceased had hired a man for the summer past, that the said Snow shall pay his wages out of the crop, and the remaining part of the crop is to be Hiram's.

"In witness whereof the said parties to these presents have each of them hereunto set their hands this day and year first above written.

"ISAAC SNOW, Guardian.

"Signed and delivered in presence of us,

EBENEZER CONVERSE,	HANNAH T. FLAGG,
ZEBADIAH WYMAN,	RUTH THOMPSON,
CALEB BROOKS,	JOSHUA SIMONDS."
BENJAMIN FLAGG,	

(See page 45.)

The following are fragments of letters written by Benjamin Thompson to his mother, while he was living at Concord, New Hampshire.

[No date.]

"I would inform you that I have been very well as to my health since I saw you, as I hope you have been.

"I can't tell the exact time I shall come to Woburn; it may be a week sooner or a week later than I have set, for aught I know. When I do come I shall tell you all about my coming to Pennicook [Concord], for 't is too long a story to write in a letter.

"So I believe I shall write no more at present, only that I am Your dutiful Son,

"BENJAMIN THOMPSON.

"I have had 106 Scholars at my School [hiatus] only have 70 at once.

"To Mrs. Ruth Pierce, in Woburn."

"Concord, Jan. [missing].

" DEAR MOTHER, — I embrace this opportu—— of letting you know that we are well in our health, as I hope soon to hear [that you are].

" I should have been to Woburn before now, as I talked of, but my business was such that I could not possibly leave home. But I hope to see you soon if it holds good sleighing. Mrs. Thompson longs to see you, and is determined to come down with me to Woburn some time this winter. Pray, let me hear from you as soon as possible, and you will oblige,

" Your Affectionate Son,
" BENJ: THOMPSON."

"Concord, Febry. 27, 17 [74].

" DEAR MOTHER, — I send this to let you know that we are all well, as I hope this will find you and yours. I am extremely sorry to hear that you have been unwell, but I hope you will soon be hearty again. I expect to come down in the Spring with Mrs. Thompson, but I believe I shall not be able before the latter end of May. I have nothing extraordinary to write you. All is peace and quietness in this part of the world. Mrs. Thompson desires to be remembered to you and Father, and to all my Friends and Relations. You must let me hear from you as often as you can.

" This from your Dutiful Son,
" BENJ: THOMPSON.

" Please to remember me to Father, Children, and all Friends, especially Natty and Abigail Thompson."

(See page 67.)

The following letter of Benjamin Thompson to the minister of Trinity Church, Boston, indicates not only some of his movements, but also the direction of his sympathies, at a critical period of his life.

"October 1st, 1775.

"REVᵈ SIR,—I came out of Boston a few days before the affair at Lexington on the 19th April, and have since not been able to return. When I left the Town I little imagined that a return would be thus difficult, or, rather, impossible, and therefore took no care to provide for such a contingency. My effects in Town I left at my lodging in Hanover Street; and my landladies (Miss Elizabeth Clark and Miss Elizabeth Nowel) who left Boston about the 20th August, inform me that when they came away they took the liberty to break open a trunk of theirs in which I used to keep my papers, and that they packed up my papers together with my clothes, and everything else they could find belonging to me, and put them all into an old square box, marked on the top C—k, N—l, and on one side or end, B. T., which box they left in the lower front chamber of their dwelling-house, under the care of one Mrs. Cromartie, to whom also they committed the care of the house.

"This Box, I am informed by a person who has lately left Boston, was safe in the before-mentioned chamber as late as the middle of August. But as it contains matters of the greatest consequence to me, and as I cannot depend upon Mrs. Cromartie's care, this is earnestly to beg your assistance in this affair.

"The enclosed letter (which I beg you would deliver as soon as it comes to hand) is a duplicate of one I wrote some time ago, which I since learn miscarried. And notwithstanding in this letter I desire Major Small to take charge of the Box containing my effects, yet if you would be so kind as to take the same into your care and possession, I should be exceedingly obliged, and would not wish to give the Major the trouble of it.

"I have experienced too much of your obliging disposition to doubt of your readiness to serve me in this affair, especially when you consider to what an unhappy situation I am reduced with respect to my affairs in Town. But whether you do or do not take charge of my effects, yet I beg that the enclosed letter may be delivered. And at the same time you deliver the letter

you will be so kind as to inform the Major whether you take
charge of them or not.

"If Mrs. Cromartie denies her having any such Box as I
have described in her possession, yet if you will take the trouble
to look yourself in the before-mentioned front chamber, I dare
say you will find it. But if she refuses to deliver it up, or if the
Troops have taken possession of the house, and dispute your
right to carry it off, or if the Box is not to be found, Major
Small's assistance will be of great service, which I dare say he
will lend upon such an occasion. If Mrs. Cromartie has left
the house, and has not left word where she has gone, I believe
you may find her out by inquiring at Mrs. Phillips' in Quaker
Lane, in whose family she has, or at least had, a daughter who
was a servant-maid, and who can doubtless give some account
of her mother.

"I have a very good Hussar Cloak faced with scarlet shalloon, with yellow mock-spangle metal buttons, and an old plaid
red gown, lined with crimson shalloon, in Town, which I
should be glad you would likewise take under your care.
These I am told are at Mr. Elias Parkman's at the North End,
near Winnisimmet Ferry ways. In what Street he lives I
cannot say, but believe you may find out by inquiring at Mr.
William Jackson's store at the Brazen Head.

"If you should be so kind as to take my effects into your
possession, you will please to keep them safe till I shall have the
pleasure of seeing you, or till you shall hear from me, or from
my Executor or Administrator. And in the mean time, if you
should leave the Town, you will either leave them with Doctor
William Lee Perkins, or some other person that you can depend
on, or take them with you, as you think most for my safety.

"The preservation of my papers is an affair of the *utmost
importance* to me, and I hope that a consideration of that, and
of my present situation, will serve in some measure as an excuse
for my wishing to give you so much trouble in this matter.

"I cannot conclude without informing you that since I left
Boston I have enjoyed but a very indifferent share of health,
having been much troubled with Putrid Bilious Disorders.

Since the 12th of August I have been confined to my room the greatest part of the time, and this is the nineteenth day since I have had a settled fever upon me, which I fear is not come to a crisis yet. My Physician gives me encouragement of getting better after a while, but I am very apprehensive it will be a long time before I shall be well.

"I have not been out of the Province of Massachusetts Bay since I saw you. Mrs. Thompson and little Sally were with me during the month of May, since which time I have not had the pleasure of seeing either of them.

"I am, dear Sir, with the greatest truth and esteem,

"Your real friend and very humble Servant,

"BENJ' THOMPSON.

"To the Rev. Mr. Sam! Parker,
  Trinity Church, Boston."

This letter was not sealed. It was probably sent, or intended to be sent, into Boston through one of the British sentries on Charlestown Neck.

(See page 94.)

In disposing of a part of his estate by the following indenture, Mr. Thompson may have had in view the purpose more clearly indicated in the account which succeeds it.

" This indenture of Agreement made this 21st day of June, 1775, between Cyrus Baldwin, of Boston, in the Province of Massachusetts Bay, merchant, on the one part, and Benjamin Thompson, of Concord, in the Province of New Hampshire, Esq., on the other part.

" Witnesseth : That whereas the said Thompson has this day given a deed to said Baldwin, of a certain tract or piece of land lying in Woburn and Wilmington, containing 20 Acres and

67 Poles; And as said Baldwin has this day drawn an order for value received in favor of said Thompson for the amount of £ 32 17 2, Lawful Money in goods, to be delivered at said Baldwin's Store in Boston: It is agreed between the Parties that said Baldwin shall not be obliged to deliver said goods at any other place than his store in Boston, and in case they are not called for, or cannot be delivered there within 60 days after sight of said Order, then said Baldwin shall deliver up the aforesaid Deed to said Thompson, upon said Thompson's delivering up to said Baldwin said Order, and paying him £ 22 5 4, L. M., otherwise all are to remain in full force. It is also agreed between the Parties that if upon measuring said Land it shall appear to contain more than 20 Acres and 67 Poles, then said Baldwin shall pay to said Thompson after the rate of £ 2 14 0 *per* Acre, for all it shall so overrun; and in case it shall fall short of 20 Acres and 67 Poles, then said Thompson shall pay to said Baldwin after the rate of £ 2 14 0 *per* Acre for all that it shall so fall short.

"*In Witness Whereof*, we have hereunto interchangeably set our hands and seals.

"BENJ? THOMPSON,
CYRUS BALDWIN."

(See page 94.)

The following account, copied from a paper in the handwriting of Benjamin Thompson, dated "Woburn, Oct. 10, 1775," was probably made out in view of his intention to leave the country.

"A State of Benj? Thompson's Affairs in the Province of Massachusetts.

"Due from Benj? Thompson, Viz' Old Tenor.
To Mr. Tho? Courtney, of Boston, upon a Note of
   hand,   95 10 10

To Misses Clark and Nowell, of Do., for about 13
    Weeks Board, at 5 £, and Washing,   75   0   0
To Mr. Andrew Dexter, of Do., on a Note, £22 10,
    and on account, about £7 10,   30   0   0
To Mr. Dehone, of Do., about   9   0   0
To my Aunt, Hannah Flagg, of Woburn, part of
    Legacy   165 10   0
To the Rev. Sam¹. Williams, of Bradford, on a Note,
    about   55   0   0

" I have not settled with Mr. Timothy Walker of Wilmington, my former Guardian, but I believe we are nearly upon a balance.

" Due to Benj ͬ Thompson.
From Mr. Cyrus Baldwin, on an Order for value re-
    ceived for goods,   131   0   7½
From Benj. Tay, of Wilmington, a Note of hand upon
    interest,   31   6   6
From Mr. Benj. Converse, of Woburn, about 15 or
    20 £,   15   0   0
From Mr. Jno. Butters, of Wilmington, on a Note,   14   3   3
For the Land which I now own in Woburn and Wil-
    mington I have been offered upwards of   750   0   0
    and it rents for 33 £ *per annum*."

I have also before me a copy of a deed by which, on the previous 14th of September, Mr. Thompson conveyed some land in Wilmington to Josiah Pierce.

(See page 150.)

From a mass of interesting documents relating to Colonel Thompson's military services in America, copied from the originals in the government offices in London, and kindly sent to me by Dr. H. Bence Jones, I select the following.

1780, June 7. — Lord George Germaine writes a despatch to Sir H. Clinton, New York, saying that Captain Murray, on the part of Brigadier-General Ruggles, proposes to raise the King's American Dragoons.

One of his propositions was that no person who shall hold a commission in this regiment shall receive any pension or allowance from government for support as an American sufferer, and no pay until half the number of privates, or one hundred and sixty-five men, are raised, and then only half-pay till the enlistment is completed.

The King ordered the plan to be sent to Sir H. Clinton.

1781, May. — Only part of the appointments for Brigadier-General Ruggles had arrived out.

1781, July. — Thompson acts as Deputy Inspector-General of Provincial forces in North America, to send out accoutrements, and the Lords of the Treasury order him a percentage which came to £120, in August, 1781.

1781, September 30. — Lord George Germaine wrote a private letter to Sir H. Clinton introducing Mr. Thompson, and thanking Sir Henry for the favor and protection he has shown Mr. Thompson in giving him the command of a regiment of Light Dragoons, "which I trust will be raised in a manner to entitle the officers of it to your approbation. Lieutenant-Colonel Thompson shows at least a spirit and zeal for the service in quitting for a time an agreeable and profitable civil situation in the hopes of being useful to his country, and by his military conduct showing himself not unworthy of the protection which you have granted to him. If you do him the honor to converse with him, you will find him well informed, and, as far as theory goes, a good officer in whatever you may think fit to employ him. I can answer for his honor and his ability, and am persuaded he will ever feel attached by gratitude to you for the very kind and obliging manner in which you have protected him and the regiment under his command."

On the 4th of October, Thompson appointed Mr. Fisher a clerk in his office, to receive his half-pay of thirteen shillings a day.

A despatch of Lord George Germaine's to General Leslie, in answer to Leslie's of December 30, says: "I am glad you will have Colonel Thompson's assistance in forming what cavalry you have. His offer to serve in your army until the season for action to the northward arrives, corresponds with that public good and zeal for the King's service which prompted him to quit his civil situation and engage in the military line."

General Leslie writes to Clinton of Thompson, on January 29, 1782: "From the unwearied attention and diligent efforts of that officer the cavalry has become respectable, and I have everything to expect from this improvement."

Thompson writes to Leslie from Daniel's Island, February 20: "We arrived without being so fortunate as to meet the enemy we came in search of."

And on February 25, the same to the same: "I did not expect, after the affair of yesterday, the enemy would so soon have put it in my power to congratulate you upon another defeat of their troops. We had the good fortune this morning to fall in with a chosen corps under the command of General Marion in person, which we attacked and totally routed, killing a considerable number of them, taking sixteen prisoners, and driving General Marion and the greater part of his army into the Santee, where, it is probable, a great many of them perished."

A despatch of Leslie to Clinton, dated March 12, 1782, says he had the cavalry, one hundred men of the 30th regiment, the Volunteers of Ireland, and sixty Yagers. He speaks of this very handsome piece of service, and adds, referring to Thompson: "I assure your Excellency that I have much regret to part with this enterprising young officer, who appears to have an uncommon share of merit and zeal for the service, and could he and his troop be spared to act in this part where cavalry are so much wanted, I am confident it would tend much to his Majesty's service."

On April 15, Clinton writes to Leslie: "Those parts of your letters to which you have referred for a more full explanation to Lieutenant Thompson I shall answer after consulting with him upon the subject."

Thompson, writing on August 6 to Carlton, says that the regiment was completed, and had twenty men over and above the number stipulated in the original proposals. He asks for the advantages promised.

In General Orders of August 29, thanks were given for services, and permanent rank assigned.

On September 12, Carlton writes to Lord North: "As the officers, by very particular exertions of activity and diligence, have raised their regiment, and have spared no expense for that purpose, I cannot help concurring with the Board of General Officers that they should have permanent rank in America, and half-pay upon the reduction of their regiment."

On December 12, 1781, General Robinson makes a

report, with instructions in case of a sudden attack on Long Island. " If an attack is made on Huntingdon, in that case the troops are to assemble at their respective alarm-posts, and instantly to march to the support of the troops attacked under Colonel Thompson. It is expected that the militia in every alarm will cheerfully assemble and co-operate with his Majesty's forces in opposing the enemy."

In a memorial dated March 14, 1783, addressed to Carlton, Thompson humbly begs that he and his corps may be employed in the East Indies, or any other part of his Majesty's dominions, and offers to raise, from the men now serving in his Majesty's Provincial forces, a very fine battalion of light infantry. This, with General Leslie's certificate, Carlton sends to Townshend, the successor of Lord George Germaine.

On the 21st of March, Carlton authorizes Thompson to complete the King's American Dragoons to six troops of sixty men each, and to raise four companies of light infantry of fifty-two rank each.

On the 4th of April, Thompson writes to Carlton asking, that, as there seems no longer any prospect of service in the West Indies, his regiment may go to Nova Scotia, there to remain and do duty, and that he may have leave of absence to go to England to solicit in behalf of himself and the corps that they may be employed in the East Indies, or in some other part of his Majesty's dominions where their services may be wanted.

Leave of absence was granted Thompson on April 11.

On the 8th of June, Thompson, being then in London, writes to Lord North, from Pall Mall Court, " Having assisted in drawing up the representation and petition of the commanding officers of his Majesty's Provincial Regiments, and having been ordered by them to solicit for them in this country that the prayer of their petition be granted, I take the liberty of troubling your Lordship. They are extremely anxious to know their fate, as regards permanent rank and half-pay."

As the result of this solicitation, and in answer to Carlton's petition of September 12, 1782, above given, Lord North replies, on June 11, that the King has been graciously pleased to approve Sir G. Carlton's recommendation. And on the 15th of June, his Lordship writes that it is his Majesty's intention that all the Provincial regiments shall be removed to Halifax, where they are to be disbanded.

On July 6, 1783, Thompson writes to Carlton, congratulating him on the resolution of Parliament to give half-pay to the Provincial officers, and telling him all he had done with Lord North and members of Parliament. He says his Majesty has been graciously pleased to approve of the King's American Dragoons having the full establishment of field officers, as was originally intended, and that I should be promoted to the rank of Colonel. He adds: " I cannot help flattering myself that this arrangement will be agreeable to your Excellency, and that I shall be returned in your list of the Provincial officers for half-pay as Colonel. The rank to me is of infinite importance, as I am going abroad, in a short time, with a view to foreign service. But the half-pay is also an object, as I have little else left to depend on except my industry."

The letter to Carlton authorizing the promotion of Thompson has been given in the text, pp. 146, 147.

On the 10th of October, 1783, Carlton wrote to Colonel Thompson, who was then on the Continent: "The resolution of Parliament to give half-pay and permanent rank in America affords me great satisfaction. Your zeal and assiduity on this occasion appear to have been such as your friends might have expected."

On the 10th of October the King's American Dragoons were disbanded on the lands appropriated for them many miles up the river St. John.

[*Copy.*]

" America and West Indies. No. 146.

" *To His Excellency Sir Guy Carlton, K. B., General and Commander-in-Chief of all His Majesty's Forces in North America, within the Colonies lying in the Atlantic Ocean from Nova Scotia to West Florida, inclusive, &c., &c., &c.*

" The Memorial of BENJAMIN THOMPSON, Esq., Lieutenant-Colonel Commandant of the King's American Dragoons, for himself, and in behalf of the Officers and men under his Command.

"Humbly sheweth, —

" That the Officers of the King's American Dragoons are chiefly Young men of the first families and connections in North America, who, at a very early period of the War, entered into the King's service.

" That, except the Adjutant, who is from the 17.th Regiment of Light Dragoons, they are all Americans, and have suffered very considerably by the Rebellion.

" That in the Event of Peace and the Independency of the American Provinces, all their hopes of returning to their former situations will be at an end, and they will be reduced to the greatest distress. Their friends, involved in the common ruin, will be unable to assist them, and having no Profession but the

Profession of Arms, in which they have been trained up from their Youth, they will be unable to provide for themselves by their Industry in any other Calling.

"That they are all passionately fond of the Service and desirous of remaining in it, and are willing to go to any quarter of the Globe, provided they can be employed.

"The Memorialist further begs leave to represent, that a great proportion of the Non-commissioned Officers and private men under his Command have been trained up in the Service from their Youth, and would prefer remaining in it to any other occupation.

"That the Regiment is completely appointed, with Arms, Accoutrements, and every article of Horse Appointments and Furniture, to the full establishment of Six Troops of Sixty men each; together with four Field pieces, with their Harness, &c., complete, for a Troop of flying Artillery.

"The Memorialist, therefore, and being himself anxious to continue in the King's Service, humbly begs that Your Excellency would be pleased to recommend him and his Corps to His Majesty, to be employed in the West Indies, or in any other part of His Majesty's Dominions where their Services may be wanted.

"The Memorialist further begs leave to represent to your Excellency, that in case more Troops should be wanted for any service, he will undertake to raise from amongst the men now serving in His Majesty's Provincial Forces, a very fine Battalion of Light Infantry, Men trained to Arms and inured to Service, and Officers all young men, unincumbered with family connections, who have been bred up in the Service, and who, from their Zeal and bravery, as well as from their Sufferings as American Loyalists, are objects worthy of the countenance and protection of Government.

[Signed]　　　　　　　　　"B. THOMPSON, L! Col!
　　　　　　　　　　　　　　　Comm! King's Am. Dragoons.

"New York, 14ᵗʰ March, 1781."

Copy of a Letter from The Honorable Lieutenant-General Leslie, commanding His Majesty's Troops in the Southern District of North America, to His Excellency Sir Henry Clinton, K. B., Commander-in-Chief, &c., &c., &c., dated Charlestown, March 12, 1782.

"Sir,—I had the honor to inform your Excellency that Lieu.^t Col. Thompson having offered his service during his stay here, I had appointed him to the command of the cavalry. He has put them in exceeding good order, and gained their confidence and affection.

"I am very happy to acquaint you of his Success on a late Excursion upon the Santee, which he made with the Cavalry, supported by a detachment of one hundred men of the 30.th Reg.^t, the Vol.ⁿ of Ireland, and 60 Yagers. He had the good fortune to fall in with a body of the enemy's cavalry under the command of Horiy, which he nearly destroyed; and afterwards defeated and dispersed with considerable loss the Force which Marion had assembled to oppose him, all that he had been able to collect on this side the Santee. I inclose to your Excellency Col. Thompson's report to me of this very handsome piece of service, and I assure your Excellency that I have much regret to part with this enterprising Young Officer, who appears to have an uncommon share of merit and zeal for the service; and could he and his Corps be spared to act in this Part where Cavalry are so much wanted, I am confident it would tend much to the benefit of His Majesty's Service.

"I have the honor to be, &ca.

[Signed] ."ALEX.^r LESLIE."

(In Colonel Thompson's handwriting.)

"*To his Excellency Sir Guy Carlton, K. B., General and Commander-in-Chief of all his Majesty's forces within the Colonies lying on the Atlantic ocean from Nova Scotia to West Florida, &c.*"

"Lieu.^t Col. Thompson begs leave to return your excellency his unfeigned thanks for all the distinguished marks of your goodness to him, particularly for the last most flattering proof

43

of your excellency's approbation, that of appointing him to the command of a body of Light Troops, which were to have been raised for his Majesty's service in the West Indies, had not peace taken place. As there seems to be no longer any prospect of service in that quarter of the World, upon a supposition that the late accounts from Europe should be confirmed, and that the plan for sending troops from home to the West Indies should be laid aside, Lieutenant-Colonel Thompson trusts to your excellency's goodness for forgiveness if his request should be improper, and he humbly begs leave to sollicit your excellency:

"That the King's American Dragoons may be dismounted immediately and their cavalry appointments be packed up and lodged with the public stores of the army.

"That the regiment may be sent to Halifax, New Windsor, Cumberland, or some other part of Nova Scotia, by the first opportunity, there to remain and do duty till further orders.

"That upon their arrival at the place of their destination, such of the men as have families, and others desirous of making settlements, have leave granted to them for that purpose, to be discharged if they require it.

"That Lieut Colonel Thompson may have leave to go to England, there to sollicit, in behalf of himself and the Corps, that they may be employed in the East Indies or in some other part of his Majesty's dominions where their services may be wanted.

"Lieut. Colonel Thompson further begs leave to sollicit your excellency, —

"That in consideration of the great Losses the officers of the King's American Dragoons must suffer by disposing of their horses at this place, they may be allowed to take one horse each to Nova Scotia, and that a conveyance may be provided for them.

"And that in consideration of the sums that have been advanced by the officers of the Regiment in purchasing Troop Horses at a higher price than has been allowed by Government (which sums, for the credit of the regiment and the good of the service, they have been induced to furnish by voluntary contributions) they may be reimbursed in the whole or in part out of the monies that may arise by the sale of those Horses, should they be disposed of in that way.

> " B. THOMPSON, L! Col.
> Command! King's A. Dragoons.

" New York, 4ᵗʰ April, 1783."

Colonel Thompson to Lieutenant-Colonel Delancey.

> " New York, 8ᵗʰ April, 1783.

" SIR, — Inclosed is an account of money expended by me for the King's service during the time I had the honor to command the troops at Huntingdon, which amount I am to request you would be pleased to lay before his excellency the Commander-in-chief. I have the honor to be, Sir,

> " Your most obedient humble servant,
> " B. THOMPSON, L! Col.
> Command! King's Am. Drag.

" L! Col. DeLancey, Adjutant-General, &c."

Colonel Thompson to Lieutenant-Colonel Delancey.

> " New York, 13ᵗʰ April, 1783.

" SIR, — I have had the honor to lay your letter to me of this day's date before his excellency General Robertson, who has added a certificate to my account, which I hope will meet with his excellency the Commander-in-chief's approbation. I am sorry to add that General Robertson seems to have some doubts with respect to the Propriety of his signing any other certificate. I have the honor to be, Sir,

> " Your most obedient humble servant,
> " B. THOMPSON, L! Col.

" L! Col. DeLancey, Adjutant-General, &c."

Addressed to Colonel B. Thompson, probably by Carlton.

> " New York, 10 October, 1783.

" SIR, — I have received your letter of the 6ᵗʰ July with the several inclosures therein mentioned, and you may be assured that the resolution of Parliament to give the British American officers half-pay (with which also I find they will all have permanent rank in America) affords me a very sincere satisfaction.

"Your zeal and assiduity on this occasion appear to have been such as your friends might have expected, and I am sensible of your attention to me in writing so fully on the subject. The American officers have in my opinion so fair a claim to half-pay, that I hope the grant will finally be made for the full establishment for their several regiments without the least exception.

"Your promotion to the rank of Colonel is notified to me from the Minister, but as he has given me no instructions respecting Major Murray, you must be sensible that I cannot take it upon myself to give him an appointment which would be considered as a grievance by all the elder majors in the Provincial Line.

"I am, &c."

(See page 585.)

The following charming letter from Dr. Franklin to Madame Lavoisier, while her first husband was still living, shows how pleasant had been his relations with that lady:—

"PHILADELPHIA, October 23, 1788.

"I have a long time been disabled from writing to my dear friend by a severe fit of the gout, or I should sooner have returned my thanks for her very kind present of the portrait which she has herself done me the honor to make of me. It is allowed, by those who have seen it, to have great merit as a picture in every respect; but what particularly endears it to me is the hand that drew it. Our English enemies, when they were in possession of this city and my house, made a prisoner of my portrait and carried it off with them, leaving that of its companion, my wife, by itself, a kind of widow. You have replaced the husband, and the lady seems to smile as well pleased.

"It is true, as you observe, that I enjoy here everything that a reasonable mind can desire, — a sufficiency of income, a comfortable habitation of my own building, having all the conveniences I could imagine; a dutiful and affectionate daughter to nurse and take care of me, a number of promising grandchildren, some old friends still remaining to converse with, and more respect, distinction, and public honors than I can possibly merit. These are the blessings of God, and depend on his continued goodness; yet all do not make me forget Paris, and the nine years' happiness I enjoyed there, in the sweet society of a people whose conversation is instructive, whose manners are highly pleasing, and who, above all the nations of the world, have, in the greatest perfection, the art of making themselves beloved by strangers. And now, even in my sleep, I find that the scenes of all my pleasant dreams are laid in that city, or in its neighborhood.

"I like much young M. Dupont. He appears a very sensible and valuable man, and I think his father will have a great deal of satisfaction in him.

"Please to present my thanks to M. Lavoisier for the *Nomenclature Chimique* he has been so good as to send me (it must be a very useful book), and assure him of my great and sincere esteem and attachment. My best wishes attend you both; and I think I cannot wish you and him greater happiness than a long continuance of the connection. With great regard and affection, I have the honor to be, my dear friend, &c.

"B. FRANKLIN.*

* Sparks's Franklin, Vol. X. pp. 561, 562.

INDEX.